Now Publishing,

*In Penny Weekly Nos., or Monthly Parts at Fourpence, each Nu.
embellished with a Wood Engraving, in addition to occasional
illustrations on Steel, an Original Romance of extraordinary
interest, entitled*

THE PEER AND BEGGAR.

A TALE OF SEVENTY YEARS SINCE.

This Work, which will be found to increase in attractiveness as it proceeds,
will form, when complete, a handsome volume copiously illustrated, containing more than the ordinary three-volume Romances at less than a fourth
of their cost.

Also publishing, in Penny Numbers and Fourpenny Parts,

BIANCA AND THE MAGICIAN;

A Tale of Romance and Mystery—of

" Rites and Revels,
Saints and Devils."

*** Three Fourpenny Parts have already appeared

☞ The Works published by T. White are not mere re-
prints or mutilated Editions of other Publications, but
original Romances and Tales of sterling merit and
novelty.

Ri: Turpin.

From a Portrait in the Tyburn Chronicle 1742.

London Published by Thomas White, 59 Wych Street Strand.

DICK TURPIN.

BY

HENRY DOWNES MILES.

—Honour, that spins
Fine curious parallels that never meet,
What says she then? First, I must right myself;
And then, not wrong the publick—rare distinction
* * * * * *
But each man's private good lurks in the publick;
Then each man take his part, and where's the evil?
Oh, but the publick is the storehouse! No:
Rather the jayl, that keeps men's private goods
Confined. I'll get mine out, and set the rest on fire.
My private pleasure is my soveraign good,
T'obey and gratifie each strong impulse
Of my own will, nor heed their squeamish cavils.
The Sacrifice, by Sir F. Fane.

LONDON:

THOMAS WHITE, 59, WYCH STREET, STRAND.

MDCCCXL.

THE AUTHOR'S APOLOGY.

IT is not the intention of the writer of the following pages to disparage the pursuits of science, yet does he think that some little explanation is due to the reader for his choice of a hero, as well as his mode of treating his history. This he feels to be the more called for from the pseudo-criticism pervading our periodic literature—a disposition on the part of our weekly and monthly scribes to write down that species of literature now so prevalent and justly popular; which, taking some well-known character as its hero, fills up the accessories of the picture from the stores of the writer's imagination. The class too, from which they have chosen their leading characters, appears to have shocked the squeamish taste of these fault-finding gentry. "They are VULGAR," forsooth! Nature is not nor ever can be vulgar—the vulgarity exists nowhere but in the mind of the critic. Boz, Ainsworth, and the great writers who draw upon exhaustless human nature for their powerful and truthful delineations, are less *vulgar* than the inane writers of the silver-fork school, who never condescend to describe the actions of personages who are not entitled to a place in the Court Guide. This trumpery objection disposed of, we will approach one deserving more consideration and respect, though equally erroneous with the former. It is urged by the writers in some publications of higher scholastic pretensions. Their censures are directed against all writings of FICTION whatever; and come from men who, with unwearied diligence pursue the study of what they are pleased exclusively to term NATURE, in the growth of a plant or the formation of an insect. They spare neither labour nor expense to stock their cabinets with the dry bones of nature, whilst they overlook the feelings, instincts, appetites and passions, which animate the whole. They anatomise, they dissect the *physical* structure, but entirely lose sight of the *mental*. Others of this class are stimulated to inquiry by every pebble that lies on the shore, or every leaf that waves in the forest, and rejoice at the return of a comet or the blooming of an aloe, more than in the birth of a Homer or a Shakspeare : air, earth, ocean, the minutest objects of *sense*, as well as the greatest and most remote, are accurately and attentively scrutinised; but though these researches are laudable and suited to the dignity and capacity of a reasoning being, it should never be forgotten that the study of the *mind* itself is one of the greatest and surest means of enlarging our reasoning and reflective powers. Endowed with superior powers of sensibility and understanding, *mind* claims to itself a duration when all around shall be destroyed; our senses are vigilant in collecting ideas from every part of the creation; memory preserves them as the materials of thought and the principles of knowledge; and imagination, sedulous to amuse, arranges them into groups and assemblages; and thus by studying the passions, desires, and promptings of the human mind, though in fictitious scenes and circumstances, we instruct while we elevate, and enlarge while we strengthen our knowledge of our fellow creatures and ourselves. Shall we then assert that works of imagination, thus exhibiting the everchanging features of our nature, are less worthy of occupying the attention than the insect produced at noon-tide and perishing with the setting sun? or less edifying than an investigation of the " *Botheratiotherium*" or some antediluvian lizard imbedded in a sandstone?

As an agent, therefore, in rectifying our opinions and enlarging our conceptions of human nature, we must study its operations in the conduct and deportment of others and this can be nowhere so well done as in well-written works of fiction; and those too of the class which are denounced on the one hand as vulgar by the lack-a-daisical gentlemen of the modern novel school, and stigmatised as worthless by the utilitarians who restrict the term *science* to their own peculiar pursuits.

We have, however, been led further a-field in these observations than we at first intended, and shall therefore hasten to a conclusion by observing that, as biography has been termed " history taught by example," the romance of real life may be styled " philosophy taught by NATURE."

DICK TURPIN.

Dick Turpin chastises the insolence of Litton Weston.

CHAPTER I.

Young, innocent, on whose sweet forehead mild,
The parted ringlets shone in simplest guise,
An inmate in the home of Albert smiled,
Or blest his noon-day walk—she was his only child.
                    Gertrude of Wyoming.

Why did she love him?—curious fool be still
Is human love the growth of human will?
To her he might be gentleness.—Byron.

IT was on one of those beautiful evenings in autumn, when the slowly setting
sun seems loth to leave the land made joyous and fertile by his beams—when
the glowing tints of his departing rays linger as it were in the gorgeous
canopy of sky so soon to change into the bleak night of our early winter,
that an elderly and benign-looking old man sat before the first winter-fire
of the season, watching the cloud-paintings as they faded and changed from
tints defying the painter's pencil to the dull grey of evening. Near him,
in a pensive attitude, sat a fair girl; her hands which rested in her lap

unconsciously toying with the bones and many-coloured worsted which, until fading day interrupted her, had formed her gentle occupation. Never did mirror image a fairer girl than Esther Bevis.

The loose train of her amber-dropping hair, fell over a shoulder as rounded, but warmer and more lovely than Parian marble: her breathing lips were unclosed, and her smooth, pure brow, where the blood slept not, seemed more beauteous at each varied feeling which memory, the fit companion of such an hour, conjured up to " the thick-coming fancies" of her mind.

But if Esther was beautiful in person, her heart was a fit jewel to repose in so fair a casket. She was the kindest of human beings ; the very dog who had once seen her, knew again the sweetness of her smile. The goodness and purity of her heart reposed on her countenance like sunshine ; in short,

> " Her face was like the milky way i' the sky;
> A meeting of gentle lights without a name."

She loved all things, and all things loved her; indeed so soft yet lively, so buoyant yet caressing, so innocently simple, though blessed with woman's shrewdness of perception, did the character of Esther appear, that the casual observer might be led to suppose that strength and shadiness of character could scarcely be conjoined with such affectionate and feminine gentleness.

Time, however, and circumstance, which alter and harden, as well as bring forth qualities and dispositions unknown even to their possessor, may show latent and undiscovered features in the character of the gentle Esther. In short she was a lovely and a *loving* girl of nineteen.

Her meditative silence, however, had lasted but a few minutes—though to Esther those moments had been months, nay years, of her yet young life— when her thoughts appeared to take an unbidden direction that threw a shade on her fair face and dimmed her sparkling blue eye with a gentle tear. An involuntary sigh escaped her. Her father turned from his contemplations. The spell was broken, and the old man thus addressed his only and beloved child.

" Esther," said he affectionately, as if conscious of the tendency of her thoughts and anxious to divert them ; " I was thinking my girl—though God forbid I should urge you against your inclination—I was thinking—" and the old man paused ; " that you should at least remain in the apartment when young Weston calls on me. 'Tis considerate and kind of him, in our fallen fortune, to look in on his father's friend : besides, he is always respectfully distant, as far as I can judge ; unless something has occurred which I know not."

" Father," said she, and her voice trembled as she spoke, " I pray you not to question me. I—"

" Tut, tut : you are silly girl. Indeed," continued the old man, half soliloquising, " I begin to think that Dare-devil Dick has turned her brain. But come, Esther, tell me—for I must have no secrets between us—how comes it, that of late I hear so many sighs, and see so many pretty little true-love knots in all the corners of your work ?" And the good-natured old man chuckled in approbation of his own acuteness and drollery.

Far different, however, was the effect of his mirth on Esther, to that which it usually had. At the mere mention of the personage whom her parent designated as " Dare-devil Dick," her countenance assumed an expression of pain, and ere the well-meaning old man had finished his jocose sally, the gentle girl burst into a flood of tears.

"Hoity! toity!" exclaimed old Bevis, starting up with unaffected alarm: "why I never saw this before! why, what ails the girl, look up, my dear, look up; it's your father speaks."

"Forgive me, dear father," said Esther, sobbing and hiding her face with her delicately formed hands, " but you know not the feelings excited by your ill-timed attempt, kindly though it was meant. But I will, I must, tell you all; I never had a secret from you, father, nor will I now."

She then proceeded to narrate with all the energy and artlessness of truth, the adventure which that afternoon had befel her; and the cloud that hung on the brow of the child was soon visible on that of the parent. As she proceeded with her little narrative the blood rushed to the temples of the old man, and rising from his chair he paced hastily the old-fashioned, though neatly furnished parlour. " The son of my old friend," exclaimed he, " behave thus to a daughter of Ambrose Bevis! Thinks he then that poverty and the loss of wealth which makes men great in the eyes of the vulgar, has extinguished the virtue of our family! But, I will go to the manor-house, and before the face of his father will I make the ruffian kneel to you, my dear, my insulted daughter, and atone at your feet for the insolence he has been guilty of—Sir Mark shall compel him to that at least; but go on, you have not told me all!"

But it is necessary to the clear understanding of this history that other personages should be introduced on the scene. The object of the old man's wrath, was Litton Weston, the only son of Sir Mark Weston, whose broad lands comprised not only the snug thatched residence occupied by the Bevises, but the surrounding manor of Weston, including the village of Hempstead, though these large possessions like those of many other old families were deeply mortgaged. The good old baronet had been for some months confined to his apartment by his hereditary besieger the gout; a sore loss to the dependents and tenantry of his demesne. The length and severity of this attack, too, gave rise to surmises and misgivings as to the probable conduct of the inheritor of the influence and honours of the venerable and respected Sir Mark Weston. At the period of our story, the young Litton had exhibited little but negative qualities: though somewhat coarse in his amusements and pursuits, his position and rank in the small circle of society of which Weston Hall was the centre, were such as in a great measure to exempt him from the censure of those with whom he associated. That this should produce in a mind inflated with the ideas of self-importance, impatience of restraint and violence where opposed, especially when unchecked by a knowledge of the world, will surprise no one. We have said that his amusements were coarse; on the day to which the narrative of Esther related, the young Litton had, with a few of the sons of the wealthier farmers of the vicinity, who felt proud in the association of the heir of Weston, attended a cock-fight in the neighbourhood of Barking; the excitement of the game, at which Litton's birds had been particularly unsuccessful, together with the pecuniary loss it involved, had by no means calmed his easily ruffled temper. Pride, however, induced him to smother the anger rankling in his bosom, and he had endeavoured to drown his mortification in an unwonted quantity of wine, at an early lunch given by a sporting lord who had been the principal winner on the occasion. Such was the man, who, though unconscious of the inequality of their position, and too proud to allow himself to entertain seriously the thought of an honourable alliance, had become enamoured of the gentle

Esther. It may easily be supposed that he was not likely to find favour in her eyes; indeed the decided coolness with which she received his attentions, had produced an undefined thirst for revenge in his ill-regulated mind, which in such dispositions, is often strangely and incongruously mixed with a strong feeling of affection. In fact, Litton felt his pride rebuked by the maiden dignity of Esther.

Riding slowly along a shady lane, where the beauteous foliage of the trees already exhibited the delightful tints of the fading year, at a turning of the road the subject of his disturbed meditation met his eye, advancing from the village. A moment's pause of hesitation, in which he felt his cheek flushing with a consciousness of the unworthiness of his thoughts towards the fair creature before him—was succeeded by a determination to accost her, with a vague intention of making an honourable proposal, and at once demanding an explicit declaration of consent or rejection; though the possibility of the latter, in the event of his so far committing himself—for such he thought it—scarcely crossed his mind. No sooner, however, did Esther observe him, than, drawing on one side of the narrow road, she showed a desire of avoiding him. This at once decided the excited Litton; hastily dismounting, he advanced towards her, and bowing commenced by some trivial remark. The reply was short, but respectful; and Esther advanced a few steps on her homeward road, at the same time courteously wishing him good day. This was too much for the temper of Litton. Following her with an unsteady step, he rudely seized her by the arm. Turning her face at this unexpected familiarity, Esther perceived with alarm the flushed countenance and angry looks of the half-intoxicated squire.

"Unhand me, sir," said the maiden firmly; "this conduct is disgraceful to you." The confused Litton regarded her with a fixed stare of admiration; and unable to express feelings which were scarcely understood by himself, and in which a desire to mortify the girl for what he deemed her perverseness, and a desire to possess her, struggled for the mastery, he, relaxing not his hold on the arm he still grasped, suddenly passed his other arm round the waist of the affrighted Esther; and, drawing her towards him, endeavoured to force a kiss. "Help," cried she. Struggling with a strength that Litton by no means reckoned on, she disengaged herself from his embrace; and at the same instant a young man bounded over a gate which opened upon the lane, and confronted the surprised squire. Anger was evident on the fine open countenance of the youth; compressing his lips, and raising his right hand, which grasped the three sticks which form the wicket of a cricketer, he advanced towards Litton. A glance showed him how affairs stood, and quick as his perception the blow descended. The terrified Esther rushed towards the new-comer; but too late to interpose. She sunk panting on his arm.

The bleeding and stunned Litton lay before them.

"Oh! Richard! Richard!" exclaimed the maiden, "What have you done! Alas! you have ruined yourself, and——"

"I have chastised a ruffian," said the youth, with an expression of determination in his curled lip, and a fire in his speaking eye, which made Esther tremble lest further mischief should ensue. The prostrate squire raised himself on his elbow, and the youth made a move towards him.

"Get up, coward!" said he. Esther fell at his feet, supplicatingly.

"For heaven's sake—for my sake, dearest Richard! desist—pray—pray—quit this spot, dearest Richard. My behaviour was the cause of it all! It was, it was, indeed!"

The young man thus adjured, casting a look of scorn at his antagonist, which was returned by a revengeful scowl—for Litton, despite his sporting propensities, dared not try a contest with RICHARD PALMER—turned his attention to the half-fainting girl at his feet. Gently raising her, he led her to a bank; and while paying her those delicate attentions which true love and a warm heart prompt, the discomfited squire rose to his feet, and, staggering towards his horse, with some difficulty re-mounted. Before, however, he put spurs to his steed, he turned in his saddle, and addressing Esther, said bitterly :—

"I am obliged to you, madam, for your declaration in favour of that boy there; and I wish you joy of your chosen; but, by ——, both he and you shall rue this day!" Muttering curses between his teeth, he then rode hastily off.

Esther and her lover walked silently to her father's house; he was, however, from home; and the circumstances here related, formed the subject of the evening's conversation, which was partly given at the opening of this chapter.

CHAPTER II.

I saw an aged man upon his bier—
His hair was thin and white, and on his brow
A record of the cares of many a year;
Cares that were ended and forgotten now:
And there was sadness round, and faces bow'd,
And Friendship's tears fell fast, while woman wailed aloud.
                                        Cullen Bryant.

Your eyes drop millstones, where fools' eyes drop tears
I like you, lads.   ——   Shakspere.

IN the midst of an extensive track of gently undulating ground, in the fairest part of the fertile and well-wooded county of Essex, stood the mansion known by the title of Weston Hall. Groves of antique pollards, with here and there irregular and sinuous ridges, or green turfy mounds, bespoke the vast dimensions of its ancient chase or park. On a nearer approach, however, the ground was clothed with magnificent timber; now dipping into smooth dells, or stretching out into level glades, until it suddenly sunk into a deep declivity, at the bottom of whose verdant slope stood the ha! ha! or barrier between the Chase and the Home Park. A slender stream strayed through the lower grounds of this enclosure, having found its way thither from a small reservoir hidden among the plantations to the left; and further in the open ground before the hall, though much below the level of the building—assisted by many springs, and restrained by a variety of natural and artificial embankments—the rivulet expanded into a broad and beauteous sheet of water. Crossed by a rustic bridge, the lake found an outlet to the level meads below; and at that still hour of early morn, you might catch the sounds of the falling waters as they dashed over the artificial rockwork which detained the placid lake at its level; while, far away, obstructed only by a few trees of giant growth, the serpentine meanderings of the slowly flowing stream might be traced glittering like a silver thread in the early sunshine—whose brilliant beams, though scarcely imparting warmth, tinged the many-hued leaves of the tall timber, and penetrating the interstices of their foliage, fell upon the light wreaths of vapour hanging over the surface of the pool. No living objects presented themselves, save a herd of deer, crouched in a covert of brown fern, beneath the shelter of a clump of trees, which stood apart from the main avenue. The

slanting rays tinged the gilded vanes and antique stone-copings of the extensive
and irregular pile, and the sparrow twittered from its ivy-clad walls, as by the
path which led through the noble lines of beech and horse-chestnut, Ambrose
Bevis was seen slowly advancing towards the principal entrance of the mansion.
Well known and respected by the domestics of Sir Mark, the old man passed
onward without question, until he had reached the foot of the principal staircase, where he encountered Stephen, the trusty steward of the baronet.   His
face wore an unusual gravity of aspect; and in answer to Bevis's enquiries
after his master's health, and his expressed desire to see him, he said—

"I fear much, Mr. Bevis, that this bout will prove too much for old Sir
Mark; the doctor has desired him to be kept quiet—yet, as I know he always
wishes to see you, I will take up your name, and return directly."

So saying he reascended the stairs, and shortly coming back, ushered old
Ambrose into the apartment of his master.

Supported by cushions, carefully arranged, to procure for him as much
comfort as his painful complaint would allow him, reclined the invalid: at his
side sat his daughter Madeline.   Bevis could not help observing the ravages
which age and illness had made on the person of his dear friend; and at once
saw, that this was no time to agitate him with a recital of the outrageous
conduct of his son, and to distress him with any addition to the physical
suffering already too visible in every line of his shrunken countenance.   Prefacing his visit with an anxious and sincere enquiry after Sir Mark's health,
which was answered in a somewhat desponding tone, Bevis sat for some
moments in sympathising silence near his suffering friend.   The invalid first
broke silence.

"Friend Ambrose," said he, in a voice whose trembling weakness alarmed
his listeners; "friend Ambrose, I have of late thought much on your circumstances.   We see more clearly the importance of settling our worldly affairs
when confined a prisoner, as I have lately been, so many tedious hours in a
sick chamber.   One, too, that would have been indeed a solitude, had it not
been for my kind Madeline, your amiable daughter, and yourself.   Old Mark
Weston, no longer dining with the foxhunters of his neighbourhood; no longer
frequenting the racecourse or county balls; is little thought of beyond his
paternal acres.   Ambrose, you will forgive me the trouble I am about to impose
on you.   By my will I have left a trifle to your Esther—a trifle more suitable
to my limited means than to her merits; and I have appointed you guardian
to my Madeline here, in the full assurance that you will not let her feel, while
you may live, the loss of a parent."   Sir Mark paused from exhaustion: after
a few moments, he continued:—"This is not a time to indulge in such anti-
cipations; yet I much fear me, that when I am gone, the girl may need a
home more suited to her than a seat at the table of my son and his associates:
and where can I look for one so well as beneath the roof of my old friend
Ambrose Bevis?"

The unwonted exertion of so long a speech was too much for the feeble
state of Sir Mark; and, as he sank back on the pillows, a change came over
his face which so alarmed Madeline that, hastening from the chamber, she at
once called the physician, who was snatching an hour's repose, having passed
the previous day and all the night in attendance on Sir Mark.   The man of
drugs hastened to the chamber.   The sloping sun fell on the features of the
patient as he at once saw, that the disorder having reached the stomach, but a
short time remained ere the possessor of Weston must be summoned to the

great account. Calling for the necessary restoratives, he so far resuscitated the dying man, as to render him capable of understanding questions put to him. The danger, however, being urgent, his son was summoned, which was at once a signal to old Bevis to retire.

Perhaps it may be as well to take a glance at how the time spent in the interview here related was passed by the heir of Weston. Smarting no less with mortification and unsatisfied revenge, than with bodily pain, that unworthy scion of a respected line had spent the greater part of the early morn tossing to and fro in his sleepless bed, devising schemes for the mortification of Esther, and the infliction of his vengeance on her favoured lover. These schemes appeared, at length, to have taken some tangible form, for hastily ringing a bell in his apartment, he desired the servant who answered it to send Dennis Sowton to him directly. Before whose arrival, it may be as well to inform the reader who was the worthy thus summarily called to the councils of his young master.

Dennis Sowton, more generally known by the name of Black Dennis, was the breeder and feeder of cocks to the worthy Mr. Litton. He had the reputation of being the most desperate poacher, previous to his present employment at Weston Hall, which the county could produce; and, unless common rumour greatly belied him, he also gloried in being the most brutal ruffian of the numerous hangers on of the cockfighting gentry. His appearance was certainly as little calculated to make a favourable impression as his character. His countenance, which had always been repulsive, was by no means improved in its expression by the loss of his dexter eye; an accident which had befallen him while practising some of the refined barbarities of his calling on an unfortunate cock. This defect, added to the remaining eye twinkling beneath a shaggy eyebrow which projected far over its deeply-sunk orbit, rendered him by no means a pleasant study for a painter. But as it is more with the deeds than the person of Dennis that we shall have to deal, we will content ourselves with this slight introduction.

He soon after arrived, and the worthy pair quickly appeared on that level which accomplices in villany must ever be. Dennis was the more anxious to replace himself in the good graces of the embryo baronet, from a feeling that the bad success of yesterday's main had rendered his office somewhat precarious. He therefore not only entered eagerly into the grievances of Litton, who did not fail to colour his story with many declarations of his own magnanimity and forbearance towards Palmer, but outstripped his pupil, by proposing several villanous plots, which the other shrunk from even seriously contemplating, much more carrying into effect. As he saw each plan rejected by the more scrupulous Litton, he jestingly threw them aside; laughing at the same time at the exquisite revenge they would afford, if executed; and finishing by a declaration that he himself thought them "too bad," yet could not help being tickled with the idea. At length, a scheme was proposd which both agreed would not only mortify the proud Esther, but by disgracing Richard for ever, compel him to quit his native village, and leave the field open to Litton. Scarcely, however, was this matured, when the latter was called to the chamber of his dying father.

On entering the apartment, the old man feebly turned his glazed eyes on his son: Litton was affected, as much as it was possible such a nature could be, and advancing towards his parent, knelt down beside his sister, as the old man motioned him to do. The nature of the interview may easily be guessed; sympathy sat awkwardly on the low-minded Litton. He had all the inclination, but little of the tact to become a finished hypocrite; and, although mechanically and uneasily submitting to the restraint which so solemn a scene must have impressed on a rightly constituted mind, he spent the major part of the painful minutes which preceeded the death of his parent, in a careful enumeration of the amount of worldly wealth which the dying man would probably leave behind him, varied by pleasant mental digressions as to how he would eclipse this or that sporting neighbour when he should become a baronet. Nor were his reflections occasionally without bitterness, as he thought on the probability of Sir Mark's generosity having led him into silly bequests to sundry grey-headed dependents, who in the estimation of Litton, had certainly been for many years neither useful nor ornamental. He was aroused from this reverie by a deep groan; the dying man's lips moved as though in prayer; feebly stretching forth his hands in a posture of benediction over his offspring, he sunk back; nor did he exhibit from that time forth, any sign of recognising those about him. Gradually as the day waned, his strength and life seemed to depart, and soon after midnight, the good old baronet, without groan or struggle, yielded up his spirit.

The amiable Madeline had been led weeping to her chamber, and none but the heir and the steward remained in the chamber of death. A sudden thought shot across the brain of Litton; he desired Stephen to withdraw. The thought was a strange but by no means an unnatural one, with a son possessing so little true filial affection as Litton Weston. It was more than curiosity; it was selfishness. He had heard hints, during the remonstrances often made by the deceased, that he should not leave Madeline dependent on him. He had, moreover, some lurking distrust of the Bevises; and as this last thought recurred to him, he decided on anticipating the due course of publishing his father's will by at least perusing its contents. More than suspecting the place of its deposit he stepped softly across the apartment to an antiquated cabinet of black oak, wherein, in an iron box, his father was wont to deposit his most valuable documents; yet, before he laid his hands upon its door, he gave a glance of furtive dread at the corpse, as though the unconscious dead might witness the unworthy deed. After a long pause, however, shaking off the fear he could not help feeling creeping over him, he opened the cabinet; before him lay the box; he raised it noiselessly, as though he feared the dead might *hear*; but what was his disappointment at finding it securely locked! He feared to carry it to his chamber, lest old Stephen, to whom it was well known, should observe it in his possession. For some seconds he stood in doubt; at length he opened the casement, and gently throwing the box on the lawn, resolved to examine its contents at a more fitting opportunity. He closed the casement, and after a few minutes of anxious listening, finding all was still, he ventured down the staircase. Making his way to the spot where he had thrown it, what was his surprise after a long and fruitless search, to be able to discover no trace whatever, of the missing box. He stood paralysed; at the loss of such documents, and at such a time too, involved him in a labyrinth of doubt and painful conjecture. It *could not* be lost. Yes! there was the window, and hereabouts it must, to a certainty, have fallen:—"I will search once more." Again and again did he look in the direction of the light which streamed from that silent chamber; and with perspiration on his brow groped, now with his feet, then with his hands, in the direction in which he felt sure he must have thrown it. Wearied both in body and mind, he at length retired to

Turpin before Sir Litton Weston on a charge of burglary.

his chamber with a determination to renew the search as soon as the morning light should permit him. The few remaining hours of darkness were passed by him in uneasy pacings of his chamber: sleep was banished from his fevered brain. Now the events of the day passed his mind's eye in rapid review, anon his busy apprehensions whispered that some fatality would arise from this mysterious disappearance of the unperused documents. He threw himself on the bed, but rest came not; and before the first streak of dawn tinged the east, he was again upon the lawn; but again were his endeavours unsuccessful. No clue appeared to guide him even to a conjecture as to the means by which it had so suddenly and unaccountably been stolen, for that it had fallen into the hands of some dishonest person he had no doubt. Fatigued with seeking, and wearied with conjecture, the agitation of his mind, combined with the weakened state of his body, for his medical attendant had abstracted blood on his return after the previous day's rencontre, laid Litton on a bed of sickness the day after his father's decease.

The news of the death of Sir Mark soon spread through the neighbourhood, and many was the tearful eye, and pious aspiration of the elder tenantry on his estate, as they related to their children, or younger relatives, anecdotes of the worth and virtues of the deceased.

———————

No. 2.

CHAPTER III.

Ah, not in youth's most blissful hours,
    Are perfect joys displayed;
They are but like our childhood's flowers,
    Bright—but ordained to fade.
A lovely, yet ephemeral wreath,
That's faded by stern winter's breath.   —Anonymous.

————Yet be careful:
Detraction's a bold monster, and fears not
To wound the fame o' the worthy, if it find
Out any blemish in their lives to work on.
But I'll be plainer with you: had the people
But learned to speak, but what even now I saw,
Their malice out of it would raise an engine
To overthrow your honour.   —Fatal Dowry

THE funeral day of Sir Mark Weston arrived, and though every search was made by old Stephen, the legal adviser who had drawn the document, and other confidential friends of the late baronet, no will could be found. Sir Litton, confined to his bed—a fact which redounded highly to the credit of his filial affection among the numerous friends of the family—expressed no feigned anxiety at the absence of the important parchment; though, as may easily be supposed, he was cautiously silent as to the real cause of its disappearance. Nevertheless, though haunted with a dread of its discovery, he was in some measure consoled by the reflection that, in consequence of the intestacy of his father, he inherited, unquestioned, the whole of his property. Curiosity, for few felt much concerned in the matter, however, soon subsided, and as days and weeks wore on, Sir Litton became easy on the subject, and all enquiry ceased.

It is strange and melancholy to reflect how the death of an individual frequently changes the aspect of the affairs of all who surrounded him, and most of those who were his dependents. But few months elapsed from the death of Sir Mark, ere the amiable Madeline quitted the seat of her ancestors to reside in a home more congenial to her taste and habits than that of which her brother had now become lord and master. Old Bevis too, scorning to remain under an obligation to one by whom he had been so deeply insulted, and more than suspecting, from his last conversation with Sir Mark, that underhand measures had been resorted to in order to defeat his kind intentions towards Madeline, his daughter, and himself, quitted the neighbourhood. Indeed the pleasant dwelling he had so long occupied he could no longer think of retaining on the terms on which he had held it of its former proprietor; and having about this time received a small accession of property by the death of a relation he removed to a distant county.

In short, the notable scheme hinted at in the preceding chapter would have fallen still-born from the brains of its contrivers had not the native malignity of Black Dennis decreed that so "excellent a plot" should not sink into oblivion. His malicious nature exulted in the sufferings of his own species as well as the brute race; indeed, were it not that we should asperse the character of the brute creation, we should have classed the worthy Dennis among the latter. They at least connect not with their cruelty a consciousness of so doing; nor do they wanton in barbarities from a demoniac joy in their infliction.

Not so with Dennis; to him the sufferings of brute or man was a luxury, and the knowledge of his instrumentality in their pangs, imparted a stern satisfaction, a pleasurable emotion, to his soul. But if his plans were unscrupulously wicked, there was a caution and an ingenuity in their execution, which displayed talents for villany of no ordinary stamp. Other motives also spurred him on. Richard Palmer, though a stripling and much his inferior in weight and strength, was, by common consent, esteemed the best cricketer, runner, leaper, and single-stick player in the village. His superior prowess in the three first named exploits, Dennis, though galled by the praises of merit of any kind, might quietly have conceded; but in the last there lay a sting, which roused his petty malignity. In more than one bout of this sort, had the active Richard (for in these village sports there was little distinction of persons) discomfited the wily and spiteful Dennis. It is true that on each of these occasions Dennis had succeeded in giving his opponent an ugly or an unfair blow, but the result of their last encounter had not only left him with a broken crown, but in the rage of the moment he had attempted so foul and desperate a mode of revenge, that the spectators had, by common consent, not only excluded him from their diversions, but resolved that he should not on any future occasion be allowed to enter the arena. This exclusion from the only sport, except cockfighting, in which he took any delight, rankled sorely in the bosom of Dennis, and he thirsted for retaliation. And now having given our readers some insight into the feelings of this amiable personage, we will turn to the object of his machinations, Richard Palmer.

RICHARD PALMER,* or as he was more familiarly called by his associates, Dare-devil Dick, had resided from his youth in the pleasant village of Hempstead in Essex, under the protection of a widowed aunt. He was the only son of Captain Edward Palmer, a volunteer, who fell bravely fighting in that extraordinary exploit of the great Earl of Peterborough, the taking of the castle of Monjuich, near Barcelona, during the War of the Succession in Spain. Thus deprived in the first years of infancy of a father's care, Richard grew under the too partial eye of an indulgent mother. His widowed parent never recovered the shock of her early bereavement, and, after lingering three years as a valetudinarian, she was removed to a happier life. It cannot be supposed that the young Richard experienced much restraint during his first years from one whose whole soul was centred in this sole remaining pledge of a beloved husband, and Richard became a spoilt and wayward child. On this event he was adopted by his aunt, on the mother's side, with whom he now lived. She was the relict of a once-wealthy grazier in Essex, whose property having been invested in the notorious South Sea scheme, had, with the exception of a mere trifle. been engulfed in the wide spreading ruin of that monster-

* The meagre biographies in the Newgate Calendar, and some other similar publications, represent our hero as RICHARD TURPIN, the son of a butcher of good reputation, at Hempstead in Essex. The name by which he was known, to which he pleaded on his trial, and which was his real one, was RICHARD PALMER. The sobriquet of Dick Turpin, was a travelling *alias*, taken after his exploits on the highway had made him somewhat notorious. There is no trace of any Richard Turpin among the registers of baptisms at Hempstead, but of the Palmer family we find many. Richard Palmer, the hero of our story, was born in the year 1705; and the butcher, or rather grazier, to whom his birth has been popularly attributed was his uncle. His paternity is not quite so clear, and we therefore deem it by no means improper to assign him a parentage equally as authentic and more probable than his reputed one.

speculation, which swallowed the estates, the fortunes, the savings of so many thousands of families.

With this parent, for such she might be properly considered, he found himself, so far as the wishes and caprices of childhood were concerned, as little checked as before. Can it then surprise any one, that he grew up a wayward and a wilful boy. Yet his gaiety of temper, attractive exterior, candid manners, fearless daring, and boundless generosity of feeling, made him a general favourite, and blinded completely his partial associates to the vices into which all virtues carried to excess are, under the conditions of our frail humanity, too prone to merge themselves. Wherever the weak was oppressed, Richard Palmer was ready, with the chivalrous devotion of a knight of old, to range himself against the aggressor, and so far did this spirit sometimes carry him, as to involve him in very awkward dilemmas. Of an earnest and vivacious temperament, Richard was endued with high feeling and sensibility. Deprived of a mother before he could know half the value of her care and love—before he could even appreciate the depth of her gushing tenderness—her smile beamed only in his recollection: but the absence of this reality conjured up in his ardent mind—possessed from infancy with but one fanciful image—a phantom such as haunts the dreamer's brain of some scarce defined object of his love. This unreal idol, peopling his imagination with a thousand visions of smiles, tears, and looks of love, dwelt on as the memories of childhood, and as fondly cherished, assumed, as manhood grew upon him, a substance, a personification, a shape distinct and positive, and when in the person of the beauteous Esther Bevis this object of his idolatry seemed to stand before him, can we wonder that the long treasured emotions of years should gush forth; that he should devote himself to her, and that she, in maiden simplicity and single heartedness, should accept him?

The departure of Ambrose Bevis and his daughter from the neighbourhood of Weston Hall was one of those events, which, as far as the feelings and self-knowledge of Richard were concerned, added years to his experience. His first impulse on learning from Esther the determination of her father, was to declare his intention of accompanying her, but he was at once checked by the recollection of his dependent condition. This difficulty no sooner presented itself to its full extent, than he at once felt how the visions of his romantic mind, which had continually deluded itself with notions of retired enjoyment with the mistress of his heart, were crushed and shattered by the slightest contact with the stern realities of this working-day world. In short, he awoke for the first time to the consciousness that he was without the position in society or the worldly means to realise his hope of wedding Esther, and his was too generous a mind to entertain even for a moment the sordid notion of marrying her without possessing the power of bestowing on her the comforts of the home from which she must be severed. Yet, young and ardent, though such reflections might intrude, they were quickly expelled by the air-built castles of his enthusiastic temperament. He resolved to earn a position among men which should make him not unworthy of the hand of Esther; and she, artless and unversed in the thorny paths of worldly trials, could not allow herself to doubt of the success of one who, in her eyes, possessed such unquestioned superiority over his fellows. His first impulse was towards the service in which his father had fallen; a natural bias it is true, but one from which not only the gentle Esther attempted to dissuade him, but to which his foster-mother was decidedly averse. Even these, however, would hardly have prevailed with him—for his resolutions when once taken, seldom wavered—had not circumstance, of which we are the mere puppets, ordered otherwise. On the evening of the day preceding their departure, Richard was walking slowly in the direction of the residence they were so soon to quit, when he encountered at a turn of the lane Black Dennis. Since last he had the honour of meeting this personage, the fortunes of Dennis had much improved. The newly made Baronet had, during his illness, decided that cockfighting was beneath the dignity of the possessor of Weston; and to this conclusion his want of success had not a little contributed. Black Dennis had in consequence become the head ranger of Weston Park, to the exclusion of an old and trusty servant, who, though holding the appointment, had been long incompetent to the active discharge of its duties.

The importance of Dennis, as well as his command of money, (for something considerable he well knew might be made out of such an office,) had wonderfully increased. Those who knew his character did not scruple to whisper that not a little of the venison and game of Sir Litton would find a market in Leadenhall, though few dared publicly to say so.

"Well, master Palmer," said Dennis, " so the old gemman and his darter, I hear be about to quit; may I be so bold, though perhaps it's no business of mine, to ax if so be you're a going with them?"

Black Dennis seemed to hesitate for a few moments, as if he doubted in what way his proposition might be received, before he continued, " Well, master Palmer, there are those that is rough outside as is none the worse inside than the smoother ones. I al'ays liked you, and if there's any way I can be of use to you, even though it's a matter of a few pounds or so, for I have them by me, you shan't find Dennis backward."

Palmer coloured deeply at this proposal; and, as he looked upon the ground, half angry and half pleased, his wily persecutor's single optic gleamed with something like satisfaction. He of course knew Palmer's temper too well, to suppose that he would accept his offer, yet aware also of the warmth of his gratitude, he doubted not that this cheap manifestation of his goodwill would purchase his favourable opinion, and render him slow of belief of any reports which might reach his ears to his (Dennis's) detriment.

The result showed the correctness of his views of the simplicity of Richard, who felt humiliated at his position; and though discarding the idea of laying himself under any obligation to such a man as Dennis, he at once fell into the snare.

Catching him by the hand, though somewhat vexed, he said, " Why Dennis, you're about the last man I should have asked, so don't think I'm going to flatter you; yet I value none the less your generous offer. And though I can't accept of it, I hope I shall one day repay you as if I had."

Their conversation had proceeded thus far, and Dennis appeared about to offer his services in some other shape, when Esther appeared slowly advancing towards them.

"Two is good company when three is none;" said the rough Dennis, following the direction of Palmer's eyes, " and so, Master Richard, with your leave, I'll make myself scarce: good day t'ye, and happy may you both be; though I daresay you'll take care of that."

So saying, he walked away, inwardly exulting at, though despising, what he termed the " greenness" of the young Richard.

The lovers approached each other—the eye of Esther was filled with tears and her look was melancholy.   Richard took her hand silently, and kissed her forehead, while a tremulousness in his voice betrayed the working of his mind.   "Esther, dear Esther," said he, while she leaned on him for support, "though I hold you in my arms,—though each nerve within me speaks that you are present—though, when I gaze upon you I see the same affectionate look you always wear—though I see and feel, and know all this—a dark oppression weighs upon my heart.   It is not superstition—but something tells me that we shall not meet again like this.   I know it is wrong for me to speak thus, and at such a moment—but some irresistible impulse impels me.   Will you promise that when —" and he paused, as the thought of the unworthy doubts he was expressing rushed across his mind.

"Richard," said the maiden, relieving his arm of the burthen it had borne, while her bosom heaved and her cheek flushed; "do you ask me if I will promise? do you then doubt me?   Oh, Richard, you do not know me if you think a thousand promises could render your memory more cherished until we shall meet again."

The youth felt ashamed, though gratified; but the very temperament of our hero forbad him to love without perpetually tormenting himself with doubts, which, though for a time dispelled, involuntarily recurred, especially when, as at the present moment, the thought of a long separation presented itself.

"Pardon me, dearest Esther, I will no more pain you with my doubts.   Yet you must not refuse me one favour; promise me —" and he again checked himself—then suddenly, as if discarding the train of thought he had been pursuing, abruptly said, " Esther, I am tormented day and night with the thought that we must part—I intend quitting home shortly, and, —" the maiden listened with breathless attention—"should I be successful in gaining a position in society; will you consent to be my bride?"

She withdrew not the hand which trembled within his, as she replied, " Richard, you know my heart well enough to spare me the pain of saying more than that I hope you will, before we quit the village, see my father.   He respects you, I know—he has seen more of the world than either of us, and loves us well—you'll speak to him won't you,—dearest Richard?"   The last words were added in a tone of gentle entreaty, for the mention of her father at once suggested the painful reflection of his own dependency, which he naturally euough expected would be prominently set forth by old Ambrose, and Dick had no taste for lengthy exordiums.   His countenance, however, cleared, to the inexpressible joy of Esther, when he reflected that the consent he was about to solicit, was contingent on the circumstance of his worldly success, on which his sanguinary temperament fully calculated.   But the conversations of lovers are proverbially uninteresting to all but those who, in legal phrase, may be termed the parties to the suit, and we shall at once cut short our report of the pleadings, by stating, that Richard assented to the lady's proposition, and that the result of the interview with old Ambrose, though a nonsuit for the present, by no means excluded the plaintiff from the chance of moving for a new trial on some future day.

They departed; and with them departed all the gaiety and spring of young Richard's disposition.   He at once became moody and absorbed; his walks were solitary; and his former frank and hearty manner exhibited occasional glimpses—more especially when his privacy was intruded on—of the fierceness to which we have elsewhere alluded.   Not a few of his companions resented this change as a sort of affront, and studiously avoided him; but if they did so, Richard certainly retaliated, by not only not seeking them, but by repelling their advances to reconciliation, and their attempts, by raillery or otherwise, to draw him from his unsociableness, with angry asperity.

The popularity which Richard had hitherto enjoyed was, like that of greater men on the theatre of the busy world, fast verging to utter extinction—if it had not already expired—when another feature in his behaviour attracted the attention of the gossips of Hempstead.

Of late, his journeys to London had been more frequent than formerly; added to this, it was reported that he had been frequently met at a late hour wandering through the grounds which formed the Chase of Weston Hall. These rumours, which owed their origin to Dennis and his associates, were of course exaggerated, as the disposition for idle gossip, or the love of slander, actuated their retailers, till the unconscious Richard—for those who are belied are ever the last to hear it—had actually, without knowing it, earned the reputation of an accomplished poacher. To confirm this impression Dennis had many admirable opportunities: springes were set, and hares destroyed, in various parts of the grounds adjoining the path which Richard often took, and which led to the grounds and house lately occupied by the Bevises.

There would he sit, wrapped in speculation as to his future career in life, and drawing fancied pictures of his success—forming a back-ground to each varying scene of domestic felicity and love, the principal figure, of course, being Esther Bevis. Need we say, that the air-paintings of one so inexperienced, partook much more of the ideal simplicity of the golden age, than the harsh unpleasant truthfulness of sketches from real life.

But we must hasten onward. Two or three months had scarcely elapsed when Dennis thought he might safely commence operations on his rival, for in such light did he view Richard. Returning through the Chase one moonlight night, accompanied by his dog—a retriever, which he highly prized as the gift of old Mr. Bevis—what was his surprise, the animal having lingered somewhat behind, on a sudden to hear the sharp report of a fowlingpiece, succeeded by a loud and painful yelp from his four footed favourite. He retraced his steps; but scarcely had he emerged into the moonlight, when two of Sir Litton's gamekeepers sprung upon him.

"So, ho!" exclaimed one of them, grasping him roughly by the collar, "who have we here? young Palmer, by the living jingo! What, so it's you as lays down all these wires, is it? I'll tell you what—"

Astonishment at this rude seizure had for the moment held Palmer motionless. The imputation conveyed by the latter part of the speech of the man was, however, too much for his hasty temper; suddenly disengaging himself from his grasp, he lent the keeper a blow on the head with such hearty good will, as laid him on his mother earth. His companion instantly threw himself on Richard. He was a stout burly-built fellow, and the impetus with which he commenced his attack at once brought himself and the young man to the ground together. Palmer was undermost; and the ruffian, who was practised in encounters of this sort, twisting his hand in his antagonist's neckcloth, and placing his knee on his stomach, called loudly to his companion for something to bind their prisoner's hands. At this juncture Black Dennis approached.

"Hollo," cried he, "what the devil are you firing for at this time of night, when you know how ill master is? I'm d—d if I don't think you're gone mad. Why, Bob," looking at the prostrate form of Palmer as the two were busily engaged in binding his hands, and pretending not to recognise him, "what the devil have you got there? I thought you was out a dog-shooting by the cursed yelping I heard."

"Why, I'll tell you who we've got, though I'm thinking you'd hardly guess it," replied the keeper, panting; "it's master Dare-devil-Dick, as has been a setting of all these snares; but I think we shall stop some of his journeys to Lunnun, for some time to come. We'll a-learn him to strike a justice's keepers on his own grounds."

"There's some mistake about this here, depend on't," said Dennis; "I think I've a-known master Dick too long to believe as he's turned a poacher. No, no! If so be as master Dick had done anything of the kind it would have been something of a better sort; a good fat buck, or so. I'll 'gage he'd never bemean himself to *wire a long*.* There's some mistake in this business, I'll pound it. Hows'ever, Sir Litton 'll have an opportunity of settling that matter. What did you see him a doing of?"

"Enough of all conscience, Mr. Dennis," replied the keeper; "when I and Robert first came out this evening, master Dick here, had only just gone by along this here way,—as we heared from the boy Sparks, he often does—well, you knows what queer things people ha' said o' late, so we quietly follows him, but he warn't in sight by no means; but going along, what should I and Joe see but three or four wires, and presently two or three more, near aways to where he had just gone along. Ho, ho, says I, here's mischief and no mistake: we must look sharp after this young gentleman. So we keeps watch till he comes back, as sure enough he did just now, and we sees his dog—and nicely he's teached him to do it, let him alone for that—stay behind, and presently on he comes agin with a summut in his mouth; and Joe, here, though I told him to wait and see what comed of it, couldn't stand the temptation, so he let's fly, and drops the dog: whereupon my gentleman begins a walking back the way he come, as cool as if nothin' had happened; we collars him, and a pretty smartish bout we've had on it I reckon, for he fights like a born devil."

During this recital, the rage of Palmer may well be conceived. He felt his heart rising to his throat, and clenching his teeth firmly, as if he feared to trust himself to speak, maintained a dogged and sullen silence. The keeper whom he had knocked down, left the party, and shortly returned, bringing with him the slain dog, and the hare which the animal had been carrying.

"See here, sir," said he, anxious to retaliate the blow he had received—"here's evidence enough, I should think, to say nothing of how he tried to get off, and the way he has marked me."

"Well," said Dennis coolly, and assuming the air of an impartial arbitrator, "I'm sorry to see this; but I should like to hear what you have to say to it master Palmer."

"You promised," said Dick, "that you would serve me if you could. Will you do it now?"

"Why, I can't exactly say, master Richard," said he; "but if it's nothing unreasonable, I'll do it."

"Unbind me, then," said Dick, "and take my word that I am innocent—however much appearances are against me. It is not that I fear the charge; but for more reasons than one I would wish not to come before Litton Weston: he and I have a score to settle, and —"

* Snare a hare.

Dick Turpin's conflict with Black Dennis.—See Chap. IV.

"Well, strike me sarcy, if that an't about the most modest speech I've heared this many a-day. Litton Weston, too; why I'd have him afore master if it was for nothing but forgetting to put a handle to his name. You don't think, though, master Dick, as we're green enough to let you go with such axing—and so much civility too, as you does it with?"

"Leave him to me, and hold your silly prate, will you?" interposed Dennis in affected anger; "go about your business—I'll see to the prisoner. D'ye hear me?" added Dennis in an authoritative tone, as the men's curiosity made them linger.

"Oh, very well!" muttered the man who had been knocked down, "if you like to try a bout with him single-handed, it's no business of mine; though," he added, turning to his companion, as they walked away into the shadow of the trees, "I should ha' thought he had had enough of that afore this time—but conceit's as good as physic for a fool; and now Dennis is his worship's head ranger, perhaps he thinks he's stronger—but he may find out his mistake though, for I'll pound it Dick don't get lugged quietly afore his old friend Sir Litton."

No. 3.

The two now stood alone. The pale moonshine gleamed on the angry face of the fastbound Richard, while the cunning Dennis kept the play of his malignant features concealed by standing with his back to the light. He was the first to break silence.

"This is a bad job, master Richard," said he, throwing as much friendship into his tone as his harsh voice was susceptible of; "a cursed bad job indeed. You see my duty to Sir Litton is sadly put to it to oblige you; for it 'ud be as much as my place is worth if it was known as I shut my eyes to such proceedings."

Palmer's brow burnt at the imputation, and he interrupted him by saying—

"Do you believe those lying scoundrels, then? Do you think that I am so sunk as to rob any one, much less my chief enemy? Why, Dennis, if you think so, then—"

"Softly, softly, master Richard," said the other, "you picks a man up afore he is down: didn't I say as I couldn't believe, and what's more, I wouldn't— as you'd so little a mind as to snare such things as that;" and he kicked the hare, which lay at his foot, with contempt: "but you don't half know me yet. I'd let you go this moment and chance it, if I thought them chattering fellows wouldn't let it come to the ears of Sir Litton."

"I should be sorry," said Richard, "to get you into any trouble on my account; but it is not fear of this charge—for I despise Sir Litton more than I fear him—that makes me so anxious not to go before him; I have another reason, which I'll tell you at another time, that will make me your debtor for life, if you will prevent my being placed in his power, by this unfortunate combination of circumstances. Will you release me? I believe I never let myself down to ask a favour so earnestly before. You will do no injustice to your master—for I call God to witness that I am innocent."

"I never was counted back'ards in doing anything I was bent on, much less in serving a friend. You shan't be taken before him, though;" and the scoundrel without another word began with teeth and hands to unfasten the rope which sorely galled the wrists of Palmer.

"There you are," said he, as he drew the loosened cord through his hands, "I don't want the humbug of being thanked, so you may spare your breath. I don't half like those meddling fellows knowing about it, though. I wish I'd ha' come first across you, and then all this wouldn't have happened. But what's done can't be undone, and it's no use fretting."

Richard and his *friend* walked from the spot whilst thus engaged in conversation, and before they had proceeded many yards Dennis was not only master of every circumstance of the encounter between the unsuspecting Richard and the baronet, but had received it embellished with all the colouring which the indignation of the excited narrator could supply. After warmly sympathising with him, and repeatedly shaking hands, they separated at the outer boundary of the Chase; and while Richard made his way homeward in no very enviable frame of mind, Dennis bent his steps towards his lodge, and having, as if by accident, encountered the two keepers, he so contrived to falsify the conversation he had just held with Palmer, as to leave on their minds no doubt of his guilt. "Let him alone," said Dennis in conclusion, "he hasn't half run his course yet. I'll have an eye on him, though, and never trust me if we shan't find him better worth taking before long's over his head. I knows these things well enough: when once a young fellow

Young Palmer apprehended for Poaching.   *Page* 19

CHAPTER IV.

West of this place, down in the neighbour bottom,
Brings you to the place ;
But, at this hour, the house doth keep itself—
There's none within.   —— As You Like It. Act 3. Sc 1.

There's no suspicion of my treason—Nothing !
The saint and devil differ in man so little.
Your open barefac'd mortals look as simply
As naked dogges, or new shorn sheep, exposed
To th' injuries and scorn of all mankind :
But I, like visiting angels, kill unseen,
Here I lye rounde and close as sleeping serpents –
He that treads on me feels before he sees me.
                    The Sacrifice, a Tragedy, by Sir Francis Fane. 1686.

Is there a land whose face is studded with happier homes ; whose **meadows**
are greener, and whose homesteads *were* (for it is more than problematical if
many *are* still unchanged) more replete with all the fireside-comforts which
make life pleasant, than " merrie Englaunde ?"   The farm-houses of our
grandsires are, alas! now nearly gone—one by one have they vanished.   **The**
sturdy " franklein," who inhabited the dwelling and tilled the acres of his
forefathers, who could say to his landlord, with the independent spirit of
competence,

The farm I now hold on your honour's estate,
Is the same that my grandfather tilled—

is now the being of bygone days.   The " small farmer" is now—but we are
not about to write an essay on the causes which have led to these changes,
nor is it our province to speculate on their probable results—suffice it
for us that they *have* taken place.   At the period to which we refer, **the**
house of a farmer, " well to do," possessed not a few of those luxuries and
embellishments now *never* found in the naked and impoverished dwellings of
their descendants, the labourers in " the big barn," as Cobbett has aptly
termed them, of the monopolising landholder, whom the facilities of modern
intercommunication has enabled to sink to one dead level of misery and semi-
pauperism ; among these happy homes, few exhibited more of comfort and
independence than the dwelling and surrounding lands of farmer Lawrance.
The neatly-kept enclosures, the well-trimmed hedges, the stackyard with its
stoutly-built stands, each burthened with its load of wheat—the substantially
built barns, and lastly, the farmhouse itself—which, though straggling in its
outward appearance, possessed within an abundance of " creature comforts"—
all spoke, even amid the desolation of winter, the wealth of its occupier.
    It was market day at Romford, and farmer Lawrance with the more **active**
and able-bodied of the servants who assembled around the substantial **fare**
daily spread in his spacious oak-beamed kitchen, were with him at the fair.
The only occupants of the house on the evening of this day, were an ancient
dame, the aunt of the farmer, and two servant-maids of his household.   Lawrance himself had taken the chair at the market-dinner ; and his labourers,
well knowing the convivial habits of their master, had resolved on enjoying
a few of the early hours of the winter's evening among their associates, **the**
farm-servants of the surrounding agriculturists.
    The short-lived sun of a winter's day had set with blood-red hue, and **was**
soon followed by the rising gusts of a sullen and stormy night ; the hearth **was**

piled and the blazing log crackled merrily; the old dame sat in the chimney-corner, and, in the social and unaffected communion which in by-past days fostered and strengthened the love between master and servant, was by turns amusing and terrifying the maidens with the legendary lore with which our unread grandames used to beguile the hours of their weariness, when a stealthy tap at the window, placed close beside the door, startled the trio. Margery, whose love of flirtation had kept more than one rustic heart in a state of "suspense and doubt, worse than a knowledge of the worst," at once concluded it must be the signal of one of her many admirers. With a rising blush, she hesitatingly inquired of her mistress whether she should unbar the door.

"It's Gregory come home, I shouldn't wonder," said the dame, "I'll warrant you won't see Tummus," for so she styled her nephew, "this side of ten; he's getting on bravely just now; and I wish we'd one of the lads at home, I'd send him off on Ball to meet him; for he'll be tidyish noisy and queer, if nothing worse, before he leaves the Bull."

The knocking was gently and cautiously repeated. Margery rose. "Go along, wench," said the dame, "I daresay Gregory has something to bring him home so soon," and observing the colour on the girl's cheek, she added, "what the dickens are you maundering about, eh? The lad's a likely lad, ay—ay—and old as you think me, I an't lost my sight altogether. I remember when I was young—ugh—ugh—" and a tickling cough seized the old lady at the recollection, "I remember—ugh—ugh—but open the door, wench. When I was young—"

The recital of the old lady's reminiscences was cut short; for Margery having lifted the stout oaken bar, which formed the only fastening of the door, from its staple, gave a faint scream, and scarcely had it reached the ears of the feeble dame, before three stout-looking men, with their faces covered with crape, abruptly entered. The first seized the astonished Margaret by the wrists; the second, without uttering a word, presented two pistols at the affrighted girl and her no less astonished mistress; while the third, as if well acquainted with the secrets of the place, went directly through the apartment, and made his way to the parlour. In a corner of this apartment, the only one in the house which boasted of a carpet, stood a japanned corner-cupboard—which, when occasionally left open, as it sometimes *accidentally* was, during the stay of some visitor on whom the Lawrence family desired to produce an impression—revealed upon its shelfs the then rare and costly luxury of a diminutive tea-service of blue and white China. Its upper shelf also displayed a capacious punch-bowl of the same transparent earth, on whose rounded sides and many-coloured pigments the eyes of many a rustic had rested with admiration. Patches of dull-looking gold, blue-boats, ditto temples, and ditto lakes, most unartistically contrasted with the lilac face and pale-red dresses of a set of most Chinese-looking personages, whose sexes it would have been difficult to have discriminated, but that the fairer portion of the pig-eyed, footless, company had each a slave as ugly and as epicene as herself, holding a parasol, as high as the heavens, over her head, to screen her delicate complexion from the evershining and shadowless sun. There a nymph (attended by a slave) was being handed into a boat as long as her leg by a swain also in petticoats, who considerately stood, so admirably was the law of perspective observed, on an island of blue about a mile distant from the object of his attentions; while here in the foreground, with the listless sang-froid of an oriental, a single boatman navigated the dry land with a small bark containing a parish-church, a few barns, a pagoda, and some other light miscellaneous articles ; and, to complete the impression produced by these wonders of " far Cathay" on the unsophisticated mind, aloft in air wheeled two mighty doves, each larger than a pagoda, junk, or island, intended by the cunning limner to image forth, by their endearments, the tender feelings of the loving couple below : the kind spectator was to suppose them billing and cooing—though their open beaks, mighty proportions, expanded wings, and general action, left matter-of-fact persons in doubt whether they were about to kiss or to swallow each other. But we have really forgot, in our reverie on the punch-bowl, the critical point at which our narrative has arrived.

" If we have any fault it is digression ;"

and as the consciousness of a failing is said to be half way towards its cure, we will proceed.

The uninvited guest strode, as we have before said, toward the corner cupboard, and found it securely locked. This was evidently no more than he expected, for thrusting his hand into his coatpocket he produced a jemmy, and at a single wrench the treasures we have described presented themselves to his view. He had certainly small veneration for the arts, as he scarcely deigned, as the gleam of his dark-lantern flashed across their glazed surfaces, to notice the Chinese rarities above described. A basin and a small round teapot—the fountain and scource of scandal to our grandmothers—for even they, good souls, talked scandal, were passed unheeded : there was, however, one which contained that " within which passed show." Gently raising the edge of the huge bowl, the robber, as if well acquainted with the *locale*, peered cautiously beneath ; a grin of subdued exultation stole across all of his face that was visible, as a small, cracked, and dusty vase met his view. This was clearly the object of his search : he clutched it, and placing his lantern on a table close by, reversed it on his other hand ; the dull metallic chink of gold met his ear, and, after a moment balancing the small red canvass bag, as if to ascertain its weight, he placed it in his breeches pocket, to which he gave an approving slap. Resuming his lantern and his search, he rummaged every corner of the receptacle, transferring to his ample coatpockets various articles, such as silver-spoons, of antique pattern and workmanship, the gifts of godfathers and godmothers to various scions of the Lawrence family ; two silver-cups, testimonials of respect from the neighbouring farmers to some of the Lawrences for services duly recorded thereon ; and finally, he helped himself from the mantelpiece to an old fashioned family watch, of about the dimensions, both in diameter and circumference, of a garden turnip. He was evidently no common thief, for he deigned not to set a foot upon the stairs, or to search the upper rooms for anything they might contain ; but, as if he had satiated his organ of " acquisitiveness," hastily returned to his companions in the kitchen, and after sundry threatening gestures of most alarming and expressive pantomime—in which presenting pistols, and drawing the edge of the hand across the throat, in most melodramatic style, formed the principal features—they bound the hands and feet of the three females separately, and finally tying them together, left the house, without even the courtesy of wishing a good night.

The unpleasant taxgatherers had not long departed, when Gregory did indeed return, pretty well fuddled ; and after knocking at the window, as the other gentry had done before, was not a little bothered at getting no answer.

The fact was that the repetition of the ominous sound at once took away the power of utterance from the fettered trio, whose fears whispered them that it was a second visit from the burglars, who had come back, doubtless, to finish the job by cutting their throats, at the least, if not something worse. Gregory at length grew tired of knocking, and never did reprieve sound more welcome in the ear of a criminal than his rough exclamation in a voice thick and guttural from the ale he had drank of—

"I'm dang'd if I'll put up wi' this here! If noobody else com'd, 'a think Margery mought. Come oot some on ye, will ye, or dang'd if I don't bust in the door."

Margery was the first to find her tongue, and the astonished serving-man opened his mouth with amazement, as she cried, "Oh Gregory, we ha' bin ruined! robbed! and undone—we're a' tied together and can't stir for the life on us! Oh Gregory, the robbers! Get in at the window, Gregory, do 'ee— Oh! oh! oh my poor wristes! Oh! oh! oh!"

The fuddled Gregory could make but little of this adjuration, save and except the request to get in at the window: he therefore proceeded to the back part of the premises and speedily effected an entrance, and proceeding to the kitchen he saw a sight which effectually sobered him for the rest of the night. Bound hand and foot, as we have before described them, lay his mistress, sweetheart, and the serving-wench; while another cord, fastened to those which bound each of their legs, was made fast to the stout leg of the oaken dresser. Drawing his jack-knife he soon released them, and after a thorough search of the premises, during which two of his fellows arrived, it was resolved that the two should convey the alarm of the robbery to Sir Litton, as the nearest justice of the peace, and raise the country in pursuit of the thieves, while Gregory should hasten to Romford to apprise farmer Lawrance of the disaster. The females, however, stoutly objected to being left alone, and their pertinacity not only occasioned considerable delay, but ended in an alteration of arrangements; by which Gregory, at the suggestion of Margery, remained at home as a body guard, while the remainder of the forces were so divided as to be rendered little more than useless, seeing that neither of them would have cared, had even the opportunity presented itself, to venture, single-handed, on molesting the housebreakers.

The messenger who had been sent to the market-town returned in due time with the farmer, who having sworn himself sober, and twenty times ordered the saddle on his best horse, and as many times been told th at his orders were already executed, finished by deciding that, all had been done as could be done, by sending to Sir Litton and the headborough. Then, consoling himself by declaring he was "glad it was no worse," and such like scraps of home-grown philosophy, interlarded sandwich-fashion with some scores of most unphilosophic oaths, he called for his pipe, and seating himself by the fire with a humming tankard of brown October at his elbow, ordered the womankind to bed, at the same time announcing his intention of sitting up to receive the reports of the scouts he had dispatched.

We must now return to Richard Palmer, of whom we have too long lost sight. It has before been stated that the spot he usually selected for his meditations was an arbour in the garden belonging to the house of the Beavises. One evening, on approaching the entrance to this favourite spot, he observed two strangers advance towards him from the side of the rustic house, who, before he had time to recover his surprise, seized him each by an arm, and dexterously slipping a pair of handcuffs on his wrists, then, but not till then, condescended to inform him that they were officers.

" D'ye see, young gentleman ;" said the elder, a red-faced and somewhat corpulent looking fellow, with twinkling eyes and legs bandy as a turnspit : " D'ye see, young gentleman, as we Lunnoners are awake to a trick or two! You're a likely lad though, but rather soft, I'm thinking, to come so soon arter the *swag.* You didn't think as Lunnon traps was as blind as yer yokels, did yer ? I fancy as how you'd better have made it right with us, and then, p'rhaps—"

" With what crime am I charged?" said Palmer : " you shall smart for this, you scoundrels ;" and struggling he in vain twisted his manacled wrists.

" Soho ! gently does it ;" said the one who had before spoken. " Don't be so restive, my trump ; I've taken many a better man nor you, clever as you think yerself.—Wo ho !—softly!"

The two officers pressed his elbows close to his sides, while the assistant passed a cord behind his back and pinioned them.

" It's no go !" continued he, " playing the innocent ; we're too downey, my cove ; so put us fly to what you've done with the rest on it, and, may be, you may get another squeak, if so be as the wictim is tender-hearted."

While thus speaking, the two London thieftakers were joined by the Hempstead headborough and his assistant, and the former, consigning their prisoner to the care of his country associates, on whose countenances pity for his condition was legibly written, proceeded at once to dig up the earth which formed the floor of the arbour. Richard regarded them with fixed attention : the ground had evidently been recently disturbed, and the whole truth at once flashed upon his mind, when the officer, pulling a small bundle from the hole, the envelope of which was a cast-off shooting jacket of Palmer's, unrolled it, and giving a knowing wink at him, disclosed to his view a number of articles of silver plate.

" Ay, ay," said he, with a chuckle, " you yokels thinks yerselves spicy coves, but it's the brown suit ven yer comes ath'art an ould one. It's a pity too, as sich a smart young chap as I'd take yer to be by the cut of yer jib, should mount a 'oss foaled by a acorn,* for sich a shabby piece of panny† work as this here. I should'nt vunder," observed he, addressing his companion, " but vith good edicating he might be vorth *snitching‡* on. Vy, lord bless yer, the vally of this shabby lot ar'n't vorth *shoving the tumbler§* for, let alone scragging."

With these professional reflections, the officer, accompanied by the constables and their prisoner, walked slowly towards Weston Hall. The news of the capture of one of the burglars spread like wildfire among the domestics, and Palmer saw with sullen rage, the crowd of servants and idlers who waited his coming. Sir Litton also, apprised of the affair, determined that the dignity of a justice of the peace should not suffer in his person, had prepared for the important occasion by seating himself in the magisterial chair and investing his person with the flowered robe in which the good Sir Mark had so often dispensed justice tempered with mercy, in the petty cases of his neighbours and tenantry. At the table which was covered with green baize, and decorated for the occasion with a huge silver inkstand and a few plethoric-looking lawbooks, sat Octavius Sheepshanks, Gent., One, &c., a pert, pragmatical, tuft-

---

* The gallows.   † Burglary.   ‡ Informing.   § Whipped at the cart's tail.

'Head Quarters of the Highwaymen—a Scene at the "White Hart."

hunting, parasitical limb of the law, who, with an eye to business and a good
dinner, had dropped in at the Hall, and volunteered his services as clerk upon
the occasion. The imposing arrangements being completed, the prisoner was
ordered to be introduced.

The interval had been passed by him in the most poignant humiliation.
Around him in the hall had assembled the household, intermingled with many
of the villagers, whose faces were familiar to him on occasions when each
and all of them wore an expression of admiration, or the smile of friendly
approval, now exchanged for looks of pity or contempt. The bitterness of
his situation was enhanced too, by the murmured sympathy of the womankind—
among whom Richard was, as may easily be supposed, an especial favourite ;
and many was the bright eye that, after gazing with wondering compassion
on the manacled hands and stern desperation exhibited by the prisoner, turned
tearfully away, in pitying admiration of the " nice young fellow."

The kind heart of woman is ever susceptible, and once or twice the countenance of Richard brightened as some warmhearted country-wench expressed
aloud her determination—for a woman, when her feelings are appealed to,
scorns to reason—" that nothing should make *her* think as master Dick ever
could be brought for to do anythink of the sort;" and while the men looked
on in stolid stupidity, more than one female voice bade him be of " good cheer,'
No. 4.

until the door of the justice-chamber closed, excluding all but the officers, the witnesses, and the prisoner.

Sir Litton, despite his assumption of gravity, started, and sat uneasily in his chair on recognising in the prisoner his late antagonist; for the wily Dennis had taken every precaution to avoid appearing in the slightest degree connected with his apprehension. The discovery disconcerted the baronet. Prefacing his question with an authoritative "hem!" he, in rather a hurried manner, opened the proceedings by demanding the name and calling of the prisoner.

The pert little lawyer interposed. "Allow me to suggest—most defer-entially, Sir Litton, as *amicus curiæ*—the propriety of proceeding according to the rules and forms observed on these occasions. It is, my dear Sir Litton, in some measure indispensable, as I have before said, (though this was the first time he had spoken,) that the formalities of legal proceedings should be observed. I would most respectfully observe, most worthy sir, that there is an informality in the method of beginning by putting questions to the prisoner, who, according to the legal maxim—*nemo sese criminare obligatus est*—is by no means bound to answer questions which may tend in anywise to crimi-nate himself—or the answers to which may possibly be used against him in another place upon another occasion. We will therefore, (if it be your good pleasure,) proceed first with the examination of the witnesses.—*Oportet omnia facere decore et formaliter.*"

Having delivered himself of this farrago, the legal oracle looked round upon his gaping auditory, all of whom, except the veteran Londoner before-mentioned, seemed dumbfounded with astonishment at the learning, and puzzled with the dog-Latin of Octavius Sheepshanks. Sir Litton too, was profuse in the expression of his thanks for the invaluable assistance thus opportunely proffered.

At this moment the London thieftaker who had captured Palmer stepped forward. Doffing his hat, he made a low obeisance to Sir Litton—a duck of the head—half deferential, though with a spice of familiarity in it—to Octavius Sheepshanks, Esq., and casting his small grey eyes, with a knowing leer, on the group around, fixed them, with a singular expression of cunning, on the person of the prisoner. He was a good sample of the race of blood-hounds which the imperfect police of former days allowed to spring up into a rankness of villany to which the majority of offenders they captured might be considered as innocence itself. The sanguinary brutality of our penal code, and its horrid and disgusting accompaniment of bloodmoney, had, as criminal records too clearly show, created a crime by which the highest offence against society, that of openly taking away the life of a fellow-creature, had been outdone. Not only were the police of the times we are speaking, traffickers in felony, and the great agents in compounding it, but in many proved instances, and doubtless many more which will never see the light, did the temptation of a stipulated sum, to be paid as the price of prosecuting a fellow-man to the death, give rise to the most coldblooded and fiendish conspiracies. Mr. Ferret, however, was no such villain; he was of course unscrupulous, or he would never have arrived at eminence in his profession; though his villany was rather the result of circumstances, (he had been a pupil of the great Jonathan Wild, then recently executed,) than of any inherent depravity or cruelty of nature. In another sphere of life, Mr. Ferret would, from his con-vivial habits, and love of joke and comic humour, have been called " a d—d jolly fellow :" as it was, his company, though avoided by all respectable men—for the officer of those days was usually himself a thief—was much sought by his brother " runners."

His statement showed, that information of the robbery at farmer Lawrance's having been transmitted to the police-office to which he was attached, he had set on foot enquiries. That these had resulted in his ascertaining the fact, that a portion of the stolen property had been buried in an arbour in the garden lately occupied by Mr. Bevis. At this point of his evidence, after two or three most mysterious winks at the prisoner, and a sort of confidential grin at his worship's clerk, he digressed into some observations, by no means remarkable for their modesty, on the impossibility of eluding his vigilance, and the extraordinary sagacity—little short, if you would take his word for it, of omniscience—with which the secret passages of all cases came to his knowledge. This flourish, was, however, cut short by Mr. Sheepshanks, who in a voice of authority desired the officer to confine himself to the point. " This is not evidence, Sir Litton," said he ; " it is irrelevant—entirely irre-levant. Allow me, my dear sir, to proceed by putting leading questions to this witness ; it will greatly tend to facilitate the progress of the enquiry, and to a—a—simplify its details—a—a—*quod non relevantia est*—a—a—but you know the rest."

The capture of Palmer need not again be detailed. The officer having com-pleted his testimony, the case appeared to be likely to come to an adjourn-ment, for the messenger who had been dispatched for farmer Lawrance, in order that he might identify the property, had returned with the intelligence that the farmer had that morning set out for London. The baronet and the lawyer conferred together, and Palmer was about to address the latter when, to his great satisfaction, he observed Dennis. That personage had hitherto shrunk behind the headborough and his assistants, but now stepped forward—and addressing himself to Sir Litton and the attorney, said—

" Please your worship, I think as I can make up some of the proof as is wanting in this here case."

" Let the witness be sworn then," said the lawyer. As the sacred volume was placed in his hand, Richard gazed at him with stupified astonishment ; a look of malignant triumph stole across the swarthy features of Dennis, and sparkled in his single eye.

Sir Litton fidgetted on his chair—he feared the character of the witness ; and looked from Dennis to the prisoner, and again from the prisoner to Dennis, with an expression of countenance which the perjurer would not heed, but which at once conveyed to the mind of Palmer the suspicion that he was betrayed. By a violent effort he mastered his feelings. Dennis proceeded.

" I believe," and here he took up the jacket in which the articles of silver-plate had been found wrapped—" as I can speak pretty positive to this here jacket. I have seen master Richard there wear it, many's the time and oft ; and the man as made it is outside. Hows'ever, I'm sorry to say it, but if it comed out afterwards I might be blamed, so I'll make a clean breast of all I knows of this ugly job. The night afore last, as is my duty, you know, Sir Litton, I was on the look out near Bevis's garden, when I see two strange men a-making that way by sneaking along the hedge. ' Hollo !' says I to myself, ' may-be you aint after mischief there.' So I watches them : one on em was much like master Richard, but as it was darkish, I can't swear posi-tive ; t'other taller. I see 'em—I only speak the truth—(he observed Sir

Litton's astonishment)—go to the arbour, and after stopping a while they comes out, one on 'em carrying a spade ; and my mind misgave me as all was not right : so I called Joe, and after telling him, he—"

"Sir Litton," observed the pedantic lawyer, who had been busily taking notes, "this statement is most important. Allow me, however, to remark, that we cannot take what he told other people as evidence. Where is this Joe?" addressing Dennis; "he will be required to complete the chain."

Sir Litton became still more uneasy: the lawyer observed it, and continued :—"I am aware, my dear sir, how painful it must be to a gentleman of your kind feeling, to be under the necessity of committing one who has grown up under the patronage of your excellent family to gaol, for an offence to which the laws of society have properly affixed the penalty of an ignominious death. But may I deferentially observe, that in these cases we must fall back on our sense of public duty, and remember that the community at large owes a debt of gratitude to those who, sinking all private and personal feelings, devote themselves, like yourself Sir Litton, to a painful function for the general good."

Dennis continued : "Well, I calls Joe, as I said afore, and tells him what I thought; and as the night was cloudy, we gets a lantern, and then we finds—Joe seeing as the ground had been dug up—these things you sees afore you. And I s'pose as Joe told the gemman as took him, when he was a going to dig 'em up—"

The blood on the forehead of Richard went and came : the unblushing perjurer stood, with an affectation of concern on his countenance, as if hesitating whether he should say *all* he knew.

"Perjured villain!" exclaimed Palmer ; at the same time springing on the table, he threw himself towards him in a paroxysm of rage. The leap was so violent that he threw down the constable at his side, and launching his fettered hands full at the head of Dennis, would doubtless have inflicted some well-deserved injury on the wretch; but the latter had watched him too attentively to be so surprised—and adroitly stepping aside, his bound victim fell violently on the floor. The constables threw themselves heavily upon him, and he was again secured. Sir Litton rose from his chair: the little lawyer had retreated in undisguised terror to the farthest corner of the room.

"Hear me! Sir Litton Weston!" exclaimed Palmer, struggling with the men. "Sir Litton, I am the victim, by heaven! Sir Litton! that base wretch —"

Mr. Octavius had returned to the table ; and having assured himself of his own personal safety, and that the prisoner was efficiently secured, seemed anxious to draw the affair to a close.

"Sir Litton, I opine that nothing more can be done until the arrival of farmer Lawrance : there is a weight of testimony clearly justifying you in remanding the prisoner; I will, therefore, with your permission," and here he dipped his pen, "make a formal order to that effect."

Sir Litton assented with a nod: and the order having been handed to the constables, Richard—after an ineffectual attempt to obtain a hearing, which was prevented by Mr. Sheepshanks declaring the proceedings terminated—was dragged from the apartment.

No sooner were they gone, than ordering the footman to withdraw, Sir Litton at once fell into a conversation with Mr. Sheepshanks, in which he communicated his suspicions of the truth of the testimony, and his doubts as to the guilt of the prisoner

Mr. Sheepshanks combated his arguments, only to flatter him the more, by falling completely into his views of the subject, with many eulogistic remarks on his discernment and the goodness of his heart. Their wine was seasoned with many speculations as to the possible result of the affair, and finally Mr. Sheepshanks declared his intention of watching the proceedings closely, in order that the prisoner "might have the benefit of any doubt" which should present itself.

Meantime the headborough had conducted his charge to the cage, the only strong place of confinement which the neighbourhood contained: it was a small brick building some six feet square, and of proportionate height—before its door stood the stocks, which now and then exhibited a sturdy beggar, and beside them the seldom used whipping post with its huge iron staples.

Dense was the crowd of old and young which followed, as the important culprit was conveyed through the village street, and numerous were the expressions of surprise at the flourishes with which the headborough and his assistants embellished their description of the scene at the Hall. The resoluteness of Dick was already known, but it now came coloured and distorted to their minds as reckless and sanguinary ruffianism.

The ponderous lock had been turned on him, and the last lingering knot of gossips had departed before Palmer raised himself from the damp earthen floor on which he had thrown himself on being first thrust into the place of his confinement. Thoughts had been whirling through his brain with an intensity and volocity that had nearly goaded him to madness. The visions of his early days recurred to him, and the most minute and trifling incidents of his life presented themselves with a painful distinctness and reality to his mind's eye. He thought of each passage of his love until every word of his conversations with Esther seemed again to vibrate on his ear—then the thoughts of their fond pictures of future happiness rushed upon him, accompanied with the idea that his present infamy must inevitably reach her, and none be at hand to contradict the false and slanderous report. He started to his feet—"She'll not believe it—I know she'll not! there at least, in her pure heart, I shall find an advocate convinced of my innocence!" The moon rode high in the heavens, and the light streamed through a small and strongly grated aperture in the wall—the night was frosty and chill, but he felt it not—the damp ground on which he had so long lain had failed to cool his burning forehead. He paced round his narrow prison—the image of Dennis occurred to him—he seized him and in imagination tore him with the ferocity of a caged tiger—he stamped him to the earth—and struggled till the cold drops of perspiration started from every pore. He sat down to breathe awhile—he cast his eyes round his den, as the possibility of an escape suggested itself; but dismissed it, resolving to brave the worst: again and again it recurred, and each time with more force than the former. He had been deprived of all weapons on his capture; it was besides necessary that he should free himself of his handcuffs. They were of the old fashioned description connected by a short shackle. In the wall opposite to the window, on the spot where the moon's rays now fell, he perceived with delight a large iron staple firmly fixed into the brickwork. He placed his wrists on each side the projection, but soon found that though by a painful and prolonged effort he could bend and partially twist the shackle, the tough and well wrought iron exhibited no sign of breaking. He persevered, however, at

each time finding the resistance weaken, and within half an hour he had succeeded in separating the link and delivering his wrists from the unpleasant
union to which they had been compelled. He peeped cautiously through the grating—the silent village slept in the calm moonshine—the fields were ever and
anon chequered by the light fleecy clouds which flickered across her surface.
He tried the bars; but their removal must evidently be a work of time. The
roof, for the place was not more than seven feet high, presented a more probable chance. Fastening his neckcloth in the friendly staple which had before
done him such good service, he formed it into a strong loop, two or three
times doubled, in which he placed his foot. He now found, after two or three
attempts that, by suddenly springing up, and placing one hand against the
rafters to steady himself, he could easily remove a portion of the planking with
which they were covered. This was soon accomplished; and Dick, releasing his
foot, drew himself upward through the aperture, and sliding down the slope,
on the opposite side to the highway, found himself once again a free man.

For a while he crouched beneath the shadow of the little building, listening
attentively; all however, was still—except the occasional baying of a deep-
mouthed yard dog, as the prowling fox, or some other light sound, disturbed
his wakeful doze. Skirting the shady side of the hedges, and occasionally
making his way along a dry ditch, at the expense of a few scratches from the
brambles, he took the direction of his foster-mother's house. He knew that this
step was fraught with danger; but he could not bear the idea of quitting the
village for ever without bidding her farewell. He went to the back part of
the house: the diamond-paned casement of her bedroom glittered in the
moonbeams. Selecting a few small and light pebbles, he threw them
cautiously against the glass. After repeating this several times, he ventured
upon trusting his voice in a low whisper. "Hist, dear mother; it is I—your
son Richard," said he. No reply, however, came from the direction in which
his voice was directed; but his ear caught the sound of the fastenings of the
backdoor being cautiously removed.

"Come in, for God's sake!" said a female voice; it was that of the girl
who acted in capacity of servant and companion to Palmer's aunt. "Oh,
master Richard, we've been so alarmed. Mistress has been to the Hall, and
is now gone to farmer Lawrance's. All the people said you were committed
to prison."

They entered the house. Palmer knew too well the value of every moment,
and the danger of his situation, to forfeit his chance of liberty by remaining
long; he therefore, after making up a small bundle of more immediate necessaries, and leaving a promise that his mother should soon hear from him, bid
farewell to his home—and again took to the fields.

There is a lingering—a hoping against hope, about the human heart, which
often disposes our actions in direct opposition to our judgment; and thus it
was with Palmer. Though well aware of the imminent risk of apprehension
he encountered, he could not quit Hempstead without one fond farewell of the
scene of his joys and woes—the garden of Esther. Tnither he cautiously
directed his steps. His way, as before stated, led him through a portion of
the Chase; he lingered in view of the spot of his first apprehension. The
house of Dennis rose upon his view: he bethought himself of revenge. While
thus lurking in the shadow of the huge and gnarled trees, he fancied he heard
the hum of men's voices; he was not mistaken: the sounds approached—and as
he lay close to the trunk of a giant of the forest, two men neared the spot.

"It's all very well for you as has feathered your nest, to talk in such a way," said the first speaker; "but I can't stand it. The swag, in the guinea way, warn't half what I hear we might have had, if so be you had'nt been so precious smart at being off. I heard Gregory say myself, that what we got was nothing to what we left behind ; besides, I can't tell, for the soul of me, what good I can get by giving up the plate-part of the *haul*—'specially as you don't come down, as you promised you would."

Palmer's blood boiled as the voice of Dennis met his ear in reply.

"Why, what a precious hurry you're in ; you're a bigger fool than I took you to be : but I'd advise you not to ride rusty with your friends. We're all in it ; and if so be you can't do as I do, I'll take care you don't get the best of me. But I'll show you as I'll act honourable. Why, the vally of what them cups and spoons 'ud fetch, now, is nothink : put your price on 'em, and I'll make up your *reg'lars ;* I'd scorn to have it said I *done a pal.* Hows'ever, when we've a got this younker out of the way—an' I think I've *spun his hemp* for him—you shan't find me backward ; but it might be as well if yer comed no nearer to the house nor this, for there's that old affair still out agin yer. Here's all I have just now, but meet me on Monday at Sam's hovel in the marsh, and I'll make it all right. Good bye."

So saying, Dennis put some silver into the hand of his scoundrel-looking accomplice, who stealthily moved off among the trees. "I don't half like that vagabond," said he, soliloquising ; "but I must sweeten him a trifle just now. I guess master Dick is sorry by this time as he made me his enemy."

He began examining the priming of his gun : at this moment a rustle among the leaves struck on his ear, and while he was looking for its cause the very object of his thoughts rushed towards him—the gun was half raised to his shoulder when, with one hand, Palmer struck down the weapon, and fixing the other with a gripe, strong as his hatred, on the throat of Dennis, dashed him violently against the bole of a tree. Stupefied by the suddenness of the attack, the ruffian made but a feeble resistance. His senses reeled, his sight swam, as Richard without relaxing his compression of the villain's throat, endeavoured to wrest the gun from his grasp, without any defined idea of even his own intentions. The staggered Dennis still however, instinctively retained his hold. The violence of his fall caused him to use one hand to protect himself, and Palmer had well nigh possessed himself of the piece ; the hand of his foe only clutching the barrel, when the trigger catching some part of his dress, it exploded, lodging the charge in the body of Dennis. The man leaped from the ground with a piercing shriek and fell heavily at the feet of Palmer. He stood gazing at his antagonist, the distorted features looked ghastly in the pale moonlight and no sound escaped him, but a low moan, as his quivering body writhed on the herbage, while the blood from his side changed the green turf to a dull red. Palmer was horror struck. He stood a moment transfixed—the noise of the discharge, and the yell of Dennis must have been heard at the Lodge, and he doubted not a few moments would bring assistance to the spot. He cast the gun from him—and feeling that HE *was* a MUR-DERER fled with a speed which he slackened not until he had placed some miles between himself and the awe-inspiring sight of his murdered victim.

He paused on a small eminence, the early breath of morn played upon his temples—and as he thought upon the ignominious doom to which the machinations of the villain would have consigned him, he felt justified in what he had done.

He now resolved to make his way into London, and taking refuge in one of the sinks of poverty and crime in the neighbourhood of Shadwell, determined, after lying *perdu* for a while; to betake himself to some foreign land.—

But few minutes had elapsed ere the groans of the wounded Dennis directed the steps of some of the underkeepers to the spot. His injuries, though of considerable extent, the gun being loaded with small shot and the discharge so close as to burn his clothes, were not mortal, and after a painful confinement of many weeks, Dennis resumed his duties with no other inconvenience than a disabled arm, and a frame weakened by the loss of blood.

CHAPTER III.—1728.

Hurrah for the revel! my steed, hurrah﹐
Thorough bush, thorough brake-go we
It is ever a virtue, when others pay,
To ruffle it merrily!

Oh there never was life like the robber's—so
Jolly and bold and free ;—
And its end ?—why a cheer from the crowd below,
And a leap from the leafless tree !
—Old Ballad

"HEALTH—a lucky life, and a merry one, to Captain Turpin " exclaimed a loud and clear voice, amid the jingling of glasses and the steams of arrack; the owner of the aforesaid voice being more than half obscured by the dense clouds of tobacco smoke which floated in wreaths through the apartment.

"Health, a lucky life, and a merry one, to Captain Turpin !" echoed a dozen voices in chorus from the throats of as motley a group as can well be imagined.

The scene of the revel was an apartment in the "White Hart," a tavern, situate at the Bloomsbury end of Drury Lane; well known as the resort of all the flash tobymen* of the day. Not a few of the company exhibited all the extravagance of vulgar finery; yet sprinkled among the lace ruffles, the satin bags, full bottomed wigs, and glittering jewelled sleeve-buttons, here and there, (for crime and misery " acquaint us with strange bedfellows,") might be seen, two or three of such villanous, ruffianly, repulsive vagabonds, as an honest man would dislike to meet on a dark night. Their unkempt heads and unshaven dirty visages contrasted strangely with the nonchalant extravagance of costume of others of the party. Pipes strewed the table : costly wine and humble malt, bowls of arrack and tumblers of diluted Geneva, stood side by side with as little distinction as was exhibited by the heterogeneous company who were imbibing them. Here sat the aristocrat of the highway, and at his elbow the " swell out of luck ;" who, driven by some unlucky exploit to temporary concealment, awaited, in skulking poverty, after squandering the proceeds of his crime, the " blowing over" of the search of justice. Others of these reckless " shabbies" were the lurchers of their more dashing associates. It was the office of these desperadoes to furnish their masters with information of the where and when their exploits might come off with the greatest profit and success. These " *touters*," for so they might be termed,

* Highwaymen.

Black Dennis dismissed by Sir Litton Weston.

skulked about the residences of the noble and the wealthy, scraped acquaintance with their grooms, stablemen, and hangers-on, and thus obtained a knowledge of the fashionable arrivals and departures, in days when yet the "Morning Post" was not. This intelligence they, of course, turned to profitable account; and some of the most lucrative robberies were "put up" by their means. These inferior scoundrels occasionally did a little on their own account on the pedestrian suit—*i. e.* as footpads. From their intimate knowledge of the movements and proceedings of their more dashing associates, they were dangerous enemies; and this enabled them, like leeches, " the blood, the blood, the very blood to suck," in a pecuniary sense; and in not a few cases, where their rapacity had been disappointed, or some personal feeling of hatred prompted them, they " peached" on the " gallant highwayman."

In a chair, somewhat elevated above the rest, sat the president; and the president was, as the reader may already have guessed,—DICK TURPIN. Among the more spicy guests who figured around the board, Captain Hind, George Fielder, Rose, and Dudley may be enumerated—the two latter also rejoicing in the epithet " Captain ;" a favourite travelling title of the bold highwayman of days bypast, and which we have just heard coupled with the name of our hero, the *quondam* Richard Palmer. Conspicuous among the more seedy group, the reader perhaps will be astonished at finding Black Dennis, and some other ruffians unknown to fame, whose deeds belong not to our history. The date prefixed to this chapter will have shown that three year

No. 5.

have elapsed since last we had the honour to hear of that person—and these
three years had certainly neither improved his appearance or his reputation.
He still upheld, in his new avocation, his character for cunning and malignity;
and there was not among his whole tribe a more useful and dangerous—a more
cruel or daring vagabond than Dennis Sowton. Though despising and
detesting him, Dick Turpin, whose morals and manners also exhibited a most
striking change for the worse, had learned to " endure, then pity, then embrace," this consummate scoundrel. The laws of the society in which they
were both enrolled, indeed recognised but *one* crime—that of *treachery to a
comrade* ; and the circumstances of Dick Turpin's discovery of Dennis, and his
own position, forbad such a thought being entertained for a moment.

While the glasses are yet jingling, and the toast circulating, we will snatch
a page or two in order to fill up some passages of the life of our hero and of
Dennis, and to narrate the circumstances which had led to their present
position.

We have before stated that Dennis had resumed his office of head ranger
of Weston Park. Intense was the dismay, mighty the consternation, of that
potent functionary the headborough of Hempstead, when, on the morning of
Turpin's escape, his snore was cut short by a confused noise of voices under
his window ; and before he had time to consult Mrs. Gubbins, as like a dutiful
husband he was wont to do, on the probable cause of the disturbance, his
name was shouted by most stentorian lungs. The great man leaped from his
bed in that state in which it has been said no man is a hero, and, followed
by a sharp volley from Mrs. G.—for, from Socrates down to the Duke of Marlborough and Mrs. Gubbins, the mighty men of the earth have been henpecked—
popped his head from the window.

The village street exhibited a scene of unwanted bustle. A small knot of
villigers was grouped opposite his house, and it was evident from their looks
and the eagerness of their gesticulations that something unusual had
happened.

" Oh, Mr. Gubbins!" exclaimed a damsel with a milking pail in her hand ;
" the pris'ner han escaped !"

" Ees ! he have got off in roight arnest," chorused a dozen others.

" Come down, will you ?" exclaimed one of Sir Litton Weston's gamekeepers, who now ran up. " Why, his worship's head ranger have just been
shot dead : the robber have broken prison, an' all's in an uproar at the Hall."

Now Mr. Gubbins scarcely yet clearly comprehended the meaning of all
this. It was his wont to mug and bemuddle himself with good stingo each
night at the Fox, and to so becloud his intellects with the fumes of mundungus,
that it took him some minutes to collect his scattered ideas.

" Bless me ! bless me !" said he, as he returned towards the bedside, " the
prisoner has broken jail—against the peace of our lord the king—his crown
and dignity. Oh, the audacity of—"

" Don't stand maundering there, you old fool !" cried the vinegar voice of
Mrs. Gubbins, " but go and see what's to do ; and make haste back to light
the fire and put the kettle on—d'ye hear ? I'll want my breakfast afore
you're back, I'll warrant. I don't know how such an old dawdle came ever
to be appointed to anything—not I."

" My dear," said her spouse, " I am summoned to the Hall : the prisoner
has escaped ; and, as his majesty's representative, Sir Litton sends to consult
with me—"

" His majesty's fiddlestick !" cried the irreverent dame ; " why, your silly-head must ha' been doited when ye undertuk anything as wanted a man to do. But make haste do'ee, and bring me back all the news afore you tell anybody else ; the headborough's wife ought to know all about public business afore any dame in the town. Make haste, you old frump you !"

With this valediction the office-bearer, having donned the inexpressibles which would with more propriety have adorned the portly person of his better half, stepped out among the crowd, with a boldness and dignity which challenged the respect of the elder rustics, and awakened awe and admiration in the breasts of the younger.

Long and fruitless was the search—for Dick was far away ere the first alarm, as the reader has already been made aware.

Dennis, upon reflection, did not regret his escape—though the issue of his plot had been so entirely different from what he had designed ; and it was satisfactory that the ruin of Palmer had been effected without the risk which must necessarily have attended a trial. His triumph, however, was destined to be a short one. We have before alluded to the desperate poacher who had been one of his accomplices. The accidental encounter of Dennis with Palmer, by disabling the former from keeping the appointment mentioned in our last chapter, had induced Ned Wheeler—for such was his name—to venture nearer than was prudent to the precincts of the Hall ; the consequence of this step was his apprehension upon a warrant for deer-stealing, which had been for some time out against him. To this crime the law then awarded the penalty of death. At that period the assizes were " few and far between ;" and the the interval of Ned Wheeler's tedious imprisonment in the county gaol, Dennis had recovered. The prisoner, relying on the friendship of Dennis—or rather calculating on his fears, had commissioned a trusty comrade to confer with him as to the best means of rescuing him from his perilous situation. The hyprocritical villain felt how important the death of Ned might be to his future safety, and therefore did not fail to transmit to him the strongest assurances of his friendship. He forwarded him the means of procuring legal advice ; though at the same time that he took care that Mr. Sheepshanks should should be consulted, and, by confidential communications, put that gentleman in possession of all the particulars—and they were many—that could tell against the prisoner. But " homme propose et Dieu dispose ;" and the cunning Dennis was in this instance fated to overreach himself. In the course of a communication between the attorney and his client, the legal gentleman took occasion to mention one or two facts which had come to his knowledge ; facts which Wheeler instantly knew could have been communicated by none but his pretended friend Dennis. He enquired the lawyer's authority ; and, though the latter evaded a direct answer, the prisoner at once saw though his professional quirks. He resolved to repay the traitor in his own coin ; and within two hours after the interview Sir Litton and the smug lawyer were closeted, and the whole particulars of the burglary at farmer Lawrance's, the division of the booty, and the perjury of Dennis, were as plainly proved as circumstantial evidence and the direct testimony of Wheeler could do. Mr. Sheepshanks proposed the instant apprehension and committal of Dennis ; but Sir Litton, though expressing his abhorrence of the conduct of the delinquent, peremptorily insisted that no further steps should be taken in the affair. The little lawyer opened his eyes :—" Why surely, Sir Litton, you will not allow your personal feelings so far to compromise your duty to the community, as to—"

"Let me hear no more upon the subject," said Sir Litton, "I insist, as you value my favour, Mr. Sheepshanks, that not one word of this conversation should transpire. I will have this man Sowton before me; but mark me, I have a motive" (the lawyer bowed obsequiously, and placed his hand upon his breast) "which renders it imperative that no more should come of this."

"Far be it from me, sir," said the man of law, "to pry into the motives of my patron. Of course, Sir Litton, you will do what seemeth right in your better judgment. May I ask, in what way I can forward your views in this matter?"

Sir Litton during this speech had been pacing the room; he turned abruptly on the lawyer—"By holding your tongue," said he sharply. Mr. Sheepshanks muttered an apology,

"Send Dennis Sowton, here," said Sir Litton to a domestic who answered the bell.

It is ever the fate of subordinate villains to be hated in the proportion as they are feared, by those whom they have served. Sir Litton had long felt the thraldom in which even his worthless menial had kept him, by having possessed himself of his weaknesses; and he became acutely sensible, as his indignation against Palmer cooled, of the degradation to which he had submitted by allowing such a scoundrel to become his confidant, and the depositary of his secrets.

Dennis entered with his usual look of assurance.

"Sowton," said Sir Litton sternly, "I have sent for you before this gentleman, that he may be a witness of my forbearance towards you. He, as well as I, possess a knowledge of your crimes—crimes by which your life would become a forfeit to the law." Sheepshanks gave an approving nod, and the face of Dennis assumed a livid hue, though its expression was rather that of rage and vexation than of shame and contrition. Sir Litton continued, "Dennis Sowton, this gentleman is prepared to adduce proof not only of the offence of perjury against you; but further that you, and your accomplices, and not Richard Palmer," (Dennis gazed fixedly on the floor, and an impatient tremor of his whole body betrayed his agitation) "were guilty of the burglary at Farmer Lawrance's. Now I—"

The hardened villain raised his head. "And who," said he doggedly, "set me on to do it but yourself? If I'm to be punished I know who'll be most talked on in the matter. Few 'ud care about me, for few likes me well enough; but what 'ull the world say to Sir Litton Weston, the son of the *good* Sir Mark, who to revenge himself on his rival for the loss of a gal, egged on a poor fellow to an offence, and when, in his zeal to serve him, he got himself into a scrape, turned round and punished him.—*I* didn't commit, Palmer to pris'n for the robbery, thank God," sneered the ruffian made desperate his situation, "knowing, as *somebody* as I knows did, as he was innocent. But if I am to suffer for this—though I believe it's all a lie of some of my enemies—why I won't suffer alone—that's all." Sir Litton was totally unprepared for this bold stroke of his servant's, effrontery. His colour went and came, for he had by no means bargained for such an exposure; Mr. Sheepshanks though endeavouring to affect a deep concern, was evidently inwardly felicitating himself on the turn affairs had taken, and the family secrets he was arriving at; he broke in, however, to the rescue.

"Upon my word," said he, "this is the most unparalleled piece of impudence, that it has ever fallen to my lot to meet withal." Dennis looked at him with a threatening glance, and he immediately changed his tone. "My good fellow, the interest of your kind master has I fear been greatly defeated by the injudicious observations in which you have just indulged—*satis verborum, sapentiæ parum.* It was, I believe, the intention of your kind and generous master, Sir Litton, to have merely discharged you; thereby giving you an opportunity of retrieving elsewhere the character you have here forfeited. Sir Litton, my dear Sir, calm yourself, pray do" (he observed that the baronet was struggling with his temper) "leave me to deal with this fellow, and you will see that *suo sibi gladio hunc jugulo*—I will cut his throat with his own sword—a-hem. Sir Litton is anxious," and he turned to Dennis, "your length of service and other motives thereunto disposing him—that the consequences of this discovery should not fall, as strict justice requires, upon your head. He therefore proposes—correct me, my dear Sir, if I should err—that you should at once leave this neighbourhood. You must know, my good man, that the punishment of this offence must fall on yourself, and moreover, when you shall be convicted, and the proof is of the clearest, no one will believe the slander launched against one whose character is so high and whose virtues, public and private, are so eminently known as your respected master." The legal parrot would have proceeded further, but Dennis by this time had become fully aware of his position, and resolved upon his line of action.

"You may save yer breath, sir" said he, "I've hit the right nail on the head; that swindling cur, Ned Wheeler, has *snitched*; well, I wants none of your palaver to tell me as I must *morris;* but there's two words even to that bargin."

"Mr. Sheepshanks," said Sir Litton, "this has already gone too far. I've determined that the law shall take its course. I will no longer endure that this villain shall father his crimes on me, because in an unguarded moment I once condescended to consult with him in an affair of which I now feel heartily ashamed. Let the worst come to the worst, the exposure, if exposure it is to be," and the baronet walked towards the bell rope which hung beside the huge sculptured chimney-piece.

"Stop!" exclaimed Dennis, "another step and"—he placed his hand in his bosom, and produced a pistol; Sir Litton paused.

"I'm in your hands, I know;" said the desperado. "But don't think I'll be slaughtered lamb-fashion. You say you've found me out; but you'll know more of me if you provoke me. I've many reasons for quitting these parts; and leaving 'em won't much hurt *my* feelings. These things is better settled with a good understanding to all parties."

Sir Litton looked at Dennis, and the latter lowered the barrel of the pistol in token of a cessation of hostilities.

"I'm thinking, sir," said Dennis viewing the alarm of the lawyer with supreme contempt; "as you and I can arrange for my leaving without this gentleman's interference." Mr. Sheepshanks moved towards the door "Stop!" ejaculated Dennis again, "not so fast, I leaves this room first of the company. By your leave," he continued, walking up to the terrified Mr. Octavius, "I'll stow you within call. Here," said he, motioning towards a closet, the door of which he opened--" you'll be so good as to step into this little room while I turns a key on yer—cos I'd rather not have yer witnessing to any thing yer might see or hear going twixt myself and master. Come-in with you!" the little lawyer cast a fearfully imploring look towards Sir Litton, as he slowly prepared to comply with the command. The baronet, who among his defects did not reckon the want of personal courage, made a step or two towards Dennis.

"Hear me, Dennis Sowton," said he, "I will not be bullied by you, nor will I submit to any indignity being put on Mr. Sheepshanks, who is my friend and legal adviser.   You just now expressed a desire that we should part amicably.—I did not send for you with any other intention; for though determined to rid myself of your presence, I still, in consideration of my own conduct, am willing to act with forbearance towards you.   But beware how you endeavour to practise on that forbearance.   I will not submit to your insolence : therefore at once name your condition, and I pledge you my word that you shall find no reason to repent trusting to my honour and generosity.

Dennis saw his cue with instinctive acuteness.

"Well, exclaimed he, in a cheerful tone of voice, "I always did respect you, sir; and many's the time when you've been back-bited by others, whom you little thinks ever did anythink but sing your praises, as they've good right to do—many's the time, as I've said, ' well, if master be a little hasty or so, he's a good heart at bottom.' "—

Sir Litton looked impatient, and Dennis finding the time was past for cajoling him, went on : "Howsever as you say I *must* go, and I knows it myself, it stands to reason as I can't do without means to live ; let me have, for there's no use in beating anout the bush—a hundred pounds and I'll go down into Lincolnshire—which I wishes to see again ; and, ease your mind on't, I shan't trouble you no more."

"You shall have it," said Sir Litton ; and the readiness with which the proposal was acceded to, made Dennis regret that he had not asked more.

" And now, Sir," said Dennis, " seeing as short reckonings make long friends, I'd like if so be you'd give me my ticket for trav'lling as soon as convenient ; for, d'ye see, it might be unpleasant to stay—besides not turning out for *your* credit." (Sir Litton winced) " So, if it meets with your way of thinking, I'll go at once."

" Certainly," said the baronet.   Stepping to an escrutoire, he drew forth a small rouleau, and breaking the sealed envelope, spread a number of guineas before him.   Dennis fixed his one eye on them with sparkling eagerness.   Mr. Sheepshanks, not knowing how his interference might be taken, stood a silent spectator of the transaction.   Sir Litton told over the stipulated number; there were some eight or nine remaining which he added to the heap, and placing them in a silken bag, he said—

" Dennis Sowton, I have acted throughout this business with great lenity towards you.   Your conduct has this day been such, that, had it not been for a regard for my own character, I should have consigned you at once to a felon's cell—as it is, take this, and never let me see your face again—if I do, you will not have to thank me for any forbearance."

During this short speech Dennis had stood with extended hand, in anxious expectation of clutching the proffered gold ; his avarice having mastered his habitual caution and self-restraint : at the close of it Sir Litton presented him with the purse, and waving his hand pointed towards the door.

His success had so elated Dennis, that he scarcely expressed his thanks. "Good bye, Sir Litton," said he, placing his hat jauntily on his head; "Good bye, Sir Litton ; and long may you live ; though I don't know, if I should prosper in the world, if I shan't show you, in some way and other, as I respects you, spite the hard words you've used to me. Good bye, t'ye, Master Sheepshanks, and hark 'ee—if you wish to die in a whole skin, and with your friends about you, don't take liberties with my character behind my back. Sir Litton I'm safe in your word—good bye!" and so saying he quitted the apartment. The last sound of his footsteps on the staircase was listened for by Mr. Sheepshanks with nervous impatience, when he immediately opened his fire. Meanness, the companion of cowardice, venomed his tongue and urged him to advise Sir Litton.

"Shall I alarm the household; and capture the robber!" said he. "It would be but right to take him with the money he has so villainously extorted: I will undertake to so manage the affair as—"

"Mr. Sheepshanks," interrupted Sir Litton angrily, "I have before told you, you could best serve me by holding your tongue—I repeat it sir—and as you value my future favour and confidence, let no man ever hear of this subject more." The little lawyer at once expressed his acquiescence.

We will now follow the steps of Dennis. Rightly did he judge that the place would soon be too hot to hold him: he feared that Ned Wheeler, having once broken the ice, would not confine his disclosures to Sheepshanks, nor did he. In the hope of being admitted king's evidence, he sent for the governor of the gaol, and informed him of every particular, and Dennis had departed but a few hours, when the officers arrived at Weston Hall, with a warrant for his apprehension—but the bird was flown. Dennis made his way to London; and, as might be anticipated from the sensual character of his pleasures, he launched into the vilest depravity and debauchery. As like will to like, and his propensities led him to the most debased associations, his illgotten store saw soon expended; new means must be supplied.. The woman on whom he had lavished the greater proportion of the proceeds of his extortion, was a jezebel of the lowest class, of strong passions, and brutal violence; she had, however, met with her match in Dennis, and after two or three contests each of which terminated in severe personal injuries on the weaker side,—that of Madge Dutton, as she was called by those who wished to be civil, though, from her fighting propensities now generally known as "the Slasher,—her paramour succeeded in beating her into a sort of dogged submission, from a fear of his brutality. By Madge, who still retained many of the charms which had first made her the victim and afterwards the destroyer of men, Dennis, as soon as his money ran low, was introduced to several of the most notorious footpads, coiners, clippers, smugglers, and duffers, which " mighty Babylon" could then boast. He soon distanced many of his more experienced associates, and at the time at which we find him, a more accomplished rascal could not easily have been found, than Dennis Sowton.

The career of Palmer was of a different complexion: yet the inexplicable destiny which presides over our fates seemed to have doomed that they should each of them, by different roads, reach the same goal.

The early dawn just streaked the east as Palmer entered London by the way of Whitechapel. He made his way through the fast assembling groups of market people; for in the High Street of that suburb—now no longer a suburb, but an integral portion of the metropolis—was the market-place of the citizens dwelling in the eastern division of London. Hastening through these, he took his way along Bishopsgate Street, passed the Monument, and as day broke found himself gazing, from a wharf near Billingsgate, on the misty river with its forestry of masts. The agitating events of the night now

first affected him with a sense of bodily fatigue : mental and bodily excitement
had as yet prevented any such feeling.   He gazed on the dark hulls of the
vessels looming indistinctly through the haze, as it curled lazily off in dense
wreaths, and then cast an eye down his person.   His trowsers were spotted
blood, which had escaped from a flesh-wound in his hand, of which as yet he
had been unconscious.   His clothes were torn and disordered, and as he reflected on the crime he had committed, he saw how necessary it was to seek
some place of concealment without delay.

Near Billingsgate, that spot so famed for eloquence and fish, still exists,
opposite the entrance to the market, and parallel to Fish Street Hill, a
narrow and steep lane, known by the name of Darkhouse Lane: it, however,
in its inward and spiritual grace, if not in its outward and visible sign, has
experienced great improvement.   A century ago, this fitly-named spot contained
several dens, then known as *crimping-houses ;* places where lurked a race of
human spiders.   These wretches subsisted by entrapping unwary and often
intoxicated young men, and having drugged them into a state of insensibility,
robbed them ; then conveying them on board a receiving-ship for the navy, or
by collusion with some recruiting serjeant, as circumstances might dictate,
their hapless victim on recovering his senses found himself kidnapped ; and
the scoundrelly *crimps* received from the authorities the bounty given in such
cases to those who procured an able seaman or soldier for the king.   In front
of one of these dens, where a " palpable obscure" reigned even at noonday,
Palmer stopped.   A mingled uproar of swearing, boasting, singing, and
laughing, broke upon his ear.   He felt faint and hungry ; the smarting and
pulsation of his hitherto scarce-noticed wound added to his discomfort.   As he
hesitated, a man staggered forth from the doorway, and was instantly followed by
three others, one of whom sported the flaunting cockade and flying ribbands of a
recruiting serjeant.   They seized the man who first came out; he resisted, and a
crowd of people soon assembled.   Palmer felt that his appearance might attract
attention, and hastily entered the dingy-looking passage of this unpromising hostelrie. He looked into the first apartment, in which were seated several men. By
their garb they seemed to be attendants on the fish market.   They were clad
in long coats of a dingy white, of immense weight and thickness, their legs
encased in huge brown gaiters of undressed leather, waistcoats of a stable-
pattern, and one or two of them sported, coiled in a twist, the blue woollen
apron characteristic of their calling.   They were busily engaged in discussing
the contents of some tankards of ale and twopenny which stood before them,
and one or two who had laid down their pipes, for they were smoking
even at that hour of sunrise, were cutting away at some cold beef, or
picking periwinkles with a pin.   The shells of small crabs and the *disjecta
membra* of half-picked shrimps strewed the tables and floor ; and altogether the
apartment, though dignified by the title of " parlour," had a most " villanous
and fish-like smell."   This room, if any mortal had ever been able to
see through its mud-encrusted panes, commanded a view of the front
street, and as Palmer's object was concealment, he made his way backward,
where he saw the house offered other accommodations.   If the first described
apartment was uninviting, the one he now entered was anything but an improvement on it,   Long narrow deal tables, bound with iron, and scooped with
holes, from which at certain hours the spilt beer was swabbed out, in order
that they might do duty as salt-cellars, and scored with mysterious lines for

Robbery of Sir Litton Weston.

the games of shovehalfpenny, or tiddleywink, occupied three sides of the room. Its fourth presented a firegrate of ample dimensions; from the lowermost of its glowing bars projected a bright grating of iron, on which stood some drinkables and eatables, keeping hot. The blackened chimney was capacious; pot-hooks, and a huge crane-formed rack for suspending kettles, occupied its recesses; while above the mantel, on two upright racks, a spit or two, and a conical pot for warming beer, were displayed. The walls were black and dirty with soot and smoke; and in one corner the discoloured and dingy face of a gigantic clock showed dubiously through the smoke-laden atmosphere. Palmer checked his step in the doorway as he hastily glanced around.

"Coom in, lad," said a smockfrocked, half-drunken fellow, who sat near the door, and whose gay cockade showed that he was a recruit. "Coom, soop, lad; thee's welcum. I zay, zargent—a' guess here's anoother loikely 'un. Woo'te zarve the king, loike us? Coom, soop, lad."

The speaker was cut short by a rising hiccup, and held out the tankard towards Richard. He took it, and placed it to his lips: the eye of the wary recruiting serjeant was fixed upon him. Without noticing the speech of the intoxicated fellow, he opened the conversation with—

"You seem to be sum'at tired, young man. Ha' ye travelled far this morning? It's no business of mine to ask, I know; but, maybe, you'll seat yourself along wi' us, and take potluck."

Palmer's pride was offended by the abruptness of the man. He, however, thanked him, and declined his offer.

No. 6.

Seating himself in a corner of the room, he desired a brawny, red-elbowed slattern, who stood in familiar gossip with two fellows near the fireplace, to bring him some meat and beer. He had not long begun his meal before the recruiting serjeant and another fellow rose from their seats, and, under pretence of lighting their pipes, contrived to place themselves near him. They kept up a conversation; and, having supplied themselves with a measure of ardent spirits, exchanged a few significant glances and signs, of which Palmer was evidently the object. The latter had not noticed their presence until, having despatched what was before him, the serjeant who had before addressed him, said:—

"Pretty good takeaway, young man, I see. P'raps a glass of sperrits wouldn't hurt'e after it?"

A glass was poured out; and the serjeant, placing it to his lips, (for he appeared to take his liquors upon the homœopathic system, in infinitesimal doses,) put it down, and by inclining the pewter measure over it, seemed to refill it for Palmer. The latter, however, strenuously refused; and after several attempts to induce him, by various stratagems, to drink, the serjeant somewhat testily left the room.

The tankard containing the ale which Palmer had ordered, stood at his elbow; and at this moment an ill-looking fellow, who stood near the fire, contrived to partially spill some beer he was warming in the conical-shaped pot. He leapt back—swore an oath—grasped his scalded hand with the other—and stamped his feet in great apparent suffering. The attention of Palmer was of course directed towards him. The moment was seized by the man we have before noticed as seated near our hero; he placed his closed fist over the ale, and suddenly opening it, scattered a powder into the liquor. He withdrew his hand; it was but the work of an instant. The man who had pretended to be scalded left the room, and the other presently followed.

As Palmer leant back in his seat, pondering what step it would be best for him to take, he first became aware of the presence of a man wrapped in a coarse white duffle coat; and who appeared, from the obscure corner in which he had ensconced himself, the slouch of his hat, and the high collar of his upper coat, to seek to avoid observation. His eyes, however, were fixed upon Palmer; he was evidently watching him. Dick felt uneasy, and mechanically laying hold of his ale, was about to raise it to his lips: the stranger rose hastily from his seat, and placed his hand on the arm of Palmer. He made a sign with his head towards the door, intimating that Palmer should follow him; and he did so. The two went out into a little back yard, and the stranger at once said:—

"It may seem curious to you, that a person you never saw before should act as I have done just now; but you're in bad hands, young man. You observed that scoundrel's trick of scalding himself; at that instant the beer at your elbow was drugged. I will tell you how to act; though, as I am myself at present in hiding, I'd rather not get into a row; but, if it comes to the worst, I'll stand by you. I see, by your look, that you suspect me also; but—and there's no accounting for it—I took a liking to you when you first came in; and I'll stand by you by G—!"

So saying, he gave the hand of Palmer a hearty shake, and continued.

"It may seem inquisitive, but I don't think I'm mistaken; your behaviour, and your choice of such a place as this, tells me that you, too, are seeking concealment. Now, there are none of the wretches who frequent here whom

I trust or hold connection with. Be frank with me, for I like your looks; and knowing, as I do, how necessary a *pal* is on such occasions, I'll have no secret from you."

The abrupt and hearty manner with which this was delivered, won the confidence of Palmer—for he was by nature candid and confiding. He and the stranger retired to an upstairs' apartment—the man was lodging in the house—and the freemasonry of misfortune soon made them sworn brothers. Palmer, having taken possession of the stranger's bed, slept soundly after the fatigues and excitement of the past day and night.

Mr. Ferret—to whom the reader has already been introduced—of course formed a most important adviser in the attempt to recapture the fugitive. On a consideration of the circumstances of the escape, he decided that Palmer had made his way to London. Thither he therefore followed; and a few enquiries on the road brought him on the track of the runaway, even to the very purlieus of Billingsgate. Mr. Ferret here lost scent: he, however, knew the locale too well to be easily baffled; and after three or four turns, and some consideration, he entered the Compasses on the afternoon of the very day on which Palmer had there taken refuge.

The latter was still asleep. Ferret sat down in the parlour; but, after a little professional "pumping," as it is termed, he found that none had seen such a man as the one he sought.

While the knowing runner was thus engaged, the stranger—for so we must still for a while call him—stole a look into the parlour when procuring something at the bar. The person of Ferret was well known to him: he hastened up stairs, and arousing Palmer, informed him of the circumstance.

"It won't do to stop here," said he; "I know Ferret too well. He and I are acquainted, though; and I don't fear him, for *we* have made it right." The officers of those days made the caption of offenders a mere trading speculation; and the meaning of this was, that a mutual understanding existed between the speaker and the thieftaker. "It is *you* that he is after; I know it."

Palmer sprang from the bed.

"Here," said his friend, producing a pistol from his coat, "take this; it may serve you." He saw Palmer's hesitation. "Why," said he, laughing, "you look at a *barking iron* as if death was in its barrel. If you had *used* it as often as I, you'd know it's more serviceable for show than mischief. Many's the scrape;" and he smiled as Palmer took it—"many's the scrape that presenting the like of this has saved me, when *using* it would have done for me. No, no!" and he shook his head, "it's what *they* know you *may* do as frightens *them*."

At this moment footsteps were heard on the stairs. The stranger stepped to the door, and placed his back against it.

"Open the window," said he.

Palmer looked out upon the sloping roof of a lean-to, some ten feet below.

"Here!" said his friend in a loud whisper, seeing him prepare to get out. "Hist, man alive! where the devil are you going to? draw the bed aside, and go through that door."

Palmer obeyed his direction. Behind the curtain of the tent-bed appeared a door, the handle of which he turned, and in an instant closing it after him, descended a flight of stairs, and found himself in the passage of the adjoining house: fear of being apprehended lent him speed; he gained the street, and once more breathed freely.   Meantime Mr. Ferret had learnt, from the description of some of the taproom guests, that the man sought had been seen in that apartment, and calling in his follower, who had remained watching outside, he at once commenced a search of the premises.

Two rooms had been rummaged in vain, when the handle of the stranger's door was tried.   To the sharp rap of Mr Ferret the inmate made no reply ; but threw himself upon the bed from which Palmer had just risen. Mr. Ferret applied his knee sharply to the door, and the catch giving way, he stood in the room.   The man started up—

"Why, Ferret, you're a d—d deal less civil than you might be," said the stranger, starting from his recumbent posture, with a braggadocio air ; "smashing into a gentleman's *private lodgings* in this way, what the devil's in the wind now, old boy ?"

" Ay, ay," said the *trap*, looking round with an air of disappointment, then stepping to the open window he narrowly examined the tiles below ; nothing however presented itself there, so he raised the valance of the bed,

> " And there he found—
> No matter what, it was not that he sought."

"Ay, ay, Mr. Fielder," said Ferret, looking rather blank ; "it's all very well to try to gammon the flats, but, d'ye see, old Jack Ferret knows a dodge or two.   It isn't the matter of a *shake* * as I'd spoil a trump like you for, but this is a slaughter business as I'm arter, and that don't allow *slumming*. †"

" I'm blessed if I *pipe* ‡ you, Jack," said Fielder ; "you're queering me now.   Who's been a slaughtering ?"

"Oh, not you ; is that enough ?" said Mr. Ferret, still peering suspiciously round ; "don't think as I'd do the thing as is wrong, but mayhap you have seen the cove ?"

Mr. Ferret then entered on a minute description of the person, and so much as he thought prudent of the history, of our hero.

"Well, that's a go," said Fielder, when he had finished.   "He's a *plucked* one though.   I *have* seen him, old boy, and no mistake.   He left me within this five minutes, and went down stairs.   Have you searched the yard ?"

"No ;" said the knowing one, completely imposed on ; "I thought I should have nabbed him snoozing ; I want him, cos, d'ye see, as it 'ud be the making on me just now ; specially since that ugly escape business of Joe Hawkins. I've been clouded not a little about that there, Master Gregory ; but we can't always serve our friends without suffering a little, d'ye see ; else there 'ud be no merit in it.   Ah! Master George, you little thinks the fencing as I have to make these little jobs right with the beak.   'Ferret,' says he to me, only the last Wednesday as ever was ; 'there's been of late one or two things as has happened I don't like the look on.   There's Joe Hawkins's escape—tho' I don't say as it was possible to help it—looks very suspicious,' says he, 'take care you don't forfeit the character you've earned as an active officer.   I've reason to think, too,' says he, 'as that robbery of Sir Digby Dawson's hasn't had all the diligence used about it since you held the warrant as I expected to see from you.'   'Your worship,' says I, 'I han't slept day nor night since——'"

"Ha! ha! ha!" interrupted Fielder.

Mr. Ferret looked serious.   "Upon my soul," said he, "every word as I tells you is as true as——"

---

* A robbery.   † Concealment.   ‡ Understand.

" It won't do, old 'un," said George, still laughing heartily ; " it won't do —you've had the best of that round already.   D—n it, don't come it so confoundedly hard ; I shall be up in the stirrups again presently, never fear ; and then I'll not forget you."

" I'll tell you what," said Ferret, who was, as far as his scoundrelly avocation would allow him to be so, a good-hearted fellow, " I didn't ask you for the lucre of gain, cos I know you can't do it now."

" You don't know that," said Fielder, with the reckless swagger of the highwayman ; you don't know that ; " you've done well by me in this business ; and if any man could ever say George Fielder was slow in returning a service, d—n me.   D'ye hear anything knock?*   Here's a goldfinch† or two as were made to fly ; and, strike me, if I know a snugger nest than this."

Thus saying, the knight of *roads* placed some gold in the itching palm of the immaculate Mr. Ferret.

We shall leave the minister of justice and the robber to pursue their characteristic talk, awhile to follow the steps of Palmer.   It had been agreed between him and his newly-found acquaintance, who was no other than the notorious George Fielder, who so long held at bay the myrmidons of justice, and set at defiance the corruptly-administered laws, that in the event of any sudden separation, a rendezvous should be understood in an obscure cottage, situated on the common of the little hamlet of Plumstead, in Kent.   Essex was, of course, unsafe for Palmer, while George Fielder had equal objections to his usual haunts at the western extremity of London.   Palmer hastened over London-bridge, and never slackened his hasty walk until the appointed spot was reached.   Avoiding Deptford and Greenwich, he took the upper road, to Lewisham and the fields adjacent, and as the night was closing in arrived at the place appointed.   His directions were too accurate to admit of doubt, and he easily fixed on the small cottage which was to be his harbour of refuge.   The spot was well chosen ; to the left a narrow and little-frequented lane conducted to the banks of the Thames, near Woolwich ; and in the event of a pursuit, the river once placed between the fugitive and his pursuers was a great point of safety ; besides a water conveyance from London was occasionally an advantage not to be despised.   The place, though completely out of the line of the road, had the covenience of being a short distance from Shooter's-hill, the line of the great Dover high-road, and the scene of many of the bold deeds of the taxgatherers of the highway. Byron has rendered deathless the fame of this spot, by selecting it for the robbery of Don Juan.   Within a hundred yards of the eastern declivity of the hill stood the cottage, at the door of which our hero gently tapped.   No voice or sound was to be heard within, and he repeated the signal.   He waited some minutes in anxious suspense ere he ventured a third time to knock.   He looked cautiously through a little window in the front : the house was certainly unoccupied ; he turned his back to the door, and looked on the indistinct clumps of broom as they shook their tufted heads, rich with rows of pendent cups of gold, perfuming the cool air of evening : a man, dressed in a coarse smockfrock approached him from among the gorse.

"Did you seek any body about here ?" said he.

Palmer immediately replied by inquiring his way to Woolwich.   The man, after looking at him suspiciously, extended one arm, as if to point out to him the direction, while he placed his disengaged hand in a peculiar manner on

---

* *Do you understand this ?*   † Guinea.

Palmer's arm. The mode of pressing the fingers at once told our hero he was with a friend. It was the token of companionship already explained to him by Fielder. Palmer returned it, by instantly grasping his hand in a way also taught him by his newly-made friend. The man smiled, and pointed to the door. Palmer understood him, and made the required signal, and the two entered. They passed through the neatly-sanded front parlour, and, entering another apartment, there found an elderly man and woman, apparently engaged in the trade of making brooms from the heath with which the vicinity of the cottage abounded. Heaps of the material, green and dried, strewed the floor. The guide nodded to the couple, and passed through; they entered a small shed, occupied by a rough-coated specimen of the long-eared tribe, whose ostensible employ was to carry the manufactured article abroad for sale, though the little cart which stood in the front of the shed had many a time and oft conveyed much more valuable commodities. The man unfastened the halter of the donkey, and led it out of its narrow stable. Kicking aside the litter on which the animal stood, he removed a tile, and grasping a ring, raised a trap. The two descended in silence a few stairs of hardened earth. The man rapped at a board, and called aloud to the couple above to put back the animal in its stable; he opened a small and strong door, so small as to make it necessary for them both to stoop on their hands and knees; and after groping several yards in this manner, they again rose on their feet at the foot of a few steps similar to those by which they had entered. His companion coughed thrice: a trap in the flooring above their heads was raised, and Palmer and his companion emerged into a small apartment, in which were seated two men, booted and spurred, busily engaged in despatching the contents of a dish and a bottle. They looked hard at Palmer, and his guide broke silence.

"It's all right," said he, "this is a friend of our *pal* George's."

"Indeed!" said one of the fellows, "it's queer that he should send a stranger here; though we can't grumble at what he does, seeing none of us has more to risk than he. Seat yourself; a friend of George's is always welcome."

So saying, one of them proffered a tumbler of spirits and water.

"It's the right sort," said he, laughing; "the Queen's mixture; though we don't let her profit much by our consumption."

Palmer seated himself, and accepted the glass. The night wore on. His companions were hearty fellows; and their free talk, though at first it slightly shocked Palmer—for in his country experience such lax notions of morality had never assailed his ears—yet there was a daring, a generosity, and a style of freedom in the character of their discourse, and the little snatches of anecdotes and adventure which enlivened it, which strongly excited his admiration. Three hours had almost insensibly slipped away in this manner, when the man he had first seen entered; and announced that it was between ten and eleven.

"Are the prads in the wood, Gregory?" asked one; "who's with them?"

"Young Redhead," replied the man; "he's a cute one is that youngster. P'raps though, you don't know as George is there too himself, Master Rose."

"The devil he is," said Rose; "why, I did'nt bargain for that. What dy'e think on it, Ned; is he come down to look after his snacks, eh? I thought you and I were to put up this affair between us."

The highwayman was evidently irritated at this piece of information. His companion made no reply; and he continued:—

"I don't think that George ever did the thing that was shabby, to my knowledge ; but this looks someting like it. Excuse me, as you're a friend of his," said he, turning to Palmer ; "but this little concern is entirely on my own account ; and though I'd cut my hand off afore I'd see a pal in distress, and refuse him half of a *haul*, I don't like the look of Master George's coming down just at this moment."

The character of Bill Rose was an anomaly. To the most reckless extravagance he conjoined a jealous and avaricious disposition ; and this arrival of Fielder, who was a master spirit among them, awakened a misgiving that some of the spoils of the enterprise were to be snatched from him. His conjectures were cut short by a whistle, succeeded by a cough, such as Palmer had heard from his guide. The men left the house by the back-door ; the conversation dropped, and the party remained in anxious expectation. Two or three minutes elapsed, and again the signal being repeated below the floor, the trap was raised, and Palmer's associate at the Compasses entered. Uncasing his legs from a pair of stiff leather leggings, and throwing off a smock-frock, George Fielder stood before them indeed an altered man. A gay scarlet coat sat neatly on his symmetrical person ; leather don't whisper 'ems, of the then fashionable brimstone colour, and the most approved cut, covered his well-formed leg ; boots, with spurs of massive silver, completed his equipment. Observing Palmer's look of surprise, he smilingly made him one of the courtly and stately obeisances of the day, and surveying himself not a little vainly, said,—

"'Fore Gad, friend Dick, I've a fancy I might be taken for a gentleman just now ? What think ye—would this do for a blood to sport at D'Osyndar's, or Wills's ? I've a bit of sport on, though I must own a little love of gain is at the bottom of it. D'ye know, lads, that your scheme is off—the Sardinian envoy has not yet arrived—his horses were countermanded three days ago at Canterbury, and your game's up. But hearken, my trumps, there's another go afoot—Dick, my fine fellow, d'ye like revenge ?"

Palmer did not exactly see the drift of all this ; he knew not the fact with which the reader is acquainted, of the regret and repentance of Sir Litton Weston, and how unwilling an instrument that person had been in the plot which had led to his present desperate situation. He looked on him as the protector and fellow-conspirator of Dennis ; and often had we wished, when thinking over the occurrences of the commitment and of his escape, that he had had the opportunity of wreaking his vengeance on the principal rather than the subordinate.

"I don't clearly understand you," said he ; "on whom am I to be revenged ?"

"Why, you're rather dull, I'm thinking," replied Fielder : "who would you like most to repay for the sufferings they've made you go through ? 'specially when you can serve yourself by so doing. Sir Litton leaves the Hall next Thursday for London : I've learned that much ; taking with him none but his steward : but there's more behind. He will carry with him for security the rents of his estate : the booty is in gold, lads—in shining gold, which even its owner dare not swear to when once shook in our purses. It must be done ; and if you're the ruffler I doubt not I shall shortly see you ; why you shall have the chance of serving him as you please. No shooting though, mark me ; no taking his life. What say you to this, Dick ?"

The proposal startled Palmer. Circumstances had led him into his present companionship; and though captivated with the wild adventurous life which they led, this proposal of robbery came suddenly and unpleasantly upon him.

"Well, if you're afraid to join us," said Fielder sarcastically, "I'm only sorry I proposed it—that's all. I thought you'd have snapped at the chance of making yourself independent, and punishing your dirty persecutor at the same time. However —"

The imputation on his courage conveyed by the first part of this speech was too much for our hero; and the more than hint at dependence—for the few shillings Palmer had brought away with him were expended—called the blood into his cheeks.

"Afraid!" said he, looking angrily at Fielder, who regarded him with a friendly smile; "afraid of what!—of Litton Weston? No! Show me the spot where I shall meet him, and see if I fear him, or you, or any other man. Nevertheless —"

"Bravo! well said!" interrupted Fielder; "spoken like a lad of spirit: but don't ride rusty; for I mean you well. I see you're a little touchy on this point, and I won't press you. Comrades, will you join us?"

So saying Fielder seated himself, and desired the man to go to the broom-maker's hut, and tell the old woman to "toss him up a bit of something." Rose and his companion would not join them.

"No!" said Bill Rose, "these are queer times: I've been d——d unlucky of late, and I can't afford to idle. Curse me, but I think they've some way of even doing us when we do chance to *nail* 'em. I've known the time when any grazier 'ud *cut up* for a fifty; but now my last three *chops* got me what?— I'm d——d if I an't ashamed to mention it—that I am."

"Bill Rose," retorted Fielder, "you're the most grumbling hound I ever met with. Why the deuce don't you sit down, and make your miserable life happy. D'ye think no one draws blanks in life's lottery but yourself?"

"I couldn't make myself easy," said Rose; "I reckoned on this *lay* as a sure one; and now, as if the devil dealt the cards, and the black suit was trumps, I'm done again. But it's no use grieving, as you say; so I'll e'en take a look at the face of Oliver* for an hour, and a canter over the hill. What say you?" said he to his companion: "there may be luck on the cards for us yet."

The last words were uttered in a more cheerful tone; and after a few minutes' bustle examining the priming of their pistols, tightening the knee-straps of their boots, and encasing themselves each in an ample roquelaire, Rose and his companion, wishing them a hearty good night, and declaring their intention, should fortune favour them, to return again shortly, left the cottage.

"I'm not sorry, altogether, that he's gone," said Fielder, seating himself: "he's a strange fellow, that. Although lavish of his money, I never saw man so graspingly eager to obtain it: he would wrangle with his best pal for a fraction of booty, and then give up the whole of it upon an appeal to his generosity. The bottle stands with you. By the bye—well thought of. I suppose you are aware that in our profession we are usually known among our intimates by some other name than the one which may have come to us by inheritance from our forefathers. You have not yet been called by name before my associates: what is your name, friend Palmer?"

Fielder laughed as he said this; and after some further conversation,

* The moon.

The Meeting of Turpin and Black Dennis.

the gist of which was, the many instances in which Fielder had found the conveniences of an *alias*, and the ludicrous mistakes and misunderstandings which his questionable identity had given rise to.

The dish had been emptied, the same office, more than once, done for the flask, though but a small time had been suffered to pass between each replenishment of the latter; and the night had grown old, before Rose returned, though without his companion. His spirits were evidently lighter than at his departure. He glanced round the apartment, then throwing himself on a chair, he laughed aloud.

"You've lost a treat, George," said he, "by not going with us. I can't help laughing when I think how grievous the old Doctor looked at taking his own physic! ha! ha! ha!"

"Laugh a little softly," said Fielder, "zounds, man, d'ye think we're on Salisbury plain. You're always so confoundedly down in the mouth, or else riding the high horse, that no one knows where to have you. Drink, and if you've anything worth telling, out with it."

"Oh, nothing for that matter," replied Rose: "I've been prescribing a little, that's all; and Bob Handley acted as my assistant. But I'll tell you: We'd only just cleared the hill, when what should we see coming after us but a cove, on a stiff cob, cutting along like a reprieve; he rode up. 'Hallo! my fine fellow,' says I, 'is it life and death business you're on? Stand! if you're a true man!' He would, I dare say, have said something, only he was too much blown; so he looked rather blue at our pops as we laid hold of his

No. 7.

bridle, and at last he found his tongue. 'Gentlemen,' says he, 'I hope you'll be merciful ; I'm only a poor serving man, and I—' 'Where are you riding to at this rate ?' 'I've been to town,' says the poor devil, half frightened out of his wits, 'to fetch the doctor for master, who's main bad wi' a' surfeit, and he's a coming down the road as fast as he can.' 'Here's luck, Bob, say's I, 'a doctor's better than nothing, though he's generally richer pluck-ing after leaving his patient than before.' We let the scurvy fellow go, and in a few minutes, sure enough, up drives the carriage. You know my way. Bob takes the post-boy, while I paid my respects to old Potion, and a pretty fair go we made of it."

The highwayman here emptied his pockets on the table. The massive gold head of the long cane which the physicians of olden days invariably smelt at consultations, a single stone ring set with a large brilliant, a heavy gold snuff box, and a valuable Tompion watch, of the same material, were among the spoils, and finally the robber jingled upon the table a green silk purse of large di-mensions, evidently well lined with guineas.

"I call that none so dusty," said Rose with a chuckle, after a survey of the booty before him. "But the best's behind. I'd ha' let the old hunks go if he hadn't tried to put the *queer* on us with his purse and ring. While handing me his ticker, with many grunts and groans, he managed to drop the *skin** and *fawney.** I twigged the dodge though ; so when he comes to fork out the snuff box and cane, I says, 'Well, my dear doctor, if ever I require your services I'll send for you, but I should like to borrow a guinea or two of you that I may be ready with the fee.' The old bilk began swearing and vowing, that he had not a shilling, that we had stripped him to the last farthing, and all that sort of gammon, so at last, finding it was no use talking, I turns him out in the road under care of Bob while I had a regular rummage of his drag ; Bob meantime borrowing his wig, and along with the rest I finds a lot of physic. Says I to Bob, 'What does the old kill-man† deserve for trying to put the *kybosh* on us in this way ?' 'Desarve,' says Bob ; 'why to be obligated to take his own physic, and I knows nothing worse.' 'And that he shall do,' says I, 'if it was only to teach him not to play tricks on St. Nicholas's clerks.' You'd have split to have seen the phiz of old Rhubarb. 'For God's sake, gentlemen,' says he, 'don't think of such a thing, you'll be my death ;' 'Depend on't then, you licensed murderer,' says I, 'you shall take every drop. If it 'ull kill you, you old wretch, how dare you give it to other folks ?' Well he began a long argufying to show how it might do good to other people, though it would p'ison him ; but I cut him short ; and by the persuasion of a slight rap or two on the head, a kick or two on the breech, and putting my popgun unpleasantly close to his listener, I made him swallow all, both out of bottles and boxes, shoved him into the drag more dead than alive, and shutting him up wished him a fine night and a pleasant journey. Ecod he's in a prime pickle by this time, I'm thinking, and 'ull want putting to bed after *his* surfeit as bad as his patient. Ha ! ha ! ha ! What do you think o'that Mr. a—a— what's your name ?"

"TURPIN," replied Fielder readily.

"And what else, if we come to be better acquainted ?" asked Rose.

"DICK," said Fielder, "DICK TURPIN, to be sure, and a staunch lad you'll find him, or I much mistake."

---

* Purse and ring.   † A cant phrase for a doctor.

Rose had talked himself into a good humour; the bottle was again filled, and as the last twinkling star paled in the heavens before the brilliance of coming day, the party broke up, and DICK TURPIN, having been shown a bed in the upper floor of the cottage, betook himself to his much-needed repose.

It has been truly said we are but the creatures of circumstance, The circle into which the fate of Turpin had thrown him, soon produced the change of character such associations were calculated to effect on his young and ardent temperament. The love of adventure was strong within him; the idea of being indebted for the mere means of subsistence to a community whose perils he shared not, and in whose exertions he took no part, was incompatible with his independent spirit. Several times did misgivings dart across his mind; and more than one scheme of future conduct did he frame— the basis of each, however, crumbled on examination, and he felt that to the success of his enterprise on the coming Thursday, he must look for the means of extricating himself from his present position.

The "heart of man is deceitful above all things" said the son of David, some two thousand years since, and the experience of later generations has justified him in adding that it is moreover "desperately wicked." Dick was no philosopher, or he would have known that there is scarcely a recorded case in the history of humanity, in which the *first* step in crime proved to be the *last*. It is not in the nature of things that it should be so. The irritating consciousness of wrong-doing, like the excitement of liquor, leads on its victim to further excesses, and the robber and the drunkard alike become the prey of the demon of avarice or of intoxication. "No man is bad but by degrees," and it is the *first* step in the descending scale which is fraught with all the danger—the entrance to crime, like Dante's gate of hell, bears on its portal, *lasciate ogni speranza,* and of the thousands who have stept within its charmed threshold, and have bitterly lamented the sophisms of self-conceit which have deluded them with the vain hope of escape from its upas influence, few are there whose resolution has enabled them to return, again to mingle, unspotted, with the white-robed children of honesty and innocence. We know the cant of preachers of "repentance" will repudiate this unwelcome truth. We know the open-mouthed clamour with which it will be received; yet, though we deny not the merit and efficacy of sincere repentance, we cannot qualify or extenuate the position, that the man who indulges himself in *one* flagrant crime, though "laying the flattering unction to his soul," that it is the *first* and *last*—has found or will ever find it so. Crime is a stimulant: the agitating hopes and fears attendant on its committal, and the dread of detection, like the delirium of the gaming table or of the grape, unseat the reason of its victim; and the moral principle, which alone rules in a sound mind and a sound body, deposed from its sovereignty, is trampled beneath the hoof of passion. The *first* crime is the irrevocable seal of man's fate—*ce n'est que le premier pas qui coute*—and though he pause and deliberate as to the *expediency* of committing his *first* offence, all after delinquencies follow smoothly in its train.

Thus it was with Turpin—the attractive piece of hell's pavement* he had so prettily tesselated, and the imaginary masonry of which showed so smoothly and attractive to his glowing fancy, was destined to be shivered by

* The Portuguese proverb says, "Hell is paved with good intentions.'

the force of the stubborn truth we have just enunciated. The Thursday mentioned in a former page came and went, and as evening drew on, the enterprise in which he was engaged produced an excitement that had all the charm of novelty. The sun was just shooting his last slant ray over the undulatory outline of the Kentish hills, when Fielder arrived at the hut; he had been to London for the purpose of procuring the necessary disguise for Dick. The spruce highwayman had become so little to be distinguished by his dress from the travelling gentleman of the day, that the safest disguise was unquestionably that which the unthinking vulgar could consider no disguise at all; namely, the fashionable costume of the time. The lappelled waistcoat and large cuffed coat, the three-cocked hat with its narrow border of silver or gold, and all the requisites for his equipments, down to the short topped boots, crooked spurs, and holster pistols, had been provided by the considerate Fielder; and within a few minutes of his arrival from town, the cart, which beneath a load of unsold brooms conveyed these and other necessaries, drove into the little yard before described. Turpin speedily equipped himself, and smock-frocks having, as a measure of precaution, been slipped over their dress, they left the cottage.

A minute's walk brought them into a narrow lane, which leading directly through the Plumstead Marshes and the wood near Welling, debouched about midway up the elevation of Shooter's Hill; the lower end led to the little ferry by which the then few inhabitants of Woolwich communicated with the opposite shore of Essex. This lane they crossed, and after diving a few paces into the wood, Fielder stopped.

"How like you, our project?" said he, with an air of raillery: "if you know any just cause or impediment, speak now, or for ever after hold your peace: as the parson has it."

Turpin was too much excited to think rightly. "D'ye think, George;" replied he, with a braggadocio swagger, intended as much to impose upon himself as his companion; "D'ye think I'm the chicken-hearted skulker to shrink from a friend? Put me to the proof, and, if I shrink, shoot me for a cur."

"You're a trump," said Fielder; "so now for it." Applying his fingers to his mouth the highwayman gave a low and soft whistle, which he followed by a cooing sound resembling the note of the woodpigeon. The peculiar "tu-whit, tu-whoo!" of the night-jar was the only reply that broke upon the ear.

"That's a born devil," said George.

"What?" said Turpin; "I heard nothing but an owl."

"Ha! ha!" laughed his companion, "why Dick, my worthy, you'll know us better some day. That younker has as many tricks as the busiest imp of his father, and he's old Nick for certain. Coo-o! coo-o!" repeated Fielder.

Again the owl was heard, though this time much nearer.

They had now reached a small cleared space of verdant turf; the sky still glowed ruddily in the west; and aloft in the quarter of the heavens still blushing at the departure of the god of day, mildly beamed the golden lamp of the solitary evening star. A few tufts of fleecy clouds, light as the gossamer, reposed tranquilly in the blue expanse; and the short sharp chirrup of insect life, and the whirr of the goat-moth as it hovered about the boughs, or the rough buzz of the cockchafer, as it blindly dashed its bulky and mail-clad body against the intruder's person, were the only sounds or signs of life that met the eye or ear. Fielder shaded his eyes with his hand as he peered curiously through the shadows of the wood : a rustling sound was heard, and through a narrow bridle path which opened on the space beforementioned, a lad advanced leading by either hand a horse saddled and bridled, each decorated with a thick sheepskin shabrack and leathern holsters.

" How now, Redhead, my lad! where's Bess? You don't think I'd give the sorrel to a friend, do you?" said Fielder, with some dissatisfaction, as he surveyed the steeds.

" Why that's no fault o' moine," replied the lad, who from the foxy colour of his caput had an unquestionable claim to the title of Redhead: " a' knows he's a bit of a shier loike, and that a' kicks noo and then ; but a' can't help that. Master Wheeler said—saving your presence, sir ;" addressing Dick, " as 'twere no great matter which on em I tuk—Sorrel or Witch—sein' as there wur no need chancing mischief to Bess wi' a green un." The fellow gave a simple grin as he said this, as if unconscious of any rudeness; though a furtive twinkle of the eye as he caught the rising expression of anger on Fielder's countenance, might have been seen by an acute observer.

" And who, the h— and d—n !" vociferated Fielder, " is to settle for me what horses I shall ride, much more how I shall mount my friends. Ned Wheeler, too, the skulking, smuggling, peaching vagabond! Come, lead us on directly, and get Bess saddled quickly; fly, jump," and he cracked his riding whip within an inch or two of the leather-cased calves of Redhead.

The lad led back the horses the way he came, and the two followed him : emerging from the wood a footpath between two hedges brought them to a turnstile ; the top of this Redhead quickly removed, and thereby afforded passage for the quadrupeds into a shed, the front of which abutted on a yard strewed with wheels, whole, broken, and under repair, rough spokes, logs, and all the other symbols of a wheelwright's trade. Passing laterally through this shed without exposing themselves by entering the yard, a small door at its side conducted them into the snug stable of a hedge ale-house. A noble brute stood at the manger; the eye of Fielder sparkled, as he rapidly surveyed her form; she was in truth a study for a painter.

Her head,—and in no part is blood and breed so strikingly developed—was small and angular; from the small white star on her ample forehead, her finely chiselled head tapered toward the muzzle, and as suddenly swelled out to form the widely dilated cartilaginous nostril, so essential not only to beauty, but to free respiration; her lips were thin, firm, and well supported. Full, large, bright and expressive eyes, bespoke her intelligence; while her small and spirited ears, placed wide apart, gave token by their constant and lively action of her spirit, temper and endurance. Her beautifully arched neck, entering the chest just above the point of her shoulder, fine and smooth above, but displaying a chiselled muscularity in its lower parts, supported lightly and without fatigue the exquisitely formed head. The starting muscles of the forearm, close-knit joints, and deep flat wiry shanks, the flexors of which stood prominently from the bone; the slanting and elastic pastern, the neatly rounded and solid foot, all spoke eloquently of speed, bottom, and strength to carry her through the severest tasks which an exacting master could demand from the noblest servant of man. A long back, broad loins, muscular gaskins and flat hocks impressed, even on the most indifferent observer, the idea of her prodigious power. Her withers, though apparently low, were fine ; sloping shoulders broad chest and depth of girth, announced her endurance to be equalled only by her speed. Beautiful in form, graceful in action, and docile in temper, she playfully evinced her satisfaction at the caresses which Turpin bestowed on her. Fielder viewed with pleasure the surprise and admiration of our hero, who was himself no mean critic in all matters of horseflesh. He was gratified by his young friend's judicious praise.

"She'll do any thing but talk, friend Dick," said he, looking at her with almost a lover's eye; "where would you see such another? not in the king's stables, I warrant you; though there's fine cattle there. Too much of the thick German blood though to show such as she: there's Eastern fire in those veins, Dick, and no mistake! Fleet as a greyhound, lively as a kitten— her age? you don't guess it, for a guinea!"

"Done," said Dick, good humouredly, "five years old; d'ye like that?"

"Your guinea, Dick," said Fielder, "but you can owe it me," and stepping to the mare's head, he exhibited her mouth.

"Three years,* by jingo!" said Dick, as he surveyed with astonishment the central permanent nippers but just developed. "Why, how's this? I'd have sworn her a full-grown mare."

"The knowing ones are taken in when they meet a phenomenon;" said Fielder, merrily; "and Black Bess *is* one. But time presses."

While this conversation was going forward, Redhead was busily engaged in transferring the accoutrements from Sorrel to the back of the noble charger. "She'll want no spur," said Fielder, "I pride myself, Dick, on the finest woman, and the best bred prad, that brass and a good figure can procure. So ho! Bess! Egad, I've forgot till this moment, to ask you whether you've pluck to mount her; she's young and skittish as a maid, and as ticklish to manage. Soho, Bess! gently." While thus speaking Fielder himself tightened the girths, measured the length of the stirrups with his eye, and gave several other little marks of attention to the equipment; finally, having passed his hand down each taper leg from the knee to the fetlock, he desired Redhead to lead her forth. They were soon in the wood, and Turpin, who among his many feats of personal activity, reckoned that of being a bold and skilful rider, crossed his steed with a vault which won the heart of the generous Fielder.

The two walked their steeds slowly in the direction of the river, and having arrived within a hundred yards of the spot, they met the returning Redhead, who, having hastened to the waterside, now met them with the welcome intelligence that the boat was ready. Fielder tossed the boy a piece of silver, and both horses were soon on board.

* "When the envoy returning from his former mission was encamped near Bagdad an Arab rode a bright bay mare of extraordinary shape and beauty before his tent, until we attracted his attention. On being asked if he would sell her; 'Why what will you give me?' was the reply. 'That depends upon her age. I suppose she is past five?' 'Guess again,' said he. 'Four?' 'Look at her mouth,' said the Arab with a smile. On examination, she was found to be rising three. This, from her size and symmetry, greatly enhanced her value. The envoy said, 'I will give you fifty tomans' (a coin nearly the value of a pound sterling) 'A little more if you please,' said the fellow apparently entertained. 'Eighty, a hundred.' He shook his head and smiled. The offer at last came to two hundred tomans. 'Well, said the Arab, 'you need not tempt me further; it's of no use—you are a rich elchel (nobleman) You have fine horses, camels, and mules, and, I am told you have loads of silver and gold. Now, added he, 'you want my mare, but you shall not have her for all you've got."—*Sir J. Malcolm's Sketches of Persia.*

"Oliver whiddles* to night," said Fielder, "a few more blinds† would be no harm."

"Ay, ay, Sir," said the man who was labouring at the long oars of the horse-ferry boat, and who was evidently no novice in the service he was engaged in. "Ay, ay, but you'll have a shower, or an hour or two's by yet, I can feel it i'the wind; and see just in its eye there, how it's thickening. We'll have a dirty night, or ould Dan's a long way out—and that's what he seldom is."

The boat grided on the gravelly causeway, and the party stepped out.

"The time and signal?" said the grey-headed fisherman, for such he seemed.

"Two; but d—n it Dan can't you have Tom here with the boat, in case time should press us?"

"No," replied the other, "that's unpossible; Tom's off on a long-shore-lay;‡ and there's no knowin' when he'll be back—at least for sartain—but I'll do the thing. Though 't wont do to have the boat beached o' this side the river."

"Well," said Fielder, "needs must when the d—l drives; so bear a hand old blue-light, and keep a sharp look out for three flashes of loose powder on the edge of the osier bed here away on the right."

"Ay, ay, your honour," replied Dan; "I'll warrant as you shan't wait."

And leading their horses on to the level causeway, the two horsemen rode smartly onward for the great high road through the forest of Hainault.

Is there anything more calculated to give a fillip to the blood, to quicken the circulation, and raise the animal spirits, then a bursting gallop on a cool night, beneath the flickering beams of a partially obscured moon? The clouds had gathered over half of the horizon, and the moistness of the breeze as it came in the faces of the riders was invigorating.

Though well mounted, Fielder found some difficulty in keeping pace with his companion.

"She's all that you can wish," said he, making an exertion to draw up to her head, "but recollect she's young, and not what she will be a year or two hence." Dick reined in.

"Here's a right sort of night," said Fielder, "another mile and we're *there*." A few slight spits of rain came down the wind.

"Bravo," said Fielder, "this will do;" again their pace was quickened, and after crossing a portion of the forest at a slapping pace, they found themselves on the desired high road.

"Hold hard," cried Fielder, and they stopped. They listened; no sound was audible, save the dropping rain from the branches of the water-loaded trees, as their tufted heads shook in the passing breeze, for the shower had now ceased. "He can't have passed," soliloquised Fielder; "'tis yet scarce ten, and his horses are ordered at the Spread Eagle§ at that time, and it'll take 'em a while to put 'em into his old clumsy drag."

Turpin felt a new and unwonted sensation of anxiety creep over him as the time approached. It was not fear; it was rather a yearning to do boldly in the business, and justify the flattering estimate of his prowess which he could not help seeing his admired companion had formed. To him the character

---

* The moon blabs; tell tales.　　† Clouds.　　‡ A smuggling adventure.
§ A well known inn on Epping Forest.

and avocation of George Fielder embodied enough of romance and adventure as completely to silence all conscientious scruples; and his generosity and frankness had so attached our hero to his fortunes, that in the ardour of his youthful single-mindedness, he would have hazarded life in his defence.   Again they listened—Fielder dismounted, and placing his ear close to the ground, said hastily, "Back, back under yonder tree; I'll give the signal. Just nicked, by Jupiter! Hark!"

Dick listened; the grating, crushing whirr of carriage wheels, as they rolled heavily along the drift road, moistened by the recent rain, grated on the ear.

"Ready, lad? eh?" said Fielder, having thrown his horse's bridle over a stake in the hedge at the road-side.   "Ride out ahead of the horses and present—then to the carriage window—I've already told you the rest.—They come."

The lumbering family carriage of the Westons neared them as these words were spoken.   The well-fed long-tailed Flanders horses which drew it made but small progress in their heavy trot; and while the carriage was yet some twenty yards from the spot where the horseman and footman lay in ambush, our hero, in his nervousness lest the prize should pass and thus overwhelm him with what he deemed eternal disgrace, emerged from the shadow of the huge elm beneath which they were concealed.

"Confound it," exclaimed Fielder, as he saw Dick advance towards the carriage, in full view of the driver, with pistol in hand—"He'll get shot— it's too late now to back, so here goes, if it is to be a fight."   So saying he rushed forward, and just as our hero, in an authorative tone, had ordered the postillion to stop, Fielder seized the horses' heads, and presenting a pistol, bade Dick see to the inside passengers.   Quick as thought he was at the window—and to his ready and decisive "Deliver," the voice of Mr. Sheepshanks was heard, declaring, in a tone rendered ludicrously tremulous by terror, that they possessed nothing to deliver.

"Open the door!" exclaimed Dick.

The trembling arm of the steward of Sir Litton was stretched over the panel, and the door opened.   Sir Litton was not within; he had commissioned his steward and Mr. Sheepshanks to convey the cash to London for deposit at his banker's.   The booty was contained in three or four stout canvass bags placed on the seat of the carriage.   The parley was short.   "Hand out," cried Turpin; "d'ye suppose I'll condescend to take it; no!   Throw the bags on the ground, and we'll spare your sneaking lives; conceal but one of them and you die!"

Three bags were thrown with great deliberation and much hesitation from the interior of the carriage, and a pause took place.

"How many?" asked Fielder, who still held the bridle-rein.

"Three!" replied our hero.

"It won't do; there are five," said Fielder positively; another bag came forth.

"Another!" said Dick, accompanying the demand with a threatening gesture.   Sheepshanks threw it tremblingly from the seat.

"Five?" demanded Fielder.

"All right!" replied Turpin.

"You may go!" said Fielder, loosing his hold of the rein.

The terrified postillion clapped spur to his near horse, while with hearty

Mr. Julap's Midnight Summons.

good-will he applied the whip to the flanks of the other. The travellers in the carriage had placed a good fifty yards or more between themselves and the highwaymen, who had just secured the bags which lay on the road, when the flash of a pistol was seen from the coach-window, and an instant after the smart crack of its report reached their ears; it was out of the range of even a better description of firearms.—Fielder laughed derisively.

"That's the lawyer's shot, I'll warrant. Foregad, the vermin has the will though not the power to do mischief. I reckon that's rather out o' the record, though——as old six-and-eightpence, my Lyon's-Inn master, used to say." [Fielder had qualified himself for his present profession by having "*followed* the law," which now returned the compliment by occasionally *following* him.] "Shall we ride after and give him a taste of the nearest horsepond; eh, comrade?"

"Say the word and I'm with you," replied Turpin.

"Off then," said Fielder.

A minute's ride brought them to the carriage: it was again stopped; and the lawyer, half dead with terror, was dragged into the road.

"For the love of mercy, gentlemen," shrieked Octavius, "don't murder me; I'm not fit to die; help! help!"

No. 8.

"Hold your cursed yell," said Fielder, giving him a hearty kick in that part of the person where honour is supposed to reside, in men of other professions; for it has not yet been proved that honour dwells in any part of the lawyer race. "Take hold of his legs, Dick, there's a horsepond handy, and he'll be in no danger of drowning, for I guess he's meant for a drier death."

At this moment a confused noise of shouting and gallopping was heard in the far distance. Fielder and Dick paused. Terror tied the tongue of Sheepshanks. The sound of horsemen approaching at a rapid pace was distinctly audible.

"To horse! to horse, lad!" cried Fielder, whose experience as yet gave him the command. Dropping the lawyer not in the softest manner in the road, and giving him a parting roll in his native mud, the comrades quickly mounted. They drew aside.

"It won't do to stop, I see," said Fielder; "these newcomers have heard the cracker—they'll smoke the rig we've been at, so morris is the word."

They struck into the wood, and pursuing their course in silence for a few moments at a slack pace they listened attentively. The halt of horsemen, for there appeared to be several, on coming to the spot where Octavius Sheepshanks still lay prostrate, was clearly heard by them. But they were not prepared for what followed.

The party who arrived thus opportunely to the rescue of Mr. Sheepshanks, consisted of the guests at a fox-hunting party given on the day in question by a sporting squire of the neighbourhood. It numbered among its members the undersheriff of Essex. Octavius soon made them acquainted with the position of affairs, and our highwaymen, who were pursuing the even tenour of their way leisurely over the green sward, to avoid the noise of their horses' hoofs, were astonished, though not daunted, by a sudden view halloo from the party of joskins as they supposed them to be.

"Yoicks! Tally ho!" sung out some of the younger ones, who cared little what they rode after so as it was a hunt; and "Yoicks! tally ho!" was succeeded by a crashing of branches, and the hollow sound of more than one horse's hoofs after a lofty leap. Crash went the underwood, hurrah! shouted the riders. Fielder looked at Turpin, the latter smiled.

"Shall we face 'em, George?"

"No, no, that will never do; now for it, follow me!"

Fielder had forgotten at the moment how Dick was mounted; instead of following, three or four bounds brought Bess a length or two ahead of her competitor. Turpin held her in, and a gallop at the top of the speed of Fielder's prad commenced. He too was mounted on a horse of great strength and endurance. Independent of the excellence of their nags, they had another advantage; the horses of their pursuers were jaded; the work had been taken out of them during the day. This was evident, by the distance Turpin and his pal soon placed between them.

"This is glorious sport," said Dick exultingly; "on the back of such a mare as this who could feel fear? she springs under me as if she carried feather weight, and I guess, George, I ride some twelve stone, or nigh hand to it?"

Still the gallop continued, with an occasional pause; but each stoppage told them the pursuit was unabated.

"Damme, George," said Turpin, "but these are plucky lads; how long will they follow without a chance?"

"They think they know of one," said Fielder; "and if old Dan isn't handy, we shall have a few dykes and drains to leap yet, before we double 'em. They know how the land lies, that's clear. We're on the roadway of Barking Level, and that's the only way to the river side; but they hav'nt put salt on our tails yet."

They were now fast nearing the river. The point to which they were directing their course was the spot formed by the embouchure of the creek dividing Plaistow Level from the broad Level of Barking, and known as Creek Point. A century since, this land consisted of beds of reeds and osiers. Our highwaymen spurred their steeds on to the gravelled causeway. The Thames, at this spot, trending to the north-east from Gallion's Point, expanded into Barking Reach, then doubling the point known as Cross Ness, stretched away to the south-east into another reach known as Halfway Reach. The shore opposite the level at whose western extremity they now stood, sloped away; they glanced anxiously along its reed-lined border. Their pursuers were but just audible in the distance. Fielder rode along the skirts of the osier-bed, through which the road led to the river side; drawing the charge from one of his pistols, he filled the pan with some priming powder and flashing it three times, looked anxiously across the Thames. No sign of recognition appeared on the opposite shore, and the flitting clouds which ever and anon obscured the moon's light, rendered objects difficult to be discerned: in vain did they strain their eyes to make out the ferry-boat; the objects on the opposite shore were undistinguishable. Fielder's heart beat anxiously as the sounds of voices came down the wind. He rejoined Turpin, and the two stood side by side on the narrow causeway. It was low water, and the shining banks of smooth mud lay on either side of them.

"If we mean to double 'em through the marshes we must go back a little inland," said Fielder.

"Let's face 'em;" replied Turpin, "a bold dash and we can ride through them: Come on!"

"No," said George, meditatively; "that won't do."

A pause ensued, during which Fielder appeared to be listening with something like indecision to the approaching horsemen who were now near enough to be counted. There were some dozen of them; including a straggler or two whose horseflesh had refused to keep pace with their wishes.

"Shall we swim the river?" asked Turpin; "or, take my horse, I'm better mounted than you. I'll check them till you can get off." Fielder looked at him with grateful surprise.

"We'll do it!" said George, as if decided by the last proposal. They turned their horses' heads towards the water.

Fielder took the bags, weighty with the precious metal, from Turpin, who had thus far carried them in a leathern saddle-bag. Carefully closing its mouth with a piece of cord, he desired his companion to note particularly the precise spot of their deposit. It was nearly low water, and Fielder, walking along the elevated platform of the landing-place until knee-deep, felt cautiously with his foot for the edge of the road-way: having ascertained it, he dipped his hand, grasping the treasure, slowly beside the planking and piles which formed its sides, and committed the weighty mass to the bottom, in water so deep as to prevent its exposure by the receding tide. Turpin watched him attentively.

"So far, so good," said Fielder; "we can do very well without ballast for this voyage ; and when next we've occasion to come fishing, may be we shall know where to catch gold-fish ; eh, Dick ?   But, by goles, here are our anxious friends coming faster than I bargained for."   He hastily leapt into his saddle.

"Halloo! hoics!" cried some of the fox-hunters whom the juice of the grape had stimulated to a temper to ride at anything.   It was a moment of intense interest.   While hope on the one hand mounted almost to delight, anxiety with our friends was almost strong enough to be called fear.   A few short, shrill, sharp notes of a hunting horn, mingled with a distant hoicks! hoicks! were borne on the breeze ; and helter skelter down the narrow ride "the field" came floundering on.   A knot of the best horsemen were far in advance—having completely tailed off the main body—who, toiling along with "faultering steps and slow" brought up the rear.

Coolly and undauntedly Turpin and his pal walked their horses into the stream: a few yards and the animals were swimming steadily.   The tide was still running down, though being near to its time of flood, the meeting waters of the mighty sea had checked its power.   They had cleared the shore some twenty yards when the foremost of the party arrived on the causeway : a broken cloud gave them a full view of the highwaymen.

"Escaped, by G—!" exclaimed one ; "shall we follow them ?"

Two or three of the pursuers rode into the water and discharged their pistols ; for at the time we are writing of, the insecurity of highways and the general practice of travelling on horseback, made it a thing of course that each mounted man should be furnished with the means of self-defence.

A bullet hopped on the surface of the water between Turpin and his comrade.

"Ha! ha!" laughed Turpin, turning in his saddle, "Good evening, gentlemen ; I wish you a pleasant ride back, unless you've a mind for a bath."

At this moment the under-sheriff rode up.   "They'll be drowned," said he, as he watched with the interest of a sportsman the leeway they were necessarily making from the force of the stream.

"No!" replied another, "they'll reach Cross Ness, or I'm mistaken."

"Well, whether they do or not," said the official personage, "I should be loth to follow them on such an adventure: besides, our county's clear of them, and if the sheriff of Kent pleases to hunt them back, let him do so ; maybe he and his merry men fancy swimming the Thames, it's more than I do.   See! see! there's one off his horse."

The gentleman reckoned without his host ; for Turpin, at this moment, with that consideration for his beast which the true horseman ever displays, slipped from his saddle, and placing one hand on the pommel to prevent himself and steed parting company, relieved her of her burthen by sinking into the stream as high as his armpits.   Fielder followed his example.

"They're both off ;" cried another of the company ; "damme but they must be mad to try such a swim ; unless born to be hanged, which we all know is a safeguard against drowning."

"There's more judgment about 'em," said a veteran sportsman who had now joined.   "Leave them alone for knowing what they're about.   When I served under Marlborough, in the campaign of Prince Eugene—I was then attached to the first squadron of Royal Dragoons—I remember we passed the Maes,—that *was* swimming, my lads—we were all heavy men, and heavily accoutred, and more than one gallant horse—"

"To the devil with your stories of Prince Eugene," uncourteously interrupted another, who was eagerly watching the proceedings of our adventurers; "I think you've one of them to fit everything that turns up. That black one's a noble animal; see how he heads his companion. One of them will go to Davy Jones and rob the hangman of his fee. The light-coloured horse will never make the point."

While this conversation was held, our hero and Fielder were breasting the rushing wave,

> "With lusty sinews throwing it aside,
> And stemming it with hearts of controversy."

Gallantly did they hold their way; Bess was the first to feel terra firma, and Dick, gaining his feet almost at the same instant, led her dripping from the stream, her black coat glancing like satin in the silver light. He turned to look for Fielder. The downward tide beat strong on the point he had gained; then, thrown off by the projecting tongue of land, rushed in a slanting direction towards the opposite bank, forming, by the oblique direction of the channel, a wide and dangerous reach. Turpin saw the imminent danger of his comrade; should he fail in gaining land at that point his situation was hopeless. The power of the rushing water must carry him to swift destruction. He hesitated not—his was not the mind to hesitate—leaving Bess, he returned as hastily as the water would allow him, and was about to throw himself in. Fielder was within three or four yards of the shore.

"Hold hard!" cried George; "I'm all right yet—Witch 'ull do it."

He was wrong. Turpin saw them within his very grasp, as he supposed, when at that instant man and horse touched ground. The animal staggered—its slight foothold, insufficient to enable it to oppose the current which bore against its side, alarmed it; with a furious snort it tossed its head in the air, then buried it to the eyes in the wave: Turpin saw the fatal movement; he rushed towards Fielder, and seizing him, dragged him into the shoal water. They stood together; the unfortunate brute, from which its master was so opportunely disentangled, unnerved by terror, again thrust its head beneath the tide, rolled over, and the next moment was seen clear of the point of safety, struggling in the rapid whirl of the eddy, which bore him from the shore. Again and again did it plunge; again and again did it blow the water it unwillingly swallowed from its dilated nostrils. With one wild plunge, and one shrill cry of agony, the poor brute sunk—and ended its death-struggle beneath the rolling waters.

"There goes old Witch!" said Fielder with a bitter laugh of vexation: "that's a bad job, Dick—but I ought to think first of you; you've saved my life, friend," and he grasped the hand of Turpin cordially; "how to repay you I know not."

"Tut, tut, man," replied Turpin; "he must be a faint-hearted man who'd see a fellow-creature drown like a blind pup, and not save him—even if he were not a friend."

They walked to the bed of reeds where Bess patiently awaited them.

"Well," said our hero, "I don't think our friends on the other side will molest us much farther: however, do you mount the mare, and I'll make my way by Plumstead marshes; I know this country pretty well."

"From this day forth," said Fielder warmly, "Black Bess shall ne'er be crossed by me. Who so worthy to own her as the man who has saved her master's life? No! I know where the means to get another prad are to be had for the seeking ; so not another word, I insist upon it, my worthy. She's your's—and long may she live to save and serve you." Seeing that Dick was about to decline, he added, " By G— Dick, we have not yet quarrelled, but we shall now ; good bye"—and he cut short further parley by hastening away, leaving Turpin standing by the horse so generously presented to him : and thus did our hero acquire a servant destined to achieve an immortality both for herself and master.

CHAPTER VI.

I do remember an apothecary,
And hereabouts he dwells.
. . . .
As I remember, this should be the house :
What ho! Apothecary!   —Shakspere.

" There is a tide in the affairs of" woman
    " Which, taken at the flood, leads" God knows where :
Those navigators must be able seamen
    Whose charts lay down its currents to a hair—
Not all the reveries of Jacob Behmen,
    With its strange whirls and eddies can compare :—
Man with his head reflects on this and that,
But woman with her heart, or—heaven knows what !   —Byron.

DAYS, weeks, and months rolled on ; and but few nights passed that Turpin and his fidus Achates, Fielder, did not take the road with various success. Returning one night from an expedition which had led them as far as Dartford, they led their horses through the wood, and stabled them, as usual, in the place described in the preceding chapter. They found Redhead couched on a bundle of fern in the shed. The lad rose on their entrance.

" An ugly job to-night, muster George," said he ; " there's a dead'un, I fear, at the cottage. Ned Wheeler and Bob be gone to fetch the doctor ; but I thinks there's small chance for 'un. He's got as pretty a charge o' buckshot in's carcase as 'ud spile any man's appetite, as wasn't a glutton all out."

" Who is it ?" asked Fielder.

" Why, that's more nor I can tell'ee ; he and some on 'em ha' been out cracking a crib, and I'm guessing they ha' gi'en 'un his gruel. You'll find 'em down yonder, though."

Turpin and Fielder hastened to the hut, and found, on entering, the wounded man, supported in the arms of two of his confederates. The blood was still flowing from an imperfectly staunched wound in his breast, and the crimson fluid had saturated his clothing. The ghastly deathlike hue, closed eyes, and sunken features, next attracted his attention ; and what was his surprise, on a nearer examination, to recognise the features of Black Dennis! It appeared from the story of the man who had brought him off, that they, in company with five others, had planned a burglary at the house of a wealthy farmer in the neighbourhood of Erith ; that their plans had not been so well laid but that some suspicion had been excited among the inmates of the dwelling they had fixed on ; and that, consequently, preparations had been made to give them a warm reception. Dennis, as best acquainted with the premises, had undertaken to effect an entrance ; but, at the very moment when their party was assembled at a back-door in consultation, they were saluted with the discharge of a blunderbuss among them, from a casement in the upper part of the house ; Dennis was the unfortunate recipient of its charge.

Fielder was already possessed of the story of our hero ; yet, though he knew Dennis well, he was so little acquainted with his history, that it never occurred to him that he was the old enemy of Turpin. Dick too, forgot, in pity for the man who now lay stretched in apparent death before him, his abhorrence for the scoundrel, and assisted, as far as lay in his power, in succouring him. Meantime, the two mounted men pursued their search for a leech.

In the retired and pretty little village of Eltham,—long the residence of royalty, and still possessing in its ancient palace, now converted into a barn, one of the most beautiful specimens of the elaborate internal decoration of our ancestors in its beautifully fretted roof, and of sylvan beauty in the remains of its dismantled pleasaunce—resided a son of Esculapius, hight Jalap. No man could better—

> Mix a draught, or bleed, or blister ;
> Or draw a tooth out of your head ;
> Or chatter scandal by your bed ;
>   Or give a glyster.
> Of occupations these were quantum suff,
> Yet still he thought the list not long enough ;
> And therefore midwifery he chose to pin to it :
> This balanced things : for if he hurled
> A few score mortals from the world,
> He made amends by bringing others into it.

The humble dwelling of Jalap, before which was a small garden with low green palings, was situated in the village street. By day it exhibited in its ambiguous window, which was a cross-bred commingling of the shop and dwelling house in its outward show—some half dozen of plethoric bulbous bottles, filled with coloured water, and displaying on their protuberant sides antique symbols of astrologic quackery. The mysterious triangle, the influential crescent, tailed and untailed planetary signs, impressed many a gaping rustic with an awe and respect for their potent contents, which would have been wonderfully abated had intelligible English inscriptions informed them what trash they really held. The interior of his repository was in keeping with its outside. A few tin-covered gallipots filled with the simplest vegetable unguents bore the crabbed inscriptions of the old and exploded pharmaceutical nomenclature ; and here and there a glass jar, filled with spirit, displayed some monstrous freak of nature in the shape of a juvenile pig with six legs, or an embryo lamb with none. These, with some poppy heads,

> And a beggarly account of empty boxes,
> With roseleaves scattered to make up a show,

completed the stock in trade of Mr. Jalap, unless we take into account the learned stores of his cranium.

The scanty practice of the thinly peopled hamlet and its vicinity, barely sufficed to enable the worthy ' doctor', as he was dubbed by the old women of the neighbourhood, to keep life and soul in himself and family ;—for the doctor was a practical anti-Malthusian, and had done the state some service by his philoprogenitiveness. A dozen of olive-branches flourished around the table of Jalap, and though in patriarchal times this plurality of offspring made a man " fear not to speak with his enemy within the gate," in these degenerate days the effect was quite different ; for the insufficiency of Mr. Jalap's income made him exceedingly chary of admitting foes or friends within his outer door, from fear of the intrusion of John Doe and Richard Roe. He had been several times "not at home" to suspicious applicants, who hesitated to declare their business to his half-starved, half-liveried shop-boy, and on this very evening, had retired to his couch, in perplexity and doubtful dilemma, as to the possibility of obtaining the wherewithal to settle a long-standing butcher's bill, for which legal proceedings were threatened.   His dreams presented to his troubled fancy long columns of figures arranged between red-ruled lines of sheets of blue foolscap, each headed with the ominous " brought forward ;" and his fancy was busily engaged in turning over the innumerable folios of some unpaid bill for bread or beef, when his dreams were scared by a lusty knocking at his outer door.   He started on his nether end, and desired his prolific partner to reconnoitre who

> With heavy fist upon his gate,
> Did knock so loud and knock so late,

while he listened attentively to the reply to her inquiry of " Who's there."

"Doctor Jalap's wanted at the squire's directly ; he's at the p'int o' death ; so tell him to look alive—we're to bring him with us," said a rough voice.

" Gracious dearee me!" exclaimed Mrs. Jalap, "who'd ha' thought it ?   Make haste, my dear, and speak to the gentlemen outside.   We're made people by this job—he'd always his doctor's stuff from London, I thought."

" Hold your prate, woman !" replied the doctor, who was gingerly getting into his well-worn and as well-mended nether garment.   " Skill is sure to be appreciated—merit must rise, eventually.   Now there's Bolus, the physician, who attends —"

" Holloa ! master doctor," exclaimed one of the fellows, " bear a hand, will you."

Jalap rushed to the window, " I'm coming, gentlemen ; coming directly ;" and in another minute, Mrs. J. having unfastened the door in the meantime, the leech issued from his dwelling.

One of the men dismounted for the purpose of helping him into his seat. " Now, sir," said he ; " with your leave, I'll manage to make the nag carry both on us."

Jalap did not exactly like this mode of travelling, but anxiety to oblige the squire prevented his making any objection.   They rode for a minute or two in the direction of Foot's Cray, then, suddenly wheeling to the left, took their way by a green lane towards the eastern base of Shooter's Hill.   " Holloa !" exclaimed the doctor, on noticing this proceeding, " where are you going to ? This is not the road to Sidcup ; you should keep to the right."

" It's right enow for us," replied Ned Wheeler; "mind your own business, and we'll mind our'n.   Pr'aps it wouldn't be inconvenient if you did'nt see any thing to frighten you, for you seem rather timersome.   Lend us your fogle, Bob, and I'll darken his peepers."

Wheeler was right; for the doctor trembled violently.   "Don't be afeared," said his nurse, as he felt Jalap shake in the saddle, "there's no harm a coming to you, if you sit quiet."   They bound his eyes ;—this added to his terror.

" For the love of heaven, gentlemen," expostulated Jalap, "don't murder me.   Consider my large family of helpless children ;   I never did you any harm, and I'm too poor to be worth robbing—only take me home and I'll—"

" Be quiet, and be d—d to you," said Wheeler.   Jalap became aware by the motion of the horse that they were leaving the road, and ascending a bank—the bough of a tree caught his head, and stripped it of both hat and wig.   "Mercy, mercy !" ejaculated the blinded doctor.   "Be still, or I'll

Turpin and Madge Dutton interrupted by Dennis.

knock you on the head," said his travelling companion; "Bob, put on old Rhubarb's wig." It was replaced as they moved on. "Have you got him?" asked a voice, in a loud whisper, as they turned again into a gravelly road. "Yes, we ha' got him," was the reply. The most horrid deaths floated through his distracted brain. What could this mean if it was not murder? and hope deserted him. Again a voice enquired, "Got him?" and again did the horseman reply in the affirmative. Jalap's heart sunk within him. "Got him," they had indeed! The thoughts of his anxious wife, and the glee with which he had obeyed this fatal summons, rendered the anguish of his mind doubly poignant. Each attempt at deprecating their murderous design was, however, stifled by their blasphemous denunciations of vengeance, should he make the slightest noise. At length they stopped, and having lifted him from the horse, led him stumbling over some dreadfully uneven ground. A door was gently rapped at, and he found himself in an apartment; thus much he could tell, though the tight bandage prevented his discerning surrounding objects. Now then, thought he, the moment of immolation has arrived; he fell upon his knees; the kerchief was plucked from his head; he gazed wildly round. In the small chamber were five or six men. "I'll neve

No. 9.

divulge anything I've seen, gentlemen, if —" Mr. Jalap was fated that night
not to be allowed to finish a single sentence.

"Man alive, don't be such a fool—you needn't be so cursedly frightened,"
said Fielder, laughing good-humouredly at the pitiable figure of the kneeling
doctor. "There's nobody here will do you any hurt, if you'll be reasonable,
—we want your assistance, man ; so look sharp, and call your senses about you."

Poor Jalap, with open mouth, looked enquiringly at Fielder. The dashing
garb of the highwayman made him think he had at any rate met a gentleman,
from whom he might hope protection. At the conclusion of his short speech,
Fielder drew aside the curtain which divided a small truckle-bed from the rest
of the apartment, and exposed the wounded man to his view. The doctor rose
from his knees, and gazed stedfastly on the emaciated countenance and blood-
stained clothes of Dennis, who lay in a ghastly swoon before him. Such a
sight might shake most men's nerves—it had an entirely opposite effect on
Jalap's. The truth dawned upon him—he was not a doomed man—no ; his
skill was only required, not his life. He was safe, his deliverance was too
astounding to be true ; he wept tears of joy, shook hands in his confusion
with two or three of the housebreakers, blew his nose tremulously, wiped
his eyes, tumbled over a chair, rubbed his hands, and then, with the air of
a man who has neglected some urgent business, drew from his coat-pocket a
small box, his surgical vade-mecum, containing lint, probes, lancets, and the
ordinary appliances of his vocation.

"I see, I see," said he, nervously ; "I see, I see ! Bless me ! Can you
procure me a little warm water? I ought to have a sponge somewhere ; confound it ; ah, here it is ! Be so good as to hold me a basin ; it's fortunate
you sent for me, gentlemen. I flatter myself you might have gone further
and fared worse. I've had some experience, gentlemen, in these sort of
cases. (It was the first gun-shot wound he had ever beheld.) I studied, gentlemen, under the great Dr. Mead. I attended all his demonstrations and
lectures. Ah! syncope ; it might be expected from the loss of blood ; hold
this. Very unskilfully dressed—you'll excuse me—how happened it? I don't
wish to be inquisitive, but—oh, ay, slugs and a blunderbuss, you say? Don't
think at present, as far as an opinion can be formed, anything more than a
severe flesh wound ; laceration of the pectoral muscles ; dear me ; man's shoulder
wounded before ; dreadful cicatrix ; hum, ha! present wound not dangerous though."

Jalap was really a man of much skill in the art of surgery as then practised,
possessing considerable judgment, though sadly deficient in nerve. The wound
was dressed, and the doctor suggested the propriety of his being allowed to go
home for the purpose of procuring a draught for the patient. This produced
some consultation among the party ; Mr. Jalap's hilarity sunk to zero when
Fielder interposed and said, "I am sorry, my good sir, to place you under any
unpleasant restraint, but it would not be exactly the thing for you to be seen
going and coming hereabouts ; and if you're a reasonable man you'll agree
with us. Therefore, perhaps you'll oblige us—here is pen and ink—by writing a note to your wife ; one of our men shall take it—it will calm her
uneasiness, and procure the necessary medicines."

The doctor, with the foolish reliance for which desperate men are proverbial,
mistook the mildness of Fielder for indecision. He rejoiced in his heart he
had found what he thought a gentleman, among the rough crew by which he
was surrounded. He prepared himself for an oration, but his unlucky star
was still in the ascendant, and he had scarcely got through the exordium of

what he intended to be a very polite address, when his old persecutor, Wheeler, who had brought the writing materials, broke in with—

"We've made up our minds, so it's no use argufying: you've brought your gammon to the wrong shop. Hold your gaf, and guv us the bit of scratch, and I'll make it all right with the old woman. I've got a way o' dealing with the women as 'ull settle their little tirrits and frights."

This speech was like a stream of cold water pouring down the doctor's back. He gave a nervous start at the very tone of his voice, and turned to look at the speaker. There was nothing in the forbidding features and marked lines of the desperado's countenance to reassure him, or to recommend him as an ambassador to the ladies. Wheeler saw his fear.

"Come," said he, handing him the pen, "scribble away, old rat's-bane, and none of your fluffery; there's them here as can make out your pen-work, if so be I can't, so no tricks; shove along my hearty; I'll be the cove as 'ull take it."

Mr. Jalap saw it would be useless to resist; so, with a deep sigh, he sat down and penned an epistle to his wife, at the dictation of Fielder, to the effect that the squire's illness was of that alarming nature as to render it impossible for him to leave the Hall; and concluding with a P.S. to his assistant (who was his shop-boy and messenger) to deliver, per bearer, the necessary drugs. This done, Wheeler departed.

It was now day. The fields and hedge-rows glittered with dew-drops, and the birds twittered from every thorn; the curling mists rolled lazily down the sides of the hills, to dwell awhile in the vales, till the ascending sun should draw them towards his mighty source of life and light. Here and there the dappled cow rose from her damp bed; the sheep nibbled their early repast as they strolled slowly; and the tinkling bell of the ancient wether struck musically on the ear. The bright daisy lifted its golden eye; the hare-bell shook its fairy plume in the breeze; and the bean-field loaded the light air with fragrance. The hare aroused from its form, bounded lightly across the pathway, and all nature sprung joyously to salute the day.

All this was passed unheeded by Wheeler. The guilty, the sensual, and the debased, are incapable of duly feeling the beauties of nature; it is only the pure in mind who can appreciate the wonders and the beauties that the hand of a beneficent Creator has spread with lavish profusion around us—it is only to those who can look "through nature up to nature's God," that this highest of man's enjoyments is vouchsafed. Wheeler was none of these; he plodded unadmiring and unseeing through the lovely scenes around him, contriving the best means of most completely blinding the worthy Mrs. Jalap, as to the real situation of her spouse. He succeeded; and having obtained the necessary medicaments, returned.

That day and the following elapsed, and towards nightfall, Mr. Jalap, having pronounced the patient out of danger, and given the necessary instructions for his future treatment, after being again blindfolded, was conveyed homewards, much in the same fashion as he had been brought to the hut; except that on this occasion, after the same sort of roundaboutations, and riding him through one or two shallow streams, they took the bandage from the doctor's eyes, in a bridle lane, some mile or two from his home. On this occasion Turpin and Fielder accompanied him; and the latter, having presented the doctor with ten guineas, to his great surprise and satisfaction, bid him good speed, and left him pouring forth a profusion of protestations of secrecy and gratitude. The worthy Esculapius hardly knew how to contain

his joy, not only at the unexpected gratuity, but at his miraculous escape
from assassination, for such he deemed it. He doubted not that he had
travelled many miles, so greatly had his journey been protracted by the dreadful suspense and agony in which the time had passed. But we must pause
awhile to notice how affairs had gone on in the interval with the good
doctor's family.

On receiving the epistle from the broom-maker's hut, in which Jalap had
certified his loving spouse of the alarming state of the squire's health, the
dame lost no time in exhibiting the document to sundry of her acquaintances,
who, on their parts, were equally diligent in spreading the news. The poor
squire was two or three times killed outright in the ensuing twenty-four hours;
and the chances of his recovery had been learnedly canvassed at the corners of the
several streets, and in the village alehouse; when a labourer who returned in
the evening from his work at the squire's, astonished his dame by declaring it
to be "top and bottom, a dom'd lie," as he had just left the much commiserated
individual in question "as well as ever a'd seed him this mony a year." The
good woman and he called at Jalap's, and the surprise and anxiety of the
doctor's rib and family was extreme. Gallipot, his assistant before-mentioned,
was despatched to Sidcup, and had not long returned to the expectant circle
when Jalap himself came in.

After the first embrace was over, Mrs. Jalap insisted on knowing where he
had really been; but the doctor, to the great disappointment of the party
assembled, politely requested them to retire. Spreading the gold on the table
—he forgot his former fears and protestations, and soon informed the inquisitive dame of the nature of the service he had been performing; and the village,
the next day, knew—though it was communicated as a profound secret by
each narrator—that Dr. Jalap had been carried a great many miles to see a
great lord, who had been desperately wounded in a duel.

Woman is an unsolved, nay, an unsolvable problem. Madge Dutton, the
paramour of Dennis, had once been the finest girl in the village of Sibbertoft,
in Northamptonshire. Of poor and industrious parents, who had paid little or no
attention to her moral or mental training, she grew to eighteen, the pride of
the village green: few girls in Sibbertoft could dance like Margaret Dutton;
and many a hard-handed, hard-working rustic sought her in marriage. Though
her passions were strong, her coquetry and love of admiration, were sufficient,
in her earlier days, to keep her humble suitors at bay. The flattery, attentions, and presents, of the good-looking son of a neighbouring farmer, however,
effected that which the honourable proposals of suitors who were her equals
in station had failed. The desire of outshining her companions, and her love
of dress, made her an easy prey to her comparatively wealthy seducer; and
before she had completed her nineteenth year she deserted the roof of her
parents, and accepted the protection of young Johnson, who, to avoid the
scandal of their rural acquaintance, provided her with lodgings in the neighbouring town of Lutterworth. Her seducer, however, had miscalculated the
character of Madge—she had no taste for domestic privacy; and but a few
weeks passed before his jealousy—for he loved her, if a sensual passion like
his could be so termed—was excited by rumours of her continual gaddings
about, and company-keeping during his absence. Her gay clothes and attractive figure drew the attention of some of the young officers of a squadron of
dragoons quartered in the town; and her rural admirer, whom the fear of his
family had prevented from uniting himself in wedlock with her, was greeted
with the intelligence, that Mistress Madge had eloped with a cornet of the

regiment, and had betaken herself, with her new protector, to the metropolis. Here her history was the old one—neglected by her paramour, she received the visits of "promiscuous" friends; and passing through the various gradations of the unfortunate or vicious, at length became the mistress of one or two of the most noted cracksmen of the day, who successively, driven from the land, or forfeiting their lives on the gallows, left Madge to the tender kindnesses of mankind in general, whose perfidy or inconstancy she retaliated in full. Such was the present Mrs. Sowton, as she styled herself. For Dennis she felt that sort of affection which arises among such beings, more from a feeling of his being necessary to her as a bully (protector she would have called it) and the pride of sustaining a character, which, even in her degraded position, she would not forfeit, that of behaving "like a trump to a chap as had stuck to her while he *had* the tin." This led her, upon hearing from a companion of the accident which had befallen "her fancy man," to declare her intention of going down to attend him—for woman, even in her utmost degradation, feels the kindly promptings of our nature—and this determination she forthwith acted on. The third night of his confinement witnessed the arrival of Madge Dutton at the cottage. This addition to the party much displeased both Rose and Fielder.

"I'm d—d but this place will become a regular resort for these blackguards and their women; what in the name of mischief could have induced Gregory to send her here? Mark me, Fielder," (it was Rose who spoke) "I'm no prophet if this don't lead to worse than you reckon on. I never knew a woman in a secret, that, sooner or later, harm didn't come of it."

Days rolled on, and Dennis became gradually convalescent. Meantime a change had been silently working in the feelings of Madge: the attractive person and pleasing manners of Turpin had raised a flame in her ill-regulated breast; and with her, once to form a design was to see no obstacle to its gratification. She still possessed no inconsiderable share of charms; and these she on all occasions displayed, when in our hero's presence, to the best advantage. She was piqued at what she conceived his indifference, and after one or two hints of her surprise that so likely-looking a young fellow as himself was still without that indispensable to men in his profession, a mistress; and some more than hints how little difficulty he would experience should he lay siege to any woman's heart; mingled with much artful flattery, and some lamentations as to her ill-assorted alliance with Dennis, all which Dick purposely pretended not clearly to comprehend; she ventured on more open proposals. Luckily for Dick's virtue—we grieve to say it, but truth must out—at the very moment when his resolution was wavering, for he was no stoic, Dennis entered the room. It was the first time he had quitted his bed. The flushed cheek of Madge, the equivocal position in which she then stood by the side of Turpin, one hand tightly grasping his shoulder, and the evident confusion of the latter, at once told him how matters stood; and his jealous and suspicious soul told him even more than had yet taken place. He was, however, tactician enough to dissemble his anger, and in reply to Turpin's somewhat confused enquiry of how he felt himself, he replied,—

"Pretty much the same, thank ye, for that part on it. Why Madge, have you been taking a drop o' anything short? You looks as red about the gills this morning as if you'd bin taking some rough exercise?" He said this in a half sneer, which increased Turpin's confusion. Madge, however, indignantly cut him short.

"Why, what are you driving at, you jealous brute, you," retorted she; "the gentleman—and his little finger's more of the gentleman in it than the whole of your blackguard carcass—was telling me—you scape-gallows wretch,—I wonder I'd ever anything to say to—"

Dennis stepped towards the woman, and, raising his unwounded arm, was about to strike her. Dick interposed. A quarrel was what Madge desired to bring about; she therefore continued her vituperation. Dennis, however, saw her design.

"Ay, ay!" muttered he—"'twon't fit; I see through it though, marm. Dick, here's my hand; I'll never quarrel with a friend for such carrion as that: take her, if she's any catch; and I wish you luck of her."

So saying Dennis quitted the room, and throwing himself on the bed, the head of which was close to the slight partition, listened, notwithstanding his previous declaration of indifference, to what passed between the couple he had left. Madge proposed, but in a whisper inaudible to Dennis, that Turpin and she should immediately leave the cottage for London; and endeavoured to enforce her proposition with all the blandishments she possessed; but the charm of her influence was broken: the form of Esther, glowing in all the charms of virgin innocence, rose upon his imagination—the spell was irrisistible—he shook off the impatient and irritated Madge, and strode hastily from the cottage. A few steps on the gorse-clad common, and a few minutes spent in reflection on the scene in which he had just been an actor, produced a feeling of self-approbation; and in a reverie on his first love, he soon lost all remembrance of the charms of the polluted syren he had quitted.

How different were the feelings of Madge!

Her first resource was tears—tears of bitterness and vexation; then rage, choking and uncontrollable rage, tore her breast; and next, revenge, deep, deadly, implacable revenge.

"Revenge is sweet, especially to woman,"

says Byron most truly. She struck her forehead angrily with her clenched hand as she inwardly muttered,

"Have I then let myself down? have I then bemeaned myself to ask a silly green boy to accept me? have I sued a —" Passion choked her utterance. "But I'll be revenged: if Madge Dutton can't have him, no other shall; I'll tighten the cord that shall strangle him with these hands first!" She held forth her clenched fists as she thought, rather than said this.

"Hell has no Fury like a woman scorned;"

and Madge might at that moment have sat as a study for a Pythoness.

The first paroxysm over, reflection came to her aid; she saw that it was indispensable, to effect her revenge, that dissimulation must be had recourse to. She rose from the seat into which she had thrown herself, and clearing her brow, arranged her somewhat disordered headgear; then practising a smile in the glass, stept into the adjoining chamber. The wily Dennis counterfeited sleep. Madge regarded him attentively though abstractedly; she saw him not, though he lay before her; the late shock had unnerved her; and she felt, for a few moments, the tenderness which is woman's heritage—as she thought of all she was, and what she might have been. She thought of her parents; of her first wooing; of her first love; he whom she had slighted, disdained, deserted; and who, as far as she had been able to learn, now, in still living, braved the perils of a soldier's life in a distant clime. She thought of this, and more, as she stood beside the couch of Dennis; and none of those who fancied they knew her best would have believed it—the eyes of the hardened, the desperate, the outcast Madge Dutton were filled with tears! She thought of the wretch she had become; of her parents, and their humble rooftree; of her sisters, and of her brothers, whom she had disgraced—and she thought of this, until, had there been one by to counsel her for good, to confirm her in the virtuous resolutions at that moment floating indistinctly, and rudely formed through her brain—who can say that even *she* might not have been drawn back into the ways of pleasantness and the paths of peace? But none such was there. Her feelings were ever predominant over her reason, and memory brought back the circumstances of her present position. Dennis lay in his feigned slumber; she touched him gently; he started, and looked at her with the half intelligent stare of a newly-awakened man, and then sulkily turned his face towards the wall. Madge seated herself, and by the aid of a few dissembling tears, and an artful statement, half persuaded the suspicious Dennis, that the confusion in which he found her was occasioned by an improper proposal on the part of Turpin; which she, desirous of preventing a renewal of their former deadly feud, had made up her mind to conceal from him: that it was by no means the first occurrence of the kind; and that her feigned anger at his entrance was caused by a wish to prevent a contest in his then weak state, but that it was changed to real, when she found how injuriously even he suspected her.

Man was ordained to be the dupe of woman, since our first grandam, Eve, lost this "great globe and all that it inherit," for a pippin. This improbable story, garnished with a few well-timed sobs and tears, and occasionally a sort of timid approach to a caress, blinded the other eye of even the cunning Dennis; and he also, though not without some misgivings as to the good faith of Madge, felt all the embers of his nearly-expiring hatred fanned into flame.

A few weeks, and the precious pair left the cottage, Dennis still feeble, for their haunts in London. Madge, before her departure, carefully noted each entrance and outlet of the spot—she had not given Dennis even the remotest idea of her revengeful feelings towards Dick. She grew, to the great satisfaction of her paramour, who looked upon it as a proof of her affection, high in spirits, talkative, good-humoured, and, as Dennis thought, handsomer than ever, as his convalescence advanced. She continually dwelt on the pleasure she should feel when he was once more "about," and they set out for the metropolis in apparently better humour with each other than usual.

"Dennis," said Madge, gaily, "you're preciously out of feather, would you mind to '*snitch for the forty*,' * providing you wasn't obligated to split on a friend?"

"I don't know what you're at, just now," replied Dennis; "I'd do a good many things just now, to put us square; though snitching is the last thing I'd do—it's not to my fancy, Madge."

"Pooh! pooh! I could put you fly to how you might have half on it, by laying others on the scent, without ever joining in the cry; there's others as 'ull hunt down the game, if you'll put 'em on the trail."

* Inform for the *forty* pounds—the blood-money then allowed by Government for a capital conviction.

Dennis didn't half like the proposal; he feared that the woman who could act thus, "might betray more men;" he looked at her keenly from his single eye, as he said—

"You're pumping me sure-ly, Madge? you arn't in arnest in this business! no; if I wants to punish an enemy, though he was my worst, I'd not go about it so sneaking a way as snitching."

This speech imposed on Madge, and extorted from her that "hypocrisy which is the homage," says Johnson, "which vice pays to virtue" Not that there was anything like virtue in either of the couple, yet Madge acknowleged even the principle of good faith implied by this declaration, by laughing as she said coaxingly, pinching his arm,

"You don't go to think, Denny, dear, as I'd tempt you to peach on any man, do you? I was only just trying it on a little to see how far your jealousy would make you go towards that conceited young monkey, with his-side-locks, at the hut there, as took such freedoms with me; but I think I've taught him to think twice afore he comes his impudence to any woman as has got a man by her side; that I have; the ignorant, upstart, Johnny Raw! I wonders at the face of boys, now-a days, I do."

Dennis was not improved in temper by this mention of Turpin; however, Madge saw the danger, unless he would come over to her views, of entrusting him with the secret of her plan; she therefore resolved not to make him a participator in its execution.

On the second day after this conversation, as a November wind howled mournfully over the bleak waste of Woolwich Common, a party of men were assembled near a clump of plantation which skirted it on the side towards the Barrack Fields, which abuts on the lane leading to Plumstead Common; they consisted of four of the Bow-street patrol with their cutlasses and pistols, reinforced by some dozen stout fellows—local constables, and sheriff's men of Kent; with them also was a female, and she, the reader may easily guess, was the treacherous Madge.

"It'll cost me my life, for certain," said she to the officer who had the direction of the posse, "if I'm seen in any way in the business; can't you all go without me, now you know so well about it?"

"Certainly not, my pretty little tell-tale," said the officer, chucking her rudely under the chin. Madge was too much used to the degradation, often thoughtlessly inflicted, which men are guilty of towards unfortunates of her profession. "Why, my pretty damsel, you've told us so much, that you must let us into a little more, afore I've any mind to say as you've arn'd the *posh.**
We shall want a little 'dentification business from yer; eh? You know most em personally, I'll warrant?" and the trap and his companions laughed. "As you're all here, I b'lieve, we'll start out of hand—now then, mistress Madge—damme, but you're a handsome wench, though a little of the devil in your eyes. Come, let's tramp it."

They set out: on reaching the corner of the common, the officer who had direction of the party (who was no other than the noted Dick Bayes, of whom we shall by and bye see more) divided his men into four companies, in order to prevent escape. They sneaked cautiously through the heather; three of those most to be relied on took their way towards the cottage, while Bayes with two more proceeded to the broom-maker's hut. The officer gave the signal, and after a short pause, Ned Wheeler issued from amongst the heather,

* Money.

The Break-up of the Plumstead gang.

through the subterraneous way by which Turpin had first seen the man who introduced him to the hut, and thence led him to the cottage. The man came close to Bayes, whose two followers crouched near by. Bayes seized him, and presented a pistol to his ear; the man said nothing, and Bayes quietly handed him over to their care. He now made a preconcerted signal to some others, and several men hurried to the cottage door. Bayes burst it at a single thrust, and with a pistol in each hand, followed by his myrmidons, entered the parlour. It was empty; and they stared around pretty considerably chap-fallen. They proceeded to the other two rooms, but no trace of a highwayman was to be seen, save a whip or two, and a pair of spurs. The thief-taker stood a moment in doubt,—the noise as of a heavy weight f on a boarded floor was heard, and the shuffling of feet, and a confuse pering. One of his followers pointed to a mark in the paint of a panel, which looked like a secret door; it was the work of an instant to burst it, and Bayes and his companions found themselves in the small room containing the trap-door, by which, as the reader will remember, our hero first came into the cottage. The trap was open, and one man was descending, and two or three stood in the apartment. They raised their pistols, but seeing the number of their enemies, as quickly lowered them. "Surrender, in the King's name!" exclaimed Bayes, "throw down your weapons, or I'll fire!"

"Oh, you needn't make so much noise about it," said Fielder, "we see there's enough of you. Perhaps you'll be so good as to tell us to what we

No. 10.

are to attribute the honour of this visit, Mister Bayes? It's as unwelcome as unlooked for, I can assure you. However, Bill," said he, turning to Rose, "it's no use being down on your luck—so Mister Bayes, if you've anything to say to us, we wait your commands."

Fielder said this with an air of mock politeness, for he was one of those humorists who view life as a practical jest; to whom even misery and misfortune assume a grotesque air, and who see something comical that disposes them to joke, even with death. The poet Prior, who penned as an inscription for his grave,—

> " Life's a jest, and all things shew it;
> I thought so once, but now I know it."

would seem to have been of this temperament. The great and good Sir Thomas More mounted the scaffold with a jest on his lips; and who does not remember the playful way in which the lovely Anne Boleyn, when at the block, smiling on the headsman, grasped her delicate neck, with a pleasantry on its smallness, and the little trouble its severance would give to the bearer of the shining implement of death. Numerous are the instances, among the wise and the virtuous, of the prevalence of this disposition; though the mighty moralist and lexicographer, Dr. Johnson, has told us, with his usual dogmatism—that Shakspere was '*unnatural!*' in depicting men shooting off quibbles and quirks, with the near prospect of death. Old Doctor Dread-devil, as Cobbett quaintly nicknamed him, was marvellously out of his depth, when he undertook to lecture Shakspere on human nature. He says, "Shakspere's characters have a conceit left them, even in their misery—a miserable conceit." Prodigious! The 'conceit' existed nowhere but under the mighty doctor's wig.—But where the devil are we wandering? We have already once apologised for digression, and beg pardon again. To return: Fielder was of the temperament we have above alluded to;—mischance could not depress, nor misfortune sadden him.

We have before said that every officer of any standing in the then state of our police, was intimate with the leading violators of the law. To his jocose submission, Dick Bayes replied :—

"You're a queer chap, George; you're a sort of Godsend though, for I didn't reckon to find you—and, what's more, I wasn't seeking you; however," and he winked his eye knowingly; unobserved by the rest, whom he at the time turned his back on; "you're our prisoner; and in order to make sure of you, we shall be obleeged to clap on the *darbies.*"*

Taking a pair of handcuffs from a bystander, he placed one on the right of Redhead, and beckoning a stout burly countryman from among the men, he placed the other shackle on his left wrist—and, having locked the snap, not only secured the prisoner but the constable, who could not let his charge go even had he been so inclined; Rose and another were similarly served; and the two men who had escaped by the underground-passage, and who had been taken, getting over the fence of the broom-maker's garden, being now brought in, they were similarly disposed of.

"Now, my man," said Bayes, turning to Fielder, "we'll purvide for you, as you're a deep 'un, by gettin' yer into a conveyance of some sort; for I supposes you won't like to tramp it to Maidstone, eh? Got any *ochre* to pay for the drag?"

* Handcuffs.

Fielder replied in the affirmative.

"Well," said Bayes, "then suppose Tom Pearce goes wi' you? I must put you on the wristbands, though. What! ain't you got no more pairs? Lord, Lord—these joskins! what a thing it is to have anythink to do wi' 'em!"

Mr. Bayes produced a piece of cord from his pocket.

"Dash it," said Fielder, "you might stand something genteeler than that." Here he drew a handsome large-sized silk kerchief from his pocket.

"Oh, anything to accommodate a gentleman," said Bayes, laughing at Fielder's particularity. "Now, Pearce, this is your prisoner; and see that you deliver him safely into the custody of the governor of Maidstone gaol. Now gentlemen," continued he, "we're ready to start. Are you sure every part of both premises has been strictly searched?"

The men who had done so assured him no corner had been left unransacked; and several articles of silver plate, a watch or two, and some miscellaneous property of value were produced. No money was, however, found—for each highwayman usually carried his specie about him, or concealed it in a spot known only to himself. Mr. Bayes, having scrutinisingly examined each article, and carefully noticed their peculiarities, with an occasional shrug, smile, or interjection, placed them all together in a carpet-bag, and the prisoners left the cottage, under the escort of the constables, for Woolwich, where Mr. Bayes had made arrangements for their safe custody for the night, until all should be ready for conveying them to the county gaol at Maidstone.

But the night's adventures were not yet at an end; the order of march was thus arranged. First went three of the sheriff's men, and then followed Rose and his yokemate; Redhead, Ned Wheeler, and another pair similarly manacled, and three or four more of the catchpoles; while Pearce, Bayes, and the Londoners brought up the procession. The foremost had reached the end of the lane, when a loud cry arose from the rear; three or four pistols were fired in rapid succession.

"Help!" roared Pearce, who lay extended on the ground with a discharged pistol in his hand.

"Which way did he go?" cried Bayes.

"There he runs!" exclaimed another, firing his pistol in the direction he pretended to see the fugitive.

"Hollo! what's the matter?" burst from a dozen tongues.

Mr. Bayes, however, knew better than to satisfy these queries too early—it might be mischievous. Not heeding their enquiries, he hastily buttoned his coat, and striding rapidly a few steps from the beaten footpath towards the point indicated by the man who had just fired, turned—and grasping another pistol which he drew from his pocket, bid the men scatter themselves to his right and left, and observe his motions. He thus occasioned still further delay.

"You keep out here on the right. Why what the devil are you about? I'll hold you responsible, master headborough, for the safe keeping of the other prisoners. Norris and Pearce, see to the men you already have. Now, my fine fellows, it won't do for either of you to come singlehanded on the cove who's just tipt us the slip—so be cautious, and make sure of him when you get him in sight. Forward, lads!"

Mr. Bayes set out with much bustle; and the heath, as well as the imperfect light would permit, was beat, as may easily be supposed, with little success, until the party arrived at Old Park Wood. To impress the rustics with a due sense of the vigilance and activity of their leader, Mr. Bayes kept up an incessant volley of directions, garnished with sundry oaths, which it would be neither edifying or proper to record; and moreover, on nearing one or two furze-bushes of questionable outline, he displayed his valour by furiously springing forward, and incontinently discharging a pistol thereat. The farce concluded by Mr. Bayes, after some swearing by way of epilogue, leading his men back across the country to Woolwich, whither the prisoners had by this time arrived.

The result is soon told. Eaton and two of the gang, against whom Wheeler was admitted as evidence, were executed on Penenden Heath. Wheeler, as the price of his infamy, received his discharge. Rose, against whom no specific case could be established, was sentenced to a term of imprisonment as a confederate of the gang; while Fielder, as the reader has been told, through the connivance of Bayes, was left to pursue his lawless career.

Our hero, by one of those lucky coincidences for which his life was famous, was in London, at the George, in the Broadway, Westminster, with Rust, Stevens, and others, whose names have figured in our criminal annals, with whom his friend Fielder had made him acquainted; and bitter was the regret of Madge Dutton, who had awaited the result at Woolwich, to find him not among the captured. Her presence of mind did not desert her, and calling Bayes aside, she represented to him how serviceable she might be on future occasions, if not "blown," as she termed it, in this affair: and the thieftaker, seeing the reasonableness of her view, after shaking her by the hand— sealing the bargain with a kiss, and promising secresy, which he was sure to observe, as it was his interest so to do—bade her farewell; Madge returned to London to the home of Dennis, which was in a small house in Sun Tavern Fields, Hackney, without even a supicion on his part of the treachery in which she had been engaged.

CHAPTER VII.

Nay, answer me, stand and unfold yourself.—Shakspere.

Peachum.—The Captain keeps too good company ever to grow rich. Marybone and the chocolate-houses are his undoing.

Peachum.—Really I'm sorry, upon Polly's account, the Captain hath not more discretion: what business hath he to keep company with lords and gentlemen? He should leave them to prey upon one another.—Beggar's Opera.

IT will be necessary, in pursuing the steps of Turpin, who had so fortunately escaped the dangerous plot of Madge Dutton, to give the reader some notion of the companions to whom his London life introduced him, the place of his abode, and the manner of his life. All these are necessary to a right understanding of this history; and unless he will allow his imagination to throw him back a century, into the period when the second George was king of these realms, we despair of conveying to him a just notion of the men and times in which the bold Turpin flourished.

Few of our readers but have seen the announcement of the first stage-coach, which "God willing," would start from York on a certain day in the year of our Lord, 1739, and which would arrive, under the same pious D. V., at London, some eight or ten days thereafter. This may serve to give some notion of the infrequency of communication ; and this infrequency threw a safety about the highwayman, which in this age of fast coaches and railroads is no more. The highwayman who took a purse on the road, had then only to ride across the country, and he was, comparatively speaking, as safe from pursuit or recognition, as if, at this time, he betook himself to some distant land. The merchant, the lawyer, the farmer, the grazier, the commercial traveller, knew not then the safety of banks, the convenience of paper currency, or the accommodation of a ready and rapid transmission of valuable securities by post. The grazier who drove up his live-stock from the north, returned, by easy stages, on horseback, in or out of company, as he might happen to be prudent or incautious, bold or cowardly, with the proceeds of his speculation in "bright red gold." The farmer took his way to market with leathern or canvass bag, well or scantily furnished, as his worldly means might permit. The commercial traveller, proceeded on his rounds, with goods of the more valuable and lighter descriptions in bulk, on packhorses or by the broad-wheeled wagon. Long after the time of our hero, even in the days of Fielding and of Smollett, we find in their life-like novels, such persons as clergymen, and men of a respectable rank in life, travelling by wagon; a conveyance now confined to the lowest and most needy of the populace. For the shorter distances round London and the great towns, there were, it is true, stage-coaches ; but these, from the slowness of their motion, were overtaken or stopped at pleasure, and thus offered an easy prey to the knights of the road. Another cause of impunity and the contempt with which the laws were treated by the violators of them, was the corruption and inefficiency of our police regulations. A more consummate set of scoundrels, as our criminal annals bear witness, could not have been found than the subordinate ministers of justice. The lapse of a few years shows us no less than seven thieftakers who ended their days on "Tyburn tree" for various desperate crimes of which they had been convicted. Need we then wonder that a brave, daring fellow, such as our hero certainly was, should run so striking a career, or that the roads in the neighbourhood of the metropolis, should be so infested, as to occasion the then Duke of Newcastle to declare, that for a man of rank and property to travel fifty miles unmolested, was so unusual that it had become the exception not the rule ! The character of Macheath in the Beggars' Opera is not overdrawn, though some modern critic has declared it to be so. The scurvy, cogging, petty larceny knave of these degenerate days of thievery can furnish no point of comparison with the dashing, well-dressed, well mounted man, who rode forth with primed pistols, and jauntily cocked hat, to take a purse, and in so doing risk his life, not so much at the gallows' foot, as by the barrel of the man whom he boldly bid to "Stand and Deliver!" Numerous are the anecdotes, and many the stories—and popular tradition is generally not far from truth in its main features—of the generosity and bravery of those modern knights-errant, Turpin and his companions.

The traveller who enters Westminster by the Great Dover Road, now an integral portion of the Great Metropolis, can make but a poor guess at the Westminster which Turpin saw. The stone bridge planned by the skill of Hawksmoor, the second only in date which the inhabitants of London beheld spanning the waters of father Thames, was not then erected.

The commodious thoroughfare of Bridge Street, and its continuation by Great George Street to Storey's Gate, was occupied by a labyrinth of mean and miserable tenements. The western abutment of the Bridge was then known as the *Great Wool Staple.* Some remains of the place where this ancient Staple was held, especially an old stone gate, fronting the Thames, were in being till 1746, when they were pulled down, until which period the place retained its original name. At the same time also was the noble avenue, now known as Parliament Street, widened and improved; until which time the only road to the houses of England's senate, was along King Street and Union Street, which were so miserably narrow, and so wretchedly kept, that " faggots were thrown into the ruts on the days the monarch went to Parliament to insure the safe passage of the state-coach."* The reader must excuse the dryness of these details; but they are necessary to picture the Westminster of our great-grandfathers. From Union Street the road continued on the western side of Palace Yard through St. Margaret's Lane ‡ to Old Palace Yard. Through this filth and meanness a spacious opening was made and houses erected adapted for the higher classes of society. The modern street is formed by this line with the addition, so says the survey, of *thirty-four feet!* of the ground on which Tudor Buildings once stood, and a portion of the Old Fish Yard, or Market of Westminster. So extremely narrow and incommodious was the old lane that a paling of four feet high was placed between its single foot-path and the carriage-way, to protect the passenger from the carriages and the mud which they splashed on all sides in abundance. The continuation of this wretched street was appropriately termed *Dirty Lane,* and the miserable hovels which lined it now bear the title of Abingdon Street. Its end led to Palace stairs, where the bishops formerly disembarked from the palaces in the Strand, at Southwark, or at Lambeth, on their way to the House of Lords; for at that time it was the custom of the Right Reverends to go to the House in state barges, rowed by servants in purple liveries. The eastern side of *Dirty Lane* was then filled by numerous sheds and outbuildings, interspersed with a public-house or two; the *Naked Boy and Star,* burnt down in 1751, and the brick building which was once a tavern, and bearing the singular title of *Heaven.* On this ground James Neeld, Esq. erected the present row of houses fronting Abingdon Street, which were built from materials purchased at the sale of Canons, the seat of the Marquis of Chandos, then lately pulled down. The stairs called Palace stairs, abovementioned, were blocked up soon after the riots of 1780, upon the petition of Mr. Delaval, whose house, situated near that spot, was much annoyed by " the vagabonds and disorderly characters who daily assembled there."

The spectator, who now, standing in front of the beautiful hall of Rufus, surveys the mighty fane where repose the ashes of patriots, poets, princes, and prelates—the gifted to whom his country owes its proud position among the nations—can form but little idea of what the hand of modern improvement has effected in the neighbourhood of the Hall and Abbey. We must confess, for our parts, that the onward course of man has more charms for our

---

* The History and Antiquities of Westminster, by J. T. Smith. This rare and splendid Quarto volume with its two hundred and forty engravings on copper, is now scarce; but it may be consulted in the library of the British Museum, No. 491. h.

‡ Now St. Margaret's Street.

contemplation than any mere antiquarian relic could possess. We are not such Goths as would destroy the beautiful in art, or the venerable ruins which time and historic recollections have consecrated; yet we do feel a little vexed at that silly veneration for mere stone and lime, which respects them in proportion to their age, rather than their utility or beauty. We have of late been treated to several Jeremiads on the destruction of the ancient cloisters of this building, or the tower of that, or the gateway of the other; though each have been standing nuisances. This has been especially the case with regard to the buildings in the vicinity of Westminster Abbey. As late as 1731, the fish-yard occupied the west side of the noble hall, where the committee rooms and other conveniences of the House of Commons and Law Courts stand, and so blocked was the place with buildings, the members of Parliament groped their way through Waghorn's Coffee House, at the south end of the Court of Requests, or through another tavern at the west end of the same building. We have before mentioned public-houses bearing the odd name of Heaven and Purgatory, near the south end of the hall; its western angle was obstructed by two others, who rivalled their neighbours by the titles of *Hell* and *Paradise;* these, says the survey, were the resort of disreputable characters, and the most raffish of lawyers' clerks. Not content with crowding the area of New Palace Yard with irregularly-built houses, our ancestors had the barbarity to erect seven mean-looking tenements before the gateway of the Hall, thus concealing its venerable front; nay, the very towers which flank its gate were built against and hidden, the one by Oliver's, the other by the Exchequer Coffee house. We have purposely dwelt in this detail chiefly on those spots which now present clear and beautiful openings for the health-laden breeze and the sunshine of heaven, rather than those spots still so unsavoury which exist in the purlieus of Duck-lane, Peter-street, the Almonry, Strutton-ground, &c. &c.; those any reader may still wander through, though even they are changed marvellously for the better, by the substitution of upright fronted brick houses, for the old over-hanging wooden tenements, whose friendly garret windows, in the more narrow streets, almost shook hands with their opposite neighbours. We need not say that this suburb of Westminster, with its dirt and its ancient privilege of sanctuary, was the resort of the profligate; for though poverty is by no means synonymous with crime, yet crime always seeks companionship with poverty. This has induced many persons to confound two things totally different; and because the vicious, with the view of concealment, ordinarily seek the haunts of the poor, there have not been wanting those who would identify the dwellings of the necessitous with the abode of crime.

In a yard, at the bottom of the Broadway, resided the notorious Nan Turner, of Golden-lane memory. She was at this period playing spouse to Bob Berry the cork-cutter, who, as the tomb-stones have it, "departed this life" at Tyburn, in 1733. Fielder and Turpin also slept in this house, which was frequented by many of their companions, Ned Rust, Bush, and others; Rose, who had served out the period allotted to his imprisonment, also joined them. Turpin and his chosen pal stabled their horses at the old Leaping Bar, in High Holborn; the fields at the end of which then commanded an uninterrupted view, from Bloomsbury northward, to Highgate and Hampstead hills, and westward along the Oxford road, now Oxford-street, and the meadows adjacent, to the Edgeware road and Harrow.

Our hero is now fairly launched on his desperate and reckless career. His name, from the number and daring of his exploits, was fast attaining a bad eminence. Yet however questionable on the score of morality might be the nature of his actions, generosity and courage, which are ever popular, were so strikingly displayed, that men almost forgot the crime of the deed in admiration of the high spirit and boldness of its execution. It would be uninteresting and wearisome to our readers to detail each of the many adventures on the road, in which Turpin was about this time engaged. His residence we have before described; but during the time he lived here, he met with an individual whose association so influenced his future life, that it would be unpardonable to omit the particulars of their first encounter.

Dick had been taking a canter on the road one evening—for it was no uncommon thing for him to leave London by way of Bloomsbury and the Oxford road, (now Oxford street), as early as noon-day—when near Alton he espied a gentlemanly looking personage, well mounted, with whom he soon rode up and commenced a conversation. His fellow traveller was slightly made, but active; his dress was neat, and possessed an aristocratic cut, which impressed Turpin with the idea that he was of rank. The equipments of his steed were remarkable for their finish and tastefulness; and his countenance, the features of which were rather too small and regular for manly beauty, bore a pleasing smile as they exchanged salutations, which spoke of the politeness and urbanity of a man used to good society. The traveller appeared of a merry and careless disposition, and in the course of their talk, more than once alluded to the exploits of Turpin, whom he expressed a great desire to see. They were as yet too near the village to be secure from molestation, had even our hero felt disposed to have done a little professional with his newly-found admirer; besides Dick, who was by no means avaricious, was amused with his frankness and apparent fearlessness.

"A pleasant evening, sir," said the stranger, courteously; "Rather finer, too, than we had cause to anticipate from the cloudy look of the day. Riding far on this road, sir?"

"Not a great way, sir," replied Dick; "I've been at Farnham, taking a look at the hop-market: trade confoundedly dull. Much afraid my steward will have a long face at quarter day, which has an awfully depressing effect on the nerves of a landlord. Rents are surely at the lowest, yet my tenantry declare that they are unable to pay even the current dues, although most of them are sadly in arrear."

Turpin looked askance at the face of his fellow traveller. He observed a meaning smile steal across his countenance, the expression of which he did not like; and still less did he understand the merry ha! ha! with which the stranger followed it. Dick looked at him somewhat doubtfully, but affected not to notice it.

"Egad, if you've at all been doing business at Alton, I'd advise you to be wary; for the whole country hereabouts, is ringing with the deeds of one Turpin, (Dick felt still more perplexed at the behaviour of his companion,) who certainly is an astonishing fellow, if half they say of him be true. Pon honor, I'm thinking he must have some little dealings with the old gentleman; for we hear of him everywhere, but catch him nowhere. Demme, but I'm of opinion there must be some half dozen of 'em. I've heard some curious anecdotes of him of late. Such as his robbing Mr. Sheldon, of Croydon, to whom he gave back his watch, in consideration of its being a family relic: his

Turpin stops Tom King.

returning fourfold to the poor woman at Ferrybridge, whom he had robbed by mistake; and several others " *

All this time Turpin felt that he was observed by his companion. His was not the heart to feel fear; yet there is many a brave man who never shrunk from open danger, who has felt perplexed, nay, agitated by something very like fear, if not fear itself, at some inexplicable anticipation. Yet there was something in the manner and conduct of the stranger which determined our hero to know more of him. The latter seemed to enjoy his embarrassment, and continued,

---

* A mere reference to one or two of the instances of Turpin's generosity, extracted literally from the meagre sketch of Turpin given in the Tyburn Records, vol. I., p. 99, may not be out of place here: they will suffice to show that the popular estimate of his character was by no means unfounded.

"Notwithstanding the dreadful scenes of robbery in which Turpin was engaged, he gave several proofs of his possessing a heart capable of feeling for the distresses of a fellow-creature, and a spirit of generosity. He once met a country dealer coming up to market on the Essex road, whom he commanded to stop and deliver his money. The poor man told him he had but fifteen shillings and sixpence, which he said was his all—and, if it was taken from him, he should be reduced to absolute want. Turpin, whose finances were quite exhausted, answered, there was no time to be lost—his money he must have; but at the same time desired him to be in a certain part of Newgate Street, on a particular hour the next day, with his hat in his hand: and if a person walked by and dropped anything into his hat, to take no notice, but go immediately about his business. The man accordingly took his station at the time appointed, and had not been there more than half an hour before he felt something fall into his hat, and upon opening the small packet, to his great joy, he found it to contain ten guineas.

"Another time he robbed a poor woman returning from Ferrybridge, where she had been to sell some commodities; and soon after, hearing she was distressed by her landlord for rent, he contrived to relieve her in the following singular manner. He found out her abode, and threw into the window, through the glass, a leather bag, containing gold and silver to the amount of six pounds."

No 11.

"Well, foregad, I'd give a trifle to see this same Turpin, for no man admires courage more than I do; though it's a queer fancy to wish to see a highwayman, except at a long distance. I've a notion that he'd be a pleasant fellow to crack a bottle with. If they should ever lodge him in quod, I'll visit him, if it was only out of curiosity, damme!"

"You need not wait till your kind wishes for his apprehension are fulfilled," replied Dick, suddenly turning his horse across the roadway, and presenting the *things*.† "I'll do myself the pleasure of drinking a bottle to our better acquaintance—though for the present, as I'm out of cash, I'll take the liberty of borrowing the money. Come, deliver your purse, and you may keep all the rest about you."

The behaviour of the stranger was singular. Clapping his hands upon his hips, he burst into a hearty laugh, a laugh so loud and clear that the neighbouring echoes rung with it. Dick knew not what to make of this; but kept his eye keenly fixed on his odd victim, for so he thought him. He laughed again. Turpin was growing impatient, and strongly suspecting some trick, was about imperatively to demand his ready money, when the stranger, having recovered his voice, though tears of merriment stood in his eyes, exclaimed,—

"What, dog rob dog? ha! ha! Why Dick, man, don't you know a tobyman from a chawbacon? Well, strike me, if that's not good! Put up your barking irons, my chuff 'un, and save your saltpetre for somebody else." Then changing his tone so as to mimic the supplicating whine of a cowardly victim, he added, "Pray, pray, good Mr. Highwayman, have pity on poor Tom King!"

Another burst of laughter followed. Turpin slowly returned the pistols to his holster, and caught King by the hand. He had met him once or twice before at the White Hart, as noticed at the beginning of a former chapter, but did not recognize him at the moment, though he had that floating remembrance of the features which still more puzzled him as to where he had before seen their owner. The greeting was cordial, and from this time forth Turpin and King were sworn confederates; and many a time did they laugh as they talked over their encounter on the road. And now, gentle reader, we will introduce you also to spicy Tom.

Who more gay at Marybone? Who more admired among the loungers of the chocolate houses? Who more smiled on by the fair frail ones of Drury, than Tom King? His character, from all we have been enabled to glean, appears to have been a curious though not uncommon admixture of the fop and the man of courage. Few sported a smarter boot at D'Osyndar's or Wills's, or a more elegant silk-clad leg at Marybone, or Cuper's, or other places of fashionable resort; and few bloods of the day could boast of greater success with the sex than Tom. Ready in conversation, pleasing and affable in manners, polite in bearing, gentlemanly in appearance, and of good extraction—he was calculated to shine in any society into which he might be thrown. A perfect master of the small sword, and of unquestionable courage—he was the looking glass of the young rufflers among whom he mixed, and the exemplar from which they modelled their follies, and, truth to say, copied not a few of their vices; in short, he was the very D'Orsay of highwaymen.

The world was ever the dupe of appearances: outside shew has always been, as it still must be, the criterion by which the many judge of mankind. The

† Pistols.

specious blackleg of the modern hell, he who by false dice, planted cards, or confederate *bonnets*, plunders the titled flats of the nineteenth century, is but the degenerate and cowardly type of the bold highwayman of the eighteenth. The latter mixed in the *best* of company, as by a strange conventional misnomer, the sprigs of nobility who ambitioned the reputation of men about town, have been called. He too ruffled, bullied, diced, drank, and ————, like the more artificial and refined thief of these days, the gambler. Yet it may be doubted if the robberies of the former class could be so destructive as his crafty successor, the chevalier d' industrie ; and though *hazard* was alike the game of both, there is something more manly, something less repugnant to our best feelings in the bravery of the highwayman, that must place him far above the scurvy, cogging, cozening knave of billiards, faro, roulette, or the card table.

King, on his first start into life, had been possessed of a small fortune : the gaieties and dissipation of the metropolis however possessed too strong attractions for one of his mercurial temperament to resist ; and Tom, in a very short time, was without a sous in the exchequer. Rings, snuff-boxes, superfluous swords, *et hoc genus omne* of the nicknackeries which made up the dandy of our great-grandfather's days, were successively parted with, until Tom found himself, one evening, with his only remaining court-suit on his back, his last guinea in his pocket, and his woman by his side, seated in the dress boxes of Old Drury. Despite his high flow of animal spirits, despite the poco-curante, devil-may-care hilarity of his temper, King had too sound a judgment not to perceive the dead lock to which he was brought. His vices and follies were too much a part of his existence to be readily or lightly parted with ; he was not the sort of man to weary his friends, to let himself down before the companions of his revels, and patch up his poverty for a time by meanly soliciting loans, with risk of a humiliating refusal. As he revolved these things, he but little heeded the scene before him ; he was recalled to the business of the stage by the loud plaudits of the audience. The play was the Beggars' Opera :† the actress who supported the pert Polly was Miss Fenton. Tom, ever alive to female beauty, soon became interested in her performance, and was gradually led, through her dulcet notes, into the impression of the reality of the scene before him, so necessary to the right enjoyment of dramatic representations. The bold Macheath figured through his adventurous career ; and so fixed was his interest and attention, that it was not until the curtain fell, King was awakened from his reverie.

"Tom, my love," said the dashing bona roba at his side, slightly pressing her hand on his arm ; " one would think you'd been dreaming for this hour or two. I'm not jealous, you know, but come, confess, dearest, don't you think

---

† In the year 1727-8, appeared the "Beggar's Opera ;" the vast success of which was almost incredible : during the two following seasons it run one hundred and twenty-six nights. It spread into every great town of England, and was played in many thirty or forty nights, and at Bath and Bristol fifty. It made its progress into Wales, Scotland, and Ireland—was acted in Dublin thirty-four successive nights, and was performed several times at Minorca. Nor was the fame of it confined to the reading and representation alone, for the card-table and drawing-room vied with the theatre and closet in this respect. The ladies carried about the favourite songs of it engraven on their fan-mounts and screens, and other pieces of furniture were similarly decorated. Miss Fenton, who sustained the character of Polly, though till then in obscurity, became suddenly the idol of the town ; her portrait was engraven and sold in great numbers—books of letters and verses to her were published—there was even a pamphlet printed containing her sayings and jests. She herself was received into the highest circles ; and finally she attained the highest rank a female subject can acquire, by becoming by marriage the Duchess of Bolton. The profits of this piece were so considerable, both to the author and Mr. Rich, then manager of Old Drury, as to make it said, that it had made Rich gay, and Gay rich.

Fenton devilish handsome ? You're a sad rake, Tom," and the syren sighed ; " I fear you're born to break the hearts of us weak women ; but mind, Tom," and she playfully tapped him with her fan ; "mind, Tom, I don't hear of your gadding about after Miss Polly—though I think you love me too well for that —don't you, Tom ?"

King turned and smiled, but replied only by a slight pressure of her hand, as he drew her arm under his, and they prepared to leave the theatre.

Many were the nods and greetings which Tom and his fair companion received as they rustled through the stiff brocades, and silks, and hoops, which crowded the staircase. Tom's gallantry eschewed the unsocial, solitary sedan ; he and his fair one entered a carriage. King was still silent and abstracted, a mood with him so unusual, that his innamorata began to feel a little real uneasiness stealing into the place of the feigned jealousy she had just played off. Again she rallied him, and with rather more asperity. She, however, had it all her own way, until, her temper being not accustomed to such trials, she exclaimed pettishly, prefixing it with a half suppressed sob, and an appeal to her handkerchief—

"Tom, I see it all—it's plain enough now—silly poor fool that I was to believe that you loved me ! But go—leave me—desert me : I might have expected this cruelty ! Oh, Tom, do not however—though you leave me— do not---"

"Zounds !" exclaimed King ; "why, what in the name of Lucifer and all his imps is the woman at now ? I was no more thinking of Polly than of my grandmother ;" the lady had thrown herself weeping on his shoulder ; "Do you think, my own, my dearest Letty, that it was the sight of a mere baby-faced singing girl that would make me treat you with neglect ? No ! no ! my mind was occupied with other thoughts."

"Then I ought to know them," said Letty, coaxingly ; "I've never given my Tom reason to mistrust me, have I ?"

"No, no, love," replied King, revolving in his mind some expedient to baffle her inquisitiveness ; for his thoughts were such as he meant not to divulge.

"I received a letter, love, conveying some unpleasant family news ; an old uncle, too, from whom I've expectations, is at the point of death—though, egad," and King cleared his brow, and rattled on in his ordinary good humour : "though, egad, you'll say that's no reason a fellow should be dull as a Dutchman. Well Letty, love, what say you to a jaunt to St. George's Spa tomorrow, or to the Punch House at Sadler's Wells ?" †

---

† "Sadler's Wells was so called from the existence of two chalybeate springs, formerly the property of a man named Sadler. From early records it would appear, that the ground originally belonged to the monastery of St. John, Clerkenwell ; and we find it, from an early survey, to have been then laid out in gardens. In the time of James I., the Wells appear to have been opened to the public ; and, from scattered notices in various works, we find the resort to the mineral waters in the vicinity of the metropolis was, at that period, as fashionable among the tradesmen—their wives and daughters, as a trip to the more distant Brighton, Cheltenham, Margate, &c. are now. Among them appear—Islington Spa, the London Spa, the Tunbridge Spa, the Dog and Duck Spa, St. George's Fields, St. Chad's Well, Gray's Inn Lane, &c. &c. In the time of Cromwell, (1652) resorting to these places were prohibited by the puritanical rulers of the land, under the pretext that they fostered superstition, and " Popish observances :" they were also denounced as " the resort of lewde and disorderly persons." In the reign of Charles II., Sadler purchased the ground on which the theatre and adjoining tenements now stand. He made several erections, principally of wood, and opened it as a place of public recreation and entertainment under the title of " Sadler's Wells Music House :" he also re-opened the two wells. In process of time it came into the possession of one Forcer, a dancing-master, who introduced, in addition to vocal and instrumental music, dancing, rope-vaulting, tumbling, &c. The son of Forcer succeeded him, and at his death came into the possession of Mr. Rosoman, (whose name is preserved in Rosoman Street, &c.) This proprietor altered the buildings into something of the form of a regular theatre ; for we find there was a stage, scenery, an orchestra, a curtain, &c. The entertainments announced were singing, dancing, tumbling, rope-dancing, and various gymnastic exercises, with occasional burlettas, or rather, musical dialogues between two or three performers at most. The

"You needn't ask me, Tom," replied she, drying her eyes; "you know I'll go wherever you please. But, Tom, did you buy me the silk joseph I priced in Ludgate Street on Saturday. I see you didn't by your looks; out of sight out of mind—eh, Tom?"

Thus the conversation went on until it again turned on the play.

"That dear Captain Macheath!" exclaimed Letty; "I don't wonder at all the wenches running after him. So bold, so handsome—I could love a highwayman for his sake!"

King smiled slightly as he handed her from the coach. "Good night, love," said he; "I've letters to write respecting the affair I told you of: I'll be with you early to-morrow. Adieu, dearest; and, mind you *dream of the highwayman.*"

That night saw a well-equipped horseman gaily cantering on the road to Hounslow; and the next day the talk of the barbers' shops and street-corners was the daring robbery of my Lord of Newcastle by a single highwayman; how his lordship, as he left Windsor from attending on his majesty, had been plundered of a great sum in gold and jewels; and how he had refused to allow steps to be taken for his apprehension, (no one had the slightest clue) in consequence of his courteous treatment, and the generous return, by the robber, of a picture of his majesty set with diamonds, his seal-ring, and his watch. Need we say the highwayman was TOM KING?

Such was Turpin's new confederate. Often after spending the day in the gaieties of the town, did they stop at night the very man whose movements they had thus made themselves acquainted with during the day. We left our hero and King, riding towards London.

"Dick, my worthy," said King, "I've often desired a closer intimacy, for damme, but I admire your mettle. That's a pretty nag under you: but that's not what I wished to talk to you about. I'm not down here without a scent; and as I don't do my business through lurchers, but start my own game, (which you'll find the safer plan), I'll let you into a secret. Dick, we are both gentlemen, and what say you if I introduce you to my Lord Coventry this evening, and make the visit pleasant and profitable to us both, eh? how like you the notion?"

"I like it much," said Turpin; "here's my hand on't; consider it as done. You must not be seen in it, Tom; he may know you, though I did not. By Jove, my buck, I have it. Leave it to me. Only detain him at the Star a few minutes, and if he 'scape, laugh at me, that's all."

plan on which the place was conducted at this time seems closely to have resembled that of many of our public concerts of the metropolis, now the resort of the lower orders. The house, though vending ale and other liquors, bore the name of the "Punch House." No admission money was paid; for, though something beyond the average prices were charged for the liquors supplied to the company, any person was at liberty to walk into the area in which the performances took place—where, it would appear, they smoked and drank, while shrimps, &c. were hawked about for sale. Rosoman eventually took a partner of the name of Rutherford, who dying, left his share to his widow, coupled with the condition that she should live single, or the property devolve to Rosoman. A friend of Rosoman's, however, won the widow's affections; she married—Rosoman became possessed of the forfeited share, and again sole proprietor of Sadler's Wells. . . . .

"It was, for many years, a custom at this theatre to sell to the audience negus and punch at sixpence per pint, as an inducement to the public to visit the "Wells." A printed ticket, one of which now lies before us, was given to each person, with the following notice:—"The bearer of this ticket is entitled to a pint of wine, or of punch, on paying an additional sixpence." This brought, at one period, a lucrative trade, and a more numerous than respectable audience to the house. . .

"The two wells, whence its original designation was acquired, still exist on the premises; one in the yard, which is arched over—the other in the cellar beneath the theatre. The water for the various exhibitions is not obtained from these wells, but conveyed through pipes from the reservoir at the New River Head."

The above account is abridged from the Life of Joseph Grimaldi, by the author of this work, where will also be found many other particulars relating to "The Wells."

"I don't approve of your having all the danger, though," said Tom, "I'll be at hand, in case of necessity."

"Pooh! pooh! never fear: dy'e think I'll sloven it? Show me the rattler,† and I'll give you the account of its contents."

Matters were soon arranged, and King rode forward to the inn at which the young nobleman was expected, who soon after arrived. He was personally acquainted with King, from a town introduction; and was then on his way to his country seat. Pleased at meeting the pleasant Tom, he ordered wine; a merry hour and a half was spent, and in the mean while Dick made the necessary arrangements for the success of their exploit.

> "The sun set, and up rose the the yellow moon;
> The devil's in the moon for mischief,"

and so would my Lord Coventry have thought, if he had known what was to befal him in the next hour. After some hearty shakes of the hand, and promises, and an appointment to meet in London at a future day, King bid good bye to his aristocratic bottle-companion.

The evening was beautiful; the broad bright orb of a summer moon silvered the foliage of the massy and majestic timber which clothed both vale and upland; there was scarcely enough motion in the air to shake the leaf of the aspen; and the nightingale poured its song from the grove. The attendants of the nobleman consisted of his valet, and a postillion. They were now entering a narrow lane. Long rows of lofty over-arching elms threw dense shadows on the roadway; they had advanced some fifty yards along this avenue when the horse on which the boy rode suddenly shied, and tossing his head, reared at some obstacle in the road: his rider spurred him on, and he fell, dragging with him the off horse, who had also stopped short. The boy rolled from the saddle, the valet leaped from the rumble, and opening the carriage-door enquired if his lordship was hurt; a question more polite than necessary, seeing that nothing had happened which was likely to hurt him. His lordship was just enjoying a doze, to which the sultriness of the evening and the fumes of the wine had disposed him, when he was awoke by the sudden stoppage.

"What the devil's the matter now, Stevens! 'Sblood, a horse down, eh? Help the lad to get him up then, and be d—d to you. Stab me, but you stare like a fool. Shut the door, fellow; I'm drowsy."

A minute after Stevens again softly opened the door. "My Lord," said he, almost in a whisper, "we can't get on; there's one of the horses disabled by his fall. One would think 'twas done on purpose; there's a small tree across the road, and so barked that it was not to be seen in the moonlight. Shall I go back to the Star, my Lord?"

"You may go to h—," vociferated the angry nobleman; for in those days the accomplishments of drinking and swearing formed a distinguishing feature in the composition of a man about town, to which character his lordship laid claim. "Strike me, but these rascally road-contractors shall hear of this, the d—d scoundrels. That extortionate numskull too, the host at the Star, to send a nobleman on with such foundered catsmeat. Demme, but I'll horse-whip him!"

His lordship having now swore himself awake, looked out of the front

† Coach.

window of the carriage with a stretch and a yawn. " Stevens," said he,—the valet hastened to the carriage-door—" Stevens, what the devil's the use of your running away ; can't the young scamp there, go as well for the fresh horses, you blockhead ?"

" Certainly my Lord," replied he : and the boy accordingly mounted the uninjured horse and rode back to the inn.

He had scarcely cleared the lane when a man stepped from behind a tree at the road-side.

" Stand, or I fire !" exclaimed he, presenting a pistol to the head of the alarmed valet, who stood near the open coach door.

" Down on your knees !"

The man knelt. Turpin's eye was, meantime, directed towards his lordship, who, having recovered his first astonishment, clearly saw how affairs stood. His lordship was no coward ; yet the coolness and assurance of the highway-man, who was now passing a cord round the wrists of his servant before his face, for the moment staggered him. He placed his hand in the carriage-pocket, and drawing forth one of his travelling pistols, deliberately levelled it at Turpin's head. The weapon flashed in the pan. Our hero turned to him with a smile —

" Upon my word," said he coolly ; " I'm obliged to your lordship for reminding me of your presence. I have to apologise for not waiting on you first."

Lord Coventry had snatched another pistol from its receptacle. Again the sharp click of the lock and the disappointing flash of the priming-powder ensued—he angrily dashed the harmless weapon at Dick, who, ducking his head, avoided the missile. His lordship threw himself back on the seat, with the air of a man who has lost all hope of resistance.

" Obliged to you for your kind intentions," said Turpin, without even changing the tone of his voice, or dismissing the smile which played on so much of his face as was not hidden by the mask.

" Much obliged for kind intentions," repeated Dick. " But, my dear lord, when next you feel inclined to shoot any body, be sure the charges of your pops haven't been drawn."

His lordship looked absolutely confounded.

" And now, if you please, we'll discuss business-matters. I must trouble you for your loose cash, my lord—(a purse was handed to him.) And now, if you please, I'll take your watch : it's a handsome one I know—(his lordship slowly drew it from his fob): that diamond on your finger, too: and I'll also thank you for the miniature you carry of a lovely lady, of whom we'll say nothing."

All but the last-named article were delivered with the air of a man who is helplessly resigned. His lordship now found his tongue.

" Gadzooks, Mr. Highwayman," said he ; " I'm sorry I didn't know you better : I take it you're a gentleman ; and as it seems (his lordship here un-buttoned his coat, and drew forth a picture) you know of this—though, stifle me, if I can guess who the h—l could tell of it—I'll make an appeal to you. The picture I'll not part with, damme (his lordship grew warm) ; and if you're the blood I suppose, you'll not insist on it. Name the terms, and I'll redeem my word as a man of honour and a gentleman."

" Why, really," replied Dick, " I've wasted more time on you than I ought already. I forgive you the attempt you made to provide for me in the other world; and as I've reason to believe your lordship has an affection for the picture, and I've no wish to disfigure it by breaking it from its frame, say thirty guineas; an order for immediate payment on your agent at Coombe, and I'll ensure its presentation before your lordship can trouble him with any advice on the subject."

Lord Coventry drew forth his pocketbook, and, extracting a leaf, wrote the required order.   Turpin looked narrowly at it—folded it—and, bowing lowly, and with an air of mock reverence to his lordship, closed the coach-door.   A low whistle was heard, and he disappeared through the hedge by the way he had come out.

All this while the valiant Stevens had knelt, with bound-wrists and piteous aspect, in the road.   His master looked out—and, despite his vexation at the untoward affair, could not keep his gravity at viewing the pale and affrighted countenance of his terrified menial.

"By G—!" exclaimed he; "may I be struck comical, if you are not the drollest picture of a goose at his last gasp I'd ever the luck to see!   Why what, in the name of all that's miserable, ails the man?   Get up with you, confound your sneaking, white-livered soul, will you?"

Stevens rose from his genuflexions.   The whistle Turpin had heard was the signal of the approach of the horses and assistance.   They came, the obstruction was removed, and his lordship proceeded on his journey.   We need not say the order was presented and duly honoured.

We will now return to Tom King, who had remained lying flat on the sward behind the hedge, an attentive observer and listener to the transactions we have described.   The twain walked hastily down the highroad, and unfastening their steeds, rode gaily across the country.   King was not more loud than sincere in his eulogies on our hero's conduct; and Turpin was equally pleased with the manners of his comrade.   They took their way towards London, in high spirits and extreme good humour, at the success of their adventure.

A day or two after their return to town, Turpin and his friend Tom were sauntering down Margaret Lane, with the intention of idling an hour at Oliver's, to learn the news of the day, when, as they were about to turn into Palace Yard, they were passed by a motley rabble of ragged boys, unwashed coster-mongers, and slipshod women, shouting most vociferously, thrusting and elbowing towards a knot of blackguards who were carrying a woman, apparently drunk, in the midst of them.

"Hurrah! for Roaring Peg," cried the disorderly mob.   "Hurrah! for the ducking stool! † hurrah! hurrah!" and onward rushed the riff-raff down the narrow nasty avenue of Dirty Lane.   Bellowing and shouting, on they passed, and turning by Purgatory, took their way to the river side.

"Shall we follow, and see the sport?" suggested Dick,   "What the deuce does it all mean?"

"Have you never seen the cooling discipline ?" asked King.

Dick replied in the negative.

"Have with you then :" and the friends followed the riotous assemblage.

Arrived at the spot, they witnessed a curious scene.   The victim of this

---

† "The Ducking-stool stood at the end of Dirty Lane, near the building called Purgatory. It was removed about 1788."—See Smith's History and Antiquities of Westminster, 4to. London, 1807. where a description of the apparatus is given.

Esther and Madeline recognise Turpin.

popular discipline was a muscular virago of some thirty-five years old, and displayed in her neglected person, and carbuncled face, the wreck of a once-fine woman, destroyed by the curse of that scorching pestilence, gin. In spite of her kicks and struggles she was thrust into a strong and clumsily constructed wooden arm-chair, and a rod of iron being passed through a hole in the extremity of either arm, she was effectually confined therein. This chair was attached by a chain to the longer lever of a huge wooden beam, and by the united efforts of a number of men the drunken scold was at once elevated in the air amid the vociferations of the mob.

"Now, my lads," exclaimed the beadle, who appeared to be master of the ceremonies on this important occasion, "stand clear there!" and he lustily applied his rattan to the shoulders of the junior branches of the bystanders. The ponderous machine swung upon the post which formed its fulcrum, and by a half revolution placed the lady in mid air, suspended over the river, which was now at high tide.

"Hurrah!" shouted the crowd.

The functionary gave the signal; the relaxed rope attached to the shorter arm of the lever allowed the chair to descend, and the incorrigible scold dis-

No. 12.

appeared, head and all, beneath the waters. Again was it elevated, and again sputtering oaths and imprecations, was its unlucky feminine appendage immersed.

"Hold hard!" cried the beadle. "Peg, will you promise not to give me and these gentlemen this trouble again?"

Peg's reply was too strong for "ears polite," so once more she was "plunged hissing hot into the bosom of Thames." This time there was a momentary pause before the ascending beam again exhibited Peg to the derision and laughter of the populace. The last dip had cooled her.

"For the love of mercy!" exclaimed she, "let me out, and I'll promise never again—"

"Land her," cried the beadle; but to this some of the malicious assistants demurred.

"D—n it, mister, let's guv her another dip; it 'ull do her a mort o' good," remonstrated they. But the dignitary knew that one concession to such demands was ever followed by others; so, to preserve the authority of his office, he peremptorily forbid it. The arm swung round; Peg was deposited on terra firma, and the beadle, after exacting a public and unconditional promise of peaceable conduct, ordered her release.

Turpin and King retired much amused from the scene, and the victim of intoxication staggered home to her hovel, with a 'tail' of ragamuffins that would have been envied even by the great Irish agitator.

CHAPTER VIII.

"—She loved me once;
Now pales and swoons e'en at my sight. She's true;
But I have stain'd the heart that once could soar
High as her own! Dreams! dreams! and yet, entranced,
Unto the fair phantasma that is fled
My struggling fancy clings. Oh there are hours
When memory with her signet stamps the brain
With an undying mint: and those were such
When fond ambition and enraptured love,
Twin genii of my daring destiny,
Bore on my sweeping life on their full wing,
To joys as bright as baseless."
                              —The Tragedy of Count Alarcos.

'Tis circumstance makes conduct. Life's a ship,
The sport of every wind; and yet men tack
Against the adverse blast. How shall I steer
Who am the pilot of Necessity?   —Idem.

THE lamps in the garden at Ranelagh shone down on "fair women and brave men," for it was the night of a grand fete. The alleys and walks were crowded with gaily-dressed people. The etiquette of court dress was then strictly observed, and the ruffles, bag-wig, breeches, and sword, were indispensable to obtaining admittance to the festive scene. The costume then adopted drew a strong line of demarcation between the tradesman and the gentleman, either real or pretended. The substantial citizen of the John Gilpin school, he who, clad in sober brown and grey worsted stockings, duly on the sabbath, headed, with his good dame, a family procession to the parish church, has no

The Robbery of Lord Coventry.   *Page 90*

successor among the modern tribe of shopkeepers; and his manners, habits, tastes, and amusements, were as dissimilar as his dress from those who are conventionally supposed to be "his betters." He mixed not with them, nor held other conversation or communion with them, than across the counter of his warehouse. For such an one to have indulged in the abomination of a scarlet coat, and its appurtenances, would have been equivalent to a declaration of insolvency. The gentleman, or he who passed himself off for one, was easily recognisable, even at a distance, from the trader or mechanic. Not so in these revolutionary and levelling days. A lord and a linen-draper, a baronet or a beer-shop keeper, when either of the latter are *out*, call for more than mortal discrimination, in most cases, to distinguish the one from the other. We are not deprecating this change, we are merely noting it as a social revolution, by which those who may be termed the industrious portion of the middle classes, our traders and manufacturers, tread so closely on the heels of our gentry, and in some instances of even our nobility, as to have broken down all the barriers of exclusiveness in places of public resort.

Turpin and his friend had several times taken their round of the lamp-lit avenues and shaded walks of this gay and crowded scene; King occasionally exchanging the smile and nod of courteous recognition with some of his numerous acquaintances; and had now seated themselves in an arbour near to the orchestra. They did not notice a small group at a little distance, consisting of a military man and two ladies, who were looking at them with fixed attention.

"The one seated on the left, I know by sight," said the officer, in reply to some observation of the more matronly lady, who, however, was still in the bloom of youthful beauty; "he is Tom King, a gentleman of respectable family and independent fortune I have heard, though I must say of dissipated habits, and not the character I should exactly wish to introduce to my family circle."

"You mistake me, Albert," said the lady. "It is the other gentleman I mean—if it be not he, the likeness is so extraordinary that—"

The younger and fairer of the females was so greatly affected, and trembled so violently, that, had it not been for the support of the gentleman who escorted her, she would have fallen. Rallying herself a little, she exclaimed, in a voice choked by emotion, and turning eagerly towards her female companion, "It is he—indeed!" The trio stood as if in doubt; the officer seemed to hesitate as to the propriety of addressing our hero and his friend, but at this moment they caught the eye of King.

"Dick," said he, "do you see yon officer with the two ladies? Egad, it's Sir Albert Denistoun—what the deuce can make them take such a particular fancy to you? You don't know him, do you?"

Turpin turned his eyes in the direction indicated by the nod of his companion; and who shall attempt to express his feelings when, at a little distance, regarding them with looks of interest, he observed a military man, to whose features he was a total stranger, supporting on the one arm Madeline Weston, and on the other his only, his early love, ESTHER BEVIS! The strong man felt as a child: he rose suddenly and unconsciously, and gazed fixedly at the little party.

"By the lord Harry!" exclaimed King, "you look I don't know how; if you were a woman I'd call for water."

"Shall we accost them, Esther?" asked Madeline, who seemed also agitated; but Esther replied not.

"I'm in your hands, ladies," said Sir Albert, bowing; "though, if I may humbly suggest, it would be more consonant with etiquette—nay, it would be only proper—that the first advance should be made by the gentleman."

Sir Albert's speech went for little; the heart spurns the cold artificial considerations of mere fashionable insincerity.

"*I* will speak to him, at least," said Esther in a suppressed voice, and with an energy that she herself mistook for resolution.

Richard Palmer, for at that moment he was not Dick Turpin, stood transfixed as the three slowly approached him.

"Egad," said King, rising and bowing; "they're coming to speak to us."

Poor Esther! she had resolved to converse with her lover—to call upon him for explanation of his conduct, which her fond partiality hardly doubted but he would give. She would tax him, but with gentleness, for his neglect; she would—in short, do and say a thousand things—such was her resolve: but she had sadly overcalculated her nerve. The blood forsook her cheek as they drew nearer, and again as suddenly returned, suffusing her fair neck and lovely countenance with crimson. Maiden modesty; the painful slanders she had heard; the perplexing position in which she now found him, mixing in good society, and his undeniable air of fashion; and lastly, the force of woman's first and only true love, to which the praise or censure of the world is as dust in the balance—bewildered, confounded, and unnerved her.

"Esther!" was the only word Palmer uttered. The tone of the voice seemed to deprive her of speech: she turned towards Sir Albert, and grasped his arm with both her hands, and the next instant sank into her lover's arms. As he tenderly supported her, Sir Albert looked with an air of perplexity from King to Turpin, as if to ask some solution of this, to him, mysterious conduct. Madeline was the first to break the painful silence.

"Albert," said she, "this is Palmer, Richard Palmer, of whom you have often heard me speak. It is not fitting that this scene should continue—we are attracting attention; Esther! dearest Esther!"

But Esther heard not. Long and severely had she suffered: strong as woman's faith had been her belief in her lover's innocence; and devoutly and ardently had she desired, ere her heart could consent to condemn him, that an opportunity should arise for his exculpation. She doubted not—what doubt can love feel?—that he was calumniated; and now she saw him, among the *elite* of fashion, mingled in the concourse of the gay and the wealthy, conviction flashed on her mind that she had been bitterly and cruelly deceived by those whom she thought most entitled to her confidence. Her first impulse was to have received him coolly—to have listened to what she doubted not to hear, his triumphant vindication of his character; and with this intent she had expressed her wish to Sir Albert Denistoun that they should approach and speak to him. But she had overcalculated her self-possession; and the sound of the voice, whose very tone she had so long treasured in her memory, brought with it torrents of rushing remembrances, which overwhelmed her fancied resolution.

The party retired; Palmer, for so we must now call him, leading gently the agitated Esther to one of the arbours. King held Sir Albert in converse, while Palmer endeavoured with all the soothing tenderness of a lover to reassure and compose the agitated maiden. King, meanwhile, with the readiness and self-possession for which he was remarkable, imposed upon Sir Albert with a plausible tale of his young friend having lately acquired a small competency through a distant relation. As Esther recovered the conversation grew more animated, and, at Sir Albert's pressing request, King and his friend promised to dine at his table the ensuing day. They parted, and the single-hearted maiden retired to her pillow with a happy heart, and her light slumbers were chequered with visions of future happiness too bright for realisation in this world of stern realities.

As for the two friends they walked silently towards their home. Even King's loquaciousness seemed checked by the scene he had just witnessed; he intruded not on his friend's thoughts, but waited for him to break the silence. At length Palmer said—

"You may suppose me weak, Tom, perhaps you'll laugh at me, but—(and he paused hesitatingly) no, I'll not say it—I'll quit the course of life I am now pursuing, and endeavour, by honest industry, and a legitimate exertion of the talents with which God has blessed me, to render myself, as far as I can, worthy of her hand and heart. I cannot bear to deceive that fair creature. I'll not go to Sir Albert's to-morrow, for it is not fit that we should meet again."

"Dick," replied his companion, "you are not just now in a frame of mind to argue with, or I could soon show you the dilemma in which such conduct would place us both. Do you not know that I have represented you as possessed of property; that I have deceived Sir Albert with a tale of your having acquired wealth, at least a moderate competency, and such a resolve as that you have just hinted at would ruin us both." Palmer relapsed into his former silence for awhile; and then, after questioning King as to the nature of his representation, said—

"For myself, Tom, I would not care at once giving the lie to any deceit that might impose on the girl I love; I would not heed exposure, nor balance for an instant the sacrifice of myself to save her from a moment's pain; but I fear that in this affair I shall be compelled to make shipwreck of my dearest hopes: yet, though I tear my heartstrings in the effort, I will persevere:—no, no; I cannot consent to deceive her."

King appeared nettled at this declaration. "Then when I wait on Sir Albert to-morrow; when I meet the fair Esther looking for the appearance of her plighted lover; I must say that he has determined never again to see her? Or, Dick, my good fellow," said he, assuming a tone of raillery, "shall I say you've forgot the appointment I saw you seal; and *perhaps* will call on her to-morrow or next day, if nothing very urgent should intervene to prevent you?"

"For God's sake, as you value my friendship, say no more," replied he, "I'll go. Oh Esther, Esther, how have I debased myself! I am surely the sport of fate; but the worst that destiny can do shall never lead me to wrong thy purity and innocence."

"Romantically said; we shall see though," said King. "Why Lord bless you, you do not know what women are; they love men the better for a spice of the devil in their composition. Constancy, virtue, purity! ha! ha! green boarding-school misses, and sighing boys, who have hardly left off eating bread and butter, talk love after that milk and water fashion; but men of the world—"

"Tom, you are my friend," interrupted Turpin; "may I beg that you'll not recur to what has passed this night. I'll go to morrow and see her—let that suffice you."

"Ay, ay, I knew you would; and you'll go and see her again. Tut, tut, don't look displeased man.; but, mind, you'll sacrifice me as well as yourself if you are not discreet. Talk to your damsel as you please, but pray leave me to manage the thing with Sir Albert."

"Pursue the subject no further, I again request you," said Dick; "I'll not betray you, at any rate. Good night."

"Villain that I am!" exclaimed Turpin as he seated himself in his chamber; "yet how can I extricate myself from the difficulty in which I am placed. I must dissemble, yet I'll not betray her—no!" and with this resolution he threw himself on his bed, but not to sleep.

Wearily and distractedly did he toss throughout the night; anxiously did he speculate on the future; and vainly, as every other mortal must, did he strive to raise or rend the impenetrable veil with which a merciful Providence has concealed the portal of futurity. Wearied, baffled with conjecture, now harassed with doubt and fear, now cheered with hope and anticipation, the hours of darkness stole on; day dawned, and with it, through the ivory gate, fled his morning dreams, and he awoke to the realities of this working-day world.

At an early hour King tapped at his door, and seemed somewhat surprised at finding him already dressed.

Dick, my lad," said he gaily, "how's this? I thought to have seen you brisk as a bridegroom, at the thought of meeting her of whom I've often heard you express a wish merely to see or hear of; and now, demme, but you look like a fellow who has prayed and waited for the death of a rich old relation, and then finds himself cut out of the will. Cheer up, my boy, you must succeed, with a woman's heart in your favour, and such a friend as I to back you. You're not offended at me, I hope; egad, you're as down as a bucket in a deep well; can I serve you—eh? if so, command me."

"I'm obliged to you for your good wishes, Tom," replied Turpin, "but you would but smile at my feelings if I explained them. That girl, Tom, is too good, too unsuspecting, too pure, to be sacrificed to such as I have become. It is the thought of the deceit I am practising on one who is guileless; one who, I grieve to say, has placed her affections, for that I sincerely believe, on so worthless a character: that makes me despise myself; however—"

"Excuse me, friend Dick,"rejoined King, "but I can't exactly see the cause of all this self-contempt; methinks such a likely young fellow is a fit suitor for any she that ever walked—ay, and an undoubtedly successful one to boot—if he only have the necessary courage—faint heart never won—eh, friend Dick?"

"I would willingly break off this affair at once," said our hero, "but I confess I do not see how, without exposing both of us to Sir Albert: I shall therefore put the best face I can on the matter, and trust to time and chance for the rest."

"Bravo!" cried King, "and time and chance will repay you for the credit you give them; or I'm no conjuror. Leave it to them, my boy, and Esther will be yours. What! don't that please you either? Damme, Dick, but I shall begin to think you're something out of the ordinary run of men. Here's a pretty woman loves you to distraction; an introduction to good company presents itself, which hundreds might seek in vain, and the perspective of a handsome wife, with, I dare say, a snug jointure; and you treat this slice of luck as if your best friend were bankrupt, or your mistress brought to bed of twins—foregad, it's the most extraordinary way of taking such good fortune I ever met with."

" "I shall go with you; let that suffice," said Turpin, to whom the conversation was evidently unpleasant.

They went at the appointed hour. The dinner passed off smoothly enough. Our hero, however, who was seated next to Esther, was embarrassed; while King enlivened the company by his mirthful sallies. Dick, though not sharing in the conversation, was frequently provoked into a smile, and Esther, before half an hour had passed, warmed into good spirits, nay even into hilarity. The ladies retired, and Dick, feeling himself called on, by courtesy to his host to exert himself, brightened up. He thought he had never seen King to such advantage as on this occasion, and Sir Albert was so delighted with his company, that before they retired to the drawing-room to join the ladies, he had exacted a half promise from our friend Tom that he would favour him with his company during his stay in London, whenever other engagements should permit him. As the evening drew on, Richard and Esther, whom the host and hostess considerately allowed to be as much together as etiquette would permit, fell into agreeable converse. He had never beheld her so lovely; the four years which had flown, since last they parted with mutual vows of unchangeable fidelity, had improved her form, her intellect, and, if possible, her heart—at least it had given that steadiness and constancy to her feelings, which, though he never could seriously doubt them, made the assurance of her affection doubly sure. Ten times was he on the point of entering upon some explanation of his present position; not that he was about to tell her the real truth as to his pursuits; he could not think of so shocking and alarming her. Should he make a mysterious declaration of the impropriety, under present circumstances, of their meeting again? No! to what injurious and painful surmises might it not give rise; he could not bear the thought of living despised in her estimation, whose good opinion he valued beyond that of all the world. Should he explicitly declare the cause, it would be still worse. He looked on her fair face beaming with smiles; could he cloud it with woe? Heaven forbid! His resolution wavered, grew weaker at each moment, and at last resolved itself, as resolutions under such temptations are wont to do, into thin air. He became animated, and they separated with promises not less truly than ardently interchanged, to meet again the following day.

Three weeks passed thus; and Sir Albert, with his lady, talked of leaving London for his country seat. This was communicated to Palmer, for so we must call him in this society. Esther and her lover sat in the recess of a deep window, looking on the setting sun. Sunset is assuredly the most dangerous time for lovers' tete-a-tetes. The calm softness of the hour disposes the soul to tenderness: at least, Byron, who may be considered some authority in these matters, has sung of sunset as "the hour of love," to say nothing of some score of minor poets, who seem to have entertained a similar opinion.

The mild and subdued light streaming through the small compartments of the deep-sunk diamond-paned casement, shed a mellow light on the fair countenance, and glancing on the golden hair of the maiden, seemed to receive more brilliancy than it gave. Palmer looked fondly upon her; the world and the world's crimes and woes vanished from his recollection as he contemplated her pensive look, for at that moment her face was somewhat

"Sicklied o'er with the pale cast of thought."

Man is a selfish creature; at least his actions are sadly so, when the gratification of his passions is in question. Palmer forgot, as his friend had prophesied, all his fine speeches about self-denial, with whatever sincerity they might have been uttered, and thought of nothing but the possession of so fair a bride.

"Esther!" said he, tenderly. Esther started, and a smile spread over her face, as if at the dreams in which she had been indulging. "Esther—will you be mine?" She withdrew not the small hand which reposed in his, but slightly averted her head. The crimson flush which suffused her neck tempted Palmer to a salute. "Answer me, Esther: for God's sake do not keep me in suspense!"

"Richard," replied the maiden in a tone of serious yet tender remonstrance, "have I not, years since, plighted my troth? Why do you ask it again of me? Have I ever given you cause to doubt me?"

"No! by heaven! But Esther, dearest Esther, are we again to separate? Will you again leave me? When you are gone, Esther, consider—"

"I've said it," replied she, turning towards him with firmness in her voice. "I'm yours---yours for ever!"

An embrace sealed the compact. Sir Albert was informed of the intended marriage, and both he and his lady Denistoun were loud in their congratulations. The day was fixed; Palmer alone of all the circle did not enjoy the prospect of approaching happiness---dark clouds hung over the future. So true is it that unalloyed joy can be felt only by the innocent; hence the proverbial happiness of

"——childhood's careless hours,
When every month is May.
When we wreathe the choice of Summer's flowers,
Nor deem they can decay."

How contrasted were now his feelings! Crime had not then written foul defeature on his soul. As he thought over the bold adventure and reckless enterprise of the last four years, their events seemed to him as a dream. Was he indeed, then, the desperate villain at whose name men trembled, though even his person was unknown to them? Was such as he a fit bridegroom for the innocent and the single-hearted Esther Bevis? Could he hope to throw off the associates with whom he was entangled, and to whom he was pledged? Was there any ray of hope, should he even do so, that exposure would not inevitably follow? His conscience answered, No!

"Beset, surrounded as I am," exclaimed he, "by adverse fate, I foresee the doom of misery to which I am dragging her; yet how to avoid it I know not. I paltered with crime, took the first plunge, and now 'tis hopeless to stem the current of my fate! I am fortune's child, and must submit to her caprice!"

With such plausible extenuations, are men, whose evil propensities and want of moral courage have drawn them into straits, which principle and firmness might have avoided, wont to "sugar o'er the devil himself." Turpin had none to blame; and therefore he talked of fate, destiny, fortune, and so forth, when a small exertion would, at the outset of his career, have saved him from the dilemma in which he now found himself. It has been said, when balancing between virtue and dishonour,

"The woman who once hesitates is lost,"

and equally true is it that when man once deliberates on the *expediency* of committing a crime, his guardian virtue leaves him.

The Marriage of Esther and Turpin.

CHAPTER IX.

Yes—twine the myrtle round her brow,
  And braid her golden hair;
And o'er the flowery garland throw
The veil whose hue may mate the snow,
And bid its soft and graceful flow
  Half screen the peerless fair.

Now strong in beauty's conquering might,
  Hope kindling in her eye;
She shows to the enraptured sight,
Like an ethereal form of light,
A being far too pure and bright
  For mortal destiny.
                Anon.

Oh, well it is youth may not see,
  'Mid the fair visions round it flung,
The shadowings of its destiny;
—Or whose the brow that would not bear
  The wrinkling stamp of joy's decay;
And the bright cheek of gladness where,
  Whose bloom would fade not soon away?
                Acton.

"Time and tide," saith the proverb, "wait for no man;" and the winged feet of the bearer of the scythe and hourglass brought rapidly the day for the celebration of the nuptials.

No. 13.

Despite the presentiment of coming evil, our hero became gay as the time drew nigh. We have before said that his temperament was sanguine and full of hope; and so easily do we believe what we wish, that he had almost persuaded himself that the fortune which had thus far befriended him, would not reverse her fickleness, but remain constant to one to whom she had shown such extraordinary favour. As for Esther, though maiden modesty might cause a fluttering at her heart, it was a throb of anticipative pleasure; she was too loving, too confiding, too hopeful, too guileless, too happy, too single-minded, to doubt, much less to fear, the future. Of *his* affection she was sure and safe; then, what misgiving could she feel? In a word, she was happy; and happiness unalloyed is a treasure which kings may covet, but cannot purchase.

The day first fixed for the marriage was, however, delayed. Esther, having informed her father of her unexpected meeting with Palmer, and the circumstances in which she now found him—after dwelling on his unchanged affection, and her reciprocal feeling towards him—claimed from her parent the fulfilment of his conditional promise passed long since. Her joy was heightened by the receipt of an answer in which old Bevis announced his intention of being present at the ceremony, and of giving away his daughter in person. A more distant day was accordingly named, and her venerable parent duly arrived on the day before that originally fixed.

There is, however, "many a slip between the cup and the lip;" and the fatigue of the journey so completely laid up the old gentleman that he was unable to proceed to church with the wedding party, as he had intended. Both Palmer and Esther proposed a further delay of a day or two; but of this the kind-hearted old man would not hear. The marriage was like most other marriages; the bridegroom looked very simple, very loving, and very silly, as most men do upon the like occasion; the bride, as far as her bashfulness and embarrassment would allow her to observe him, thought, however, (if she could think at all) that he looked marvellously interesting. Tom King was all smiles, good humour, and joke; while Madeline and her husband, as became staid married people of a twelvemonth's standing, looked on with most edifying seriousness.

Our hero took his bride, at the earnest invitation of old Bevis, to spend the honeymoon at his house, until a small cottage in Bloomsbury, which he had taken, should be furnished and prepared for the home of his wedded wife. Thus far,

> "All went merry as a marriage bell."

Esther was too happy to notice, for the first few days, the occasional pang which shot across her husband's face, as he fondly gazed at her. Indeed, he for a time succeeded in concealing from her his uneasiness, by the most endearing assiduities and fond attentions which a sincere affection could dictate. The honeymoon passed, but saw no abatement of their affection, and the couple removed to town, to occupy their new abode.

Sir Albert and Madeline, or, as we ought to call her, Lady Denistoun, had now left London for their seat in the north; and almost the only visitor of the new-married pair was their friend, Tom King. From him, Turpin had, of course, no secrets; and often did they confer on the subject uppermost in his mind, the course it would be advisable for him in future to pursue. Neither of them possessed any knowledge of business, and it may therefore be supposed these conversations were anything but satisfactory; indeed, they usually ended, like the history of the Prince of Abyssinia, in "a conclusion wherein nothing is concluded."

"What say you," enquired King, after one of these undecisive colloquys "to a stroll to White's? There's good company there. Our little confab has quite given me the blues; besides, 'I can't help suspecting that you're running low; don't try to conceal it if the case is as I suppose, for you know where you can draw so long as there's a stiver in the exchequer."

Dick looked at him thankfully; he knew the sincerity with which the offer was made, and acknowledged it warmly. They were still conversing, when the girl whom he had engaged to attend Esther, and assist in the household duties, made her appearance with a letter, which she stated had been left by a woman, who said it required no answer. Turpin broke the seal, and read as follows.

"Dear Dick,
      I've been seeking you everywhere, but the deuce a bit of find could I make of it. At last I met Madge Dutton, who let me into the secret of your getting married. I've something worth your notice, if you'll drop on me at Bob Berry's, in George Yard, at ten this evening.
                Yours, and no mistake,
                    GEORGE FIELDER.

"There," said Dick, tossing the letter to King "I'll go; for to tell you truth, I've not a guinea of my Lord Coventry's left; much less can I say of a few shiners I had intended for the comfort of my fireside. I'm a dreaming idiot, Tom, or I should not have put myself in the cleft stick in which I am now fast."

King smiled. "Thumbscrew me, but I never knew the married man who didn't repent the deed, as soon as he had time to come to cool consideration. 'Marry in haste, repent at leisure' is as old as our grandmothers, and not the least true of their sayings; but if you are going to Berry's, I'll accompany you. What say you?"

Our hero assented; and as darkness approached, the twain set out, arm in arm, for the appointed place.

They threaded their way by the wretched twinkle of the oil lamps, which here and there,

"Like angels' visits, few, and far between,"

glimmered at the court yard gates, or before the front gardens of the detached mansions of Bloomsbury. The night was dark, and, besides a cold damp fog, a fine, drizzling rain, rendered the road slippery, and clogged the shoe at every step. They crossed Oldbourne, towards Monmouth Street, then, as now, the favourite locale of vendors of cast-off garments, and took their way, little molested by the sons of Israel, for the night was an unpromising one for "cushtomers," towards Soho, at that time a wilderness of tenements in course of erection. They were threading their path through heaps of mortar, and picking their steps over boards and puddles, when, at the corner of an unfinished street, they passed a man closely muffled in a horseman's coat. He stood aside to allow them to pass: they had left him some dozen paces, when he hastily followed them, and saluted them by name.

"Dickon, my trump," said he, addressing Turpin; "I've been asking two or three of our friends after your health. How goes it?"

Turpin held out his hand as he recognized the voice of Fielder.

"I got your note," said he. "I and Tom were just off to the place of meeting."

"Whose note?" asked Fielder. "I was told by Dennis, that you were married; and if I hadn't feared intruding where I might not have been welcome, you'd have seen me at your snuggery long before this."

Turpin looked at King with surprise.

"Then am I to understand you sent no message to me to-day?" enquired he.

"Not a bit of it," replied the blunt straightforward Fielder; "I'm not given to writing letters where I can do my business in person."

"Egad, that's droll," said King: "let's step into the Marlborough here, close at hand. You've the letter, Dick."

The three stepped into the tavern, and over a glass discussed the probable motive of the writer—Fielder at once repudiating its authenticity. The hand was unknown to all parties.

"There's mischief meant here," said Fielder; "though from what quarter it's to come I can't even make a guess: you'll not go, Dick?"

"Not at the appointed time, certainly," replied Turpin: "if there be traitors in our camp, though—and this looks like it—it is better they should be at once found out. I'll disguise myself, and watch the neighbourhood."

"Let's all three keep together," suggested Fielder.

King assented, and they left the tavern: it was now near the hour of ten. Dick having furnished himself with a cap, and a supplementary beard and bush whiskers, and his companions having also effected considerable alterations in their outward appearance, they again set forward.

A dense October fog was spreading its volumes of mist over the clumps of irregular buildings which formed the thoroughfare to Charing Cross; and, although the hour was yet early, few persons were abroad—not only owing to the disagreeableness of the night, than the danger of the spot to the foot-traveller. Arrived at Charing Cross, they entered upon the dirty and ruinous conglomeration of houses forming the heart of Westminster. The street by which they took their way, was lined on either side by wooden sheds, which jutted out with great irregularity, and but little regard to the sanctity of the highway, which in many places was inconveniently narrowed by these encroachments: intermixed with these were wooden houses, with their quaint gables and grotesque carvings—varying in size, height, and ornament, according to the taste, caprice, or wealth of their occupiers. A stack of bare wooden boards, black with age, and mouldering with the rot, stood beside the rudely-carved and newly-painted front of the wealthier tradesman, or private person, and in these small sashed windows occasionally took the place of the leaden casements which distinguished the poorer tenements—while here and there a stone-building, of some pretension and antiquity, might be seen; but in every instance the buildings were constructed without that respect to public convenience which, in modern times, has been secured by law. Yet, miserable as was the aspect of this locality by day—still, when viewed by night, with a clear sky, and the moonlight streaming upon it, the sharp outlines of the roofs, standing forth in the clear expanse, every angle and peculiarity brought out in strong relief, and the broad masses of gloom below, produced by the various projections of the houses, gables, and sheds, it presented—bold combinations of lights and shadows, and a picturesque effect which we seek in vain amid the straight formal lines, and uniform brick piles, which have ousted the habitations of our ancestors. Such was the road pursued by them. They had now arrived in the neighbourhood of the spot, and stopped to hold a consultation as to the best plan to acquaint themselves with the design of their enemies—for that mischief was meant they had now no doubt. The drizzling rain still fell—the streets were almost deserted; and the watch, generally scanty and always idle, were nowhere to be seen: the damp fog hung overhead, or nestled in the corners of the streets, and save the candles which glimmered through window and lattice, or the red smoking lamp which marked the situation of some tavern—the night, as we have before said, was dark. The distant lamp, viewed through the misty medium, seemed like some beacon flickering in the far horizon; and the towers of Westminster Abbey, indistinctly seen through the shifting vapour, loomed gigantic and undefined in the distance.

"A pleasant night this, 'pon my soul," said Tom; "what say you to my going and reconnoitring Nan's premises? I've a guess that, as it isn't me that's invited, that might be the safer course."

They were standing beneath the projecting shelter of a roof, which cast a deep shadow, when they became aware of the approach of footsteps; the party advanced in silence, or at least, their whisperings were too low to enable the friends to distinguish the purport of the dialogue.

"Stand close," said Fielder as they approached.

Foremost of the party came Bayes and another officer, accompanied by Madge; and behind them not less than half a dozen of runners all well armed: they halted within a few paces of the spot where Turpin and his friends stood concealed. Fielder pressed Dick's wrist significantly; and they listened with breathless attention to the following dialogue.

"I've been a seeking for you on this lay, Mister Bayes, for a long time. I see'd his fine madam up yonder this very day. He's sure to come, for I've planted it on him as George wants to give him the office for a put up; and I dessay he's at the trap afore now. You've no need, as I told you last time, to let me be seen in it: that brought you a pretty good lump of the rowdy,* but this 'ull be a better take. Mind you, Nan especially must be kept dark as to me nosing † on her crib."

Mr. Bayes promised secresy; and Madge, bidding the party good night, returned by the road they had come: while the officer and his myrmidons, having darkened their lanterns, went up a narrow alley, the rear of which communicated with the yard of Nan Turner's abode.

"Split me!" exclaimed King, as soon as the party were out of hearing, "if you're not a lucky dog, Dick. A very prettily contrived trap, upon my soul! By the bye, what might be the cause of the great interest that very communicative damsel, who is going to do it better this time than the last, seems to take in your welfare—eh, Dick?"

"I don't know whether to believe my eyes and ears," interrupted Fielder; "why, that's Madge Dutton. It's clear now, how that unlucky Plumstead job came off; d—n me, but I could find it in my heart to follow this jezebel, and knock her on the head."

---

* Money.   † Informing.

"Hark! they are at it," exclaimed Turpin.

The crash of a window was succeeded by a shrill female scream, and the clashing of swords, intermingled with oaths and execrations, was plainly audible. The report of a pistol was followed by a rattling of glass, and a man rushed hastily down the narrow entry by which the officers had entered, pursued by two or three of the thieftakers. They were too close on his heels to allow him a chance for escape; he turned upon them, but the unequal combat must soon have ended in his death or capture, when King, who stood nearest to the contending parties, stepped behind the officer who pressed hardest on the man, passed his sword suddenly through the muscular part of his arm, and as suddenly withdrew it. His limb fell powerless by his side.

The wounded man dropped his weapon, and grasping the disabled arm with the other hand, let fly a volley of curses on the clumsiness of his nearest comrade, to whom he attributed his wound. He, feeling himself innocent of the charge, dropped his point, and leaving the remaining man to press the fugitive, walked up to his wounded companion, and with some asperity, enquired the meaning of the charge. The altercation, however, was cut short, for Turpin, recognising in the man now exchanging cut and thrust with the remaining officer, his old acquaintance Bill Rose, despite a warning check from King, rushed from his ambush, and confronting the officer, drove him up the narrow entry from which he had emerged, at the same time bidding Rose to fly. He did not need twice telling, for seeing King and Fielder, who now came forward, he at once darted down a dark alley, and in a few seconds they lost the sound of his retreating footsteps. It seemed, nevertheless, likely to go hard with our hero, for scarcely had Rose made a clean run of it, when the officers, perceiving the assistance which had so opportunely arrived, retreated, shouting aloud "a rescue! a rescue!" and the cry was instantly followed by the approach of hasty footsteps. The parties, by mutual consent, appeared to have drawn off; but this prospect of a rein-forcement induced the thieftakers to make one desperate push to disable or take one or other of the party. Turpin was a little before King and Fielder, and him they singled out for their rush.

"Stand to me," whispered one of the fellows; "strike the taller one on the leg, while I hold him in play."

The man assented with a nod, and the superior officer, who was our old friend Pearce, flourishing his cutlass, advanced on Turping, exclaiming,

"Surrender in the King's name!"

Dick retreated a pace or two, and the officer, mistaking his forbearance for cowardice, pressed upon him.

"You're rushing on danger," said Dick, coolly, as he parried one or two of the ill-judged cuts of Pearce. "I shall prick you if you come closer."

Two other officers now came up, whom King and Fielder assaulted, but they, after exchanging a few thrusts, fairly turned their backs and fled. At this moment, Turpin was surprized with a blow on the wrist, given by the other fellow, who had, unperceived by him, passed under the shadow of the buildings, and come behind him. The sword dropped from Dick's grasp, and the officer sprung upon him. He had, however, reckoned without his host; for Dick, wounded as he was, catching him by the wrist of his sword arm, at one twist threw the weapon from his grasp, and seizing his throat, flung him prostrate in the muddy roadway. The other fellow now rushed upon Turpin, but just as they had closed, Fielder and King returned to the spot. The former, without a moment's hesitation, lent the runner a blow under the ear which laid him senseless.

These occurrences took much less time in acting than describing. Tom Pearce was, however, a man of judgment; and observing from the rut, where he softly lay, the mischance of his comrade, he at once saw that in the present case the better part of valour would be discretion; he therefore prudently held his peace, and lay apparently stunned, waiting till further assistance might make it advisable to recover from his stupor.

"Warm work," said King, "and awkward fighting, this night skirmishing. Damme, but I think we've cleared the coast of them. Hadn't we better be off though? They take us for rake-helly bloods or Mohocks, I know, by the exclamations of those two cowardly rascals that I and George have made skip off so nimbly just now. I wonder where Bill Rose has bolted to, and who they've nabbed at Nan's. But come, it won't do to enquire about here; so let's drop into the nearest tavern, and talk over our adventure."

" I'm wounded," said Dick, as they walked rapidly from the spot, taking one or two of the circuitous turnings in the neighbourhood of the Almonry. "That scoundrel, you so opportunely floored, George, has given me an ugly cut on the arm."

" The more reason we should adjourn to the tavern," said King; "I hope it's nothing serious; my old pal, Ned Fitzpatrick, lives hard by, and there we can procure a private room, and the necessary attendance."

To Fitzpatrick's they accordingly proceeded. A surgeon was sent for, and the cut in Turpin's arm, which was a severe flesh wound, having been dressed, the party, after enjoying a bottle, proceeded to learn the news in the common room. Here the principal topic was the betrayal of a gang of highwaymen, by one of their accomplices, and the capture of the principal man; among whom the names of Turpin, and several others were confidently enumerated. Not a word, however, seemed to have transpired of either a rescue or an escape. Indeed, though it was stated by those who professed to know best, that in the desperate resistance made to the officers, two or three of the latter had been severely wounded, the thieftakers had too much judgment to report their own partial failure. The men taken consisted of Bob Berry, the cork-cutter, who was desperately wounded in the encounter, and three of his associates—Rose escaping, as we have seen. Berry and two others suffered in 1731 at Tyburn*; while Nan Turner, notwithstanding the promise given to Madge by Mr. Bayes, was sentenced to a long imprisonment.

We must now request the reader to revert, in imagination, to Bloomsbury, and the dwelling where the gentle Esther waited the arrival of her husband and his friend. She had just completed a few of those little fireside arrangements, in anticipation of his return, which, by their very delicacy and minuteness, glad the heart of man—showing, as they do, even more unequivocally than greater things, the affectionate remembrance which in absence prompts the heart of the wife to forestall even the smallest of his wishes—when a loud ring at the front gate lighted her fair face with smiles, and she hastened to the entrance to welcome him to a warm heart and a warmer bosom. The servant, however, returned alone across the small forecourt, as her mistress listened, with a sigh of disappointment, for the wished-for step.

* See 'Newgate Calendar,'—Life of Turpin, p. 17.

"A female, in a close hood and cloak, wishes to see Mrs. Palmer, ma'am," said the maiden.

"Indeed!" said Esther; "'tis late, and a strange night for a visit: bid her enter."

Then seating herself in the little parlour, she gave way to some anxious feelings—for true love is ever anxious—first for her husband, then for her parent.

The visitor entered, but stood near the door, as if in doubt whether she should seat herself, although requested to do so by Esther. She appeared a stout-made woman, rather above the middle size; and the cloak that she wore, from its flaunting colour—although exhibiting marks of ill-usage rather than wear—was hardly such as a lady would have arrayed herself in at that season of the year, and in such unfavourable weather. Esther waited awhile for her visitor to begin; she felt uneasy and alarmed at the strange and bold scrutiny which her unknown guest bestowed upon her; and in vain tried to recollect her features. At length she broke the silence by enquiring to what she was to attribute her visit.

The woman seemed to be lost in reverie, for instead of replying to her question, she slowly muttered, as if communing with herself,—

"She's pretty, certainly pretty!—and more, she's innocent; yet she is doomed to misery, where I could find happiness! Young woman, do you know who and what your husband is! Do you know that he is not fit to mate with such as you? By this time he is—if not slain—"

Esther, alarmed by the woman's manner, started from her seat, and uttering a low cry, exclaimed, "If you know anything, my good woman, that has happened to my dear husband, pray do not keep me in suspense, but show me to him—show me where he is, do not trifle with my feelings—"

"I pity you," said she; but the sternness of her voice contradicted her assertion. "Your husband should have been mine, but he scorned a heart whose love was as strong as yours; despised and cast away a woman who was suited for him; spurned contemptuously the affection and the devoted services of her who would have been faithful to him in good and in evil, in danger and in prosperity, in life and in death; and preferred your sacrifice to the denial of his own appetites; married you to deceive and destroy you— (passion choked her utterance; after a hysteric sob she went on, while a demoniac gleam of triumph flashed from her eyes). But that's all past; and if you can still love, and wish to see the man who has betrayed you, betake yourself to Newgate, and there, in the felons' cell, enquire for RICHARD TURPIN THE HIGHWAYMAN!"

Esther stood petrified with horror and amazement. She gazed with absorbed interest on the woman before her, as if clinging to some vague hope she would contradict or recal the dreadful words she had spoken. The pause was dreadful. So bitter and intense was the expression of woe on her face that Madge, for she it was, felt for a moment something like compunction; the feeling was but too transient, and she forgot it had ever existed in her bosom, when Esther, with an energy and composure for which Madge was totally unprepared, stepped towards her, and grasping her by the wrist, earnestly exclaimed,—

"Tell me, I conjure you, what has happened to my husband. You speak as if knowing of some fatal event which has befallen. I implore you to lead me to him—my brain whirls so that I scarcely comprehend the meaning of your dark and fearful speech. (Madge regarded her in silent amaze-

Esther commands Madge Dutton to leave her house.

ment.) Tell me, I insist, (and she raised her voice imperatively) has anything fatal befallen my husband, and I will forgive you for the pain you have inflicted."

The last part of this sounded so much like a command, that it at once reassured her. She smiled with scornful indignation, and her lip curled with bitter satisfaction, as she thought how beyond her blackest hopes the barbed shaft of her woman's vengeance would rankle in the heart of the man who had slighted her. The love of Esther was, indeed, what she might have expected; but she was unprepared for a manifestation of it so much after her own heart. She almost admired her rival, as with beaming eye, flushed cheek, and a look of dauntless enquiry, she gazed in expectation of her answer.

"Silly girl!" said she at length, (her voice trembling with the eloquence of excited feeling) "You too are doomed—I see it, in your countenance. Is it not enough that I, a base, abandoned thing—an outcast, should have fixed my affections on a felon—have chosen from my associates a lawbreaker, whose desperate career will close at the gallows' foot—but that such as

No. 14.

Esther Bevis, the young, the innocent, the admired—sought by her equals in station and in character—should be crushed, sullied, made miserable in life and hurried to a melancholy death, ere time has stolen half the beauty from her cheek, that a reckless highwayman may boast for a few short weeks or months, a bride whose first and last tears will be those she sheds over his unlamented death? Can you—will you love the man, who has so cruelly deceived you; who will—I speak the words of sad experience—leave you the gibe of a cold-hearted world; the mark of scornful observation; one at whom the finger will be pointed, and the gaze of curiosity be fixed, as the WIDOW— must I repeat it—of TURPIN THE HIGHWAYMAN? Do you understand me now?"

She felt the hand of Esther tremble as it rested on her arm.

"See here," continued she, marking the effect of her speech, "here is a purse—a braided purse, and here a ring. Know you these baubles?"

Alas! Esther knew them too well; they had been early love-tokens between her and Palmer; and more than once since their ill-starred union had her husband regretted their mysterious loss, during the period of their long separation. Little did he think that Madge, having by chance appropriated them at Plumstead, had first kept them from affection and afterwards from hate. Esther paled as she looked on them; a spasm seemed to crush her heart, and she feared she knew not what. Madge, with bloodshot eye, and her fine face distorted with a malignant sneer, continued—

"What you know them, do you? These I will never part with; they are the only relics, the remembrances of a love in which he you now own as husband swore as fervently, and vowed as sincerely, to her who now stands before you, as the heartless seducer has done to induce your innocence and girlish simplicity to ally itself with his hypocrisy and wickedness. If you desire to save yourself—if you are not too firmly wedded to the will of the impostor who has entangled and ensnared, and will destroy you, break off at once—"

"Woman!" exclaimed Esther, in a tone that checked and startled Madge; whose vehemence had increased with the supposed ascendancy she was acquiring over her victim; "Woman! I know not how I have allowed myself to converse so long with you on such a subject—anxiety for my husband can alone excuse me: if you refuse to tell me the nature of the misfortune which has overtaken him I shall owe you no thanks, but will seek him myself. Tempt me no more with fiendish insinuations, I believe them not; depart this house, never again to enter it—and remember, that weak as you may think me, I have a fortitude which shall bear me through with the vow I have sworn at the altar to cleave unto him, who is my husband in the sight of God and man, till death shall part us."

Madge stood petrified. Her experience of human nature, and of woman's affection, had pictured it to her mind as selfish sensuality; the gratification of vanity; the triumph of jealousy; or the promptings of caprice. She knew not the proud disinterestedness, the high feeling, the sustaining force, the pure, the self-abjuring single-heartedness of wedded love. Madge looked silently at Esther who deliberately and firmly stepped towards the bell; which, having rung, she seated herself and composing her features, with a firm voice desired the servant to "show the lady out." The whole proceeding so completely took her by surprise, that she mechanically obeyed the curtseying maid, who stood, with candle in hand, prepared to light her to the gate.

Slowly following her conductor, she was outside of the premises, and in the darkened street, before she was well aware of it. She turned and reapproached the small gate. Ungovernable fury possessed her.

"Fool, idiot, coward that I am, to allow the haughty insolence of that green girl to daunt me! I'll return, and show her what it is to insult her equal—ay, her mistress. I'll—"

She stood for a few moments irresolute with her hand raised in the act to knock, when, at a short distance, she heard the voices of some approaching passengers; for the patter of the rain from eave and casement prevented their footsteps from being distinguished on the drift causeway. They were coming towards the spot; she therefore postponed her purpose for the moment, and stood under a small lime-tree, which overhung the low green paling. The persons approached and knocked at the gate: they were three in number. Her very eyes seemed

Made the fools of her other senses,
Or else were worth them all;

for among them, (he had changed his disguise, for an obvious reason,) she recognised the man whom she had in imagination securely lodged in the dungeon of the Gatehouse—the object of her *affectionate hatred*—DICK TURPIN!

We will now turn to the interior of the home which the jealous vindictiveness of Madge had transformed from a dwelling of happiness to the abode of misery and distrust.

Esther listened to the departure of the destroyer of her peace; then, throwing herself on a seat, buried her face in her hands, and wept bitterly. The return of Turpin, which, half an hour before, would have gladdened her confiding heart, now struck upon her ear as if she were guilty—as if the consciousness of crime in her husband had transferred the load of guilt to her own bosom. Suddenly starting from her seat, she summoned her energy—and, drying her eyes, she endeavoured to receive him with composure. Her averted head and trembling voice alarmed him—and, taking her tenderly by the hand, he inquired the cause.

"Has anything occurred during my absence?" he enquired. "Esther, dearest, you have been weeping: why this agitation; am I the cause?"

She dared scarcely trust herself to speak.

"A sudden indisposition—a severe heart—I mean a painful headache, has—"

She paused, and King looked on anxiously.

"Shall I seek assistance?" asked her husband tenderly.

"No, no!" she replied; "I shall be better presently; pray do not distress yourself. Pardon me," said she, turning to King; "let me not disturb you; I will retire to my chamber for a few moments, and return again."

She left the apartment, and Turpin followed her to the door; but, in compliance with her earnest entreaty, returned to keep company with his friend.

Agitating surmises confused her brain as she recalled each phrase, each word, of her mysterious visitor. In her quiet and secluded life the name of Turpin had never reached her ear; yet, that something dreadful, because undefined, was attached to it, she more than suspected. The woman was a jealous, a disappointed woman—abandoned and infamous by her own words: she had told her too, that her husband, with whose name of Palmer she appeared well acquainted, was a highwayman; but then, had she not also assured her that he was in a felon's cell for his crimes? That, at least, was untrue;

and might not the rest be so?   Was she insane? she caught eagerly at the
hope, but the broken reed pierced her as she remembered the ring and the
other token of affection which the woman had shown to her—coupled with the
assertion of her husband's baseness.   At length she decided to return to his
presence.

"I will not believe him so heartless—he has been ever kind—and upon
what evidence am I about to convict him?   Would a man of respectability
and character—though, I must own, rather too gay and volatile—be his bosom
friend and constant companion, were he such an one as the malicious frenzy
of that desperate woman has represented him?   No! though, alas! my heart's
confidence is shaken, my hand shall not be the first to plant the bitter weeds
of unhappiness in our hitherto happy home."

With this resolve she checked her tears, and rejoined the friends.   The eye
of her husband was bent on her with anxiety, that was instantly displaced by
glistening pleasure, as he marked the change in her aspect.   The frugal
supper was despatched amidst many pleasantries from King—who wished, as
he said, to dispel the low spirits he was pleased to attribute to the temporary
absence of her spouse.

"'Pon honour," said he, "Dick, you're the happiest fellow unhanged;
(Esther started at the word, as her husband looked anxiously at her, though
the action was unobserved by King.)   "You've a treasure in Mrs. Palmer,"
(and he bowed gallantly to the lady) "which wealth cannot purchase, and
but few of the most fortunate of our sex can hope to—"

He paused—a livid palenesss chased the colour from the cheek of Esther.
He involuntarily followed the direction of her eyes, and at once perceived the
cause of her emotion.   The ruffles which decorated the wrist of Turpin were
saturated with blood; for although he had carefully removed every stain from
his person, the exertion of his wounded arm, in his endeavour to conceal the
accident from her observation, had caused it to bleed afresh.   Turpin, too,
caught the expression of her countenance; but before he had time to enter
upon any explanation, the wretched Esther, who saw in these sanguine spots
the confirmation of her worst forebodings, had sunk senseless from her chair.

The little party was now broken up; King took his leave, and Turpin, on
his wife's recovery, soothed, as he thought, her agitation, by a plausible lie,
as to the accidental injury he had received.   Esther feigned to believe him;
and thus was confidence, the firmest bond and cement of wedded love, shaken,
crumbled, destroyed, and replaced by a feeling of mutual distrust, disrespect,
and alienation.

From this time forth Turpin no longer met his amiable partner with the
open smile of sincerity; and she, whose joy it had hitherto been to minister
to his slightest wants, to anticipate a wish ere he had time to frame it—still,
it is true, performed the duties of a tender wife—but oh! how changed in
manner!   A sad pensiveness, a mild abstraction of manner, pervaded all her
actions;   kind, uncomplaining, and attentive, she still welcomed him—
but it was no longer the sunny smile of guileless joy which glowed on her
features and sparkled in her eye; and her pleasure (for she did feel pleasure
on each occasion of his safe return) had become subdued and matronly.   Turpin
saw the change, yet dreading the explanation to which an enquiry might give
rise, he watched, in painful silence, the grief which robbed her cheek of its
rose, and her eye of its lustre, until her increasing weakness and sinking
strength forbad him longer to pass her state unnoticed.

She was now too, in a situation which, though upon its first discovery it had rejoiced his heart, now added to her claim on his tenderest and most considerate sympathy; and the knowledge that he was about to become a parent brought with it pangs of the bitterest reflection and self-reproach. With Esther too, the pride and joy of the mother seemed chastened by a secret sorrow; and though a faint smile might mantle across her face as the subject was delicately alluded to by her husband in their conjugal *tete-a-tetes*, it was so suddenly dispelled by an earnest seriousness of expression, and a suffusion of her bright blue eye, that Turpin for some days had scarcely dared to speak even on the most indifferent topics.

They sat one evening beside the brightly-burning fire; his gentle helpmate silently engaged in preparing some necessary or ornament for the little stranger now soon to be expected; the flickering blaze threw its fantastic shadowings on the pure white ceiling; the smooth-skinned cat, with half-closed eyes, dozed and purred in happy slothfulness on the rug, or with curved and moistened paw ever and anon sleeked her glossy head; the cricket chirruped joyously from his warm chink in the chimney corner; day had died out, and darkness had stolen on, while Esther, to whom the subdued gleam was more congenial than the glare of candlelight, had continued her task without noticing, or at least appearing to notice, the transition. How changed were her thoughts, how altered her views of the future, from the waking dreams floating through her mind on the evening which, in our first chapter, introduced Esther Bevis to the reader. How contrasted, too, was even she with her former self. The sanguine, the hopeful, girl, had become the pale, the unhappy mother; and the very event, her union with the man she loved, which she had fondly pictured as the fount, the source of purest happiness—of happiness such as none of earth's children shall enjoy, and none but the inexperienced can hope for—had poured the devastating torrent of the black waters of adversity over her heart, and laid its pleasant feelings and its sunny prospects waste, cold, and desolate. A deep, but partially suppressed sigh, heaved the bosom of Esther, and she raised her mild eyes to her husband's face as he said,—

"Esther, dearest, there is surely some deeper cause for this settled melancholy than the slight wound I received some month ago. I have hitherto refrained from pressing an enquiry, in the hope that you would spare me the necessity. But Esther, dearest, can I thus see you daily withering, pining, fading before my eyes, and not seek the cause of the corroding canker? Surely it would be some comfort, some consolation, to impart your griefs to him who loves you best; and thus, by sharing, relieve the burthen which now weighs down your spirits and your health. Surely," said he, in a tone of mild remonstrance, "there is no secret too weighty or too sacred to confide to the keeping of your husband; a husband, too, among whose faults, and they are many, (Esther sighed deeply, not unnoticed by Turpin,) a want of affection for you cannot be reckoned."

Esther's eyes filled with tears, and dropping the trifle on which she had been employed, she clasped her hands, and looked supplicatingly in his face.

"Richard, do not, I entreat you, I conjure you, press me to disclose what I had hoped to carry with me to the grave!"

Turpin's hasty temperament was slightly roused; he bit his lip, and frowned slightly. The indication increased the distress of Esther.

"Richard," said she, "I fear you. Why look so darkly and angrily upon me? I cannot bear your frown—do you distrust me? Urge me no further, I implore you, as you value our future happiness, to disclose a secret, which must, I fear, produce our eternal separation."

The last words struck on the ear of Turpin like the death-knell of departing happiness. His affection for Esther had rather increased than abated; and his soul, though familiar with crime, still bowed in homage to the majesty of virtue. No man is wholly good or wholly bad; and the villains of romance and melodrame, who are as free from weaknesses as from virtues, and whose crimes are unredeemed by a single trait of goodness, are as far from nature and from truth as the

"Faultless monsters which the world ne'er saw,"

which our modern novel-writers are wont to picture as the lovers and heroes of their duodecimos.

Turpin was neither the one or the other of these creatures of a morbid imagination—he was a mere man, and therefore possessed the frailties and the virtues, the vices and the good qualities, the weaknesses and the good resolves, which go to make up the character of frail humanity, in all its shades and diversities of character. His passions were strong, and his affections correspondingly so. Unused to controul, and courageous even to a fault, ready to resent insult, yet easily pacified, he possessed all the requisites of a great villain and a great hero, characters which have a closer affinity than the flatterers of conquerors, and such like enemies of their species, are ready to admit. The reflection of Esther on his frown instantly shamed him, and his eager and reproachful tone of enquiry changed to painful regret at the harshness, for so he felt it, of which he had been guilty in thus questioning her. To her concluding supplication, and the dark hint it contained, he replied not, otherwise than by rising from his chair and pressing the gentle petitioner to his breast. Esther again burst into tears—and, relieved by them, and this silent, though to her eloquent mark of his affection, she gently said:

" Think not, dearest husband, that my love for you has decreased; no! the vow which I have pledged before heaven was needed not, but as a form. Yet, yet—a something, it may be—(and her heart misgave her as she uttered the deceit)—it may be lowness of spirits has lately—my health is not what it once was; and—and if you and I could visit my father, of whom of late I have thought much and sadly, it would gratify me."

The little *ruse* succeeded: Esther weakly imagined it might be the means of separating him from the companionship she so much feared: her ignorance of the heart of man, and of the meshes, stronger than gyves of iron, with which crime fetters the bodies and the souls of its victims, whispered her that he she so fondly idolised, might yet be plucked from the brink of the gulf of destruction. Her husband seized eagerly at the proposal; he saw, or thought he saw, in it a hope of relieving her oppressed mind, and restoring her impaired health; and Esther, with a cheerful look, drew the table near, and having placed writing materials, proceeded to indite a letter to prepare her father for their acceptance of his invitation, long since received.

CHAPTER X.

————I'll example you with thievery:
The sun's a thief, and with his great attraction
Robs the vast sea: the moon's an arrant thief,
And her pale fire she filches from the sun:
The sea's a thief, whose liquid surge resolves
The moon into salt tears: the earth's a thief,
That feeds and breeds by a composture stolen
From general excrement: each thing's a thief.
The laws, your curb and whip, in their rough might
Have unchecked theft: love not yourselves!
Rob one another. Away! there's more gold, cut-throats !
All that you meet are thieves. To Athens go,
Break open shops: there's nothing you can steal
But thieves to lose it.
—Timon of Athens, Act iv. sc. iii.

In the purlieus of Drury Lane, between Holborn and Queen-street, stood Lewkner's Lane, or rather still stands, under the title of Parker-street and Cross-lane. In this district, comprising Charles-street and the many wretched culs-de-sac adjacent, redolent of filth, festering with dirt, and disgusting both to sight and smell, still reside the refuse of London prostitution and misery. Here the victim of vice and of gin, the poor and the criminal, the profligate and the penniless congregate; and if such be now the state of this region, let the reader imagine its extent greater, its filth and poverty as great, and its crime aggravated tenfold, and he may picture the Lewkner's Lane of the time when Macheath flourished on the stage and Turpin on the road. In a low pothouse, the resort of the seediest of thieves, the scourings even of the gaols, were seated a motley mob of dirty and brutal ruffians, with their slip-shod women. It was scarcely past noon, and newly risen, they were cooling the raging thirst of the overnight's debauchery by draughts of twopenny from earthen jugs, or in more cases, bolting from the glass the " leperous distilment" of soul and body-destroying juniper. The men, unshaved, open-throated and ungartered, needed but a glance to convince you of their pursuits ; the bully and the thief were as strongly written on their countenances as though nature had branded them ; such power has man's vice and debasement to mark signs on its slaves. Here and there a cadaverous pimp, the scheming cowardly keeper of one or more of the low brothels in the neighbourhood might be seen; a wretch, who by living on the wages of some miserable abandonnée, perhaps long since consigned to an early grave by her licentiousness and excess, had scraped together wherewith to " furnish" some wretched tenement, some den of robbery to the intoxicated or the unwary, where he lurked spider-like supporting an existence " stinkingly depending" by sucking the blood and seizing the lion's share of the plunder of the miserable, profligate, and reckless females, whom he styled his " lodgers."

At the bar, or rather counter of this flourishing hostelrie, stood several juvenile candidates for the halter ; each of these boys, (shame to the society which tolerates such nurseries of crime, and such still exist among the *licensed* houses in several quarters of the metropolis,) though few had yet seen fifteen summers, was accompanied by his " fancy," a slatternly, dram-drinking outcast, often double his age. These specimens of the softer sex were also strikingly characteristic in their costume. They sported, in most cases, a dirty cotton wrapper of a staring ground or pattern, from which, however, the colours

had fled ; but to make amends for its neutral tint, or filthiness, each sported
about her neck, either twisted rope fashion, or more modestly spread over her
shoulder a brilliant-coloured specimen of bandanna. Soiled stockings, still bearing the marks of the preceding night's perambulations, were dragged 'a-la-cork-
screw,' o'er each ungartered leg ; and not a few displayed at the heel of the trod-
den-down slipper, a portion of the natural integument, which has been vulgarly,
though aptly, termed "a potato." It is but justice, however, to state, that
this was owing to the earliness of the hour. Later in the afternoon, having
drunk themselves into a state of sufficient bestiality, the female part of the company
would retire to their holes, and having "rubbed out" their hose, and hung them to
their own fire, if they had one, or if without one, before that of a more lucky
fellow-lodger, they, after a stretch on the bed for an hour or two, would sally
forth much improved in the outward appearance of their "understandings"—
the potatoes aforesaid having disappeared into their high-heeled shoes, by a
cunning process called "coaxing," which must be understood as an ingenious
substitute for the more respectable expedients of "grafting" or darning. The
neighbourhood was of a piece with its inhabitants. Among its rows of irregular, dilapidated, wooden houses, there were few but exhibited some calling
in its low rectangular shopfront. In these lower tenements—for each floor
possessed one or more distinct "holding,"—glass-windows appeared a luxury
unknown, and their place was at night supplied by rudely-formed, ill-fitting,
black shutters, sliding in a grove of wood. The windows presented a curious
assortment of stock. Fried flounders and dabs, periwinkles, a few shrivelled
oranges, cobbled secondhand shoes, damaged fruit, and a few dull-looking
Dutch herrings, the coarsest of flatfish, and the refuse of the slaughterhouse
in the shape of tripe, livers, and the hearts of various animals, seemed the
staple commodities of the district. Here and there, swathed in most unhealthy
coloured calico, dangled the black doll which pointed out the residence of the
dealer in rags and phials, a personage whose trade included that of purchasing
"bones," in other senses than the compilers of dictionaries have given to the word.
Other signs, too, appealed, by their symbolic language, to the unlettered
minds of the ignorant dwellers in Lewkner's Lane. A large red box,
crossed with yellow bars of extraordinary dimensions, spoke more in-
telligibly to them than the inscription of "MANGLING DON HEAR," traced
beneath in ill-shaped letters of the same vulgar, brimstone colour. A
cow of most unearthly proportions, and red as red ochre could make it, marked
the milk-house ; and in front of the dens of one or two pawnbrokers creaked
the three golden balls of the Lombard. The houses all presented their gables
towards the street, and their iron-framed and lead-divided windows, opening
casement fashion, swung each on its iron gudgeons and pintles, fashioned
like those on which the rudder of a vessel is shipped. From not a few of
these projected the primitive contrivance of a superannuated hair broom or
cashiered mop, standing out horizontally, steadied by a clothes line attached
to its extremity and describing an acute angle from its end to the respective
fastenings on each side of the window ; this centre pole and its two lateral
hempen stays formed an extempore clothes horse, from which floated in the
black-laden air, mutilated remnants of shirts, tattered shifts, gowns embroi-
dered *en gobblestitch*, footless stockings, and the miserable coverings of the
half-clad, squalid children, who rolled on the pavements, squalled in the passages, or made dirt-pies in the gutters of this savoury region. The ear of the
explorer, for none but those whom business or curiosity brought into the

Lewkner's Lane in 1781.

district, were likely to see or hear much of the " domestic manners " of these inhabitants of the back settlements " of Babylon, was struck by peculiar slang, or disgusted by the blasphemy and obscenity of speech, in ordinary use among its denizens.

The writer is not unaware that the squeamishness of modern pseudo-morality will turn reprovingly from such details as this. He will not ask pardon for offending or retorting on such fault-finders. He goes further than denying the validity of their position, that it is not proper, nay, that " it is dangerous to expose vice, lest we should contaminate the imagination of those who are as yet pure ; " or, as some more timidly have put it, " that it is at any rate, not expedient to open the eyes of those who are as yet, fortunately, ignorant of the corruptness of society." What is this sickly sophistry but saying in other words that ignorance and innocence are synonymous? It is a libel on virtue; for it goes to prove that it is only in the absence of the knowledge of crime that mankind eschew its commission! These precious providers of fig-leaves for human weaknesses see not the " Serbonian bog " into which they are travelling. The hermit who withdrew himself from the world, and who committed social suicide by removing himself from the duties as well as the temptations of sinful society ; who fled the field of contest, and shrunk from the trial ; according to these sages, would be worthy of reward from him who said, " it is not good for man to be alone." No ! says reason, award that to him who, wrestling with the difficulties without and the frailty within, achieved that partial triumph which must be accounted victory to imperfect humanity. " He who conquers himself is greater than

No. 15.

he who takes a city," said one of the wisest of the ancients. Our modern
sages would assert the same of him, who, to use an Irish figure of speech,
runs away from himself. The sagacity of the ostrich, which plunges its head
into a bush, seems to be the type of their deduction, that innocence is ignorance; to which, may we not add, as a natural consequence, that knowledge
is crime? "Oh no; we don't say that, that's unfair, that's monstrous, absurd.
We have always approved of the principle of that healthy morality which
induced our old preachers to call things by their right names. We know that
the change of manners has rendered what then was allowable in good society,
inadmissible." Our reply is that what was right then is right now; and though
we properly purge our language of its coarseness, we cannot consent to fritter
away principles; and therefore hold with the Spartans, who intoxicated
their helots, to deter their youth from drunkenness by showing its degradation and bestiality; and contend, though their practice is unfitted for modern
manners, the intention was one which the moralist must approve.

The word morality is easily pronounced, but not so easily understood; and
it is because we have allowed ourselves to be mystified by these wordmongers
that "tot homines, tot sententiæ," can be applied to this subject. Truth,
however, is the foundation of all morality; and paltering, or equivocation, are
to it destruction and death. There can be no such thing as "qualifying"
truth, for "qualified truth" is absolute falsehood. Truth changes its very
nature the moment we adulterate it, and cannot exist but as one, indivisible,
and unalterable. Viewing truth then as moral beauty, we cannot for the life
of us feel anything but contempt for these *couleur-de-rose* moralists, who
would tell us to keep truth at the bottom of her well; whose purblind
morality would hide the sun with their blanket, because being a "god and
kissing carrion," there is danger to corruption in his rays; whose ricketty
virtue fears the exercise necessary to its developement, and who censure the
pictures which the observer of human nature presents to them, on the ground
that, "though they are true, and though they cannot deny they exhibit vice
the seamy side without, yet it would be better, for the innocence of society,
not to permit them to be exhibited." Pshaw! that virtue, which only waits
for its first temptation to fall, is but a negation of vice; and we are convinced
that, by "showing vice her own feature, and scorn her own image," by painting
truly, forcibly, and naturally, the *misery*, the *poverty*, the *suffering*, the *degradation*, the *disease*, and the *remorse*, which haunt vice even as its
shadow, the interests of true morality are more efficiently subserved, than by
the pretty plaything pictures of the pleasures of virtue with which these triflers
in ethics propose to displace them. The observer of human nature must
admit, that the large majority of the younger criminals who crowd our gaols, are
the offspring of ignorance. This work is not the place for statistical data,
but we could show that the check of education is an effectual one—ay, though
it be even secular learning as contradistinguished from spiritual or moral instruction. A still larger proportion of the painted victims, who, by the glare
of gaslight, in faded silk or tawdry cotton, solicit the wayfarer in

Decent London, when the daylight's o'er,

owe their present position to an ignorance of the world and the world's ways.
There was a time when each of these creatures was innocent—(or ignorant,
as these vice-suppression gentry would say)—but for want of that mental
training, which would render them capable of estimating the value of a good

name—of appreciating the beauty (nay, set it on a lower scale, the *expediency*) of virtue, were easily seduced by the first villain who solicited them; while others, equally ignorant, wanted but the promptings of their own vanity and love of dress to debauch their innocence—or ignorance—into a belief that the life of a courtezan contains pleasures and luxuries which toiling virtue cannot hope for. Would not many of these, had they known the misery of vice, have shunned such a course of life—had they known that what seemed flowers in the distance would, on a nearer approach, prove sharp thorns and poisonous weeds? Would they have joyously and heedlessly have entered a land whose sparkling streams were black with woe and bitterness? whose fruits, though delightful to the eye of inexperience, are

> Like to the apples of the Dead Sea's shore—
> All ruddy gold without, but ashes at the core?

Would they, we ask, have made the plunge which placed a great gulf between them and society—which made them outcasts, which forced them to abandon all the sex's charms in order to procure a wretched, a precarious, a degraded subsistence? Would they have done all this had they been forewarned by a knowledge of the results of the fatal step, instead of being guarded by the " innocence of ignorance," contended for by these morality-mongers?

But, methinks the reader exclaims—" my dear sir, where in the name of all that's rigmarole have you got to? You left me in Lewkner's Lane some half-hour ago, and I'd thank you to leave off prating and philosophizing; if you've nothing to shew me, just take me out of this; for it's not the place any person of taste would choose to stand still in." Softly, gentle reader,—readers are always gentle—I have not yet done with you; I will shew you, if you please to accompany me, something more valuable and instructive to him who can read it aright, than can be learned in the precincts of the palace, or amid the frivolities of the drawing room; aye, or even within the walls of your parish church. In the two first-named places—where *ars est celare artem*, the manners are as unreal, the sentiments as artificial, and the expressions as false to nature, as the bloom on the cheek of the withered demi-rep of quality, or the pretended honour of the aristocratic " thief,". (to whom even discourtesy applies no stronger terms than those of "swindler," or "blackleg,")—it would be absurd to look for it. And in the latter, though you may hear a glowing and energetic picture of the beauty of virtue, it will fall but coldly on the sense, and prove but feeble in its effect, if compared with a sketch of the hideous deformity of vice, bold, truthful, and from the life. And now, apologizing for the detention, we will proceed.

The puddles in Lewkner's Lane, formed by the hill and dale facetiously termed " the pavement," shone all bright with the gay colours of putrefaction, as a woman with basket and key in hand, followed by a man, emerged from one of the overhanging doorways. The man in all the " dignity of dirt," was smoking a short pipe; the woman's handsome countenance glistened with that peculiar distension of the integument which drinking and excess produce in many females. The fervid heat of the skin, too, by fixing the soap used in the washing she had just given herself, increased this glossy appearance. She wore a flashy sort of morning dress; her high-heeled shoes were handsome, little worn, and of a bright colour; and her whole appearance was rather superior to the inhabitants of "the lane." They took their way towards "The Punch Bowl."

"Madge," said Dennis, for he it was ; "how's the blunt stand ?   B—t me if I've a skurrik.   I s'pose we can mix it up for a trifle, though ?"

The woman replied only by opening her hand and displaying a seven-shilling piece and some silver.   Dennis's look brightened.

"All right," said he.   "Madge, old gal, you're in a lucky box just now."

"Here," said Madge, "don't look shabby.   Let 'em see *you* pay," and she presented him some silver.   "There's enough on 'em a d—d sight too ready to make remarks, when they sees a man down."

They walked into the den of drunkenness described at the beginning of this chapter; and leaving them there, we will turn to a conversation going on outside.

"Biddy !" exclaimed a voice from a first-floor window, "the top of the morning to you—how's trade."

The speaker was a slovenly woman of immense stature, some five and thirty to forty years of age.   All of her person that was visible, as she rested her huge muscular arms on the sill of the casement, consisted of a proportionate pair of shoulders, covered with a bright yellow handkerchief : her uncombed head exhibited, in its coarse black locks, here and there a straggling grey hair ; her marked features bespoke the determination of her character, though the bloating of liquors, and a life of excess, had imparted an expression of sensuality to her mouth.   The person addressed by her was a commonplace-looking creature, a vendor of oysters, who was wheeling a barrow, on the top of which a board, with raised edges, exhibited small heaps of the coarsest oysters, allotted into pennyworths and ha'porths.   Even costermongering has its revolutions ; and the oyster-woman with her barrow, so common in old pictures and old songs, is gone.

"Och, misthriss Mary, an is that yerself?" responded Biddy ; "small rason ha' the likes o' me to crack about thrade, an' the ould man afther braking his leg off a scaffild yesternight."

The miseries of the poor are too frequent and too ever-present to excite more than a passing thought, and "misthriss Mary," as Biddy respectfully termed her, though she was one of the vulgarest and coarsest of the cyprians of Lewkner's Lane, without noticing the tale of Biddy's troubles, leaning herself forward, went on in a loudish whisper—

"Biddy, I want you to do me a job."

The oysterwoman expressed her willingness.

"It's no go for me to be twigged at Westmister.   You was never there, wor you ? (Biddy shook her head.)   My flash man's in quod, and that's the whole on it ; and p'raps they'll *lime** me if I go.   You heerd the whole of the dodge, I s'pose, at Bob Berry's last night ?"

"'Deed, an' troth, I'm innycent of knowin' a word ov it," said Biddy : "it's a bad hearing though, that Bill's lumbered ; sure an' I'd not be the woman to turn my back on him an' he in throuble.   But maybe, I'd not be able to get the sight of him."

"I'll put you fly to that," said the woman ; "Ben Gibbs—you know Ben, the *black-cove dubber*,† he's an old flame o' mine—he giv me this fogle," pointing to the handkerchief on her neck ; " only he's tipt me the office not to go near just now, cos it isn't with him to do nothink.   Ben's a good 'un, but my old man wor al'ays *yellow*‡ whenever his name came up ; so maybe it

---

* Detain.   † Turnkey.   ‡ Jealous.

'ud be as well not to ax him anythink as if it comed from me, cos it may breed *bate*,* if so be Bill should 'scape *Darby's fair*.† Bill wasn't a bad 'un," continued she ; " an' I'd like to hear what the quodcull ‡ has to say of his chance."

" Och sure, an' I'll go with all plasure in life," replied Biddy ; " small blame to ye for saying he was the good 'un—and Biddy Hoolahan's heavy curse on the grab as nailed him, say I. Sure, an' how might it have happened ? Sore's myself at heart to hear ov the same."

The woman proceeded to give her an account of all that she had as yet learnt of the occurrences of the overnight, with which the reader is already acquainted ; and having talked herself into a heat, ended with—

" I've heerd summut though, that I'll make some smoke for. Stevens says as he knows Madge Dutton 'peached. S'elp me —" and she wound up her declaration with an oath of vengeance against the object of her suspicions.

" I'm after guessing," replied Biddy, who was a sort of female ticket-porter in the district, " Madge wouldn't be trustin' her life in the lane, providin' she'd bemaned herself to that same. I see her within these two minits, with these blessed eyes, go into ' the Boul' with her man."

" You did, did you ?" eagerly asked Moll Rhodes, by which name she was generally known ; and starting from the window, she in a moment appeared at the door. Her countenance was distorted with the fiercest rage.

" Will you stand by me, Biddy ?" asked she, " and I'll tackle her ; it's true, Biddy—she sold him, an' I'll have her heart out."

Biddy commenced what she called " spaking rason ;" she might have spared her breath.

" Sure, an' now, there's a good woman, misthriss Mary ;" but her remonstrances were lost, for with hasty steps Moll Rhodes made her way towards the Punchbowl. " Hurroosh, there she goes ! sure an' there'll be wigs on the green, an' no one to lift 'em," said Biddy coolly, as she looked after her; " Moll's a divil's-limb for a skrimmage, an' it's a pity I tould her. Tim Lurgan, jist give an eye to my barry and things," said she ; and leaving her stock in charge of a translator,§ who stood smoking his dudeen at his door, she hastened after, not to lose the sight of the sport.

Meantime, the bar of the Punchbowl had been the scene of altercation. Madge was surprised, on going into the house, to find the bustle which her appearance created. Five or six women, who were assembled drinking, formed themselves into a knot, and after some pretty loud murmuring, one of them addressed herself to the landlord. The man came round his bar, and spoke to Dennis, who was looking with a scowl at what he thought the marked intention of the women to quarrel with Madge—

" Dennis, I'd advise you, if you've no wish to make a fight in my house, to take your woman out of this." Then applying his mouth to the man's ear, he said, " She's been 'peaching I hear ; mind, I don't say it's true ; only stall her off quietly, there's a good fellow.—I won't have no disturbance here," he continued aloud.

Dennis looked hard at Madge—she quailed for an instant ; then with the blood mounting to her face, she turned on her assailants, exclaiming—

" Show me the woman as 'ull say that to Madge Dutton's face, and I'll—"

---

* Quarrelling.   † The day when felons used to be removed to Newgate for trial.

‡ Gaoler.   § A vamper and vendor of secondhand shoes.

The party, neither of whom dared a contest, had they even been sufficiently interested in the affair, shrunk back at her bullying tone and manner; Dennis looked perplexed, for he had strong suspicions of the truth of this unexpected accusation. Further 'fending and proving was cut short, for at that instant Moll Rhodes entered. With the spring of a tigress she flew upon Madge, and with one powerful blow felled her to the ground. Dennis seized the infuriated woman, and endeavoured to drag her from his paramour, in whose hair she was knotting her hands.

"Leave me alone," screamed she; the other women tried their best to tear Dennis away.

"Shame!" exclaimed one; "let 'em alone. Moll knows what she's about. I'd murder her myself if she'd sarved me so."

"Come off, Dennis," said the landlord, dragging him away. Madge lay senseless; her head had struck a settle, and she was bathed in blood. Moll, excited to frenzy by the conflict, now turned on Dennis, who in her blind rage she set down as a participator in the treachery, and who had further aggravated her by the blows he had bestowed on her arms, in his attempt to rescue the head of Madge from her grasp.

"You one-eyed ——," panted she. "I'll do for you too;" and she sprung at him. He, however, stepping aside, caught her by the wrists.

"Take her away," cried he, merely standing on the defensive, but no one interfered. Moll threw herself on her knees, and in the paroxysm of her rage, venting curses, fixed her teeth in the hand of Dennis. The pain compelled him to liberate her arm; and the disengaged hand was immediately fixed, like the claw of some ferocious animal, on his face. Dennis swayed back to avoid the blow, and Moll, rising to her feet, bore him with violence against the wall. The great strength and weight of Moll, and the momentary hesitation of Dennis to act vigorously, had given her a temporary advantage, and she followed it up with the vigour of a fury.

"Go it Moll; slog him," cried half-a-dozen.

"Take her away, or I'll do her a mischief," exclaimed Dennis.

She now released her other hand, and twisted it in his long hair. Dennis passed his hand into the breast of his coat, and opening the blade of a large clasp knife with his teeth, struck her suddenly on the side. The woman uttered a shrill scream, reeled backwards, and fell heavily. None saw the nature of this movement of the spiteful Dennis.

"Take that, Mother Rhodes," said Dennis, savagely, as he cunningly slipped the knife from his right hand, and dropped it into his ample coat pocket. "I'm thinking that's your gruel."

Two or three women hastened to raise the prostrate Moll. She groaned deeply; and turning on her side, drew up her limbs with the movement of one writhing under severe pain.

"Well, b—t me," said the landlord, to whom such scenes were of everyday occurrence; "that *was* a floorer, anyhow. I fancy Missus Moll won't tackle the black 'un agin in a hurry. She carries heavy metal, but she's got her match this time, and no flies."

Dennis slipt out at the swing door, and made his way hastily down a narrow court that led into Holborn.

"Hollo!" cried the landlord, looking out, "why he's cut and left his woman here; I'm bless'd if he hasn't. Madge! come old gal, pick yourself up; here's money bid for you," and he raised the half-stunned woman to the settle. She put her hand mechanically to the back of her head. "Ay, ay," said he, seeing the blood, "it was a nobber. I'll doctor it though: here; Sam, some water; let's see what harm's done."

He was just going to wash the head of Madge, when his attention was called off by the exclamations of the party which surrounded Moll.

"Fetch a doctor," was the cry; "why the villain's murdered her—she's stabbed. Stop him, Mr. Stubbs."

"I'm supposing," said Stubbs, who had left his patient, "as the cowardly varmint has mizzled. He's far enough by this time. I was rayther puzzled at his hopping the twig so suddent. Howsever, if she is to be a stiff 'un, 'twon't do to have my house called in question; that can't do no good to her nor nobody else."

This reasoning appeared to be assented to by the whole of the company, and amid many execrations on Dennis, the wounded Moll was carried to her lodging.

A neighbouring apothecary, by courtesy termed "the doctor," was sent for; and the wound, if not mortal, was made so by injudicious treatment. Even the iron constitution of Moll Rhodes could not stand against three such assailants as want, disease, and neglect. The wound, which was both wide and deep, degenerated into an open sore; gangrene ensued—and the day that Bill Stevens attended what was then termed the "Sheriff's Ball" at Tyburn, Moll lay a stark corpse in her miserable tenement in Lewkner's Lane. The coroner, it is true, assembled a jury, *pro forma*, and "the doctor" gave evidence that the deceased was wounded. Nevertheless, after attributing, in mystifying jargon, the fatal result to drinking, and giving it as his opinion that deceased could not have lived, even had she not been stabbed; (by which ingenious representation he washed his hands of all the future trouble consequent upon a prosecution of the murderer)—the "twelve honest men" decided, with the accuracy for which "Crowner's Quest Law" is famed, that the twice-slain woman died "By the visitation, &c."

Taking his way across Holborn, and through the "Field of Forty Footsteps," Dennis pushed on toward Highgate, and rested that night in Caen Wood. With the dawn he again started, and avoiding the highway until he had cleared some twenty miles, struck into the northern road on this side Hertford; thence, passing through Bedfordshire and Huntingdonshire, he, on the fourth night, reached his native place near Sleaford, in Lincolnshire. We have before said that Dennis had been a daring poacher: an absence of seven years had, however, he flattered himself, worn out the memory of the affray which had occasioned him to leave that part of the country; and moreover, he hoped, that his intimate knowledge of its localities, and his old associates, should any still remain, would assist him in eluding the law. He was not long meeting with kindred spirits; and few months elapsed, from the time of his arrival, before the increase of petty robberies and predial outrages, bespoke an unwonted activity and daring among the lawbreakers of the county of Lincoln.

CHAPTER XI.

An English landscape! to my heart
  Fraught with a deeper spell,
Than in far prouder works of art
  For me could ever dwell;
My eye their charms might more approve,
On this I gaze with silent love.

'Tis but a vision! yet its bliss
  Is sober, pure, and true;
To think how many a spot iike this,
  As fair in form and hue,
With it in quiet beauty vies,
For English hearts to love and prize.
                              —Bernard Barton.

————Upon his brow
The damps of death are settling, and his eyes grow fixed
And meaningless; she marks the change
With desperate earnestness; and staying even
Her breath, that nothing may disturb the hush,
Lays her wan cheek still closer to his heart,
Haply to catch a sound betokening life.
It beats—again—another—and another,
And now—'tis still for ever.

"An English landscape!" The pencil of Salvator Rosa may dash off the sombre sublimity of the brigand-haunted passes of the rocky Apennines; the warmth of Claude may image the gorgeous sunset of a southern sky; the transparent Canaletti may place before us the "still life," the rows of palaces, and the translucent water-streets of the widowed queen of the Adriatic; the sober Dutchmen may limn with truth and minuteness their cattle, their flats, or their fishing boats; but could any or all of these give to the eye or to the heart "an English landscape?" Its charm lies not in the striking features which arrest the painter's attention, but in the harmonious blending of tranquillity and comfort—that word so truly *English*—which we look for in vain in more romantic lands.

Here, nothing strikes us with surprise,
  But peaceful and serene—
New landscapes smile before our eyes
  Like some remembered scene—
And bear the fascinating grace
Own'd by a loved, familiar face.

Such was the scene on which a thatched cottage, embowered like a bird's nest amid luxuriant foliage, peeped forth. Its snow-white walls were variegated with the clustered rose, and the creeping honey-suckle hung its fragrant calices, moist with stores of nectared sweets, around the light green latticework which formed the porch; clusters of the golden stonecrop adorned its roof; and from the window sills the fragrant mignonette breathed its perfume through the rustic dwelling. Its small garden exhibited, in every part, the traces of a delicate and inexpensive taste. A small and elegantly formed stand, on either side of the entrance, was crowded with Flora's favourites. The odorous geranium in its various hues, from the crimson outvying the painter's tints to the faint blush of lilac, alternated with the waxen flower of the succulent balm, and the modest leaf of the lemon-scented verbena. Thrift, the London-pride, and the bright-coloured garden daisy, bordered the neatly-kept walk, and confined within their bounds the coloured pea, the azure iris, the peony, and the taller and larger flowers clustered round the glossy-leaved rhododendron, which seemed, by its central situation in the group, there to hold its floral court.

The Robbery at Ambrose Bevis's determined on.

Nor did the fair flowers of this sequestered scene waste their sweetness on an unworthy mistress. Fair, fragile, and beautiful as they, was the gentle being who daily tended on them, who rejoiced over their growth, and with a pensive regret, that was not sadness, watched their decay. Between these, one or two feathered pets, and her attendance on her aged father, did the fair Esther divide her time. Within, too, the comforts of taste and competence were visible: the opened book, the harp, and the unfinished drawing, which met the eye in the little parlour, told the indoor relaxations of the occupant. In this lovely retreat, for some weeks, had old Ambrose been blessed, for to him it was indeed a blessing, with the presence of his daughter. The quiet retirement of the spot had done much for the health of Esther; and though a settled melancholy pervaded her thoughts and actions, the old man saw nothing in her behaviour which he did not think accounted for by the absence of her husband, who, after placing her safely in the hands of her parent, had returned to London, after a stay of a few days, on the plea of urgent business. The congeniality of her occupations and position to her taste and wishes, had their effect in restoring placidity to her mind, while the healthy breeze and sweet air recalled the bloom to her cheek, brightness to her eye, and elasticity to her step. Her occasional anxiety of look, and abstraction of mind, only called forth the quiet facetiousness of the fond old man at the, to him, glad prospect, as he phrased it, of "making him a grandfather." The only other dweller in this abode of peace, was a serving girl: not one of those pert coquettes, who, with slipshod feet chatter at door to the baker's man, and with flaunting ribbands and fancy caps, trip into the next publichouse to bandy half-indecent jests with the barman; or who carry on practical flirtations

No. 16.

with John the footman in the passage, or on the staircases of their master's dwellings—but a plain, unsophisticated, neat, trustworthy girl, the daughter of a neighbouring widow. And now, having introduced the reader to the household of old Ambrose, we will resume our narrative.

On a lovely evening, the old man, still hale and active, sat beneath his honeysuckled porch, watching with a pleased eye his daughter as she busied herself in watering her little garden. Old Bevis was evidently revolving something in his mind, and appeared once or twice to be upon the point of giving utterance to his thoughts; at length, the progress of her task brought his daughter nearer, and he thus addressed her :—

"Do you remember, Esther, the family of the Rentons; or rather the old lady and her daughter who visited us in Essex some years since ?"

" Yes," replied she; "and now you remind me, did not the elder lady request your permission for me to accompany herself and daughter, on a lengthened visit to their dwelling in some distant part of the country? Though our acquaintance was a short one, I formed a strong affection for Matilda Renton; and until her departure with her mother for France, where I heard she took the veil, (Esther saddened at the thought) many were the letters that passed between us. I have them now, and read them over only last night, with melancholy recollections of the happy hours of childhood we passed together. Poor Matilda !"

" Pshaw," replied old Bevis, in a cheerful tone; " upon my word, Esther, you're getting needlessly sad upon all points—brighten up, child; her lot's not so dark as you've painted it. Taken the veil, forsooth! why who told you that silly story?"

" Her schoolfellow, Madeline; I beg her pardon—Lady Denistoun; but it was many years ago—when she and I were at Hempstead."

" Taken the veil—taken fiddlesticks!" said the old man, merrily; " why she lives near Lincoln, is married to a substantial man, the junior partner of one of the wealthiest bankers in the county, who is brother to a member of parliament, and has some half dozen of the rosiest, merriest, nicest little curly-pated children you've ever had the fortune to see. Taken the veil, ha! ha! ha!"

" Well," said his daughter, brightening up; " I'm sincerely glad to hear it; but why should Madeline have been imposed upon by such a story?"

" I can tell you, little simpleton," said her father, gaily tapping her cheek, as she now stood leaning on the arm of his chair; " I can tell you. She was in a convent for education, which is against the law, dearest.* She is of an old Catholic family; and after a year or two spent on the continent, she returned; and I know none would she more warmly welcome than her former playmate and the daughter of her husband's friend. But I have more to say. Some money, which I have to pay over, as trustee under the will of a friend, has lately fallen in, and is now lodged in the hands of the firm of which her husband is the acting partner. I expect the attorney of my ward here shortly, with the necessary authority for receiving it. To-morrow I shall go to Lincoln, and if my Esther has patience to travel with her old father, he will be proud to introduce her to Mrs. Stourton."

---

* The statute against Catholic seminaries, imposing the penalty of forfeiture of lands and chattels on any one who should send a child to the Continent for education, was at that time in full vigour.

Esther, as might be expected, gave a joyous assent to the proposal, and the following day but one witnessed the mutual greetings of the two friends, and the renewal of their long-interrupted intercourse.

After a stay of a few days, Esther and her revered parent returned. The old man in high spirits, Esther gladdened by the warmth of Mrs. Steurton's affectionate kindness, and anticipating her promised return of the visit by a call at their pleasant home.

We must now turn to a far different scene. In a dark room, the low ceiling of which presented bare and smoke-blackened rafters; at a rudely fashioned table sat a party of four reckless, desperate-looking ruffians. At their feet crouched several wire-haired mongrels and lurchers. Beside each man, leaning against the bench on which they sat, rested the poacher's companion— his gun. They were smoking, and by the eagerness depicted on their villanous features, seemed earnestly discussing some matter of great interest.

"I'll tell 'e whot," said a bluff, muscular-looking desperado, in whose face there were traces of a bold fearlessness. "I'm dang'd if I mind e'er a keeper in Notts, Lincs, Hunts, no, nor Laystersheer naythur, but a' doan't 'xactly loike this here job. Carn't we do it 'athout cracking the crib; let's stcp un at Crossferry—eh—there 'ull be ne'er a soul to help un, an we can black our faces."

"You're a greater natural nor I thought you," said Dennis with a sneer. "Don't you know---" "A'll tell 'e something wi' a clink o' your head, Muster Dennis," replied the angry fellow, rising at what he considered the insult, and slapping a fist about the colour and size of a shoulder of mutton on the table, "who do you go to call nat'rals, cos they doan't think all along of you, and doan't loike to put their necks i' the halter, and mischief them folks as never meddled wi' them. I woan't do no harm nayther to th' ould man nor his wench; but a' woan't say as much as a' woan't do it thee, if---"

"Stash* this here, Roger," interposed the others; "if you don't like the job, you needn't make a shine."

"Oh," said Dennis, "who knew the personal prowess of Roger well enough, yet was equally aware of his influence over him; "I'm danged if ever I saw anybody yet so snappish as you grow; who the devil ever talked about doing a mischief to either on 'em. I don't know," said he, winking at his comrades, "whether I shall have anything to do with the job myself, on second thoughts; which they says is best. Roger, give us thy paw;" the good-natured fellow did so; "an' if what I said sticks in thy throat, wash it down wi' a horn o' beer." The beer was called for and dispatched, and after a short pause Dennis again opened his battery.

"Well, lads, as I've told you afore, this ain't no common catch; I know summut o' the way of finding out these here things, d'ye see—I warn't in Lunnun all they years for nothink."

Dennis's London experience was always alluded to whenever he had a mind to impress his companions with a due sense of his superiority.

"As I said afore, its in Lunnun as a man gets awake to these here things. Well, I finds out—no matter how," and here he again winked his one eye mysteriously, "as the ould man has drawed a power o' goold from Squire Sturton's; I have heered as its sumwhere to the tune of five hundred pounds."

---

* Put a stop to; cease.

He paused, after deliberately uttering the sum, as if to read the effect of its announcement in the faces of his auditors. He was not disappointed: they looked one at the other in astonishment.

"Five hundred pounds!" repeated Roger, as if taxing his powers of calculation to take in the amount; "why, darn it, that 'ud 'mount to two hundred apiece, or thereaway:" and he commenced a perplexing notation of units on his fingers.

"Yes," repeated Dennis; "five hundred pounds, in red gold, mark you; and it's to be had for asking: but we mustn't smash the door in, eh Roger?" said Dennis sarcastically, as he looked at the brown study in which the rustic was involved. Roger either did not comprehend, or heeded not the sneer.

Ready assents were given by the other two; and, after some further conversation, the pitcher was refilled, and the party broke up at midnight. On parting Dennis said—

"Now, mind my trustys, this very coming night we meet at Forster's Gap at twelve—you know the rest; and, if you behave like trumps, you're made men for life."

The slant rays of a clear moon streamed through the snow-white curtains of a little bedroom, and fell upon the features of a venerable old man, who slept quietly and profoundly. Beside stood a swarthy villain, who, pistol in hand, scrutinisingly surveyed his features by the aid of a dark lantern, the gleam of which, as he unclosed its slide, he passed suddenly across the sleeper's face. The examination seemed satisfactory; and, turning the lantern around the apartment, he singled out a small polished escritoire of dark wood, which formed the upper part of an old-fashioned chest of drawers. Stealthily and on tiptoe, he crossed the room. A severe and narrow examination of each fastening seemed somewhat to disappoint him. Directing an anxious look towards the bed, he drew from his pocket a small heavy hammer, the handle as well as the head of which were formed of iron. The implement was of that description known among mechanics as a *sheep'sfoot*, from its handle having at its end a sharp-edged wrench, split like the foot of the useful domestic animal from which the implement derived its name. Silently he prised it, but the stout fastenings yielded not; again and again did he strain it. He paused, muttering curses on the artisan who had framed so obstinate a lock.

"Swearing won't open locks, though," said he in a low voice.

Another and more violent wrench was given, and with a smart report a splinter of the stout hard walnut-tree flew from the edge of the lid. Perspiration stood on the forehead of the burglar as he paused and again looked anxiously towards the bed—the clothes moved, and the old man woke. Dennis stood back in the shade of the curtain, and placed his hand on a pistol in his breast.

"Who's there?" asked old Bevis.

Dennis held his breath to preserve the silence, and waited in expectation of the old man again composing himself to sleep. Old Bevis, however, was thoroughly awakened: he listened—the thought of the charge he had suggested itself. A minute or two of anxious suspense was followed by Dennis again venturing to move; and the first rustle of his footfall was the signal for old Bevis, who held the handle of the bell at his bed's-head, to ring it violently.

"D——n!" exclaimed the ruffian. Dashing the curtains aside, he dragged the old man out upon the floor. "Silence, or by G—d I'll brain you."

Old Bevis fell on his knees supplicatingly. At this instant a shrill scream from below assailed his ear.

"As you hope for mercy in another world," he exclaimed frantically, "harm not my daughter—take all I have, but oh!"—another, but fainter scream was heard; the distracted old man, not knowing the effect of his appeal, added—"Can I believe it? Dennis Sowton, for the love of heaven interpose—"

"What!" said the ruffian sternly, whom this recognition seemed to paralyze for the instant, "you know me, do you?"

"Yes, I—"

The unhappy old man spoke no more—the heavy weapon of the murderer descended on his grey head, and crashing through bone and brain, he fell a gasping corse at the villain's feet. Dennis, ruffian as he was, stood appalled; —he gazed at the body as it lay in the cold moonlight—a deep groan burst from its breast—he put his hands before his eyes, as if to collect himself; at this moment a noise was heard on the stairs.

"Stop her!" exclaimed the voice of Roger, from whom his charge had escaped; and Esther, who from below had heard the death-groan of her parent, rushed wildly into the room, and threw herself on the body of her murdered father! Roger and one of the men who had watched below, followed her. Dennis stared at the new comers with a half-stupified look; the appearance of Esther momentarily unnerved him; he was, however, spared small time for consideration.

"Thee dom'd villain," said Roger—but before he had time to utter another word, Dennis had disappeared from the scene, and leaving the house, was hastening across the country with a speed that nought but mortal fear could have imparted. His companions, base as they were, looked pityingly, first at the scene, and then doubtfully at each other.

"We shall some on us swing for this, I'm thinking," said Roger. "For myself, I'll leave these parts as quick as my legs 'ull carry me. 'A wish 'a could do summut to help the poor cretur, but that 'ud be slipping our own necks into the cord. So here goes—" and the poacher left the room, followed by his comrades.

Hours elapsed—the sun rode high in the heavens; yet still and insensible on the floor of that chamber of death, lay the fair girl, pale as the snow-white night-dress in which she was attired, and corpse-like as the white-haired man who slept the long and ghastly sleep of death in her relaxed embrace; one taper arm, white as monumental alabaster, encircled the neck of her parent; and her hand lay unshrinking and unconscious, dabbled in the pale bright gore; on his breast lay her head, and a torrent of fair hair, escaped from the slight band which confined it, glittered in the sunbeams as it fell into the pool of blood below.

Bright and joyous was the scene without this cottage of death and woe. The flowers smelt fragrantly, the little birds twittered from its eaves, and even within, the pet canary made the desolate home of its orphan mistress musical with its song. Nature looked brightly on that mournful spot, as if to tell poor perishing man the eternity of his Creator, and to bring home to his heart the conviction, how like a dream his memory shall vanish, and his place be no more found; how like a shadow he shall pass away from the face of that earth he so arrogantly calls his own.

We have before mentioned a servant girl, who formed one in the household of old Bevis. It is time we should notice her. On the first entry of the burglars, one of the men, after compelling her to rise from her bed, had thrust her into a small wood-closet adjoining the kitchen, and there, after the most dreadful threats of instant death, should she give the slightest alarm, he fastened the door upon her. Here, in darkness and in terror, did poor Mary pass several trembling hours, ere she could resolve to endeavour an escape. Her irresolution might not have lasted so long, but when once terror has seized the mind, the slightest and most absurd circumstances are capable of increasing or prolonging it. Now it so happened that the robbers had not, like good boys ought to do, shut the door after them; indeed, their precipitate retreat had so far detracted from their characteristic politeness, as to have rendered them, in this instance at least, unmindful of one of the little courtesies of life. The bad hinge of Mr. Shandy's door has been celebrated by Sterne, and that creaking hinge had its fellow in the door of Mary's kitchen. Now it is known to most students in natural philosophy, that one of the properties of doors is to swing backwards and forwards in the breeze, when left unfastened; and that such swinging, though anything but pleasant, is nothing very terrifying taken *per se*. Nevertheless, to a panic-struck young female, locked up in a dark closet, and assimilating each noise to the stealthy tread of some sanguinary cut-throat, a creaking door may possibly "grate" something worse than even "harsh thunder;" and so it was with poor Mary, who would doubtless not have ventured forth, had not a friendly gust, somewhat harder than the rest, lodged the door in such a position as to prevent its further vibrations; some quarter of an hour after which Mary ventured a push, and encouraged by that, another, until she was once more free.

Peering fearfully into the parlour, where all appeared undisturbed, she next repaired to her mistress's bedroom, and finding it also untenanted, she crept cautiously up stairs. The nearest apartment was that used by old Bevis as a library, and writing or reading room: here, too, nothing had been meddled with. Mary felt herself encouraged by having met with nothing as yet of an alarming nature, and stept suddenly into the only remaining chamber. What was her horror at the spectacle which presented itself! Her heart seemed to rise with a sudden spasm, and she was compelled to seize a chair to prevent herself from falling. She gazed a moment mute and horrorstruck—then, with a sense of sickness and of suffocation, she tottered to the stairs, and sat down to collect herself. She soon, however, rose, and looking back towards the apartment of death with an undefined feeling of superstitious terror, she slowly left the house. No sooner had she cleared the porch, than with a nervous panic she rushed towards the gate, and hastily unfastening it, ran, with streaming hair, down the little lane which led to the high road, with an intention to alarm the village. Fright, horror, and excitement lent her speed; the distance, however, was considerable, and the poor girl was nearly spent with exertion, when she spied a carriage approaching her at a rapid pace. She stopped beside the road for a few moments in order to recover speech and breath to tell her tale of horror. A lady from its window, observing her gesture and cry, ordered the driver to stop. It was Mrs. Stourton, who, with two of her children, were coming, as we have before mentioned, to visit the Bevises. A few incoherent sentences from the panting girl made Mrs. Stourton acquainted with the dreadful occurrences, with the addition of the murder of Esther to that of her venerable father. After some consideration, the horrorstruck friend of Esther, taking the terrified maiden into her carriage, drove at speed towards the rectory, whose occupant was also a magistrate. He communicated with Sir Albert Denistoun; and so rapidly did the news fly, that within a few hours the whole county was aroused in pursuit of the miscreants.

The arrival of a surgeon, and the proper authorities, soon showed the real state of the affair. Esther was conveyed senseless from the scene of death to the mansion of Lady Denistoun. It was long before she recovered the shock. She woke, it is true, but not to consciousness—happy for her that she did not; not even a trace of the horrid scene seemed written on her memory; a low muttering delirium, in which the care of her birds or her flowers seemed her constant topic, was varied with imaginary converse with her parent, of whose dreadful death she seemed unconscious; occasionally her thoughts seemed to take a different direction, and her attendants—amongst the most assiduous of whom were Mrs. Stourton and Lady Denistoun—were shocked and perplexed by continual allusions to her husband, coupled with, to them unintelligible, fancies of a felon's death.

For several days did she thus linger: towards the evening of the fifth day, the medical man having abstracted a quantity of blood, she fell into a deep sleep, and awoke refreshed. In the last stage of weakness, reason had now resumed its throne; and, after thanking her two kind friends for their attention, she expressed a hope that her husband had been written for. A cold shudder came over her as she alluded to the dreadful death of her parent; then collecting herself by an effort, as if to perform some high duty, she desired that Sir Albert, or some other gentleman who might be proper to receive her statement, might be called.

" It is my dying deposition," said she faintly to Madeline, " I feel it to be a duty I owe to my murdered father—to—to disclose his murderer. Madeline, I shall never live to return your kindness; I am going from this world of woes to a brighter sphere; yet pray that I may be spared to see my husband before I die."

Madeline endeavoured to reassure her; but Esther, casting aside hope, looked steadily and almost joyously towards the prospect of that unknown world, at which sages and heroes have in their last hour shrunk inwardly appalled.

Sir Albert, with the reverend magistrate before spoken of, were quickly in attendance, and the deposition duly made out, wherein Esther positively identified Dennis Sowton as the man who with weapon in hand had been seen by her to stand over the corse of her murdered father.

This disclosure gave new vigour to the pursuit; yet, although they succeeded in apprehending Roger, the mere fact of whose absconding occasioned his capture in a distant part of the country, Dennis still remained undiscovered.

Meantime Turpin, to whom the dreadful tidings had been communicated, hastened from town. On his arrival at Lady Denistoun's, on the evening of the fifth day, an affecting interview took place: it may easily be supposed what was its nature; it is therefore unnecessary we should record it. The most forcible appeals were made, and the most solemn promises given of an amended life; and Esther appeared calmer and better than she had hitherto been. All congratulated him on the prospect of the approaching recovery of his wife.

The pursuing parties had returned unsuccessful, and Dick, burning with abhorrence and indignation at the dastardly Dennis, set out with a determination of leaving no exertion untried for his discovery, to which he rightly flattered himself, though he was silent on this head, none other possessed so good a clue.

But the deceitful hectic which glowed on the cheek of Esther was like the flickering light in a charnel-house, only the signal of the still blacker darkness to succeed. Still she was cheerful, and was evidently supporting a struggle with decaying nature, to prevent the pain her illness inflicted on her sorrowing friends. The remains of her father were consigned to the grave, but from the hour of the disclosure above-stated, the unrepining victim rapidly sunk; and ere one short month had elapsed, the mother and her still-born babe followed her murdered sire to that peaceful home, where the "wicked cease from troubling, and the weary are at rest."

CHAPTER XII.

For good acts Conscience seats
The mind in a rich throne of endless quiet—
But being clogged with guilt, its evil deeds
Like leaden weights still sink it as it soars,
And plunge it deep in horror. Conscience, stained,
Is like a fretting ulcer that corrodes
The part infected. There's no punishment
Like that to bear the witness in one's breast
Of perpetrated evils when the mind
Beats it with silent stripes, with whips of steel,
And scourges it with scorpions.
       The Microsom, by Thos. Nabbes, 1637.

—Let me go!
Art thou there, traitor! Oh
For a little breath to vent my rage!
Give, give me way, and let me loose upon him.
   —Yes, I deserve it for my ill-timed truth.
Was it for me to prop the ruins
Of thy fallen reputation?
To place myself beneath the mighty flaw,
Thus to be crushed and pounded into atoms
By its o'erwhelming weight. 'Tis too presuming
For humble knaves to keep that virtue
Which brings its own destruction.
              Dryden.

WE will now turn to follow the steps of the murderer.

On rushing from the scene of his crime, Dennis had thrown from him, into a shallow pond near the house, the implement with which he had perpetrated the murder. This had since been discovered, and was preserved as evidence against the criminal.

Taking his way across the country, the flying wretch slacked not his sneaking and tortuous course by ditch and copse, until the setting sun gave signal of approaching night. With the cessation of his bodily exertion, and the failing of his physical energies, came the thought of the horrors of approaching darkness. Darkness and solitude! the hardened ruffian shrunk as he looked on the setting orb of day, as if, with his departure, fled the last stay and support of his animal courage. He looked on the earth, the glowworm in the hedge transformed itself into the cold, dull, ghastly eye of a corpse; and his fevered imagination furnished out the rest of its lineaments. Yes! there it lay, stark and bloody! He closed his eyes—it was still before him. He lay down—it was there. He tried to reason himself into a belief that it

The Capture of Dennis by Ferret and Turpin.

was delusion. He buried his face in the damp grass—it was beneath! he turned and gazed upwards; for a moment the appalling vision melted into air, and he breathed freely—he beheld the moon moving in her majesty, and the stars shining in their brightness; but anon, the planets furnished eyes to the ghastly stare of his victim, and the still cold visage of the old man, dabbled in gore, eclipsed the face of material nature. He started to his feet, and shading his aching eyes, staggered a few yards without knowing whither he bent his steps. He looked on the fields—each pollarded tree assumed some fantastic or horrid form. He walked hastily onward, as if striving by bodily exertion to shake off the cold fear which struck like a bolt of ice even to his very heart. Fatigue forbad his further progress, and he looked around with a shudder as he pursued a path leading to a barn, which he now saw at a short distance before him. The door was secured only by a latch—he entered; and, after a short examination, threw himself on some hay. He slept; if sleep that can be called when the tormented spirit beats madly in the prison of the brain.

He dreamt. Again did that white-haired venerable man kneel before him; again did he inflict the crushing blow; the features changed in their dying contortion—and before him lay, the corse of Esther!

A change came o'er the spirit of his dream;

he sat heavily ironed on a dungeon-floor; grinning faces of blood-red demons gibed at him, as they danced with demoniac glee around the ever-present corse of the old man; the bell tolled—he was led forth to execution; the upturned faces of a thousand spectators met his gaze as he mounted to the

No. 17.

fatal tree—but not one look of sympathy; and, as he looked on them, the features of each face in that staring crowd gradually assumed a resemblance to those of the murdered old man. He felt the hangman's fingers busy at his neck; the cord tightened—his brain swam—and, with starting eyes, and a gasp that seemed to burst his bosom, the wretch awoke. He raised himself on one arm, and stared around him; cold perspiration bedewed him, and seemed to penetrate his very bones. He rose—further rest he dared not try; and again set forward on his journey.

There is a fatality by which criminals seem chained to spots which would seem to all but themselves most dangerous. And this fascination, like that of the heedless moth who perils its brief existence by the candle's flame, may be only another illustration of the great truth of nature's poet, that

> Murder, tho' it hath no tongue,
> Will speak with most miraculous organ;

and that

> There's a divinity that shapes our ends
> Rough-hew them how we will.

This fatality, or whatever your metaphysicians may please to term it, led Dennis to direct his steps to London; the great vortex which absorbs both virtue and crime; which hides, amidst its ocean of humanity, alike the good deeds and the evil ones of man; which shadows in its human forest alike the good deeds of virtue and the crimes of monsters; the retreat of struggling poverty, and the home of splendid villany. To London he bent his way; and toil-worn, travel-spent, and hungered, lurking till friendly night threw its shadows around, he stealthily crept into a low publichouse, after disguising himself as far as his means would permit, on the evening of the sixth day from his leaving Sleaford.

Meantime our hero, as we have seen, had hastened to the metropolis; rightly judging, from the unsuccessful result of the search which had been instituted in the neighbouring districts by persons well acquainted with the vicinity, that the fugitive would most probably seek concealment in the "great city of refuge." The most careful enquiries were unavailingly instituted on the road; and his search had been prosecuted with the energy and perseverance which marked his character for several days previous to Dennis's arrival.

We have before had several occasions to remark the close intimacy existing between the officers of justice and known criminals. The former frequented the same places of resort as the latter, and we find, from the life of Jonathan Wild, the disclosures of Mr. Hinchman, the city marshal,* and other contemporaneous publications, that this intercourse existed to an extent which, to those who are acquainted only with modern police, must be wholly incomprehensible, if not incredible.

On his arrival, therefore, Turpin hastened to the White Hart, and having retired to a private room, despatched a messenger to the house of our old acquaintance Ferret, requesting him to immediately favour him with a confidential interview; a few minutes brought that worthy, who happened to be still in bed, to the appointment.

* These, and many other works of the early part of the seventeenth century, display a curious picture of this mutual understanding. In "A Trip to London," 12mo, 1724, in the British Museum, we find a list of the coffeehouses, and the characters of their frequenters; after enumerating some twenty or thirty, the writer says—"Let the country visitor avoid the taps of Stacey Street and Drury, where cozeners, thieves, rogues, and their doxies do most resort, and the officers of the justices are found—knaves, who do profit largely by the pillage of the thieves, as the last do by the pillage of the countryfolks."

A bumper of stiff Jamaica having been swallowed by Mr. Ferret, as " a morning," that important personage took a seat; and preparing himself by a hem and a hawk, and two or three twitches of the cross-barred pudding which encircled his plethoric neck, observed :—

" Well, Mister Dick, what's the go now? summut serus by yer meloncholly phiz—eh? Curus go I dropt inter last night at Bob Redding the buzman's: you've seen a tall, queer, lanky, wide-o sort of a chap, as I used to —"

" I beg your pardon for interrupting you, Ferret," said Dick; " but perhaps, when you've heard what I have to tell you, you'll guess I'm not in the humour for talking; it's a murder, and that the most horrid, upon which I have sent for you to consult with me."

Mr. Ferret immediately put on the countenance which he was wont to wear when giving evidence before their worships; which, from its grotesque expression of gravity and concern—contradicted by the cunning twinkle of his little grey eye—we shall call his official or police-office phiz; and composed himself with an air of solemnity to listen to Turpin's communication.

As our hero proceeded with his brief narrative, which he gave with all the energy and excitement of his nature, Ferret was once or twice uneasily affected; he fidgetted—rose from his seat—fumbled the head of his twisted stick—and scarcely gave the narrator time to conclude before he exclaimed—

" You've said enow, my good fellow—give us your hand: d—n it, but I'm glad you'd the thought to tip me the office in this here affair; old Jack Ferret's your man; I knows the ill-looking, vun-eyed, cut-throat varment: it's the like as he as brings disgrace on purfessional gemmen. I al'ays thought him a savage hound, but I'd not reckoned as he'd cum to *two hundred weight** so soon: there vos gallus though, in his looks; leastvays, in the eyes of they as knows a thing or two; and 'mong them sort o' people I reckons ould Jack Ferret. Let that pass, howsomever, and take my advice; don't let nobody know in Lunnun as you're on this scent, nor nothin' else about this; I'll write down a few 'ticulars o' this consarn, and guv it i' the proper quarter, vereby I shall serve both myself and the inds o' justice, d'ye see—eh? don't hallo about this here or you'll frighten the birds. It's a shockin' job though," said Ferret, having concluded the professional part of his advice; "shockin' as ever I heerd on. Poor ould genelman! It's a sarvice ve owes to society, Mister Turpin—a sarvice ve owes to vun another, to bring such villins to the halter. Maybe you'd be so kind as to guv us these 'ticulars in black and wite, as I can't crack much o' myself in the way of writin', d'ye see."

Turpin complied; and Mr. Ferret, after many other expressions of condolence, promises of vigilance, and queries by which to guide his endeavours at discovering Dennis, took his leave; and making his way towards Westminster, had the honour and credit of communicating at the chief office the first intelligence of the murder, and receiving the warrant for the apprehension of the perpetrators, whoever they might be : for, of course Mr. Ferret, with his usual caution and assumption of mystery, did not choose to reveal *all* he knew, or his means for pursuing the inquiry, further than by allusions to, and hints of his almost superhuman sagacity.

For two days and nights was a strict but fruitless watch kept on the lodgings of Madge Dutton. At the end of that time Mr. Ferret, who had several times held communications with Dick, resolved upon honouring Mrs. Margaret with

* The reward, in atrocious cases, then usually offered by the Secretary of State.

a call. After the occurrences related in our eleventh chapter, it may be supposed that Lewkner's Lane had become too hot to hold her; and she had now shifted her "beat" to the neighbourhood of Whitechapel. Mr. Ferret, accordingly, after a communication with his follower, from whom he learnt that she had not yet left her home—such as it was—walked deliberately down the opposite side of the street; a dirty muslin half-curtain rendered objects indistinctly visible from the other side the way. A dim candle burnt in the room, and by the shadow cast on the ceiling, Mr. Ferret could perceive that Madge was busily engaged at her toilette, which she was making by a glass laid on the table at the window: he could make out pretty well her various movements; she was certainly nearly dressed, and was now engaged in the arrangement of her hair. Another shadow passed on the ceiling; but, whether that of a man or not, was not discoverable. Ferret gave a low whistle, and his follower approached him.

"Run up to the 'Lion'," said he in a low voice, "and send Bill Johnson to me."

The man obeyed, and another officer joined Ferret.

"This is a desperate slasher, Bill, as I'm goin' to grab," said Ferret; "and I mustn't give no chance avay; so, do you vait on the *mounter*[*] vile I goes in, if so be I can do it vithout a *crack*;[†] and ven I cries "Var hawks," do you show yerself. Is yer irons primed?"

Bill answered in the affirmative; and Mr. Ferret—buttoning his coat, then feeling in his breast, and giving that sort of long inspiration which men are wont to do when going on some exploit which requires determination and courage—slapped his hat tightly on his head, and quickly but noiselessly entered the house. Mounting the stairs two at a time on the points of his feet, he suddenly turned the handle of the door, which was not otherwise fastened, and stood in the apartment of Madge Dutton. A half-dressed female, who was engaged in lacing the stays of Madge, gave a faint scream of surprise, and the latter turned in astonishment. Ferret, without uttering a word, looked searchingly and cunningly round the room: there was nothing denoting the occupation of the apartment by a man. No article of wearing apparel, save those belonging to its female occupants, was to be perceived—not even a stick, or any other questionable trace, could he see. On the table before-mentioned, beneath the window, lay a fragment of a looking-glass, of a shape which would puzzle a geometrician to designate. It had once formed a portion of a larger mirror; and now, propped slantingly against an old brass candlestick, its surface specked with unreflective spots, occasioned by rubbing off the silvering, did duty at the dirty toilette of Madge and her fellow-lodger. On the dingy deal table lay a collection of appliances which would have perplexed a fine lady to apply to their several uses. Half a dozen of japanned hair-pins, and some soaped and floured bunches of hair, soiled ribbons, a broken comb and filthy brush, lay there. In a small pasteboard box, the crazy sides of which would have parted company but for the threaden ligaments wound round it, exhibited several small lumps of red-looking chalk, intermingled with little balls of whiting; Dutch pink, for so was the cheap pigment styled, and domestic whiting, procured in ha'porths from the nearest huckster's, being the only false colour now procurable by Madge or her companion. Mr. Ferret took all this in at a glance. Closing the door and fastening it, he made a bow of mock politeness, and thus spoke:—

---

* Staircase.   † Forcible entry.

"Don't be frightened, ladies; no intention to be rude. Needn't be so modest, Missis Dutton; you ain't the first women by some hundreds as old Jack Ferret have seen not quite drest for company. Beg pardon, I'm sure, but it's business I've comed on."

Madge's companion looked at her as much as to say, "Shall I leave the room?"

"P'raps we could talk it over better 'tween our two selves—eh, Missis Margaret?" said Ferret, assuming an air of great familiarity.

"Well, then, I'll leave you two together," said Madge's fellow lodger, and hastily gathering up her gown, stockings, shoes, &c., she left the room and went upstairs to finish her toilet in the apartment of a sister unfortunate.

Mr. Ferret and Madge had a long confab. The officer held out to her great hopes in the event of her furnishing such information as might lead to Dennis's apprehension. Madge, however, could not very well enlighten him, inasmuch as she most assuredly knew nothing of the affair herself. She had been for some time in expectation of hearing something regarding Dennis, whom she had not seen since the hour he left her senseless from her contest with Moll Rhodes, in Lewkner's Lane. Her feeling towards Dennis had never deserved the name of attachment. It had been one of circumstance and convenience, and now, the information which Ferret had just given her was repaid by a full statement of the cause of the death of Moll Rhodes, by which Mr. Ferret became possessed of the means of identifying the perpetrator of another murder. He saw the great advantage he had acquired, and in the excess of his joy and generosity he drew forth some coin, and protested he would "stand summnt handsome;" nay, he went so far as to bestow sundry kisses and gentle slaps on Madge, who merely made that short show of offence followed by a laugh, which is always interpreted as encouragement. They were getting on the best possible terms, when a smart knock at the door stopped Mister Ferret's dalliance.

"I say, old buck," exclaimed the voice of Bill Johnson, "when next you want to visit your woman, don't send for me to mount guard at the door, that's all," and the steps of his comrade were heard descending the stairs.

"Confound it, Moggy," said old Ferret, jumping up and unfastening the small bolt beneath the latch, "I'd forgot Bill was there. D—n the bolt. Holloa, Bill! Here—"

"Well," replied the runner, who had gone but a few stairs down, "you don't want me any further, do you? You're a werry nice old gemman, I don't think, to bring me out to wait on this here dark ladder, while you does the loving vith another cove's doxy. I'se ashamed on you, Mr. F.," continued he, chaffing. "I wos jist a-goin' to drop in on the old woman at home, and let her know a summut; give her the lady's address, or so. D'ye twig, old nosey---eh?"

By this time Mr. J. had walked himself back into the room where Madge and Ferret were. He winked to the former, then bowed, hat in hand, to the latter.

"Hope I han't spil'd sport; wouldn't wish to interrupt anything as my friend Mr. Ferret might—"

"Stow *yer whid*, you chaffing wagabone, will yer?" said Ferret, "and listen, if you can keep that d---d rig o' your's to yerself for half a minnit. I've been on bisness vith this lady," and the old fellow grinned and leered, as if willing his words should be misconstrued.

" Dessay, no doubt on it," interposed Bill, laughing.

" I haven't told you afore, but I've every reason to believe, from information I have got o' this lady, might be the means of you and me doing the job tidily, by convicting the wagabone as murdered Moll Rhodes, done two or three months agone.   I know as the crowner returned a verdict of nateral death ; but that's nothink, cos I can get people as 'ull swear that down.   Vell, this here good looking lady has guv other information, and as it's as vell for us to run in kipples, as far as ve can, I'm going, Bill, to make you my partner in this here job.   So, if you've a mind to do the thing as is right, you shall hear all on it, over a drop of the righteous sort.   Jist call up Stevy, who is a visitor outside ; he'll fetch the lot."

This arrangement, however, was at once overthrown by the apropos appearance of Madge's companion, who had been listening on the stairs on hearing the arrival of another man.

" Did you call me, Margaret?" enquired she, entering, having now completed her attire.   " If you want anything fetched, I'll go for it," added she, looking significantly at her companion.

Mr. Ferret was not so green as not to be awake to this manœuvre.

" It's all very vell," said he, shaking his head and laughing, " to come that ere over the sappy vuns, but that cock von't fight here, my pretty vun.   I pays for vot I likes, as a purfessional man ; but vot I don't git I doesn't tip for, d'ye see.   No, no, you mustn't try it on for no cull-money * at this shop, my sveetest."

" This is Mr. Ferret, an old friend of mine, 'Till," interposed Madge, who saw that the lady was about to give anything but the retort courteous.   " He's a hofficer, old gal, and so's his friend ; (Miss 'Till's manner changed,) and he's a very good chap too.   I don't like to impose on good nature," said Madge ; and without further objection, Mr. Ferret's follower being called up, he was dispatched for liquor.   Miss Till did the amiable to Bill Johnson, who couldn't do less than stand his " fire ; " then the two worthies tossed who should stand the next round ; and finally, they adjourned to a neighbouring public-house, from the bar of which, after treating Madge and her companion, they departed westward.

It was a dull cloudy evening, as Madge was picking her way along the Whitechapel Road, for the day had been a rainy one. She observed a decently dressed man coming towards her ; she accosted him, and he stopped. A beggar who had been skulking under a gateway came up to them, as they conversed beneath a lamp.   The man was crippled of one leg, the knee of which rested on a wooden crutch ; he wore a tattered sailor's jacket, with canvass trowsers, the plaited petticoat, then common to all classes of seamen, and his left eye was hidden by a huge black patch.   Uncovering himself, he displayed a strong and plentiful crop of grey hair ; and humbly solicited the gentleman's charity.

" Pray, your honour, be so merciful as to bestow a trifle on an old seaman as has lost his precious limbs, and more preciouser eyesight, in the sarvice of his king and country.   I sailed seventeen years with the great Sir Cloudesley Shovel ; likevise the noble Sir George Rooke, at the siege of Giberaltar, where---"

---

* Profit obtained by the keepers of houses of ill fame, by retaining the change of moneys sent out for liquors, by enhancing the price of the same, or by bringing a short quantity.

Madge was vexed at the interruption, and hastily said, " Give the poor fellow something, and let him begone."

The gentleman, turning from the supplicant, thrust his hand in his pocket in search of some coppers. The extraordinary behaviour of the beggar attracted the attention of Madge, as he slunk a little behind the gentleman, and stared with his single eye at her intensely ; then, coughing slightly, he said in a different voice,

" I'se well known, yer honour, by the bold Captain Naylor ; and his discharge vith a 'stificate, vot I received ven---"

Madge recognized the voice ; and the gentleman having now given some halfpence to the pretended sailor, Madge told him, in a tone of feigned anger, to leave them, at the same time making him a sign of recognition. Dennis, for he it was, hobbled off to a spot where he could command a view of the road, and yet screen himself from observation.

In a few moments Madge joined him. During the day she had been exercising her ingenuity a thousand ways iu devising plans to effect what now seemed thrown into her way. A conviction that events were fast bringing her and Dick together, though in what way she could not at present even guess, took possession of her mind ; and to effectuate this, the removal of Dennis, and the service she should render to Turpin, seemed to hold out a promising opportunity. Dennis was, sooth to say, in a most pitiable condition. Conscience " that doth make cowards of us all," had joined with bodily privation, and mental exhaustion and terror, to reduce the stalwart ruffian to a wretched state of weakness. His haggard countenance betrayed in its deep-seamed lines an expression more repulsive than mere physical suffering could impart ; and the whitening, to which for the purpose of disguise he had subjected his hair, in conjunction with the wasting of the last week or so, would have prevented any one but those most intimate with his voice and manner from recognising him. He commenced his tale of suffering to Madge— who listened with feigned surprise—by a story of a desperate affray with some gamekeepers, in a part of the country where he had been sojourning since his unfortunate encounter in Lewkner's Lane ; which latter, of course, he attributed entirely to the lengths to which his anger had carried him, as the defender of Madge. The woman listened, and saw it would be wisest to conceal her knowledge of anything since he had last left her. Dennis declared that he would not, even after he had revenged her on her assailant, have left her, had not the landlord promised his protection.

" Besides," said he, " if it was to do agin, I'd do it, Madge, rayther than see you put upon by one on 'em."

They now went into a public-house, and after some further conversation, Madge proposed to Dennis to accompany her to her lodging. To this, however, he demurred.

" No, no," said he, " there's too many *noses* * about they sort o' places ; and you see I might get blown about Moll's bisness. This 'ull blow over presently, you'll see, Madge, and I'll come out again fresh as a four-year old. Hark, wasn't that a scream ? "

" Yes, to be sure it was. Why you look as queer and turnip-faced as a gal —it's only a sing out—some shindy—or belike some bilking dodge a-going on down the Fields. † "

---

* Tale-tellers, blabbers.   † Goodman's Fields.

"Hark!" exclaimed Dennis, who appeared to be listening with absorbing attention. "There—there was a cry of murder! There it is again."

"Well, and what if there is," said Madge, looking upon him with something like disgust, "I don't s'pose as they's very particular what they sings out just hereabouts."

"True, true," said Dennis, in a tone that indicated his absence of mind; "you're right, Madge; they don't mind. I've something to tell you, and I shan't be easy till—not now though. Good night—there's another scream! Damn the woman's throat. If you desire to see me, meet me here to-morrow night. I'll follow you, though, to your place, for I'm weary of sleeping out of doors, an' I'll be away early; it can't signify one night, surely."

Having made this arrangement, Madge turned through various narrow courts and streets, all at that time without even public lamps, and in a few minutes reached her dwelling. Here, having admitted herself by the ingenious contrivance of a knotted string, which, suspended through a hole in the door, drew back the spring lock, she left the entrance open; Dennis shortly arrived by a different route. The wretch slept that night the sleep of fatigue and weariness. Scarcely, however, had morning dawned, than with aching limbs and fevered blood he awoke, and to the great disappointment of Madge, who had lain awake part of the night revolving schemes for his betrayal, declared his determination to depart immediately, while yet few persons were stirring. Madge was too well aware of his cunning and suspicious temper to carry her persuasions to stay beyond a mere request; which, meeting with a refusal, she changed her position, and feigning to agree with him as to the policy of his precaution, advised him to depart—not, however, before she had arranged to visit him with some sustenance at a barn in the vicinity of Bow, which had for some nights been the lodging of Dennis.

He had scarcely departed when Madge leaped from her bed, and in another hour was closeted with Mr. Ferret at his abode near Long Acre. Madge was desirous of accompanying him on his visit to Turpin, but this Mr. Ferret, from a desire of enhancing his own services, strenuously opposed. She was, therefore, compelled to submit; and according to Ferret's advice, to return as quickly as possible to her lodgings, where he promised to bring our hero in the afternoon.

Mr. Ferret hurried out on his mission, but arrived at a most mal-apropos moment for business. Ringing at the outer gate of Dick's cottage, he was rather bothered, as he would have expressed it, by the delay which occurred in answering it; and when the girl did appear, her eyes were red with weeping; and to his enquiry whether her master was within, she replied no otherwise than by guiding him to his presence.

Dick heeded not his entrance. He sat with his arms folded, and with a stern expression of grief, mixed with stronger passions, in his rigid countenance, severely and fixedly gazing on an opened letter, which lay before him. Ferret regarded him with inquisitive surprise; and scraping a bow, said,—

"No wish to interrupt bisness, Mr. T.; but if so be as your sarvant had been so thoughtful as to tell me you was engaged, I'd ha' waited a bit afore I took upon myself—"

"There needs no apology, Mr. Ferret. If I before had a vow sworn, deep as mortal hatred and revenge for those I loved best could make it, how must I now feel at the murder of one—do not start (Mr. Ferret looked perplexed; this accumulation of murders quite staggered him) I say murdered—

Black Dennis exposes Turpin.

who was but too good for this world—I mean my wife, Ferret—who has been foully murdered by the hand of the incarnate fiend who butchered her venerable father."

Mr. Ferret was completely dumbfounded at this; his matter of fact comprehension did not enable him to interpret bold figures of speech, and therefore to his literal understanding, how this murder could be committed, when, as he well knew, the suspected criminal was some hundred miles from the spot where it was perpetrated, was totally beyond his powers of conjecture. At length he found his tongue.

"Vell! it may be as he did it, but I can't unriddle it, for here he's bin in town these three or four days; and may I be so bold as to ax ven this here vos committed? 'cos I thinks he couldn't very vell have bin at that ere place and in Lunnun at the same time."

Dick answered him by silently handing the letter in which Madeline communicated the sad tidings of the death of Esther. The officer, who was no great scholar, slowly puzzled out the meaning, and having spent a few moments in apparent perplexity, drawing his coat-sleeve across his eye,—for his profession had only case-hardened him---he observed,

"Shockingest thing as ever I've heerd. Vell, altho' I never seed the young lady, I carn't help thinkin' as I could take the life o' that ere wretch myself; though it would be a disgrace on a hofficer to take Jack Ketch's birth, yet, sink me, if I wouldn't do for Mister Dennis afore I'd see his honour the Sheriff vithout a substitute. Vy, it's downright horrid; it's vorse nor a play;

No. 18.

poor cretur! But I knows, Mr. Richard, vere to drop on the murd'ring thief; think o' that. I've got him as safe as if he vos here;" (and Mr. Ferret clutched his hand emphatically, in the style of griping a prisoner;) " he's limed, tvigged, nail'd, boned, lumbered and fixed, beyont the art o' man to save him, and no mistake!" concluded he, emphatically striking his clumsy hand on his thigh, by way of emphasis.

Dick stood in stern silence; he made no sign of attending to Ferret's words, though he drank them all in, and the latter ones eagerly. He walked to a buffet, and drawing from it a pair of handsome pistols, carefully examined the locks; having deposited them about his person, he, with that calmness which ever marks a determined mind, strode towards the passage, and taking his hat, beckoned Ferret.

" Rather short about it, though," thought the officer; " we'll have a chat yet, for there's two words to the bargain; and I don't see as the king's hofficer is to be treated as if he vas nobody."

"Pardon, Mister Turpin," continued he aloud; " but mayhap it vouldn't be more nor the respect which is due to my hoffice, if you vas to tell me vot you're jist now goin' after. Cos, d'ye see, the management of this here veighty affair belongs to me, and my experience in this here line gives me, in course, a great deal of visdom in managing 'em, so as they mayn't be made a mess on. You starts off like a young colt, Mister Dick, vich is very nateral for one at your time o' life; but as ould 'uns knows as the fastest tires first, so, if you pleases, ve'll go about the job arter the fashion of chaps as don't throw away a chance ven they've got it."

Dick displayed much impatience during the sagacious discourse of Mr. Ferret; he, however, saw that, to effect his object, he must be content to humour the importance of the thieftaker. He accordingly placed himself under his direction and guidance; and after a couple of hours of the most painful suspense and irritating delay on the part of Ferret, who spent the time in feeding, drinking, and gossipping, the infliction was put an end to by the functionary declaring that it " vos time, seein' he vorn't the best o' valkers, for 'em to cut their vood, as he should have a person ready to join 'em, vich vould make the happrehension safe as a trivet." Dick, however, overruled this; and Ferret, considering that the fewer of his tribe were employed the larger would be his own share, assented to his view of the matter; especially as Dick's determination to effect the apprehension was so manifestly sincere.

They set forth, and in due time reached the lodgings of Madge; Turpin started when he saw her. They had not met since the scene at the cottage on Plumstead common, with the exception of the short glimpse he had obtained of her on the night of the apprehension of Berry and his associates. He knew not of her treachery, further than it related to that affair, though he had a suspicion of it as related to the former one. His gentle wife had carried to her grave the secret of her knowledge of his guilty career; and Madge was now scheming in what way she could expose the character of Dick, without committing herself, in the supposition that in his degradation and separation from his wife, lay the only hope of compassing her ends. Short and unsatisfactory was the interview, so far as Madge was concerned. Ferret talked a few characteristic common-places; Dick was taciturn, and looked so truly miserable, yet vindictive, that Madge dared not intrude upon his thoughts, and at Ferret's request, led the way towards the barn, where Dennis awaited the traitress's arrival with refreshment.

The shades of evening were fast approaching, as an emaciated wretch was seen crawling from amongst some broken trusses of straw, which lay in a heap in the corner of a dilapidated shed. The haggard look, the sunken yet preternaturally bright eye, the wasted flesh and shrunken features, told a tale of suffering and of misery, which might excite pity for any criminal but so atrocious a murderer. He walked with unsteady steps to the side of the barn, then, sinking on his knees, applied his eye to a hole in the planking which formed its sides, and looked intently forth from his spy-hole on the country without. Long and anxiously did he gaze; at length, sinking from his position on the hay which strewed the floor, he heaved a deep groan—a groan so sad, so expressive of heartache, that had it sprung from repentance, or aught but selfishness, might have weighed much against even *his* sin.

"She's like the rest," said he, querulously; "just like the rest," and a bitter curse passed his lips, for the exhaustion of his body had subdued the strong ruffian to the weakness of complaining childhood. "P'raps she's right not to come till it's dark; it's a long day though, and my thoughts is no companions. No—I'd not have believed it; I'd have laughed at it, if any one 'ud ha' told me as Dennis Sowton 'ud have feared a shadow, an old wife's fancy —but I've seen *him*—" he shuddered and looked fearfully around. "I've seen him a hundred times. He comes with the dark, and lies on me with his leaden face pressed closed to mine, and draws my breath as I sleep, and kneels upon my chest," he drew his breath strongly at the mere thought of the dreadful nightmare. "I've often laughed at people who've give themselves up for crimes; I've often gibed at piety and remorse---now I dread the night---no, I shouldn't fear it but I'm *alone*, and then he comes to me, and prays me not to——" His face quivered with anguish; he waved his hand as if to dispel some illusion from his sight, and shaking his head despairingly, endeavoured to divert his thoughts, and occupy his vision, by again looking forth from his place of observation.

A long path lay across the flat fields which stretched towards the eastern outskirts of London, and along this he expected to see the approach of the bearer of the sustenance he so much needed. The sinking sun gilded the brown line of the pathway which led through the bright green fields; his glorious orb was slowly sinking behind the spires and domes of the great city, casting through the smoky vapour a blood-red beam, and his broad face seemed magnified by the medium through which he shone. Dennis's attention seemed suddenly attracted by some approaching object, and his looks assumed an expression of intense anxiety.

"Some one 's coming," muttered he to himself; "there is three of 'em; if it was but one by himself, p'raps I might relieve myself by easing him of a trifle. One's a woman, and strangely like Madge too. But who's that with her? Tis Ferret by G---; and, can I b'lieve my eyes, Turpin! How can I 'scape?" He sat himself down. "I'll not try---they can but hang me; better so than live thus," said the desperate wretch. "Shall I sell my life? Madge too--I see it---she's Palmer's ———; that's plain; I'll be revenged though---" He drew his trusty knife from a small case, wherein he carried it for ordinary purposes, tried his thumb against its edge and point, and slunk among the straw which had before concealed him. "I needn't give a chance away," said he; as if excusing to himself this proceeding, so much at variance with his former declaration of determination and despair.

He had scarcely effected this, when Ferret, followed by Dick, cautiously entered. Dennis had calculated upon stabbing Madge; but now, suddenly bethinking himself of the hopelessness of escape should he do so, his love of life overthrew the resolve, and replaced it with a suggestion of the practicability of another plan—namely to bestow the favour on our hero instead of his paramour, and endeavour by a bold push to escape from Ferret. The two entered. The officer made directly towards the spot where Dennis lay; this frustrated his intention; he hoped to have been approached by Dick, which would have enabled him to bestow upon him the *coup de grace*. Ferret, grasping a huge leaden-loaded bludgeon, which he thrust violently among the trusses of straw where Dennis lay concealed, had already bestowed upon him some smart pokes in various parts of the body; as he proceeded he turned over the straw, and though Dennis had contrived to shift a little from the spot, and retreat farther into the recesses of the heap, his situation was hopeless. Neither could he now see the position of his enemy. Panic terror seized him; and in an attempt to rise to his feet, he suddenly exposed the upper part of his person above the straw. His appearance, knife in hand, for he still almost unknowingly grasped it, was the signal for the descent of Ferret's cudgel with such heavy good will, as to prostrate him senseless in the hole from which he had risen. It was fortunate for him that this happened, for simultaneous with the blow was the discharge of a pistol from the infuriated Dick. The ball whizzed past the very spot which had the moment before been occupied by the head of Dennis. Dick followed up the action by a revengeful spring towards the spot, and drawing forth his other pistol, levelled it---Ferret seized his arm---

"D—n it!" cried he, "you're too hot upon it; if you wants to punish him, don't put him out of his misery so soon."

The slightest check gave Turpin time to recollect himself. The sight of the monster who had thus " shivered his household gods" around him; who had rendered his cheerful hearth desolate; who had made the house of joy the house of mourning; who had left his heart a joyless blank; who had, with his vile hand, crushed that tender flower, "ere yet her morn of bloom had well begun," whose form and fragrance—although our hero felt them unfitted for his companionship and bosom—had left a painful sting, a numbing woe, in his heart; who——but at sight of the villain the figure of that venerable old man, and his heart-broken daughter, rose upon his mind, and with an impulse of uncontrollable rage he sought to wreak his and their revenge. The hand and speech of Ferret recalled him, and he became ashamed of the crawling reptile who lay before him. Dennis slowly rose, and looked with piteous supplication in his abject eye on his captors. Dick turned from him with disgust and abhorrence.

"I dare not look on him," said he, returning his pistol; "lest it should make me forget myself again, and rob the gibbet of its due. I cannot scold."

Ferret was busily engaged in slipping on the handcuffs, to which Dennis made not the slightest resistance; he submitted, still kneeling, with a look of fear and hopeless despair, as if seeking commiseration even from the man he had so deeply injured. He looked indeed

> ———————A man as bruised in spirit,
> As broken-hearted, and subdued in soul,
> As any breathing wretch who deems this day
> Can bring no darker morrow.

The party left the barn—Mr. Ferret expatiating, in no measured terms, on what he termed his sagacity and knowledge of " human nater," as exemplified in the craven behaviour of their fast-bound captive—taking the whole credit to himself; though it may be doubted if, singlehanded, he would have been at all taken even by the renowned Mr. Ferret. Dennis, however, seemed to revive—at least some sign of spirit, though it was of evil spirit, imparted itself to his looks—when he spied Mrs. Madge, at some distance, evidently awaiting their arrival. He cast the look of a chained tiger at his manacles, and gnashed his closed teeth, indications of temper not unobserved by Mr. Ferret.

" Cum, cum, Mister Cut-throat, none of that ere : Mr. T., vill you obleege me by taking this?" presenting a small strong cord which he had fastened to the shackles of the handcuffs, and held by its other end. " Now then, sir, I vould'nt wish to inconvenience yer," said Ferret sarcastically, with a wink at Turpin, which the latter noticed not; " but raly you looks so very pleasant just now, as I thinks it part o' my duty to see as you don't lay. vi'lent hands on yerself, nor nobuddy else, more 'specially the vomen-kind."

While thus talking, Ferret produced a cord with a slip-knot, with which he pinioned his prisoner. Madge now joined them; but her presence rendered Dennis so violent and excited that, at Ferret's request, she left the party.

The same night Ferret and his prisoner, accompanied by Turpin, who firmly refused to quit Dennis until he had seen him safely lodged in gaol, set out in a postchaise for Lincolnshire. The journey was tedious, though executed with all the despatch possible in those days of sluggish locomotion; and in about the same time that it had taken Dennis to reach London on foot, the party, putting up every night at an inn,—for no man then dreamt of posting after dark,—arrived at Sleaford.

The news soon spread far and near of the apprehension of the atrocious criminal; and as the carriage passed through the streets of the little town, the many-headed mob gathered like a rolling snow-ball, swelled by the accession of villagers from the country around. Having alighted at the principal inn, a messenger was despatched to Denistoun House, with the information of the capture and arrival of the culprit.

An unexpected visitor returned with the messenger. Dick, who doggedly refused to quit his post near the murderer, either by day or by night, was seated in an arm chair, near the window of the apartment; the prisoner was lying on the floor at the further end of the room, with his head pillowed on a cushion, a position which he had assumed in preference to an upright one, as more suited to his exhausted mind and body. Mr. Ferret sat at a small table, spread with a huge fragment of boiled beef, bread, a flagon of foaming ale, pickles, mustard, and other condiments, to which he was paying his most assiduous respects.

" Vy dont 'e do as I do?" enquired he of Dick, who sat musing, with his eyes fixed on the ground. " Vy by the time you gets to my time o' life, and sees as much o' the vurld as I have, you'll say to yourself, 'vell, old Jack Ferret vos right ven he—' "

The door opened; the lump of beef on Ferret's fork was arrested on its way to his mouth; Dennis looked scowlingly at the new comer; and Dick, after a moment's steady gaze, started to his feet in surprise.

" Sir Litton Weston, as I live!" said our hero, as if doubtful what should be the character of their salutation; but the baronet set him at ease by advancing with extended hand. Dick took the proffered mark of amity, for his recent mightier woe had, " like Aaron's serpent, swallowed all the rest ;" and he could not now stop to remember feelings or troubles so long past as those of Weston Hall.

It appeared from the explanation of Sir Litton, that his sister had written to him upon the dreadful occurrence, and had followed that by another letter announcing the dangerous illness of Esther; that family connexions—the circumstance of old Bevis's business-connexions with old Sir Mark, and other considerations, had brought him to his sister's house. His manner, nevertheless, was anything but frank and cordial; and it was clear that neither of the parties were anxious to prolong the interview, or render the connexion more intimate.

The prisoner was soon placed in a conveyance, and amid the hootings and execrations of the infuriated crowd, conveyed before the magistrates at Denistoun House.

Sir Albert sat in his drawingroom in the magisterial chair; by his side was Sir Litton, who, though not of the commission of the peace for the county of Lincoln, was of a rank, and had an interest in the case, which entitled him to the courtesy. The circumstances of the crime were related; the dying deposition of Esther produced; and the confession of Roger, which also went to prove Dennis to be the actual murderer, was remarked on. The evidence seemed fully sufficient for the commitment of the prisoner. Turpin had, during all the time, maintained a silent attention. Mr. Ferret was rather vexed that *he* had not been called upon to relate the particulars of the apprehension of the criminal. He therefore determined to break ground; this, however, led to a scene which none present had at all calculated upon.

Ferret scraped a low bow. " Please your verships," said he, " I hopes you'll pardon the 'trusion, but as the pris'ner han't admitted nothink, not even his name, I'm thinking as ve an't yet see'd no evidence as he's the werry hindividyal as done this here murder; leastvays, I han't see'd no 'dentification on him furder than this—as you all seems agreed he is the rale Dennis Sowton. Now if so be as you'd allow me, or this here genelman," pointing to Dick, " to jist speak to his being the right 'un, spoke on in that ere affecting paper, as he mayn't prove no *alibi*, nor nothink o' that sort, it 'ud be more reg'lar."

Mr. Ferret, who was quite the orator of his profession, from his great practice as chairman of various free-and-easies, looked round with the air of a man who has imparted instruction.

" It is scarcely necessary, I think ?" observed Sir Albert to a county magistrate, who sat near him. The magistrate said, it might be as well to take such evidence of identity.

At this juncture our hero stepped forward.

" If there be any need for the identification of such a villain as Dennis Sowton, I can easily furnish it," said he.

Turpin then proceeded to swear to his long acquaintance and perfect knowledge of Dennis's person. The culprit's eye glittered with a bright ferocity as he proceeded; and, for the first time, he showed outward emotion. He thought of the scene he had interrupted at Plumstead; of the night of the betrayal of Bob Berry and his companions, in which he now fancied he saw a plot for his (Dennis's) betrayal; and of the last crowning act of Madge's perfidy. His jealous mind put them together, and he jumped the conclusion, that the man who stood before him was her accomplice; and that, cunning as he thought himself, he had been duped by a woman, and was about to be destroyed in the pitfall he had first contrived for his enemy. He roused himself; and as Dick concluded, addressed the bench with a request to speak "a few words," which was complied with.

"You've heerd me identified, gentlemen," said he, with a scowl at Turpin; "it's now my turn to identify."

Ferret winked stealthily at our hero, with a significant nod towards the door. Turpin looked with indignation and disgust on his accuser, who smiled bitterly in return.

"Sir Albert," said Sir Litton, who feared that he might be unpleasantly involved in the affair; "I think that we may as well close this sitting, and remove the prisoner —"

"May I be allowed," interposed Dennis, "to say, Sir Litton, that what I've now to tell hasn't nothing to do with yourself—nothing whatsomever. Sir Litton, your carriage was robbed of four hundred and fifty pounds some five year since, in Essex; there stands the robber, and I'll prove my words."

Turpin moved slightly back in the group, and placed one hand in his breast. The magistrates sat astounded, as if expecting our hero's reply.

"Oh," continued Dennis, "I'm not afeard: I know you've pistols, and that you use them. I'd take it as a favour at your hand if you'd do so much for me;" the villain sneered; "but I've not done yet. Perhaps the Earl of Coventry and many others would like to see the man who robbed them. There is one who now sports in London, and is called Tom King; do you know him, Sir Albert Denistoun?" Sir Albert seemed petrified with surprise; "the other stands before you; Richard Palmer—I beg his pardon—Dick Turpin the Highwayman!"

The assemblage, even down to the footboy, looked aghast.. Sir Albert gazed enquiringly on Turpin, when Sir Litton Weston, suddenly rising, exclaimed, "Officers, seize him!" Old Ferret very judiciously grabbed hold of his charge, Dennis. One bumpkin, rasher and more inconsiderate than the rest, advanced to do the baronet's bidding, but instantly measured his length on the floor. Turpin, with his face towards his enemies, pistol in hand, slowly retreated towards the door. A servant stationed there, who made a slight offer to prevent his egress, received a vigorous compliment on the head, which laid him sprawling. His determined aspect and gesture, and the unexpected discovery of his name, paralysed the energies of the bumpkin constables; and before they had recovered the consternation which the announcement had produced, Turpin had gained the outer court, leaped on a horse, of which three or four belonging to persons within doors stood saddled at the gate: clapping spurs to his steed, he made a bow to the gaping grooms and stablemen, who bowed in return, and in another instant was careering at full gallop towards the great high road.

Meantime, dire was the confusion in Sir Albert's hall. "Stop him!" sounded from every throat, but no one started in pursuit. Turpin had placed a mile and more between him and his late friends before a party was formed to follow. Indeed, the name of Turpin had struck a surprise among them which induced the one or two first in their saddles to delay their start until some half-dozen had mounted, for none of them seemed ambitious of being the first to come up with the daring robber. Sir Litton and Sir Albert, having now joined and mounted, forward they set, the farmers and men of peace, however, keeping pretty well together, and leaving the honour of precedence to the good steeds and impetuous haste of their leaders and superiors. They might all have spared themselves the trouble; so cool in temper, and so quick of eye was Turpin, that in the short moment before mounting he had chosen the strongest and best-bred horse which the group presented him. It was a hunter of great bone and mature age. He laughed within himself for the first time since the late sad events; for to him adventure and excitement were necessary stimulants; and dangerous enterprise, to his fearless spirit, was a pastime and a sport.

He rode on thus for some ten miles, when having mounted a slight hill, he looked back—no pursuers were in sight; he struck into a cross-road, and took his way towards Folkingham.

CHAPTER XIII.

Lear.—What, art mad? A man may see how this world wags with no eyes. Look with thy ears. See how yon justice rails on yon simple thief. Hark in thine ear—shake them together—and the first that drops, be it thief or be it justice, is a villain.
*   *   *   *   *   *

I tell thee 'tis the usurer hangs the cozener.
Through tattered clothes small vices do appear,
Robes and furr'd gowns hide all!
                          —Lear, Act iv., sc. iv.

There's a black gibbet frowns upon Tappington Moor,
Where many a gibbet has frowned before;
    And murderers there,
    Are swinging in air,
By one and by two and by three.

                          —Master Thomas Ingoldsby.

It was assize-time at Lincoln: the court was crowded. In the dock appeared Dennis Sowton, Roger Haynes, and a third person, by name Michael Clark, who had been apprehended in the intervening period from Dennis's examination, detailed in our last chapter. On the bench were seated, besides the judges of the king, several of the leading nobility and gentry of the county. Sir Litton Weston too, from his intimate connexion with the deceased, had been accommodated with a place within the privileged portion of the court, and had taken his seat beside his brother-in-law. Mixed motives gave rise to the anxiety he felt in the issue of the case, the predominant one of which was doubtless a desire to relieve his mind by a certainty of the destruction of a man whom he deemed dangerous, and who had long given him much secret uneasiness. The trial had concluded; the jury retired; and, after a solemn pause of breathless expectation, the foreman returned into the box, followed by his eleven brethren. The silence was painful; each spectator held his breath; there was but one feeling, that of thirst for blood, pervaded the vast auditory.

"Guilty, my lord," deliberately uttered the foreman; "Dennis Sowton as the murderer, and Roger Haynes and Michael Clark as accessories thereunto."

A buzz of applause murmured through the dense multitude, which was

Dennis charges Sir Litton Weston with stealing the Old Baronet's will.

instantly checked by the officers of the court. The judge assumed his black cap, and thus addressed the first prisoner :—

"Dennis Sowton! you have this day been found guilty by a jury of your country, of the highest crime which man can commit against his fellow-creature. Have you aught to say why the sentence of the court should not now be passed upon you?"

Dennis turned towards the bench. All eyes were riveted, and all ears open as the prisoner thus spoke :—

"My lord, it is useless, I knows, for me to say anything to delay the punishment of my crime. I don't deny it; I don't ask your mercy; no, no! but I ask you to believe what I now say. Since I've been in prison, I've many times begged that man there (he pointed to Sir Litton Weston, who started slightly, but instantly recovered his self-possession) to grant me, as a man shortly to die—and not likely to ask a trifling favour---to give me a meeting. He has refused it; he has come here this day, armed with his rank and consequence, to see and delight in the death of one he fears even more than he hates. But though I now stand on the side of my grave, I'll show you, my lord, that

No. 19.

there is a man here whose villany would have been equal to mine, had he the same temptation. Sir Litton Weston, I---"

" My lord," exclaimed Sir Litton, rising angrily, " will this court listen to the slanders of a villain, whose unlicensed tongue seeks to spit its venom on those who---"

The judge interposed : "I advise you," said he, addressing Dennis, " though I am anxious to extend indulgence to any prisoner in your awful situation, to confine yourself to the one point : your reasons why sentence should not be passed."

Dennis bowed ; he had evidently been collecting his energies and his wits for this last display. Sir Litton had turned a deaf ear to his applications ; and he had determined, in his malignant soul, that this last cup of bitterness should be sweetened by revenge.

" My lord," he continued, " I've a duty to do ; I care not, why should I now? for the frown or ill-will even of Sir Litton Weston ; and I will do at least one act of justice to atone for my crimes. My lord, I owe one thing to the man who has deserted me after leading me into guilt ; (it suited Dennis, cunning to the last, thus to put his case, though he was both vicious, nay criminal, before Sir Litton first knew him ;) to the *honourable* baronet, I say, who sits near you ; who thinks I'll be hung tamely, like a dog, and that with me will die the accomplice of his guilt. But, no, my lord, Sir Litton told, and told truly, that *I* had committed the robbery at Farmer Lawrance's ; but he has not told you who encouraged and incited the condemned wretch who now speaks to you to that act, that he might, by charging it upon his rival, Richard Palmer, punish a girl, who had rejected his dishonourable proposals, for her good taste in preferring a bold man, who meant honourably, to a base seducer. Sir Litton Weston sneers. I'll yet tell more. He has not told you that, to fix the guilt on that Richard Palmer, he contrived this very robbery ; and that he gave me, in presence of one Octavius Sheepshanks, whom I do not see here, one hundred pounds, never to divulge what I---"

Sir Litton could contain himself no longer. " My lord," exclaimed he to the astonished court : " my lord, I appeal to you if this indecent scene can be suffered to continue. This measureless liar, my lord ; I beg pardon, but my indignation must excuse my want of decorum ; is now endeavouring---"

The judge rose with dignity in his seat, and waving his hand, commanded silence, without noticing the speech of Sir Litton. He endeavoured to continue ; but his lordship, with cool impartiality, thus gave his decision :—

" Sir Litton Weston, the court has not assembled this day to try the truth or falsehood of the charges which the prisoner has so irrelevantly and extraordinarily made. If they be made, which will be easily provable, with the view of occasioning a short delay in the extreme rigour of the law, the prisoner will find himself wofully deceived. He must hold no hope that the short time allotted to him will be extended on account of anything he may now say which may criminate other persons. It is with his crime, clearly proven, and his punishment, we have now to deal. Prisoner, it is the practice of the judge to allow persons in your extremity the greatest latitude of speech ; yet, remember, this course can in no wise avail you."

Dennis listened with respectful silence to the address of the venerable judge. He was not, however, to be turned aside from his purpose ; and the tone and abuse of Sir Litton fixed him in his resolve. He thanked his lordship, and proceeded :—

"I believe Mr. Sheepshanks could prove all about that—if he dares; but there's more behind." (Sir Litton rose angrily, and was about to quit the court; but a slight groan of disapprobation, which escaped some of the crowd, induced him to resume his place.) "I'm glad you're not gone, Sir Litton; you refused me assistance, and forgot me: I'll show you I've a better memory. My lord, the late Sir Mark Weston *left a will.*"

"Liar!" muttered Sir Litton between his clenched teeth; then checking himself, he said—"My lord, it is notorious that my father died intestate. Will you, my—"

The judge motioned him to silence.

"My lord," resumed Dennis, "the late Sir Mark Weston *did leave a will.* My lord, I confess it—for to conceal a small fault will not now help me—I *hold that will!* Don't go, Sir Litton; I'm not done yet. Do you recollect the night of your father's death, eh? does that sting you? On that night, my lord, I was crossing the lawn of Weston Hall, when I heard a casement opened: I stood aside, and by the light saw Sir Litton moving within the room; he stretched his arm from the window, and dropped a small box on the grassplot beneath: that box I secured, thinking it might one day serve me; and had Sir Litton made a friend of me in this my last extremity, instead of thus deserting me, the despised Dennis Sowton would not have proved him, in open court, a robber. No! nor have compelled him to disgorge his illgotten wealth to his wronged sister Madeline, and to others; nay, more—had he not connived at my destruction—had he not have lent his guilty hand to crush his humble accomplice in villany, I should not this day have shown him before this assembly a defrauder and a liar."

While Dennis, to whom excitement lent energy and rude eloquence, was delivering the last sentence, Sir Litton quitted the court-house. Counsel, jurors, and the crowd, stood wondering what was to come next, and gaping as if expecting further disclosures. Dennis relapsed into his former quiet indifference. The judge enquired if he had concluded; and in reply he handed up a paper. His lordship read it attentively; it contained directions for the recovery of the long-lost documents.

"Is this all?" said his lordship.

Dennis assented by a bow.

The question as to sentence was put to the other prisoners, who severally replied in the negative. The judge proceeded to the solemn and impressive duty of passing the last dread fiat for the infliction of the extreme punishment of death, then so lamentably and disgracefully frequent, but which a milder and more enlightened age has humanely and wisely expunged, in numerous cases, from our penal code; and concluded with the last solemn commendation of their "souls to that mercy from their Maker which they must not hope from man."

The extraordinary disclosures of the prisoner formed the town-talk of Lincoln, not only among the lower, but among the higher circles. Sir Albert, who had been in court throughout the proceedings, was congratulated on all hands on the extraordinary accession of property to his wife: he hastened to his house. Sir Litton had in the meanwhile left the town in a postchaise; and spared neither horseflesh nor whipcord until he arrived at his paternal acres. Here he intended to collect a large amount in ready money and valuables, and then betake himself to France, there to watch what proceedings would emanate from these unlucky disclosures. Sir Albert found

Madeline, whose good heart never harboured an ill wish toward another, rather pained than rejoiced at the accession of wealth, coupled as it was with such disgraceful exposure. Nevertheless, she felt indignant at the baseness of her brother. She placed the whole affair in the hands of Sir Albert, first exacting a promise that he would be as tender as possible of her brother's name; and that, as he would unquestionably surrender the ill-acquired property, no ulterior proceedings might be adopted. Sir Albert, having obtained from his lordship the paper which contained Dennis's directions for the recovery of the deeds, set out for London in quest of them.

The clouds loured gloomily in the wind's eye, and the large drops which precede a thunderstorm fell heavily at long intervals, with measured splash on the dried earth; yet the threatening of the sky, which gave every token of a coming deluge, could not damp the eagerness, or daunt the curiosity of the dense crowd which assembled on the sloping side, and in the flat bottom forming the base, of a hill, on which a huge black frame of wood reared its ominous form. It was with difficulty that the "specials" and "locals," for it was the morning of the execution of Dennis and his accomplices, could prevent the curious and mischievous assemblage from fairly carrying off or demolishing the little cottage, before whose door, according to a practice then not uncommon, the murderers were to expiate the crime they had there committed. Beneath the huge squared timbers stood a large country waggon, containing the doomed wretches, the executioner, and the clergymen; beyond these, the attendant sheriff, and a few gentlemen of the county. There was but one feeling pervaded the mass—a brutal, fiendish, savage, and blood thirsty exultation. Here might be heard the ribald, indecent, and profane jest: there echoed the horse laugh; while in a third place, a vender of Geneva, or of ballads, bawled lustily in the exercise of his vocation. And this was the scene almost daily presented in a civilized Christian land!

It was for this that men preached, prayed, wrote, and prated about *law*, as "the perfection of human wisdom." Such domestic dramas as this did our grandfathers, nay our fathers, call "examples." They pandered to the worst and most debased impulses of humanity; fostered its vilest and most sanguinary propensities; ay, lent the majesty of justice, and the sanction of authority, to excite the worst passions of a brutal and ignorant multitude, and then talked of "example," of "vindicating the majesty" of "law!"---of law whose footsteps were blood-prints; and fondly imagined that humanity could be taught by a sacrifice to a judicial Moloch! Yet it is scarcely out of the recollection of many, even of the present generation, when "learned lawyers," and callow "statesmen," twaddled in our senate about the danger of washing from our statute book these foul and crimson stains of barbarity and ignorance! Let us not be mistaken, however; it is not to such a crime as that of the villain whose closing scene we now faintly depicture, that we would extend even sympathy. We are speaking of the hecatombs which the "law" has slain; the myriads of murders which speechifying legislators have committed through the instrumentality of ermined judges and ignorant juries, for crimes against society, which wealth first made, and then, by the right of might, punished, even to the shedding of a fellow-creature's blood. To such cases as these—where weak man for a little dross, a false signature, or an appropriated animal, took the life he cannot give,—spilt that blood of which heaven has declared, "Whoso sheddeth man's blood, by man shall his blood be shed,"—to such as these are our remarks intended to apply; for such, in the sight of the God of mercy, and the man of reason, are---MURDERS.

The wavering multitude reeled to and fro; the pinioned Dennis stood listening with a sort of dogged stolidity and indifference to the sonorous exhortations of the clergyman beside him; the ladder was placed, and the hangman proceeded in his task of adjusting the ropes. He had already carried the end of the first over the cross-beam, and drawn it to nearly the height of the unfortunate Clarke, who was the first to ascend the ladder—Dennis, as the highest criminal, being allowed the enjoyment of witnessing the sufferings of his fellows, by way of additional privilege—when a loud roar, succeeded by cries of "a reprieve, a reprieve!" arose among that part of the crowd which commanded a view of the high road. It was followed by a horseman, who, holding a paper high above his head, rode furiously through the crowd, which gave way on either side, towards the officials. These advanced among the people to meet him: the dread operations were suspended. Dennis glanced nervously towards the sheriff; his eye twinkled, and he shuddered: the feeling was but momentary; he shook his head despondingly, stamped his foot on the board, then forcing a grim smile, looked around him. The unfortunate man, Clarke, had been allowed to descend from the ladder, the rope having been loosened for the purpose; his feelings had overcome him, and he sunk half-fainting on his knees. Roger Haynes stood staring with a look of wonderment, rather than fear, upon the sheriff.

"Roger Haynes," said he, slowly, "my lord judge has mercifully selected your case as fit to be represented to our gracious king, in consideration of your early confession and surrender to justice; you will, however, remain in custody, till his majesty's pleasure be known."

Haynes turned towards his fellow culprit, as if expecting he too was included in the reprieve; the miserable wretch, with straining eyes, looked as if possessed with the same hope. The sheriff, the principal director of this sanguinary scene, was a humane man, such power has habit and custom; he slowly folded the paper and turned away, in signal that he had communicated all its contents. With a piercing shriek the doomed victim started to his feet, and instantly fell senseless, and was in this state placed by the executioner and his assistants beneath the beam; happily for him, the ladder was withdrawn, and eternity opened on him, ere he knew he had quitted this scene of that cruelty which passes all other cruelty, "man's inhumanity to man." As for Dennis, he died as he had lived, "loving nothing, fearing nothing, and believing nothing:" and dying thus, his memory was long preserved by the old, as the best actor in that bloody drama; "zeein' as he died game, an' wur a most owdacious trump, to be zure;" such was the high tone of English morality and philosophy inculcated by these exhibitions of the "wisdom of our ancestors."

CHAPTER XIV.

———

Lolllo.—You've a fine trade on't here: madmen and fools are a staple commodity.
Alibius.— Of course; we must eat, wear clothes, and live.
Thus at the lawyer's haven we arrive;
For still by knaves and fools we both do thrive.
                    The Changeling. By W. Middleton and Thomas Rowley. 1602.

1st. Outlaw.—Stand, sir, and throw us that you have about you;
If not we'll make you sit, and rifle you.
Speed.—Sir, we are undone! These are the villains
That all the travellers do fear so much.
                    Two Gentlemen of Verona, Act iv. sc. i.

Two months had now elapsed since Dick Turpin had arrived in London, where it was his first act to seek out King, to narrate to him the stirring events with which the few weeks ensuing their separation in London had been fraught; concluding with the late exposure by Dennis, in which King, as well as himself, were so deeply involved.

"Egad!" said Tom, "that's a very pretty little history, that same. Quite romantic, extraordinary, horrible, and dramatically wound up. Don't look serious, Dick; I felt perhaps more than I showed outwardly at one part of your story; but it isn't my way to look at the dark side of things. Sad, I know, are your recollections; but, dash it, Dick, ' grieving's a folly, boys,' says the old song; and I agree with it. Mourning won't bring back lost pleasures, and make worse present disasters, eh? that's my philosophy: so let's dismiss the dumps, and tell us what you think best to be done; for make ourselves scarce we must, as soon as this ugly affair gets wind. I admire your escape, though; Dickon, my trump, give us your hand on't. Yet I'm sorry you couldn't give an ounce bolus to that wretch, just by way of good-bye. You expect your old friend, Sir Litton, in town upon your trail, I suppose?"

"Certainly not, I should say; he will stay at Denistoun Hall until the trial of the murderers, which will be some six weeks hence; and I have some reasons for suspecting, that from personal motives, he will either purchase or connive at the escape of the chief miscreant—should my suspicions prove true, even though the pursuit of my object should bring me to the dungeon or the scaffold; depend on it, neither Sir Litton, nor his accomplice in bygone villanies, shall escape from exposure, or elude my revenge."

"Very good; capital," said King, smiling; " your feelings do you honour, though I must say they are rather too chivalric for my comprehension. If *I* do anything that chicken-hearted folk call bold and adventurous, it is that I may live in ease and enjoyment for a time. A present for my lady fair, the wherewith for a bottle with my friend, a suit of spicy togs, or a neat prad, are to me enjoyments of life; and he who would not risk a little for enjoyments such as these, is a skulker, a coward, and no philosopher, say I. Who'd starve in quiet, or herd with filth and poverty, when there are so many fat-pursed, heavy-brained, chicken-hearted clods, who know not how to enjoy the wealth they possess, and wait only the word of command, ' Stand and deliver,' to hand over tamely, and without trouble, their gold, to such roaring blades as St. Nicholas's clerks—eh, Dicky, my boy?"

Turpin had fallen into a slight fit of abstraction during this rattle of his volatile friend; the question put in the last few words, however, roused him,

"Upon my soul, Tom," he replied, "you're a most inexhaustible fellow. I'd give a trifle for your spirits; but let that pass. I was just contriving a nice little plan, for I see you have booked me for the road again; and as it's no use doing things by halves, here's my hand on't—we're pals, and share and share——"

"Done!" exclaimed Tom, with the eager heartiness of his nature. "It would be a sin such a noble spirit should rust—here's with you for good and for bad—an adventurer's wedding, like a matrimonial spec., 'until death do us depart, ha, ha, ha!'"

"Leave off your rattle, Tom, for a minute," said Dick, "and listen. The last place in which the bloodhounds of the law would seek me is certainly that of my birth, from which a long interval of time, and other circumstances not worth repeating, have so entirely severed me. When a boy, (and his voice unconsciously and unintentionally assumed a melancholy tone,) I was thought somewhat daring,—somewhat venturous. Within a few miles of my birth-place was a naturally-formed cave; and in my rambles, many a time, excited by tales of robbers I had read, did I imagine how proudly and heroically I might issue from such a spot, to levy 'black mail,' as I've read of its being termed, on trembling and dastard travellers. Time," said he laughing, "and a better knowledge of men and things, has, however, made another sort of thing of a robber from the creature of the old romantic legends of my youth. Yet there is one point remains feasible still in my idea, and that is the conversion of that same cavern into a stable for our nags. It is——none of your laughing, Tom—unless the country is much changed, known only to some few bird-nesting urchins. In a word, friend Tom, we'll e'en take a trot down this night, if you will, and survey the premises."

"Dick," replied his comrade, "done! for the second time. But I like to keep a good thing to the last. Suppose I've sold your bonny black Bess, though, what then? Oh, don't look serious before it's time. I've sold her to a very good tune, but don't mean to part with her; however, what you've told me just now will hasten the affair."

Tom then proceeded to relate, in his usual lively and gossipping style, the following adventure.

"Since you've been flaring up out o' town, and all that sort o' thing, of course, Dick, as I'd your permission, I've kept your black mare—and a splendid creature she is—in exercise. Well, more than once, as I've sported my figure in Pall Mall, Piccadilly, or the Oxford Road, have I had offers made for her, and enquiries as to price; these, however, went for nothing, till a bright idea struck me on Wednesday last that something like a cool *three hundred* might be made, and the mare not parted with after all: do you smoke how that's to be done, eh—Dickon, eh?"

Turpin expressed his inability to solve the question.

"It will take a little manœuvring, a little impudence, and a little bounce—I won't say courage—to do it neatly: yet I shall manage it, never fear. I'll tell you how I mean it to come off; and as we're *going out of town, you know*, eh? (and Tom facetiously nudged his auditor) I've no need to be quite so scrupulous. Don't be impatient, I'm coming to the point. Captain Willoughby—you don't know him; he's an empty-headed, full-pocketed maccaroni—has been boring me to sell the horse till he has put a scheme into my head, tho' I'm sure he never could have one in his own. It is this: he proposed to me to raffle the horse; and has promised me that he will procure among his acquaintances six subscribers of 50*l.* each, The knave's half cunning, and therefore one of your best flats. 'Now,' says he, 'I'll tell you what I'll do. I'll take one share; and I'll sound the others to see if the winner won't let me have his winning for another 50*l.*, in the event of his being fortunate: and then, don't you see, besides my own chance for 50*l.*, p'raps I shall get it for a hundred.' I saw the sap's cunning, and mean to bite the biter. I'll have their three hundred, but neither of 'em shall have Bess; and what's more, the winner shan't dare to talk about his being bubbled. What think you of that, Dickon? Come with me to 'The Turk,' and you shall see it done."

The friends strolled off towards Charing Cross, and entered a coffeehouse, where many well-dressed men sat sipping their wine or coffee, exchanging their snuff-boxes, or gossipping over the news and scandal of the day. King looked around, and after exchanging nods with several, fixed on a knot of three young bloods, congregated in a box at the upper end of the room. Before them stood the remains of a broiled fowl, a few cigar-ends, some olives, a plate of anchovies, and two or three snuff-boxes; and amid this heterogenous mixture, on the sloppy table, was a bottle of black strap, a ditto of sour German wine, and an awkward squad of glasses, tall and short.

"Ah! Tommy, my rattler, there you are! Consume me, if we weren't just talking about you and that dem'd fine mare of your's. Come on, my buck, and join us. Shove up there, Phipps," said he, to a companion; "make room for Tom and his pal—Tom's friend is sure to be a rum un. Shove up there!"

The speaker was the Honourable Captain Willoughby, a choice sample of the aristocratic blackguard of the earlier part of the eighteenth century. Picture to yourself, reader, a sallow whey-faced young man, on whose features dissipation and debauchery were written in lines that all might read. A wig of questionable shape, the curls of which bore scattered stains of red wine or blood, the one as likely as the other, was stuck carelessly on his head. He was attired in a handsome court suit of mazarine blue, edged with silver lace, but loose at the knees, soiled and slovenly; while wrinkled stockings of tinted silk, shoes half-drawn at the buckle strap, and a patch of black plaister on the cheek, to hide a wound received in a sword brawl on the preceding evening or morning, completed the picture of this Waterford or Waldegrave of 1730.

Turpin and Tom were soon on the best possible terms with the party; the bottle was replenished; oaths---for swearing was then deemed a mark of manhood and good-breeding---and obscenity, which passed for wit, formed the staple of discourse; spiced with some narrative of how some valorous dozen of Mohocks pinked a chairman in St. James's, or a Charley in Covent Garden: with various other lordly amusements of a similar character.

Tom suffered the current of conversation to take its own course: as it began to flag, however, he imperceptibly led it to the matter in hand.

"Well thought of Willoughby, split me, but I'd forgot. Didn't you drop something about the black mare I was trotting t'other day in the 'Dilly? We can talk it over now, tho' I couldn't then. My friend here, Mr. Newton, (alluding to Turpin,) is the owner of her. I've told him your proposal of the raffle; but I suppose you haven't thought of it since?"

To this feeler Captain Willoughby replied by drawing from his pocket a book, and opening it on the table, he selected from a group of applications

King and Turpin return the money to Captain Willoughby.

from industrious tradesmen, each supplicating as a favour "a settlement" of his little account, and a soiled and crumpled letter of paternal advice. On the back of this, the dutiful son had made an entry of four names; the rest of its top and sides were covered with figures, containing calculations of the doctrine of chances, as applicable to gambling speculations; such being with Captain Willoughby, as with not a few of more modern gentlemen of University education, the only practical purpose to which mathematical studies are ever applied. Spreading the letter before him, he went on—

"D'ye think I'd forgot it? No, no! Here are four down—three of them, Phipps, Levinz, and Harcourt, are here. Mr.—a—a—whats your name?"

"Newton," said Dick, bowing.

"Oh—ah—Mr. Newton. 'Gad that *is* a mare of your's. Phipps, you saw her. Stab my vitals, but she's an angel—a black 'un though. What shall we do for a fifth? Phipps, Levinz, Harcourt, and self—wouldn't Sir Lumley Pluffington make one, eh? Harcourt, you know him best: ask him, my boy."

Dick here, as previously arranged with King, observed that it was impossible to protract his stay in London beyond to-morrow; therefore, "anxious as I

No. 20.

am to oblige the friends of Mr. King, I shall keep my horse, unless something decisive is done to day."

"Then," exclaimed Willoughby, who was anxious not to lose his prize, "Harcourt, my boy, I'll tell you how we'll do it. Come to Sir Lumley's— I'll ask him first. Mr. Newton, will you show the horse with your servant before Sir Lumley's window?—he's a prime judge; and Harcourt, you'll second me."

" Pooh, pooh !" replied Harcourt, "don't make any fuss about it, I'll make Lummy post his fifty; you mustn't gaff it about town though, but my uncle the old bishop, (he'll cut up nicely when he goes to heaven) holds half Lummy's lands on mortgage, at least his lawyer does, for old Spintext always pretends he's as poor as a church mouse, he! he! Come on, my carnation, I'll do the trick. Mr. Newton, just let your prad be down in the Mall, will'ee? at— what the hell's the time now—oh two—at three o'clock. I'll manage it. Good bye."

The wine had certainly got a little into the head of the bishop's nephew, or more probably had never got out of it since dinner the previous day ; and forth he sallied with his friend Willoughby, to the residence of " Sir Lummy," as he familiarly termed him.

Turpin and King took their way to Holborn, and shortly after Bess, rode by a helper from the stables, was trotted gently past the residence of Sir Lumley.

That fashionable personage at the time of his two friend's arrival, was under the hands of his frizeur, an important individual in the days of perukes, pomatum and powder; he however, gave them the entrée, and promised his name to the list, provided his connoisseurship in horseflesh should find itself warranted in so doing by a personal inspection of the animal.

The affair was thus far conditionally arranged ; and the man of tongs and grease, having finished his torturing on the caput of Sir Lumley, the noble brute was, according to agreement, paraded by the window. Sir Lumley admired her action, but desired a closer inspection ; and the three went down into the street, where, after a rigorous examination, and having seen her put through her paces, Sir Lumley added his name to the list ; and proposed accompanying them to the Park.

One name yet remained, and Turpin and King having joined the party, Mr. Newton (Turpin) at the suggestion of King, who thought delay might be dangerous, proposed to take the remaining chance for himself. This was agreed to, and the raffle was at once proceeded with. Captain Willoughby proved the fortunate adventurer. He was congratulated on his good fortune, the two hundred and fifty was pocketed by Turpin, and after a few more glasses of wine the Captain, who was eager to obtain possession of his prize, proposed to accompany Mr. Newton, for the purpose of receiving the horse.

Dick was not a little puzzled to conjecture what would be the next move, and despite his confidence in the address of his friend Tom, began to think Bess in some jeopardy. The other members of the party, feeling no farther interested in the affair, stuck to the bottle.

It was dusk as the trio, Captain Willoughby, Turpin, and King, set out towards Bloomsbury, they passed up the Haymarket, until they had arrived opposite the spot, where afterwards stood the " barn," of Foote, known as the " little theatre in the Haymarket." King looked behind, there were no passengers in sight. He dropt the arm of Willoughby, and thus addressed Turpin.

" Dick my lad, we've carried this joke far enough to my thinking; hand me here Captain Willoughby's ' fifty.' " The fuddled Captain was rather puzzled at this speech—Turpin handed over the cash to King.

"Sir," said King, again addressing Willoughby; "you first proposed this raffle to me, and it's as well to be candid in these affairs. I want cash; your original scheme looked so much like a swindle for fifty each on at least three of the parties whom you *honour* by the title of " friends," that you must see I have your character a little in *my* keeping. (The Captain stared but said nothing.) I presume you consider me a man of honour, so shall I you, unless obliged to declare otherwise. (The Captain laid his hand on his sword, but his arm was arrested by Dick.) " Pray Sir, don't be hasty," said Tom, laughing, at the same time unsheathing *his* rapier; " I beg you'll not let this little affair lead to worse. I suspect you know that at the fencing school I can give even you a hit or two." The thought of King's known superiority seemed to have an effect on the sudden valour of the Captain, for he dropped his weapon quietly into its scabbard, saying,

" Well, you're a funny fellow, Tom ; but, blind me, if *I* can make out what's the meaning of this. Mr. Newton, Sir, I presume you'll deal fairly in this affair, but I've had my honour impeached Sir, a soldier's honour, Sir, damme! Nevertheless, Tom, we'll cry quits; I'm hasty you know, Tom." The Captain offered his hand, which King accepted. " And now," said he ; " show us this d—d out of the way Bloomsbury hole, where you've stowed away the mare. Come along Mr. Newton."

" Don't hurry yourself," interposed King, " the plain fact is, Willoughby, you'll get no horse at all. Don't stare man, I mean what I say."

" What!" exclaimed the Captain, who was roused by the idea of losing his cash ; " you won't swindle me out of both horse and money ?"

" Not a bit of it, my dear boy," returned King ; " only do a bit of ' diamond cut diamond.' Here's your ' fifty.' I think that's pretty honest. And now, mark ye, Willoughby,", said King assuming a serious look and tone. " I, and my friend Newton wanted a little cash, for we're leaving London for a short time ; you wanted a horse—you haven't got the horse, but you have your money, so you've lost nothing but not a word of this. I won't threaten, for I believe you are a brave man, and fear not personal danger: (this was a piece of most adroit flattery on the part of Tom, for he knew the Captain to be both bully and coward.) But, Willoughby, think of *your* reputation my boy ; for by the sharpest six inches of steel that ever man took into his stomach against his will, if you breathe a syllable about this, other than I tell you now, I'll not only call you to account, but I'll blaze to Harcourt, Phipps, and Sir Lumley, your own pretty little plan. Mr. Newton, mind you, has *bought back your bargain for another hundred.* You understand me—eh ?"

King took Turpin's arm, and they strolled leisurely towards Piccadilly; King nodding familiarly to the Captain as they moved off. He was so confounded at the consummate impudence and coolness of the pair, that he stood irresolute; discretion however whispered his valour that it would be very unsafe to attempt personal revenge in a case where the odds were so seriously against him ; moreover his courage was of that " swash-buckler" breed, which requires very peculiar circumstances and the presence of many spectators to excite it. He had no idea of throwing away so precious a commodity, of which, he possessed so small a modicum, in private combat ; so, after two or three muttered curses, he looked at the cash returned to him; deposited it in the pocket of his braceless unmentionables; whistled a pensive air; and sauntered down the Haymarket in the direction of St. James's Palace, cogitating how to revenge himself, without exposure, on the pair who had so neatly outwitted him.

Gaily and hilariously did the two friends chat over the day's adventure, as they walked to "The Old Leaping Bar." Dick especially was boisterous in his laughter, as, once more on the back of his gallant Bess, 'they trotted down Holborn. A fine bright moon shone cheerily as they clattered gaily along, and one short hour brought them to a roadside alehouse.

"There's a stable here, Tom; 'tis but a short mile, and you shall see my whim, or whatever else you may please to call it—the cave, Tom—though, I dare say, like all other objects of our boyhood, it will appear shrunk and small to our travelled eyes. Soho, Bess!" The couple dismounted, and a rough fellow, who did the menial work of the little establishment, proffered his services. To him the horses were consigned, and Dick and Tom, after taking a glass of ale, strolled forth. The night was beautiful; they walked some hundred yards down the road, Turpin narrowly examining the hedge row as they went on: a bridle path presented itself. "I have it," he exclaimed; and starting at a smart walk, they pushed into the wood. The startled game rose with a whirring sound as the footsteps of the intruders approached their roosting places; the frog hopped from the damp grass, and leaped with a lumpish splash into the ditch, or rather drain, which bordered the path; the bat wheeled heavily close above their heads, and ever and anon the downy wing of the white owl bore him noiselessly in his sweep among the branches of the low trees.

"A very pretty little bit of a man's land this seems to be, for so near town, Dick," said King. "The approach to your castle isn't very majestic, though. Curse it!" ejaculated he, "what's that?" as he knocked his foot against and stumbled over the foot of a tree long since hewn down, and concealed by the tall grass. Turpin laughed.

"I see you don't manage this sort of travelling as well as I, Tom," rejoined he, as they struck through some hazel bushes into the thicket: "Look to your feet, Tom; don't be staggering; it won't do to walk here as you would in the Park: mind your ten toes,—that's the principal thing, or you may chance to find yourself in a hole or a drain. It's necessary, too, to mind your eye, for a lash from a twig in one corner of it will make you wink, or a salute from a briar on your cheek may damage your beauty; besides, scratches look suspicious, Tom, specially to the women. I've not forgot the road, you see," said he, stopping at a small space of ground where the trees so stood as to leave an open space of some three or four yards in front of a tuft of underwood. King looked about him.

"Devil a cave do I see; and those who do must have good eyes, I'm thinking," said he.

"Who intended you or any one else should, till I showed them," replied Turpin.

Dick passed between the bushes of the thicket, thrusting their boughs to the right and left; and after three or four turns in different directions, after the fashion of the entrance to the "maze" of an old garden, he stopped before two tufted, bushy-headed trees, of some fifteen feet in height.

"D'ye see it now, Tim?" said Turpin laughing. King expressed his inability. "Then follow me," said he; and slightly stooping, he passed into the partial obscurity, occasioned by the thick foliage. Three steps plunged them in deep darkness, and King placed his hand on the back of his comrade to guide his steps. Turpin went on a few feet; then taking King by the arm, he turned him round, and both companions stood looking towards the opening by which they had entered. The flickering leaves as their bright surfaces shook in the night-breeze glanced in the moonshine, was visible from the position in which they stood; the little light, however, which found its way into the cavern did not enable them to distinguish any object around them. The extent of the excavation, if such it was, or the nature of the material forming its sides, were undiscernible.

"What d'ye think of it?" asked Turpin, as he stamped his foot on the ground, which sounded hard beneath them. "It's dry and pretty deep. The ground rises backward hereabouts, and this opening, whether made by man, or fashioned by nature, is in the side of the bank, at the place of its most abrupt rise. There's worse stables than this, Tom, ay, or lodgings either. But perhaps, as I'm to show you over the premises, you'll require some particulars before you enter on them; so here goes for a light."

Dick produced from his pocket a piece of vegetable tinder, and placed it in the pan of his pistol, after drawing the charge; one click of the flint on the hammer of the weapon communicated a spark, a sulphur match was applied, and behold, in almost as little time as with a modern congreve or lucifer, did Dick produce a light from this characteristic tinder-box. King looked on and smiled. "You're a shrewd fellow, Dick," said he; "I'd rather have one ready-witted chap than a dozen hard-headed strong-fisted blackguards. But how go rent and taxes in these parts, as you seem to have the letting of this snug retreat?"

"I'll tell you," said Dick, assuming an air of business-like gravity. "The rent must be collected by the tenant; and as he no doubt, in a great measure, will act as tax-gatherer for the district himself, he will be asked to pay no other dues than those of friendsqip; and should none eject him until he who lets it shall endeavour to do so, then he may reckon on a lease to the day of judgment. Nay more, his landlord will share his tenement, make common cause with him, and the bold fellow who attempts to drive him out must do it over Dick Turpin's body."

The friends shook hands, and taking their way towards the ale-house, mounted their prads, and slept that night at Epping.

A few days' active exertion of Turpin and King, for they deemed it prudent to trust no one with the secret of their retreat, sufficed them to collect the necessaries for making the cave available as an occasional retreat; and thither, preparation having been made for their reception, they removed their horses. Considerable ingenuity and much thought were expended on making its approach and exit, which were by different circuitous routes, and as little likely to excite attention as might be. The sides were of a light yet somewhat tenacious loam; and they resolved to leave its outer entrance as little altered from its natural state as possible. Three or four days were spent by them in excavating a small lateral chamber, and the earth removed therefrom they deposited against the sides of the larger or entrance chamber near its mouth, thereby materially narrowing it, leaving only space through which a horse might enter. They also began burrowing a small passage, to creep through on the hands and knees, by which, in case of a watch being set on their main portal, they might escape. The perfecting this was necessarily postponed, as future time and leisure might serve for its completion; its termination being contrived in a small thicket of dense underwood, some fifty feet from their subterraneous abode. And here we will leave them to return to Sir Litton, whom we left hurrying from the scene of his exposure and disgrace.

We have said Sir Litton Weston spared neither horseflesh nor whipcord until he again brought in view the vane-surmounted and turreted; roof of Weston Hall. Small time for tarrying did he there allow himself. The consciousness of guilt made him, like "the wicked, who flee when no man pursueth," resolve to retire to the Netherlands, for awhile to watch in security the turn affairs might take. A little reflection suggested to him that it would be advisable to make, if practicable, the worthy Mr. Octavius the companion of his flight. That obsequious individual could not yet be acquainted with the unfortunate affair; and Sir Litton, knowing his man, reasonably suspected that it would be injudicious to allow him to remain behind, for he feared that the little lawyer might tell some unpleasant tales. He therefore summoned him to the Hall: he obeyed the mandate without delay.

"Mr. Sheepshanks," said Sir Litton, "I've sent for you to consult upon an important piece of business."

The lawyer declared his entire devotion to his commands.

"I'm about to take a journey to the continent, respecting some peculiar private business, and I am desirous of availing myself of your professional advice and assistance," said Sir Litton. The neatly-contrived lie completely threw the cunning little latitat off his guard, and he declared his readiness to accompany his patren.

Sir Litton speedily collected the most valuable and portable of his family plate and jewels, and having drawn a considerable sum in cash from his agent, started on his journey towards the coast; he resolved, however, to avoid suspicion as to his destination, to avoid the more frequented route, and travelling by Colchester, and thence to Harwich, to trust to some small vessel to convey him to the opposite shore. This resolution led, however, to a most unlucky recontre.

It was Saturday night, and a party of farmers and graziers, small tradesmen, and the upper servants of the neighbouring gentry, were assembled in the parlour of the Eagle. The ruddy fire burned brightly, and the smooth and dark oak-panels warmly reflected its cheering glow. Into this snug room did Turpin and King enter, and having been supplied with a glass of spirits and water and a tray of tabacco, selected each his yard of clay, and took their seats. The "talk was of bullocks," as might be expected; and this interesting topic exhausted, miscellaneous subjects followed.

"Didst hear the news, Geoffrey?" asked a burly franklin of an acquaintance on the other side at an opposite table: "Sir Litton Weston ha' coomed to the Hall; and young Jenkins—he that be fag to Muster Sheepshanks—did tell me as his master and the barronit be gwain to sum furrin part; it be a secret, tho'."

"Ugh!" grunted the party addressed, taking his pipe from his mouth, and spitting deliberately in a small triangular wooden box, filled with sawdust, which stood at his foot; "ugh; 'tisn't much his people hear about 'un, 'xcept when they be back'ard in their rent. A doan't think it much matters if a' be at the Hall, or onywhere else, for the good a' does."

None of the party seemed to be disposed to champion the good name of the

Baronet, for the disparaging speech of the blunt farmer was succeeded by a short silence. Tom looked significantly at Turpin.

" Ah," observed another of the party; " if that ould Sheepshanks be goin', wi 'un a' shouldn't guess as anybody 'ull grieve about that 'ere, neyther. Ould Gilly told me, this very day as gone, as Sheepshanks called on 'un, and drawed 'un o' forty pound, and as he wor main pressin', too. A' told 'un as the Baronet wor goin' to take 'un wi' him on a job as wor o' main weight, an' that he might tell 'un in confidence, as he mun ha' the money out o' hand; for it wor a great lawsuit, or summut o' the sort. He told 'un too, as he wor goin' off ther very morrow as ever is."

" Maybe;" observed a gamekeeper; " for Job Tyler have been all day up at Weston, putting a chain and doing odd jobs to the travelling coach."

The conversation changed; and after staying another hour, Turpin and his companion left.

Their consultation was long on the important information they had thus acquired. They had arrived at the spot where they usuly dismounted, and looking along the road lest they might be observed, were about to lead their horses into the wood, when they heard the distant clatter of horse's feet approached them.

" Shall we mount?" asked King.

" Yes," replied Dick, " and ride a little distance from this spot at any rate. It may be game," added he, examining his holsters.

They rode slowly on: the horseman gained upon them; and the companions drew up between some trees at the road-side. The traveller came on—he had certainly seen them, for the road was level—and on nearing the spot, slackened his speed. The night was clear; and as he approached, both King and Turpin together recognised their old friend George Fielder. Their greeting was hearty; and after some conference between King and Turpin, they resolved to make him a sharer in the adventure already resolved on.

The residence of Octavius Sheepshanks, Gent., one, &c., was one of three brick residences with which the village was distinguished. The other two were the parsonage and a boarding school. Wood, wattles, or groutwork, formed the materials of the remaining structures. The green door of the abode of the man of law was distinguished by his name, in large white letters, painted thereon, and the dusty appearance of the large squares of glass in the parlour windows, for that apartment was used as a counting-house, gave a business aspect to the house altogether distinctive from the neater dwellings on either side. Other anomalous features did it exhibit,—a round orifice, enriched with a brass escutcheon, was visible in the green door aforesaid, intended for the insertion of a latch key; and the rustic applicant who for the first time applied to the knocker, stood startled and abashed at the entrance, at the magic process by which the aforesaid door opened itself, without hands, in reply to his " knock and ring;" the wonder aforesaid being brought to pass by the agency of a wire pull suspended above the head of Jenkins the clerk, in the office before-named.

" Is muster Sheepshanks at whoam?" asked a shockheaded rustic as he entered the little office of Sheepshanks on the following day. The question was addressed to a pert, lankhaired, seedy-looking youth, who, perched upon a high stool, was copying some law-form at a desk within a little railing.

" What's your business, my good man?" asked the youth, sticking his pen behind his ear.

"Whoy, said the man, scratching his head, "a's a little advice to ax; a' wants to *lawyer* ould farmer Gubbins, an' a'd like to see 'un."

"Mr. S. is at the Hall on important business," said the youth; "but I can do as well. What's the nature of your complaint against Gubbins—eh?"

The man hesitated.

"Can a' see him if a' call i' th' arternoon?" asked he.

"Indeed you can't," returned the clerk; "he's a-going to the Continent this very day on matters of great consequence."

The man again resorted to scratching his poll.

"When will he coom back?" enquired the man.

"Why—a—a—you see," said the youth, "if you want justice against Gubbins, I can do as well as Mr. S. himself; therefore, my good man, if you'll step into the private room, I'll —"

"Noa, noa," said the joskin; "a' must see un; maybe if a' went up to the hall—"

"Certainly not," said Jenkins, whose dignity was hurt by the rustic's pertinacity. "You don't suppose, my good man, that Mr. Octavius Sheepshanks can be disturbed when engaged in important consultations with counsel from London, about your little affairs? Go up to the hall, indeed!"

"Well, then, a'll call agin," said the man, sauntering out.

"D—n your impudence," muttered Jenkins, *sotto voce*, applying himself again to his task.

The rustic walked some twenty yards down the road, and struck into a bye-lane. There was a meaning smile on his countenance, singularly at variance with the assumed simplicity it had worn during the conversation with Mr. Sheepshanks's factotum. A man stepped from a stile by the road-side.

"Well, Dick," enquired Fielder, who awaited the countryman's return; "how goes it?"

"All right," replied the seeming countryman; "he's off this very afternoon—but I'll go up to the hall to make sure."

"No, no," said Fielder; "give me the smock-frock and wig. I'll do that part of the business, and join you in half an hour behind the church."

There's many a slip between the cup and the lip. Fielder was walking slowly up the road towards the Hall, when, to his no small surprise, he met the carriage of Sir Litton, containing that gentleman and the lawyer. He hastened across the fields to apprize Dick of the unlucky circumstance. He was not at the spot he had left him; he ran to the place appointed, but Turpin, who had taken a circuitous route, had not arrived.

"Confound it," exclaimed he. Five minutes, to him an hour, elapsed, but still no signs of his comrade; ten more were spent in the same way "It won't do to leave this," said he. He looked out on the road in vain. Three quarters of an hour passed, and, boiling with very rage and disappointment, he started off at a sharp walk towards the cave, where King awaited their return.

A few words sufficed to explain the unfortunate state of affairs.

King refused to start on the adventure, except in conjunction with Dick; and George was by no means pressing. An hour elapsed.

"He'll be at Colchester and give us the slip, by Jupiter!" exclaimed Fielder, who was pacing impatiently the small chamber, in a sort of fisherman's walk, that is, three steps and a turn.

The rendezvous in Epping Forest. Turpin and King preparing for an expedition.

King meantime had busied himself in preparing his own horse and that of Turpin for their adventure; and, lest any time should be lost upon Dick's arrival, he had thrice examined every buckle and strap, and stood now impatiently tapping his riding-whip against the leg of his jockey-boot.

"This is a pretty turn-out, Georgy, my buck. I'm of opinion that it might almost be as well to start at once—he'll follow us, surely; and we can leave a slip of paper to tell him——but no," continued Tom, checking himself, "correspondence is dangerous; no man should trust himself in black and white, where —"

A whistle was heard outside.

"There he is at last!" said Fielder and King at the same moment: "better late than never."

Turpin hastily entered.

"Why George," exclaimed he, "how happens this? I've sworn a good half hour away at the place of meeting behind the church. Ready and saddled, eh? and not a bit too soon either, I suppose."

"Indeed not," replied George; and he briefly explained the circumstance of his meeting with the carriage, and his hastening to the cave in search of Turpin.

"Well; "I met with a strange chance," said Dick; or I would have been here before. Sauntering down the road, I cast my eye on the 'Old Weston Arms;' the creaking sign looked dusty and dim, but a new name on a bright ground showed staringly beneath it; so I e'en lounged in. While

No. 21.

taking a glass of ale, a man alighted, the bearer of a letter for the Hall.
He had just executed his errand, and stopped to wet his whistle; so I
was unexpectedly the listener to a curious conversation between the landlord
and the new comer. The affair of my discovery and escape from Denistoun Hall
was talked of; it is, I find, no secret here. The man, who had come from Lincolnshire, added to the village news intelligence of an extraordinary kind. It
seems that the villain, whose execution took place some week or so since—"
Turpin paused momentarily; "but that's passed—I'll think of it no more—
did one good deed before he forfeited his life. He has exposed the Baronet as
the thief of his father's will, by which a large share of the property was
secured to Madeline Lady Denistoun—and under which even I possess a claim as
the representative of her who—in short, Bevis and his daughter are also claim-
ants, and I alone am left to enforce their rights; and as sure as Sir Litton Weston is a knave—if no worse—shall he find me a creditor not to be fobbed off.
Now, as you understand the state of the business, you don't wonder at the
hurry he shows to be off; and, as we're something like two hours behind them,
let's be off too. I've been maundering, confound it, about the neighbourhood,
looking at old scenes and recalling old times: but this is no time to think
of *them*. However I don't know that there's anything I've met with to im-
prove my opinion of the worthy Baronet. We must not stand prating here,
though; and what's more, it won't do at all for the three of us to go gallopping along the road. What do you think of my scheme? I'll ride forward
and look after the Baronet—he'll certainly not clear more than twenty miles
this evening—and do you follow me, either by cart, on foot, or any other
mode which may best serve your need. Our first place of meeting shall be
Chelmsford, for to that town I am convinced he has gone. At any rate we
can't be much out of his track, from what I learnt by chance half an hour
since."

King and Fielder assented, and Dick was soon on the road. Sir Litton,
however, had made no great speed; and after a smart ride of fifteen miles,
our hero found the post-horses, which the Baronet had discharged, standing
at the door of the inn where he had dined and changed horses. He had the
satisfaction too, of learning that he had scarcely departed ten minutes; and
on gallopping to a rising ground saw the carriage rolling leisurely along.
The next stage, as he knew the country well, he was aware would present no
opportunity for their enterprise; he therefore retraced his road, and had the
satisfaction of shortly meeting his two comrades, making the best of their way
in a light cart to the place of rendezvous. The position of affairs was soon
explained. After a short consultation, it was decided on that Fielder, whose
person was unknown to both Sheepshanks and the Baronet, should ride on
and put up at the inn where Sir Litton might stay for the night.

Fielder sped well. After watching at a cautious distance the progress of
the carriage, it stopped at the principal hotel in the town of Chelmsford.
Fielder scraped an acquaintance with the valet of Sir Litton; and before
midnight, on the plea of anxiety to arrive at Colchester on important business,
he, with many expressions of reluctance at leaving such good society, quitted
the company, and in a few minutes joined his companions at an obscure
publichouse.

"Well, my Britons," said he on entering a small room, where none but the
pair were present; "the thing's as good as done. Old Parchment and the
Worshipful will be off with the morning's light. Up with the lark, lads, and

off. They're going to France; and I'm much mistaken if there's not more than either of us guess in their cargo. Four or five portmanteaus, the plate-chest, and an imperial stuffed full of something, are in an out-house, while one or two smaller boxes are stowed in the apartment of Sir Litton himself. The valet has the valuables I first spoke of in charge; we might manage them, perhaps, by the morning—what say you?"

"Certainly not, George," said King; "what's most worth and least bulky is within; besides, we should only rob Boniface by borrowing the things on his premises; and the cream of the jest is lost if he can get back his property by prosecuting the innkeeper. No, no! we'll do the thing another guess fashion."

"The early morning will suit us best," observed Dick; "leave it to me."

The first grey of dawn had not yet streaked the east as three men stood in earnest yet low converse beneath the shelter of a huge oak, distant some twenty yards from the roadside, within a short mile east of Chelmsford. They had not waited long before one of them, walking to a slight rising-ground, gave signal of the approach of a carriage; and with hasty steps rejoined the men he had just left.

The heavy coach neared them at a lazy trot; it passed a turn in the road which concealed it from the view of any traveller who might approach from the direction leading from the town. The valet slumbered soundly on the box of the vehicle, and withinside the passengers were also enjoying a comfortable nap. The postilion was immersed in a profound cogitation, the gist of which was, to decide the colour, quality, price, and quantity of riband he should purchase at Colchester as a present to the wench on whom he had fixed his affections. An occasional twinge of jealousy arose as the thought intruded itself how the damsel aforesaid had accepted, with alacrity and seeming pleasure, a red-leather housewife from a rival, the ostler at the Lion: and that too, though he had, out of pure and disinterested friendship, previously cautioned her as to the faithless character of the man. He was jogging on, seeing nothing and absorbed in self, when he was brought up "all standing," as sailor's would phrase it, by a salute after the following fashion:—

"Stand!" and he suddenly became aware of the presence of two masked men, who had each possessed himself of the bridle of one of his horses. Nor was the suddenness of the surprise less with the inside travellers. They too, were enjoying a sleeping nap as profound as their driver's waking one; and arrived at a sense of their situation by an equally laconic address.

"The Lord have mercy on us!" exclaimed Sheepshanks, seizing the slumbering Sir Litton by the arm. The coach-door opened, and displayed a pistol, with its muzzle pointed at his head.

"Sit down, you yelping cur," said the unwelcome visitor, "or I'll give you the contents of this."

Octavius needed no second bidding. Sir Litton, whom long travel and a harassed mind, had soundly locked in the arms of

"Tired nature's sweet restorer, balmy sleep,"

snored on.

"Come down, sir," said one of the men at the horses' heads, to the valet. The man, seeing resistance was useless, obeyed. He was ordered to betake himself to a bank, and seat himself by the roadside: this order too he complied with. A general rummage of the trunks behind the carriage, beneath the box, and on its top, followed; this was carried on by George, and most heartily did he pursue the search. Articles of massive plate and other valuables were cast on the road as he proceeded, but the amount of cash found was next to nothing.

"We must disturb the gentleman, I'm thinking," said Dick, leaving the horses, from which they had compelled the postboy to dismount. "Keep your iron pointed at the sleeper," whispered he to King; "never mind about the smirking lawyer;" and Turpin stepped into the low and wide carriage. On the seat beside Sir Litton lay a small iron-bound box, and on the opposite one a large leathern portmanteau. The former Dick handed out to his companion, and was in the act of laying hold of the latter, when he saw the little lawyer deal his master a sharp kick on the leg. The Baronet muttered an oath, and Turpin, in his momentary anger, dealt Sheepshanks a blow with the back of his hand.

"Murder! murder!" shrieked the terrified coward.

Dick placed his hand on his bleeding mouth to stop his cries. Sir Litton awoke, and unconsciously seized Turpin by the collar; the place was too confined for anything but a close struggle, the portmanteau was dragged from the carriage by King, and at the same instant the Baronet awoke to the fact that he was being robbed. He was a powerful man, and Dick, who wished to disengage himself from his grasp, though unwilling to do him a serious injury, tried in vain to disentangle himself. The Baronet roared lustily for assistance, and his valet, who was no coward, seeing King and Turpin with their hands full, rushed to the rescue. Snatching a massive flagon from the ground, he aimed a desperate blow at Fielder; he had better remained where he was; for King, who still held the portmanteau at one end by its handle, raising it suddenly, swung it with all his strength against the shoulders of the man, and laid him sprawling on the road. Meantime our hero was sore beset. The little lawyer, seeing his master in close struggle with the highwayman, mustered courage, and attempted to seize Turpin by the legs, in the hopes of pulling him down, but received so hearty a compliment in the stomach as sent his diminutive person plump into the lap of King, who was just advancing to the coach door. Tom repaid the salute by a kick in his backside, followed by a hit in the back, which laid him also prostrate; and seizing Sir Litton by the leg in his turn, dragged him and Turpin, of whom he would not release his hold, out of the carriage. Dick immediately regained his feet.

"Villains!" gasped Sir Litton, "do you know——"

"Exactly so, my dear Sir," laughed Turpin; "but there are other villains beside highwaymen. Call your constables, my dear Sir Justice. 'Seize him,' I believe you said, last time I'd the honour of seeing you in Lincolnshire, eh?"

"Turpin as I live!" exclaimed he. "I throw myself on your mercy. You are a bold, and I hope a generous man, and will not harm me now I'm in your power."

"I've only come to claim my wife's legacy," said Dick, "that you'll own is mere justice, though I shall of course expect a trifle to reward these gentlemen, whom I have professionally engaged to assist me in its recovery. I believe Mr. Sheepshanks that's correct. I can't at the present moment stand here to tax the bill of costs, but if there's any more than they think right, why we'll return the balance."

The highwaymen laughed, and the Baronet stared in mute astonishment.

"This baggage will be heavy, my good sir," continued Dick to Sir Litton, "and will take time for its removal. Blindfold the gentleman," and he made a sign to Fielder. The operation was quickly performed, amid loud remonstrances from the baronet. His hands were tied, and the same kind offices performed for the valet and Mr. S., which they patiently submitted to.

"And now, my good sir," said Turpin, addressing the post-boy, "we'll proceed to provide for you." A handkerchief then passed over his eyes; and the highwaymen consulted apart from their prisoners for a few moments.

"Leave the carriage to me," said Dick; "I know the cross-roads well. I'll take the post-boy to drive me; and with the aid of Sir Litton's travelling robe and cap, I'll manage to convoy the swag, never fear. Meanwhile, do you and George escort our blindfolded friend—his servant, and the lawyer, to yonder sand-pits. But don't, if you can help it, leave 'em for two hours; by which time I'll undertake the thing shall be done clean, or don't trust Dick Turpin again."

Dick's plan was assented to; and the three prisoners were moved off, under the escort of King and Fielder. Dick watched them as they skirted a hedge near the common. No sooner had he lost sight of them than, unbandaging the postilion, he bad him mount his saddle; and promising him an instant bullet, should he attempt any trick or treachery, he directed him to the right, down a cross road, by which, making a detour to the south and west, he might regain the highway, some miles on the London side of Chelmsford. Having effected this without interruption or suspicion, his next care was to secure the more valuable portion of the property. This was soon effected; and giving strict injunctions to the postilion to drive slowly towards town, Dick left him, after transferring the money and plate to a hiding place in the forest; taking the precaution however, of again blindfolding the postilion and removing him to a dry ditch, where he could not observe the proceedings, before so doing.

We will now return to follow Sir Litton and his two unlucky fellow-travellers. They moved on in utter ignorance of the way they were going until they arrived at the cartway leading to some disused sand-pits. This was the spot selected by the highwaymen for their sojourn until the booty should have been conveyed to some place of safety; and here they compelled their three prisoners to lie down, each on his back, under strong threats should they attempt alarm or escape. It may well be supposed that Sir Litton was in no very enviable frame of mind. He preserved a sullen silence. The valet had most to say for himself; and was loud in his declarations of indignation at the ungentlemanly treatment to which he was subject. Fielder was immensely amused. He and King kept up a running fire of joke on the piteous aspect and bearing of the little lawyer, which seemed by no means calculated to abate his ill-humour: indeed, his spleen seemed more than once to get the better of his fears, for he replied now and then to their jestings with a bitterness which added vastly to the merriment of his tormentors.

"Did Dick ever tell you," asked Fielder, in an undertone to his companion, "how that little venomous reptile once tried to shoot one of us—I suppose he didn't care which—when we stopt him near Snaresbrook?"

"Ay," replied Tom; "but is this the real, the identical little cheat-devi' who tried to pop off our bold comrade? If you are sure of it, it would be pity not to give him some little joke to tell, if it was only that he might remember us as friends of gallant Dick."

" What say you to ducking him?" suggested Fielder ; " here's a shallow
pond hard by, and it would be only following up what we meant to do on that
occasion, if we had not been interrupted. Mr. Sheepshanks," continued Fielder,
" a friend of mine has just proposed that a ducking, which has been a long
time overdue, should now be paid. I suppose you remember firing a pistol at
one of our friends on this road some few years ago, and some passers-by fortunately rescuing you from a taste of the next horse-pond, eh ?"

Mr. Sheepshanks replied not. He was convinced that silence would be
discreet, and therefore, like a detected thief before a committing magistrate,
he wisely " reserved what he had to say for another place." Fielder had
certainly a genius for a practical joke. A few words passed in a whisper
between himself and King ; the latter laughed heartily, and said :—

" Split me, George, but you're a droll fish. 'Pon honour tho', it would be
rather too bad ; for the fright might kill the chicken-hearted little scoundrel.
But do as you like ; he deserves a drill for his conduct, on more accounts than
one."

" Sirrah lawyer !" exclaimed Fielder, throwing a determined sternness into
his tone—though, if poor Octavius could have seen the speaker's face, he
would have beheld it struggling to maintain its gravity,—" Sirrah lawyer !
it has been represented to me that you have been guilty of attempting the life
of an honester man than yourself. Now, this is a sad crime against society :
had you blown out your own brains for a rascally knave, none could have
grumbled ; but it appears you have more than once attempted to shorten the
existence of the brave Captain Turpin ; you are therefore sentenced to be
thrown from the highest cliff into the next adjoining gravel-pit, and the Lord
have mercy on your wicked soul !"

Mr. Sheepshanks listened to this address in bewildered fear. Fielder made
a sign to King, and taking hold of poor Sheepshanks, each by an arm, they
raised him to his feet ; they then led him about among the small sand-heaps
in the bottom of the pit for a few minutes, to produce upon his mind the
impression that he had walked some distance. The alarm of the lawyer was
increased by their placing over his head a cloth which completely enveloped
it, and fastening the same round his neck. Meanwhile Fielder gave vent to
the most horrid imprecations of revenge. The two hours stipulated between
the highwaymen had now expired. They walked slowly up the cartway by
which they had entered, and led Sheepshanks, more dead than alive, to the
side of the pit : it was scarped and perpendicular, but not more than ten feet
in depth at that part ; and nearly at their feet lay Sir Litton and his valet,
still bound and blindfolded. " Shall we throw him over here ?" asked Fielder,
in a low whisper, with a wink of the eye at King.

" No ! curse him," growled Tom ; " that would be too good a death for
the wretch ; let's—" The rest was lost in horrid indistinctness.

" For the love of Christ ! Oh ! mercy, mercy, pray, for the love of heaven !"
shrieked Octavius, in a paroxysm of terror : " Spare me, and I'll swear ; spare
me, and I'll never—Oh Lord ! Oh Lord ! I'll pray for———"

Fielder had much ado to keep himself from a horse-laugh. " We must
not dally," said King, in a voice which would have made the fortune of a
Coburg-theatre assassin. " Blood for blood ! Stay, we'll leave him time for
repentance—time while he can hang over this brink and pray to the heaven
he has outraged." The two highwaymen seized him by the shoulders, and
thrusting his legs over the side of the pit, lowered him gradually. " Now

hold fast," said Fielder, thrusting the fingers of one of the lawyer's hands into the turf; while King did the same by the other. The terrified Sheepshanks swung his feet to and fro within the pit—no support met them. He was fully aware of his dreadful position: he clung to the earth with the gripe of despair, and prayed, in the intensity of his agony, with a fervour that might get even a lawyer into heaven.

Fielder and King departed with hasty steps, while poor Octavius, who could spare no hand even to release his eyes, clutched with straining sinews the moist ground. His bodily strength was never great; and, though his carcase was by no means heavy, he felt sure that all must soon be over. He listened —his assassins were surely gone: his faculties were sharpened by terror, and he distinctly heard the bloodthirsty villains' laughter borne on the cool breeze. They were running away—there could be no doubt of it. He collected his remaining energies for one mighty effort, and he struck his toes against the perpendicular wall of sand; but the faithless, friable dirt, crumbled, and refused a foothold. "Could I but once raise my knee to the surface level," thought he, "I am saved! Shall I cry aloud? No; they will return, and murder me! I'll try it!" exclaimed he, desperately. The perspiration poured down his forehead, as he worked up his resolution for the dread attempt. He sprang upward: his digging fingers stuck firmly in the soil; and with one knee he had reached the top of the bank, when a huge fragment of earth gave way beneath the pressure of the limb; he slipped downward; a larger piece, the sole support of his grasping hands, detached itself; and, with a scream, the wretched victim fell back into the abyss.

"Hell and fury!" exclaimed Sir Litton, struggling to his feet, as the staggering and bewildered Sheepshanks deposited his seat of honour plump on his countenance, while a rattling shower of loose earth followed the uncourteous salute. "D——n! what's the meaning of this?" and he dealt a stumbling kick on the prostrate lawyer's carcase, and fell; he plucked the bandage from his eyes, and, to his astonishment, beheld at his feet his fainting and senseless legal adviser. "Linton," said he to his valet, "get up." The man obeyed.

"They're gone at last, I believe," said Linton, looking round apprehensively.

"I see they are," said his master, "but what the devil's the meaning of all this? I thought they were murdering poor Sheepy here, he's been making so many supplications for mercy, and they've finished by throwing him into the pit this very moment, so they can't yet have got far; yet, unarmed as we are, it would perhaps be wise to be still a bit. I'm a ruined man any how," muttered Sir Litton to himself, as the thought of his loss obtruded itself. "See to Sheepshanks, Linton; I hope he's not seriously hurt."

Some cold water was thrown on the face of Octavius and his friends had very soon the satisfaction of seeing him restored to animation. He had received no injury; but they were for a long time in some doubts of his sanity, so strongly was his imagination impressed with the idea of having fallen from an immense height. The valet after several reconnoitrings of the common, having announced the coast to be clear, the trio took their way towards a farm house some mile or so distant from the solitary spot where they had spent three such memorably unpleasant hours.

CHAPTER XV.

—Unreasoning reason,
To set perverseness on its heavenly throne
As man doth use : banishing the sun's light
To walk by smoky lamps. Oh yes, ye brutes,
Ye are our betters, and I bow to ye ;
For ye have used your talent to the full,
Poor though it be ; while with our higher one,
And godlier—we've buried it in mire,
An outcast jewel.—

                        Ernest.

The prophet wept for Israel ; wish'd his eyes
Were fountains fed with infinite supplies :
For Israel dealt in robbery and wrong ;
There were the scorner's and the slanderer's tongue ;
Oaths, used as playthings or convenient tools,
As interest biass'd knaves, or fashion fools ;
Adultery neighing at his neighbour's door ;
Oppression, labouring hard to grind the poor ;
The partial balance, and deceitful weight ;
The treacherous smile, a mask for secret hate ;
Hypocrisy, formality in prayer,
And the dull service of the lip were there.
    *   *   *   *   *   *

The temple and its holy rites profaned
By mummeries, He that dwelt in it disdain'd ;
Uplifted hands, that at convenient times
Could act extortion and the worst of crimes,
Wash'd with a neatness scrupulously nice,
And free from every taint but that of vice

                        Cowper.

In a narrow street in Houndsditch dwelt Moses Solomons, one of the despised and scattered race of the sons of Israel. It was the Sabbath night ; and the door had been kept closed, in compliance with his creed, during the day—for Solomons, though within an unscrupulous scoundrel, was ceremoniously precise in making clean " the outside of the platter." A rap at the small hatch of his dwelling called him forth. A woman desired a little private talk on business ; and she was shown into a small parlour behind the frowzy-smelling shop. The visitor was Madge Dutton : her dress was dirty, and her looks squalid.

" Vell, Mishtriss Madge," said Solomons, " vat's de bishness now ? S' help me but a'm very poor : dat vash a pad bishness dat last I did for you, as I'm a shinner. A' hope, ma tear, you've not got no more of dem dere copper sheals, nor coot-for-noting vatches. Let's see the lot, tho', and if a can deal a vill, tho' a musht borrow de monish of a neighbour if a do. Let's see de pargain. Cot help ush ! a give too mush monish for everyting : but you're an old cushtomer, Mishtriss Madge, and if a can do bishniss vid you, vy a vill."

" I've neither gold nor silver, Mr. Solomons," replied the woman ; " but I've that which may bring both. You've heerd o' the *topping** of my man— eh ?"

Mr. Solomons affected ignorance, though he knew well every particular.

" Cot persherve us !" exclaimed he ; " is it de truth a' hear ? Vot, mishter Torpin, vot a' heerd vos takin' a fancy to ye ?"

" No !" said Madge, testily ; " not he : who told you *he* had taken a fancy to *me* ?"

" A'll not be shure vere a' vos heerin it," said the wily Jew ; " but a've heer

                      * Execution.

Madge selling the Weston Papers.

as it vosh all along mit you, as he vosh leaf his vife and come to Lonton. Put dat ish notin to de purposh ; vot ish te coots if dey are needer cold nor shilver ?"

Madge replied by drawing from beneath her dirty shawl a packet tied with green silk riband, having an outer covering of white vellum. She glanced at the door of the room suspiciously as she did this ; and Mr. Solomons, taking the hint, rose from his seat, secured it by a small square bolt beneath the lock, and resumed his chair.

The woman proceeded to state that, though unable to read the contents of the parchments she held, yet she had no doubt of their being of great value ; a conclusion to which she had come from many mysterious expressions of Dennis, to the effect that their possession would one day make his fortune. He had, moreover, upon more than one occasion declared to her that, in the event of circumstances rendering it necessary for him to fly the country, these papers would always be a reserve to which he could appeal for the means of so doing ; that these declarations he had always associated with dark hints of the power he possessed over the character of his former

No. 22.

master, Sir Litton Weston ; and she wound up the whole by saying that, having no resource left but these documents, and not knowing in what way to render them available for the relief of her present pressing necessities, she had applied to him (Mr. Solomons) as a likely person either to assist her, or to put her in the way of turning into money the writings, should they prove upon examination to be valuable.

The Jew listened with eager attention, though pretended indifference, to Madge's statement ; shook his head doubtfully, and said :—

" Vell, a' can't say as a' see anyting dat can be done. It vould be vorse nor a pig in a poke—and a' vouldn't like to puy von any vay—to gif hard monish for poor ould sheepskin, vot no von can tell is vorth anyting."

Meantime Solomons had clutched the packet, and untying the riband with his teeth, threw out several tape-bound packets on the table. He opened the largest of them, and stared perplexedly at the large engrossed heading. Mr. Solomons, like most of his race, was extremely illiterate, though eminently shrewd ; the cramp engrossing of the law-hand completely puzzled him ; and " 𝕿𝖍𝖎𝖘 𝖎𝖘 𝖙𝖍𝖊 𝖑𝖆𝖘𝖙 𝖂𝖎𝖑𝖑 𝖆𝖓𝖉 𝕿𝖊𝖘𝖙𝖆𝖒𝖊𝖓𝖙," in the text-heading, was all he could decipher. He looked over one skin after the other, for there were several in the instrument ; and gazed earnestly at the various seals and signatures to the document and its codicils ; but saw no clue to their contents, save the repetition of the old Baronet's signature, and the impressed coat-armour by its side.

" It's shum nobilman's vill," said the Israelite internally, " and may be of vally ; but how am a to tell ?"

Madge watched the selfish features of the Jew anxiously, as he pursued his examination. Solomons, by a sidelong glance, caught her eager expression ; he threw down the parchment, and leant back in his chair with his hands before him.

" You see, mishtress Madge," said he, with an air of indifference, " dat a'd like to do anyting as ish reasonble to obleege you ; but it ish neshessary—for dese ish pad times, fery pad times—for everypody to look to demselves. A'm shure it's creat rishks vot a' runs every day to sherve ma cushtomers. Dere's mushter Wild, Jonathan I mean, vosh lose his life, clever as he vosh, all trough dis meddlin vid writins. A vish it vosh anyting else you vished to shell—anyting in de regler vay, a might get te monish ; but you see none of my peoplsh vill lend me noting on dese ould papers. If you vill leave dem here for to-morrow, vich ish de firsht day of de veek, a vill shee a shentleman as has got monish ; an' maybe he may do someting for you."

To this Madge sturdily objected. She knew Mr. Solomons too well to trust the deeds out of her sight ; she therefore replied—

" Well, I see you and I can't deal ; so it's no use losing time. I've not broke fast since yesterday, and I'll go and call on mother Jacobs in Petticoat Lane : she'll stand a bob* or two on 'em, and chance it, till I can release 'em."

So saying she caught the documents up in hasty anger, and passing the riband round them, walked towards the door. Solomons eyed her in silence, until he saw she was really bent on going ; and then stopped her, when her hand was on the lock, by saying :—

" Vell, a think you might ha vaited till a said vether a vould lend you a

* A Shilling.

trifle, afore you shtarted off in dat manner. Mother Jacobs vill lend you noting on 'em, a know vell enough; beshides, if you must go borrow till you can take 'em up agin, a didn't say as a vouldn't lend you noting; put you're so very short ven von means noting put right, so you are."

Madge returned to the table, and Solomons went on:—

"Now a'll tell you wot a'll do; and dat's more nor mishtris Jacobs, as you're so fond on, vould do for yer if she seed yer shtarvin. A'll shend for ma friend mishter Aprams, de lawyer, and he shall look at de tings; and if so be anyting is vorth havin', vy a'll give you all he says is the vorth on 'em—dere!"

The last monosyllable was delivered by the Jew with an emphasis, as if to express even his own astonishment at the incautious liberality of his munificent proposal; Madge, however, knew her customer too well to be in the least moved from her ordinary composure by the generous announcement.

"I don't mind who I sells 'em to, providing I gets the money," replied she sulkily; "an' I suppose you won't buy without you gets money's worth. So, if so be this mister Abrams is handy, I'll wait for him; but I won't leave the writings, and that's flat."

"Rachel, ma tear!" cried Mr. Solomons, opening the door; and a small, black-eyed, cunning specimen of Hebrew humanity presented herself. She came into the room; and Mr. Solomons, holding the door to with one hand—a habit acquired by continual suspicion and illegal traffic—directed the child to the house of Mr. Abrams, with a message that her father desired to see him. That personage, ever alive to business, returned with the messenger. He was a heavy, fleshy-faced, sensual-looking man; and the brutal expression of his thick countenance was not much improved by the leering and sinister expression of a pair of deep-set eyes, which had never been known to look straight in the face of man, woman, or child. He was attired in professional black, and wore a white pudding neckcloth; and in lieu of the stocking, the ordinary costume of the day, his huge calves were encased in black cloth gaiters. Mr. Abrams had the reputation of being the most successful (which means the most unscrupulous) Old Bailey attorney of his day. He had the credit of having defrauded justice of her due in more glaring instances of guilt than any other man; and, having amassed wealth in the respectable calling of defeating and rendering inoperative the laws which society has framed for the protection of honesty and industry, was respected accordingly. It is true that he was pretty generally known to have taken a share in the compounding of numerous felonies, but then they were of that important and extensive class which, from the amount of property involved, could afford a respectable commission on their arrangement: cases where the plunder was ruin to the parties robbed, unless some such public benefactor as Mr. Abrams stepped in to negociate its return for "a consideration." He was, besides, eminently distinguished for his ability in assisting the escape of felons (who could pay him), by his extraordinary astuteness in discovering a flaw in an indictment—some misdescription, or an erroneous orthography; slips which, in the eye of a lawyer, break down all distinctions between innocence and guilt, or right and wrong. Such was the wealthy, and therefore the worthy, Mr. Abrams—the thieves' attorney; and had it not been for the unfortunate bar of Judaism—who knows (since Judaism *was* then a bar) but that the prosperous lawyer, grown fat on the spoils of robbing robbers, and plundering the plundered, might not, as " an eminent professional man," have arrived at high public honours—nay, have aspired even to the magisterial chair of the great city which was honoured by giving him birth. As it was however, in those days of illiberality, his religious profession (not his worldly one) prevented his rising beyond a private station; and the rich Mr. Abrams vegetated among his "peoplsh" in the obscurity of Houndsditch. This important personage shot one of his sinister glances at Madge—slightly nodded his head to Solomons—and said, in a brattling voice—

"Evening, Mishter S.! jist 'bout to take a littel turn of a valk ven your Rachel came—noish little shild dat Rachel, marm—" turning to Madge, "verra 'cute—Rachel's very mosh a favourite o' mine."

Having thus introduced himself, Mr. Solomons stated to him the business upon which he had sent to solicit his advice, occasionally treating Abrams with a wink, unobserved by Madge, to convey the fact that she was necessitous, and might be imposed on: though the speech of Mr. Solomons was artfully filled with professions of his great anxiety to deal, not only justly, but even generously in the transaction. Indeed, to have heard the worthy man, one must have concluded that nothing but a sympathy with the necessities of the applicant could have induced him to meddle in a transaction so certain to produce nothing in the shape of profit, and so fraught with danger to himself. While the Jew thus spoke Mr. Abrams slowly inspected the various documents. Lavater himself could have read nothing in that countenance varying from its habitual cunning and villany. He scanned over the various writings with as little expression, either of satisfaction or disapprobation, as if their figured surfaces had presented one continuous blank. Having gone through the whole, he said,—

"A hardly know vot to say to dis. They may be of some value to the rale owners, but a don't tink 'em of no vorth to no von else. Dis von (taking up an unimportant draft of an agreement which, by its conditions, had long since expired) might be of some use to de owner if it vosh stamped; but de resht is noting. Neverdeless, as Mishter Solomons says he vishes to befriend you, and you seem a goot sort of voman, I will give a ginny, upon the repayment of vich a vill let you haf dem all back agin—but den a musht haf 'em redeemed vithin von month, or else a vill haf cut dem all up for tailors' measures."

Madge was in no position to refuse money; and it appearing doubtful to her whether more could be made of them, after a little haggling she accepted the coin, a light one, and took her departure; Mr. Abrams previously hinting by a conversation *at* Madge, but addressed *to* Mr. Solomons, that the penalty of transportation to Antigua would be the result of discovery to her, but of course not making the remotest allusion to any punishable offence as regarded their part of the transaction.

No sooner had Madge's footsteps died away than the respectable Mr. Abrams altered mightily in his manner. He closed the door—examined its fastenings—then, drawing a chair, he seated himself on the opposite side of the fire to Mr. Solomons, and stirring the wood with vigour, till it shot into a cheerful blaze, trimmed the lamp. Solomon watched him with an expression of inquisitiveness on his filthy and selfish face.

"Lishten, cousin," said Abrams, "our fortin ish made; but you must give me something more den half in dis affair, for vidout me you would have got noting."

Mr. Solomons objected *in limine* to this proposal, and in a few minutes the two Jews were engaged in an arduous battle of the wits, as to which should *do* the other "in a business way;" for upon the "honour among thieves" principle, it was only by an admitted advantage on the one hand, or oversight on the other, that a "coot pargain," *i. e.*, an unfair adjustment, could take place. The documents were, as the reader may already know, the last will of the good Sir Mark Weston, which Sir Litton had purloined on the night of his death, and which had so singularly come into the possession of Dennis, together with other deeds of the Weston family of great importance; and Mr. Abrams and his client did not separate until a late hour—so keen was the encounter of their wits, and so numerous the projects of their fertile brains, as to the best means of procuring the largest possible profit from this lucky windfall.

We left Sir Albert Denistoun, who had possessed himself of the paper of instructions for the recovery of the deeds, dictated by Dennis, on his road to London. That paper stated Madge to be the depositary of the documents, and gave directions for her discovery. Sir Albert was desirous of avoiding any personal communication with his brother-in-law in relation to the recent disgraceful affair, for he feared lest his indignation at his rascality might betray him into some act which might inflict pain on the estimable Lady Denistoun; he therefore set about the search in person. He sent for Ferret, who had become known to him in connexion with the apprehension of Dennis, and consulted him upon the affair; and that worthy undertook to do his utmost, being stimulated thereto by a large promised reward.

But we must return to Sir Litton. The three unfortunates made their way to the farm-house before spoken of, and the good people, upon hearing the disaster which had befallen them, not only ministered to their immediate wants, but, on ascertaining the rank of Sir Litton, turned out their best vehicle and "crack" horse; and, under the charge of "joltering Giles," nightfall saw them again under the roof of Weston Hall. The recent loss had determined Sir Litton to stay; and further reflection on the posture of affairs suggested to him that his sister's good heart might be so practised on as to confine the mischief to the mere exposure, and to a small sacrifice of property on his part.

Numerous were the consultations between the Baronet and the lawyer, as to the most advisable course to be pursued. The first advice of Sheepshanks was to address Lady Denistoun, and endeavour to make the best possible bargain in the way of restitution; but this was rejected: and as time and their councils went on, and no intimation arrived, either from the legal adviser of Denistoun, or directly from Lady Madeline, their schemes assumed another complexion.

"D'ye think," suggested Sheepshanks, "that they've got that will at all? Might we not strike a bold blow for its possession and destruction? This woman must be poor—she is, of course, to be bought. Leave it to me to search her out, and I'll contrive it so that we may stand upon terms with them till we are in a position to defy them to the proof—which rests as yet upon the unsupported declaration of a mere felon."

Sir Litton at length assented to place the affair in the hands of Sheepshanks, and the little lawyer, ever zealous to recommend himself, was seen to enter the lodgings of Madge, the afternoon of the Monday succeeding the Saturday's interview with Messrs. Abrams and Solomons, above-mentioned.

"Here's a gentleman wants you, Mistress Dutton," exclaimed a female in the front parlour or shop, for it was both, in reply to Mr. Sheepshank's enquiry. Madge, slipshod and in dishabille, peeped down the narrow stair-case, and beheld in the passage a smart and dapper little man, most unexceptionably attired. She hastened back, thrust a cap upon her head, and desiring that the "gentleman" might be shown up, stood at the door of the back room on the same landing, into which she retreated, after taking a look and bestowing a smile on Mr. Octavius, as he was shown by her landlady into the front. A couple of minutes were spent by Mr. Sheepshanks in surveying the whitewashed walls and patchwork quilt in this den of vice and misery; and the same portion of time was consumed by Madge in dragging on a pair of clean stockings belonging to the woman in the said back room; dilating, as she did her slovenly toilette, on the "old swell," and calculating the probabilities of the douceur of a guinea or a seven-shilling piece. This hasty speculation was concluded by a decision in favour of the latter, drawn from the gentlemanly appearance of the visitor; and with a request to her pal, who was still abed wearing off the effects of a gin fever, that she would "wish her luck," Madge tripped smiling and smirking into the apart-ment where Mr. Sheepshanks sat gingerly poising himself on the most solid corner of a ricketty rush-bottomed chair. The little lawyer rose at her entrance, and pulling a grave face, said---for he feared a misunderstanding,---

"My good madam, I have called on you on important and serious business.'

Madge stared, as if half doubting whether he was in earnest; but seeing no smile on the face of her visitor, she dismissed her own, which in truth was a forced one, and prepared to listen with becoming gravity to the stranger's communication.

Mr. Sheepshanks, with professional circumlocution, impressed upon her the importance to her future prospects of placing herself, in the business he was about to broach, entirely under his guidance; he then spoke of the affairs of Dennis, and gave confidence to Madge by showing the intimate knowledge he possessed of them; and last of all, offered her a large reward, on condition that she would give up to him, as the agent of Lady Denistoun, (he thought this lie most likely to baffle enquiry,) the documents deposited in her care by Dennis, and of which he gave her an accurate description.

Unluckily, Mr. Ferret had already been with her, and, in the excess of his munificence, had presented her with a crown, for which reward she had already acquainted him, under a promise of secresy, where he might find the missing documents. She had no doubt but that the cunning officer had duped her, and was himself about to reap the golden harvest, the right to which she had thus igno-rantly parted with. She therefore held her tongue as to the former negociation, and after coquetting with Octavius for some time, which rendered the lawyer more eager, she, upon the advance of fifty guineas told down, and a promise of the other fifty on the recovery of the deeds, not only informed Sheepshanks of the whole transaction with Solomons, but undertook to show him the house. This, however, Sheepshanks, who, as we need not tell the reader, was an arrant coward, declined from a fear of treachery, but appointed the following evening to meet her, and with "a friend" go down to Houndsditch together to repurchase the parchments.

The little man flew on the wings of exultation to inform his employer of his success, and the Baronet announced his intention of accompanying him in disguise on this important negotiation.

CHAPTER XVI.

I'm in, and now no hope of safety's nigh.
I'm sore beset; yet like some bold merchant,
Who, when his long-tossed laden vessel hits
Against some rock, and with loud horror splits,
First grasps one casket, which does all contain,
Then, desperate, plunges in the foamy main;
So I to thee, my prize, my stake, my all,
While life shall last will cling, nor quit thee till I fall.

Hannibal's Overthrow. By Nat. Lee. 1694.

Here's a conjunction of the planets! By St. Christopher this meeting's a rare one; a pretty mingling of sweets and sours; all the devils of contradiction couldn't have made a nicer dish of hell-broth ; no, not if they'd set Lucifer himself with his long ladle to stir the cauldron.

Diego.—Yes: peppered, on my life: much good may it do him. I'd not have my hide so riddled for my cap full of double pistoles.

—The Spanish Gipsey, by T. Middleton and W. Rowley.

THE cash which Mr. Sheepshanks had given to Madge was not suffered to lie idle; and silks, velvet, cheap and showy jewellery, paint, perfume, patches, powder, and fine linen, had so changed the dirty trull of yesterday to the fine lady of to-day, that none but the practised eye of the man of the world would have suspected them to be one and the same person. We have said Madge was handsome, or rather of that large order of beauty to which the epithet of "showy" has been aptly applied; and now --- shining in silk, rich in velvet, and attired in all the pride of splendid-coloured silk stockings, with deep black clocks, shoes edged with silver lace, a bright satin joseph, and a diamond-quilted petticoat of gaudy brocade---she sailed along Whitechapel, admired by the butchers, and envied and sneered at by the women, a striking illustration of the homely proverb, that "fine feathers make fine birds."

Gentle reader, we will let you into the secret of all this unwonted display, or rather into the motive which, superadded to personal vanity, (the last passion which dies in such a woman's breast,) prompted this careful decoration. The slight hint of the designing Mr. Solomons had sunk deep into her mind; and though she knew the systematic lying and deception of her informant, she positively argued herself into a conviction of its entire truth.

"What we wish we easily believe;" and Madge, having satisfied herself that the Jew could have no motive of gain in telling her a falsehood on this point, concluded that Turpin had really been enquiring her out. True, at their last interview, he had been short and abrupt; but that was excused, she thought, by the dreadful circumstance of his wife's death, and her connexion with the murderer. Yet that ought not to weigh against her, inasmuch as she had not, nor could have had, any participation in the awful deed. She was walking on, picking her steps, self-absorbed, and unheeding the winks, stares, and occasional nudge or beckon of the impudent or idle passer-by; for Madge's beauty and attire were deeply stamped with the je-ne-sçai-quoi of her profession; when her attention was fixed by a man, who after twice staring her rudely in the face as he passed, placed himself directly in front of her, saying,—

"D—n it, Madge! won't you speak? S'pose you're above it, though," and he glanced down her attire with a smile. "Coming out not a little, I see—how the deuce it *is* done I can't guess—ha! ha!"

Madge looked full at the speaker, and recognised the features and voice of George Fielder. She brightened up at the thought of the clue thus opportunely given her, for she doubted not that George could give her information of our hero. George proposed a treat at the bar of a neighbouring liquor-shop, and the woman assented. He was, however, suspicious of Madge's character, and therefore prudently denied all knowledge of the whereabout of Turpin.

"Though to tell you the truth," added he, "you are the very person he has commissioned me to look after. (Madge could not conceal her gratification.) I suppose it's an old story to tell you all about the black 'un's speech, before they sent him to dance upon nothing, and be d—d to him—so I'll cut that short. Dick has a claim under the will—but setting that aside, for he's some odd notions, he's taken it into his noddle that it would be mighty generous and only proper for him to get back those parchments, and give 'em up to Sir Albert Denistoun; which he says he should do out of heaven knows what sort of feelings of duty, and respect, and all that sort of thing; which neither you nor me pretend to know much about. Now comes the dodge; give me the papers —I should like to surprise Dick, and it would please him too—and here's ten as bright guineas as ever came out of old George's mint. What d'ye say to it? Am I to have 'em—yes is the word."

Saying this, Fielder, with his hearty bluntness, drew forth a canvass purse, such as those in ordinary use among farmers and cattle-dealers, and shook it significantly in the palm of his hand. Madge, with the ostentation of her precarious profession, had no idea of being outdone.

"You're very flush of your *ochre** jest now, Mister Georgy; but don't think as you're to get all the world in a string in that way. Brag's a good dog, you know; but there's as good as he: I'll show with you (and lifting the skirt of her dress, she dived her hand into some mysterious recesses in her petticoat, and drew forth a long, netted silk-purse, with sliding rings). What d'ye think of that?" said she, knocking its heavier end on the counter, while through the meshes of the other she displayed a note or two; "eh, Mister bounceable? If I give up the writings it 'ull be to the right owner hisself, and I thinks him Mr. Richard, and no one else; so it's no use trying to put the come-over on me with your shabby ten *quid*."†

George, after fruitlessly attempting to elicit something more satisfactory, was fain to submit to her views; and Madge, with many asseverations of fidelity, and of her respect for Dick, prevailed on Fielder to promise to bring them together that evening, Turpin being then in town; first, however, stipulating that it should be at a place of his own appointing, and not hers; and exonerating himself from all blame in the event of Dick's refusal.

Turpin unhesitatingly assented to the meeting: he was heart-whole, and had looked on the woman with feelings of perfect indifference; and towards night-fall Fielder, Turpin, and Madge, met at a publichouse near Bow.

We have before said that Dick was no hero of the novel-school, but a mere man, who felt strongly and acted strongly. Of a bold and impetuous temperament; "sudden and quick in quarrel;" but easily appeased. Madge was

---

* Gold   † Guineas.

Fielder's Encounter with Madge Dutton.

all smiles, pleasantry, and frankness; she excused to Dick her deposit of the documents with the Jew—for their sale she did not admit—on the score of her ignorance of the contents; and did not forget to place her disinterestedness, in the refusal of Fielder's ten guineas, prominently before him. She, moreover, displayed the greatest earnestness in her endeavours to promote the views of Dick in obtaining the papers: and lastly, laid open to him the fact of Mr. Sheepshanks' visit of the day before; though, of course, knowing no better, she represented him as the messenger of Sir Albert. The large sum, however; the anxiety she described him as having displayed; and the arrangement by which she was to guide him after dark, on that very evening, to the house of the Jew; seemed to him so unlike the proceedings of a respectable professional man—and such he felt assured Sir Albert would employ—that Dick began more than to suspect all was not as it should be. He therefore questioned Madge closely as to the personal appearance, manner, and dress of her generous visitor; all which Madge faithfully described. Turpin looked significantly at Fielder as Madge concluded a somewhat caricature portrait of the man of law.

No. 23.

"Sheepshanks for a thousand!" exclaimed Fielder. Turpin laughed.

"I should think it asked no conjuror to guess that," said he: "why, George, we're in luck's way again; poor latitat will think we deal with his master—the old gentleman below—ha! ha!"

More wine was called for; Madge warmed into exuberant spirits; and Dick, who was no stoic, after declaring he never thought her half so handsome, bestowed on her a hearty kiss, to which it may be supposed the lady offered small objection.

"And now, my dear, if you'll accept my arm," said he, "we'll see you as far as the rendezvous. You shall have your other fifty; the right owners shall take the documents from the false knaves;" and here—truth compels us to declare it, despite the constancy and all that sort of thing which young ladies dream about—Turpin repeated a stronger and closer kiss, improved by the addition of one arm round the waist of the half-resisting Madge; "and you," added he, "shan't be forgotten."

Madge saw herself at the goal of her manœuvres; and composing her head-gear, with smiling face led the way from the house. They chatted merrily until they had completed half the distance to the appointed place of meeting; when Madge, having described the house, where Sir Litton and Sheepshanks were already waiting, left them to follow her footsteps in such a way as not to excite suspicion.

Two men, enveloped in riding cloaks, joined her; she led them through narrow entries and dark lanes to the street where Mr. Solomons dwelt; and having pointed out his residence, which was a low-fronted old clothes shop, she, at their desire, waited at a distance. They were no sooner admitted than Dick and Fielder joined her: it was, however, indispensable that they should obtain possession of the documents; and Madge was also to get her promised fifty, before anything could be done. A considerable time had elapsed, and the parties were growing rather impatient, when three men passed them in the direction of Solomons' dwelling.

"That's Ferret," said Madge in a whisper to Turpin; "and the other's Bill Johnson; what can they be at?" She trembled as she thought of what she had communicated to the officer; and feared, not without cause, the destruction of her hopes. "Who can the other taller man be?" added she.

"I think I know him," answered Dick; "but wait here an instant; I'll walk before him, and get a look at his face." He hurried forward a few paces, and crossing their path diagonally, entered a doorway; the party passed him, crossed the road, and, after conversing in a low tone for a minute or so, the taller man rapped, left them, and entered the passage of Solomons' house. Dick returned to Madge.

"It's Sir Albert Denistoun, as I live!" exclaimed Turpin; "what can all this mean?"

We will now turn to what was going on within. At a baize-covered table in the first-floor room—for this affair was too important to be transacted in the little back-parlour—sat Mr. Abrams, Mr. Solomons, Mr. Sheepshanks, and Sir Litton—the latter disguised with false whiskers and a wig. A quantity of cash lay upon the table; and Sir Litton, having obtained possession of the documents, was again examining their genuineness with eager eyes, when a footstep was heard on the crazy staircase, and a smart rap with the knuckle on the room-door followed. The whole party started; Mr. Abram's red-purple countenance changed to a livid blue, Mr. Sheepshanks' parchment skin to still uglier yellow, and the blood rushed from the cheeks of Mr. Solomons as rapidly as it flew to the forehead of Sir Litton. Mr. Abrams, however, with great presence of mind, scraped the cash, with the dexterity of a gaminghouse croupier, on to a cloth hastily placed in the table-drawer, and immediately closed it; while Sir Litton deposited the parchments under his ample cloak.

"Let them in, whoever they are," said Sir Litton; and Solomons, turning the key in the lock, a tall man of commanding figure entered.

"Let no one stir!" said the stranger authoritatively.

Sir Litton looked at him with a scowl of desperation—it was his brother-in-law! He could not know him in his present disguise—should he make a dash for it? and, without calculating consequences, the Baronet made towards the door. Sir Albert placed his sword across, to bar his exit. Sir Litton saw the emergency; he dared not speak lest his voice might betray him: he drew his weapon, and suddenly striking down the barrier, sprung towards the landing. He was not so quick, however, but that Sir Albert, by a smart blow with the flat of the sword on his face, drove him back: the indignity maddened him. At this instant Mr. Sheepshanks, who of course knew both parties, uttering a scream of terror, and extinguishing the lamp by dashing it on the ground, sought refuge beneath the table. Sir Litton profited by the darkness: he made a desperate lunge, and Sir Albert fell, crying—

"Officers, below there, look out! the villains are escaping."

The sound, however, had scarcely reached their ears, when Mr. Ferret, who was ascending the stairs from the passage, where he had been keeping watch, received such a tremendous blow on the mouth, from the hilt of a sword, as sent his heavy carcase with dread momentum down the stairs—jamming, with crushing effect, the unlucky Mr. Johnson, who was close behind, in an angle of the narrow staircase. The unseen aggressor bounded past them; a spluttering cry from Ferret, who with a mouthful of loose teeth and blood was not very distinct in his delivery—and a bursting groan, which was driven out of Johnson by the concussion, were all that Sir Litton heard, as he bounded with one leap into the narrow passage, and rushed forth into the street. The clash of swords, the cry of Octavius, and the smash of the lamp, coupled with the knowledge Dick possessed of who was within, led Fielder and himself towards the door at the instant that Sir Litton, sword in hand, rushed forth.

"What ho!" cried Dick; "stop!"

Sir Litton looked a moment at his audacious opponent. It was but a moment: he had fleshed his sword; and, like the tiger who has tasted blood, he struck at Dick with mad fury. Turpin gave way for a moment; and Sir Litton slightly galled his sword-arm; then, despising pass or ward, rushed at him. Dick gave point; his incautious assailant threw himself on the keen steel, struck at him ineffectually while it was yet sheathed in his body, and fell mortally wounded at his feet.

"'Twas his own fault, whoever he is," said Dick, looking at the prostrate stranger, for there was no lamp within many yards of the spot.

Sir Litton groaned.

"Bring me some water," said the dying man faintly; "do not let me die here; convey me somewhere from the street. Richard Palmer—you are avenged."

Turpin started at this address. Madge had now advanced into the road-

way.   So silently had the rencontre come off, and so deserted and un-
watched was the street at that hour, that the two men carried the Baronet
into the entry of Solomons' house unobserved, save by a single passenger,
whose curiosity was satisfied by Madge, who readily replied, to his enquiry of
" What's the matter ?" by saying that " the gentleman was drunk."

Mrs. Solomons now came down, with a face of terror and a long six, to enquire, in like manner, into the cause of the disturbance; but did not get quite
so commonplace an answer.   She first came upon Sir Albert, who, leaning on
one arm, held in his hand a handkerchief, saturated with blood; vainly endeavouring to staunch the blood flowing from a deep wound in his thigh.   After a
feminine squeak or two, and once dropping the candlestick, Mrs. Solomons, the
two discomfited officers, Dick, and Fielder, formed a consulting circle around Sir
Albert; while an outer one was made by a whole tribe of little Solomons, who in
yellow-white nightgowns, stared, with their large black Hebrew eyes preternaturally dilated, on the bloody stains and fine clothes of the prostrate gentleman.
Meantime Mr. Abrams, who had secured the cloth containing the cash, had most
judiciously beat a retreat in the confusion; and not caring to face the dangers
which might beset him below stairs, he stealthily sneaked up; where, having
with some difficulty, squeezed his fat carcase through a trapdoor, he was now
enjoying a cool meditation on the adventure, in a gutter on the house-top.
Turpin was the first to speak.

" Let a surgeon be sent for," said he to the staring and terrified Solomons.

At this moment Mr. Sheepshanks, recognising Dick's voice, foolishly attempted to skulk by and pass down stairs.

" Halloo, my lucky little lawyer," cried Fielder; " you musn't come this
way."   Sheepshanks sneaked back into the room.

Mr. Solomons' tongue clave to the roof of his mouth as he gazed on the
four armed men: he gave himself up for lost; and mentally invoking
all the patriarchs of his religion, he repented of his sins, stedfastly purposing
amendment.   A lively vision of Jonathan Wild's last kick, and that ugly square
erection where so many of his clients had been suspended, floated before his
mind's eye.   He eyed Turpin with a stupified stare, as the latter threw off his
coat, and seizing his shirt, which was of strong linen, by the shoulder, tore·
away the left sleeve; then kneeling beside the prostrate baronet, passed the
fragment tightly round his thigh—thereby preventing the effusion of blood,
under which he was fast sinking.   Sir Albert recognised him, and thanked
him for his attention with a surprised look.

" Sir Litton Weston lies dead below," said Turpin, as, kneeling, he
pressed his hand on Sir Albert's wound; " and it was he, doubtless, who
has done this."

" No! no!" faintly replied Sir Albert; " 'twas not he; I saw the villain
who stabbed me, sword in hand, the moment previous to the extinguishment
of the lamp; and 'twas not my brother-in-law.   Base as he is, he would not
strike but in fair fight."

Turpin shook his head, and Sir Albert, smarting with vexation and pride,
added—

" You doubt me ? the blood of the Westons with which I am allied, is not
so degenerate,—Sir Litton's fame is identified with—"

The flush of anger rose on Turpin's cheek; for the high military pride of
the aristocratic Sir Albert was, even in his then disabled position, getting
the better of his judgment.

" May I beg you not to irritate yourself on your present dangerous state, said Dick, checking himself; " though not of the high blood of the Westons, as you term it, I receive not the lie. George, know you the corpse that is below."

" So sure as it's dead, so sure it was once Sir Litton Weston," replied Fielder.

Sir Albert seemed sorely perplexed; he was silent for a few seconds, then added—

" I see but one way to avoid the exposure which this unfortunate affair must bring with it; and Mr. a-a-(Sir Albert hesitated to pronounce the name of Turpin) Mr. Palmer I mean—may I rely on your honour, and that of your friend, to prevent this disgrace to the name of my wife's race—now first dishonoured in the person of the man who has paid the forfeit of honour with his life—from becoming public talk ? (Dick assented by an inclination of the head ; and the wounded man continued) Let me be conveyed to my house ; Ferret, go call my carriage, which waits in Bishopsgate."

The surgeon was consulted ; and upon discovering the rank of the sufferer, and being made acquainted with the unhappy circumstances of the affair, he agreed with Sir Albert in the expediency of concealment ; accordingly, on the arrival of the coach, the body of the luckless Sir Litton was secretly deposited therein ; and the wounded baronet having been placed on the seat, the wondering coachman drove off with all practicable speed for his master's mansion.

The severe wound of Sir Albert, and the confusion consequent on such a scene, had diverted the attention of the parties from the origin of all these mischances. The rattle of the carriage, had scarcely died on the ear, when Turpin drew from his pocket the fatal parchments.

All this while Mr. Ferret and his men had kept a sharp eye on Solomons and Sheepshanks.

" Here are the papers," said our hero, looking upon the packet, which was saturated with the blood of its late unfortunate possessor ; " here are the papers which have caused so much bloodshed. He was a desperate—"

" Sorry to hinterrupt sich a moving discourse," said old Ferret, with a quiet grin of his damaged mouth, for the blow had spoiled his usual good temper ; " sorry to hinterrupt—but ven you're done I'll take them ere in custody along vith these two gemmen here ; as I'm thinking as I may have to produce all three on 'em—I means the parcel, the lawyer, and the Jew—at the sessions, d'ye see ?"

It was in vain that Dick urged the exposure which must take place, Ferret was inexorable. His mouth, too, prevented much argument, and his replies were ill-tempered in proportion to their shortness. He therefore handcuffed the pair, took possession of the parchments, and, having procured a coach, carried off his prisoners. Turpin, Fielder, and Madge, took their way towards Bow in silence, for the recent events were too extraordinary for street converse ; and in half an hour from Sir Albert's departure, the house of Solomons was as quiet as though no such scene of death, treachery, and blood, had ever frightened it from its propriety.

As for Mr. Ferret, having once taken the pair of culprits before a magistrate, where the influence of Sir Albert procured a private hearing, it became necessary to follow up the affair; and the purchase of the documents by Solomons, their felonious sale, with the subsequent transactions arising out of it being clearly

proveable, without making public the manner of the death of the Baronet,—
that circumstance was carefully suppressed. Sir Litton consequently rested
with his ancestors, as the baronet " who was killed in a duel." The prosecution
and collection of evidence were left entirely to the discretion of Ferret. Mr.
Abrams, as might be expected, *contrived to abscond for awhile;* but the worthy
and charitable Mr. Solomons, and the accessory lawyer, after being pilloried and
slit in the ear, were turned loose upon society, decidedly not improved, either
in character or respectability, by the discipline of " the law."

CHAPTER XVII.

Aurelia.—I'm plagued justly :
And she that makes a fool of her first love,
Let her ne'er look to prosper!—Sir——
   Andrugio.—O falsehood, thy name is—woman.
   Aur.—Have you forgiveness in you? There's more hope of me
Than in a maid who never yet offended.
   Andr.—What! make me your property!
   Aur.—I'll promise you
I'll never make you worse: and sir, you know
There are worse things for women to make men·
But by my hope (and sure that hope is lawful)
I'll be as true for ever to thy side
As she in thought and deed that never erred.
   Andr.—I'll once believe a woman ; be it but to strengthen
Weak faith in other men ; I have a love
Doth cover all thy faults.

     More Dissemblers besides Women. By Thos. Middleton. circa 1603.

Welcome, comrade, to our ring,
  Make rhymes, we'll give thee reason ;
" Canary" bees thy brain shall sting,
  Mull-sack did ne'er speak treason.
" Peter-see-me" shall wash thy nowl,
  And " Malligo" glasses fox ye;
And if thou toss not bowl for bowl,
  Thou'lt ne'er deserve a doxy.

     The Spanish Gipsy. By Middleton and Rowley. Act iii. sc. i.

THE autumnal wind howled mournfully across the bleak common, and sighed
in the forest glades as it whirled the shrivelled and discoloured leaves in
rustling eddies around the stems of the forest giants, now wellnigh stipped
of their summer livery. The night was cold, dreary, and cheerless ; leaden-
coloured masses of dense clouds hung their pall before the obscured moon ;
and spits of intermittent rain added a chillness to the moisture-laden air, more
searching and depressing than the colder temperature of actual winter. But
though such was the night without, the snug party to whom we will now
introduce the reader, felt none of its discomfort.
. In a small arched cavern sat three men ; the apartment was low, and in its
shape resembled the cellars of the innumerable modern streets, which within
these few years have stretched their ramifications, like the arms of some giant
tree, in every direction around our great metropolis. Yet though small, and
certainly not boasting any architectural attractions, it was not without its
creature comforts—and something more. The sides and roof, for it would
have been difficult to define the line of distinction between them, were curiously decorated. Here hung a horseman's coat, and there a "dreadnought"

cap, or south-wester; beside a pair of jockey-boots and bright spurs dangled a prime small ham of the true Westmoreland shape and complexion; while bridles, dried tongues and Bolognas, a carbine resting on two hooks, whips, some kipper salmon, and a German pipe, completed the medley ornaments, or utilities, on the walls. In one corner stood a huge demi-john in its basket covering; and this larger receptacle was flanked and surrounded by several minor bottles, pitchers, and flasks, which spoke mutely eloquent of the care that had been used for the liquid as well as solid comforts of the occupants of the retreat.

In a recess, hollowed out at the upper end of the chamber, glowed an iron grating, whereon blazed merrily a bright wood fire. Before it stood a woman, who was busily engaged in superintending the culinary operations, while a savoury steam rose from a kettle, suspended in the stream of flame; before the grate, amid the wood ashes raked upon the stone slab, lay roasting a goodly company of the tubers which old Cobbett anathematized as the "accursed root." The female turned, with glowing face and a pleasant smile, to the three men seated at the rudely formed table; and disclosed—the features of Madge Dutton! Crime, (which is misery,) " acquaints us with strange bedfellows;" Madge was now directress of the bed and board arrangements of our hero. In a word, circumstances had installed her in all the privileges of Mrs. T., though without the rite ecclesiastical. And here we will pause to reflect on "world thy slippery turns." So little yet is man advanced in that knowledge, which the old Greek told him some two thousand years ago was the summit of wisdom,—the "knowledge of himself,"—that we are justified in doubting whether the pratings of sciolists and the cobweb-weaving of metaphysicians, be anything more than a game of intellectual pushpin; the fancy toys of children of "larger growth." "The child is father to the man," says Wordsworth, and upon this Irish principle it is possible for a man to be his own grandfather, and none the wiser for it. But, jesting apart, there is something inconceivably absurd in the way in which thousands of writers of works of fiction go on systematizing; dividing personages of history or of romance into (positively not relatively) *good* and *bad*. Nor is this violation of truth and nature confined to authors; reviewers, too, under pain of their critical condemnation, will admit no action into the life of any character, but such as comports with this imaginary consistency. The result has been a deplorable and pervading misconception, not only of *ourselves*, as painted in fiction or the drama, but of *others*. Mixed beings act mixedly, from mixed motives; and the microcosm is no more constant in its sunshine or cloud—no more ever smooth, or ever ruffled—no more uniform in construction or persistent in destruction—than the great world around us. Our limited comprehensions forbid us from appreciating the *good* of *evil*. Yet that *that* exists, and must have had an origin, we all see; and the same being whose inimitable wisdom has formed antagonist elements in the material world, has shown his power, and, doubtless, his wisdom, in the world of mind. Yet to his omniscience and perfect judgment—which has formed us mixed creatures, in whom now passion now reason holds alternate sway—bat-eyed man would prescribe laws to suit his own purblind views of right and wrong; would carve monsters of consistency from a mass of contradictions. But we must quit this theme; and, having given the hint, leave the reader to follow out the argument here faintly and incidentally advanced.

The very woman of whose treacheries we have been the chroniclers;

was, it would seem, under such circumstances as should call forth its exercise, capable of devoted attachment; and now, though linked with a highwayman, and surrounded by men who owned no moral restraint, was faithful, incorruptible, and constant in the performance of that part for which woman was formed—the comforter and the companion of man. In fact—alas for consistency, and constancy!—in the few wreks succeeding the occurrences related in our last chapter, the indifference of our hero had warmed into respect; respect into esteem; and esteem had given place,—

> " Even as one fire doth drive out another—"

to warm affection.

"Now," cried Madge, in a cheerful tone—while her flushed cheek, glistening eye, and bright smile might have recalled, (though robbed of the freshness of youth and purity,) a remembrance of the Margaret Dutton who had once been the pride

> " Of all the gay lasses that danced on the green—"

" now, Richard, all's ready: come, bustle, Georgy, you're in the way! There, that'll do." Thus saying, she hastily cleared the board of its bottles and horns, replacing them by a coarse but white cloth; bread, smoking meat, and well roasted potatoes followed, flanked by several savoury grills, on turned trenchers or bright pewter. Beer of the best, in brown stone jugs; for as yet Wedgwood had not framed the convenient and cleanly queen's ware, which adds elegance and comfort to the modern table, completed the substantial fare.

Madge seated herself, and for the next ten minutes little was heard, save the rattle of knives and forks, or an occasional word, as one pledged another of the party in " brown October." Supper dispatched, the kettle was placed on the fire; rummers took place of the drinking horns; pipes were filled; and a new disposition of the company took place. Placed in a semicircle around the hearth, of which the upper centre was occupied by the end of the table before mentioned, the company set themselves in for an evening's enjoyment.

" What say you to a song, Dick?" asked King; "you ought to be inspired by the bright eyes I just now see turned so affectionately on you. I can't unriddle it for the life o' me; but you're deuced lucky with the women.—I love 'em all alike, it's true, but that's in self defence, for they're such a fickle lot, that they now and then return the compliment, and like all others as well as me, when I'm out of sight. But it won't do to philosophize about the ladies; they're not fit subjects for anything, but unfortunate victimized men to adore, and not question—eh! What think you, Mrs. Margaret?"

The flight of Dick was somewhat too high for Madge; she had, however, been so long in the practice of answering speeches without understanding them, that she replied at hazard by assenting to Tom's remark; then added—
" I should like, of all things, Tom, to hear your song, I've been told that you sing delightfully all ' Polly's '* new songs; do favour us!"

Tom laughed, raised the glass to his lips, put it down, and sung the following, to a then fashionable air :—

---

* Miss Fenton, before mentioned.

Death of Sir Litton Weston.

FAIR IRIS I LOVE.*

Fair I-ris I love and hour-ly I die, But not for a

lip . . nor a lan-guish-ing eye; She's fic-kle and false, and

* The author does not think any apology necessary for presenting these specimens of the song-writing of our ancestors: they are all antecedent to the time of Turpin. The writer of this first, which was long popular, was the great Dryden, of whom it is superfluous to say more than the name; the music is from his masque of Alexander and Amphytrion. The others are respectively from the pens of Matthew Concanen, of the time of Queen Anne, and James Bulteel, who published a poetical miscellany, in the reign of Charles II.; for the airs to which they were sung, the author is indebted to the rare and curious supplementary volume to Ritson's Old English Songs. London, 8vo. 1783.

No. 24.

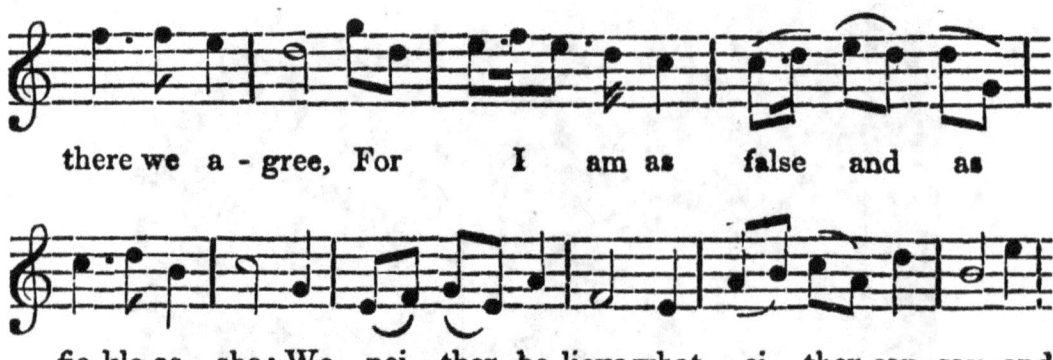

there we a - gree, For I am as false and as
fic-kle as she; We nei - ther be-lieve what ei - ther can say, and

nei - ther be - liev - ing we nei-ther be - tray·

II

'Tis civil to swear, and say things of course ;
We mean not the taking for better for worse ;
When present we love—when absent agree—
I think not of Iris, nor Iris of me:
The legend of love no couple can find,
So easy to part or so equally join'd.

"Bravo! bravo!" exclaimed Fielder ; "but we must hear mistress Margaret : it's cursedly out of order this, to leave the ladies behind."

Madge declined with an affected simper, and King interposed.

"I believe it's my *call*," said he; "and if the lady (and he gallantly bowed) will condescend so far as to favour the com—"

Madge's politeness was of a very questionable colour, for she interrupted him with—

"Oh, la! Mr. Tom, you flatter me, I'm sure ; I never, in my whole life," &c. &c., though we may observe, *par parenthese*, that she was not a little proud of her vocal abilities. Her inward mortification was therefore great, when the blunt George Fielder thus broke in :—

"Well, when I'm called on, nobody can say I keep the company waiting ; it's all very natural though, for females ; they think you don't want them unless you press them. I'll volunteer—so here goes :" and off he did go, in an old rambling ballad, making up for some defects in time by a clear and powerful voice.

THE GOSSIPS.*

Two gos-sips they mer - ri - ly met, at nine in the morning full

* This ballad may be taken as a *prima facie* contradiction of those who attribute a twinbirth to tea and scandal ; our grandams could destroy reputations over canary, to the full as goodnaturedly as their descendants.

soon ; And they were re-solv'd for a   whet, To   keep their sweet

voi-ces in   tune ;   a - way to the ta-vern they   went ; Here,

Joan, I do vow and pro   -   test, That   I   have a crown yet un-

spent ;   Come, let's have a   cup of the   best.

" And I have another, perhaps,
    A piece of the very same sort ;
Why should we sit thrumming of caps—
    Come, drawer, and fill us a quart !
And let it be liquor of life—
    Canary, right sparkling wine !
For I am a buxom young wife,
    And I love to go gallant and fine."

The drawer, as blithe as a bird,
    Came skipping, with cap in his hand—
" Dear ladies I give you my word,
    The best shall be at your command."
A quart of canary he drew,
    Joan filled up a glass and begun—
" Here, gossip's a bumper to you ;"
    " I'll pledge you, girl, was it a tun."

",And pray, gossip, didn't you hear,
    The common report of the town ?
A squire o' five hundred a-year
    Is married to Doll of the Crown."
" That draggle-tailed slut ! on my word,
    With her clothes hanging ragged and
        foul ;
In troth he would fain have a bird,
    That would give a good groat for an owl."

" Well, she had a sister last year,
    Whose name they called Gallopping Peg,
She'd take up a straw with her ear—"
    " I'll warrant her, right as my leg !"

" A brewer he's got her with child—
    But e'en let them brew as they bake ;
She always was wanton and wild—
    But I never meddle nor make."

" Nor I, gossip Joan, by my troth ;
    Though, nevertheless, I've been told,
She stole seven yards of broadcloth,
    A ring, and a locket of gold ;
A smock, and a new pair of shoes ;
    A flourishing madam was she :—
'Twas Margery told me the news,
    But it ne'er shall go further from me."

" We were at a gossipping club,
    Where we had a chirruping cup
Of good humming liquor, strong bub—
    And your husband's name there it was
        up,
For bearing a powerful sway—
    All the neighbours his valour have seen,
For he is a cuckold they say—
    A constable—gossip, I mean.

" Dear dame, 'twas a slip of the tongue,
    No harm was intended in mind ;
Chance words they will mingle among
    Our others, we commonly find :—
I hope you won't take it amiss."
    " Sure no, that were folly in us ;
For if we sometimes get a kiss,
    Pray what are our husbands the worse ?"

"And now, my Madge," said Dick with a smile, as the jingling of the glasses following Fielder's merriment subsided; "I often hear you humming snatches of songs; you *can* sing I'm sure."

Madge hesitated, cleared her throat, requested them to excuse her if she should fail, and then, in a rustic style, sang the following:

THE COUNTRY WEDDING.

Well met, pret - ty nymph, says a jol - ly young swain, To a

beau- ti-ful shep-herd-ess   cross - ing the plain ; Why   so much

in haste, (now the month it was May,) Shall I   ven-ture to   ask

you, fair mai-den, which way ? shall I   ven-ture to   ask you, fair

mai - den, which way ? Then straight to this question the nymph did

re-ply, With a smile in her look and a   leer   in her eye, I am

come from the village, and homeward I go ;   And now, gentle shep-

herd, pray   why would you know ?

II

I hope, pretty maid, you won't take it amiss
If I tell you the reason of asking you this;
I would see you safe home, (the swain was
    in love,)
Of such a companion, if you will approve.
"Your offer, kind shepherd, is civil, I own,
But I see no great danger in going alone;
Nor yet can I hinder, the road being free
For you as another, for you as for me."

III

"No danger in going alone, it is true,
But yet a companion is pleasanter, too;
And if you could like (now the swain he
    took heart)
Such a sweetheart as me, we never should
    part."
"O! that's a long word," said the shep-
herdess, then—
"I've often heard say there's no minding
    you men:

You'll say and unsay, and you'll flatter, 'tis
    true,
Then leave a young maiden the first thing
    you do."

IV

"O judge not so harshly," the shepherd
    replied;
To prove what I say, I will make you my
    bride;
To morrow the parson—(well said, little
    swain)—
Shall join both our hands, and make one
    of us twain."
Then what the nymph answered to this,
    is not said,
But the very next morn be sure they were
    wed.
Sing hey diddle, ho diddle, hey diddle
    down,
We ne'er see such courtship and wedding
    in town.

"That's all," exclaimed Madge, laughing, as she finished her ditty; "and now Dick, dear, we're all attention:" and she playfully pulled him by the sleeve.

Dick's manner, however, had of late much changed; he was occasionally absent, and during the singing of the last song, puerile though he considered it, a melancholy stole over his face, and a sternness, that was almost morose, settled upon his features. He shook it off, and forced a smile, as if ashamed of his absence of mind—then seizing the goblet, drank deeply and eagerly; a custom to which he had only lately addicted himself, for hitherto he had been remarkable among his companions for abstemiousness.

"Why, friend Dick," exclaimed King, "your thoughts seemed gone on a voyage of discovery, just now."

Turpin smiled again, drank again, and said—

"Well, don't say I spoil harmony. I suppose it's my turn for a song—eh, Madge?" and he pinched her cheek sportively; "well, I'll not keep you waiting;" and in a fine bass he began:—

HAD NEPTUNE WHEN FIRST.

Had Nep-tune when first he took charge of   the   sea, Been as

wise,   or   at   least been as   mer - ry   as   we, He'd ha'

thought bet-ter on't, and in - stead of his brine, would have

filled the vast o-cean with gen-e- rous wi . . . . . .

. . . . ne, Have fill'd the vast o - cean with

gen - er - ous wine.

What trafficking then would have been on the main,
For the sake of good liquor as well as for gain !
No fear then of tempests, nor dread e'en of sinking—
The fishes ne'er drown that are always a drinking.

The hot thirsty sun then would drive with more haste,
Secure in the evening of such a repast ;
And when he'd got tipsy would have taken his nap,
With double the pleasure, in Thetis's lap.

By the force of his rays, thus heated with wine,
Consider how gloriously Phœbus would shine ;
What vast exhalations he'd draw upon high,
To relieve the poor earth, as it wanted supply.

How happy us mortals when bless'd with such rain,
To fill all our vessels, and fill them again !
Nay, even the beggar, who has ne'er a dish,
Might jump in the river and drink like a fish.

The stars, which I think don't to drinking incline,
Would frisk and rejoice at the fumes of the wine ;
And, merrily twinkling, would soon let us know,
That they were as happy as mortals below.

Had this been the case, what had we then enjoyed !
Our spirits still rising, our fancy ne'er cloy'd !
A plague then, on Neptune, when 'twas in his power,
To slip, like a fool, such a fortunate hour.

"- "Foregad !" exclaimed King ; " I didn't suspect you'd such a voice for a Bacchanalian, Dick.   Here's to you—a toast ! a toast !"

"I've finished the round of songs, I believe," said Turpin ; " yet I'd begin it again with you, but I have just thought of a neglected piece of business. I will ride this morning, before the people are stirring, into London, and leave some documents, I still possess, in the hands of Sir Albert. Though their value has become nothing, as Lady Denistoun is now the heiress of Weston in her

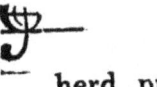

herd pi

own right, yet as business is best done whilst thought on, I'll e'en at once to saddle."

"Then take my bay, Dickon," said King; "Bess is a remarkable animal, and may be observed, for it will be day before you return—be advised."

Dick assented: the bay was soon saddled; and taking the parchments from a small portmanteau, he mounted and rode forth.

The first grey gleam of dawn streaked the east, and the face of nature shewed tokens of the fury of overnight's storm, in the bright patches on the dark bark of some of the largest trees, which marked places where mighty limbs had been tore from them by the wrathful blast. The boughs were laden with moisture, and the surperfluous water which hung in gem like drops on every blade of grass, soaked through the traveller who attempted to make his way through field or copse, with a searching celerity exceeding the heaviest rain. Dick looked at the quarter where the sun gave promise of soon appearing. The twinkling stars still shimmered in the wide and clear expanse of sky—there was a mild freshness in the air, and the rosy east grew minute by minute more warm and cheering in its colours—every omen spoke to the weatherwise in promise of a fine day. Our hero mounted and was soon on his road from King's Oak.

But if merriment was the order of the night, at the highwayman's retreat, theirs was not the only party which kept it up,

> "Till morn in russet mantle clad,
> Walk'd o'er the dew of the high eastern hills."

The dining parlour at Squire, or as he was more generally termed, Justice Asher's, was the scene of revelry not less hearty, and to the full as coarse, as that of our outlawed hero and his associates. The guests consisted chiefly of "sporting" characters. There was the wealthy landholder, the red-nosed, three-bottle descendant of a long line of Shallows who, like Shakspeare's deathless justice, had written "armigero" to their name any time these hundred years; there too were the owner of the neighbouring pack of hounds and the rosy incumbent of Boozle, who was also the vicar of Soakingham, of which his worship held the presentation. As the younger son of an influential family, Mr. Tithe 'em had been bred to the clerical profession; he was a staunch member of the "state church," an excellent fourth at "a rubber of long whist," a very Ajax at backgammon, "old dog at theology," and

> "——As thirsty a soul,
> As e'er tossed off tankard, or fathom'd a bowl;"

yet his punctuality in the execution of his pastoral functions halted lamely if compared with the exactness and promptitude of his attendance and delivery of grace at a patron's dinner, from which he was of course never absent. With such qualifications for the ministry can his success be wondered at? The party—at least such of them as gout, hard drinking, or the infirmities of age had not prevented from joining the sport—had had a "glorious" run that day; and it had taken I don't know how many dozen of port to do justice to the exploits of some forty men, who had, with horses, horns, and dogs, run down a single, unresisting animal; nay, each of them felt how incumbent it was on the achievers of such heroic deeds to drink hard, that each might be able to speak in terms sufficiently glowing of his own bravery; conscious that without such maddening stimulants as should shake reason on her throne, no sane man could listen to, nor rational being narrate, such unblushing exaggeration and distortion of mere acts of folly into feats of superhuman gallantry and heroic daring.

The hours rolled on, and the company rolled off—their chairs we mean. The parson had fallen into a prosy disputation with a plethoric powdered old gentleman with a purple face, who sat next him, sleeping with his dull gooseberry eyes wide open, staring directly in the face of the divine; the obfuscation of that reverend personage's faculties leading him to interpret an occasional snort of the uneasy apopletic slumberer as a grunt of assent to some major or minor of his learned and logical propositions. Other groups surrounded the board. Mighty men, the terror of poachers, ale-bibbers, and itinerant scrapers of catgut—men intolerant of wakes, fairs, foot-races, and fiddlings; and all of whom could assume the severity of a Cato the censor, and turn up their eyes in abomination at the enormities of Hodge or Roger, when Sir John Barleycorn led these vulgar offenders into some temporary indiscretion. Some of these "custolorums" were sleeping, others prosing, some boasting, while here and there an overturned chair told of the departed, who slept the sleep of drunkenness beneath the mahogany, the face of which, covered with apple-parings, walnut-shells, broken glass, knives, dessert plates, decanters, upset olives, and filthy slops, told the good deeds of those who reposed beneath "in mere obliviousness." These prostrate drunkards lay nowhere so thick as in the neighbourhood of the reverend priest, whose cloth had procured him the honour of the right hand of the now vacated chair. Among these somnolent wine-bibbers was one who yet retained his perpendicular; he was a military man, and had evidently followed Bacchus to the last charge, for "strong wine had slain him," and now—with the last glass of claret spilt before him, and the fragments of its broken receptacle scattered in the ruby stream, his head reclined on his breast, and a helmet of paper stuck on his head by some freakish companion—the "gallant officer" lay,

> Like some warrior taking a snooze,
> With the foes he had slain around him.

But we will turn from the upper end of the "justice's" table to the lower; near this end sat a group of talkers; the one, a middle aged man, was Mr. Major, well known on the turf as the owner of Whitestockings, and several other celebrated racers; he was evidently much more sober than either of his companions, who were young men, attired in bright scarlet coats, with broad skirts, buckskins, and short riding boots, the very pink of hunting costume of the period:—

"I'll tell'ee what, Major, old boy," said one, a thick, podgy, homebred specimen of two-fisted squirearchy; an unlicked cub, who might have sat for Goldsmith's Tony Lumpkin, in every point but dress:—"I'll tell'ee what, if Grey Grizzel carn't clear double dyke and rail wi' onything in your stable, I'll eat her—done for fifty as I'll jump her 'cross Dainsbury's dyke, and that's a good thirty foot i' the clear, now, if ye like—I've done it back again and over to-day—say the word and it's done for fifty!"

The elder man smiled; he knew that Grey Grizzel was at that time unable to wag a foot from the day's hard riding; he was, however, about to reply when the third took up the argument.

Turpin shoots Whitestockings and robs Mr. Major.

"You're thundering nutty," exclaimed the legisletor *in posse*, "on that Grizzel o' your's, master Bobby, but you should ha' seen my Rusty take the ditch and quickset at Westerham ; last Wensday three weeks, that was—he's a horse if you like."

"Your Rusty ! ha ! ha !" ejaculated the individual addressed as Bobby, with a laugh of derision, "your Rusty leap—I like that—ha ! ha !—h—" The laugh was suddenly checked, for the owner of Rusty, to use a vulgar phrase, suddenly "rode *rusty*," and dealing the disparager a blow on the face, over he went, chair and all. His blood was up, however, though his body was down, yet such was his state of intoxication, that he was only able to bring himself to his knees, the lower part of his *understanding*, like his *upper* one, having lost its functions. In this pious posture he placed his fists in a boxing attitude, and spluttered a defiance at his aggressor, who, equally drunk, reeled towards him with half clenched fists, and both the "scions of a noble race" went rolling on the floor together. Mr. Major rose from his seat, and separated them, as they lay swearing, scrambling and tearing each others clothes : and having succeeded in his friendly interposition, he left the two helpless champions of their nobler brutes, and walked to the upper end of the apartment. The chair, as we have before said, was empty, for Squire Asher had retired some two hours since to his chamber ; but had left his guests, as was the mode, to enjoy, *i. e.* brutalize, themselves unrestrainedly.

"Dr. Tithe'em," said Major, to the parson, who still sat mumbling some unintelligible gibberish, and sipping his port. Dr. Tithe'em however, was too much

No. 25.

absorbed in his theological mystification with the snoring Oxonian (for the sleepy little gentleman in the cauliflower wig, had been his fellow-commoner at the University,) to hear the address. The speaker opened the shutters and admitted a flood of light on the edifying scene : this seemed to startle his reverence ; and Major continued :—

"Dr. Tithe'em, I shall not stay here to-night—so, if you wish for company on your ride, as I see the morning is clear and fine, I'm the man to see you to the rectory." This proposition, however, by no means squared with the worthy doctor's notions of decorum—for Dr. Tithe'em never forgot what was due to public appearances ; he thought, though he did not say so, that it would be rather undignified and unclerical for the rector of Fleece'em, who was " a D.D., and, moreover, an A.S.S.," to be seen, at such an unseasonable hour, jogging home, cheek by jowl, with a notorious turfite and fox-hunter—no, no, the doctor knew too well what was due to his cloth thus to scandalise it. He, therefore, evasively declined the friendly offer, pleading that he feared taking cold ; then, drawing a huge, old, chased "Tompion" watch from his poke, he exclaimed :

"Bless me, Mr. Major, is that day-break I see yonder? Five o'clock !—dear me ! How *can* the time have flown—really I and Dr. Syllabus, here, have been involved in such an animated and interesting controversy—you know my dear Mr. Major, that Syllabus and I were contems at Brazennose—bless me ! why Syllabus is asleep—well, well—I'm quite ashamed of the hour —but when congenial spirits meet to enjoy

'The feast of reason, and the flow of soul,'

Mr. Major, eh ?—"

And thus twaddling on, the reverend divine staggered from the table, bearing a candlestick ; and calling, with a guttural grunt, for his servant, who was enjoying a snooze in the ante-chamber, he placed his hand upon his shoulder ; no doubt rather as a mark of confidence, than with any design of steadying his steps, and thus conducted, toddled off to the bed-room appointed for his use.

The guest looked round the now silent chamber. The snuffs of the expiring candles flickered, flared, or smoked offensively in the sockets of the chandelier, which hung over the centre of the table. He looked around— of the noisy gathering of a few hours since, none remained but the dead drunk or the sleeping ; and the whole scene bore striking testimony to the glories of what people who ought to know better, sing and celebrate as " old English hospitality." This was "worshipful company ;" these were the legislators, the teachers, the exemplars of society—the class who were scandalised at the idea of education—who feared the light, as well they might, which an advance in the social and moral condition of the masses must bring with it ; in short, these were the " fine old English gentlemen"—the " venerable Tories"—whom designing men would hold up to challenge respect and veneration for their posterity, as the descendants of the " old families."

"I'll start off," said the guest musingly ; "faugh ! the room smells filthily ; I think a ride would do me good this morning."

He walked out, called his servant, and communicated his intention of riding home.

"However," said he, "as the horse I rode to-day is in the stable here, and no doubt very stiff, you must see to him, Robert, and stay here till to night. Let Whitestockings be saddled—make haste."

" Ay, ay, sir," replied the man.

Whitestockings was saddled, and Mr. Major took his way along the avenue leading from the justice's mansion.

The "balmy breath of incense-breathing morn" commended itself wooingly to the fevered blood of the horseman; he slackened the pace of his steed as he reached the high road, and with open mouth inhaled the moist air, to cool his palate, dry and parched from even his moderate share in the night's debauch. The morn was lovely; it was one of those fine day-breaks which late Autumn shews, as if Summer, cooled in its fervour, still mildly disputed its cheering sway against the rigours of the approaching tyrant— Winter. The bright clear sun rose cheeringly, and blandly smiled on' the fresh-smelling earth, and the stirring air rustled with breezy freshness amid the partially-stripped boughs of those trees which earliest yield their leafy vesture to the winter's blast. Mr. Major rode leisurely on, with loosened rein. His steed was one which from its training and pursuits might be said to have but two paces---a walk and a gallop. We need not tell the sporting reader that the race horse of a century since, though not equal in speed to the " finer" bred animals of the modern turf, was an animal of far more bone, and lasting strength, than the present racer; hence, he was more readily convertible to the purposes of a hunter, and master of greater weight. In short, the old " King's plate " horse of the days of which we are writing, though unfit to compete for short distances with the higher bred nag of the present time, made up in bone and endurance what he lacked in blood and swiftness. The current of the rider's thoughts, which had rambled desultorily over the events of the preceding day and the talk of the night, suddenly, he hardly knew why, became fixed on arriving at a topic which had been agitated at the board he had just quitted. It was, the increasing danger of the roads, in the county of which many of the company were magistrates; the daring with which several recent robberies, particularly those of Mr. Bradele and his wife, near Loughton; that of Mr. Thomas Ashton, within sight of his own house, at Woodford; and several others, had been accomplished. The advisableness of a communication to the Secretary of State had been mooted, and a suggestion made of the expediency of an application for the aid of a troop of dragoons; then a not uncommon mode of patrolling the roads in the neighbourhood of London.*

Whilst thus musing, the regular sound of a horse at full speed rose on his ear; the rider was evidently going the same road; namely, that towards London.

" Here's company, at any rate," said he, " and pretty well mounted, if I may guess from the pace."

The horseman came up, and courteous salutations were exchanged.

" Fine morning, sir," observed Dick; for it was our hero. " Going far on this road?"

---

* From this employment of the army, the state of the highway and police may be imagined. Several instances of their being engaged to patrol the roads may be found incidentally in the Sketch of Turpin in the " Malefactor's Register," in the life of " Gentleman Harry," who was executed at Tyburn, 1754, London, 8vo., 1754; in the London Magazine, and in numerous contemporaneous tracts.

"Some four miles; nearly to Plaistow," replied Mr. Major. "Early out this morning; that's a pretty beast of yours."

Turpin replied merely by patting his horse's neck, and the conversation turned on indifferent topics. Nothing was further from Dick's mind than doing what he termed "business" with the gentleman whom he thus met at the very entrance of the small village of Laytonstone. They rode on amicably, and in reply to an enquiry on the part of Mr. Major, Dick informed him that his name was Cutler; that he resided at Ware, in Hertfordshire, but having occasion to call on a relation at Epping on his way to town on urgent business, he had slept there, on account of the unsafeness of the roads, and had started with the morning's dawn. The frank manner of Dick, and his manly bearing, prejudiced Mr. Major in his favour; yet being like most sporting men, not a little given to braggadocio, he could not forbear laughing at our hero's apprehensions.

"I never had the luck," said he, "to meet any of these fire-eating blades; yet, as the gentry hereabouts have requested me, I've put my signature to the requisition for the military. If I knew two or three whose staunchness I could rely on, damme, but I'd have a try to trap some of these knights of the road. There's Colonel Asher, the justice's brother; 'tis true he's a military man, but I don't value him a straw. The humbug, when I asked his opinion, prated as if he were about to open a campaign on the Rhine against King Louis, instead of nabbing some three or four scurvy desperadoes. No, no! he's no good. It's one Turpin (Dick turned his head to conceal a smile) they talk about most, and I've more than a guess that there's something in the notion that he's a lurking-place in the Forest here. I should like no better sport, if they'd let me have three or four of the troopers—though I suppose that would be contrary to military etiquette—than to unkennel them, with a hound or two."

"You may unkennel *one* of them without red-coat or hound," cried Dick, suddenly turning his horse against the shoulder of his antagonist's. "Deliver! and go home safely to tell your friends, the justices, that you met DICK TURPIN!"

Mr. Major reined back his horse, for the salute was so sudden that he hardly understood its import; there was, however, no mistaking the look and gesture of Dick. Mr. Major did not lack courage; he dashed aside the presented pistol with the butt of his riding-whip, struck spur into the flank of White-stockings, passed Dick at a single bound, and had cleared some three strides ere our hero could give chase. Turpin had not fired his pistol—indeed, so desirous was he not to do mischief, that its being upon half-cock alone secured it from discharge when struck aside by Mr. Major.

"Stop! surrender! or I'll fire!" exclaimed Dick.

Mr. Major, relying on the excellence of his horse, put still more ground between them.

"By G—!" muttered Dick between his teeth, "I'll be as good as my word; he's best mounted, but he shan't escape me!"

He raised his horseman's pistol to his eye, and took as deliberate aim as his position would permit. A bystander might easily have seen, however, that his practised hand was directed far below the level of the flying rider before him. Whitestockings shrunk momentarily, but on a hint from the armed heel of her rider, again "laid out." A trickling stream of sanguine colour showed itself down her broad buttock and muscular thigh, and threaded its way, in bright scarlet, down her fine white shank. Turpin eyed it with a smile. Still, nevertheless, though his horse was at its utmost, did the mare not only hold her own, but was fast running away from him : and what was worse, they were within a short mile of a clump of houses, and a road-side inn. Turpin drew his remaining pistol.

"Stop! I warn you!" exclaimed he in a determined tone.

The only reply the fugitive deigned to this summons was to place one hand behind him and discharge a pistol, without aim. Dick raised his weapon to a level with his shoulder ; but let it fall again, as if hesitating whether he should throw away his last shot.

"No, I'll not—he *must* escape—I'll chance it !"

Again was a low aim taken ; again the sharp crack echoed—the smoke curled along the air—two bounds upon three legs—a sob—an abortive attempt at a spring—and over fell Whitestockings, sending her rider rolling on the road before her. Dick rode up to Mr. Major---the bullet had taken effect in the hock, and the panting animal lay piteously eyeing her flanks. Mr. Major was on the ground slightly bruised, but by no means seriously hurt, and Dick, keeping an eye on him, quickly reloaded his pistols.

The prostrate gentleman had now recovered his feet, and was about, in his confusion, to make his way to his wounded horse ; this, however, Dick prevented, for he doubted not that another pistol remained in the holster.

"Another yard nearer, and I'll shoot you!" said he. The half stunned and smarting gentleman stared at him stupidly. "Come, quick, hand out---look alive ! Your watch I'll take first, that's handiest, besides mine don't *go* just now, but I'm sure *yours will*."

Mr. Major complied sulkily---he could not relish the jest ; and cast a look at his wounded horse.

"D——n," muttered he ; "I wouldn't mind my purse---but to lose my White-stockings---Fellow," said he, turning angrily to Turpin, (who with one hand extended, and the other presenting the muzzle of the "*little persuader*" at his head, sat waiting the delivery of the gold,) "you've done more mischief than you can mend---I'd gladly give five such purses as this to have saved her life."

"I've no time to argue," said Dick, looking warily along the road ; "tho' as we seem pretty much by ourselves, I'll tell you---that brooch in your shirt frill, if you please---that I'd the choice between you and your horse, and I seldom miss. Thank my forbearance it's no worse: Whitestockings or yourself---for you will observe I've hit her twice---I'll thank you for the studs from your ruffles and the clasp from your hat—*must* have fallen ; I took my choice, and wherever you mention this little affair, be sure to set against your regret for Whitestockings, the recollection that you owe your life to the forbearance of Dick Turpin."

So saying, our hero clapped spurs to his steed, and three quarters of an hour after he was riding through London on another horse, having changed his dress, and left his steed safe at the dwelling of a cousin of Tom King's, of the name of Street, who kept a livery stable in the neighbourhood of White-chapel.

CHAPTER XVIII.

Ferdinand. To prison with 'em both: what! call himself a gentleman, and play the ass! He's an impostor.

Leon. If all gentlemen that play the ass should to prison, you must widen your gaols. Have not your gentry leave to be fools in this land, that they must therefore be thus maltreated?

Soto. Alas, our comedy's turned tragical—the tables are turned, and we true men are become the laughing-stocks for the knaves.   —Shirley.

San. My lord, what part play I?
Fer. What part do'st use to play?
San. If you have ever a coxcomb, I think I could fit you.
Alo. And if you've ever a justice, I. For in the banquet scene I can guzzle, and talk big too a scurvy cogging knave, with ever a fat paunch of them all.
San. Or, by Mars, a soldier's part I could play bravely. Your marches and counter-marches, retreats, charges, sieges, and sallies; your tantarara and sa! sa! O, I could carbonado the enemy rarely. A soldier's part, by all means.   Old Play.

THERE was astonishment in the parlour, and alarm in the servants' hall, at Mr. Justice Asher's, when, in the afternoon of the day on which Mr. Major had been robbed, that gentleman returned on a borrowed horse, and related the particulars of his adventure.

"By the lord Harry!" exclaimed Major, as he ended his narration to the justice, who had summoned his brother the Colonel, Dr. Tithe'em, and one or two other of his guests, who had not as yet quitted their bedrooms, as a council;— "by the lord Harry, but the knave's a rare one. He's a fine fellow, too; and I could find it in my heart, if he hadn't shot Whitestockings, to be sorry such a bold blade should stretch a rope. I'll remember his parting words, Dr. T., and damme if I'll wag a finger against him—if I do, may I—"

"My dear sir," remonstrated the doctor; "you are most assuredly losing sight, in your improper admiration of this outlawed ruffian, of the duty you owe to the social community, of which—I speak it in humility, and under due correction, as not being a secular man—you are a member. The duty towards our country, and towards the interests of order and the protection of property, are twofold; firstly, the duty towards our country, as loyal men and subjects of our most gracious prince, whom heaven long preserve, with all who are placed in authority under him—"

"'Pon my soul! doctor," interrupted the colonel, "I'm somewhat drowsy, I heard a good deal o' that on Sunday---and---you understand me," added he, with a knowing wink, observing some of the servants grinning as their converse. "I would advise," added he, "that the immediate march of a cavalry detachment into these parts be urged on his Grace of Newcastle."

"And I," rejoined Dr. Tithe'em, who had a high opinion of pecuniary temptation, "that a large reward should be offered, both by the hundred, and by government, for the apprehension of the offenders."

"And the issue of a proclamation, more especially pointed at this daring villain," added Justice Asher.

"I'll direct the operations of the troops," said the Colonel.

"I'll place my name as the party by whom the reward will be paid, on the lodgment of the felon in one of his Majesty's gaols," said the parson.

"And I'll undertake, if the means are placed at my disposal, that there shall be no lack, either in form or in evidence, to convict the audacious thief," said Justice Asher.

To this colloquy of their worships, Mr. Major listened with a smile.

"Well, well," said he, "I wish you all the success your energy and good intentions deserve; yet, though I am bound by no promise whatever to the bold-faced rascal who has plundered me and killed my horse---confound him for that same---yet, as I before said, I'll not wag a finger to do him harm--- for I admire the fellow; and if I had him before me with a troop of horse at my back---damme, but I'd give him 'law,' and a fair start for his life. I'd not kill him in cold blood, master parson---it's not my creed."

The reverend doctor was preparing a formal reply, but Mr. Major cut it short by leaving the room. The letter, signed by the magistrates, was duly despatched; the official reply that the representations it contained had been " submitted to the proper quarter," was returned; and the next week, to the huge delight of the colonel, the dragoons arrived, and were placed at the disposal of the military magistrate. Mighty was the bustle at the justice's; the troops were quartered at various inns on the road, and so judiciously were they divided and subdivided, that, except where a regular patrol of the principal highways was made by them in something like form, they were utterly useless, from their scattered and isolated posts; which, exempting them from all surveillance, rendered them formidable only to the beef, bacon, and ale, of the houses where they were billetted; and much less dangerous to the active "clerk of St. Nicholas" * than to the virtue of the rustic serving wenches.

It was evening as two men, in the garb of farmers, stood conversing near h e door of a small ale-house. On the form beside the door sat a toil-and-travel-stained man, in a tattered sailor's garb; he was of great stature and of great strength, and appeared to have lately tramped it from the coast. His face was bronzed by exposure to the sun, his muscular throat was unconfined by a neck-cloth, a worsted Guernsey frock supplied the place of shirt and waistcoat; and with a jack-knife in one hand and a lump of bread and bacon in the other, the man seemed contented to let the world e'en wag its own way for him. The two men were Turpin and King, who had assumed this disguise with the view of procuring information of the whereabouts of their friends, the dragoons. Turpin eyed the sailor closely; he gave a slight shudder, and an expression of dislike passed over his face.

"Tom," said he, in a whisper to his companion, "that's Roger Haynes, one of the murderers of my sainted wife!"

King was surveying him attentively when the man raised his head; the fellow looked confused.

"Come away," said Turpin. "He was the least to blame of the wretches; indeed I believe he tried to save her,---but I'd rather not have---"

"As you please," observed King; and they walked slowly down the road.

The man seemed struck with a sudden thought; he followed, and overtaking them, bid them "Good day." Turpin would fain have avoided him---he did not like his suspicious and enquiring looks; and in the hope of getting rid of him, said---

"My good fellow, if 'tis charity you seek, there's a shilling. Begone; this gentleman and I are engaged on business."

These sound of his voice appeared at once to remove all doubts from the man's mind. He suddenly advanced towards Turpin, and taking his hand, exclaimed---

"A'd a laid a thoosand as it wor thee, tho' a've zeen thee but twice avore---

---

* The Highwayman.

PUBLISHER'S NOTE

P.160 SHOULD READ AS P.200.

wunst when 'ee didn't zee me, and wunst at Justice Denistoun's. A've but
one thing on my mind, and that's a thing a'll not say a word on, for a' zee it
vexes ye, but no mortul breethin' daur zay as Roger Haynes——thof that's a neam
as mustn't be spoke——ever did harm, not even in his mind, to *her*. Will'ee
forgive———a' doant suppoze 'ee can vorget———(Turpin writhed at the allusion):
a's as innocent as the babe as wor never born——a'll zwear afore G———."

Dick looked displeased; but his disposition, as we have oft said, though
violent, was placable.

"I can't forgive," said he; "but go; your life *must* be the forfeit if you
are discovered, I know that. Go!"

"A'll not," said the man doggedly. "A don't vally my life; it's been no
great catch anyhow zince that misfortunate job———a'll not rame it ag'in——A've
heerd o' your name zince I've been in these parts, and bin a longing to zee
ye———and if you'll take zarvice from one who's don'ee no harm o' purpose,
Roger Haynes will stick to 'ee back and edge."

Turpin looked doubtfully at his comrade, and Tom returned to the full
as dubious a look. Roger watched them with an anxious eye, and seemed,
as far as his rough features could express it, much hurt by their distrust.

"We'll strike into this wood," said Dick, pointing to a thicket by the
road-side, "and talk more of this: we may be overlooked;" and the three
men left the highway.

In a few words Haynes explained to them the danger of their position———he
had overheard a conversation in the ale-house passage, from which it appeared
that arrangements had been made for their capture; that close and accurate
descriptions of the persons of Dick, King, and Fielder, were in possession of
the magistrates; that from information they had received it was gathered
that these highwaymen, wherever they lurked, had the means of stabling
their horses; and lastly, that a woman, a stranger in the neighbourhood,
who had several times been watched to London, and who had there made
purchases, and had been lost sight of, as she unaccountably disappeared from the
highway, when near Waltham———was suspected of being an accomplice of the
robbers. That the communicant of this information to the publican, (who
had retailed it, with additions of his own to a guest or two,) was Mr. Thompson, the principal ranger of the forest; and that he had hinted his knowledge
of the retreat of the highwaymen. This conversation, he told them, had
scarcely ended, when they came up, and he feared that this Thompson, who
had hastily left the house on their arrival———was gone for assistance to capture
them; as he thought from his manner that he had recognized them, spite of
their disguise.

"By Jupiter, Dick," said King, with a smile, "this is sharp work; it
would be a pity though, as they seem determined to serve an ejectment on us,
not to give these clever men-hunters some token teo remember us by. D———e
but it's a reflection on our bold profession, Dickon, to hunt such as
us like badgers.———Say the word, friend; shall we take this fellow———he's
a rough-looking one, but there's something tells me we may trust———him
to our sanctum."

"Ay, certainly," replied Dick; "I'm not often deceived in those I
trust. Come, no protestations," and Dick pressed Haynes's hand, "I'm an
outlaw myself, and I can feel for those whom society has thrust forth.
Pursued by men, I'll not refuse shelter to a man in the same strait as
myself. Come on; you shall see how we highwaymen live, though I

The Robbery at Justice Asher's.

distrusted you at first, I never do things by halves; we're comrades from this time forth."

For the next two days Turpin and King kept snug in their retreat. Madge, too, was cautioned not to stir out, an injunction she readily obeyed. Fielder and Roger Haynes, as the parties least likely to be recognised, were the only persons who left the cave in search of information or necessaries. Turpin, however, soon grew tired of this inactivity; excitement and enterprise were to him life, and on the third day, completely disguised, he and his friend Tom ventured on an excursion. They soon possessed themselves of all necessary information as to the force, position, and operations of their enemies; nay, one evening they met a party of dragoons, going with a petty officer to post certain men at the public houses in their immediate neighbourhood, upon whom they so completely imposed by their disguise and address, that they not only wormed from them every thing they wished to know, but received a courteous good night, with a proffer of escort, which favour of course they politely declined.

" And where were these redcoats going to?" asked Fielder of King, on his return, when he related the circumstances of their meeting.

" Let me see:" said Tom, " I'll tell you : I could not help laughing in my sleeve, when the fellow told me all their arrangements. He had left a man at Chingford, another at Low Street; and two at Sewardstone—the last I must say is a deuced deal more close to us than pleasant—and of the remaining five, two were for Walthamstow, two for Epping—and I know not where the devil he didn't tell me rest of their troop were scattered about. We shall have to cut these parts, Georgy my lad, that's clear."

"It's more than likely," said Turpin gaily; for he had a heart whose courage warmed, and a head whose coolness and determination rose with the dangers which surrounded him. "It's more than likely that they may hunt us to 'earth' —but we're not such fools, I hope, as to have but one hole to start to. No! no! we'll astonish 'em yet, before we leave these Essex calves in quiet possession of their grazing grounds. I've a scheme which will require all our force to execute; to-morrow I will myself ascertain whether its execution is practicable."

Fielder, who had taken a mighty fancy to Roger Haynes, with whom he had been conversing in an undertone, now said:—

"I've a scheme of mine too, Captain; I and Roger have been talking it over, and if you don't want us for your business to-morrow, why, I think we too may show 'em some sport."

"Don't get yourselves into mischief then," said Dick jokingly; "and you may have holiday till the night after next at twelve. But, remember, *then* we must meet all together at the oak to the right of Copthall green—twelve's the hour; no later."

"Ay, Captain," said Fielder, "we'll be with you. It *will* be rare sport, Roger: *we'll* manage it prettily, ha! ha!" and he laughed heartily at his own conceit.

For some days the duty of the soldiers had been dreadfully harassing; no less from the formal fooleries of old Colonel Asher than from the false reports of robberies, perpetually spread, not only by Dick and his companions, but even by the lower classes; with whom the gallant highwayman, who robbed only the rich, was a special favourite. Their duty, indeed, had been no sinecure; at one time intelligence was received by the soldier-magistrate, who had fixed his head quarters at his brother's house, of some petty depredation, and no sooner had his soldiers departed on an excursion after the delinquent, than a daring robbery was committed in the very place they had left; while his "merry men all," after a fatiguing gallop across the country, returned to quarters only to find they had been hoaxed. The worthy colonel grew splenetic and violent as these disappointments and mortifications increased. True it is that he, or rather individual soldiers, succeeded in driving from the country the notorious Gregory * and capturing or dispersing his desperate gang of footpads and burglars, which had long infested the neighbourhood of Brentwood, Billericay, Horndon, and the

---

* Samuel Gregory, who was styled Captain of the "Essex Gang," was, after absconding from Essex, taken at Winchester, and, after a desperate resistance, conveyed to London, "chained under a horse's belly, guarded by eight armed men." He was executed this year (1735) with three other malefactors, Lewis, Hughes, and Sutton, for robbery and rape. Herbert Hayns, and others of his gang, were executed at Chelmsford in the same year, on the same day with Margaret Onions, who was burnt alive for the murder of her husband. Joseph Gregory lay at that time desperately wounded in Winchester Gaol.—See Monthly Register, in London Magazine, for 1735, pages 282 and 391. The proclamation issued by the Secretary of State, after reciting the robberies of Mr. Split at Woodford, Mr. Eldridge of Walthamstow, Mrs. Shelley of Layton, the Rev. Mr. Dyde of Parndon, Sir Cæsar Child (who, resisting, had his nose shot off,) &c., offers a reward of £50 to any person who shall lodge in gaol any one of the offenders; and during the session an act was passed making it a penal offence for any person to travel the high road, disguised or otherwise disfigured.

lower parts of the county; but these were mere low-lived offenders, and though their crimes were atrocious, they were not the men he was most anxious to capture, inasmuch as their depredations were rarely committed on gentry or nobility; and it was in favour of those classes chiefly that the sympathy and zeal of the justice were most readily excited.

At Sewardstone was a small alehouse, once known as the Plough. It was a little gable-ended structure of framework and mud, with a coating of shells and pebbles; before the door stood the indispensable horse-trough, and on the top of a stout pole, in an iron frame, swung a dingy board of mysterious colours, on which an ancient and clumsy contrivance, intended to do duty as a plough, had once been limned by unskilful daubery of the village house-painter, whose admiration of the cunning of his own right hand in this higher department of the art for several years induced him (he now sleeps with his fathers) to take many a pot of strong ale beneath the shade of this pictorial achievement. The kitchen or tap of this humble hostelrie was entered by a latched door from the small space of hoof-indented ground which intervened between the house and the roadside. The stabling, or rather long shed, for the accommodation of four-legged beasts was in a line with the front of the premises, one half being devoted to the purposes of a cart or chaise shed, the other to horses. In its front stood an empty dung-cart with its shafts raised high in air, looking, in the dubious dusk of evening, like the horns of some monstrous animal; behind the hedge which continued the line, was the kitchen garden, and in the rear of the house the piggery of the holding. The household consisted of the landlord,—once coachman to a neighbouring gentleman, but who had for many years changed the spruce powdered grandeur of my lord's coachman, into the jolly, ungartered, slip-shod, tun-bellied Boniface; his wife (formerly the still woman of my lady)—who was as strikingly metamorphosed from the prim propriety of the wearer of a bunch of keys at "the great house"; a shock-headed stable boy; and a red-elbowed, bare-legged, slatternly serving wench, with cheeks like "thumping red potatoes," overfond of romping behind doors and in passages with the half-fuddled rustics who patronized the Plough.

In the kitchen of this hostel sat two dragoons; in a corner stood their huge iron-sheathed swords; they were busily masticating brown bread and bacon, which they washed down with copious draughts of home-brewed, while their noble black horses were similarly engaged with oats and water in the shed beforementioned.

"What think'ee of this here Gregory?" enquired one, of his comrade; "he's a rum 'un; why I hear as he swore at the parson, sung all the way as he rode to the gallus, and shied his shoes among the mob for good luck:* dang me, but I likes a spirity chap: he *was* a game 'un."

"I'm not sure as his brother warn't as good as he," said the other; "they do say as he wounded three of the sheriff's men, if he han't killed one on 'em, afore they took him. Why did'nt they cut 'un down, or shoot 'un; I'd stand no repairs with such desperate varmin."

* Fact—see the account of his execution. An order had been made by the Lord Mayor and sheriffs, that same year, forbidding any persons, under a heavy penalty, to supply any culprit, on his road to execution, with any intoxicating liquor—thus abolishing the well-known St. Giles's bowl: " there was therefore," observes the writer in the " Monthly Register," anno 1735, "no reason to suspect, as in many other cases of indecent behaviour, that the unhappy man was intoxicated."

"I'd like mainly to get a crack at this here Turpin," said the first speaker; "he's what I calls a nobby sort of a chap; there's two hundred on him, catch him that catch can: domme, but I'll go down into the country, if I get it, an' live like a genelman—I will."

While this talk was going on, two other guests entered the room; they were clodhopping-looking fellows, in short-worked smocks of a greenish colour, laced ankle-boots, and worsted stockings; each wore a white round-crowned hat, of coarse brown woollen, with a turned-up rim, and they were soon busied in toasting two rashers of bacon before the fire. At the mention of Turpin, they exchanged glances of peculiar meaning; their faces, however, were turned from the speakers. Having called for bread, and a pitcher of humming ale, they commenced their repast.

One of the newcomers was of large stature, and wore a black wig; the shorter one concealed his dark brown locks beneath a well-made sandy crop of hair, and a pair of red whiskers. They were not long in scraping acquaintance with the soldiers, and as their pouches seemed tolerably well lined with shillings and groats, the men of war, whose capaciousness of swallow was certainly out of all proportion with the scantiness of their purses, by no means discouraged their advances. The shorter countryman proposed a toss for a tankard—the troopers assented; and the stale game of " most heads or most tails" being proposed and agreed on, the rustic so managed it that either himself or his clumsy companion lost in almost every turn. Their money, nevertheless, as well as their patience, seemed not easily exhaustible: the soldiers laughed and drank heartily, so elated were they with their extraordinary success, while the countrymen scratched their heads and cursed their hard luck, as with feigned desperation they hazarded again and again the fortune of the coin, occasionally doubling the venture to two pots. The red-coats were too eager and too thirsty to notice, farther than by a passing remonstrance, that the strangers, though raising each time the vessel to their mouths, cleverly avoided taking their share of the drink. The evening drew on, and some dozen of quarts of the " right stuff" had been swallowed before the soldiers cried " hold, enough," and proposed to their new acquaintances a temporary adjournment of the sitting, on the plea that it was their duty to ride, from seven till ten, from Low Street to Waltham Cross.

"That's dom'd unlucky," exclaimed one in his feigned accent; "can't one o' ye go, and so take a turn about for a hour—eh?"

The soldiers assented; but as some altercation ensued as to which should take the first hour's turn, it ended by their mutually agreeing that there was no need, provided they kept their own counsel, to leave the fireside and nappy at all.

> The night drave on wi' sangs and clatter
> An' ay the ale was growing better;
> The landlady and Tam grew gracious,
> Wi' favours secret, sweet, an' precious;
> Kings may be blest, but [they] were glorious,
> O'er a' the ills of life victorious.

Ten had struck, and by this time the rough familiarity of the drunken troopers had more than once procured for them a hearty thwack from the mutton fist of the sturdy kitchen-wench; the landlord too, left the table, where he had been helping off, in the way of trade, not a few pints of the reckoning; when the two countrymen desired to know whether they could be accommodated with a bed. The dragoons were in the occupancy of the only spare one, but so delighted were they with the liberal joskins who had so gloriously filled them with nut-brown ale, that they swore, in the fulness of their hearts and stomachs, that they should have theirs; and to this, with pretended reluctance, the strangers agreed.

All was silent within and without; the cricket chirrupped in the chimney chinks; the dying embers yet glowed on the slow-cooling hearth. Within a barricade, formed by an overturned bench, which sheltered them from the keen draught admitted beneath the door, enveloped in their horsemen's cloaks, lay the sleeping soldiers. The care of Dolly—for so was the wench called—had, however, sufficiently marked her preference; for while one of the loud-snoring drunkards lay, with unprotected head, on the bare flooring, the younger and slighter one reposed his on a hay-pillow from the wench's bed, and was carefully covered by a horse-cloth; nay, had not his helpless state of intoxication annihilated all his powers of locomotion, it is questionable whether the son of Mars might not have occupied the bed itself. With noiseless steps and stealthy tread the two countrymen entered from the passage, and were soon busy about the persons of the heavy sleepers. They disencumbered them of their cartouches, crossbelts, and swords; and one of them, having unfastened the door, took charge of the various accoutrements, went out, and returned. The few halfpence remaining in the pockets of the soldiers were taken, when the shorter man, in a low whisper, said—

"Roger, bring the saddles, bridles, and pistols: hist! the joke will not be half completed unless we take their horses. Go softly out—and give the signal when all's ready. I'll watch here."

He left the room: the man who stayed behind stood for a few seconds in the attitude of listening; he looked on the faces of the slumberers, and a smile stole across his features. Stepping on tiptoe to the fire-place, he selected from the embers a piece of wood perfectly charred, and after ascertaining it to be cold, smutted their faces in the most ludicrous manner—he stopped and smiled —again and again did he touch and retouch the "visnomies" of the slumberers with true Hogarthian zest, grinning all the while " consumedly," till a low whistle brought him on his feet, and he too left the place. The companions, after breaking the troopers' swords, deposited them in the dungheap; the horses were rode off through the forest in the direction of Chingford Green, and there cast loose; and before two in the morning, Turpin and King were laughing heartily at the merry narration of Fielder and Haynes of their evening's diversion with the dragoons.

Let us now return to the justice's mansion. At a library table in the drawing-room sat the Colonel; before him lay spread a large county map; on its surface were traced in red ink many mysterious zigzags, doubtless considered by the profound and puzzled tactician who had drawn them as evidences of military skill and sagacity which must immortalize their projector. He was evidently ill at ease, both in body and mind—for his foot was swathed in flannel, owing to an attack of his old besieger, the gout; while the indignity put upon the troops under his command--and of which the particulars had but just been reported by his nephew, a young officer, who stood respectfully by his chair---had by no means soothed his natural irascibility. Muttered curses struggled to his moving lips, but decorum forbad their coming to full growth.

"And so, Bennett, these scoundrels suffered themselves to be made drunk and robbed by a couple of bacon-fed rustics—eh? They shall be flogged, Bennett. I'll court-martial them to-morrow, by G—. Sure such disgrace was never before suffered by the army of our King—God bless him. I shall write this night to the Horse-Guards—are they under arrest---in safe custody---eh?"

The young officer replied in the affirmative, and the Colonel fell into a brown study.

"I see how it is," said he, thinking aloud. "This infernal gout which has so unluckily taken me in *toe*, will be the ruin of the campaign. The horses, you say, were found on Chingford Green?"

"No; in the church-yard, sir," said the officer.

"And their swords in a dung-heap," muttered the Colonel, choking with indignation.

His nephew assented by a bow.

"By powder and shot," continued he, "I swear I'll give no quarter, while grass grows or water runs, to these insolent scoundrels, till this indignity to our profession is wiped out. I've received information this very day from Thompson the ranger--who's certainly (with the co-operation of the military) very active and useful in hunting out these scoundrels---I've received information, as I said before, that two of these audacious villains are the very dogs who robbed that convicted rogue, lawyer Sheepshanks, of some hundreds of pounds of Sir Litton Weston's rents. They'd a narrow squeak for it that time; 'tis some years ago; and the fellows only escaped through my horse being knocked up, for we had been all day out with Sir Marmaduke's hounds. By gad, they must have been cursedly frightened, Bennett, for 'between the devil and the deep sea,' they chose the last, and swam the Thames to Plumstead Marshes; they must have been damnably afraid of us to chance their lives---but they shall die a drier death yet, Bennett, so sure as I hold his majesty's commission. Did I ever tell you, Bennett, how I proposed to cross the river after 'em, and hunt 'em through Kent, but none of the party would volunteer?"

The young officer, who balanced his large expectations from his bachelor uncle against the infliction of his tedious harangues, had become an admirable listener, a qualification indispensable to expectant legatees, but one most painful and patience-trying in its acquisition; he accordingly, by a nod, implied the gratification which the narrative, to which he had listened some hundred times, would impart on its hundred and first repetition.

The old gentleman, however, paused. Nature had not blessed him originally with any peculiar perspicacity of intellect; and an over-indulgence in black strap, the conceit engendered by easy circumstances, with the non-contradiction of his whimsical absurdities, had by no means strengthened a mind weak *ab ovo*.

"Where the devil was I," he soliloquised; "ah, ah—about swimming the river---yes---I told 'em then, when I was under prince Eugene—I was a younker at that time--how our heavy dragoons forded—swam I mean; oh, ah—Bennet, just shift my footstool," said the old man querulously; "you might have seen me uneasy for this long time, but you don't care, not you. Well, about these insolent fellows, who have dared thus to insult his Majesty's troops; look here, Bennett---(the young man smiled as his uncle turned his body to the map). Here, you see, (and he drew his forefinger along the red lines)---I'm afraid though, boy, that you, having never seen the combined operations of the great Marlborough, or of Eugene, will not be able to understand what, on a small scale, I have here done in imitation of their grand campaigns. Here you see, at Chelmsford, I post my extreme right; while this dotted line, extending, you observe, across the country to a little southward of Stratford-le-Bow, may be considered as the base-line of the operations, by which we shall sweep the county, at least those western hundreds which it is the plan of my campaign to clear of this enemy. The hundreds of Becontree, Havering Liberty, Chafford, Barstable, and Chelmsford," said the old gentleman, drawing his finger slowly along the map, "I consider as already cleared; and the hundreds of Ongar, Waltham, Harlow, and Dunmow, will form the next series of operations."

A lurking laugh played round the lips of the young officer as he thought, that in these cleared districts, or those in what his uncle called "occupation," the whole of the recent depredations had been committed. He repressed the smile—and the old Colonel went on :

"As to those drunken villains—I've scarcely patience to think of it—who have subjected our arms to this disgrace, I'll see them pickled---and the outlawed villains who were the instruments of this indignity shall expiate their crime—aye—I'll cut down the best oak on my estate to build their gallows, and I'll have its remains made into an easy chair, in which I'll sit and tell how I avenged the affront done to my cloth. I remember, Bennett," said he, in reply to some soothing remonstrance from his nephew, "when Marshal Tallard dared to boast---that was when I was with Marlborough, not long before Blenheim ---I remember when Tallard boasted that with three thousand men he would---"

"A man waits below stairs with a letter from Mr. Thompson, of the greatest consequence, sir," said a servant entering.

"Bid him send it up," replied the Colonel.

"He says, sir, as it is so vastly pressing as he must give it into nobody's hands but your own."

"Show him here then," said the colonel, for he observed military brevity in his conversations with subordinates.

The man came up, scraped a bow, and delivered his commission; the Colonel broke the seal, and read as follows :---

Navestock, Saturday evening, 7 o'clock.

Honoured Sir,

"I hope the urgency of the occasion will excuse my troubling you with this, but if your arrangements will permit you to place two or three of your men under my guidance, I have not a doubt but that I shall be able, before morning, to bring before you the noted Turpin, as well as other two of his associates. I write this in haste, as I have applied to the nearest station at Stanford Rivers, but the men refuse to stir without written orders under your own hand.

"With the greatest respect and veneration,

"I remain, Sir,

"Your most humble servant to command.

"JOHN THOMPSON."

The old gentleman brightened up as he read the letter, but on further thought, his countenance fell.

"D——n," grumbled he, thinking aloud; "how's this to be done? it *is* stonishing how these jacks-in-office---I beg the authorities at the Horse-guards' pardon--- it is astonishing how we commanders are crippled by this ill-judged economy, this niggardly denial of means to effect the most brilliant services. I remember my Lord Cadogan---he commanded the cavalry in Flanders ---used to say---he said once to me---Asher, says he, I wish those red-tape-tying fellows in London had to———"

The young lieutenant pointed to the man who stood waiting an answer; and the gesture recalled his uncle's tongue from his ramble in the Low Countries.

"Oh, aye, the man waits an answer---yes---you come from Mr. Thompson?"

The man replied in the affirmative.

"Damme, if I've got any men---who's below, Bennett?"

"There's your orderly, uncle, and a trooper---and couldn't I go? I'll go with pleasure, if you will spare me. The three of us, with Thompson, are surely enough---and if my wish has any weight, dear uncle, I would add my request, that you will allow me to take some more active share in this business, than merely writing orders and acting as your secretary."

"Ay, ay; no doubt you're tired enough of staying with a gouty old man," said his uncle testily; "you'd like a great deal better, I dare say, to be galloping across the country, than getting the more important knowledge which an intimacy with the practice of combined operations will give you; ay, ay--- headstrong, shortsighted boys, think war's all fighting, but grey-headed old veterans know better; they know the head's stronger than the arm, boy; and so will you, if you live to see the service I have seen. But you shall go, nevertheless---you shall go, and old Thomas shall wait on me; no one shall say the public service suffered for the convenience of old Colonel Asher---no! no! Send up the two men, John, (he addressed the servant)---send them up; for it will be necessary I should instruct them myself as to the duties they are about to perform."

The young lieutenant left the room, and soon returned fully equipped for his excursion. The man left with them, and the party, took the direction, through the forest, towards Navestock.

It was about ten o'clock on a dark and uncomfortable night when they set out, and young Bennett, who knew but little of the country, (his two troopers knew nothing), was obliged implicitly to trust to the knowledge of their guide. They rode in single file, at a slow pace, for about an hour, along an intricate bridle-road.

"And where is this Navestock, friend?" asked the young officer of the messenger.

"Some seven mile yet," said the fellow coolly; "it 'ull be near twelve, I'm thinkin', afore we're there. I wish as how Mister Thompson had ha' gotten some 'un else for this here job, for I shall be main tired a' time I gets back."

They rode on, until they came to two diverging roads; their guide paused in momentary hesitation, and muttered something as if in doubt.

"You're sure of your road, I hope?" asked young Bennett.

"I'm pretty sure it's the right hand road," said the fellow, "but it's so darn'd dark as I cant zee a pig from a hollybush. Oh, ay, I've got it---yes, yes," and he rode forward at a slow and cautious pace, the young officer keeping close by his side.

They had now gone about five hundred yards along this road, which seemed

Turpin shoots the Ranger.

to become more and more intricate, tangled, and less beaten at every step, when the man again stopped.

"Dang it," said he. "this is main queer; there's the oak, else my eyes doan't sarve me, wi' a white blaze on the bark on't; d'ye see it, zur? but it's to the right hand, 'stead o' the left on us. I'm a thinkin' there's some mistake about us—I doan't know though, 'xactly," and the man lifted his hat and

Scratched his ear, the infallible resource
To which your puzzled people have recourse.

The young officer's blood rose at the fellow's stupidity and coolness.

"Curse it," exclaimed he, "you've brought us on a pretty fool's errand : push on into the nearest highway. Put us into some civilised road, out of this infernal wilderness, my good fellow, and leave us to enquire the way for ourselves. We've tongues in our heads, and there's surely some dwelling or alehouse to be found, where we may get put right. I wonder what the devil Mr. Thompson could be about to send such a dunderhead on an important service. So you don't know the road after all, you infernal blockhead !" exclaimed the young soldier, who was provoked by the fellow's silence, for it was so dark from the shadows of the clouds which overspread the sky, and the thick and lofty trees around them, that he could not see his face.

"I think ye might be civil when a chap's a-doin' his best," grumbled the fellow; "I know my way well enow; ye an't near no highroad, as I knows

No. 27.

on, till ye get out o' this wood. I've a bin doin' all as I could to take ye a short cut, but if ye like to go back to Theydon Gernon—them's the houses and church we passed some time agone—p'raps we might do better by gettin' in the road ;· for it's at Kelvedon Hatch as we're to meet Muster Thompson, d'ye see."

"Confound the fellow," said Bennett ; "lead us somewhere out of this, and be hanged to you! Don't stand shilly-shallying here—show us a road out of this devil's hole, and I'll answer we'll gallop to this—how d'ye call it ?"

"Kelvedon Hatch," said the man sulkily ; "this here's called Beachet Wood ;* thof if I can't hit the road it 'ull be sadly out of our way, I must say—it's so very dark too, you see."

The officer's patience was exhausted : he burst into a volley of execrations on the fellow's perverse dawdling.

"Lead us out of this, or I won't answer for your bones," said he peremptorily.

"Well, zur, I'll do that the shortest way : just let's go back as far as the fork of this here road, and I'm zure as I'll put ye in the train. Ay, ay," muttered he, "it's all right ; yes, yes—there's the tree wi' the blaze on the bark as I told ye on."

The officer strained his eyes, but it was too dark for him to see. They were now, by having passed their men in the narrow way, about half a dozen yards in advance ; beside the road, or rather pathway, was a deep ditch—beyond it, on a bank, a quickset hedge. The last speech of the countryman had directed Bennett's attention to the bole of a huge tree, the branches of which overhung the road ; and the young officer was stooping over his saddle-bow, shading his eyes with his hand to strengthen his sight, when the countryman by his side, taking advantage of his position, adroitly slipped his foot from his stirrup, stooped and seized the officer by the back of his ankle, and by one sudden lift cleanly unhorsed him. An exclamation was all that escaped his lips ere the lieutenant lay at his length in the long rank grass ; and the first idea that anything was amiss was conveyed to the astonished troopers by the crash of boughs and the simultaneous exclamations of George Fielder and their officer.

"Good night, gentlemen," shouted the highwayman, as he dashed through the crashing thicket ; "good night, gentlemen ; keep the road to the right, and look out for the blazes on the trees—ha ! ha ! ha !"

"Fire ! shoot the scoundrel ! fire !" thundered Bennett, as he started to his feet, and rushing knee-deep into the wide drain, endeavoured in vain to scramble up the steep-scarped clay-bank on the opposite side, over which Fielder's horse had lightly carried him. The carbines of the soldiers rattled, and their sharp report awoke the echoes of the wood, as the harmless bullets glanced against the trees from the random discharge.

"Pursuit must be useless," exclaimed Bennett bitterly, as he stood with folded arms in the pathway. "How can I shew my face again ? Damnation !" and the young man ground his teeth. "My uncle's a cursed old fool, I begin to think—why we shall be the laughing stock of every chaw-bacon in the country ! One night they make our men drunk, and rob them ; the drunk-

---

* The reader must bear in mind that the small patches of timber now dignified by the title of woods, are but little segments of the great forest of Hainault, which formerly covered the face of south-western Essex.

enness, though no excuse for *them*, in some measure wipes off the indignity put on the troops—but what shall *we* say—in our sober senses, to be thus fooled ?"

The rustling of boughs died away and a joyous halloo was heard in the distance.

"I'd give the brightest—but no! Roberts! hold my horse."

The two dragoons had sat still as statues during this soliloquy. The system by which the modern soldier is reduced to a mere machine, (neither bravery bringing promotion nor enterprise fame, condemned to one dead level of irresponsibility, except so far as the *machine* duty of soldiership requires,) rendered them perfectly indifferent to the success or failure of any adventure they might be engaged in. True it was that they fully possessed that animal courage and national pride which is inseparable from the English character, and that they would fight well and boldly when the occasion called for their arm and sword ; but they had no stimulus for seeking fame, therefore did no more than what they called their *duty*, and having no share in the responsibility they entered not into the feelings of their officer ; in short, there was no sympathy between them ; so, without a word of regret, except a whisper that if " they'd ha' known it they might ha' collared him an' got the reward," they set about retracing their steps to the highroad.

" The letter is a forgery ; that's clear," soliloquised Bennett, " so it can be of no use going on to Kelvedon. I wonder where this Navestock really is. I shouldn't wonder if that's a humbug too, and Thompson don't live there. Well, turn out how it will, I'll not go back to the old Colonel till I've done something, as I've broke bounds for once."

They rode on, but such was the perplexedness and intricacy of the path, that in ten minutes they found themselves again approaching the same spot.

" I'll return to that gap, leap the bank, and follow the track of that villain," said the officer.

This proved their wisest plan, for within three hundred yards they found themselves at the side of a lane, through which they gained the road, and soon arrived at a small public house, where we shall leave them, seeking information to guide their search.

The clock had just struck eleven ; and the worthy Colonel, having imbibed a stiff glass of " hot with," sat dozing in his well-stuffed chair. Old Thomas, too, with the familiarity of " antique service," was enjoying a cat-sleep in a chair, placed at a respectful distance behind his master. The other servants of the house had retired to rest in the various offices attached to the mansion, for, except on " boozing days," the household maxim was " early to bed and early to rise." The Colonel, however, among his other freaks, had lately made a practice of sitting up all night, or rather sleeping in a perpendicular instead of a horizontal position, from a notion that this change in his mode of resting must have some mysterious influence upon the issue of what he called "the campaign." A fat little spaniel, the property of his niece, lay on the thick worsted hearth rug, its pink nose snugly sheltered between its fore feet, and its long silken ears of brown contrasting beautifully with the gay colours of the carpeting. The last named member of the trio was certainly the most vigilant ; and he it was who first became aware of the approach of visitors. A creak was heard, and Pompey raised his head, shook his ears, turned his nose enquiringly towards the door, and gave a most suspicious sniff. The intelligence thus nasally conveyed was far from satisfactory, for Pompey followed it by the vocal enquiry of a sharp short bark, at the same time walking leisurely from his lair.

"Lie down, Pompey!" grumbled Thomas; but Pompey's instinct was not to be put down by old Thomas's veto. He gave two or three calls for explanation so shrill and imperative that the drowsy Colonel snuffled out,—

. "Thomas, turn that dog out; d——n him, he's been barking all the night."

Thomas seized the offender, who was now close to the door, and had just consigned him to a large closet which led from the room, when the door of the apartment opened, and three men with crape on their faces, stole softly in. One stepped lightly to the table, and secured the arms of the Colonel——not his weapons but his bodily appendages. The old gentleman opened his eyes.

"What Thomas——eh? God bless me!" and he became aware that somebody was tying his limbs to the elbows of his chair. "Eh, how!"

"Hist! silence!" said the intruder.

The Colonel stared, and saw within a short twelve inches of his head, the muzzle of a pistol. The man clicked the hammer as he drew the weapon to full cock,

> "It has a strange quick jar upon the ear,
> That cocking of a pistol, when you know
> A moment more will bring its sight to bear
> Upon your person—"

says Byron; but the bard's unpleasant sensation supposed "twelve yards off, or so," as the space between your head and the "explosive tube." Now it must be admitted, in this case, that the unpleasantness was dreadfully aggravated by the reduction of the twelve yards to twelve inches, and the proximity interfered greatly with the restoration of the Colonel's mental equilibrium.

That something dreadful was going on he saw, but his awakening, with the omission of the "tweaks" and "thwacks," was as slow as that of Sir Hudibras from his "swound." He fixed his eyes with a stolid seriousness on the gaily dressed robber before him.

"Hoy, Thomas! why, what——"

"Another word and you're a dead man!" said the masked robber in a low determined voice.

The Colonel was silent.

Thomas had meantime been safely bound by one of the other men; and they were soon actively employed in managing the place. The massive family plate, which shone on the sideboard, was rapidly transferred to a sack by one, while the other stuffed his pockets with the various valuables which an examination of the repositories, drawers, escritoires, &c. presented. The evolutions of this small body of *rifle*-men, though displaying great skill and readiness, were by no means gratifying to the old soldier. He had watched their proceedings in silence for some minutes, when one of them, among some other articles of jewelry, pocketed a large ring set with pearls, then his tongue became loosed——

"You seem," said he to the holder of the pistol, making at the same time an uneasy shift of his head to place it out of the line of the barrel, "to be the leader of these scoun———I beg their pardons—these a—a—a—"

"I perfectly understand you, sir," replied the stranger; "you are right. I *am* the leader of those a—a—a---a's you say."

"That ring contains the hair of a dear relation, and I value it far beyond what you would get for it if—"

"Say no more, sir," said he of the vizor; and making a sign the ring was given to him, and he placed it in the hand of the Colonel.

The old gentleman stared, as well he might.

"And, now sir, before we go, perhaps we might as well let you know how you come to be honoured by this visit. You received a letter from me---ah, here it is, (and the man took up the epistle which still lay open upon the table,) I promised you here, I see," said Dick smiling, "tho', by the bye, I've signed another man's name—(the Colonel's eyes underwent a saucer-like expansion as the true state of affairs dawned on him)—I've promised, I see, to bring before you the noted Turpin, and other two of his companions, and as I seldom bark without biting, say what else you like against me, you can't charge me with breaking my word."

The Colonel at last saw clearly---and his fears were immediately awakened for his nephew rather than himself. For the old man had some good qualities; he did not lack courage, venerated the memory of his sister, and though continually scolding his nephew, as indeed he did every one about him, had a strong and sincere affection for the young man. Seeing some symptoms of departure---one of the men was tying the mouth of the sack---he said,

"For God's sake tell me if anything has befallen the lad---the officer I mean ---who left this night on the information of that letter. If he is, as I fear, in your power, gentlemen, release him unhurt, and I'll undertake to recompense you in any way that you---"

"Make yourself easy, Colonel, on that score; if I didn't well know the man who brought you this, I should fear for *my comrade's* safety; but I know be has mother-wit enough to tip your dragoons the slip. Your nephew is somewhere wandering in the Forest, with his companions, and I've no doubt will be here in the morning as soon as they have light to see the way---for I don't reckon they'll be able to *feel* it. Now lads, bustle, look alive, we musn't overload ourselves; adieu, my dear Colonel---compliments to Marlborough and Eugene; all stratagems fair in war, you know, and when next you plan a campaign, take care the enemy don't visit you at head quarters. Good bye!"

So saying, Turpin walked through the doorway, turned to make a low bow to the fast-bound Colonel, who sat biting his lips in silence, and hastened after his comrades.

CHAPTER XIX.

The flying rumours gathered as they rolled,
Scarce any tale was sooner heard than told—
And all who told it added something new,
And all who heard it made enlargement too—
In every ear it sped, on every tongue it grew.
　　　—Temple of Fame. (Pope's paraphrase.)

The bold and active conquer difficulties,
By daring to attempt them; sloth and fear
Shiver and shrink at sight of toil or hazard,
And make the impossibility they dread.
　　　—Rowe's Stepmother.

I hold a mouse's wit not worthe a leke,
That hath but one hole for to sterten to,
And if that faille then is she alle ydo.
　　　Chaucer—The Wif of Bathe's Prologue.

THE country was now thoroughly roused, and dangers and difficulties thickened round our hero and his companions. The audacious robbery of Mr. Major, almost within sight and hearing of a town-end; the ignominious usage of the "bold dragoons;" the befooling of the self-appointed commander-in-chief by an impudent forgery; the daring overthrow of the young officer, by which the supposed countryman effected his escape; and lastly, the crowning audacity of Turpin's burglary at the justice's, and the binding of the Colonel, set all tongues going, and commanded the attention of all public functionaries, to these alarming infractions of the law and defiance of social order. Not only did the magistrates of Chelmsford issue their manifestoes in borough, village, and market town, offering rewards, and announcing the means taken for public security—some of which present a curious picture of the state of intercommunication and police a hundred years ago—but the good citizens of London took the alarm. Among the proceedings of the Court of Common Council,* we find the following :—1. " An act of the Common Council for the better enforcing the laws relating to rogues, vagabonds, &c. &c. ;" 2. " An act for the better regulating watch and ward ;" 3. " An act for enforcing the apprehending and committing to jail loose and idle persons unable to give account of their livelihood, &c. &c. ;" and much discussion took place on a plan submitted to the Corporation for rendering the trainbands efficient, and establishing a *system* of watch and patrol for the apprehension of robbers in London and its suburbs, which scheme appeared in the form of a thin octavo, London, 1737. But to return to our narrative.

Hot was the search, and untiring the quest of horse and foot after suspicious and disreputable characters, but more especially the perpetrators of the late daring offences. Gentlemen and yeomen rode the highways, and constables and headboroughs searched the alehouses and lodginghouses ; beggars were put in the stocks, pedlars committed to gaol, vagrants whipped and carted to the town-ends, and woe betide the stroller or gipsey who could not or would not give an account of his or her way of getting bread. The gentry, especially the younger ones, took to horse-patrolling ; which, in the absence

* These Acts will be found under the article " LONDON," in Cat. Brit. Mus., where they are arranged chronologically, anno 1736-7, *et seq*.

of other sport, proved jovial amusement; and the innkeepers reaped a glorious harvest from this general bustle. As for Turpin, he had come to the conclusion that King's Oak was no longer a residence for him, and that his "occupation was gone" so far as the county of Essex was in question; he accordingly made every preparation for "flitting," and now only waited a favourable opportunity. He had settled in his own mind to effect his escape across the country to Nazing Marsh; thence, under cover of night, to pass the boundary of the county near Broxbourne, where, being beyond the jurisdiction of the magistrates of Essex, he anticipated pursuit would most probably cease, and thence to continue his journey through Herts and Huntingdon, and so crossing the north-eastern end of Northamptonshire, fix himself in Lincolnshire. Several considerations moved him to this, which we may hereafter notice. A light cart had been procured, in which, with some of the lighter valuables, it was purposed that Dick and his *cara sposa*, disguised as countryfolks, should make their way to the rendezvous, which was fixed to be Mob's Hole, near the river Rhee, at the junction of the three shires of Herts, Huntingdon, and Cambridge. There was policy in this, as in those days the mere slipping from county to county gave a *chance* in favour of the fugitive which was worth consideration; King, travelling as a country gentleman, was also to meet them there.

All was now ready for starting; Dick and Madge were the sole occupants of the cave, for Fielder was in London, with Haynes, turning their late booty into cash among the Israelites of Bevis's Marks and Monmouth Street. The plate and other property obtained by their late adventure had been concealed on the morning of the robbery, in the Marshes near the White House, a little below Sewardstone, and having since been cleverly smuggled across the Lea, was now fast melting in the crucibles of the sons of Abraham.

But the best-contrived plans occasionally miscarry, and Dick was fated not to escape so easily as he had reckoned :--- Success---

> "———the mark no mortal wit,
> Or surest hand can always hit;
> For whatsoe'er we perpetrate,
> We do but row, we're steer'd by fate,
> Which in success oft disinherits
> For spurious causes, greatest merits,—" *

was in this case to be purchased only by blood.

We have before mentioned the name of Mr. Thompson, the ranger of Epping Forest. He was certainly one of the most active, fearless, and efficient of the many persons who engaged in the endeavour to apprehend Turpin and his comrades. His intimate knowledge of the intricacies and the general features of this extensive forest rendered him well calculated to direct the proper measures for its thorough search, and he had already offered to direct a party in the most certain way to discover the existence of the robbers' place of concealment, which was more than suspected to exist somewhere within its boundaries. This, however, had been declined by the dunderheaded justices of the peace, in deference to the proposition of the old Colonel; upon the principle that a civil justice of the peace being a concentration of sagacity in civil affairs, a military just-ass must be the quintessence of wisdom in matters where soldiers were engaged. Mr. Thompson, therefore, though highly praised for his zeal, and receiving the bow of thanks from several large and thick powdered heads,

* Hudibras.

"in petty session assembled," was rejected, and left as an individual to pursue his own measures; one of the magistrates kindly informing him that the large reward they had so liberally offered (out of the county rate) was "as open to him as any one else." Mr. Thompson, who had been for some days engaged in a narrow scrutiny of hedgerows, thickets, copses, and banks, throughout the patches of forest in the northern hundreds, without success, had taken to his councils one Sutton, a higler, who to his ostensible avocation of a hawker of poultry, added a little dealing in game, (then a most dangerous calling.) This man, from his mode of life, was of course well acquainted with the country; and Thompson had engaged him to explore the forest in the neighbourhood of Pinner's Hall, Copped Hall, and King's Oak, while he himself examined the more western parts. The higler soon possessed himself of most important information; while lurking near a hedge in a bye lane he espied Madge, who had ventured cautiously out, drawing water at a small spring, concealed among the trees some hundreds of yards from their retreat. He watched her as she dived into the thickest parts of the wood, and by dodging from tree to tree, never entirely lost sight of her until she entered a thicket, when she suddenly disappeared.

"Ho! ho!" said the higler to himself, as he stealthily crept towards the spot, stopping ever and anon to listen, and cautiously avoiding the least rustle. "I've found the place!" A few straggling twigs of two hazel bushes lightly crossing each other, and some dried leaves thrown loosely and carelessly on the ground between them, without a sign of footmark on their top, gave no token of the passage.

The higler shook his head and looked puzzled, as he glanced round with a lurking fear of some ambuscade; for the cunning as well as courage of the robbers had inspired a general terror.

"She certainly sneaked in here," said he.

He listened—all was silent; he carefully raked aside a few of the leaves and found beneath them the stems of a few hazels cut close and level with the earth.

"Ah! ah!" said he; "I'm not the first person as has been hereaways, wild as the land looks. Here's a scent, and no mistake; I'm a Dutchman, if she han't some way of getting into the ground---she was a likely-looking wench too, by gosh!"

He peeped among the bushes; still keeping his posture on hands and knees, and then crawled softly through; a small path among the low grass was tracable by the practised eye, and following it round a small clump of underwood, the higler beheld the object of his search; a large branch of a bare tree lay before the aperture, and crawling to one end of it he saw six or seven descending steps cut from the clayey soil and covered with turf; at the bottom was a small door smeared with clay; the higler saw this, but farther investigation he did not dare. He had found what he thought the entrance to the robbers' den: but he had found one of them only, for this was merely the outlet, or sort of postern, of which we have before spoken. The fellow delighted with his discovery, crawled back, and no sooner did he reach the road, than full of joy he posted off, as fast as his legs would carry him, in search of his employer.

Mr. Thompson was smoking a pipe at Godling Hall; he had spent his forenoon in riding, and was enjoying his Indian weed, after a hearty dinner, when his "finder" arrived, breathless and blown, from his expedition.

"I've done 'em, Mister Thompson; a's track'd 'em home at last: the vixen

Fielder apprehended by the London Thieftakers.

fox, and a' dessay the dog ain't far off! Let I alone for dodging 'em; it's a poor scent as I can't lay on; but I caught it breast high this morning."

"The devil you have: and where is it they kennel at last?"

"They don't kennel at all, I tell 'ee, they burrows: dang me if I ever see'd a cunninger contrived thing in all my born days. But, mister, we musn't scare the birds—we're as safe on 'em, sir, as thof I had 'em tied by the legs in kipples."

"Hold your tongue," said Thompson, "will you, you silly fellow: don't you see that wench has left the room to spread the news among the servants that the robbers' den is found out. Confound your stupidity, you'll spoil all; run after the girl and send her here. You musn't whisper anything, even to a brick wall, about these fellows, or they'll get hold of it and tip us the double after all."

The girl was brought in, and having been properly cautioned by Mr. Thompson to keep silent as to what had been just said, she promised obedience; and performed her promise by communicating the whole, and rather more than the whole, of what she had heard (always under a strict promise of secresy) to seven females and one male of her acquaintance; each of them, however, to her credit be it said, being persons in whose discretion she had more confidence than in her own; and they, good souls, proved their title to such confidence by each circulating improved versions of the story; so that by nightfall every pothouse in Theydon, Debden, Loughton, and the

No. 28.

neighbourhood, had undeniable assurance that Sutton the higler had found the robbers' cave ; that Mr. Thompson, with a troop of dragoons, had taken Turpin and his gang, after a desperate fight ; and that the prisoners and wounded had been seen by somebody—who had told somebody else, who had told the narrator—passing through somewhere on their way to Chelmsford.

"And now," said Thompson, after his informant had made an end of a minute though rather confused description of the features, natural and artificial, of the entrance to the cave; "I think I can't do better—you're not afraid I suppose to act as guide?—than go and examine this cave myself. The entrance, if it be such as you describe it, can't lead to the place where they stable their horses ; that they do that somewhere hereabouts is now plain enough ; for the guards at Stratford and at Waltham, are sure that they do not bring their horses from town, and I'm equally sure that they don't put them up at any inn in these parts ; so we must find out more before we let them know we have found out anything, else they'll give us the slip again. Now, Sutton, as I won't put it off beyond to-night, delay's dangerous, you and I will start for King's Oak. I'll leave my chaise there, and we'll go and see what further is to be learnt."

In a few minutes they were on the road, and in an hour were crawling on hands and knees among the thickets near Turpin's cave.

Stealthily, and with cat-like caution, they crawled and listened, and crept and crouched, as they threaded their devious way through the tangled undergrowth. At length they reached the spot where the former search of Sutton had ended. Thompson scrutinised it long and closely.

"This is no go," whispered he to the higler in a tone of disappointment : "it may be a lurking hole, but it can't be their stabling."

He looked carefully at the surrounding features of the place, and after some study his face brightened, as he said—

"Well, well ; this is a glorious find, at any rate, Sutton ; but there's more yet to be learnt. I'm not quite certain, but I've some notion, that I've heard hereabouts of a cave of some size, used many years agone by robbers ; sure-ly it's somewhat near hand. It's strange—though it's some years since to be sure that I heard on't—that I shouldn't have thought of this place before. Let me see. Do you know the ground well hereabout, Sutton?"

"Can't say as I do," replied the higler ; "but if so be as they've another place beside this here, I'll pound it, it arn't a longways off. She wor as nice a wench as you'd wish to ha' seen, as slipt in at that little—"

The ranger grasped the whisperer by the arm, as a signal for silence ; a slight noise was heard, as of the withdrawing of a bolt, and the two men, retreating on all fours into the bushes, hid themselves in breathless apprehension in the friendly covert. The door opened, and they had scarcely ended nestling and settling down in their concealment, when a man, in a countryman's dress, emerged from the hole. After looking cautiously round, he passed through the bushes ; on reaching the outlet between the hazels before-mentioned, he made a long and anxious pause, and they could imperfectly see, by peeping between the stems about their place of concealment, that he was engaged in a close examination of the spot. Something had certainly attracted his attention, and they watched his movements with eager anxiety and palpitating hearts. They felt assured that, though they might succeed in slaying the man before them, yet within call were several, they knew not how many desperadoes, (for report had exaggerated their number,) whose only chance of safety would lie in the sacrifice of their lives, and who, they doubted not, would swarm forth from their hive on the first alarm of a shot. The man continued for a minute or more, to them an hour, to linger about the place; at last, after throwing the twigs into their usual disorder, and sprinkling some loose leaves on the spot of his egress, he walked hastily off. Thompson drew near his companion.

"We'll take that fellow, if he gives us a chance," said he; "he's ours; but we must let him get a little further off the den. Hark! do you hear his footsteps? I don't."

"No," said the higler, who had been laying his ear near the ground; "I'll get up and take a peep."

The man rose to his feet, and peered through the upper twigs of the bushes. "I don't see aught on him," said he.

"It'll never do to stay here, Sutton," said Thompson; "I'll tell you how we'll contrive it, as soon as we're out of this. We'll have 'em, never fear."

They crept along till they came to a pathway through the wood.

"I'll tell'ee what," said the higler, looking carefully on the ground as they walked slowly along; "here's a hoss bin this a-way, and not long since neither;" and he fell on his hands and knees and peered knowingly along the pathway. The marks of horses' hoofs were here and there visible.

"There's a strong stile at the end of this, Sutton," said the ranger, musing; "and the only other way to get in is by the three posts, opposite the Bell. By Jove, this *is* queer; no horses—and if ever horse was shod, that's the print of a shoe, ay, and there's the calkins—ever could come this way, unless—"

"Look here, look here," whispered Sutton, beckoning his master, who was carefully tracing the footmarks; "one, two, three, four; and this is another foot, for it's broader in the bar, and not so round as t'other. One, two, three, four, you sees; and here, under this big oak, they walks over the hard soil into the wood."

They passed a piece of loose gravelly ground, beneath an oak, and "walked as though they trod on eggs," until, after threading the labyrinthine windings described in our first notice of the cave, and discovering at every step fresh proof that they had hit the right track, they came to the small open space, before what might be called the entrance to the covered way which led to the mysterious retreat of bold Dick Turpin.

While peeping from the bushes, before venturing to cross this small lawn, a stealthy step caught their ear, and the man they had before seen, after putting aside a bough or two, appeared from the opposite side of the area. The fact was, that Dick had discovered the passage of the two men, who were ignorant of the precautions used by the gang; and knowing that Madge had lately left the place and returned, he attributed the appearances to her neglect, and was now making his way back to the principal entrance, to caution her to be more guarded.

"We're between him and his den," said Thompson; "he's coming this way; he'll discover us: let's put a bold face on't, and seize him."

During the whole time Thompson had kept his gun slung at his back; he now unstrapped it, and stepping out of the thicket, advanced towards Turpin. The latter had seen Thompson before, when in disguise. He knew him; he approaching him with readiness, in an off-hand manner enquired if he was looking for rabbits? The ranger replied in the affirmative.

"I shouldn't think this a likely place," remarked Dick, with studied care-lessness; for he strongly suspected the ranger's object. "Have you found any?"

"No!" said the ranger; "but—" and he caught at Turpin's collar, "I've found a Turpin!"

He had *found* him it's true, but it was another thing to *keep* him; for the act of extending his arm exposed his side, in which Dick dealt him so severe and bursting a blow as sent him, though a strong man, reeling, with his mouth open, gasping for breath; and the higler at that moment showing himself, Dick, with one active bound, dashed into the wood. The first act of the ranger was to put his hand to his side: he was a bulky man, and so severe was the blow that he feared he was stabbed. He drew a long and painful breath and gasped out, "Why--didn't--you--seize him, Sutton?" for not doing which the higler gave a most satisfactory reason—"'cause he couldn't." Meantime, Dick hastily entered the cave, and seizing a carbine which hung against the wall, exclaimed, "We're hunted to earth, Madge!" and rushed out. She followed. The two men yet stood in the small open space, and at this moment, the ranger, spying Dick's hat or Madge's cap move among the bushes, in his haste and excitement inconsiderately raised his gun to his shoulder and fired. The smoke curled among the bushes, the swan-shot rattled, and the next moment Dick appeared at the opening. Thompson, holding his gun by the barrel, rushed towards him; Turpin raised his carbine, the trigger moved, and the whole charge entered the breast of the unhappy ranger. One short cry, a heavy groan, and the murdered man lay on the turf before them. The higler, who was only armed with a stick, no sooner saw the fall of his master, than he sought safety in a hasty flight. Turpin looked at the face of the dying man.

"Bring him some water," said he, in a hoarse voice. "He sought it—I did it not—it was self defence.

Thus does villany of the blackest dye ever seek to excuse to itself the consequences of its own previous crimes—not considering, or caring to remember, that it is the small crime which leads to the greater, and that when man once transgresses the eternal principles of right and wrong,—once commits those great offences, which all nations, times, climes, and creeds have accounted crimes against society, he has lost the power of self-controul, and can never say to himself, "thus far will I sin, but no further;" a countless scorpion progeny of sins rise hell-engendered from his first great crime.

Turpin, it is true, regretted the stern necessity, for such he tried to persuade himself it was, which had compelled him to this deed of blood; and almost argued himself into justifying the slaying of a fellow creature who was engaged in the performance of a duty he owed no less to the community than himself—namely, the enforcement of those laws without which might must dis-place right, strength supersede justice, peace and order lie strangled amid anarchy, bloodshed, and confusion, and the *sic volo sic jubeo* of powerful tyranny stand for the peaceful supremacy of that social law of which Hooker has truly said, "The public power of all societies must ever be above every soul contained in them; and the principal use of that general power is to give laws unto all that live under it: which law it is the duty of each and every to obey and enforce; * * * because, except our own private and but opinionable resolutions be by the law of public determination overruled, we take away all possibility of sociable life in the world." * * Then, with a burst of eloquence which even the quaintness of the old philosopher's scholastic style cannot obscure, he declares, with a sublimity only exceeded by its truth, "that we may briefly add; of law, [order] there can be no less acknowledged than that her seat is the bosom of God; her voice the harmony of the world: all things in heaven and earth do her homage; the very least as feeling her care, the greatest as not exempted from her power: creatures of what condition soever, though each in different sort and manner, yet all with uniform consent, adoring her as the mother of their peace and joy.*"

"What!" exclaims the reader, "you are 'at your old lunes again?' Twice have you apologised for these digressions. Though you mayn't be aware of it, I can assure you that these 'unutterable ponderings' are anything but amusing, and if they be instructive all I can say is, that they are confoundedly misplaced; nay, I consider them a fraud, although perhaps a *pious* one, a sort of sermonising clap-trap, which the readers of the life of a bold highwayman never calculated on purchasing, and therefore a foisting off of morality under false pretences." Such was, in effect, the criticism, as he called it, of a "kind friend;" and though I shall, perhaps, if I like it, take his advice and eschew these vagaries, I won't beg pardon where I believe myself right: yet as a book must consult the taste of its readers, or it will not sell; and if it don't sell can be of no earthly use, either to public, printer, or author; I'll 'hold a candle to the devil,' waive digression, though it be the only part of my book worth reading, and as Jonathan has it, "go ahead."

Short time for tarrying now remained for Turpin. This last and deadly encounter had entirely destroyed his plans. There had been a witness to the shedding of the blood which was now sinking into the thirsty earth of the cave—for thither they had dragged the body—and there could be no doubt that an hour or two would bring its avengers with a force that must look down resistance. It was by this time long past noon, and the short twilight was fast coming on.

"We must take time by the forelock, Madge," said Turpin, endeavouring by an assumed cheerfulness of tone to shake off the depressing sense of blood-guiltiness, and actively knocking about everything at hand, though apparently with no fixed purpose; Madge's feelings were of another and more selfish class; the fear of caption was uppermost in her mind.

"Oh, for mercy's sake, Dick," said she, looking on the corpse, "let's get away from this place; they'll be here presently, sogers and all. Oh, if you don't leave this place directly, I shall—"

"Do what?" said Dick, endeavouring to force both a joke and a smile.

Madge was silent.

"I shan't stay here any longer than I can help, I promise you," said he. "We must leave a good many things behind, Madge; this will be a bolting the moon sort o' job at last; the cart is at the Grange, and I can't get it at a moment's notice. I have it," said he, suddenly. "Get your basket and disguise, that beaver slouch I mean, the bright kerchief, linsey petticoat, and the rest—ruddle your face, my Madge, a little," and he tried a laugh; "come, be brisk about it, or else I shall—run away, as I suppose you were going to threaten just now."

Madge, who had the highest admiration for, and confidence in Turpin, smiled in her turn, and sought, by active exertion, to shake off the suffocating

* Eccl. Pol. book 1, sec. 16, *ad fin.*

load she felt weighing on her chest.   They were soon prepared, and Dick, after leading his horse nearly two miles by the most unfrequented paths, was joined by Madge in a by-lane, who mounted a pillion behind him, a mode of travelling then so common as not to draw the attention which even a common chaise cart would excite.

> "———— Light thickened,
> And the crow made wing to the dusky wood,"

as Turpin and Madge struck into a seldom-travelled by-way.   For the thorough knowledge which Dick possessed of the country enabled him to avoid the high road, now unsafe for *his* travelling, as the reader will be at no loss to conclude.

They rode on their silent way; the fears of Madge pressed with leaden weight upon her spirits, and forbad much speech, while the thoughts of Turpin were turned to the mistakes and misadventures to which this precipitate flight might give rise.

"Madge," said Dick, "why you're mute as a fish.   They say women are shrewd at a difficulty—so let's have your advice, girl.   George and Haynes will be at King's Oak to-night or to-morrow; and I've more than a guess they may light on other visitors besides friends.   Now I should never forgive myself for betraying a pal, still less such a one as Fielder—how's it to be done; how *can* we give him the office, Madge?   I can't say I just now see; do you?"

"*We* musn't stay in this quarter, anyhow," replied the woman; "and if he *is* to be taken, why he *is*.   I'd be sorry to hear of any ill-luck happening to George, but it can't do him no good for others to suffer as can't help him out o' the hobble.   Besides, we can help him best when we're t'other side the Lea, 'cause there's no dragoons on the roads there; and belike he hasn't left London, and if so, we can give him warning not to go to the Oak— eh?"

These arguments, backed by Dick's wish to believe in their cogency, silenced his scruples.   Now and again they stopped to listen, as the formation of the country reverberated from some rising ground their horse's footfall, and bringing to the ear the echoing sounds, told of some other horseman near them.   At each such sound they halted; until satisfied that none but themselves travelled that road, they resumed their way, grateful, with Nature's poet, that

> "Dark night, which from the eye its function takes,
> The ear more quick of apprehension makes,
> And where it doth impair the seeing sense,
> Still pays the hearing double recompense."

Thus they journeyed until the tower of the church at Nazing greeted their eyes, for now the night had changed its features, and the friendly darkness, which had hitherto hung its thick clouds over them, was exchanged for the, to them, dangerous glitter of starlight.   The glorious expanse above brought no pleasure to their eyes—crime and the beauties of Nature have no sympathy :—

> "The floor of heaven
> All thick inlaid with patines of bright gold,"

was inwardly cursed by their guilty minds, with the impiety, but not the sublimity, of Milton's fallen angel.

"It won't do to pass the bridge by this light," said Dick, in a tone of vexation, as they stood in the shade of a large tree, in a lane some fifty or sixty yards from the main road leading to the bridge. "Madge, can you hold on? we'll go up beyond the marsh and ford the river."

"Oh, anything," replied she, "to be out of the reach of those dreadful fellows. I'll trust to you—I'll not be afeerd. Hark!" said she, her hearing sharpened by her fears.

The heavy trot and iron rattle of a horse-soldier was heard: the relief-challenge at the bridge was followed by the hasty walk of a couple of horses down the road, and the laugh and talk of the fellows who were riding off to their quarters.

"It's all up there," said Dick, with a smile at Madge, and chucking her under the chin; "that's our friends, did you hear 'em?"

"Oh yes," said the frightened woman, in whom fear had absorbed all other feelings: "pray put me down here, and leave me to make my escape myself, if you're going to face those men. Don't, pray—you'll be shot; and then—" and she finished her incoherent speech with some suppressed sobs and a flood of genuine tears—poured out chiefly for her own situation, and partly at the thought of the dreadful scene she had conjured up.

"Why, you don't think me such a d—d fool as to throw myself in the way of those fellows' carbines, and with a woman at my back too, do you?" said Turpin. "No; no! you shall see though. You're nearer 'em now than you ever shall be again; at least with my consent. Hold fast!" and Dick walked his horse slowly down the lane they came up, increasing at each step the distance between themselves and the high road.

He now dismounted, and led the animal cautiously beneath the shade of hedgerows; these, however, were soon exchanged for willow, pollards, patches of reedy grass, and the usual accompaniments of a wet heavy soil. The beaten way disappeared. The river bank, or rather the shelving shoaly side of the stream was gained; and after a cautious inspection, both up and down the open space on which they were about to expose themselves, he led the steed into the gravelly bed. There was a sharp stream running, but the place for fording had been well chosen; the current there being broad and shallow, rippled over its natural bed unconfined by artificial embankments. They passed, unmolested and unobserved, to the Hertfordshire bank, and continued their journey,

"Till, like a lobster boiled, the morn,
From black to red began to turn;"

viewing which beauteous sight we shall leave them, to look after the fortunes, or misfortunes, of George Fielder.

We have before mentioned that Fielder was in London, turning into current coin the plate and jewels of Justice Asher; this he had done with considerable success, and with replenished purse was now making his way towards King's Oak. The high road by Stratford he knew to be carefully guarded, and accordingly he and his companion, Roger Haynes, separated, and singly made good their return into Essex on the very day of the death of the unfortunate Mr. Thompson. Fearing communication with even the casual passengers, they shunned the highways, and plunging into the more wooded parts of the country, made the best of their way towards King's Oak, the neighbourhood of which they reached at nightfall. The whole country was alive; and they were not a little alarmed at finding the soldiery were hastening in all directions along the roads in the neighbourhood. After lurking a while, Fielder resolved on leaving Roger, and venturing to mix among a group of countrymen whom he saw in deep talk before the public house at Sewardstone. Here he learnt the just discovered murder of Thompson, the arrival of the soldiery, and the ransacking of the cave; of which one of the fellows was giving such a description to his companions as left no doubt on his mind that all was over; he was, however, gratified at hearing that Dick and Madge were not as yet taken—

"Though," said the bumpkin, who was retailing these wonders, "they won't be long afore they has 'em. Cos d'ye see the sogers is everywhere arter 'em; and if so be they hasn't dealings wi' the ould gentleman—and some do say as Captain Turpin have sold hisself to 'un, to have his own way for ten year—they'll be hung up to dry, the whole on 'em, herring fashion; and I'll make one to see 'em."

Fielder slipped away from the group unobserved, and hastening back to Haynes, communicated the unlucky tidings. They divided the cash between them, and at once began their flight.

Haynes was lucky enough to pass the river unobserved, but not so Fielder. His travels in town had come to the knowledge of some of the officers of police, to whom the Jew receivers, on condition of being left unmolested, had given not only a portion, in the shape of cash, of their illgotten wealth, but had "split" upon the robbers; and upon condition of not being implicated in any disclosures which might ensue, they 'planted' their 'goot friends' the thieftakers on the very men whom they had just victimised "shent per shent," in what these most detestable of thieves termed the "way of bishness."

This affair was thus managed: the officers who had got scent of the whereabouts of Fielder, received the hush-money; and then, without disclosing the receivers whom they had detected, put a brother officer in the way of doing what they could not do without danger of compromising themselves; thus effecting the apprehension of the felons, and obtaining the reward; of course stipulating for their "regulars," as they termed their share of the "blood-money." In consequence of this information, two expert London thieftakers had tracked the two robbers from London, and were now "beating the bush," in conjunction with some soldiers, in the neighbourhood of the spot where Fielder and Haynes had a few hours before passed the Lea. George, to whom the country was imperfectly known, had decided on returning over the border, at the spot where he had entered Essex, and this proved his destruction. He had made his way in safety, just as day was breaking, to the bridge, without meeting a living creature; and confident in his disguise, was jogging along the road, when he was accosted by a man, whom he well knew as a London officer. The man having courteously addressed him, they walked together a few yards; and Fielder was just contriving a bold push for an escape, when another man sprung from the hedge-row on the opposite side, and the two simultaneously seized him. A whistle was given, and from the bridge foot, where they lay in ambush, three guards with their corporal appeared.

"Here's the leftenant, lads!" cried the thieftaker.

The man pointed their pieces at Fielder, and the handcuffs were immediately slipped on.

"Your captain's not far off, I suppose?" observed the 'trap' with a grin; "so we'll make you safe, and see if we can't find you some company in your

The Golden Lion at Boston. Mr. Newton the Horsedealer.

new lodgings. Artful dodge, though—and werry nice you did it at the price. Well, well," continued the officer, as he locked the handcuffs, " we has all our time when we're cotched a-napping ; p'raps it wouldn't be the worse for you, if so be you was to do a little *splittery*—summut in the *nosing* way I means ; cos, d'ye see, if so be we could wind up this mornin's job by grabbing the Captain—you needn't try to look hinnocent, you knows well enow who I means. Come, come," added he in a confident coaxing tone ; " do the ready thing, and I'll guv you a lift before the beaks as 'ull save your *squeeze*. Eh, vot—you're crusty, are yer ? If there's any hoath among ye—as I knows you're a plucky one, Georgy, as 'ill try to do the thing that's right by a pal— vy, you can give us the ticket and sarve yerself, without saying —"

" It's your turn, Mr. Johnson," replied Fielder, whom not even the peril of his position could cast down ; " but save your breath to cool your porridge, my boy ; you'll get nothing out of me, 'xcept this—that ' the Captain,' as you call him, is more lucky than me, for he's out o' your reach, as I wish I was. Why the dickens," continued he, (looking towards the soldiers, who still stood with military preciseness, with pieces at the " present,")—why don't you drop those ' fire-irons?' They're ugly playthings, and enough to make a fellow nervous. (The corporal gave the word, and the men " recovered.") Ay, now you do look a little less dangerous. Come, Billy Johnson, just walk us off some where : here's a house, and I'll stand a drop, for I'm cursed thirsty."

" I shall jist help myself for that matter," replied Johnson. " So, you
No. 29.

won't say nothing about your Captain—well, it 'ull be worse for you.   Corporal, leave your men here; there's two more on 'em on the lurk somewhere; and Sam, you stay with the sogers, while I, and the corporal, and Mr. Fielder, as he says he's thirsty, just take a rosin.* "

The officer looked closely at the handcuffs, passed the prisoner's handkerchief behind his back, and before his elbows, and having thus secured him, they walked a few yards to the public house at the foot of the bridge. Here, over the glass, a long conversation took place, in which Johnson vainly voured, by various allurements and promises, to draw from George some clue to the whereabouts of Dick; and strongly urged, now that all was up with Turpin, who, he said, would not long escape, that Fielder should make his peace with the law by furnishing him with the information, necessary to his capture.   To all these fine promises, however, George turned a deaf ear; and at last the thieftaker, finding all his rhetoric in vain, lost his temper, and threw off his feigned civility.

"This here will all fall on your own head, I tell you." said he, angrily. "It's the captain as the justices most wants, and you might get off, if so be you worn't so precious headstrong.   But it's no use talking; I've tried to stand your friend, but you won't let me,—so, Mister Corporal, with your assistance, I'll sarch the prisoner."

The rummaging of Fielder's pockets, his hat, his boots, &c., was soon completed; but nothing more than a few shillings was found.

Bill Johnson looked blank.   Again and again he passed his hands over the highwayman's person, no money was there.   The disappointment sadly ruffled his equanimity—Fielder jeeringly said,

"What would you give, now, to recover some of the rhino that has made you so 'cute in this business, Billy my boy, eh ?"

The officer raised his hand.

"Don't strike a man as can't pertect himself, yer cowardly feller," said the soldier interposing, "fair play's a Hinglishman's motto; and I von't see him ill used."

Ill-humour at the grievous disappointment of missing the rich booty he had such certain intelligence of, inclined the officer to be quarrelsome, and he turned angrily on the soldier.   He was a blunt fellow; and as Bill Johnson looked at his open face and broad athletic shoulders, and his unshrinking though good-natured, careless look of defiance, he felt his courage, like Bob Acres', "oozing out at his finger's ends."

Johnson offered his hand, which the soldier accepted.

"It can't be far off," said the latter; "and if there bees all the gould as you talked on this morning, afore we lighted on this here gentleman, why it can't be stowed in a snuff-box nor the bowl of a 'bacca-pipe.   P'raps, as fair words does more than foul—leastways, they al'ays does with me—this here gemman, as so much ready can't be of no manner of use to him, will put us in the way of getting hold on it, without the trouble of sarching for it—provising we tips him his fair whack on it, and divides it reg'lar Yorkshire."

This did not at all suit Mr. Johnson's notions of justice; he estimated highly his own professional skill, and had never calculated on more than a guinea as the share of the redcoat; and as to "your paying back," Falstaff did not "hate" it more fervently; he therefore exclaimed—

* Wet.

"Vot, give a third of vot I've yarned by my skill and gumption to you, and another large vack to this here sulky tell-nothing varmint; vell, I'm jiggered, mister lobster, if I can make a guess vere you vos dragged up: I thinks you vasn't behind the door ven 'cheek' vos sarved out, or you vouldn't go for to propose to a Lunnon hofficer to guv up his perquisites, and divide reg'lars with a redherring and a limebird* as —"

Fielder saw, with a pleased eye, that the reflections on his profession, and the nicknames which the vexed Mr. Johnson had made use of, brought the blood into the soldier's face. However, the man seemed to suppress his indignation, and twisting up a piece of a printed bill, he lighted it at the fireplace, and to the no small vexation of the prisoner, waved it beneath the table at which they had just been sitting. It will be necessary to apprise the reader, that Fielder had suspended the bag of guineas round his neck by a string of sufficient length to allow the bag to hang below the tight waistband of his unmentionables—at that day worn by all classes without braces; that while seated in the corner, he had contrived, by leaning against the table, to stretch the slight cord to breaking, and cunningly and quietly letting the bag gradually down to the ground, between the calves and ankles of his legs, had silently driven it with his foot into a dark corner under the settle.

"Oh! oh!" cried the searcher, jocosely, as he caught sight of the precious deposit: "finding's keepings!" and thrusting his rattan into the corner, he struck the bag, which gave forth the dull but most musical chink of gold. The eye of Mr. Bill Johnson had sulkily followed the movements of the soldier; he saw the bag, and heard the sound and the exclamation of the finder, who was preparing to drop on hands and knees to crawl under the table.

"'Vast, there," said the greedy thieftaker; and he seized the soldier by the shoulder to thrust himself before him. The fellow, gathering from what had just dropped from the officer, that his share of the gold was likely to be but small, if he trusted to his generosity, caught Mister Johnson by the leg, and dropped him on his broadest end. Fielder watched the movement with a smile; and at the instant Mr. Johnson's seat touched the floor, he sprung through the open doorway, ran through the long passage to the back yard, and made the best of his way across the fields at the back of the house. The corporal jumped first to his feet, and following close, kept him in sight, as he put his best leg foremost in pursuit; and Bill Johnson, shouting at the top of his voice "Stop thief!" followed hard in his wake.

"Hoy, halloo!" shouted two or three early labourers who were mending the road near the river side, and with picks and spades they joined in the pursuit.

The soldiers and constables on the bridge heard the cry, but little guessed its cause, till hastening on to the wooden structure, they saw their late prisoner, at "topping speed" heading "the chase," as a turn of the road brought him in view: but he was too far off for a shot, and in a few seconds more they saw their corporal, who was a young and active man, followed closely by Johnson, struggling in pursuit. They hastened to the road, down which the fugitive and his pursuers were holding their headlong course.

The shackled condition of Fielder was sadly against his chances of escape. He could not, with his bound hands, venture on a cross-country dash; stile or fence must be his destruction; swimming the river, too, was out of the question:

---

* Prisoner.

we have said before that he knew but little of the country, yet his speed and wind were good, and the thought struck him that if he could find the ford by which he and Roger had passed, and which could not be far off, he had yet a chance left. A bend in the road which followed the windings of the river, now placed him out of the immediate view of his pursuers, whose cries and footsteps were, however, much too near to be pleasant. Fielder nevertheless felt that he had scarcely, if at all, increased the distance between himself and the corporal who was an active young fellow, and had considerably headed the rest of the party.

"I shan't be able to hold this out long," thought he ; " and I'm just now running without a chance, for I shall surely meet somebody presently, and I shall be stopped and retaken. Huzza—!" cried he internally, as another bend of the way showed him the very white house by the ford, which he before had noted. Hope gave him fresh speed ; he laid out, and pressing his arms with all his strength forward and against his sides, the handkerchief tore at the knot, and with one more violent wrench the shackle of his handcuff gave way. He had not yet reached the fording place by some yards, but an exclamation of delight escaped his lips as he hastily and imprudently leaped from the bank : it was very suddenly and unpleasantly checked by finding himself, head and all under water—he struggled and rose—but the precious moment and equally precious had spot been missed. He had leaped into the well of a fish preserve and his staggering feet were hardly assured of ground beneath them, when his pursuers appeared within twenty yards of him : it was his last effort —fortune and activity might yet befriend him.

George's courage did not forsake him : on came the corporal, armed only with his cane, and quick as thought plunged in. He was, however, no swimmer, and George was now in midstream ; he was confoundedly puzzled, nevertheless, at not finding the shoal water he expected, and affairs looked very serious when Mr. Johnson walked rapidly into the river without sinking deeper than his knees, by judiciously entering some half dozen yards lower down : what made it worse too, was, that he was fast coming, in an oblique direction, towards the spot where Fielder was now struggling up a steepish bank into shallow water. The three were now within a few yards of each other—Fielder in the middle, Johnson below, and the soldier some little distance higher up. The bloodhound of the law was now close to his prey ; in his right hand he grasped a pistol, in the left he clutched the bag of gold, which, throughout the chase, he had held with characteristic pertinacity. Towards him, as the most pressing danger, and the man whose pursuit he most feared, Fielder boldly advanced.

"Surrender, George, or I fire !" cried Johnson, with levelled pistol.

"I do," gasped Fielder, with dissembled exhaustion, sinking on his knees in the water, with a pretended stumble. It was cleverly done. George ducked his head as his face neared the surface, caught the thieftaker's legs beneath the water, and he fell, discharging his pistol in the air. Gentle reader, did you ever try a tumble in three-foot water ? If not, do it, and see how awkward you'll find it to regain your legs. Moreover, imagine the additional awkwardness of receiving at the same time a blow on the head, with right good will, from a strong and desperate fellow--the said whack being rendered emphatic by the accompaniment of a heavy handcuff—and you will see good and sufficient reason why Mr. Bill Johnson did not pick himself up very quickly. Fielder turned—he was yet far from safe :—one look at the soldier who was close to him—a rush—and he disappeared below the surface into a deeper part. The red coat tried to stand still, but he was up to his armpits, and the stream refused him foothold. He looked around him as he walked with the current, and turning his face up the stream endeavoured to hold his ground, for he felt sure that it was *up* and *against* it that the fugitive had gone. At this moment George's head appeared for a moment, as he drew breath, some three yards off; the corporal made towards it. The soldiers had now come up.

"Present, lads!" cried the corporal, "and shoot him if you see him."

A few seconds and again the head of George appeared, this time close to the opposite shore, and near to a steep bank. The three men caught sight of it—the levelled tubes swept slowly towards the point, the priming hissed, the bullets whizzed to their destination, and the rattling explosion of the muskets struck on the ear, mingled with the short bubbling death-cry of George Fielder, as his shattered head sunk beneath the waters. All the balls had struck him; two, with deadly precision, tore through the brain, and the third struck his spine, just below the base of the skull. His death was merciful and instantaneous.

"He's done for, lads!" said the corporal, with professional coolness, as he watched the death-spring and the struggling sink of the highwayman. The body soon rose, and was drawn ashore and laid on the bank with the same pleasant smile which had curled round the lips in life. The peculiar relaxation which marks a death by gunshot wound may not be known to the reader; unlike most other modes of violent death, the victim's countenance assumes a placid tranquillity; every passion seems at rest, and the face, if of pleasant expression during life, seems as of one who dreams happily—and such was the countenance of George Fielder.

It may be guessed that such an unusual noise as the nearly simultaneous discharge of three muskets at so early an hour, not only "awoke the echoes," as the poets have it, but aroused the inhabitants of the "thereabouts." In a very short time, some dozen or two assembled. Mr. Johnson was dragged senseless from the river, with his nose and one eye dreadfully damaged, and minus his darling money bag, which, strange to say, could never be found; while the body of poor George, with the head weighing some two ounces heavier than at any former period, was conveyed to the nearest alehouse, there to await the crowner's quest.

Poor fellow, he deserved a happier fate—the creature of impulse, the sport of circumstances, education—the first duty of every government deserving of the name—did little for him; his birth in a civilised community still less; and example, more powerful than precept, had, in his case, done worse than nothing: his crimes were great, his redeeming qualities many; and had not *others* neglected *their* duty, who are overpaid as *public teachers*, a few words in season, and a few moral lessons, might have made the reckless highwayman a valuable member of the social community, which first neglected, then corrupted him, and at last shed his blood for outraging the laws it had never taken one step to teach him to respect or to observe.

CHAPTER XX.

The last's a serious chapter—but 'tis not
My cue for any time to be terrific;
For chequer'd as is seen our human lot
With good, and bad, and worse : alike prolific
Of melancholy merriment, to quote
Too much of one sort would be soporific :
Without, or with, offence to friends or foes,
I sketch your world exactly as it goes.

OUR hero and his companion reached the rendezvous on the Rhee, mentioned in the last chapter, without question or adventure, where they were joined by King. The following night brought Roger Haynes. He related to them the circumstances of his escape, and the particulars of his separation from Fielder. The next day and night passed, and the party grew anxious at his protracted absence : Roger Haynes volunteered to seek if any hap-hazard information might be procured on the road to Broxbourne, and returned in a few hours with the lamentable particulars of his death.

The news threw a shade over the party; the flow of King's cheerfulness was checked ; and the thoughts of Dick reverted to his first adventure, and the few though chequered years of crime which had flown by since the pleasant comrade, now a stark corse in the hands of his enemies, presented him with the black colt now matured into his noble Bess. He thought too of his hearty good temper, his boldness, his truth, his merriment,—and, to his comrades, his honesty.

"He was the first," said Dick, shaking off his feelings with an effort, "with whom I took a purse—and damme, Tom, if he shan't be the last."

King stared.

"I've a few shiners, Tom, and I'll turn to another account what motherwit I have. I'll betake myself to Lincolnshire—quit the road and its dangerous pastimes, and turn honest man. What's to prevent me?"

"That you are Dick Turpin," replied Tom. " Stab me, if you're not coming it conventicle fashion, friend Dickon ; turn honest man—ha! ha! why your best friend could not wish an honester fellow than you are already—what the devil's come across you—eh? Show me the fellow who dares say Dick Turpin's not honest, and I'll give him no chance to repeat the lie. Cheer up, Dick, old fellow—poor George has escaped a higher and drier death ; one that would have been more tedious and painful, yet as unavoidable as the unlucky shot which cut short his joys and troubles."

"I'd give something more than thanks for your spirits ; but jesting don't always suit me, Tom, (and he offered his hand to his comrade.) This is no new thing ; I've thought long and seriously since that unlucky shot of mine at King's Oak—and so, if *you* are determined to keep the road, or rather make the road keep you, then, Tom, our ways lie different ; you shall always find a friend, but no longer a comrade, in Dick Turpin. My fireside, and I hope soon to have one, shall be your own; my purse at your service ; but I have resolved, and Richard Palmer will keep his word, to renounce my outlawed life."

"Well, well," said King in a subdued tone, for he knew that in these tempers Dick was immoveable ; " I suppose you know best ; I've prophesied though, once or twice before, and I've not been wide of the mark, when these sudden moralities come over you, that you'd find 'circumstances alter cases,' as the old women say—and some of our grandmothers were no fools. But are *you* really bent on cutting us all dead at this spot, eh? Mrs. Margaret," said King, with an engaging smile. "We must really get you to intercede with the Captain, as common report now styles him, not to —"

But the gay Tom's rhetoric had been forestalled, for the power to which he appealed had already been consulted, and the late taste of the perils and precariousness of a robber's life had made her not only assent, but strenuously exert herself to strengthen the resolved amendment of Turpin. The death of Fielder too, as related by Roger, lent her additional weight; so to King's appeal she replied :—

"Indeed, Mr. Tom, if you reckon on my word in this business, you're much mistaken : do'ee think as I'd take upon myself to advise Mr. Palmer against his own good? I've no idea, not I, of a gentleman like you doing as *my* Richard—(and she laid a stress on the *my*). We've made it up long since to go down into Lincolnshire, leave the whole on ye, and live quiet ; besides, for you to advise —"

"Will you oblige me," said Dick in a vexed tone, "by leaving myself and Tom to ourselves?"

Madge was too accustomed to Dick's voice not to know that this desire was a command ; she therefore left them.

"And now, Roger," said Dick, "have you a mind to take service, or will you follow your present life?"

"I'll follow you," replied the rough fellow, "go where 'ee will, so long as yee 'll let me. Ize main zorry though, for poor Master George ; he wor a jolly trump, and thof our 'quaintance wor but short, 'twos a merry one. Many's the time he brought the tears i' my eyes wi' laughing at his sayins and his doins—but he's goan ; " and Roger finished the funeral oration of his facetious friend with a shake of his huge head.

"Then I'll take you at your word," said Dick. " And now, Tom, farewell ; and if ever you come to Brough, for there it is my intention to settle, after buying a few horses on my road down ; I shall feel offended, if you forget your old friend—who was once Dick Turpin. Good bye!"

Twelve months had rolled by — it was market day at Boston, and a busy group of the more respectable graziers and farmers crowded the principal room ; a large panelled apartment, on the walls of which hung hats of every shape and size, and coats of every material and colour, from the showy upper "Ben," of the flashy horse-chaunter and coper, down to the coarse heavy blanketing of the sturdy farmer. The group was not less motley than the garments. Here two sporting-looking kiddies adjusted the difference between pounds and guineas in the price of a high-bred "bit of blood," and there farmer Wiggins settled wi' Gregory Gubbins the money "to boot" which should effect an exchange between "ould Ball" and his grey galloway, "Trusty;" while Mr. Flower, the miller, who never thought blindness an unsoundness, was chaffering for a sightless animal, which he had heard had been struck by lightning, and thus rendered almost useless for the pack-horse work of Mr. Swap, the carrier.

In the midst stood Mr. Newton, a most "respectable" horse-dealer, at least common report said so ; for he always paid what he promised, dealt shortly and liberally, sported a great deal of ready money, was off-hand in his settlement of accounts, liberal in his manner, sang a good song, and last, though not least, always paid for the "odd bottle," in a reckoning. He moreover kept a natty gig, had rather a dashing wife, and was therefore, of course, highly respectable and respected. Yet few knew whence Mr. Newton came; but as he "owed nobody nothing," as the saying was, "nobody need care;" and accordingly nobody *did* care, or trouble themselves, himself, or herself, about the private matters of Mr. Newton.

"I'll tell'ee what," said a hearty-looking man with whom Mr. Newton had just before entered, and who had now finished a bargain, "I think I've ge'en 'ee such a large figure for that animal, as you ought to stand summut hansome—I do—"

"With all my heart," said Mr. Newton; and they turned towards a small table to seat themselves.

At this table sat two men; they were dealing for a horse, and the purchase money had just been paid down. The face of the purchaser was turned away from Mr. Newton, but he could not fail to recognize the fall of the shoulders, the genteel riding coat, and the precise gentility and active person of his old friend, Tom King.

He stepped forward so as to get a sight of the man's face; at that moment the man turned his head, and a meaning smile stole across his features as he glanced at Turpin.

The farmer and Mr. Newton were soon joined by Tom.

"Ah! Mr. Newton, how do you do? Glad to see you—just come from Scarbro' myself; been drinking waters for benefit of health—saw servant on road, Mr. Newton,—said I should most likely find you at the Golden Lion—dem'd lucky to drop on you. Take a glass of sherris, friend N., do as we do, eh?"

To this rattle Mr. Newton replied by accepting the proffered glass; a bottle was discussed; the old farmer left the room, the company thinned, the young fellow of whom Tom had made a purchase departed, and the two friends were left nearly alone. A lazy-looking waiter loitered about, wiping up slops and rubbing tables; candles were brought, and at length the waiter aforesaid, having finished his dawdlings, retired to a little box or hole, fitted up for his convenience in one corner of the apartment, there to occupy himself in sundry deliberate gyrations of his fingers in the bell-shaped rummer glasses, which operation, though there was no dust in the glasses, he termed "dusting."

"I suppose Dick," said King, when they were left alone, "that you can't assist a fellow on a pinch in this part of the world—eh?"

Turpin did not look displeased. And here we must apologize for preferring nature to the statutes of novel-writing "in this case made and provided." We have before had occasion to avow our heresy, and declare our intention not to yield for an instant the precedent of melodrame and romance, where observation and truth tell us they belie nature. Turpin had good motives, but what avail are they against the evil bias of the human heart, when crime has become habitual? He had no fixed principle. He meant well yet acted ill. He saw the better and took the evil way; and then silenced conscience by "the tyrant plea, necessity." We have said that to such a soul as his action was life; with such spirits, it is the good or evil direction of their energies which makes them eminent for good or for evil. They cannot live and die like the commonplace plodders, who hug themselves mightily on their common sense, prudence, propriety, &c., &c.; they are the active and superior geniuses, who, figuring either as conquerors or cut-throats, hierarchs

Captain Scott robbed by Turpin and King.

or highwaymen, bishops or burglars, poets or pickpockets, princes or prison-breakers, monarchs or murderers, "carve" for themselves a name, by genius in the study, eloquence in the pulpit, valour on the battle field, or hardihood on the "bad eminence" of the scaffold. Of such mould, though differently directed by birth, education, time, temperament, and circumstances, are the men who, incapable of mediocrity, outstrip their fellows; who blot or illustrate the page of history; who live famous or infamous in the memory of their race; and who, whether as glorious objects for veneration and example, or beacons for evitation and abhorrence, *must* excite interest, whether figuring among the princes of the earth on the scroll of history, or "damned to everlasting fame" on the records of crime. Thus a "deathless hero," who "leaves a name at which the world grows pale," and a desperate villain, who lends an absorbing interest to the history of "notorious criminals," are but various studies of our common nature; forms, slightly differing, of our common clay, and nearer links in our common humanity than the conceit of sciolists, and the pride of philosophers dare own, even to themselves.

King waited his comrade's answer. Turpin was evidently undecided for once. The ruling passion for adventure had been long restrained; many a time had he felt an inclination to take a trip to town to see his old companion; and now he was thrown in his way. Dick was certainly ill-adapted for trade. The hasty generosity of his nature was no match for the wily "Yorkshire tykes," with whom he was continually dealing. He was, perhaps, as far as judgment was concerned, as good a judge of horse-flesh as most of

No. 30.

them; but his judgment was neutralised by the absence of that wary and patient cunning by which they would, as Sam Slick says, "get hold of the "end of a bargain:" consequently, as his character became known, his impetuous liberality was practised on; and, though he got the best off with his eyes open, Dick, with his liberal and spendthrift habits, had already exhausted his little capital. The failure of his means was not, however, accompanied by any retrenchment in his expenditure; nay, as his resources decreased, Dick, as might be expected from his temper, became more profuse, and what people called "liberal," or rather reckless. To King's question he replied,

"Can *I* assist you at a pinch, Tom, do you say? A word in your ear—here's twenty-five (and he drew out a small canvass bag) and five are thirty, (producing some loose gold and silver from his pocket,) take what you want."

"Why look ye, Dick," said King, with a slight expression of hurt feeling in his tone; "I *did* suppose you thought better of me than that I'd sponge on even *you*; though I know your purse is as free as your heart. No, no; 'tis not for money that I asked your assistance—but I've a question, which I know you'll excuse, and then we'll talk about t'other business. How go matters—business matters—prosperously? I know we've no secrets."

"I'll tell you, Tom," said Turpin, lowering his voice, "these thirty guineas you see there, are the full half of all I possess in the world, and twenty of that's the produce of a mare and foal which belongs to one Tom Creasey, of Bullingbrook; 'twixt you and I Tom, I must take Bullingbrook in my way, and call on that fellow; he's a shrewd chap—an ugly customer in the way of lying, cheating, and all the other accomplishments which go to make a prosperous dealer in these parts. You haven't seen so much of 'em as I have. I'm sick, heart sick, of the meanness, scoundrelism, and roguery of these slow-blooded, chaffering knaves, who talk of their 'honesty,' while they are always sailing within a doubtful point of the law. A set of vagabond cheats who only avoid felony in their dealings because their cowardice blenches at the thought of danger to their own worthless carcases. I've many a time, Tom," continued he, his choler rising as he spoke, "many a time been tempted to right myself by robbing some scoundrel who had taken a dirty advantage of me, (all, as he called it, in the way of trade;) it's no use blinking it, Tom: I wasn't meant for this d—d plodding, dirty cheatery, and what's more, I'm determined to have done with it—so out with your scheme—and if you've need of him, Dick Turpin's once again your man."

"Bravo!" exclaimed King, grasping his hand; "there spoke Dick himself. Good bye, Mr. Newton"—(and Tom bowed, with much gravity, towards the door, as if bidding some one farewell.) "The plot's this:—Didst ever hear of Dicky Scott—Captain Scott of Scarborough-Spa—'The Governor,' as they call him? (Dick replied by an affirmative nod.) Well, p'raps, by way of explaining, I ought to tell you I've been doing the dash there for this season; and being, I flatter myself, a pretty fellow of my inches, I began the campaign tolerably well: I was flush-blunted too, so ran on pleasantly enough; for you see, thus far north, I hadn't the honour of being known. But all play and no work will never do, Dickon; and I must say that I've sadly lost sight of business in my pleasures. Among my acquaintance there, I've become rather intimate with the Captain, and an oddity he is; he took a marvellous fancy to me, by-the-bye:—well, though I wasn't looking for anything of the sort, I picked up a few little bits of information, that may be of professional service ; and one of them is, that the Captain makes it a practice to keep the greater part of his property in cash—and from his prompt payment, has got the name of ' Ready-money Dick.'   Now, at the end of the season, on leaving Scarborough, he takes with him a large sum to his residence at Pickering, mostly in gold.   What say you, Dickon, to a few hundreds of the gold the worthy ' Governor' has collected from the visitors at the Spa ?"

Dick assented by a squeeze of the hand, at the same time laying upon the table a heavy-handled horsewhip, which he now usually carried : King's attention was attracted to its massive mounting.

" I see you like to distinguish yourself even in these parts," said he ; " egad, such a whip as that would astonish the horsemen at " St. James's :" (Tom read the inscription.) ' To James Newton, Esq.'—damme, they've 'squired you too—' as a testimony of their respect, this whip is presented by the members of the Buckleigh Club ;' very good ; ha! ha! and who may this same ' Buckleigh Club,' as they call themselves, be ?"

" A mere set of hawbucks," said Dick, " though convivial dogs they are, as far as that goes ; they presented me this whip—which, I must own, shows their good feeling much more than their taste—in consideration of some slight serivces rendered, and the remembrance of some pleasant hours.   But when, for this is idle talk, do you ride?--'tis some seventy miles, or more—to Scarborough? and you've not told me when the *pigeon* flies."

" On Monday next," answered King ; " five days are surely enough for the distance : we must not travel together, and I'll meet you on the road.   And now, Dickon, we'll take a cheering cup, and cast dull care behind us."

The hours flew merrily, and it was late before the smirking chambermaid, with bright candlestick in hand, was called to usher the ' two gentlemen in the travellers' room,' to their Nos. 8, 9, 10, or whatever their rooms might have been inscribed ; for as *de minimis non curat lex*, so will not our history record these minute details.   Suffice it to say, that there they slept till

——The morn,
Waked by the circling hours, with rosy hand,
Unbarred the gates of light.

An early breakfast, and the lure of two cobs was despatched, and Turpin and King rode towards Brough.

Three nights after, again on the back of his " coal black steed," with the " friend he could trust beside him," Dick stood beneath a tree on the side of the road between Scarborough and Pickering.   The similarity of the position, for the day had been rainy, to that in which, years agone, he had entered on his first robbery, rushed on his mind.   Where was their companion, the mentor, the instructor in crime, to whom he had looked up?   How different now his feelings !   The emulous, eager tyro, had become the cool, the dauntless, the self-possessed master of his hazardous pursuit ; and had so far distanced the knights-errant of his reckless profession, as to leave vulgar robbers immeasurably behind.   And what were now his feelings?   The *omne ignotum pro magnifico* again illustrated.   He thought, as all such men do, little or nothing of himself, or of his acts, and wondering why people should be astonished at that in which *he* saw nothing to wonder at—hummed a tune impatiently, and turned to King.

" 'Tis seven o'clock, Tom ; I hear the bell : I've no notion, when I start on such a spec. as this, to make a miss of it.   You say he stops at the ' Garter' to change—why, d—n it, I'll take a push off, Tom, and look for him."

So saying Dick dismounted, and drew his saddle-girths; then patting his matchless mare on her bold arched neck, he remounted.

"Stay here, Tom, till I return," said he; and he cantered gaily towards the inn spoken of, which was distant some mile and a half.

As he approached the hostel, he saw no chaise, as he had reckoned on, standing at the door; he therefore gave his horse to the stable-boy, and entered the coffee-room.

There he found himself not a little at fault. Direct questions might have excited suspicion, and after a few commonplaces, he left the room and adjourned to the bar, where, after ordering his horse, on the plea of intending to ride some five miles further, he fell into chat with a rosy-lipped buxom damsel, who claimed paternity from the landlord of the Garter. A few jests from so good looking a customer, and some soft things from so "nice a man," —for Dick had that prepossessing exterior which, like a scarlet coat, allures womankind, when real merit, and that which passeth show, is naught—placed them on the best of terms. To record this "small change" of conversation would be tedious and foreign to our purpose—suffice it to say that, after some rallying as to her numerous sweethearts, a "soft impeachment" which never offended even the veriest prude, Dick said,—

"And so you dare to tell me, Marian,—your's is a pretty name; excuse the compliment—(Marian smirked)—that none of the dashing London gentlemen from Scarbro' ever took your fancy? Come, tell me, don't you dream now and then, Marian, of a Captain Darcy, who was here some months ago?"

The girl's colour changed momentarily, and, with a toss of the head, she said,—

"I'll thank you, sir, to mind your own business—Captain Darcy, indeed! I never trouble my head, I'm sure, about any such fellows."

Her mortified tone belied her words, and female curiosity triumphing over her affected indifference, she added,—

"Do you know anything about the Captain? He promised—" then checking herself, she looked at Dick, and with the arch smile of a coquette, continued, "but all you fine London gentlemen think nothing of promising us silly conntry girls, and then leaving us—"

Their chat was interrupted at this point by a long and loud ring at the yard bell, and a stumping countryman, who entered the passage, exclaiming,

"I zay, missus, here's a foine to-do just a t'other soide o' the hill. They ha' brokken doon wi' the Guvner's ould cwoach, and hur wants Robin, and zum help to lug the ould lumb'ring thing to the smithy—an a poastshay to Pickering, d'ye see."

The non-appearance of their intended prey was now fully accounted for.

In ten minutes the Captain arrived, and having ordered supper, declared that he should stay there that night; and Dick, having found out the exact time at which the chaise was ordered for the morning, hastened back to his comrade.

"Tommy, my boy," said he, "this will be a peep-o'-day job—my best chops have generally been early morn ones. We must put up for the night somewhere; you're too well known to show at the Garter, I find. Egad! Tommy, you've been turning the girl's head there, for she looked all carnation when I named Captain Darcy—you're a sad dog, Tom, however---so we'll ride back to the next village, and return to this by seven o'clock, about which time I've made an appointment with myself to meet Captain Scott on matters of business—eh?"

"By all means," said Tom, laughing. "I too have a loan to negotiate with the same gentleman; and with your consent, Dick, I wish to have you as a witness of the transaction; so, at seven, we'll wait the arrival of our kind provider, under this very tree."

They rode off, and stabled their horses at an alehouse on the road; then retired to a private room.

It was a dull and cloudy morning, as the two highwaymen repaired to the spot fixed on. The chill air was loaded with a damp fog, which rendered it difficult to discern objects, even at the distance of a few yards.

"Cheerful day this, Tom; one would think it made on purpose for our job. Hark! here he comes!"

The posters came on at a shuffling trot, and the chaise was opposite to the tree, when King commanded the post-boy to "stand," which ominous order he obeyed, even with the hair on his head, which stood erect with fright as he eyed the barrel of the long horseman's pistol in a line with his skull.

The Captain, however, was quick and ready; he was well armed, and among his eccentricities, "discretion," which Falstaff has pronounced the better part of valour, was certainly not to be found. The word "Stand!" was followed by a flash from the window of the chaise, and a bullet whizzed across the cheek bone of King, flittering the yellow worsted wig with which Tom's natural hair was covered, and carrying away a love lock, about the size of an opera glass, which had long been one of the objects of his assiduous cultivation. Tom raised his hand to his head, down which the blood was trickling, felt his left ear, and was about to return the compliment with interest, when Dick, who was near the coach window, cried out,

"Don't fire, Bob—no bloodshed; come, surrender, or—"

The chaise-door opened, and there stood Captain Scott with another pistol in his hand.

"Come, come, gentlemen—I beg a parley," cried he, on seeing that he had two armed men to deal with. Dick, who carried the heavy horsewhip before mentioned, had no notion of treating thus with a presented piece; so with one sudden and sharp blow, he struck the weapon from the Captain's hand. The unfortunate gentleman saw all resistance must be worse than useless; he therefore tried, by resigning a part of the large sum he had with him, to retain the rest.

"Well, gentlemen, I see I'm at your mercy—what say ye to a gift, a free gift of a cool hundred? I'm not going to behave shabby---that'll be a good morning's work; and I'll give you the word of a man of honour, you shall neither be pursued nor molested, nor will I ever—"

"Can't think of it, my kind sir," said Tom, bitterly, still feeling the side of his head which had suffered the never-sufficiently-to-be-lamented bereavement of his lady-killing curl; "Wouldn't have taken the small sum you mention for the deprivation of my —"

Captain Scott's astonishment, during this speech, may be supposed; he was, however, cunning enough not to betray the discovery he had made, for Tom, in the unaffected grief at the loss he had suffered, had quitted his assumed stern tone, and fallen into his natural speech and manner, and had confirmed his identity with *the* Captain Darcy of Scarbro' notoriety, by the exposure of his hair, which he had made by pushing up the wig from the wounded side.

"Can't positively take less than two hundred and fifty, in consideration of personal damage, and don't include my friend's claim in that—What, you know me, eh?" said Tom, suddenly recollecting himself, and perceiving at the same time a peculiar meaning look steal across the face of the Captain: "Oh! very well; Captain Darcy's compliments to Captain Scott, if it's come to that, and will thank him to honour *this* draft for five hundred, or—" said Tom, bringing his horse close up to the chaise-door, and clapping his pistol close to the Captain's head.

This *argumentum ad hominem* was undeniable—there could be no mistaking its meaning; yet the captain did not show any intention of leaving his treasure.

"Come out into the road, sir, immediately," said Dick, in a tone that made the gentleman start; he still, however, hesitated: he loved his money bags, and stood

> Like Adam, lingering near his garden.

Turpin saw his hesitation.

"Come out, sir, or by G—," and he accompanied the oath by again raising the butt end of his whip.

Captain Scott saw that affairs were hopeless, and stepped into the road.

"Take care of your friend, Captain Darcy," said Dick, and proceeded on the search. A small leather travelling desk lay on the seat of the carriage, and told, both by its weight and sound, of its precious contents. "Here's what we want," continued Dick.

The Captain looked at it with a despairing sigh.

"You're fortunate," said Dick, with what the Captain thought the most unpleasant facetiousness it had ever been his lot to hear; "you're fortunate in falling into the hands of gentlemen; we shall not take your watch, and shall leave your loose cash, &c., but you must consent to a little arrangement for our safety, which may be rather inconvenient."

Dick dismounted; and having bound the hands of the Captain, in spite of all remonstrances, he transferred the shawl from his neck to the traveller's eyes. Having completed the same kind offices for the postboy, who begged hard for his life during the ceremony, they led the pair through a gate into a field, where, laying them both on the grass, they promised them worse treatment should they stir for one hour; then, after toggling the horses' forelegs with the reins, left the chaise by the roadside.

"The chance is, there'll be nothing by this way for some hours—at any rate, we shall have a fair start; that was devilish unlucky that recognition; I must cut these northern parts, for I don't think the air of them agrees with Captain Darcy's constitution. However, I don't know it goes for much; only I must drop the Darcy, and keep out of the way a little: what say you to a trip to Holland? I forgot, there's no need—you can return to Brough, nobody will ever suspect the unsuspectable Mr. Newton."

For the last half minute, Dick had been inspecting the handle of his whip with a troubled look.

"There's worse to come of the matter, I fear, than even the discovery of Captain Darcy, which is no discovery at all. Mr. Newton must disappear, and that without delay; it will never do to ride back now—no, no; look here, Tom, that's awkward, I should say:" and Turpin held the whip-handle towards King, who now saw that the silver decoration inscribed with Turpin's assumed name, and that of the club who had presented it, was broken off.

" There's something there they may make *a handle of,·'* said Dick, with a bitter jest ; for desperate danger, which unnerves many men, lent him presence of mind: "Mister Newton mustn't even call at Bullingbrook now, I should say, unless he's a mind to commit *felo de se :* so "here's for London, Tom, and when there we must leave the rest to the chapter of accidents. I go no more to Brough—that's certain."

A few changes in their disguises were effected, and the following Sunday Dick and his gay companion were once more in mighty Babylon, snugly ensconced in the back slums of Westminster, in the privileged hole called " The Sanctuary, on the " *lucus a non lucendo*" principle, that its precincts contained more crime, and consequently less *holiness*, than any equal space in the sinful city of London.

CHAPTER XXI.

To what results will fell revenge not lead
The human mind; the heart inured to guilt
Shrinks not at murder to attain its ends.
Oh dreadful thirst for blood, that canst destroy
Our kindlier instincts, and the soul imbue
With a desire of annihilation,
Hence from this bosom keep; and be my fate
To banish malice, and forgiveness teach.　　　—Old Play.

THE fame of the robbery of Captain Scott, by an adventurer who had been known for a few months at Scarborough, as a Captain Darcy, and the unequivocal testimony of the engraved whip handle, which had broken off when Dick struck the pistol from the Captain's hand, and was found amongst the straw in the post chaise, as to the participation of Mr. Newton, the " respectable" horse dealer, in the affair, had astonished the country far and wide. The sudden disappearance, too, of that worthy gentleman, decided the fact of his penchant for highway exploits ; and within a week, not a doubt remained on people's minds that the redoubted captain of Essex, the far-famed Dick Turpin, and the liberal horse dealer of Brough, were one and the same. The Captain declared in all companies where he narrated the particulars of his loss, his conviction that Captain Darcy was *the* Tom King, and stoutly maintained that he had had the honour of being robbed by the two most accomplished thieves in Christendom. Daring, even though in a bad cause, ever charms the multitude ; and the dashing courage and bold generosity with which many of the offences of Turpin were accomplished, had positively rendered him popular, especially with the lower orders. There are several instances recorded in which this admiration led the people, even at personal risk to themselves, and in the teeth of the temptation of a reward, to shelter and assist, or connive at the escape of a " bold highwayman." Nor is this to be wondered at—for the sympathies of the poor were not with the class who were robbed by the mounted man—and that irrepressible respect which daring contempt of danger ever commands, made, in the eyes of the vulgar, a hero of the criminal.

Dick remained for some months perdu,* and Madge, returning to London, took apartments at a small house at Holloway.

It may be guessed that the officers watched her movements narrowly, but a liberal supply of Captain Scott's gold enabled her to sweeten those she feared, and completely hoodwink those she despised; and after two or three months, during which her every action was studied to make it appear that she was as ignorant as themselves of the whereabouts of Turpin, they gave up the job for a bad one, and the quest ceased.

The reader will remember that some chapters since we noted the escape of Rose, the capture of Berry the cork-cutter, and the treachery of Madge which led to the death of the unfortunate paramour of Bill Stevens, in Lewkner's Lane. Vice rarely fails to bring its own punishment; and Madge had many an uneasy hour when the past came on her mind, as she thought of the vile plots to which her ill-regulated desire had prompted her, and how lamentably she had failed—yet their very failure had saved her from the misery of revenge. She trembled whenever she thought of the possibility that some chance or other might put Dick in possession of her perfidy and infamy, of which he was still ignorant. Her apprehensions, too, were painfully increased when she reflected that his present hiding place was in the very heart of the scene of her treachery—and that many of the off-scourings of society in that neighbourhood must be well aware of the whole details of her villany---and what she feared most soon happened.

Dick, protected by false hair and whiskers, and a dyed skin, now occasionally ventured forth. He was seated, one evening, in a publichouse near the Broadway, at no great distance from the scene of the rencontre on the night of the capture of Berry. Turpin, as we have before said, sat in the drinking room of this thieves' hotel. The company consisted, for the most part, of young fellows. Jackets, decorated with a profusion of pearl buttons, kneebreeches, and bright blue worsted stockings, seemed the favourite costume; but there was a singular shrewd expression of low cunning in most of their eyes, which showed the " snapper up of trifles;" ankle shoes of a neat cut, and well adapted for running, fastened by a long tongue-strap, and a small white metal buckle, seemed in general favour; and each sported " around his squeeze," a bright blue or yellow fogle, of a bird's-eye pattern. The loose negligence of the tie, and the absence of anything in the shape of a stiffner, were characteristically *degage*, and so artlessly artful, as to show that this part of the costume was highly regarded. They were mostly youths of vulgar features, and many of them wore long sidelocks, curled in the corkscrew fashion, down the cheek, in the mode so much affected by theatrical sailors. Yet, although most of these " young hempseeds" were commonplace enough in their features, there was a something in the restless twinkle of the eye, and a peculiar shrewdness in the look with which a stranger's least action was watched, which fully spoke the avocation of these candidates for transportation and the gallows.

" Vy, lively, my kid," said one of these slangsters to a pal, who sat smoking an ostentatiously large yard of clay, while watching a game of

* All the lives of Turpin, (at least *three* published shortly after his execution) agree that for the two years previous to his execution, all trace was lost of him; during part of this time he resided at Brough, in Lincolnshire, where, as appears from the evidence adduced on his trial, he bore a reputable character until his sudden disappearance from the place.

Nan Turner assaults Madge Dutton.

shovehalfpenny ; " vy you seems to me in **Tow-street**(1) just now.   Vot, anothe^r tweiver ! (2) vell, blow me, but you're dropping the Stephen ;(3) vot'ill the old hen say to this here ?"

The speaker was dirtier and older than the majority of the company, and though clothed much in the same style, displayed none of the flash smartness of his juniors.   The man he addressed, who looked about his own age, was not only dressed in a more respectable manner than the rest, but had an air of swagger about him, which spoke the thief of a superior class.   He had been betting on the chances of the game, and had lost several shillings to a fellow who, like himself, a looker on, had been taking his bets on the events.

" Don't 'xactly see vot bisness 'tis o' yourn," replied the chap, in a half-earnest, half-chaffing tone, " vot my old 'un ses 'bout the grease ; (4) for don't s'pose as I lets her go like your hen vith rum rigging on the morning lay : that ere area-sneak suit vos rayther queer—is it true, my rum 'un, as they guv you a vooden ruffle for buffing(5) on that ere suit ?   Vell, don't look cagged ;(6) it vos all correct to try to double the lumber coves for the old voman, cos she vos doing the rightus thing ven the haccident (7) fell in."

(1) Getting into a dilemma—being deluded, or helplessly led by the nose.
(2) Shilling.   (3) Money.
(4) Money.   (5) Got put in the pillory for perjury.   (6) Angry.
(7) Detection.

No. 31.

To this severe stroke of chaffing satire, the fellow seemed to have little to retort.   He grinned with affected indifference, and observed :——

"Vell, if I did look out o' the pictur' frame, I didn't show half so hugly a hindex(1) as a kevaintance of our'n, ven he vos stagged in coming the kimbau,(2) for the yack and onions,(3) and yelped to the grab, asides shelling out the ridge ;(4) for all vich he vos revarded by gettin' the jigger dubbed(5) on him. Vo ho, ses I, ven I heerd on it, vot a muff he must be :—did you hear anything knock(6)——eh, Lively ?"

"Very tidy that ere, from a cove vot's vorn a Norvay neckcloth,(7) I don't think," responded Lively, who, though he had the best of this encounter of Tyburn wit, seemed to consider his antagonist beneath him ; he therefore continued———

"Vell, Harry, there's no use you and I chaffing, so stow yer whid (8) on that suit ; asides, I varn't nabbed pricking the vicker for a dolphin,(9) cos the old voman's all right right for scran.   Howsever, bite yer name in that ere," said he of the broadcloth coat, handing the pot ; "and if yer for a Field-lane duck,(10) I'm the cove as 'ull do the dodge."

Turpin had listened with some amusement to the slang of these two minor practitioners in the " art of appropriation ;" the one, he plainly saw, was the thief *in* luck, and his familiar was the same character *out*.   The dainty to which the thief had invited his comrade was quickly produced, smoking hot ; for the landlord of this boosing-ken, like many others in low neighbourhoods, supplied sheeps' heads hot each evening.(11)   The poorer and seedier thief seized the knife, and dipped it into a hollow of the thick table, where some most suspicious looking mixture, of ambiguous colour, lay heaped, and proceeded to sprinkle the variegated dust on the steaming morsel———for this receptacle was the only saltcellar the landlord dare trust to his light-fingered customers ; nay, it was the peppercaster too ; which accounted, in some measure, for the dirty aspect of the powder, though it would not be safe to vouch that no other dirt but trashy black pepper had a share in detracting from what once might have been the pure whiteness of the salt.

"Cut avay," said the patron and provider.   "I don't vant any ; I'se agoin to get a relish———a Yarmouth capon,(12) or summut o' that like———vill yer have some panum, eh ?"

"Lively," as he was called, left the room, but soon returned, carrying one

(1) Face.   (2) Was detected in an attempt to defraud.   (3) Watch and Seals.
     (4) Gold.   (5) Door locked.   (6) D'ye take the hint ?
          (7) Another term for the pillory.   (8) Hold your tongue.
          (9) Robbing a baker's basket.   (10) A baked sheep's head.

(11) This was an ordinary practice——now no more.   Covent Garden has this very year 1839, been forcibly bereaved of its coffee (once saloop) stalls ; which formerly, (as the following couplets from a " A Covent Garden Eclogue," published in 1737, will show) were devoted to curious uses in the edible way.   The writer, after going through the various scenes presented by each successive hour of darkness, thus paints the dawn of the morning :——

> " Now Phœbus gilds the square, all cabbage strown,
> And should'ring porters 'neath their burdens groan :
> The stagg'ring blood reels homeward with his trull,
> And dirty ruffs and faded silks show dull ;
> Stalls thickly gathering o'er the open ground,
> With ' Hot ox-cheek, and barley-broth' resound !" &c.

(12) A red herring.

of those piscatory delicacies, and called a boy-prig, with an air of superiority, to " guv it a toss on the grill."

Harry had by this time stripped the bones of the sheep's head, whose rows of dingy teeth seemed " horribly to grin a ghastly smile ; and Turpin, who, in a dark corner, had fallen into a reverie, was awakened by something to the following effect in the course of their conversation.

" Vell, Harry, vot's bin along vith yer, o' late ? I ain't seed nuffin o' Hoppy 'Till sence she and you vos a livin in Vitechapel. My eyes !---I know'd there vos summut as I vonted to get light (1) on. Vot cum'd o' that ere Madge as vos a lib(2) to the vun eyed 'un as vos nubbed ? (3) She vor a spicy Moll. vot's cum'd on her ?"

" Vot, vorn't you fly to all that dodge.---eh ? By nabs," said the fellow, shaking his head, " she vor a spicy vun---if so be you calls it spicy to nose it on the cove as she gammoned she fancied. Vy, lor bless yer, I'll tell 'ee vy she nashed (6) to the Chapel : fust she nosed on Bob Berry, Bill Stevens, and the lot here hard by, vich vos the cause of a lot on 'em got spoke to.(6) A spicy vun I think you said ?---vy there never vos a more artful card. She gammoned the vun eyed 'un---he vos no ketch for sartin---but that's nuffin : vell, she gets him in a line to take a downer (7) at her crib vere 'Till vos,--poor gal, she vos a trump, I'll say that for her, though she has hopped the twig (8)--let me see, vere vos I ?---Oh ! about Madge. Vell, she know'd from old Ferret as her cove had been at a cracking consarn vere squeaking had 'a bin done,(9) so she draws from him vere he vos a hiding, and in the morning early, she ikes off to the traps, makes it all right, and nails the cove for a *ground sveat.*" (10)

" D---n her———" growled the auditor, between his teeth, while Dick listened to the narrative with astonishment and curiosity.

" Vell, as I said afore, he was crapped. You knows ven I vos vith Bill Pearce in that ere consarn in the George here ?" The other admitted his recollection of the circumstance with a nod. " Vell, I vos lumbered for a lunar,(11) though there vos nuffin agin me ; so I owes her vun, two---she's a knowing vun. Vy vot d'ye think she does ?---she ketches hold ov an old rattling gloak,(12) and makes ridge (13) out on 'im like dirt, tips him turnips, and vithin a veek, she logs (14) herself on vith Captain Turpin---you needn't stare, it's true vot I'm a tellin' you--ay, vith Captain Turpin, the high tober gloak ; (15) cuts the veeds of a hempen vidder (16) and I dessay 'ull go on vith him as long as the corianders vill last,--and then, vy, if she doesn t git nicked afore, vy she'll slip the prime 'un's jemmy into the rope vinder, vere them as looks through can't feel the floor."

" Vell, that's a rummy story, if half on it's true," said his listener. " Sluice yer ivories, Harry, but vot's queer to me is as she should ha' tried to snitch on the Captain, and she so gallus fond on him."

" Vy you're soft my Lively, I'm a thinking—though I ought to ha' told yer one thing. Ven she tried to put the kybosh on the cove that owns her now, he

(1) Information.   (2) Left-handed wife.   (3) Hanged.
  (4) Hanged.   (5) Ran away.   (6) Cast for death, passed sentence on,
(7) Sleep, go to bed.   (8) Or, as an Irishman would phaase it, " gone dead."
(9) A burglary where murder has been committed.   (10) Got him taken for a crime
       which forfeited his life.   (11) Imprisoned for a calendar month.
  (12) A simple old dupe.   (13) Gold.   (14) Attaches herself to, hangs on.
  (15) Dashing highwayman.   (16) Wife of a man who has been hanged.

vos swished; (1) vy, 1 heered Madge say vun night, in this very crib, as she'd go the last kick to be the death on her." (Turpin's gorge rose. There was too much of the coherence of truth in the thief's story to allow of a doubt of its main facts.) "Vy, she vos in here vun night, vile you vos in the mackery,(2) a swearing as she had nosed out vere the lawful vun hung out,(3) and how she had been a-giving her a turn, and a little 'un in for herself; and how she didn't know, till she told her, as how Dick vos a toby man, vith a lot more on it; and how she'd ha' done this that and t'other, oney the cove hisself kim ben,(4) jist in the nick. None of us know'd then---though the grabbing at Nan Turner's came off that very night---as Madge know'd about that 'ere, till it vos blown here at the Gate,(5) by some of the coves as did the nose (6) Vell, she nammused, as you may guess, but fust poor old Moll Rhodes got a chive (7) in her breather,- and there vos others owed her it, but as she vos a right 'un to 'Till, I couldn't split on her. However, since as she bolted vith the nobby cove vot gathers gravel-tax,(8) she arn't know'd nobody." "Vell," said the thief, taking a swig at the pewter, "ve sees queer ups and downs, Lively. I passed her t'other day, rigged out like a madam; and them as didn't know her vould never ha' thought as she was used to have her home in the paviour's vorkshop,(9) and didn't she give me the topping eut(10)---my eye! But I'll be vun on her tibby yet."

"There's more asides you as has promised that much. Nan Turner dropt into Golden Lane, arter her three years' spell, this very blessed day---and I heered her svear about part a' vot you vos telling me, and she vos axing arter ---if she should come across her---var hawks! I'd like to be there to see."

Turpin rose from his seat and left the room hastily, but scarcely breathed till he reached the open air. He looked right and left from habitual caution. Thieves' virtue, the honour of villains, that strikes all crimes but treachery from its moral code, had not so entirely taken possession of his faculties, as it had of these plebeian robbers. He stood in doubting reflection on the pathway, or rather the sloping accumulation of drift-like mud, some three feet wide, which rose at an angle against the front wall of the public-house he had quitted. He was thus standing, when footsteps approached, and a woman in a heavy hood and cape passed him. He stood aside to allow her to go by, but she stopped, and lightly touching his shoulder with her finger, said "Richard!" in a low voice, and walked slowly on, for she did not dare a more open recognition, lest she might be watched, and thus unwillingly betray him, for to *him* she was really faithful. She walked on, without turning her head, to the corner of the next turning, doubting not but Dick would follow. There she stopped, and looked cautiously around her--no suspicious person was in sight---she looked down the street, and, by the dim flare of the smoky lamp, saw Turpin still stand in front of the house, immoveable as a statue. She watched and waited, but he stirred not. He could not have recognized her signal---it was assuredly him---it must be! She had visited his lurking

(1) Married.   (2) A slang phrase for the country; applied to being in prison, at which time the thief was supposed to be out of town.
(3) The wife lived.   (4) Came home.   (5) The Gatehouse Prison.
(6) Give the information.   (7) A knife.   (8) Money obtained from travellers on the highway.   (9) The street so called for an obvious reason.
(10) The cut consequential.

place, and he was not there---she felt a fear of something, she knew not what, which restrained her for a few minutes from again accosting him.

"She's perhaps just now serving me as she's served so many others," said Dick, and he smiled bitterly as he felt in his breast for the weapons without which ne never stirred. "Well, well, it will come when it will, I suppose, and now as well as any other time. But they shan't take me easily. I see no one about; maybe I'm judging her wrong; wrong or right, I don't fear her, but I won't trust her,---no! no!"

He had got to this point, when Madge again came down the lane, and Dick advanced towards her.

"Well, Madge," said he, in so cool and altered a tone that the woman started; "you're come to look after me---very anxious, no doubt, about my health?" added he, with a sneer he could not repress, as the thought of what she had inflicted on Esther Bevis recurred unbidden; "have you brought any friends with you to visit me in my troubles, as you did the day I was not at home, some years since---eh?"

Madge's heart leaped to her mouth---she tried to speak but could not--- it was, however, a chaos of mingled feelings---revenge towards the unknown divulger of her cherished secret---mortification at a discovery which she feared would degrade her in the eyes of the only man she cared for---and lastly, a lurking devil prompted her to retort, so cuttingly cold was Dick's tone and manner; her conscience, too, told her that to him at least she was devotedly true, and this barbed the shaft of his contempt. She stammered a "Thank'ee," or she knew not what, and gave a curtsey that was intended as a mock. Dick went on,---

"I've unfortunately mislaid your note, madam, to the appointment you so kindly made, the evening you honoured my humble home in Bloomsbury with ---pshaw!" exclaimed he, as he turned away with a motion of disgust, "I can't stand here prating with a woman; go, Madge, good bye---here's money, *and unless there's somebody waiting for me*, we had better not meet again."

Thus saying, he thrust a purse into her hand: the woman received it passively, looked on it with a vacant eye, then dashed it into the roadway. Dick had taken but three strides, when Madge rushed madly after him, and seized him by the arm; at the same moment, the two men whose low talk we have already chronicled, came up the step which led from the publichouse into the street. Madge noticed them not as she eagerly said,

"Richard! for God's sake, if we must part, don't part thus! Richard, dearest Richard, you may spurn me, but you shall not shake me off, till you have heard me out. They're lies, cursed lies, by——; I never harmed you, or wished to---"

Dick put one hand on her mouth as she poured forth this, and pointed significantly to the two men, who stood amazed spectators of the scene. Madge took the hint, for she suddenly checked herself---and darting a look of fear and apprehension at the men, both of whom she at once recognised--- she gently pressed Dick's arm, who obeyed the motion, and the two walked hastily away.

"Vell, blow my nose!" said the elder; "you can't guess who that is, I s'pose, can yer?"

"Don't I, Harry," retorted his pal; "cos I vos rayther nutty on her myself afore she slipped off so mysterously: vy, that's Madge Dutton, or my glims is queered."

"The right nail, and no mistake," said Harry; "and t'other---didn't ye hear vot she said, eh?"

"Not 'xactly," replied Lively.

"Vy, t'other's the bold Captain hisself---Dick, and no mistake; and ve vas gabbing over his family 'fairs afore him: vell, that is a go, to be sure---ha! ha! and he a going to giv her turnips(1); vy, she'll lumber(2) him, or there's no darbies in the stone pitcher. He's an out-and-outer, the Captain, and if ve could only give him the office to keep out o' mischief, I'd chance a little to do it. Let's track 'em, Lively; come on, my tulip," and away went the two prigs together. They watched the pair till they were housed.

"Now, Harry," said the one, "keep a sharp look-out, and I'll go back to the ken; if you sees anythink queer, or the hen comes out, tip me the knowledge, and I'll jine yer, for I'm cock sure there's some snitching(3) a goin' on this blessed night."

Mister Lively was here, however, quite out of his reckoning, for there was nothing of the sort in agitation; other events of equal importance, nevertheless, were in embryo, which the night was fated to bring forth.

We have long lost sight of Roger Haynes; he had been the servant of Dick, and had since been employed as the go-between of his whilom master and mistress. On the eventful night of which we are now writing, Roger had accompanied his mistress; but, by her instruction, had remained at the end of Duck Lane to watch, lest she should have been tracked in this her first visit to Dick. How differently had that visit resulted, to what Madge had calculated on! How were her air-built castles of happy greetings and fervent salutes, crushed, annihilated, by the unforeseen knowledge of her infamy which Turpin had acquired! Absorbing self, "like Aaron's serpent, swallowed up" all smaller thoughts, feelings, and hopes; and she had forgotten even the existence of the patient and faithful Roger, who still stood watching at his post, and occasionally walking a few yards in the direction of Dick's lurking-place---soon, however, to walk back to his former station. But now a new actor appears on the scene.

Nan Turner, as we have already heard, had within a day or two been discharged from the gaol to which the treachery of Madge had consigned her. As might be supposed, she had many acquaintances, and from having for several months rented a thieving brothel in Golden Lane, was well known to all classes of those who live by preying on the unwary, vicious, or intoxicated. Since her discharge she had not even found leisure to be sober, and now, in a state of excitement from liquor, fast verging to frenzy, she had made her way to the bar of the George, and was there treating some of her whilom unfortunates; for Nan had many friends and more acquaintances, and was not unprovided with cash.

Lively, as the better dressed thief was called, entered, and as he passed Nan and her two companions in the narrow passage, a mutual recognition took place.

"Vy Nan, strike my blessed daylights if it arn't better nor good luck to see yer—tip us yer mauns,(4) Vot are you sluicing your ivories vith—eh? red tape(5) Vell, I stands the next brown—vy you looks in as prime tvig as ever!"

(1) Get rid of her.   (2) Get him apprehended and imprisoned.
(3) Treacherous informing.   (4) Give us your hand.   (5) Brandy, Cognac.

"Give your red rag a holiday, Master Lively, and speak to them as speaks to you," replied Nan, "that Spittleonian and bit of lamb's wool,(1) seems to make you forget yerself. Keep your treats for them as axes 'em. Ven I comes out on the cadge, I'll not drop the civil (2) to such as you—so shove your trunk, and keep your own company."

With this polite request to take himself off, Mr. Lively complied, saying,

"Vell, vell, she's a-come out jist as bounceable as she went in, and I've screwed a pig (3) by that suit, and arn't lost my carackter for civility nay-thur;" he walked into the room before described.

The interview between Dick and Madge had been much more protracted than pleasant. Dick coolly and quietly declined saying more, after briefly relating to her what he knew. Madge entreated, as such a woman would do, to be confronted with her accusers, but Turpin refused to be a witness to any such disputation, and coldly and calmly ended her remonstrances by saying,—

"I have not the vanity, Madge, to think that I can change into a faithful and attached woman, one who has thus acted. Go!—perhaps you have already done it—and betray me. Your worthy friends, the officers, to whom you are so valuable a tool, will reward you for it. But—" (he compressed his lips with anger,) "they shall earn the blood-money before they take me. Go! but I'll take care it shall be too late for them to seek me here—farewell!"

So saying, Dick passed into another room, and sliding back a pannel in the side of a deep cupboard, discovered a large chimney, applied to an use never contemplated by the builder. It was a capacious old-fashioned flue, and here and there, at short distances in its sides, a brick had been removed, and its place supplied by a square of wood, the end of which slightly projected on each side into its cavity. Turpin stood within, and after closing the pannel, rapidly felt his practised way down ten steps, and catching hold of a piece of wood projecting farther than any of the others, he swung by his hands. A drop of two feet,—a stoop,—and he emerged in a desolate-looking lumber room, in the rear of the adjoining house. The highwayman drew a lantern from his coat, which he placed, with the readiness of one who knew the local-ities even in utter darkness; he then produced from his breast a small strong iron box, much similar in size and appearance to those in which some tars stow their tobacco, and took from it a spring steel; one smart stroke against a gun-flint screwed in the edge of the box gave a spark to he German tinder it contained, and put Dick in possession of a light; he unclosed the slide of his lantern, and scrutinized each corner of the apartment. All was right; and darkening the candle, he gently unclosed the casement, crossed a small yard, hastened down an alley, and stood, in a few seconds, in Union Street, West-minster.

But we must now return to Madge. When Turpin left the room and passed into the next, she was sitting near the doorway, which commanded a view of the stairs; and the suspicion never for a moment entered her mind, that the direction in which Turpin had gone commanded the means of exit. She sat for a few seconds with her face buried in her hands, making herself sure that her humble and penitent posture was under the eye of Turpin, and hoping

---

(1) Silk neckcloth.　　(2) Make a curtsey.　　(3) Saved a sixpence.

that the contrite expressions she was pouring forth might induce him to relent. She listened——no sound met her ear; she looked up, with a timidity that was half true and half pretended; he was, however, gone. Woman's wit told her that, as he was in the next room only——for that he had not passed her to descend the stairs, she knew——it would be most advisable to wait a short time ere she ventured again upon an appeal. She peeped slily through her tear-wetted fingers: he was not within view, though a light burned in the next apartment. She listened; all was silent as death: he was assuredly not there. She rose, and stealing towards the door——which, though open, hid two thirds of the room——peeped through the crack between the post and hinges; the room was tenantless! She entered, and was convinced he was gone. A minute's irresolution followed: " I'm again scorned——again deserted; fool! fool!" and she struck her forehead violently, as the blood mounted to her temples. " Oh what would I give;" and she gnashed her teeth, and stamped her foot in the paroxysm of her rage, " to be revenged on the wretch who has told him this. He told me, now I recollect, that I had *friends* at the George, who knew more of me than he did; why didn't I prevent his ever coming to this cursed spot---fool! fool! fool!" She looked again around the place, then staggered, rather than walked, toward the stair head, and the next moment stood in the street. She rapidly revolved in her mind the most probable hiding plans in which she might find Turpin, for to see him again she was resolved. After so long an absence, with a little disguise and caution, she might venture into the George, and doubtless might there learn the source of the mischief. She had gold; and she felt sure, that for that she could not only buy counter-testimony, but if need should be, produce the very babbler himself, to contradict and eat his own words. " I have it," said she; " I'll ferret it out, and get the very cove hisself---for I dessay he's not nice; none of the lot were when I knew them---to say that it was all chaff---a mere line that he was getting his companion into. I'll manage it;" and away went Madge to a neighbouring dealer in female wearing apparel. Here she left her bonnet, cloak, &c., in pledge for the return of some seedier and more suitable habiliments for her adventure; and having put on a false front of much lighter colour than her natural hair, and by whitening her eyebrows, slightly altering her complexion, &c., she soon effected the desired change in her outward appearance. Thus equipped, she walked into the George.

Nan, and one of her companions, despite the sneering tone in which the first offer of Lively had been received by her, had joined that personage. She was by this time far gone in liquor, with violent exclamations of rage, each of which received applauding reception from the assembled ruffians. Ever willing to see a fight, they nevertheless preferred one where an informer might be punished, for on such offenders retribution "came home," as the newspaper scribes have it, "to every man's business and bosom" in the assemblage. They egged on Nan in her resolve for revenge; at this juncture, the Jewess to whom Madge had applied for the change in her dress, entered, and whispered very strenuously across the table to one of the thieves.

" Unpossible," exclaimed the fellow, withdrawing his pipe from his mouth, and squirting the saliva on the sanded floor; then, looking hard at the woman, he said, " that cock von't fight, Mother Josephs; how d'ye sell your *string?*(1)

---

(1) A rather untranslatable phrase, meaning, I'm awake to your hoax; or rather an intimation that the speaker sees through the trick sought to be put on him.

Turpin recognises Tom King and the Barmaid of the Garter.

do yer see anything *green* here?" added the fellow, drawing up his eyelid so as to submit the *white* of the eyeball more clearly to the inspection of Mrs. Josephs; "ax sum vun else to go to the counter to look at Madge Dutton, and there make 'em stand Sam; (1) it von't fit here—Valker!" and the accomplished and ingenious youth applied the end of the thumb of his left hand to his nose, while he agitated his extended four fingers in the air.

'Mother Josephs,' nettled at this imputation on her sincerity, retorted; and the "gag" was getting up, when Lively chimed in. The woman then proceeded to narrate circumstantially the visit and proceedings of Madge: the thief went to the door and took a survey.

"It's she for sartin," said he, returning; "kious(2) Nan, and we'll git her in. Now, no touting," continued he, to the scoundrels around. "or you'll spile the sport."

Lively left the room, and very shortly came in, accompanied by Madge, who was secretly rejoiced at what seemed ·to her the happy success of her scheme. She seated herself by the fellow, and was soon engaged in an artful conversation.

"And so, my pretty 'un," said Lively, still pretending not to recognise the masquerader; "you vos last at Lincoln, eh?"

Madge replied in the affirmative; and after a few minutes' talk on indifferent subjects, she skilfully contrived to lead the conversation to the subject

(1) Pay for the liquor called for.   (2) Be quiet.

No. 32

uppermost in her mind.   The blood of Nan Turner, who was at a table behind that where Madge was seated, was boiling with rage, and it was with no small difficulty that the two fellows who sat by her could restrain her from breaking out into immediate violence, despite the instruction of Lively, that she should await his signal for the discovery.

"I dessay," said the thief, "that vile you vas in them parts, you see'd the bold Captain oftens?"

"O yes," replied Madge, entirely off her guard.

"And maybe you might ha' knowed his moll(1), a spicy, swellish sort of a bit o' muslin, as he took vith him ven he made hisself scarce from Hessex, eh?"

Madge gave a short hem; there was something in the leer of the speaker she did not like, but she dissembled her apprehension, and said, gaily:—

"Oh ay, let me see—Madge what's her name—I never saw anything so very spicy about her.   I was always told, though, that she was his wife," said the woman, her vanity getting the better of her discretion; for if there is one thing more than another upon which the class of unfortunate females pride themselves, it is the assumption of the title of a married woman.   Nay, though abandoned by or separated from her husband, however worthless a criminal he may have been, or even though she herself may have deserted him, still does the " married" *abandonnee* look down with a ludicrous assumption of supe-riority on such of her companions as have never vowed at the altar " to obey." There are, mental peculiarities which seem to accompany every class and pursuit in life, and no observer of the world and its ways, can have avoided noticing this anxious desire of almost every female outcast, however degraded, to lay claim to having been " in holy wedlock bound."

This empty vanity betrayed Madge's secret—or, at least, furnished Mister Lively with a hint for her exposure.

"Swished to her—gammon!" responded he: "vot, swished to a 'peaching, snitching varmint, as vos common as ditch-vater all through the 'Minster!— Lord, how this vorld is guv to lying!"

The woman's colour rose; the retort was too keen for endurance; she gulped down her rising passion, but the keen eye of the knowing thief caught her's, and its cunning twinkle expressed his acquaintance with her secret;--- Madge saw she was discovered.

"P'raps Missus Turpin vould condescend," said he, in a chaffing tone, " to let us into the secret? come, Madge, my rum 'un, show us the marriage lines. 'Richard Turpin, Esqvire, to Madge'—no, that von't do," said the thief, facetiously pretending to read from the back of his hand, which he held before his eyes, in the way of holding a paper---" Richard Turpin, Esqvire, of Gam-mon parish, to nosing Madge Dutton —"

"Take that!" cried Nan Turner from behind, dealing an ineffectual blow at Madge.

She had been bursting with passion for some minutes, and now rushed by the two men with whom she had been sitting.

"Come out! come out!" screamed the infuriated and intoxicated virago.

Madge shrunk back.

"Don't let me spile sport," observed Lively, as he shifted out between the settle and the table, so as to render of no avail the protection Madge had

(1) Woman.

sought by retreating to the upper end of the table, and near to the wall: "now you can go in, my rum'uns; and I hope the best voman 'ull vin;" and Mister Lively, withdrawing his interposing body, permitted Nan to get at Madge; who, unnerved and astonished at the dilemma in which she found herself, shrunk back to avoid her.

On the table stood one of the old heavy tankards with a lid, this Madge seized as a weapon of defence, but it was instantly snatched from her grasp by an arm from behind, and as instantly transferred to her assailant. Thus armed, Nan seized her by the hair—Madge's false curls and head-dress soon strewed the floor, and twisting her left-hand in her strong black hair, the right hand of Nan descended on the head of the unhappy woman, inflicting a fearful bruise or gash.

"That's the ticket," exclaimed some of the ruffians around. The landlord, used to such noises—for Madge uttered at first no cry—did not leave his bar, being engaged, at that very time, in serving some customers. The brain of Madge reeled beneath the stunning and cutting effects of the blow, and seizing her adversary by a part of her dress near the bosom, she slipped beneath the table, dragging Nan with her into such a position, that her blows failed of effect. Here the two she-fiends scratched, clawed, and swore; but Nan, whom a long prison diet, an unusual quantity of drink, and more advanced years, had reduced below Madge in physical strength, was fast getting the worst of it. Madge had got possession of her head, though undermost, and was getting her into that critical position known among pugilists as "being in chancery," while Nan, from sheer pain and drunkenness, had lost her "hold of vantage," by relaxing her grasp of Madge's long hair. This state of things suited not the spectators.

"Pull 'em out," said one of the thieves, with perfect *sang froid*, "Vy the rightus 'un 'ell git tocus—don't yer see how the whiddling (1) warmint is printing her ten commandments(2) in Nan's squeeze (3); kim out!" cried he; and suiting the action to the word, he grasped the leg of Madge, and dragged her out from beneath the protecting table. She now lay defenceless on the floor. No time was given her, for Nan maddened with liquor and the conflict, sprung upon her, and with one knee firmly planted on her chest, struck the miserable wretch with murderous violence on the forehead. Again and again the blow descended.

"Skewer the jigger (4), carn't yer," cried Lively to a pal, "don't let's have it spiled arter all—slog (5) her, Nan; that's the cheese."

The blood of the wretched woman spirted on her assailant, and sprinkled the room around.

"Mercy! Mercy!" she gasped faintly.

"She's a crying 'cavi," said one of the brutes with a grin; and then an ill-aimed blow or two descended, for Nan Turner was now nearly exhausted.

One of the ruffians approached the combatants, and dealt the prostrate wretch a kick in the side. She writhed and screamed with pain—the door burst open simultaneously with the kick, and the unmanly brute lay stunned against the corner of a table hard by.

"Dom yer murd'ring eyes," exclaimed the new comer, looking at the bloody

(1) Informing.   (2) Her finger and thumb nails.   (3) Throat.
   (4) Fasten the door,   (5) Smash, strike heavily.

woman, and then glaring savagely around the room, after dragging Nan—no
difficult task by the by—from off her victim.

"Nail him (1); quoit him out," cried Lively, striking with his foot at the
intruder's leg.

The man would have fallen, had not a friendly table conveniently received
his huge latter end; so the trip, though cunningly tried, failed of its object.
The thieves at once assaulted the new comer, who was for a moment staggered
—it was however but for a moment.

"Sew up his sees" (2), cried Lively, as he and two of his pals made a
simultaneous rush.

The stranger, who was of huge stature, rose from his semi-reclining position
despite their blows. One smashing hit deposited Lively in the fire-place,
with the symmetry of his countenance wholly deranged; another thief, fearing
to hold his head up, rushed at his legs—but one kick from the hob-nailed boot
of the intruder deprived him of more front teeth than he cared to spare, and
he too lay on the sanded floor. The other fellow liked not this specimen of
the prowess of Madge's champion, who, having thus disposed of his first two
customers, stood with his strong arms extended---

"How many more on ye, ye cowardly vagabones! Dang it—whoy doan't
'ee cum on: ha' ye had enuff?"

The thieves clustered at the door, and a woman, who was in the room, ran
screaming to the bar.

"Cum, stow this shindy," said the landlord, entering; "cum, shove your
trunk; (8) let's ha' none o' this." (He addressed the stranger.)

"Tell they murdering sneakums to toddle—I shan't. Look'ee, Muster
landlord—see;" and he drew the man's attention to the bleeding and senseless
Madge. "Domme, but I'll—" cried he, as if irritated by the disgusting sight,
and again advancing, with a threatening look, towards the three fellows at
the door. The specimen he had just given of his capabilities was, however,
so full and satisfactory, that they must have been far more sceptical than wise
to seek any further proof; they, therefore, took themselves off at his first
advance, and left the room to the undisputed occupancy of the stranger, the
two women, the landlord, and their prostrated comrades.

"What d'ye call all this here?" asked the landlord of the den.

"A'm danged if a' knows," replied the man: "this is very purty doins
tho'. I heerd a screech of a woman; so, thinks I, they're ill using on her,
and a' wanted to cum in and zee---but the door wor fast; so I shoves in, and
sees that dom'd villian a' kicking of she, whoile t'other wench wor a lacing
away wi' the stoup; so a' catches her off ov 'un, and guvs he a kick-like in
return—that all a' knows: git some water for the poor thing, will'ee, Muster?
A' wish a'd bin here zooner, dang me but I'd ha'—whoy---no, it can't—yes it
is—whoy it's missus! by the livin' daylight!"

The change which, as we have seen, had been effected in the dress of Madge
since Roger Haynes, for it was he, had seen her, had prevented his recognising
in the prostrate female his quondam mistress. Instinctively, too, in order to
escape the dreaded blows, she had turned her face, covered with blood, and
disfigured with scratches and contused wounds, towards the ground; and this,
added to the other injuries, put immediate identification of the wretched
object of their brutal maltreatment, out of the question. Roger raised the

---

(1) Seize him.   (2) Black his eyes.   (3) Go; be off.

head of the senseless wretch in his arms, wiped the gore from her face, and satisfied himself the victim was no other than Madge. The landlord entered with a bowl. Nan---for she had not come off scatheless---lay panting on a settle, still venting curses, not loud, but deep, on the object of her implacable revenge.

"I'll have her soul," growled the drunken fury; "let me at her;" and she scrambled towards Madge, with the pewter still grasped in her hand.

Roger was kneeling beside Madge; he caught the reeling Bacchante by the leg, and she fell heavily and stunningly against a settle.

Mister Lively had gained his feet and sneaked out, and the other thief quietly followed his example. Madge was partly recovered with a supply of brandy. The landlord sent into King Street for a conveyance, in which, having safely deposited the wounded woman, Roger, by his advice, had her conveyed home. The wounds were many and severe; but Madge's temperate mode of life for many months, and her strong constitution, triumphed over the injuries; and leaving her gradually to attain convalescence, we will return to follow the steps of other actors in our motley scenes.

CHAPTER XXII.

I know how to love, and to make that love known,
But I hate all protesting and arguing;
Had a goddess my heart, she should e'en be alone,
If she made many words to the bargain.
Long courtship's the vice of your phlegmatic fools,
Like the grace of fanatical sinners,
Where the stomachs are lost, and the victuals grow cool,
Before men sit down to their dinners.
—Matthew Concanen.

That was your business.
No artful prostitute, in falsehoods practised,
To make advantage of her coxcomb's follies,
Could have done more.
—The Orphan.—Otway.

SEVERAL months had rolled by, and Time, in its revolutions, had brought, as it ever has done, change to all the dwellers on the ever-rolling earth.

The barmaid at the Garter, near Scarborough, will perhaps be remembered by the reader, as an admirer of Captain Darcy. A coquette rather from circumstances than disposition, her situation in a well-frequented inn was, perhaps, the most dangerous that could well be supposed for one of her temperament. The poet has libelled the softer sex, by declaring that

Every woman is at heart a rake.

Without assenting to the sweeping libertinism of this assertion, we may safely say that Marian Glover *was* one. She was of that class of women who wait only to be wooed and won; and disappointed of Darcy, (who had certainly awakened what with such a woman passes for love, though a less dignified name would better become it,) she had resolved to follow him to town on the first opportunity which should present itself; for thither he had told her he was going, when he had last kissed the ready-tear from her eye-lid at

their parting. That she was vain, fond of dress, and accessible to flattery, **were**
her failings; but to balance these, she was generous, frank, and warmhearted; and lastly, to her own misfortune, she possessed a pretty face, of
that order of female beauty which may be termed the *piquant:*—a beauty
which attracts only while the brilliancy of eye and bloom of cheek are retained—a beauty, which, depending not on regularity of feature, or intelligence
of expression, ceases to attract so soon as vivacity abates, the first fresh dew
of youthfulness exhales from the lip, and the fawn-like elasticity of the step
sobers down to the gait of staid womanhood. Marian, once resolved to see
London, did not wait long for an opportunity to put her scheme in practice.
She possessed not those quiet domestic affections which render a separation
from home painful to the young heart; no---she panted for what she thought
liberty; became querulous at parental control, however mildly and considerately exercised; fancied every restraint irksome; and resolved to take the
first offer that might present itself, to free herself from what she considered an
ignominious thraldom, unendurable by a woman of her spirit and beauty; for,

> If ladies be but young and fair,
> They have the gift to know it,

was no less true in the time of the philosophic Jaques, or in the reign of the
first George, than it is in the reign of the first Victoria.

In this state of mind, Marian pursued the usual tenor of her way, flirting
and coquetting with every visiter who might make an advance; and in such
a place it would have been wonderful indeed if so silly a moth had not singed
its wings. A dapper Lieutenant, who had taken Scarborough on his return
from Edinburgh, where his regiment lay, sojourned a few days at the Garter.
Like most of his profession, especially in those days, Lieutenant Crosbie
possessed little cash, and, as far as women were concerned, less principle.
He was a soldier of fortune, and acted up to the maxim of finding a wife
wherever opportunity offered. The forward and tempting Marian confided
to him her desire of seeing the great city: and the gallant Lieutenant not
only encouraged her design, which jumped with his own desires, but offered
to escort her thither. The offer was accepted, and Marian, after packing up
a few trifles from her wardrobe, and making free with a considerable amount
of loose cash, gave her plethoric, bottle-nosed papa the slip, and, under the
protection of the gay Lieutenant, sought the metropolis.

The characters of Marian and her paramour were, of course, not calculated
for a permanent cohabitation. Nay, nothing could be farther from the
intention of both parties than a life-long union. Marian wanted a protector
on her voyage of discovery, and had no objection to the lieutenant; though
her preference was strongly rooted for Darcy, to seek out whom was the main
object of her visit to London. She had, however, miscalculated the doctrine
of probabilities and possibilities, which a better acquaintance with the human
wilderness would have taught her; viz., that to look for such an individual as
our friend Tom in London, bore no comparison, in the chances of success, to
the figurative search so popularly described as " seeking a needle in a bottle
of hay." Luck, fortune, chance, or what you will, however, did better for her
than she had a right to expect.

The lieutenant, now cooled in his first ardours, began to remit greatly in
his attentions, and to look, as such *roue.* ever do, on women, who thus,

> As men should do a cucumber,
> Just throw themselves away;

indeed, he scrupled not to let Marian see that he regarded her as an encumbrance,
—a let on his pleasures, during his short leave of absence from his duties. A few
private sparrings sufficed to mature the distaste into aversion; and after a quarrel
rather sharper than usual, the "ill-used" Marian, for so she thought herself,
withdrew from the "protection" of Lieutenant Crosbie, and took lodgings
near Chelsea, in the vicinity of Ranelagh, where she encouraged lovers

——In the plural number,
Not finding the additions much encumber.

One night, as she returned from the scene of folly and dissipation, unaccom-
panied, save by her own thoughts, which were depressed in proportion to the
exuberant hilarity she had forced during the evening, she was overtaken, near
the turning leading to her lodgings, by a well dressed man, who politely
offered his escort. Marian first looked at the lace of his coat, and the glittering buckles on his instep---then the hanging buttons from his wrist ruffles, and
lastly at his smart cocked hat and cut steel sword. Her professional survey
told her that these bespoke the gentleman; one, at least, who was "good for" a
guinea or so. As her finances were sadly diminished she refused not, but
accepted his proferred arm; they repaired to her home—and there the
gentleman discovered himself as---*the* long-sought Captain Darcy. The next
day was past pleasantly. Woman's preference is a strange and wayward thing
---a problem which the man who shall attempt to solve---a mystery, which the
man who shall say he can fathom—must be labouring under an extraordinary
amount of delusion and self-conceit.

The pleasure of Marian, at meeting the object of her girlish choice, was
not less sincere and ardent, for that she had, since first that preference was
awakened, become a "vile polluted thing;" and now she discovered in
her quondam lover, a reckless outlaw, her affection seemed to be excited to a
stronger heat, and she thought that she could love—even more warmly than
she had ever done the dashing Captain Darcy---the bold Tom King, the
highwayman. Such a paradox is woman!

We will now leave Tom in amorous dalliance with his ladye-love, to look
after our hero.

From the purlieus of Westminster, on the night of the affray at the George,
Dick betook himself to the old scene of his earlier revels. He threaded his
way through the half-lighted streets near Covent Garden, occasionally rendered still more gloomy by the horn lantern borne by the watchman, or some
casual passenger: the dirty and scorched sides of these apologies for lamps,
being rendered still more opaque by frequent blotches of brown, imparting
a tortoise-shell hue, the said blotches being occasioned by the falling of the
inclosed candle against its sides, from the sleep, intoxication, or carelessness
of its bearer. One of the ancient watchmen, those drab-coated, peripatetic
horologes, was shuffling along before him through a street which led to Long
Acre. This phenomenon, whose murky lantern, "the light of other days, has
faded" and "paled its uneffectual fire" before the blaze of lucent gas—whose

Mighty pole
Has been uprooted from the firm-set earth,

to make way for the succinct *lignum vitæ* of the policeman's truncheon—was,
in the time of Turpin, a thing of life—

Doomed for a certain term to walk the night;

but now, alas! slain by the hand of Peel, no more permitted to

   Revisit the pale glimpses of the moon,
   Making night hideous

with his unmelodious announcement of the march of time. We love the memory of the ancient Charley; there was a *bonhommie* even in his scroundrelism, as displayed in the song of Dibdin; (which by the bye we have always considered a libel on that ancient race;) but we hold no sympathywith the spruce blue-coat of the modern policeman. *He* speaks not of patient vigils, he looks more like the soldier than the patrol; that spry, act*ive*, red or black whiskered gentleman, with a stiff stock, chatting at the corner with Sally our servant maid, *cannot* be the *watch*man! No, no, tell that to the marines: he does not look like one, or the English language has lost its meaning. He belongs to the " *force,*" and what Englishman can associate, how can he amalgamate the idea of *force* with the mind's eye picture of a watchman? We feel grateful, when the " last of the Charlies" expired by act of parliament, Sir Robert had the cruel mercy, the assassin-kindness, to spare the last blow; and while annihilating the dynasty, did not allow the usurpers of their " beats," to continue *their* style and title :---" constable," if you please, though that sounds oddly, but not *watchman.* We look along the vista of memory, and see the dim shadowing of drab-coats, the huge red comforters and woollen night-caps, the misfitting shoes, the mighty crabsticks of " the days that are gone, and the men who bore them:" we think on the low crowned hat, stuffed with a wisp of hay, enveloped in a cloth, furnished by the ancient crone who " bore the honoured name of wife," to the sleepless old man—the aforesaid hay being a prudent protection to the head of the watchman against the blows on the pate which perchance some Corinthian Tom or Jerry Hawthorn, on " frolic mischief bent," might inflict on his dull cranium: we see the Diogenes snoozing cosily in his small and tub-like domus, with lantern by his side ready, like the philosopher of old, to look for a " honest man:" seeing that it was his principle, like his mighty prototypes Dogberry and Verges, to " comprehend" the honest men, for " to have to do with false knaves were indeed a pity:" we scent the odour of cheese and onions, with perchance the flavour of a " dash of jimakey," from the small pocket pistol, brought at eleven by the ministering hand of her who owned him: we hear his strange unearthly voice---a voice so contrived, as not to distress his wheezing lungs, loud, yet indistinct, and unvarying: throughout the night punctually doth the wanderer announce unintelligibly an announcement wherein nothing is announced, save the existence of some living creature—yet methinks

    No creature
   But a wandering voice;

and thus year after year, " through summer's heat and winter's cold," did that " old man wonderful" discourse sounds without articulate word or meaning: we see his coat with its literal inscription---its " S. P. C." or " S. M. L." with its subjoined number—and we look with scorn on the one letter which bespeaks the divisional degeneracy of these later days: we miss his red pauper-face at Christmas, albeit he came among many duns; and seeing and hearing all this with the eyes and ears of memory, can we look on the trim file of soldier-booted, oil-caped, whalebone-hatted, formalities, now marching past our windows, and say " there *go* the watchmen?" Alas! No—

Dick Bayes's visit to Marian Glover.

they *are gone!* Home Secretaries may prate, committees report, honourable members speechify, and utilitarians bray about improvement; but we have yet a corner in our heart for the watchman with which our mother threatened us when refractory, and whose drowsy voice, heard " oft in the stilly night," gave a charm, even in the idea that there *was* a waking thing beside yourself, which the "dumb dogs" who have displaced them must have many yet undiscovered merits to counterbalance. In short, we liked the old parish watchman; it is our prejudice, and we will keep it—our hobby, and we will ride it. He had many failings, but his habits and his manners spoke of the " irregular freedom" of England, not the formal, centralized despotism of France; and in " the deep damnation of his taking off," modern innovation has much to answer for.

Sir Thomas Browne quaintly denounceth those " rascally ancients who have stolen our best thoughts from us;" the reproach of those who have truly occupied the field and engrossed the highest glories of literature, is, however, (with all due deference to the learned and facetious author of "Vulgar Errors," and that delightful book on " Urn Burial,") more plausible than true. Originality, the stamp of genius in the highest degree, is eternal and inexhaustible; and even in the lower walks, the observant eye will never lack subjects in the ceaseless mutations of manners, laws, customs, politics, feelings, opinion: in a world where everything is uncertain save the certainty of change, fresh food for thought, fresh material for the pen, and new fields for the investi-

No. 33.

gation of science, will never fail, 'till rolling years shall cease to move.' And
now, having overtaken not only our ancient Charley, but even given the go-
by to the times in which he _lived—such power has the "fine essence" of
thought to annihilate time and space—we will let our hero overtake him too,
at least so far as the physical part of him is concerned.

Turpin stepped to the side of the muffled guardian of the night. A sudden
thought had struck him, that, in the event of Madge intending to play false,
it would be unwise to resort to the White Hart; for it was but probable that
there she might seek him.

"That old rap," said he, mentally, "knows every place of accommodation
about here; the simplest course, in these cases, is generally the deepest and
safest."

He tapped him on the shoulder. The old man peered beneath the brim
of his battered hat, and seeing a well-dressed person, touched it respectfully.

"Can you direct me to a bed about here?" asked Dick.

A wheezing cough attacked the ancient rogue—for experience had taught
him the wisdom of the serpent. Profound was the meaning of that old
man's cough; it covered a design worthy of the celebrated shake of the head of
the great Lord Burleigh---and that design we will now disclose.   Firstly it was,
that the well-dressed questioner might be moved thereby to "stand a summut"
to liquor his distressed throttle; and secondly, to gain time for calculating,
from the manner, appearance, &c., of the querist, the character of the house
of entertainment to which he should usher him—seeing that this was an
important consideration, materially affecting the probable gratuity for his
civility.

"Humbly ax pardon, your honour—ugh--ugh--ugh—afeard it's that I am,
as the best houses on the whole entire beat is jist shut up—ugh--ugh--ugh—
maybe, but they is rayther high in the way of comin' it over sthrange gint at that
same crib—hot-el I mane---ugh--ugh--ugh--ugh--ugh;" and this time the
queasy gullet of the afflicted old fellow rattled and shook in a way that might
have "made milch the eye of heaven," so acutely asthmatic were the tearings
and hawkings of that poor old man.

"You've a bad cold, friend," said Dick; "show us a house, and I'll stand
something warm; for there's a vile fog, which I've no doubt you would
wish to keep out."

"God bless and persarve yer honner's wurtchip, and glory to the last day
in your honnerable life, and after that's over, ses Terence M'Grah;" and he
gave a short cough just to save appearances.   "Here's an illigant house all out,
jist down beyant here—troth, in the same's a house as won't turn its back on
any one in the Garden, or elsewhere for that matther, in regard of the liquors
they kape.   This way, yer honner: long life t'ye!" and Terence, with obsequious activity, lighted the steps of Turpin, by walking a little in advance of
him, and throwing the glimmer of his lantern on the footpath immediately
before him.

They turned from James' Street into Hart Street, at the top of which was
situated the "night house," spoken of by Terence.

It was a low building, with an overhanging front, the shutters and door
were closed, but a dull light which appeared through the dirty glass over the
doorway told that the inmates had not yet retired to rest.   Terence applied
his ear to the key-hole, looked at the light before mentioned, then, shortening
his hold of his huge crabstick, he dealt three distinct talismanic knocks on

the oaken door. The bolt was drawn, and Terence bowed our hero to the bar. The first, and most important affair, (at least so Terence considered it,) was despatched, namely, a half-quartern of jimakey, to relieve the "configurashun," as he termed it, and Turpin looked around. Pallid prostitutes, whom the bright carmine and skin-eroding ceruse rendered ghastly to all save the hot-blooded intoxicated rakes who were plying them with liquor, stood in little groups before the counter, on which were several small rough and unpainted kegs, bearing the inscriptions of "Right Nantz"—"Choke-devil Schiedam"—"Madam Gin," and, lastly, "Old Tom," the only name which has survived the mutations even of drunkenness. Between the casks were placed three iron candlesticks, each containing a flaring dip, and from the ceiling depended a lamp, fashioned like an oil-can, and nearly resembling those still seen in the lowest market-stalls of London. Striking was the contrast which the place offered to the splendour of a modern gin palace. The appearance of Turpin was the signal for one or two of the nymphs of the *pavé* to quit their swains—whom they had discovered to be pennyless, or unwilling to furnish them with more liquor—and to besiege the stranger with importunities. Terence did not interfere with them, for many a sly sixpence did he pick up from these unfortunate outcasts as the price of his blindness or deafness to their peccadilloes. Turpin, however, cut them short by enquiring for a bed, to which the landlord assenting, he, after ordering a treat, to the extent of a shilling's-worth of juniper, for the unfortunates, got rid of further annoyance by stepping into an apartment inscribed "Parlour," to which the females were not allowed the privilege of the entree. Though it was so late, a group of three men still clustered about the fire; they were seedy, yet their habiliments had that smartness of cut, their hair that extravagance of growth, and their hats that knowing half-swellish cock, and their looks that *un*gentlemanly assurance, which bespeaks a blackguard out of the common and vulgar run—a rapscallion, in short, of a somewhat more intellectual breed than the mere duffer, thimble-rigger, or prig. Turpin soon found, from their large talk, vulgar consequence, parroted quotations, and empty assumption, that he had fallen among some strolling players, who were bent the following morn on a voyage to Greenwich, then and there to enact some horrid and unexampled tragedy.

"Well thought on," said Dick, mentally; "I'll go to Greenwich myself." He finished his glass, and retired to bed.

Dick, like all other great men, (do not smile, reader, if word-mongers have taught you, for their own selfish and anti-educational purposes, to confound the terms *good* and *great*, and *great* and *good*,) was an early riser; and before any of his snoring fellow lodgers had yawned off their first drunken slumber, and, like the sluggard of Solomon, had turned themselves with a cry of a "little more slumber, a little more folding of the hands to sleep," he started eastward. Arrived at Wapping, he "cast his slough" at a Jew slopseller's, and in a new skin stepped on board a fishing smack, which, at "top of tide," now waited the chance of making a few shillings by dropping passengers to Greenwich, on this great festive occasion, for it was now Easter Sunday.

Let not the Agnewites start: we say *Easter Sunday*. Your advocates for the *bitter* observance of the Sabbath; your pharisaic, uncharitable, neighbour-annoying, thank-God-I-am-not-as-other-men humbugs; your prating, preaching, canting, street-corner-praying ignoramuses, who measure religious fervour by intolerant excitement, spiritual gifts by the lack of practical charity, and their heavenly acquirements in an inverse ratio to their ignorance ; these mischievous meddlers, (for "fools rush in where angels fear to tread,") will tell you that God's judgments (of which *they* are the interpreters !) are rife throughout the land, because of the desecration of the Sabbath day.   The author has now a writer before him, who describes the houses of entertainment in St. George's Fields, at Chelsea, and other places, crowded with drunken men and women on the current Sabbath days ; while on Easter Sunday, the principal street of Greenwich was full of men who, with bottle in hand, invited " the sailors and their punks" to take a glass of " right Geneva ;" and the highway was filled with fighting drunkards, " both men and women."

But it is necessary, even at the risk of tediousness, to describe the attire of our hero.   Before leaving Wapping, he had equipped himself in the quilted petticoat, the broad leathern belt, and the hat with flying band of ribbon which marked the sailor in the time of Sir Cloudesley Shovel ; long woollen stockings, buckled shoes, and a stout stick beneath his arm, completed the " rig-out" of our jolly jack tar.

The scene, however, which we have above adverted to, had not yet filled the street.   Indeed it was not till noon, or after, that the motley group of holiday-making mechanics, apprentices, thieves, prostitutes, hawkers, spirit vendors, and gambling sharps, would get into full play.   Now and again a lad and lassie gay, were met as he strolled into the principal street from the " Ship Tavern " stairs, now obliterated and rased from the book of things that be, by the new landing-place and steam-pier.

Turpin rolled up the street, his appetite whetted by a dram he had taken with the skipper, and was casting his eyes about in search of a house where a luncheon might be procured, when he observed a dashing specimen of the feminine gender linked arm-in-arm with as dashing a ditto of the male sex as you would wish to criticise on a fine day.   He looked dubiously at them as they approached—doubt gave place to certainty—it was Tom King ! and she —it must be she—he had seen her before, but where ?

A courteous bow from Dick, was acknowledged by a stare from the lady— and a grasp of the hand from Tom.   To see Dick in a disguise, did not astonish him ; but to meet him thus, was both gratifying and surprising.

"My friend, Mr. Lindsay," said Tom readily, with a wink at Turpin.

They were soon housed ; a jolly lunch, a stinging glass of ale, a digester of Cognac, and a minute's whisper, put the two friends in good humour with each other and the world.

To tell how they enjoyed the sports of knock-'em-down, the fortune-telling on the Heath, the down-hill rollings of the Park—and how Marian was delighted with the tragedy and the " mechanical motions," to see which Tom treated her, with the jokes, practical and verbal, of the merry and licentious mob, and the fiddle and hop at the " Ship," with which the night's amusements concluded, would be tedious—suffice it to say that, through that and the following three days, they " kept it up ;" and on Thursday returned, less merry, less rich, and no wiser, to the great city.

King had gone, by appointment, to the Red Lion in Aldersgate Street, to meet Dick, " anent and concerning," as the Scotch lawyers phrase it, certain "acts and deeds to be done and executed ;" and Marian sat alone in her chamber, at the furnished lodgings she then occupied.   Tom, though her " fancy," was by no means lord and master thereof ; at least, not to that extent of seignory that a "friend," who might visit the fair Marian, would be excluded from a visit. A rap at the door, and an enquiry for "Miss Groves," showed that the gentleman knew her "travelling name;" and the party was, at her request, desired to walk in.

He was a vulgar-looking man, though showily dressed—but Marian had learned not to be squeamish; for she had found that ladies of her profession were indeed slaves; and that there was no limit to the degradation which woman entails on herself by the *one* false step. She therefore tried her blandest smile, and placed the gentleman in a seat.

"Will ye take a glass?" said he, abruptly, thrusting a hand into the pocket of his leather riding-breeches; "I've got a crown as never was spent—beg your pardon, Miss;" and the fellow rose, and popping himself down on a sofa by the side of Marian, placed his arm behind her. "Why you don't mean to say, as because I'm a friend o' your friend, as that's any reason why—" and he stole a kiss. Marian pretended offence. The stranger again dived his hand into the pocket, and pulled out some silver, mixed with guineas and seven-shilling pieces. She caught sight of the gold. "He's a hawbuck," thought Marian; and she resolved to make use of him accordingly. Liquor was brought in; as they drank, her objection to the visitor wore off, and they fell into commonplace chat. Marian preferred punch, which the stranger, on the plea of his great skill in compounding it, mixed himself. Its effects were extraordinary; for scarcely had Marian drank a second or third glass, when she felt herself in a whirl of intoxication. The truth was, that the cunning scoundrel had drugged the mixture; and she became, without being aware of it, immensely talkative. The stranger plied her with the liquor; and the silly woman was soon so far beside herself as to chat with him as if he had been her most confidential friend.

"I shouldn't wonder," observed the man, still doing the amorous, "that you thought me a rum sort of chap; I'm a good 'un though, when I take a fancy. Ask Tom if I ain't—why, lord bless you, many's the time that he and I and Dick have been out together, he's said to me says he, ' Bill—'"

"What, do you know Dick, then, as well; dearee me, I never thought—now you won't tell, will you?"

"Me tell!" said the visitor, reproachfully; then kissing her; "Me tell—do you think any of the right lot ever—"

"Then *you* won't tell if *I* tell," said Marian; "do you know Tom only left me this morning—we've been these three days at Greenwich, and had such fun; oh dear, how my head swims!"

"Take a little water," said Bayes, proffering a glass; for he feared he had overdone it.

"I didn't reckon though as he'd have gone away this morning without waiting for me, seeing he'd promised not to go till I came. However, it's all for the best, as the old song says, for when the cat is out the mice may play; and so can you and I, pretty Marian."

"I'd thank you to keep your distance, sir," said Marian, repulsing his familiarity, with assumed indignation, for the water had slightly sobered her. The stranger tried some coaxing, and the woman was soon soothed.

"When do you expect Tom back?" asked he, as if it was a matter of indifference.

"Oh, there's no fear of that," answered Marian, quite mistaking the object of the question. "He and Dick are going off for a day or two. He promised I should meet him this evening in Aldersgate-street."

" I'm sure they'll both be cursedly vexed that I'm not with 'em. My name's Rose, Bill Rose ; you've heard 'em speak of me, no doubt ?"

Marian did not clearly remember whether she had or had not. But the name seemed familiar, so she said " Yes."

" Oh, do you know that my Tom—I always call him *my* Tom ; he'd be jealous though, I shouldn't wonder, if you went with me to the Red Lion, so we wont go together."

The stranger had arrived at the information he desired, and withdrawing his arm from the waist of Marian, fidgetted about, urged her to drink more, which she declined, and exhibited such unequivocal signs of an intention to depart, that Marian grew vexed that she had shown such entertainment to so shabby a visitor. All her hints at expecting some compliment were parried by the strange gentleman ; and he took himself off rather abruptly, with a promise that he would see her again on the following day—important, though till that moment, forgotten business, compelling his departure.

The door was slammed soundly after him by the indignant slattern, who acted as servant maid ; for a recognition of the gentleman by that personage had put out of question any request for a gratuity.

The girl hastened up stairs to Marian.

" Lord bless me, doesn't, you know who that swell is ; eh ? I didn't see him, for missis let him in ; and she should ha' let him out again for me if I'd ha' twigged him. Please to remember the servant ! I was just going to say, till I jest looked in his ugly face—why that's Dick Bayes the grabsman ; what could he want with you, miss ?"

Marian was alarmed, her head was by no means clear in ordinary cases of difficulty, and this piece of information paralysed her. She tried to recollect what she might have said to the man, but she could only recal one point ; viz. that she had divulged to the pretended Bill Rose the place at which Turpin and King would meet.

She stood a few seconds with her head grasped between her hands.

" Oh say you're mistaken, Kitty ! what, what, shall I do ? they'll both be taken and hanged ; my foolish tongue will cause it all !" and she burst into a flood of tears ; for Marian was easily excited and easily appeased, like all persons who want strength and decision of character.

" It ain't no use saying I'm mistaken, when I ain't," replied the servant, who stood with dirty face and sympathising look, as much perplexed as her mistress ; " I've seed him scores o' times, when I was slavey * at missus Jacobs's in Shire lane. Law bless you he was used to be there with old Polly Bedford as died i' the Lane years agone, when I was a kinchin†. I knows Dick Bayes too well ; he nabbed my fancy man, and I've liked him like pie ‡ ever sence."

" Tell me what I shall do," exclaimed Marian, ; " he knows all, they'll both be taken—and I—," and Marian, really mistaking herself for a woman of intense feeling, fell down on the sofa and sobbed hysterically.

" What ! the captain ?" asked the girl. " Captain Darcy ?" for his liberality and good looks had made him a favourite. " Have you stoppered § him. Where is he—I'll put him down to loap ‖ the grab yet."

* Servant. † Child.
‡ A slang metnoymy—signifying that the speaker would have no objection to stick a knife in the party spoken of.
§ Cut short the career of.   ‖ Get away from. Give the slip.

"No! no! replied Marian, starting up;" I'll go myself. I shall yet be in time to put him on his guard; run, Kitty, and bring me my clogs, and my hood. I'll go myself: oh my poor head—how could I be such a fool?' Mmuttering self-condemning incoherences Marian attired herself for her adventure; and with swimming head and confused brain set out from Brompton [on her endeavour to repair the mischief she had thus unwittingly committed.

CHAPTER XXII.

What mighty ills have not been done by woman?
Who was't betrayed the Capitol? a woman,
Who lost Mark Antony the world? a woman,
Who was the cause of a long ten years war,
And laid at last old Troy in ashes? Woman.
Destructive, damnable deceitful woman!
Woman, to man first as a blessing given,
When innocence and love were in their prime,
Happy awhile in Paradise they lay
But quickly woman long'd to go astray,
Some foolish new adventure fain must prove,
And the first devil she saw she changed her love,
To his temptation, lewdly she inclined
And for a single apple damned mankind.
                                                Otway.

O malignant and ill boding star,
Away! vexation almost stops my breath!
Thus sundered friends greet in the hour of death,—
——-Farewell! no more my fortune can
But curse the cause— I cannot aid the man.
I'll tell thee now, how, thou shalt make escape!
By sudden flight, come, dally not, begone.
                                Henry vi. act. iv. sc. v.

MARIAN walked briskly on, through lanes skirted with quickset, and through the grounds of the great market gardens, then covering the space now occupied by the formal and uniform brick houses of Chelsea, Sloane-street, and the ditto Square: for all the places, rows, and streets rejoicing in the name of Cadogan, as yet were not; and the mighty congregation of bricks and mortar now loading that portion of the clay of our common mother, known as Brompton, Chelsea, Kensington, &c., as yet took no place among the things that be. The ground was, to a great extent, as the maps of the environs show, dotted with the residences of noblemen and gentlemen, whose names still live in the rows and places which have disfigured the spots once sacred as the grounds of my Lord This or Sir Erasmus That. Much, however, of these lands were laid out in market gardens; for 'tis easy to tell when profit battles with the pride of peerage, artichokes with aristocrats, or cabbages with coronets, what will be the result of the contest. Pride succumbs to pence, bricks weigh down the baron, applewomen outvote ancestry, dukes are postponed to demand, marquises cede their pleasant places to murphies and retire before the energy of industry to preserve *procul profani* the empty dignity of exclusiveness in some more remote part of the land.

Through this suburban district Marian had hastened, and now having passed Hyde Park Corner, was wending her way along Piccadilly, when she became aware of some person walking close behind her; the man, for it was a military tread, kept close for a few yards, and then, as if half-assured of her identity, stept up to her, and peering beneath her bonnet, said, " Bless me, my dear Miss Groves (such was Marian's travelling name), how charmingly rosy you look this morning. Stap my vitals, but I never a saw such a goddess, 'pan hanner. Will you deign to accept-a—of the arm of your devoted slave-a," and the beardless Lieutenant D'Eresby, (by courtesy Captain,) enlocked the hand of Marian within his elbow.

Captain D'Eresby was a silly youth---a scion of the aristocracy, and neither wiser nor better than such spoilt cubs of fortune usually are. Character he had none, in either of the senses of the word ; but cash he had, and he put it to the vilest, the silliest, and the most profligate uses. He aspired to the character of a blood, though naturally a coward : had made the acquaintance of Marian incidentally, and was just now, for want of some more useful pursuit, persuading himself into the idea that she was a paragon of beauty, and desperately fond of his own insignificant self. Marian, equally empty, undecided, and vicious, felt flattered, as well as profited by so rich and foolish a cull---he prided himself in being seen promenading Piccadilly with a confessedly fine woman, and she, having an eye to number one, postponed feeling to lucre and convenience : inwardly, however, resolving that she would make her best haste, as soon as she could decently get rid of him, to the rendezvous of King and our hero. They chatted rapidly until they neared Burlington-gardens. At the corner of Bond-street stood a confectionary and soup house ; and into that, after some persuasion, her squire persuaded her to enter. Here a short half hour was spent : when Marian, now recovering from the effects of the drug administered by the cunning Dick Bayes, insisted upon leaving the Captain—and she did so.

* * * * * * * *

" Vill you puy any rhuparb, shpectacles, or sheals ?" said a miserable looking Jew to two men, who sat in earnest conversation in the back parlour of the Red Lion in Aldersgate-street.

" We don't want any, my good fellow," replied one, nettled at the interruption. " Can't you take an answer---or must I ring for the waiter to turn you out ?"

" Praps de oder shentleman, vould puy ?" said the pertinacious Israelite, shoving his box before him.

" Isn't my friend's telling you to go, enough, and be hanged to you ?" retorted the other.

The Jew turned away, and moved towards the door ; yet whoever had seen the demoniac twinkle of his black eye, and the mean expression of treachery, and selfishness on that contemptible face might have read mischief. The pedlar was our quondam acquaintance Mishter Solomons, of Houndsditch : and the companions were Turpin and King.

" Tish all as right as a trivit, Mshter Bayes," said the jew, as he joined three men, who waited at the corner of an inn-yard, some little distance from the house. " Dey're both on 'em a talking at de table in de left hand corner of de roomsh : plesh me, I vaited and vaited viles I could get dem to shpeak, for I knows Mishter Dick's shound of de voish vell—and shall never forgit it," added the Jew, *sotto voce*, with a shudder, as he thought on

The Death of Tom King.

the night of Sir Litton's death and the pillory, and plucked the cap over his earless scull.

"What the devil keeps Bill Johnson and his runner I can't think," said Bayes, testily; for truth to say, he feared the consequences of an attempt with the force then present, to capture the highwaymen. His two assistants he might depend on, but upon the Jew he could not calculate—he knew him to be a thief, and he doubted not he was a coward. Besides, it would be necessary to have one man to guard the exit from the rear, while he, with at least two others, should enter at the front. He stamped hastily and vexedly—steadily eyeing the door of the house from his post of observation. Muttered curses occasionally escaped him. "Hallo! what the devil's coming here?" said he, as a man in sleeves and a striped stable waistcoat led two spirited horses from the corner of St. Ann's Lane, (then debouching at the lower end of the narrow part of St. Martin's-le-Grand.) The man, who was no other than Street, Tom King's cousin, stopped a few yards from the corner, and consigning the steeds to a shoeless urchin, walked towards the Red Lion. "Why, d—t—n!" growled Bayes; "that's Dick's black mare. Follow, Rob, I must nail that fellow, or he'll blow the gaff,* and all the fat 'ill be in the fire at last."

Thus saying, Bayes, followed by his subordinate, hastened across the street, and intercepted the man who had brought the horses, just at the

* Betray the secret.

doorway of the Red Lion. "Stop!" said the officer, displaying his crowned staff—"you are my prisoner."

Street changed colour ; as he looked at Bayes and his man.

"May I go in?" asked he, "to tell the gentlemen as their horses is—" then recovering his surprise, he said, "but what am I your prisoner for, I'd like to know?"

"There's no need," said Bayes, sarcastically, "to trouble the gentlemen, as you call them, till *I* announce their horses are ready: come, come, Mister Street, I knows you ; and if so be you've a mind to save your own scrag, you'll give me, and these gemmen with me, as little trouble as need be; 'complices, you know, can be made safe, if so be they'll assist in windicating the law upon the principals—eh, Mister Street, do you twig?"

Mr. Street did twig, as Bayes termed it ; for he walked quietly across with them, to the gateway, without resisting.

"Now, Mister Street, d'ye see, there's enough on us here," and Bayes pointed to Solomons and the other man, "to make all safe : you'll excuse me, however, when I say that, to prevent mistakes, I must trouble you with the ruffles ;" and Bayes handcuffed him ; a precaution rarely neglected in those days. "We're waiting, Mr. Street," said the superior officer, with a wink, "for a couple of friends, who will lend us a hand ; as I don't wish the affair to come off any way but so as 'ull do credit to the skill of Richard Bayes, —dy'e see?" and Dick Bayes winked and gave a chuckle at his own wit and sagacity.

"You see, Mister Street," continued he, still in a chaffing tone ; "as my force can't nicely spare a man just now ; and moreover, as our acquaintance is too short for me to trust you—you see I knows you—and it's no go to try a shirk, I'll leave Sam with you, while I, Rob, and Mishter Solomons, just take a look at the premises. Confound those fellows!" added he, in another tone ; "where the deuce can they be!"

Mister Bayes looked up and down the street—no Bill Johnson nor his man was in sight—he swore and swore again, but they came not. Two chairmen, carrying a hack-sedan, trotted briskly by, the stout ash poles springing beneath their load as they kept the active and measured step, which marked the practised sedan-bearers.

"That's a James's Street chair," said Bayes, as he looked after it—"Why, what the devil does this mean?" exclaimed he, as the strapping Irishmen deposited their burden opposite the door of the Lion, and one of them, with polite activity, raised the lid and unclosed the door of the little box in which they had brought the fare.

Bayes walked hurriedly across, and so contrived to pass the party as she alighted, as to obtain a view of her person. The start was mutual as their eyes met. Marian Glover saw it was Dick Bayes, and Dick Bayes beheld Marian Glover!

"Confusion!" growled the thief-taker, as he recrossed the road at a jump and three strides—"Rob, and be d—d to you, stick to my heels—Sam, keep close—d—n the prisoner! Come on, Solly!" and the four hurried towards the Lion, leaving Street unguarded and alone, a spectator of what might happen next, but too much interested even to attempt escape, which, he felt assured, must only lead to his recapture under less favourable circumstances.

We will now look into the parlour, where we left our hero and his comrade.

"Street's late with the prads," observed Dick, looking at his watch—"'tis past five, and he's seldom behind his time. We've a long ride before us—three hours I should say—and we must not meet these people nearer than St. Alban's."

"It's my notion, Dicky, that the fellow has been taking some precious circumbendibus for fear of being watched—couzin Bill's rather lily livered, though he talks large ———" The room door swung open suddenly, and Marian, pale with terror, and gasping for breath, caught Tom by the arm.

"Hey-day, my Molly-Ann!" said King, surprised at her looks—"what in the name of Moses's mother does all this mean—show us the ghost, and we'll ——— "

"Fly! fly! Tom, for my sake—Bayes and a posse of officers are at the door—and ——— "

Dick looked at King with a bitter smile, and producing a pistol, quietly cocked it.

"Rather unpleasant, I should say," said Tom, placing his back against the room door, and doing the like with consummate coolness. "How many, of 'em are there, my pretty Marian, eh?"

"Oh don't ask me—I don't know—I've seen none but him—oh the odious wretch. I knew him again the moment I saw—"

Turpin gave a meaning look at Tom, and said, in a tone of reproach—"These women, Tom, these women. This is no time to ask for explanation—but Mister Bayes would not try it on alone—no, no; take time, by the forelock, Tom—and— "

"Your horse stands at the corner, and yours," said Marian; "I saw a boy holding them both."

"Bravo," said King; "that's the best news I've heard these five minutes. Come on, Dick."

"Softly," said Turpin, arresting his arm; "stay a moment—a boy holding them did you say?"

"A ragged boy," answered Marian.

"Street is taken Tom, I see it now. One dash, Tom—down the first that stops us—and to saddle—once mounted, and we'll forgive them if they take us. Come!"

The friends walked suddenly into the passage. Entering the doorway was the worthy Mishter Sholomons; who, urged by the threats of Bayes, and the hope of reward, was about again to enter the room to gather information, in his character of pedlar. A short cry of alarm and surprise escaped him, as he met the highwaymen in the narrow entry.

"Take that, you Jew-thief;" cried King, dealing him a back-handed blow on the mouth with the butt end of his whip, the pistol being grasped in his left hand. Mishter Solomons measured his length on the ground.

Three yards from the door stood Bayes and his myrmidons. The cry of the Jew and the rush of Turpin and King into the street were simultaneous. They saw their horses, and made towards them.

"Nail 'em, boys!" cried Bayes, and the officers flew at their game, rendered desperate by the chance of losing the valuable prize.

Rob had possessed himself of Dick's collar, while Bayes and Sam did the same courtesy to King. There was a short and sharp struggle.

"That's for *you*," cried Turpin, as he threw his man heavily against the large stone which stood on the edge of the hard pathway, for the convenience of horsemen arriving or departing from the Red Lion; for Aldersgate Street was not then regularly paved.

The fellow lay stunned: Dick ran to his horse—grasped Bess's glorious mane—vaulted into the saddle—and rode towards where Tom was scuffling with the officers. Bayes was incomparably the stronger man, and had brought our merry friend Tom into an unwonted position—he was on his knees; and the other thieftaker was trying to loose his hands from their grasp on Bayes's collar.

"Hold out!" cried Dick in an encouraging voice; "I'm here and safe;" and edging Bess close to the group, he delivered a blow on the sconce of Sam, that sent his head spinning, and brought sparkles from his eyes.

"Oh Lord!" ejaculated the fellow; and losing his grasp of King, he raised both hands instinctively to his head, staggered a step or two, and fell.

The blow, however, cost Dick his weapon. The stout stock of his holster pistol broke short to the barrel with the concussion, and Dick threw the barrel at Bayes; it struck him between the shoulders without serious effect. Turpin drew his remaining weapon, and King sprung to his feet.

"Bullet him, Dick!" cried King, making a desperate effort: Bayes bore him down, and they rolled struggling in the road. It was now dusk, and a turn or two on the ground rendered it difficult to distinguish friend from foe.

"Fire, Dick—damn it, fire!" gasped Tom, for he felt how much he was overmatched.

Dick raised his weapon, and looked with steady eye along the barrel, for he feared much, in their continual shifts, he might hit his friend. A whistle was given, and a voice, some dozen yards off, shouted "Hoy! hoy!"

"Here, Bill, here!—help! help! a rescue!" exclaimed Bayes, holding King between himself and Turpin, who, with finger on trigger, sat eyeing his opportunity to fire. Another struggle and the men turned. There was no time for hesitation—succour was at hand: the flint descended and the heavy charge of slugs passed the ear of Bayes, lacerating it dreadfully, but buried themselves in the breast of King.

"Done for, by God!" cried King, in a tone of anguish, as he grasped his left shoulder with his right hand. Bill Johnson, with two other officers, came up. "Fly, Dick; it's all up with me," and he sank into their arms. "Farewell, Dick! love to——" the dying highwayman gasped—the death rattle struggled in his throat—a shudder, a groan, and the gay Tom's expressive features settled into the changeless quietude of death.

"Fifty extra to the man that nails him!" cried Bayes, as he rushed towards Bess's bridle. Turpin swayed his horse with a curvet, dashed his pistol in the face of Bayes,—one spring of Bess cleared the officers, whose bullets whizzed after him, and "away, away, on pinions that outstrip the wind," dashed Dick and his gallant steed.

CHAPTER XXIII.

On we went—I took no heed,
  How such a strange career would end:
I urged my barb to meteor speed,
  But cared not where that speed might tend.
He sprung, he flew, as though he knew
  A frenzied wretch was on his back;
And kept his pace, for goodly space,
  Upon his own free chosen track.

What an unthought of goal I'd won;
  Mercy! what wild'ring race I'd run.
'Twould soon be o'er—my failing horse
  Was strangely wheeling on its course.
His strength was out, his spirit flagged;
His fire was spent, he faintly lagged;
His dripping flanks and reeking neck
Were white with rifts of foaming fleck.
His laboured breath was quick and short;
His nostrils heaved with gasping snort:
He tottered on, his will was good,
His work had not belied his blood.
Another mile—and then he fell;
His part was o'er—he played it well:
With snapping girth, and reeling head,
He groaned and sunk—my steed was dead!
                    Melaia: by Eliza Cook.

The Pursuit.

THE shop-windows in the wide street called Goswell Road, exhibited but feeble lights in that dark age; and the rude, thick window-frames threw huge and magnified shadows on the roadway, which rendered it difficult to distinguish objects, with certainty or clearness, even at the distance of a few yards. The gravelled road rung loudly to the rattling gallop of the gallant Bess, and the bright sparks flew brilliantly from the flints imbedded in the drift; for the unfrequent carriage traffic allowed such soft material to be used to bind the large coarse gravel with which the highway was repaired. The passing horseman excited but a passing thought, and Dick held on his course toward the Angel at Islington: satisfied with the speed he had made, he pulled up.

We have before said that, of late, Dick had relaxed much of his early abstemiousness. His mouth was parched, yet he asked not for drink to quench it. "He's dead!" said he, as Bess drew toward the mounting-block; "but I did not think mine should be the hand to deal his death-blow. Alas! poor Tom! They'll surely follow," added he, thinking aloud; "'tis not safe to dismount. No! no! this saddle is my throne, and I must not quit it. Hallo!" and he called to a rough-headed ostler; "brandy here! d'ye hear?"

"Aye, aye," responded the fellow, lounging into the old-fashioned hostel. The landlord came forth, bottle and glass in hand.

"'Tis right Cognac," observed the pursy fellow, as he proffered the dram. Dick despatched it.

"Fill this," said he, presenting a canteen. "Now a glass."

"Another!"   It followed.

"Another!" he again presented the glass.

"Another!" and "Another!"

A heavy gallop sounded in the direction of the City Road—Turpin turned his head; he threw a guinea to the man.

"Good bye! and keep the change till Dick Turpin returns!" cried he.

The astonished Boniface stood, with bottle in hand, until three men rode up.

"A man on a black horse?" eagerly asked the first, who was mounted on the animal once owned by the light-hearted Tom.

The host pointed along the road—the sounds of Bess's hoofs yet ringing on the ear.

"Forward, forward, lads! a race for a thousand—he's worth it; forward, forward!" and the trio—Dick Bayes, Bill Johnson, and Pearce, with whip and spur, urged onward in pursuit.

Turpin felt that dogged determination and self-confidence which smiles at the darkest frowns of fortune. He laughed scornfully, as with scarcely an effort, and without call for the use of hand or heel, his gallant Bess bounded forward, the shouts and gallop of the pursuers growing fainter at every stride. Leaving the church of Islington to his left, he took the Lower Road, passed Ball's Pond, and was soon breasting Stamford Hill. He slackened his pace: the sounds of his enemies were borne on the light breeze. Through the Wash at Edmonton, by the church, across the brook, and by the ancient conduit, he sped: the venerable cross at Waltham rose on his view, silvered by the bright moon; Hertfordshire is gained—Theobald's passed, and Dick breathed freely. The stake was too large, the reward too great, and the bloodhounds too staunch, to forego the pursuit without a struggle; and Dick, with the nonchalance of fatalism, now suffered them to gain considerably on him. As he cantered, rather than galloped, through the street of Brockton, and by Burton Mill, the cry became, however, too close.

"We must lay out again, awhile, my Bessie," said the highwayman, patting her smooth neck: the noble beast answered with a snort; and, as if interpreting the wish of her master, turned her beautiful and active ears on their elastic pivot. The sounds from behind reached her; and Bess, who suffered nothing to overtake her, again laid out.

Brockton and Hoddesdon are cleared a mile, and the hill surmounted; the cross-roads to Hertford and Stanfield passed, and the opposite acclivity gained. Turpin turned in his saddle.

"Ha! ha!" cried he; "'tis well I'm prevented from brooding on my mischance: these fellows are obstinate—one, two, three, four—egad, there's a reinforcement—well, the more the merrier. We'll try their horseflesh, Bess, and give them such a night's ride as shall serve them for talk to the end of their lives; what! take Dick Turpin in his saddle—and that on Bess—ha! ha! Halloo! Halloo!" cried Dick, as he placed his hand to his head and gave an encouraging view halloo to his eager and panting pursuers. The clear strong shout was borne on the wind :—

"D'ye hear the murderous varmint?" said Bayes savagely, "he's mocking us, by G— ; may I never see home again, if I have him not this night, dead or alive; forward, lads, forward!"

The blown horses were forced onward by lash and curse and armed steel. Thus crossed they the aqueduct of the public-spirited Sir Hugh Myddleton, and reached Ware, where they succeeded in procuring fresh horses. The loss of time, however, fully countervailed this advantage, and they crossed the Lea without seeing or hearing the fugitive. But if they had lost time, Dick did the same not farther on; arrived again on the Lea, he paused a few minutes near Ward's mill, at a publichouse, where again he had recourse to brandy.

"Rest I cannot bear," muttered he; "what matters my flight; I've murdered the truest, kindest, the best friend man ever had—the world contains not a soul I care for, and see—they're coming on again. I thought they had had enough of this," added he, as the sound of hoofs once more rose on the ear. "Well, well, good bye! for the third time!"

He shook the rein on the neck of Bess, and away she went. The hills between here and Collier's Well, added an excitement to the ride, which cheered the heart of the fearless highwayman. Each successive acclivity enabled him to judge accurately of the pace of his foes, and regulate that of his matchless steed accordingly: again and again did his jeering cry strike on their ears, replied to, each time, by muttered curses. On, on, however, they strained; but their ardour abated, or their steeds flagged, as fagged and weary they toiled up the hill, and by the windmill, two miles on this side Royston :—

> Up the green hill he climbs,
> Stops on its brow awhile, scornful looks back
> On his pursuers pricking o'er the plain.
> Again he flies, and with redoubled speed
> Skims o'er the ground—still the tenacious crew
> Hang on his track, aloud their prey demand,
> And chase him many a league. †

Thus held they on until the moon was "walking in her brightness." The night was glorious, as Dick mounted the hill before entering the town.

"We can play with them like a cat with a mouse," said he to his gallant Bess; "we must encourage them, or they'll give up and spoil the sport."

Turpin checked her head, and slackened her into a walk. The ruse had the desired effect.

"Now, or never!" cried Pearce, who was the best mounted, to two grooms, who had joined them at Ware; "his beast is lamed—hurra! hurra!" and they goaded the flanks of their panting horses.

At a smart trot Royston was cleared by Bess, and Cambridgeshire entered.

"Halloo, gentlemen!" cried Dick, as he passed the boundary, scarce fifty yards before them; "welcome to Cambridgeshire: any business in Hunts? happy to ride with you—pleasant night; good bye—no nearer, if you please."

The distance was impracticable; but Johnson fired his blunderbuss in mere rage, as Bess again bounded off.

The mare bestrode by Bayes, and which he had procured at Ware, was a staunch and good animal; but the thieftaker's horsemanship, though he was a bold and stouthearted rider, had nearly beaten his horse—unlike our hero, who rode so as scarcely to allow his matchless steed to feel him. The two grooms who had joined them at the change, inspired by the promise of ten guineas from Bayes, might have proved more formidable competitors in the race, had they not kept with the ruck for deficiency of weapons, and per-

---

† Somerville's Chase, b. iii.

sonal apprehensions rendering them loth to be the first to encounter the famous Turpin ; they prudently kept neck and neck---and no more---with those whose profession entitled them to the honour of the first shot from the highwayman's pistol.

'Tis nine o' clock, and forty miles have now been covered.

"A consultation, lads," cried Bayes ; and rising gingerly in his saddle, he checked his horse, nothing loth, into a walk ; the rest of the party did the same.

"'Tis the pace that kills ; he's better mounted than us, and be d—d to him," said the officer, striving to hide his mortification. "I'll tell you---we can procure horses, he can't---let's track him slowly ; tomorrow we'll find him, even if he should slip us now. His mare's a trump, but she can't last much longer : easy, lads ; slowly forward to Arrington ; there we'll take a rest and a whet, and remount to follow the slot of this buck, should he run to the land's end."

His company assented. The two assistants, however, declining to follow further, and grumbling at the guinea, which Bayes proffered them, they turned their jaded steeds southward, and swore their weary way back to Royston, whence, they returned in the morning to Ware, with a thousand maledictions on thieftaking and thieftakers, as many protestations never again to engage in hunting a highwayman, and as many aspirations that, (as they had not taken him,) our hero might baffle the shabby scoundrel's hope of getting the reward.

The officers rode on easily, so far as pace went ; and now they sniff the cooling breeze which sweeps the glassy surface of the classic Granta. What is that figure stationary on the bridge ? 'tis the object of their hopes and fears seated quietly in his saddle.

The pursuers gnashed their teeth with vexation.

"He's laughing at us, by G---!" said Bayes. "'tis no use to spur ; keep easy, Bill, I say ; the daring scoundrel knows his Bess can run away from us when he pleases. But, if it costs me fifty, I'll have a horse presently that shall put you to your tether, my lad, or my name's not Dick Bayes."

"Now then, loitering again, gentlemen," cried Dick, as he could plainly distinguish the shuffling trot into which the trio now urged their horses. His voice came clear on the silence of night.

"Let's try another burst : we're but a mile from Arrington ; an accident may yet make him our prisoner."

"Done !" cried Bayes, and once more they dashed off into a gallop. Their first stride was the signal for Bess and her rider. In the night the good folks were startled with the clatter of hoofs through their main street, mingled with the shouts of men. But like the lightning's gleam, which, "ere a man can say behold ! it is gone," so soon fled the sounds in the distance : yet many a year did aged garrulity report the story of that chase ; and many a withered ancient so embellished the oft-repeated lie, that at last, by the mere force of iteration, not a few believed they could describe---aye, and more, they did describe---the person of the bold Dick Turpin.

On---on---and now the hill on this side Wimple rises before him : up its sides

See his swift courser strains : her shining hoofs
Secure and steady beat the sounding earth. Now

Turpin invites his pursuers to a ride through Cambridgeshire.

Down he sweeps, as stoops the falcon bold
To pounce his prey. Now, up the opponent hill,
By the swift motion flung, he mounts aloft;
So ships in wintry seas, now sliding sink
Adown the steepy wave—then, tossed on high,
Ride o'er the billows and defy the storm.

Wimple is passed—the stream crossed ; and still, as " darts the dolphin from the shark," the vigorous chase holds her own. Leaving " the beauteous groves of Stowe" on the left, he spurs through the wooded road and mounts the hill; but, where are his pursuers? Dick looked back ; slowly they emerge from the wood, still urging their over-ridden beasts in vain pursuit, and arrived at the hill on whose steep ascent they view once more their tantalising enemy.

" It's of no use," said Bayes, for the first time speaking in a desponding tone.

" Hold on to Caxton—cheer up !" cried Pearce ; " we've a chance on the cards yet. Don't let 'em say we had a highwayman in sight all night, and couldn't take him at last. No, no ! follow, lads, follow !" and once more he urged his horse forward through Caxton ; and, led by Pearce, who was by far the best rider, the party followed Turpin, who rode steadily on. Papworth St. Agnes, and Papworth Everard—four more miles—and lash, and steel, and curse are powerless to urge their over-marked brutes to greater exertion—

No. 35.

The panting courser now, with trembling nerves,
Begins to reel; urged by the goring spur,
Many a faint effort makes: he snorts, he foams;
The big round drops run trickling down his sides,
With sweat and blood distained.

"Done! by G—d!" cried Bayes, mad with vexation, as the rattling fling of iron rung on the hard road.

Leaning aside, he looked anxiously down his horse's legs: the foot in which the worn nail still remained galled her, and she halted cruelly.

"Give her a warming, and she'll forget it," said Pearce, ignorant of the nature of the mishap.

"She's cast a shoe, confound her!" cried the thieftaker. "Never mind: hold on! hold on!" and he forced the wretched animal to speed; with reeling steps, and heaving flank, the tortured beast staggers on: the steep ascent by which Huntingdonshire is entered rises before Turpin, who now

—Looks back and views
The strange confusion of the vale below,
Where sore vexation reigns: see yon poor jade:
In vain th' impatient horseman frets and swears,
With galling spur harrows his mangled sides—
He can no more: his stiff unpliant limbs
Rooted to earth, unmoved and fixed he stands,
For every cruel curse returns a groan,
And sobs, and faints, and dies. †

"There goes twenty pounds," growled Bayes, as he disentangled himself from his dying horse.

The others gathered round him.

"Are ye hurt?" asked Pearce, as his discomfited brother officer rose to his feet, and beat the dust, for the road was dry, from his person.

"Hurt!" retorted Bayes angrily; "aye, in reputation, and mind, and pocket: follow, Bill—follow and shoot him—never take him; lend me your horse, if you're afraid. Look at him!" exclaimed he, as he pointed towards Dick, who had again reined up, and sat in the calm clear moonlight, his jet-black mare contrasting strongly with the white chalky road. "Look at him!" repeated he, hoarse with passion, and shaking his fist with impotent rage.

"What shall we do?" asked Bill Johnson, as, holding their panting beasts, they joined in council with their chief.

"Do! why give me your horse; I'll not return alive without Turpin;" and, in the fury of his disappointment, he sealed his determination with an oath.

A few minutes' consideration, however, materially cooled his ardour; and, at last, he assented, with pretended unwillingness, to the proposal of Johnson, that they should endeavour to reach Papworth by the Roman road, and give up farther thought of overtaking our hero.

Dick sat, as we have said, in the calm moonbeams, looking at the group.

"There's one down, by jingo!" said he gaily: "ho! ho! the others dismount; I hope he hasn't broke his neck for the sake of his chance of catching us—eh, my Bessie!" and he patted her neck affectionately. "We can't afford to lose ground, can we?" he added, as if consulting with his four-footed favourite; "or we'd step back to ask after their healths. Catch you, Bess! ha! ha! or take me on your back! ha! ha!" and he rode her on to the grass

† Somervile's Chase. b. iii.

by the way-side; and, with silent steps, drew nearer to his foes. Lowering his head beside her muscular neck, he listened anxiously to her breathing—it was strong but clear—accelerated, it is true, yet regular; he looked at her skin, not a hair was turned; he touched her mouth lightly; the fine trumpet of her short round ear turned actively and playfully; he checked his rein; she swerved her head, and looked steadily at him with her full, round, placid eye.

"My pride, my only friend," said the highwayman, transported at these signs of temper and endurance.

He pressed his face against her neck, and the faithful brute rubbed its head caressingly, as if acknowledging the kindness. He was now within such a distance as his experience in pistol practice told him could not with safety be diminished, and had halted to pursue his scrutiny, when Johnson spied him in the shadow of the hedge.

"Why, the audacious scoundrel's coming back to us!" cried he; pointing towards Dick. The eyes of his companions were directed to the spot.

"He'd only laugh at our firing; he's too far off," said Pearce, doggedly.

"I'd give ten guineas for a shot at him, at a reasonable distance," muttered Bayes.

"What the deuce is he at?" asked Pearce, who was more short-sighted than the others.

"'At?' I think you said, old Blinkey; why, having a laugh at us, to be sure."

"Hallo!" cried Turpin; who saw he had attracted their attention: "I invited you, gentlemen, to a ride into Cambridgeshire, and I thought you promised to accompany me into Hunts. Can I be of any service, eh? Saddle-girth slipped, eh?—Shoe cast, eh?—smith at Hilton, few miles further on.—Bellows to mend, perhaps," added he, still laughing; "respectable tradesman in that line, too, in the same town—if they're not quite past repair." Bayes raised a pistol in the excess of his vexation.

"It's no use," said Johnson, putting his hand on Bayes's arm, "he's out of range, and the thief knows it."

"Leave me alone," said the irritated superior, and the report of his long horse pistol echoed along the hill-side.

"Obliged to you, much," said Dick, waving his hat with mock politeness, then drawing a canteen from beneath his riding coat, after inviting them to drink, he put the bottle to his mouth. He was yet drinking, when Pearce, suddenly getting under shadow of the roadside bank, crouched, and ran some dozen yards in a stooping posture. Dick, who had finished his pull at the brandy-flask, was surprised to see but two men beside the fallen horse, and was trying to discover what had become of the third, when a flash from the hedge-bank caught his eye, and a bullet striking the tip of Bess's ear, passed obliquely by. Dick saw the sanguine stain, as Bess shook her head violently and raised her fore-feet slightly from the ground. "Pretty pistol practice," cried Turpin, moving towards Pearce, whom the flash of his pistol had betrayed. The officer ran back to his comrades for safety, but not so quickly as to escape a return of his shot from Dick; the ball struck his arm, and with an outcry of pain, he sprang towards them, and sunk beside the fallen horse. Bayes and Johnson had drawn their weapons, when Dick, wheeling rapidly, retraced his path. Two bullets followed him at an ineffective distance. "Good bye! good bye!" sounded on the ears of the discomfited thieftakers, and away, as though the speed of thought were in her limbs, springs the gallant Bess, and bounds

O'er rough, o'er smooth, nor heeds the steepy hill,
Nor falters in the extended vale below.

The Ride.

Away! away! and on we dash,
Torrents less rapid, and less rash,
'Twas scarcely yet the break of day,
Yet on he foamed, away! away!
Mazeppa.

" Hurrah for Huntingdonshire," cried Turpin, as at a sounding pace his mare crossed the bridge over the Lesser Ouse; " hurrah for Huntingdon! More counties shall yet hear of us, my gallant Bess!" her firm and active ears alternately turned to catch the sound of her master's voice, then playfully lowering them, as though in the act to bite, she tossed her noble head, curveted sportively, and without hint from hand or foot, beyond a slight pressure from her rider's leg, sprung into a gallop. Hilton, Beggar's Bush, a hill—and the beautiful embattled tower of the ancient church of Godmanchester rises heavenward, rearing its venerable spire in the calm and stilly night air, a monument of the piety of the men who sleep the long sleep beneath its shadow; and pointing, with mute eloquence, toward that home to which man's best thoughts and wishes should be directed. Not such, however, as should be ever-present to the mind of a reasoning and accountable being, were the thoughts and feelings of our hero—the world-defying scorn of the outcast had thrust from his soul the feeling of love for his kind, which, when lost, makes man no longer social. The irregularities of an uncurbed lawless career had obliterated from his mind those right principles, and emancipated his actions from those moral restraints, which are as essential to the happiness of the individual himself as to the order of the community of which he is a member. Misfortunes, (so he termed events which were but the legitimate and inevitable results of such crimes as his,) had so dogged his steps, that he felt himself justified in warring on mankind.

" Every man's hand is against me," thought he, in the very spirit of the Arab; " so shall my hand be against every man."

Alas! poor human nature knows not itself; at the very time he thus poured forth against human kind the bitterness of a crime-stung soul, he was anxiously caring for his horse!

The bell told eleven as, crossing the ancient stone bridge over the Ouse, he rode up the main street of the city rendered memorable as the birth-place of the Protector Cromwell. Arrived in the spacious market-place he drew up at a house of entertainment which seemed well lighted.

" All pursuit," said he " is far enough behind: they've had enough of it: we'll have our ride out though, as they've put us on our mettle."

He felt that reckless spirit which scorns concealment, that desperation which, daring the worst, is rather madness than true courage.

" I'll show myself a bit this night—they shall talk of us, Bess, in time to come—we've lost ground though sadly in the last two hours—we're going to York, Bess; once there let the future take care of itself," and he drained the last drop from his companion-flask.

" Hallo! house! within there!" brought a waiter from the door.

" Be pleased to dismount, sir," officiously snggested the polite napkin-bearer, steadying the stirrup of the horseman.

Dick declined his assistance, but dismounted.

" Walk in, sir," said he of the cotton stockings and thin shoes, for silks were then only sported by the lace-guarded lacqueys of the first nobility.

" No, no," replied Turpin, smoothing the fetlocks and the mane, and rubbing dry the flanks of Bess; " fill that, (he handed him the flask), and send the ostler to me." He came.

" Can you scald me a mash—a sweet one—a small quantity, eh?"

The fellow replied in the affirmative. The brandy was brought—the mash eaten—and Turpin again in the saddle.

" Waiter!"

" Yes, sir!"

" Pay your master for the brandy, and keep the change. Sam! take that; and when your companions talk of the horses they've seen, tell them you've had a guinea from Turpin for grooming Black Bess. Good bye!"

" There goes as good a trump as any in England, let the next be where he may," said Sam, as the regular sound of Bess's canter grew fainter in the direction of Great Stukely: " 'taint every day, no, nor week neither, as such as we sees such gentleman's conduct from them as, I dare say, think 'emselves good enough to look down on Mister Turpin. Well, well, if he do get his money lightly he parts wi' it lightly, and where's the odds? good luck to him, ses I; and those as don't like it may lump it. I'll go an' drink his health in the best as is in the cellar."

" And I'll join you, Sam," said the waiter to the head-ostler, " so soon as I've given master the keys of the smoking-room; there's ne'er a customer there, and no coach till to-morrow."

Sam agreed to wait a few minutes; and leaving the pair quaffing their stingo, and each, as the brain-inspiring liquor mounted, inventing or exaggerating the exploits of their bold benefactor, we will take a gallop after the subject of their discourse.

By Alconbury Inn, nor to right nor left he turns, but straight onward by the Three Sawtreys, and through the town of Stilton—name dear to epicures in cheese—he holds his way. The fenny country, once the forest resort of dappled deer, now lies before him, one marshy level, flat and cheerless. Norman Cross, Water Newton, Sibson—the Nene bridge is crossed, and Northamptonshire lies before him. The moon is down, and the bright stars twinkle, while the planets, with steady and various coloured ray, look down on the peaceful earth; no sound is heard save the hoof of the steed, and the strong breathing of herself and her rider. By Thornhaugh and Whittering, through a country dotted with white gleams of mere-water; and now she sniffs the cool air, and hears the ripple of the broad Welland: the boundary of Lincolnshire is entered, Stamford traversed, and Rutlandshire reached within two miles. Great Casterton and the Guash are to the left, Bowland's Gibbet to the right; Stretton, and the woods and windmills beyond, are passed, and Lincolnshire again entered. To his left flows the Witham, winding peacefully 'mid grove and mead, till, crossed again, he sees it rolling on his right. He looks on the bosky shades which mark the river's course; and crossing the rill on this side the road which diverges towards Basingthorpe, he reads inscribed on the ancient stone, " 100 miles from the Standard on Cornhill."*

Turpin could not repress a cheer—" Hurrah, hurrah, for the hundredth !" cried the highwayman. A pull at his flask, and forward.

Still travelling parallel with the sedgy Witham his gallant steed covers the ground with steady stride, and now, gleaming across the flat and swampy land, he views the extended plain

> Spread through the shadow of the night ;
> And onward, onward, onward, seem
> Like precipices in a dream,
> To stretch beyond the sight.

Strong and steady, and with unflinching resolve, his horse bounds on ; what beauteous spire is that rising from the tufted trees, the mellow white of its stone-work contrasted with the dusky green of the massy foliage sleeping in the imperfect light—'tis Grantham.

The town is passed, and Bess toils among the windmill-crowned hills 'twixt it and Gunnersby ; toils for the first time, for no mark of exertion, not to say exhaustion, had yet appeared. Her crisp short ear lopped, and with erect tail she laboured up the steep ascent of Hoocliff Hill. Turpin was too good a horseman, even in his then excited state, not to mark the symptom ; six miles of open road is rode at a pace to save distress, Bernyngton is neared, and now Bess weighs heavily on the sustaining bridle-hand of her rider.

> Some streaks announced the coming day ;
> How slow alas! he came !
> He thought that mist of dawning gray
> Would never dapple into day,
> So heavily it rolled away,
> Before the eastern flame
> Rose crimson, and deposed the stars;
> And culled the radiance from their cars,
> And filled the earth from his bright throne,
> With glorious lustre all his own.

At that still hour, the steam rising from her flanks, with the first white foam clinging to her bit, Bess and her rider entered Bernyngton. Turpin dismounted at the inn.

" 'Twill never do," said he internally, " to let her stiffen."

He had not eaten since the noon of the previous day, yet he did not ask for meat.

" Is your ale good?" asked he of a drowsy fellow, who with ungartered legs, lounged from a side door to answer the summons of the early wayfarer.

" Aye, aye, sur, sure it be, and 'tis a-singing i' my head noo"—and rubbing

*It may be as well to observe here, that the writer, throughout the ride, has used the scarce and curious itinerary, entitled " The roads of England and Wales, from actual survey, by J. Ogilby, improved by J. Senex, London, 4to, 1719." The road " from London to Barwick," (Berwick,) via York, being engraved on 42 copper plates, in columns, to imitate scrolls. He has also referred to some other contemporary topographical works, such as " Rocque's Survey," 1736, which will account for the miles here incidentally mentioned differing from the present. The route also occasionally deviates from the present one, but not materially ; all distances in contemporary authorities are computed from the Standard at Cornhill, and not from Hicks's Hall. He has preferred resorting to them, though the modern road-books would have saved him much time and trouble.

his eyes he gazed toward the gorgeous east—"Early abroad this morning, sur?" said the man sulkily, and stealing a suspicious look at the smoking Bess;—"and travelling all night, too," thought he, though he kept that part of his observation to himself.

"Mind your own business," said Dick tartly; once more engaged in rubbing down his favourite. "The ale, fellow."

"Oh, aye!" and he sauntered in at the doorway.

Five minutes passed, and the man returned with the tankard—

> In the full glass the liquid amber smiles,
> Our native product.

"Drink yourself," said Dick.

"Thank'ee, sur. That went down hissing, master, for the copper's hot. I'se little bit queery this mornin'; and there's nothing like a hair o' the dog as bit 'ee overnight to set 'ee roight i' the mornin'."*

"Warm the rest on't, and you shall have a shilling to drink my health: sugar it—but mind ye, no ginger."

"Aye, aye;" and the fellow, returning to the kitchen, removed the cake from the top of the unextinguished peat fire, and blew its embers into a glow.

"Now, my Bessy," said Dick, as he presented the warm ale in a small piggin.

She thrust her nose eagerly into the vessel, and drank of its contents. Her crest rose, her eye brightened, and the pawing forefoot told her impatience.

In saddle again, and freshly and gaily they career along. The border of Notts is passed; and Barnley-in-the-Willows, with Newark, are to the south. The Trent has twice been crossed, and hills and windmills left behind, and now—

> Up rose the sun; the mists were curled
> Back from the soundly-slumb'ring world,
> Which lay around, behind, before;
> What boots it thus to travel o'er
> Plain, forest, river?

The sun shone brightly on the frequent waters which traversed their road, as Sutton, Weston, and Tuxford appeared on either side; the beacon hill is in view—'tis reached; and Turpin's horse *walks* the ascent. Dick shook his head as he observed this. The strong, laborious breathing of an over-tasked animal, though yet not blown, sounded ominously.

"My Bessy," said he, as they surmounted the hill.

Her ears momentarily pricked at the sound of his voice, but fell, more especially the wounded one, as he ceased to speak. Again he spoke, and the high-couraged animal mended her pace.

"I fear I've overmarked her," said Dick as, passing the Twin Oaks, he saw the 137th mile-stone. "Well, well, what must be, must be; I know my end approaches, but none beside Dick Turpin shall ever cross Black Bess!"

He struck the spur against her side—fired at the unwonted indignity, her blood and courage rose, and with a speed few fresh horses could have rivalled, Bess covered the ground for the next eight miles, clearing the dreary moor of Barnby and the villages of Tarworth and Ravenskel; nor slackens she till Scrooby is in view. "Bravo! bravo!" cried Turpin, as with straining

---

* A north-country proverb, implying that the debauch of over-night is best remedied by a draught of the same liquor on getting up.

speed she held her way—" 'twill cost thy life, my Bess; but we must all die once, and as well now as any time." They passed a farm-yard—spruce chanticleer, strutting before his dames, in the pride of his shrill throat, gave forth his clarion of defiance, and was answered by his feathered rivals of the country round.

Dick looked at the stout-hearted bird, as he passed along, "I've surely heard, or read somewhere, that the entrails, including the heart, of a true game cock, will inspire the courage of a failing steed—'tis but a trial : pshaw, it's foolish superstition—an old woman's story.*   I'm getting silly." he drew his bottle and took a long and strong pull—it would not do, the idea had presented itself and would not be dismissed. He drew Bess towards the road side, it would be unsafe to shoot the animal with the house and its inmates so near. He stole cautiously towards a hedge, crossed a stable-yard, and coming upon the spouse of dame Partlet, while he and his harem were concealed from the house windows by an intervening haystack, at one grasp twisted the neck of the vain-glorious polygamist. His pocket-knife did the rest, then cleansing the entrails in a running brook, and rinsing them with diluted brandy, he wrapped them round the bit of Bess. The animal closed her lately open mouth—

"She'll do fifty yet" cried Dick; and his leg had scarcely crossed her when the unconquerable animal once more went forward.

Over the river Idle, and Bess---for she was a Yorkshire foal---treads her native soil; and as though, Antæus-like, her mother-earth gave renewed vigour, springs strengthened by each straining stride. Bawtrey, the wood and the open country bear witness that she belies not her race—the hardy old English hunter with a dash of the eastern blood. Of the spectators of a modern race-course few know the sacrifice of muscular power, endurance, and utility, at which the short-distance speed of the race-horse of these degenerate days has been purchased. The old hunter, and the old four, six, or even twelve-mile king's plate horse,† with their short limbs, open chest, expanded

*This is an old prejudice; in some early books on horsemanship, great feats are narrated to have been performed by the aid of this restorative, and the traditionary accounts of the ride of Nix from Gad's Hill to York, as well as that of Turpin, mention either fowl's entrails or raw beef thus used.

† It is notorious how soon the limbs of the modern racer give way : a single race, nay, the preparation for one, often breaks him down. Had the old standard been steadily maintained, by which our early racers were tested, the modern ones would never have been permitted to deteriorate in respect of qualities, which, being natural, can only be renovated by a recurrence to nature. The modern racer assuredly has not lost speed—he is swifter than our earlier horses; but he no longer possesses that form, or those qualities, which denote vigour, endurance, or utility.

The approach to the form of the pony's head, in the old portraits of hackneys and hunters, is remarkable; and we need not say a word of the greater proportionate power of a small compact horse over a long and large one It may not be uninteresting to the reader, who is in the habit of daily reading accounts of the breaking down of racers, on or after a mile-and-a-half or two-mile course, to give, from authentic records, two or three examples, from among many, of the performances of old English racers, when stoutness was not entirely postponed to speed, and a honest distance was required as the test of superiority. They are of the time of Turpin.

1718, Newmarket. Twenty-three matches in all. 8 st., four miles ; Duke of Wharton's, Chanter, won. Duke of Wharton's Galloway, 8 st. 10 lb., against Lord Hillsborough's Fiddler, carrying 12 st.; six miles. 200 guineas.

In 1720, at the same place, there were twenty-six matches, some four, some six miles ; and weights that would frighten a modern jockey. In Oct. 1720, the Duke of Wharton's Coneyskins, carrying 11 st. 10 lb., beat Lord Hillsborough's Speedwell, carrying 12 st. Best of three heats, four miles each : twelve miles : for 10˜0 guineas.

In 1737, Black Chance, five years old, 10 st., won the King's Plate at Durham, distance four miles. Ladies' plate at York, same year. In 1738, King's Plate at Guilford ; do. at Salisbury ; do. at Winchester : do. at Lewes ; do at Lincoln ; in one season ; every race four miles, and each contested ; and in October of same year, started for King's Plate at Newmarket, but fell in the running, and was beaten. In 1739 he won twice ; in 1740 at Wrexham, Shrewsbury, and Oswestry, carrying 13 stone ! at Denbigh 12 stone ! In 1741 the same horse was victor at Chester, Manchester, and Hereford ; 1743 received premium at Chester, and won at Manchester ; in 1744 walked over for plate at Farnden ; thus running and winning, with heavy weights and long distances, for seven years consecutively.

It would be useless to multiply instances. Another racer, Johnay, won or received forfeit twenty-five times ; distances, four, six, and twelve miles. What would our modern jocks say to this ?

The Death of Black Bess.

ribs, wide hips, fine head, muscular neck, powerful arms, thighs, and stifles, and above all, broad and strong loins, can now only be seen in the portraits by Marshall or Stubbs; and though we cannot deny the swiftness of his light, feeble, weedy successor, the sacrifice to art has no compensatory advantage.

But we are digressing. The town of Doncaster, near which his noble mare first tugged the teat or nipped the tender grass, nine springs ago, is seen by Bess for the last time.

"I'll not pass through," said Turpin; for her elastic spine, no longer rising with the spring of the tense bow, bent slowly beneath the weight of her rider. A mark of speedy-cut too, was visible, and the trickling blood stained the dark bone of her fine hard shank.

"Here's the Don at hand," said Dick, as he diverged across meadow and open ground, into a bye lane towards the shining river: "a cold bath, my Bessy, for we're both doomed, may restore you a while. York I *will* reach, and you *must* go with me."

Arrived at the river, one plunge, and

It is no dream,
The wild horse swims the wilder stream,
The bright, clear, river's gushing tide
Sweeps winding onward, far and wide.

The cool wave laves her smoking side; and, braced by the shock, she breathes more slowly, as with short motion her still active limbs propel herself

No. 36.

and her rider towards the opposite shore.   Dick did not hurry her, but looked at her head, with the careful eye of a practised horseman.

"It's nearly out of you, I fear, my Bessy," quoth he, as

> With glossy skin and dripping mane
> And shivering limbs and reeking flank,
> The strong steed's sinewy nerves now strain
> Up the repelling bank.

Turpin, sanguine and hopeful as was his temperament, and strong as was his confidence in Bess's prowess, desponded too early.   Like some hasty stream, awhile dammed up, did she now foam along with fresh recruited might, as though the breathing pause of the short time spent in crossing the stream, where she first had slaked her thirst, lent new vigour to her limbs.

Away! away! Cusworth is to the left, and Scausby; he turns his head, and looks along the ancient streetway which leads to Wakefield—the well which owes its name to bold Robin Hood is near.   Bess stumbled; never before had her sure foot failed—she recovered.

The sun is high in heaven, and shines hotly on the dry and dusty road; Dick looks back, and views, with a shudder of alarm even human blood had not occasioned, a sanguine stain marking the dry chalky dust.   She overreaches; and this time a wide and crimson wound gaped on her springy pastern.   The highwayman dropped his rein.

"'Tis done," said he.   Again his flask was produced: he drank, then wiped the perspiration from his forehead.   The skin of Bess, once smooth, was now rough and staring; and the veins, always prominent, started from its surface, bound her over-strained muscles as with cords of searing fire; the rosy pink of her dilated nostrils is replaced by the bright scarlet of the vital fluid, which bursts from every pore of the tender membrane; and her mild bright eye is suffused with the scalding tears which trickle down her noble face.   With reeling step she now holds on---deep sobs heave her labouring sides---"A few more yards, and then," said Turpin recovering himself, and with desperate heel he tears her side—the whip descends, and on, staggering, feeble, and faint * * * But see her erected crest and mane, and trembling spine---she sways to and fro like a drunken man—her near leg strikes her off---she stands—a pant—and now a heave that stretches "her leathern coat almost to bursting"—the girths are broken, her rider dismounted, never again to cross the steed who has served him so well—and with one mighty sob the gallant Bess rolls on the chalky road!   The highwayman stood watching the last fierce struggle of that strong brute in the yet stronger grasp of Death: he loosened her head-stall, and slipped the bit from her mouth; her own efforts had saved him the task of doing so by her other incumbrances. He stood, we said, watching her last pangs: the bit is removed, and with gaping mouth and wide-strained nostrils the wretched animal seems to devour the air---her flanks heave—a spasm draws her round ribs, and bends her powerful spine---her head is raised from the earth---and, flexing her near leg, she rolls her forequarters from the ground; the off foreleg paws the road in vain—the trembling sinews shake—they weaken, the power to rise is gone; another groan—she rolls back prostrate---one sob—a gasp---a choking rattle: and she pours from her nostrils the spark of life, in a gush of blood, at the feet of her too-well-served master.   Her heart is broken!

Turpin stood gazing on that protruded eye, as its preternatural and bloodshot orb glazed over with the dull film of death, till the stiffening limbs and sinking sides, the shrinking veins and dingy coat, could convey to the casual observer but a feeble idea of what that mare was in the hey-day of her pride and beauty.

"'Tis idle to stand here," said he; "the last being that loved me or cared for me is now gone—nay, the last that I shall ever love or care for."

He stood beside the prostrate corse so late instinct with life and vigour; the faint steam ever and anon curled in a tiny wreath from the rough, staring, and unsightly skin, once beautiful and black, now brown with travel-stains, and rough with clammy sweat; he watched the steamy wreaths growing fainter and fainter as the fast-cooling body lost its natural heat, even in the hot rays of the noonday sun. He started from his reverie: the life of that gallant and faithful brute had passed before his mind's review; the exciting and adventurous career they had run together—Fielder, King, Esther, her venerable father, rose from their graves and passed, like Banquo's shadowy line, across the mirror of his fantasy. Fatigue, excess, excitement, exhaustion, had worn the strong man down in mind as well as body, and, at that instant, had not pride forbad, and fear of the world, and the world's scorn, (though he deluded himself into the belief that he despised it,) been a stronger trial than he dared to brave, he would have repented: but no—he had gone too far for reflection. His best friend had fallen by his hand: he looked at that hand, as the thought arose, as though he expected to behold some crimson stain, and felt surprised at its absence—he thought of *her*, the innocent, the guileless; of her---

"who loved not wisely, but too well:"

of the murdered Bevis; of the treachery of Madge, whom he now suspected to have been the cause of the apprehension of Street, the death of King; and the cause of this ride, in which last feat only did he now feel pride. Anon the gibbet on which the bones of Dennis yet swung creaking in the passing wind, presented itself. "And such," said he, as the dreadful apparatus of death arose, "such will be my fate---I feel it, I know it: where now are—"

The whirr of wheels, afar off on the road, now saluted his ear: he looked across the vale.

"I must retire awhile; they'll see the horse, though."

The chaise approached, and Turpin, taking with him the bridle and saddle, walked behind a stone wall out of sight of the party.

What now were the feelings of the bold highwayman, whom the ignorant or superficial youth, looking through the vista of romance or the drama, may imagine a hero? He was man, and therefore felt as one; conscience may be despised, and its warnings neglected, but it cannot be stifled; the "still, small voice" can own no shorter life than the pulse of the heart to which its counsels or its warnings are addressed; and those counsels, those warnings, disregarded or defied, it shall not cease to sear the soul with remorse till they or it sleep in the grave, "where there is no repentance." The bold villain felt---he had felt it before, but never so strongly as now---that vice has no need of bitter in her cup beyond that supplied by her votaries; and that he who embraces sin, lured by the beauteous wreath which hides her temples, shall feel the sting of the snakes they hide; and sooner or later, when

The piercing spear in laughing flowers concealed,

smites his heart, shall find that sin, misery, and remorse, are inseparable. These thoughts hirled through his brain ; he started to his feet, and draining the flask, sought oblivion in intoxication. He drew a pistol from his holster, and examined the priming, as he held it with unsteady hand. The desperate thought of suicide suggested itself---the next moment he laughed loudly and long.

"Ha ! ha ! well, I'm getting an old woman ; finish a life in whose end the hangman has a fee simple, with half an ounce of my own blue lead---ha ! ha !"

A horseman, at a steady trot, was seen some mile off. "Ho ! ho ! shoot myself---ha ! ha !" cried he, as he gave another ineffectual suck at the flask. " 'My courage is out,' as the bold Macheath said ; pshaw, Tom King, Polly--- what the devil is my brain running on—gone by G---d, all of 'em, but *I'm* left. D——e, but this isn't a bad one coming, I know by his action," said Dick, as he watched the approaching rider : "that fellow don't know there's a gentleman waiting here to borrow his horse---ha ! ha !"

"Stand !" was the next word spoken, as Dick, with levelled pistol, walked slowly to the centre of the roadway.

The stranger drew rein. The salute was so bold, so sudden, and so extra-ordinary, at such a time and at such a place, that the rider was inclined to consider the whole a jest ; more especially when he saw the flushed counte-nance, the disordered dress, and strange manner of the highwayman.

"You are disposed to be facetious, sir, this morning," said he.

The gesture and language of Turpin, however, soon convinced him to the contrary ; and being unarmed, he was forced, after many manœuvres to gain time, to dismount, in compliance with Turpin's peremptory demands.

"I shall not take your purse, sir," said Dick, when his search had finished ; "but I shall require your horse for the day. To-morrow, if you will pledge me your word as a gentleman---which I see you are by the papers about you--- not to proceed farther in the affair, the animal shall be left at stables in the city of York, of which I shall give you notice. Adieu, sir, for the present ; and don't forget you have lent---*lent*, mark me. for I shall not want it long--- a horse to Dick Turpin : farewell !" and in a few minutes the favourite hack-ney of Sir William Lamb was seen by its owner, at its best pace, ascending a hill in the direction of Upton.

At Wentbridge a whet, and on, over stream and river, to Ferrybridge and the Ack---the cross-roads to Hillum, Burton, Farborne, &c., to the hundred and seventy-third mile stone ; a spanking trot up Betteress hill takes some of the con-ceit out of his new prad, and he breathes her through the open country to Milford. At Sherborne the flask is replenished ; the bloody field of Towton, where England's best blood was shed in civil strife, is passed ; the beauteous Wharf is seen stealing in shining silver its course among sylvan shades ; eight more miles: Ringhouses is left behind ! the windmill is to the left, and through the Micklegate—YORK IS REACHED.

CHAPTER XXIII.

There's a divinity that shapes our ends,
Rough-hew them how we will.
—Shakspere.

In the days of our forefathers, the hardy sons of toil restricted their labour to the hours which Nature herself points out. The night, "when no man can work," was respected, if we may use the term, at both ends; and the morning's sun was allowed to obtain undisputed possession of the sky, ere adult, much more infant, labour was begun. No factories vomiting smoke, and glaring with gas, then dragged infant misery, from its humble pallet, to their stifling work-rooms, before darkness had withdrawn its veil; while the shuttle or the comb, the spindle or the reed, were cast aside, by old and young, before Sol's broad face sunk behind the western hills, or quenched his radiance in the crimsoned wave. Then was the dance led up beneath the ancient tree on the village green; the quoit hurled, the football kicked; and some manly and healthful recreation succeeded the sedentary employment of the day: or, should the weather prove unfavourable, the ancient ballad, whose lengthened narrative riveted attention, even though recited for the hundredth time, alternated with the jest, the story, the tradition, or the " auld wife's tale," as the grannam sat in the chimney-corner, "fast by the ingle." Such was, in those days, the manner of life of the inhabitants of the great northern districts, where the staple manufacture of cloth was carried on. Has it improved? The dame who spun, and the man who wove or carded, performed their tasks by their own hearthstone : he did not crawl an emaciated, gin-besotted, half-starved slave to the huge prison-looking, soul-crushing mill of the manufacturing Moloch; but in a cleanly cottage, with the wife of his bosom singing at her wheel, and the children of his heart playing around, he pursued his task: the thatch of his cottage peeped from the trees, marking the abode of industry, health, and contentment. Utilitarians may sneer, but these things *were* so; and neither the statistics of M'Culloch, the arguments of Adam Smith, nor the twaddlings of an universe of *poleetecal* economists and Scotch *feelosofers*, can gainsay the truth, that, if gold has been gained, if tables of imports and exports have been swelled, if laden argosies have multiplied on the face of the waters, yet contentment, independence, morality, and above all, *health* and comfort have decreased among the wealth-producing classes of the community: and shall gold weigh in the balance against these things? We pause for a reply.

But if such was the position of the labourer, equally or still more easy and otiose were the days of the small trader---the dweller in the city or the market town. 'Tis true that on *two* days, or perchance *three* of the seven, he was in what he would have termed " a bustle," seeing that market-day was a busy day; but at other times he enjoyed himself, literally *enjoyed* himself, as with nut-brown jug, and pipe with " lip of wax and eye of fire," he sat at the polished oak table, and

Drank the mighty ale,
And told the merry tale;

while jollity, and mirth, and social chat, banished the few cares of a simple trading concern, which procured for the numerous tribe of small traders a sufficiency for the creature-comforts of life. Where now are these races of men? where are the classes of society which have succeeded them? what transformation have they undergone? The labourers have been swallowed up, engulfed by the black throat of the factory fiend; aye, even " childhood's self, as at Ixion's wheel," has been crushed, the fair flower of blooming infancy has been polluted and withered in the foul atmosphere of the gas-heated bastile; while the small traders, the independent, sturdy burgesses, have merged into the sleek-headed, cringing, quill-driving, degenerate race of upper clerks, half-salaried serviles, in the great " establishment" of the " opulent firm" of Wiggins, Spriggins, Dobbins, Dowling, Thorneycroft, & Co., high and mighty lords in cotton, and traffickers in white slavery.

It was before such evil days fell on the land, that a group of substantial shopkeepers, traders, and their friends, were assembled on the bowling-green of the York Arms, enjoying the healthful diversion to which it was appropriated—at least, the middle-aged and younger ones were doing so: the elders of the party, with long pipe in mouth and tankard hard by, stood in a knot near an open alcove, relating their own feats of by-gone days, and passing strictures or jests on the game going forward.

A handsome looking man, in a riding frock, came from the house; his smart London coat attracted attention as he walked down the green with an unsteady step, and on his nearer appoach it was evident, from his flushed cheek and general bearing, that he was intoxicated, or nearly so. He bowed politely to the assembly, but declined the proffered October. The reader will not be at a loss to guess that the new-comer was our hero. A few minutes' attention to his toilette, with the assistance of the boots and the waiter, had removed the stains of travel and the marks of his long journey; but mere dress or cleanliness of person could not conceal the nervous excitement, aggravated by intoxication, which was manifest in his every word and gesture. The game proceeded: the bets of mere groats and sixpences—or at most, the venture of a tankard of ale, were as little suited to the then temperament of Turpin as the prosaic dulness of their broad provincial talk.

Dick's irritation was of that kind which, like jealousy, increases " by the food it feeds on." The excitement of drunkenness had become a necessary adjunct to his then state of existence. Madness, that worst of madness, which man *himself* wills—the madness which like its continual consequent, suicide, is man's own act and deed—had hurled reason from her throne.

" Brandy," said Dick, to the staring clodhopper who waited upon the frequenters of the bowling-green and skittle-ground.

" That's rayther strong drink to take by itself," said a prosy old gentleman in a striped woollen waistcoat, a brown Welsh wig, and a soft three-cornered, felt hat, so much in fashion with the substantial burgess of 'tis now a hundred years since.

Dick gave him a look that made the old gentleman start even to the huge square-plated buckles of his square-toed shoes.

" Keep your opinion until you are asked for it," said Dick with a waspishness which the innocence of the remark by no means called for: " Brandy, fellow! What are you gaping at?

" I'se not toald how much, zur."

" A quart! a guinea's worth!" said the highwayman testily, throwing a piece of gold bearing the head of the last queen who adorned the throne of

Britain, now made happy under a third female rule---the peaceful triumphs of which, GOD grant! may eclipse and cast into the shade the blood-stained glories of an Elizabeth or an Anne.

The fellow took up the gold with the grin of satisfaction which may be supposed to pass over the face of a Yorkshire tyke upon clutching so unexpected a payment. "A'll git a hog out o' this flash chap; he's a-thrawing his shiners about rarely---he's a-given Sam the waiter a dollar for his boots---he's a-cooming oot---A'll put on my best purliteness." So saying, Rob made his way towards the house, and soon returned with the liquor and change.

Turpin had now shifted to another part of the green, and Rob, who generally guaged his customers, seeing his state, deposited the bottle of brandy and glass upon the table, and forgot, with true North-country shrewdness, to return the silver which he had received from the landlord.

"I'll bet you twenty," said Dick to a staid, puritanical looking man in a snuff-coloured coat with broad skirts, who had ventured to question his opinion as to the bias of a bowl. "D——n! do you take me for an ass?" The man to whom he spoke was at that moment poising the oblate sphere of wood in his hand, and cocking his eye, with much more conceit than skill, towards the small ivory globe, so many times unsuccessfully aimed at, and which reposed unharmed from thumps near the centre of the emerald carpet of the bowling ground. The man, we have said, was poising the bowl; but, at the very moment of launching his projectile, it was arrested by the hand of Turpin, and snatched from his grasp with a rude abruptness which dumbfounded the orderly and sedate woolstapler. Strong, however, in tho pride of his respectability, and the countenance of his fellow citizens, the burgher, though at heart a man of peace, resented the insult offered to his social importance, by seizing the arm of Turpin, in an endeavour to regain the bowl.

. He had not calculated the consequence of interfering with an intoxicated, reckless, and desperate man; suddenly was he prostrated by a back-handed blow, and Dick, without noticing its consequences had, before the bystanders recovered their astonishment at the uncalled-for outrage, delivered his bowl with such precision, as to strike the jack, and follow it so as to place beyond dispute the claim of his play as the winner.

"There, old boy," said he with a braggadocio of inebriety; "where's your twenty?---fork out!"---and he turned, unconscious of the effect of his thrust. What was his surprise on seeing the elderly man, whose turn he had usurped, just raised from the ground, with his face bleeding slightly from the rough salute he had just received. The countenances of the bystanders spoke their indignation; but, though their looks were threatening, no one dared to give utterance to his feelings.

The landlord by chance approached the spot, half a dozen tongues were at once let loose. "Mr. Hall!" exclaimed a leash of voices, "do you allow your regular customers to be insulted and aggravated by bullying chaps from Lunnun, acos they wears jimmy coats, and calls for brandy?"

"Turn him out!" vociferated the company.

It is one thing to say and another to do: not one of the open-mouthed roarers seemed, however, inclined to give effect, so far as venturing his own person was concerned, to this unanimous vote of expulsion; and, Dick, who though intoxicated would still have been a formidable antagonist, placing his back against a fence which enclosed three sides of the green, exclaimed, "If you mean rough play, I'm ready!"

The firm planted foot, the slightly bent back, the muscular shoulder, and the extended arms, well up to the head, in the style of Broughton, had the effect which might have been expected on these men of peace. The host, whose natural anxiety not to disoblige a good customer combated with his wish to oblige the smoke-a-pipe party of neighbours who thus claimed his interposition, accordingly tried conciliation; and Dick, after an apology to the man he had struck---for that individual's honour was easily satisfied--- ordered punch, drank more brandy, and was rather tolerated than welcomed by the players. The game went on, when an unlucky accident disturbed the lately restored harmony.

It so happened that the host of the "York Arms" owned a splendid game cock; and if there was one living creature in this world which Boniface prized beyond all others, it was this feathered biped. Cockfighting then ranked high among the sporting world, and Mr. Hall was, like most other inhabitants of Yorkshire, mightily addicted to the sport. Dick was becoming impatient of his companions, and looking about for something to divert the uneasiness of thought, when this unlucky bird, springing from an adjoining yard on to the low fence, clapped its wings, and crowed loudly.

"He's down, for a hundred, with a single ball," said Dick, looking at the bird.

Some of the party who considered their dignity had not been sufficiently consulted by the landlord, felt gratified at the prospect of turning that person's wrath against the drunken stranger. Dick drew a pistol from his vest, and cocked it. "Who'll take my wager?" hiccupped he; not putting his query to any one in particular.

"You can't do it---nor no other man," said he who had been struck.

Dick raised the short tube at the challenge----looked along its shining barrel---steadied his hand----the light blue smoke curled off, and the gallant bird lay fluttering its last on the gravel walk which skirted the fence.

"You'll have to pay through the nose for that joke, anyways," said one. "It was a good shot, though; Mister Hall vallys that ere bird at more than I'd like to give for un. Squire Dixon offered him ten guineas, and---"

Rob, who had been a silent witness of the act, ran into the house with the tidings of mischief, and the next moment, foaming with rage, his master burst into the ground. The company receded to right and left, as the infuriated publican advanced towards the transgressor.

"How dare you, sir, to---;" he paused as he saw the ire of Turpin was rising at his abrupt address. "Will you pay," he continued, "for the damage you've done?"

"Don't flurry yourself, old boy," said Dick; "what's the damage, eh?"

"Damage!" iterated the landlord; who was ever awake to business, and who saw the easiness with which profit might be made even of this untoward event. "Damage! why I can get twenty pound from Squire Nixon any time: the bird was worth that gold anyhow: but, as you seem a gentleman, I---"

"Twenty devils! d'ye take me for a flat?"

"Ay, ay," retorted the angry Boniface; "or twenty days you're like to get in quod. Have you any taste for anything in that line----eh?"

Turpin advanced towards the landlord with clenched fist; but was seized by half a dozen arms.

Turpin shoots the Game Cock.

A swing released him from their hold: another moment, and Mr. Hall would have got a harder blow than he bargained for, had not Rob caught our hero an awkward trip: it was an under-leg one, and he dropped; Rob closed him.

With Dick's activity and sober caution, Rob's brute strength would, most probably, have been below par; but now, when sleight, sudden effort, and stratagem were gone, the yokel's weight and power told fearfully. The tyke threw himself on Turpin with a bursting fall, grasped him by the throat, and pinned him to the earth.

"Fetch Mr. Grougham! fetch Mr. Grougham!" exclaimed the landlord, echoed by his customers.

Now Mr. Grougham was the constable to whom the taking and keeping of all offenders against "the king's majesty, his crown and dignity," were entrusted by the parish in which the York Arms was situate; and Mr. Grougham's name was no sooner mentioned than two or three bystanders, glad to be out of what seemed a serious row, started off in search of him. He was soon found; and in his charge our hero—who confined his anger to remonstrances against the indignity to which he had been last subject; namely, the unmanly advantage taken by the rustic waiter of his prostrate condition, and the cruel maltreatment of the "long odds" of some ten on one man, seasoned with much commonplace braggadocio as to what, under other circumstances, other times, and with other people, he might, could, would, or should have done—was walked off, drunk, desperate, swearing, and imbecile, to the

No. 37.

cage ; and thence, after some minutes' delay, escorted to the house of Mr.
Thomas Jordan, citizen and grocer, he being the nearest justice of the peace.

The examination was short : Turpin, intoxicated and enraged, refused to
give compensation or apology, and further offended the dignity of the alderman by doggedly declining to furnish that functionary with his name, address,
or standing in society.

"I can't help saying, Mr. Hall," observed the mortified magistrate, "that
the prisoner is the most disrespectful and audacious that I ever saw in all my
magisterial experience, and I've been one of this ancient corporation these
thirty years.   He looks like a gentleman, too," said he, hesitating ; "maybe
some arrangement—a--a--understanding—might be come to yet.   Perhaps if
you retired—you see, sir, I wish to temper justice with mercy—(this was Mr.
Jordan's stock-phrase, and it had carried him through many a dilemma)—
tempering mercy with justice, sir, is—a--a—do you see, doing—I would recommend you to compensate the prosecutor Mr. Hall, who is a most respectable
man, and I dare say he will not be exorbitant : you have committed also two
assaults, for which apology and reparation are required ; and sir, sitting here
as a magistrate desirous to temper justice with —"

The rigmarole of the fat-brained justice was here for the third or fourth
time interrupted by Dick, who declared much more plainly than courteously,
that he'd give Mr. Hall a guinea; but added, he'd see the whole of the company at a place whose name must not be mentioned to ears polite, before he'd
make other reparation ; and as to apology, he'd see them in the warm
quarters before alluded to, and even then---he'd make none at all.

"Then you must take the consequences of your contempt of this honorable
court," said the mortified great man, swelling with slighted importance ; "Mr.
Grougham," the constable bowed, "remove the prisoner ; keep him in safe
custody till tomorrow, and let him be brought before ourselves at the Guild-
hall; and I doubt not, when sober, he'll repent having abused my condescension and forbearance in this matter : for though I, as a justice, and a member
of this ancient corporation for thirty years, say it as shouldn't say it, I always
temper justice with mercy.—Remove the prisoner, Mr. Grougham !"

That evening and night our hero slept soundly in the lock-up of the Castle,
appropriated to drunken and disorderly characters ; his money and appearance,
however, procured him a bed and other attentions from the gaoler which ordinary or pennyless prisoners never received ; and it was broad day before the
events of the ride, the altercation of the bowling-green, the examination before his worship, and his committal, presented themselves with sufficient distinctness to his returning senses, to enable him to form a clear notion of his
position.

"Why what, in the name of all the devils, could have maddened me to
fight and brawl with those fellows; and—yes,—surely that was what I was
charged with.   I shot the landlord's game cock, I remember, just to astonish
a gaping set of old buzwigs ; why I'm becoming fool as well as braggart, as I
get older.—Hallo ! gaoler, some drink here, I'm parched with thirst."

The man came, and for an extravagant price, furnished his charge with
some ale.   The hours rolled on, and Dick, in due time, was placed at the
bar of the civic police office ! the charge was proceeded with, Mr. Hall had
agreed to accept an offer of five guineas, and all was going off smoothly,
when a most unexpected termination to the case was occasioned by the entrance of a middle aged gentleman in a brown riding suit.   He looked long

and steadily at the prisoner, who quailed not at the scrutiny. Some whispering took place on the bench; several of the myrmidons of justice clustered between Turpin and the door; he looked round the court; escape was out of the question; he therefore stood calmly, betraying by no outward emotion the recognition which was certainly mutual—for he saw in the newly arrived gentleman his old acquaintance, Captain Scott, of Scarborough!

The next night was passed by Turpin, heavily ironed, in the gloomy dungeon of York Castle.

CHAPTER XXVI.

Troth, sirs, the clouted shoe hath oft-times craft in't,
As says the rustic proverb; and your citizen
In's grogram suit and chain, and well-blacked shoon,
Bears under his flat cap oft-times a brain
Wiser than dwells beneath a casque and feather,
Or seethes within the statesman's velvet night-cap.
—Old Play.

'Tis not in mortals to command success.
—Shakspere.

THOUGH no railroads ribbed the land with iron, no tunnels perforated nor viaducts spanned hill or valley, that news, merchandise, and travellers might be transmitted from one extremity of " broad England" to the other, with meteor-speed, yet good or ill news, provided it were worth the carrying, was slowly and surely conveyed. A fortnight had elapsed, and Dick, upon a second remand, awaited further identification in the gloomy keep of his fortress-prison. Thomas Creasey of Bullingbrook, of whom the reader may remember some mention was made at the period when Dick left Lincolnshire rather more hastily than convenient, had been one of the sufferers by the non-settlement of Mr. Newton's affairs, and happening to be in Yorkshire purchasing stock, he was soon on the spot, and sealed the fate of our hero by procuring his commitment. But we must leave York, and return to London, to look after some other personages who have figured in this our veritable history. The death of King, and the escape of Turpin, were too notorious and exciting in their nature to escape becoming the chat of taprooms and barbers' shops; but the interest of the variously-told story was wofully flagging, when the intelligence of Turpin's capture being transmitted to the proper quarters by the magistrates at York, public attention was again excited and renewed.

" On est etranger a son voisin," observes Mercier, speaking of life in Paris, and it is assuredly as true of any other great city. Men know but little of what is going on around them; and this indifference, amounting almost to ignorance, is peculiar to the denizens of every " populous solitude." You may know a countryman, or a newcomer, by his evident surprise and gaping curiosity, excited by objects and occurrences which your citizen notices not, or notices only to wonder at what the yokel sees in it to wonder at. Yet the *nil admirari* of the cockney is but a proof that, accustomed to view a variety of noticeable objects at an age when he lacks understanding to appreciate them, reflection seldom arises in after life upon matters with which the senses are already familiar.   London would indeed be a magazine of marvels to the man who could only walk, with the eyes of his understanding open, from one end of the city to the other; but how few men, possessing the necessary amount of knowledge from habitual residence, are competent to such a task?

What extraordinary places are those colonies of one and two-story tenements, which in the last fifty years, but more remarkably in the last twenty, have covered the swamps of Lambeth, St. George's Fields, Walworth, &c.—the prolific brick and mortar progeny of the masses of masonry at Blackfriars and Waterloo!   What a peculiar squalor strikes the eye of the wayfarer as, passing from the crowded and trading city, after crossing the ever-repairing pont of Blackfriars, he turns to the right, and explores westward from the line of Surrey Street!   What lines of slightly-built houses, decaying even in their lath and plaster infancy, mark out the miry and cut-throat streets covering the ground of the gardens of the Halfpenny Hatch and the neighbourhood of the St. George's Bunhouse, from the Riding School even to the back settlements of the Victoria theatre.   It is in summer only, or in a hard frost, that these unpaved defiles are to be considered passable ; after dark, the pedestrian wayfarer looks dubiously, from the gas-light at the corner in the " Road," into the fog and gloom—resolves, then re-resolves—then doubts if the road " by the Obelisk" is not as near.   Lamps are few and far between in these marshy fastnesses of prostitution and pilfering ; the policeman at the corner glances at you suspiciously, and slowly follows your steps, for he sees you are a stranger in the land—and you wade on your muddy way, now up now down, speculating, as you pass each puddle, on who can be the people, of what means or what order, who reside in this paradise of pigs, dog-carts, and dilapidation.   'Tis dark, or at least, the only light visible is the feeble gleam given from almost every window uniformly blinded by dingy calico ; and within, by the occasional movements, you see the shadow of some female form engaged in the arrangement of her hair, or her apparel, by a solitary dip ; in another hour you shall meet her, after crossing " Waterloo" or the " Minster," on foot or in cab, as fortune may provide, smiling through rouge at the theatres, or promenading the purlieus of the Strand, or of Covent Garden, in all the glories of velvet, feathers, and silk.   But if there be varieties in the styles of the several locales of the metropolis, if its various *quartiers* exhibit each its peculiar features, not less worthy of observation are the manners of its inhabitants : nevertheless, so bound up are mankind in their business or their pleasure—so formidable is the distance of one suburb from the other—and there is such apathy about seeing novelties among a people who cannot help seeing them every day, that there are thousands of people in mighty Babylon who would never hear of the dwellers in another of its sections save through a newspaper ; nay, there are hundreds even among the dwellers of Islington who never crossed London or Southwark bridge, and whole parishes east of the Royal Exchange, in which a dweller at Brompton would be as little at home as if set down in the wastes of Kamschatka!   It is not only, however, that you meet different *descriptions* of people at different points, distinguished by certain habits and manners peculiar to their calling—grooms and coachmen about Hyde Park and Grosvenor Place ; foreigners and grisettes about Leicester Square ; droves of merchants and clerks in the Poultry and Cornhill ; and sailors, crimps, &c., about Wapping and Limehouse—to the observant eye, the very *people* themselves have a distinct expression of feature--a decidedly different cast of countenance---in Aldgate or Piccadilly.   Can any man look at the Spitalfields weavers---men, women, and children---and say that they re-semble any other body of people in the metropolis? If sceptical, walk some Sunday afternoon in the neighbourhood of Whitechapel and Bethnal Green, and you shall scarcely meet one handsome female, when, more westward, you would meet twenty. The race has deteriorated---snub-noses, small stature, sunken eyes, wide mouth---the population is obviously inferior both education-ally and physically. But Rome was not built, nor can London be examined, in a day, so let us return to our Lambeth peregrinations. In a small house near Cuper's Gardens, in the spot known as Petty France, had Madge Dutton fixed herself; the vicinity of that once-popular place of amusement, now existing but in name, rendering the quarter eligible to one of her precarious profession. The unsuccessful pursuit of Bayes, and the wounding of Pearce, she had heard from rumour; and her knowledge of Dick's character led her to suspect that, in deep disguise, he had returned to some lurking place in the metropolis. The baffled officers seemed to have formed the like conjecture, with the additional suspicion that Madge probably knew the place of his con-cealment; and consequently, for the day or two preceding the time of which we are writing, she had been besieged by several offers of large reward on con-dition of betraying a secret which was not in her possession. She was sitting musing on the most likely plan by which to come at the desired knowledge, when Roger Haynes, who had recently hired himself at the neighbouring alehouse---then, as now, bearing the sign of the " Three Loggerheads,"* hastily entered.

" Eh, Mistriss Margaret," said the rough fellow, " here's a foine to do wi' measter, as I'll ever ca' un; there be two vellers at the Heads,' as ses they've knowledge of his bein' took, and as he's in York Castle, and a sight more on't."

Madge turned pale. " Give me my bonnet—what sort of men are they? ---I saw it on the cards, so I know it's true—it came up four times—trouble and a dark man, from a distance," and muttering incoherent allusions to the appeal to the cards, adopted by such females in their endeavours to dive into futurity, she hastened to the ale-house, where she found the subject occupied all tongues.

" Well, he's stagged now I s'pose," said one; " he's done for this turn; they do say, he's ridden from Lunnun to York, a matter of two hundred mile, in ten hours, or thereaway."

" Unpossible!" ejaculated his companion, who seemed to have more definite ideas on the subject of equestrian performances, " 'taint in human natur', no, nor hanimal natur' neether, to do no sich a thing. Two hundred mile in a night! no, no, tell that to the marines."

" Well, he's safe in York Castle now, anyways, and if he gets out o' that he's a clever un. I see Bayes, yesterday, he was on the dodge arter an old flame o' Dick's as hangs out hereaways, for he didn't have the knowledge then as the nobby chap had sold hisself at York. He'll have a bit of a lay there, and plenty o' time to settle his worldly bisness, for it 'll be some months afore 'sizes yet."

Madge, who had been an attentive and interested listener to this talk, drew Roger from the room.

" I'll go to York: will you come with me? I'll see him; perhaps I may be able to serve---perhaps to save him---God grant---." and the woman, bad and

* The homely wit of the sign consists in *two* grinning heads, with the inscription, " We *three* loggerheads be;" which whoso passes may read aloud---if he pleases.

base as the world would deem her, prayed ; do not smile reader, prayed that she might be able to serve, in his dire necessity, the man who had abused, scorned and neglected her.

Roger Haynes scratched his ear perplexedly ; not that he was in doubt, not that he hesitated, or feared the risk, but purely from slowness of thought and utterance.

"You 's taken the words out o' my mouth, missus ; a wor a goin' to perpose as a should goa to York mysen, a knows t' ould Castle well, a does ; a's seed it mony and monys the time. There's the Ouse and the Foss j'ines, d'ye see, and th' new jail* stands o' th' square---a doan't mind tellin' it to 'ee, but a knows every nick and cranny o' th' place, and if there's vartue in file or saw, or strength in this," and the burly fellow looked at his clenched fist, "whoy a ses it, and a'il do it. But talkin' isn't doin', missus," said he, checking himself, "how's 'ee to get there, missus? it's a distance, worse luck; a've two guineas and that's all in this 'varsal world."

Madge promised to see him in the evening, and she did so. The next morning they were on the road, Roger mounted on a stout heavy horse, and Madge seated on a pillion behind him.

It was the evening of the sixth day that the majestic towers of the gorgeous minster of York greeted their eyes ; as the splendent rays of the setting sun fell on pinnacle, spire, fret-work, and tracery, glancing on the elaborate carvings, rendering more beautifully prominent the projections, and casting into picturesque shadow the receding portions. It was dusk when they entered ; and having taken up their quarters in the Ousegate, Roger, who knew the city well, went out for the purpose of gaining the information necessary for the execution of their project.

"There's a house some'ere hereabout, if a'm not mistook, as is used by Dave Clank, th' under-turnkey---ay, ay, I'se roight agin," said Roger, as he entered the alehouse he was in search of, and his ear was greeted by a drinking song, roared out with right good will by the rough yet not unmusical voice of the very man he was seeking.

Dave Clank, or merry Davy, as he was more commonly called, was a singular character. He was a boon companion, never shirked his ale, and was generally liked, despite his odious profession, by the rude and low society with which he mixed. Originally a blacksmith, he had acquired his present post by the interest of a nobleman to whom his trade had incidentally introduced him : he was naturally shrewd and penetrating, yet easy and good natured, and lacked not judgment, though easily won by soft words. Dave was, in short, a honest man. The writer doubts not this character of a gaoler will startle the readers of romances and melodramas---upon that he calculates ; but may he not put it to the man of the world, or the man of reflection, whether such a character is not to the full as natural---nay, that it is much more natural and true---than the ridiculous pattern-card ruffians and wily knaves pictured with such ridiculous, punctual, and unmistakeable uniformity as the gaolers or turnkeys of prisons. Gentle reader, did you ever see any one of these pictures realised? It is amazing how

---

* That is the new jail, which was erected in 1701. The ancient fortress was dismantled by Cromwell, afterwards seriously injured by fire, in 1685, and then converted into a prison. On its site a new jail and court-house were built, in the year first-named. The present jail of three stories, with its cupola—and the County hall, with its hexastyle portico, are respectively of the dates of 1807 and 1777.

much we are the creatures of education and of impression. The powerful imagination of some master-spirit writes on the *tabula rasa* of our brain---the blank sheet of our early mind is marked indelibly with the talismanic characters of the poetic wizard---and all villains are referred to the great type which has filled our conceptions, until we care not to imagine human nature as it is, though its thousand inconsistencies lie daily before us; but, wedded to system where there is none, frame a fancied character, and require probability ---aye, and even fact---to bow down before the unreal image of our fantasy.

Dave Clank was, as we have said before, an honest fellow, and a good blacksmith. Too fond, it is true, of a drop, but by no means what might be termed " a soft one!" Long since, Roger and he had been boon companions, and together they had more than once violated the game laws; an offence which no countryman looked on as crime.---Nay, a little poaching, among a certain class of society, was regarded as a sort of test of spirit---a proof of personal courage; so little had those iniquitous laws, power against common sense which tells men that the *feræ naturæ* are the common gift of the Great Provider of all. On the score of former acquaintance, therefore, Roger had a fair claim to introduce himself. His remarkable stature, and renown for bodily strength rendered him no common-place personage, and, consequently one not readily forgotten by his rustic comrades. His entrance was the signal for a general recognition.---" Whoy! here's Roger Haynes, by gum!---How beest thee, my mon, th' soight o' thee's good for sore eyen.---Coom, wet thee whustle, ould chap, or wool 'ee loike summut else better;" and similar expressions of kindly feeling, which might shame more polished society, were uttered by the assembled North-country-men.

There is a fervour of attachment, an endearing, an abiding consistency of friendship or of hate, among the northern inhabitants of the earth, which is a problem in psychology that the most acute metaphysicians cannot solve. They may tell us that the passion easily excited, is like the "hasty spark struck from the flint, which straight is cold again," or that the young man's anger is like the blazing stubble, the old man's like red hot steel; but this does not meet the question, why, with cool judgment, hasty temper should anomalously be joined; or why the coldest and least excitable races of mankind should exhibit a warmth of feeling as friends, and an enduring " faithfulness of antique service" as dependants, which we look for in vain among the more ardent, fervent, and therefore loveable, men and women of climes nearer to the sun. But this is digression.

Hearty was the welcome, and boisterously friendly the salute, which greeted Roger Haynes; and his only difficulty was which to choose of the proffered seats; his mission, however, was uppermost in his mind, so he placed himself beside the laughing Dave Clank. The conversation turned, even sooner than he expected, on the important prisoner now in durance vile in the stronghold of the once-capital and court residence of England's sovereigns.

" A'll pound it as they hang 'un afore next Candlemas," said one of the fellows; " I hear as the king hisself ha' sent a letter to the judges as is to try 'un, so there's no hopes no how."

" The king ha' doon nothin' o' th' sort," said another; " they woant hang 'un at all, I tell 'ee; vor the Duke o' Newcastle, as manages they things for the king, promised 'un when he robbed him, as he'd save his life when he sent him a ring as he gave 'un."

"Ay, ay," responded a third; "but I wor tould quite different; and as how Mr. Hall did say as he'd zee 'un wor hanged for shootin' his geam cock."

Such were the comments and conversation of these unlettered bumpkins; and he who thinks these absurdities are over-drawn, and that, even at the present day, in this land of pseudo-enlightenment and civilisation, where every man is supposed, by a legal fiction, to take cognizance of the law, such ignorance is not rife, knows little of the social state of his countrymen. The writer of these pages accidentally heard a discussion among a set of stable-men in the immediate neighbourhood of London, whether the last-named offence, namely, the *shooting a game cock, was not the crime for which Turpin was executed!* And yet, in such a state of popular ignorance, parson-justices and education-opposing prelates hold up their hands in astonishment that maniac Courtenay, socialist Owen, or the political fanatic Frost, should find dupes and followers among the benighted masses which bigotry and intolerance have fostered to become their own scourge.

> Thus even-handed justice
> Commends the poisoned chalice
> To their own lips;

and well would it be if the indiscriminating fury of the masses, whom they have wilfully bred up in mental blindness, spent itself only on the caste at whose door lies the crime of their ignorance; but, unfortunately, for national sins, the whole people suffer, not alone in the persons of the deluded, but in their general liberty---and freedom receives a wound from the trenchant sword which the law uplifts to smite rebellion.

The chat went on; Dave Clank grew talkative, for Roger was liberal in filling his horn with the humming stingo, and he, in the heat of debate---for Dave was a sort of legal authority on all matters relating to the 'sizes---did not notice the frequent repetition of the exhilarating cup.

"He's a gentleman, all out---and who says no!" exclaimed Dave; "one o' the right sort, and a good looking chap too. I've heard, though I don't know it for certain, as he's a son to some great nob---only it's kept a secret; and that, if he do come to be hanged, he'll have none but a silken cord."*

"I'd a-like mainly to zee this same Turpin," said Roger; "I've a half nction as I've a-seen him in Lunnun."

"Thee shalt see 'un, my boy," rejoined Dave; "but I musn't let 'ee in till the morn; coom at ten, and thee shalt zee 'un, so sure as my name's Dave Clank, but to-night's Jan Reeves's turn at the lock."

Roger returned to Madge highly delighted with the success of his scheme; and at the appointed hour he presented himself to his friend Dave.

"I've told 'ee as ye shuld see Dick," said Dave, as the ponderous key turned the huge lock which formed the entrance into the press-yard of the gaol; "we've had several gentry, I can tell 'ee, to zee 'un; and a main deal o' likin' they seem, 'specially the ladies, to feel for 'un; 'tesn't in natur to see sich a noice swell of a chap cut off i' the flower, as one may say, w'out wishin' 'un a 'safe deliverance,' as his honour the judge ses when he knows as they a-goin' to hang the poor devil i' the dock."

* A popular prejudice that the son of a nobleman, if hanged, is entitled to a silken cord from the sheriff. In the account of the execution of Earl Ferrers, for the murder of Mr. Johnson, his steward, it is stated that platted silk cord was used for the purpose.

The escape of Turpin frustrated.

They crossed the quadrangle, and entering another strong oaken door, plated and studded with iron, Dave showed his friend along a narrow and dark stone passage, a few steps brought them to a landing, into which a small grated window threw a stream of light, which was again transmitted through another strongly barred aperture into the prisoner's cell—other ingress for air or sun there was none. This gloomy cell, in which the prisoners charged with felony were then confined, even before trial, was deemed the safest and strongest in the castle-jail; and the renown of our hero had earned him the unenviable distinction of its occupancy. Its form was that of a casemate—a low arch of massive masonry formed its roof and sides, and its back was the ancient flanking wall of the fortress, of enormous thickness, and impenetrable from the adamantine hardness which centuries had lent to the flinty groutwork of which it was built. Dave pointed silently to the grating; and Roger, whose immense height enabled him to dispense with the assistance of the log of wood which lay for the convenience of shorter men, peeped through.

It was not until the eye became accustomed to the imperfect light, that the visitor could perceive objects with anything like clearness; and Roger stared for some moments into the dusky hole, rendered still darker by the interposition of his own huge head, before he could clearly make out the prisoner. Turpin raised his eyes, as the darker shade passed between himself and the scanty light, his long linked fetters rattled, and without recognizing his friend, indeed it was difficult he should, turned his back, as if resenting the frequent impertinence; then slowly and painfully drew the ring attached to the ankle of

No. 38.

his chain along the round iron bar which Roger now saw traversed the apartment from side to side, where it was firmly set in the solid modern stonework. A sigh escaped the rough fellow, and he wiped a moisture from his eye with his coat sleeve—Dave Clank had little idea of the thoughts passing in the mind of his quondam friend at that moment.

"If a' wor to gi'e little Dave a douse o' th' head, 'twouldn't be no use to un, poor feller," thought he, as he looked at his whilom master; "*That* 'ud only be a-making trouble worse; a've a spring saw in my pouch—but a' can't gi'e it to un: dang it! a' must goa back as a' coomed, an' talk this here oaver wi' missus—they wimen be 'cuter nor us.—Poor feller," said he, turning to Dave, and speaking aloud, "he aint th' man though as a seed once in Lunnun, as they ses is Dick Turpin," added Roger, casting his eye cunningly into the cell. The prisoner started at the sound of his voice, and looked toward the grating. Again the ring grated on the bar, and the chains clanked gently, as Turpin, with a brightened countenance, shuffled near the window, to make sure of the identity of Roger. We have said that Dave was too short to look in, unless mounted on the log, even had the small window permitted more than one gazer at a time : Dick raised his shackled hands, and significantly rubbing his forefinger on the chain, as if in the act of filing, told his desire.

"Coom, coom, Roger lad," said Dave, who thought the peep had lasted long enough. Roger was just watching an opportunity for slipping the cloc-spring saw through the bars, when Dave destroyed his hopes by opening the small turnwheel in the door, through which, at stated hours, the prisoner received his gaol allowance. As he drew back the hinged shelf on which stood a small brown pitcher and an untouched oaten cake, the turnkey obtained a view of his prisoner, who turned away with affected indifference :—Roger saw there was no present chance, and though loath to depart, depart he did, for fear of awakening his friend's suspicions. They retired to the turnkey's lodge ; whence, after standing a mug or two in consideration of Clank's civility, Roger hastened home to his mistress.

Deep was the distress of Madge, and painfully ludicrous the perplexed consolations of Roger, as they talked over the hopeless situation of Turpin.

"Could not I get to him, Roger ? if once I get in I'll answer it he shall not again need to ask for saw or file---I don't care for anything they can do to me, even should they detect me. Couldn't you get me a sight of Clank, and say that I am the prisoner's wife ?---Wouldn't they let me see him then ?"

"They mought, to be zure, do that much," said Roger; "but then they'd search 'ee goin' in an' coomin' out, be sure on't; so how 'tis to be doon a doant zee, no more nor a pig zees th' wind."

"Show me the saw you've made ?" the saw was produced; it was some five inches in length, by half an inch in breadth, and rolled up easily into a small circumference.

"That's what ull do th' ir'ns, missus," said Roger, looking complaisantly at its serrated edge,—"an' if they can be coomed over, a'll do th' rest, never fear me, or a'll swing for un, that's flat," and he emphasised his asseveration by a thump on the thigh that might have broken the leg of a dancing master.

"Then I'll do that," replied Madge, with a forced gaiety. "We'll free him yet, Roger.—You don't know what I dare do : you shall see soon, though ; and unkind though he has been, I'll yet save him, and we'll all go abroad, Roger, and be happy. I'll work my fingers' ends off; but he shall never, never more risk his life if I can prevail on him, and I think I can," said the silly short-sighted woman; pursuing the building of her air-built castle. The thought, absurd and extravagant as it was, cheered and inspired her ; and a blessing it is for frail humanity, that hope is left to brighten the gloomiest prospect——and that still, in spite of reason and experience, she shines forth, even though delusively, in the darkest storm of life. We have said Madge was cheered ; she saw, or thought she saw, a chance of *his* deliverance, and she set about the necessary preparations in earnest.

That very day she waited upon Mr. Jordan at his house, and found the worthy alderman, who was, *ex officio*, one of the visiting magistrates, dozing in an easy chair; for though it was yet not far past noon, the wealthy trader had already dined. The apartment had an air of old-fashioned comfort and substantiality about it, which we may look for in vain in the rooms of modern rich men. The walls were pannelled with dark oak, and the heavy mantel piece of the same wood, was elaborately carved, as were also the legs of the polished table, and high-backed chairs, the stuffed seats of the latter covered with brilliant needlework, the patient domestic triumphs of some Dorothy, Grizzel, or Maud of the house they adorned. The walls, too, were not without ornament; a large, dull, oval looking-glass hung in the pier between the windows, and on the other side two similar oval frames contained each a most astounding attempt at pictorial display. Here stood a mighty tower on the *top* of a river, instead of beside it, displaying a multitude of smaller towers growing out of its top, in all possible and impossible directions, bearing a mighty resemblance to a milestone run to seed; and beside it two marvellous proper swans, each as big as the castle, sailed along, stuck against its wall, so admirably was the perspective observe l : the designer had, however, condescended, by means of a bright yellow and red line, to typify that the said swans, or whatever else they might be, were not swimming upon nothing. The other frame was rather less Sphynx-like in its contents : it displayed a huge jar, or vase, out of the top of which grew a collection of brimstone coloured roses, blue apples, red lilies, and a brown daisy or two, as big again as either roses, apples, or lilies ; wondering at the floral phenomena you approached, and in gridiron-looking characters, which at first sight an orientalist might take for sanscrit, you read—"Agatha Jordan, aged 16, her work, done in the year of our Lord, MDCCI," and again found that the pencil of our industrious great granddames was their needle.

"Uncle, dear," said a light, fair-haired, rosycheeked damsel, as she placed her hand gently and affectionately on the old man's shoulder, to draw his attention, " there's a young woman down stairs, wishes to see you on business, she says ; by her talk I take her to be London."

" Aye, aye," said the old gentleman, rising, " send her up, Lettice," and Madge Dutton entered, dropping her best curtesy.

"And so you're the unfortunate prisoner's sister, you say, eh?" said the old gentleman, as Madge concluded her application, "and you wish to see him—I'm sorry for you, indeed, very sorry; it's quite natural you should see him, quite natural, and as I love to temper justice with mercy, d'ye see ; and like to do justice, and to temper it with mercy," said the old gentleman, and drawing a silver standish towards him, he dipped the pen. Mr. Jordan, though rich and respected, was by no means great in caligraphy, indeed his chief efforts in that way had seldom gone beyond figures on a slate, to assist his mental calculations. After some difficulty, however, he got through the desired scrawl, requiring the jailer to admit the bearer, the sister of Richard Turpin, to see him at a proper hour.

Madge soon contrived her part of the scheme. The impression produced on her mind by the hard diet to which he was restricted presented itself.

"I dare say I could bribe the jailer to let me take him in a little something?" Roger seemed to think the idea feasible. "I'll tell you the way we'll do it, Roger. I'll make a small pork pie, without a dish and put this saw into it, and I'll ask Clank, as a favour, to let him have it: will that do, think you?"

"Noa, noa," said Roger, "offer un summut i' the way o' some money, that's the way to they chaps' hearts:" Madge agreed. "An' a've better news still," continued Roger, "I ha' bin watching slily aboot th' ould castle, an' a'll tell 'ee a secret:—there's a big drain runs from th' poomp i' th' jail-yard into th' Foss; and there's th' grating as covers it to get up from underneath—a spied it oot this mortal day, an' its that-a-way as 'ull gi'e um th' slip ofore they can say trapsticks," and Roger snapped his finger and thumb as if despising all obstacles to his plan.

"There's your seester be coom," said Clank, as he opened the door of Turpin's cell on the following morning to make a few arrangements of straw, &c —Turpin stared but said nothing. "She be a toydyish looking wench, 'pon my sowl—she ha' gotten an order fra' his worship as she's to see you; an' old Missus Reeves is overhaulin' her jist now, to zee as she ha' brought nothin' as is'nt allowed: I'll bring her in a'most directly."

Turpin was perplexed, but his perplexity gave way to a feeling of indignation, as Clank again entered, followed by Madge Dutton. Madge started, her colour went and came, and she leaned one hand against the wall for support; while Dick, after a moment's stern scrutiny, turned his back in angry contempt.

"Richard, pray do not turn from me," said she "what have I done to deserve this? True I have been a betrayer, but not to you ---Do the rules of this horrid place allow us to be left alone?" said Madge, looking at Clank: the man did not reply; but Madge, interpreting his meaning, slipped a seven-shilling piece into his hand. Dave touched his forelock, and retired without the door, muttering—"He doan't seem vary looving to his sister ony hows— I'd ha' show'd her more manners, I'm thinkin', if so be a wor in his place, an' she had a-coom two hunderd mile to see me."

We will not detail the interview. Though Madge but half convinced Turpin, he was not in a position to throw away a chance: the tool was left in its dough covering; and the next night, at eleven, fixed for Roger's attempt. Madge undertook to furnish a disguise, and Turpin waited anxiously the arrival of nightfall to begin the task of freeing himself from his fetters.

*   *   *   *   *   *   *   *

"Two gentlemen fra Lunnun wishes to see his worship the mayor, on 'tickler matters," said a bumpkin footman, in worsted lace, opening the parlour door of the civic functionary.

"I'm at dinner, Darby," was that important personage's reply. "Stay, Darby, what like be they—tradesmen—eh? if so, they can wait," added his lordship: "people pestering for orders, I shouldn't wonder; I'm at dinner, say, and will see them in the afternoon at my counting-house;" and the mayor resumed his operation of picking his teeth, which the entrance of Darby had interrupted. The servant soon returned.

"They ses as how your lordship must be seen, for 'tis gover'ment bisness as they is on."

The aspect of the mayor changed.---Draw up the table, Darby---place the standish---here, give me that book," the 'Guide for Justices of the Peace,' was placed on the table---" pens, here---quick and send Mister Robins word to step up from the office.---Shew them in---an important communication from the Secretary of State, no doubt---how did they come?"

"In a poshay, my lord."

"Ay, ay, king's messengers, no doubt.---show them in, Darby---bustle, man! look alive." The strangers were ushered in.

They were vulgar-looking fellows, on whose countenances were stamped cunning and villany. Mr. Thrapston did not much admire their looks, for though little of a physiognomist, he plainly saw they were not gentlemen.

" Servant, your worship," said the foremost; a stout man of forbidding aspect.

" Be seated, gentlemen," said his lordship, as Darby placed them chairs.

" No, no, your worship," replied the fellow, " Dick Bayes knows his place too well to sit down afore a gentleman in his majesty's commission o' the peace. 'May be you ha' heerd o' Dick Bayes, sir, the vigilant London officer? but if you ha'n't, that 'ere, your worship, will fully 'quaint you with our arrand." The speaker tendered a long, narrow strip of printed paper, the blanks of which were filled up with a pen; his lordship knew the look of such documents, well. He read its contents, authorising the bearers to apprehend and lodge in any of his majesty's jails, the body of our hero; and straitly charging and commanding all justices of the peace, constables, and other loyal subjects to be aiding and assisting therein. His lordship smiled pompously.

" The day after the fair, in this matter, entirely, Mr. Bayes; the vigilance and zeal of the magistrates of York have already executed that object; Richand Turpin is now, and has been for some days, safe in York castle. My servant, Darby, will show you to the kitchen, though, where a glass of good ale awaits you, after your long journey, which, I feel proud to say, our activity has entirely got the start of."

Dick Bayes and his comrade Bill Johnson knew their cue too well to interrupt the magistrate before he had entirely said his say. And his lordship was surprised, when he waved his hand, to find his offer not accepted with the alacrity he expected, or the accustomed thanks returned for his liberal condescension. Bayes stood, crushing his hat between his hands, and making a scrape with his foot, as if preparing something in the way of disclosure.

" Beg your lordship's pardon, but we London men flatters ourselves as we knows a thing or two---and we're not so blind as we carn't see a hole through a ladder. I should say your prisoner ain't by no means so safe as he might be made, if so be one or two more was jined with him in other rooms o' the same stone pitcher."

" You speak in riddles, man," said his lordship.

Mr. Robins, the mayor's factotum, entered, with a smile on his face and a pen in his hand.

" Your lordship's pleasure?" said the confidential clerk.

" Take a seat at the table, Robins. These are two officers from London, come to apprehend Turpin; and," continued his lordship, " once well done, gentlemen, is twice done, d'ye see; he's safe enough in our keeping, I should say, Robins, eh?"

Robins reflected his master's grin, and obsequiously echoed a faint dupli-

cation of his master's laughter, as he looked at the thieftakers with second
hand importance---as much as to say, "d'ye take the lord mayor of York and
his clerk for ignoramuses?" The two fellows, however, stood the proof of
their facetiousness without moving a muscle.

"Your worships, (for they were not aware of the quality of Mr. Robins,)
will hear us out, I hope, for the sake of the king's service; and when we've
done, may be you may think otherwise from what you now does. We knows
well euough all about the taking o' the prisoner; sich things we has the
'arliest knowledge on: but there's a sammut behind your worships dossn't
know. Two 'desperate 'complices o' Turpin is now in this very city; we
tracked 'em down; and 'tisn't for no good as they're lurking about here, anyhow."

Mr. Thrapston looked at his clerk, and his clerk looked at him, while
Bayes went on :---

"Notorious characters, I can assure your worships; let us alone for knowing o' their movements; she---for one on 'em is a woman---has been a kind
o' tin pot---a mistress I mean, saving your worships' presence--- to Turpin
this long's past; and as for him, he's an out and out cracksman, and has been
a poacher. Well these two leaves Lunnun, a week ago, in a clandestine way,
and takes 'em two selves down here; aye, and more than that, I've heard as
she was known to say, afore setting out, to a woman of her own sort, as how
she'd have the prisoner out, or else she'd not come back alive; so I want's
your worships' warrant like, and I'll answer for proving the rest on't."

His lordship looked perplexed.

"Ring the bell, Robins."

Darby entered.

"Run to Alderman Jordan's, and request he will favour me with a few
minutes of his time: make haste."

The footman departed, and the worthy alderman who lived only a street
off, soon joined the trio. He listened to the tale as retailed to him by Mr.
Robins, amplified and illustrated by various interruptions from Bayes; but
when he arrived at the point where the woman was mentioned, he appeared
remarkably uneasy.

"You know this woman, eh?" said Mr. Jordan, turning to Bayes.

"I should think so, your worship: a stoutish, good-looking—what we
calls, saving your worships' presence, a crummy piece, and rayther—"

"Whew!" said Mr. Jordan, with a most unmagisterial whistle, or rather
an abortion of one; "why, brother Thrapston, this is the very hussey that
called on me yesterday, with a story of her being the prisoner's sister; and
cried very naturally too, I can assure you; and as I always desire to temper
justice with mercy, brother Thrapston, why, I've given her an order for admission at all proper times to see him."

"Then I wouldn't wonder at all, if Mister Turpin isn't off by this time in
a pair o' petticoats and a bonnet," said Bayes, tartly; "and you've Madge
Dutton in his stead, who'll not be quite so much sarvice to the ends o' justice
as the right 'un, seeing you can't very nicely hang her for Turpin's robberies,
whatever else you may do. Oh, I knows these women, your worshups; they're
queer craft, and do rum things when they're once put on 'em."

Doubt and alarm were pictured on the faces of the civic magistrates, and
his lordship suddenly changed his tone.

"Really this is most important information, Mr. Bayes," said the mayor; "hadn't we better send for the gaoler, and put him on his guard not to let that woman in. I don't see how we can give warrants, though, against these people, if you don't swear to some offence."

"Leave that to me : here's my companion can swear to his suspicion, and summat more, as to a burglary at one Squire Asher's; and I can swear to a genelman's watch as she——But furst, your worships," said he, "allow me and my comp. here jist to step down to the gaol, and take a look unbeknown at the prisoner—we both knows him—and after leave it to us to trace and make safe this here kipple o' bad 'uns. Put the bisness in our hands, your worshups, and it's all safe as a trivet."

"I'll go down with them to the gaol myself," said Mr. Jordan.

They went, and there learned that Madge had had a long interview with the prisoner. Bayes was, however, too fond of making his own knowledge mysterious, to breathe a word to Clank of Roger Haynes, until he had made further inquiries : they saw Turpin without his seeing them, and found their conjecture incorrect—the right one was still safe. They returned to the mayor, and were armed with the necessary warrants.

It was now dusk ; yet Bayes, after a caution to Reeves, (Clank was away,) commenced their inquiries. Madge's lodgings were easily and soon found, but neither she nor Haynes was within. In fact, they were both abroad, making preparations for their stratagem. Bayes and his comrade returned to the prison, wearied with their search. It was now nearly ten o'clock ; and they were in the very act of advising Reeves to vigilance, when the latter remarked, that it might be as well if one would step down to the alehouse hard-by, and request the presence of his brother turnkey, who was there drinking. Johnson went. On entering the alehouse before described, what was his surprise to hear a voice, not easily mistaken, exclaim, "Coom, cut along! none o' your heel-taps, Mister Dave ; it won't go down here, I can tell 'ee. Lord, man, I never zeed sich a poor un at yale. Landlord, another jug. Coom, drink, lad, will ee ?" "Here's look to us," said Clank, "I'll gie you a song, Roger, lad ; here goes :——

THE DUBSMAN'S CHAUNT.

Come, booze, jolly pals : ne'er shirk the brown ale;
 He's a fool who would doze o'er his gatter;
Tho' a dubsman (1) I be, yet I'll pitch you a tale
 Shall beat th'autem-cackler's (2) queer patter.
   Then list to the dubsman's chaunt, (bear a bob,)
   Then list to the dubsman's chaunt.

The ingler (3) so downey, he plays off his tricks,
 And the gulpins (4) he bites, till, at last,
He cuts it too fat, drops into a fix (5),
 So the stone-jug's his lodging at last.
   Then list, &c.

---

(1) Gaoler. (2) Methodist parson. (3) Swindling horse-dealer. (4) Soft ones. (5) Gets into a scrape.

The sneaking clyfaker (6) first nims a wipe,
  Grows chuff (7), and goes in for a yack (8),
Comes it strong for a while, but grabb'd when ripe,
  For a teazing (9) he turns up his back.
      Then list, &c.

Your clippers and smashers (10) in Tip-street (11) shine ;
  But, grown bolder, they scorn the low dodge ;
The clipper turns caster (12), and goes the nine (13),
  Till he's sent to the sheriff's to lodge
      Then list, &c.

The buffers and duffers, and divers and pads,
  Run their course for a time, while they've tin ;
But, queer'd for the dimmock (14), and lost for the brads,
  Thro' a Norway cravat (15) how they grin.
      Then list, &c.

The high tober (16) derricks (17), so spicy and flash,
  His prime doxy in satins to deck ;
But his reign is cut short ; for, in spite of his dash,
  He must lose his last race by *a neck*.
      Then list, &c.

Then list to the dubsman, and gather this truth—
  Though your flash coves may look very slap,
Beware of the *cross* in the time of your youth,
  Or you're book'd for the ruff, lag, or crap (18).
      Then list to the dubsman's chaunt, (bear a bob,)
      Then list to the dubsman's chaunt.

Bill Johnson waited to hear but half a verse of what we have here given ;
and Dave had not finished the last roll of the chorus, when Johnson, accompanied by Bayes, came back, and, without being seen by Haynes, or the unsuspecting turnkey, who was fast becoming intoxicated, assured themselves of
the identity of Roger.

"Ho, ho !" said Bayes, as he gently withdrew Johnson from the house ;
" I smell a rat. Never mind taking this fellow now. No, no, I've a higher
game in my head. This very night, Bill, it's to be done. Ay, ay, and the
turnkey's drinking—hum, ha ! Come along wi' me to the mayor's. I'll show
'em where the long odds lies in favour of us Londoners. Come on."

In half an hour, Bayes and his comrade were at the prison, having at their
disposal eight stout specials.

" It'll be a try on, depend on't, and this night ; so be sharp. Bill, stay
here while I tout the big 'un ;" and Bayes left to watch the alehouse.

Dave was now drunk, and slept with his head reclined on the table, and
Roger quitted the house. He looked cautiously round. The night was dark,
with slight spits of rain, prevented from increasing to a shower, by the freshness of the wind, which moaned and whistled among the chimneys and sign-
boards of the houses.

(6) Pickpocket.   (7) Saucy.   (8) Watch.   (9) Public flogging.
(10) Utterers of bad coin.   (11) Being in Tip-street, is being flush of money.
(12) Coiner.   (13) Assumes high consequence.   (14) Destitute of hush-money
to purchase the connivance of the officers.   (15) The board of the pillory in which
the culprit's neck was fixed.   (16) Dashing highwayman.   (17) Sets out on an
adventure.   (18) Ruff—a pillory ; lag—transportation ; crap—hanging.

Sir Albert and Lady Denistoun's visit to Turpin in York Castle.

"A prime night," thought Roger, as he took his way towards the bank of the Foss, Bayes cautiously following. It was too dark to see clearly his movements, but the thief-taker tracked him to a low shed, where, to his astonishment and satisfaction, he heard through the decayed planking a whispered conference, which he felt assured, for he could not see the speakers, was held with no other than Madge Dutton.

"Good bye, missus, and wish us luck—a' knows th' ground well—th' ould drain is up under th' wall at furder side—a fistfull o' minutes ull do th' job—doan't 'ee be froightened—a' feels sure on un gettin' free as if he wor here." So saying, Roger crept warily from the shed, carrying with him a stout and thick club of wood to assist his passage of the deep, narrow river, and a crowbar. Bayes rubbed his hands in extacy, and hastened to the prison-gate.

"Have you ever a sewer as opens in the gaol?" asked he hastily of Reeves.

"Aye, zure: but what o' that?"

"Show it me—quick—immediately." Bayes surveyed the strong iron grating. "This is the road out and in," said he to the surprised gaoler.

"Whoy d'ye knaw where that opens to?"

"Never you mind," replied Bayes, "send me two of the specials here."

They came, and the thief-taker posted them within a door, which opened on the quadrangle, within a few feet of the drain: three others were planted at another door which opened on the yard; while Bayes and Johnson stood in a dark angle of the square, with their lanterns closed.

"They'll be here in no time, and there's not above two on 'em, I reckon, if more nor one," said Bayes in a whisper to his brother officer.—"Hark!"

No. 39.

Chink! chink! chink! sounded from the stonework in which the grating was embedded, as the man below struck his crow-bar into the interstices, to secure a leverage for his instrument. Reeves stealthily joined them.

"Silence," whispered Bayes "they're at it."

The ponderous grating rose slowly, in obedience to the mighty strength of Haynes.

"That ain't done by one arm, Mister Bayes," said Johnson, in a voice scarcely above his breath. A partial gleam of moonshine through the scudding rack, showed the drain already pushed away, and the huge form of Roger was dubiously seen dragging himself through the opening.

"We shall top him nicely, at any rate," whispered Bayes.

"Hark!" said Reeves, grasping tightly the officer's arm.—click! click! click! click! the noise was from another quarter of the yard. "What the devil is that?"

The turnkey sneaked along by the wall, towards the spot whence he feared these ominous sounds proceeded: he had, however, cleared but a few steps, when, to his great surprise and alarm, he saw a door open, and a man cautiously stepping out.—

"Hist!—A friend?" it was Turpin who spoke.

"All right!" was the whispered response of Roger. Dick was within three yards of the hole.—

"Down with 'em" cried Reeves, at the same moment dashing at Roger.

"Fly, measter! fly!" It was too late; for Dick, seized from behind by Bayes and Johnson, half manacled as he was, was instantly thrown. Roger aimed a blow at one of the officials, who fell with a broken arm, and was turning upon another, when Reeves dealt him a smasher on the top of the head with a huge padlock; he staggered, but strove to drop down the drain-hole---another heavy blow, and, with fractured skull, poor Roger pitched headlong into the aperture. The constables, with torches, approached the spot.

"There's that one gone the way he kem," said Reeves, holding his ankle with pain, "he's broken my leg tho', I'm believin';" and he swore with pain. "Oh Lord! Oh Lord!" groaned the special, "a doctor, a doctor, for mercy's sake, I'ze killed ootreet!"

Turpin was carried back to his cell---a blacksmith was sent for, who furnished him with a new suit of irons, far heavier and more irksome than his old ones, and safely bolted; and chained by a double ring and swivels, we must leave him cursing the unfortunate miscarriage, and wearying himself with fruitless conjectures, as to the probable cause of the failure of the attempt.

"Time," said he, "can alone explain it, but I can see no clue, save the double treachery of that foresworn traitress who brings death to all who trust her."

The body of the hapless Roger was drawn from the sewer, and though life had not fled, he never spoke again; the fracture was extensive; consciousness returned not, and before the following night Roger Haynes lay a corpse in the gaol.

Madge's anxiety was soon unpleasantly terminated. Footsteps stealthily approached her place of confinement, she ventured forth a few paces, in the nervousness of impatience, and was received in the unwelcome embrace of Master Dick Bayes who, 'mid the jests of his companions, introduced her a second time to the interior of York Castle.

CHAPTER XXVI.

———

2nd. Gent.—I do not think that he fears death?
Ist. Gent.—   Sure he does not,
He never was so womanish: the cause
He doth a little grieve at.
                Shakspere. Henry VIII, a. ii. sc. i.

                Is not punishment revenge?
The momentary violence of anger
May be excused. The indignant heart will throb
Against oppression, and the out-stretched arm
Resent its outraged feelings—
And nature will almost command the deed
That nature blames. But will cool reflection
Plead strongly with soul-emoving eloquence
For the deliberate murder of Revenge.
Would you, Piers, in your calmer hour of Reason
Condemn an erring brother to be slain?
Cut him, at once, from all the joys of life,
All hope of reformation! to avenge
That deed his punishment can ne'er recall?
                Southey's Wat Tyler.

True it is that nothing great can spring from the dead level of apathy; that there is grandeur in the storm, sublimity in the earthquake, and a pleasing horror even in narrations of plague, famine, or murder; and tragic representations charm by their excitement: but the stern realities of all these things bring with their actual presence, or the inapplication to our own selves, far other feelings than those induced by their distant contemplation, or the narration in speech, in prose, or in verse. Thus that brutal, degraded, debauched, drunken, ignorant thief, the desperate, precocious villain, Jack Sheppard—his repulsiveness softened down by time—his deformities concealed by distance, shines forth in the pages of an Ainsworth, a humanised, nay, a loveable being; metamorphosed by the touch of the enchanter's wand, and purified in the refining alembic of the author's imagination, this object of legitimate loathing comes forth imbrued with the attractive qualities of his creator's mind; and as with romance, so it is with history. Prejudice and party feeling are not the only things that time wears out; fault, nay crimes great and unpardonable, are dwelt upon, talked of, canvassed, and denounced until human nature, ever on the search for novelty, nauseates the thrice-told tale, and welcomes, with joy, the skilful or daring untruth which a master-mind embodies and adorns in the life-like colours of fiction. And thus is it with our hero, as well as many others; be they statesmen, warriors or princes. No man, it has been said, with as much philosophy as truth, is a hero to his *valet de chambre*, and a right estimate of the true stature of men's minds—excuse the phrase, is among the desiderata of human knowledge.
    The

        " Fears of the brave and follies of the wise"

are proverbial, and as all courage is comparative, so is the depth or the heigh of human knowledge or wisdom, which

        "Is but to know how little's to be known.

" *Mais a nos moutons,*" as Voltaire has it.
    The first feeling of annoyance over, like the first plunge of a bather, the

seeing and being seen, even in so melancholy a situation, became a relief---a pleasure to Turpin; for the conversation of his visitors, though prompted by mere morbid curiosity, relieved him from the pressure of his own thoughts, and he watched anxiously through the hours of solitude for the time which should bring even these idle gazers. The tardy course of justice then left the unfortunate prisoner in a lengthened suspense, far less endurable than the certainty of the worst that fate can do, to the man of resolved heart.---Resolved heart! the phrase is common, but false and foolish as common; what, under such circumstances as his then were, is "resolution?" It is the physical power of controlling inward emotion—the strength of nerve which can prevent outward manifestations of the struggle within: for, in nine cases out of ten, the "hardened" offender, (as your newspaper scribes call him), feels even more acutely than the pusilanimous wretch who, with tears, sobs, and exclamations, bemoans his cruel fate, or with frantic horror shrinks from the frown of death. Such weak minds, such nerveless bodies, can never feel the depth, the intensity of that agonistic struggle by which the strong mind o'ermasters the bitterness of death, and looking on the fleshless phantom with undaunted eye, outfaces his terrors. 'Tis true that such whining imbecility passes with a multitude of well meaning persons for a proof of a fit state of mind for the awful change; but those who look deeper, and consider the structure of human minds, must know that no man is a *hero* to *himself*; and that in such a strait as that of suffering a felon's death, there lurks beneath the coolness and collectedness of the courageous man, the sharpest pang—a pang sharper, from the pressure of concealment, than the complaining lachrymose driveller is capable of. His tears and complaints are but the outward signs that he has struggled with the inward torture common to humanity, and has fallen in the fight.

The manner of our hero was cool, collected, and worthy of a better occasion than that for which it was assumed; we say assumed, for such stoicism is not *natural*—it is the triumph of fixity of purpose, pride, or what you will, over the common feelings of humankind.

In the lapse of the seven weeks during which the important prisoner awaited the arrival of the Chief Justice, Sir John Chapple, at the assizes, Madge had been tried before the quarter-sessions, for her offence of aiding and abetting the escape of a felon; but the indictment failing on a technicality, she was acquitted, and remained at liberty, though under surveillance, and, as might be expected, denied all access to the prisoner.

Dick sat one day in his cell, counting the moments, as they rolled onward, to bring the hour for the admission of visitors.—The iron tongue of the Castle bell had told him that, at its next clang, the huge key would grate in the lock, when he was surprised, some half hour before the appointed time, by the opening of the door, and the appearance of a gentlemanly man, whose bearing bespoke the soldier, on whose arm leant a placid, mild, and melancholy female—they were Sir Albert and Lady Denistoun. The stout-hearted man felt this indeed a hard trial.

"Do not think," said Sir Albert, advancing towards him, "do not think mere idle curiosity has brought us hither. Madeline!"—he turned to Lady Denistoun—"it is to your persuasion that our presence is attributable; you came with a proffer of service, as far as we can legally and consistently do, yet you speak not."

The kind, the generous heart of Lady Denistoun was overflowing; tears suffused her eyes—the remembrance of former friendships—of the old thatched cottage of the Bevis's—her escape from a brother's unkindness—she thought of the generous, the open-hearted, and the impetuous youth, now the dreaded, the ruthless robber—she thought of the white hairs of the murdered old man, and the fair form of *her*, her first and earliest friend, now mingling with our common clay—she thought, till thought became a pain, and her woman's heart, and woman's sympathy, found vent in a torrent of tears.

Sir Albert looked on, half displeased, for he knew not how to interpret this burst of feeling. Though a kind, he was a proud man ; and he could not help considering this outburst as derogatory, to say the least of it, to Lady Denistoun. " Madeline," said he, with as much coolness as he could assume, " this is unbecoming your rank and station. Think you that I would have come here to witness this ? Had I known the method in which your tender of service would have been made, I can assure you that—Mr. Palmer, may I beg you to accept our—"

" Sir Albert," said our hero ; " your kindness, I fear, is too late—even if I deserved it—but I do not. I desire but your sympathy, and your belief that I am not altogheterthe desperate villain which rumour and vulgar exaggeration has painted me.—May a felon—do not start, lady—present a token, a token that will remind you of one too good for the best, yet whose misfortune it was to be linked with the worst—" and while speaking, he drew from a small red case, a paper enclosed in silk, and proffered it to Lady Denistoun. She opened it with a trembling hand, and there fell from it on the floor, a ring— the gift of Madeline Weston—and a rich tress of fair hair, the brightness of which spoke of sunshine, though the head which it once adorned now slept in the damp dark grave.

Dick turned to Sir Albert. " To you, Sir Albert, my gift must be different, The pistols, which —but it matters not—the pistols of Dick Turpin may possess some interest in time to come ; and, as I give them you *before* my conviction, for I know well my fate, and dread not to confront it, the sheriff will, doubtless, grant the trifling favour of handing them over to you. I had forgotten that there breathed a living being who cared for the fate of Dick Turpin, until you appeared : but now may I ask that the last requests of my will, or rather my best wishes, may be complied with ?"

Sir Albert promised to see them carried into effect to the utmost of his power, and, after some further conversation, he departed ; Dick firmly refusing all assistance for his trial, and declaring his fatalism to have deprived him of even the wish to live.

The day of trial drew on, and the prisoner was placed at the bar to plead to no less than five indictments: the first two being for the capital felony of horse-stealing. A curious fact came out in the evidence on the trial, namely, that Turpin had lived for two years at Brough, Welton, and other places in Lincolnshire, where his character stood high as a liberal and gentlemanly dealer :—one of the witnesses for the prosecution declaring, that he " paid for everything freely, and he looked upon him, (though a stranger in those parts), as a gentleman." The first indictment set forth the robbery of the mare and foal of Thomas Creasy, of Bulling-brook ; and its sale, a day or two before Turpin absconded from Lincolnshire, to a Captain Graham, of Ashby, was clearly proved, while the foal had been purchased by an inn-keeper at Welton. The testimony was conclusive, and the identification complete. Several persons swore positively to Richard Palmer and Dick Turpin being one and the same person : and a witness from Beverly showed that the shooting of Mr. Hall's game cock had been the proximate cause of his apprehension and subse-

quent detection and identification—hence the popular tradition of the game-
cock for which Turpin suffered.

A second indictment, also for horse-stealing, was proceeded with; the jury
again found him guilty; when the learned judge, considering that it would
waste the time of the court to proceed with the other charges against the prisoner, seeing that those already proven made his life a forfeit to the law, called
on him for any reason he might have to offer why judgment should not *now*
be passed on him.   Dick merely replied, with the same cool steadiness he had
shown throughout the protracted trials,—

" My lord, I had expected that my trial would have taken place in Essex—
I was so advised by my friends ;—which accounts for the absence of my witnesses this day.   I am in your hands and those of the jury."

Sir John Chapple replied :—" You have assuredly had abundance of time
to prepare your defence.   Whoever advised you that you would be removed
hence to take your trial was very wrong and much to blame.   You have been
convicted on the clearest and most unexceptionable testimony, and as you
have no other reason to offer, the court will at once proceed to pass the awful
sentence of the law."

Breathless silence pervaded the vast auditory, as the grave expounder of
a bloody and brutal law, invested himself in the black cap, as the symbol
of the black deed, which barbarous *custom*, the idol of the vulgar and unthinking many, had sanctified in the eyes of a people pretending to civilization.
Perhaps there was not one, even in that great assemblage, such force have
habit and education, who despising the mummery and formalities of wigs,
gowns, and law jargon, could see beneath them, a poor, weak knot of frail
imperfect men, committing in the face of heaven a *murder* on their weak
and erring fellow, because forsooth, he did " feloniously, and with force of
arms," (or some other such foolery) " deprive another man of a *horse!*"

" Property *must* be protected, sir !" exclaims some prosaic old wigsby, " and
if you do not inflict severe punishments society cannot be kept together."   It
is a problem *now* solved, thanks to the Romillys, the Beccarias, the Mon-
tagues, the Whitbreads, and other great and good men, that blood defiles,
defaces, corrupts, and demoralises society, instead of cleansing it; that
revenge is not and cannot be the aim of enlightened legislation, even were
there not the paramount consideration, that there is but one crime, that of
murder,—" whoso sheddeth man's blood by man shall his blood be shed"—
which calls on a citizen, either as legislator, judge, or juror, to imbrue his
hands (for it should not be lost sight of that in either of these capacities he
does so,) in blood, or to violently take that life whose issue the great Giver has
declared to be in HIS hand alone.

The learned judge went on, his equanimity disturbed only by the slight
feeling which custom, prejudice, and human fallibility had not yet entirely
extinguished in his heart.   The dread words were concluded, and " the
Lord," with impious solemnity, beseeched " to have that mercy on him
which he must not expect from man !"   The prisoner bowed, and left
the dock, with the sympathies of the female portion of the assembly, ever
the last to allow sophistry to obliterate the better feelings of our kind.

The learned judge left the town without any notification of his intention
towards the condemned, a practice equivalent to a death warrant, and the
awful preparations for the closing scene were hastened forward.   The few days

which now intervened, ere time, as far as our hero was concerned, should be swallowed up in eternity, were not passed in a manner well calculated as a preparation for the solemn scene.

It is curious to dwell on the social usages of our ancestors, as displayed in their own homely, and matter of fact narratives.

The frequent recurrence of the punishment of death had so familiarized not only the populace, but the upper classes of society, that public executions appeared to have become a sort of public amusement; and privileged persons seem to have regarded notorious criminals as legitimate objects of curiosity, nay, of patronage. Thus Claude Duval, during his confinement in Newgate, was not only visited, admired, and caressed, for his courage in defiance of the laws, but received presents to a considerable amount, in money, &c , from the nobility and gentry who visited his Newgate levees, which he squandered in reckless profusion among the turnkeys, his fellow prisoners, and the prostitutes who frequented the gaol. His portrait was engraved on fan-mounts, and in like manner, Bew, Whitney, Hinton, Captain Evans, Dick Low, Will Chance, and others, appear to have been elevated into a quasi-heroism by the good taste of our nobles and gentry of the reign of William, Anne, and of the first George. Such was the high tone of morality, the aristocratic taste of the period ; a proof that sanguinary laws degrade the people, and that capital punishments invariably defeat the grand object of all penal legislation—the protection of society—by calling forth a sympathy so strong, that at length the abhorrence of the culprit's crime is lost, utterly merged, in pity for the sufferer, and detestation at the barbarity of the punishment.

We have said that multitudes of the wealthy and the noble visited our hero in his last confinement, and among them not the least welcome, were Sir Albert and his lady. To the hands of the baronet Dick entrusted the written paper in which his last requests were contained, and *nec temere nec timide*, awaited the day which should bring this " great change."

It came, but the relation of its events, and of the behaviour of the principal actor, throughout the stirring hours of the last closing scene of " life's fitful fever" shall be reserved for the concluding chapter of the eventful chronicle of RICHARD TURPIN.

CHAPTER XXVII.

Cowards die many times before their deaths,
The valiant never taste of death but once.—
Of all the wonders that I yet have heard,
It seems to me most strange that man should fear;
Seeing that death, a necessary evil,
Will come, when it will come.

                     Bleared sights
Are spectacled to see him : your prating nurse
Into a rapture lets her baby cry,
While she eyes him : the kitchen-malkin pins,
Her smartist lockram round her reechy neck
Clambring the wall to eye him : stalls, bulks, windows,
Are smothered up, leads filled, and ridges horsed
With variable complexions : all contending
In earnestness to see him : and proud dames
Commit the war of Damask, in
Their nicely-gawded cheeks, to the wanton spoil
Of Phœbus burning kisses, but to gaze.

                                      Shakspere.

THE sun shone brightly on the gay crowds which poured from York Gates toward the then marshy plain of Knavesmire, now arched and chained into the smooth green of the race-course.   It was clear that something unusual had called forth the dwellers in that ancient city,   Nor was the bustle and stir confined to the citizens alone ; in every direction the roads were thronged with groups of country folk, all verging to one point.   In one place the brawny bumpkin " tooled" along, urging Ball or Dobbin into an unwonted trot, stimulated by the anxiety of his living cargo of men and women, to procure a good sight of whatever was to be seen: while in another the spruce light cart of a traveller rattled past the heavier and slower vehicles. Mounted men and pedestrians, all were flocking to Knavesmire, for it was the day of the execution of TURPIN.

Mighty too was the bustle, and loud the hum of curiosity, without the walls of the castle, and near the gate through which the condemned was expected to issue.   Though it was yet but nine in the forenoon, and twelve was the appointed hour, the eagerness and impatience of the populace had already crowded every " coigne of vantage," whence even a bird's eye view of the cavalcade could be obtained ; and loud was the shout and great the commotion of the many headed monster as, at ten o'clock, the sheriff, with several other mounted gentlemen, attended by a band of javelin men entered the massive and frowning portal.   In the large quadrangle, before noticed as the scene of Roger Haynes's death, and of the culprit's frustrated escape, stood a group of gentlemen of the county ; magistrates, land-holders, and persons of quality ; and amongst them, at the request of Turpin, Sir Albert Denistoun. The topic of their conversation may be easily guessed : it was the life, character, and crimes of the unfortunate man that day doomed to suffer.

There stood the old fashioned, clumsy, cart, in which the condemned was to be conveyed to the fatal spot, some two miles from the city.   The executioner was already seated in the vehicle ;—he was a swarth and surly-looking fellow, a prisoner in the gaol, who had volunteered as the sheriff's substitute in this odious office, in consideration of a remission of a portion of his sentence of imprisonment, and a gratuity in hard cash.   The prisoner came forth ; his step was firm, and his carriage as erect as the heavy fetters with which he was

The Burial of Turpin.

encumbered would permit. Before him walked the two turnkeys, beside him, on either hand, the governor of the Castle and the chaplain, followed by a body of officials and javelin-men, bearing the ancient partizan or halbert. Thus passed they into the quadrangle, amid the gaze of the privileged visitors assembled there. Dick looked around : anxiety, but no dismay, sat upon his determined countenance, though in its deepened lines and the compressed lip you might trace all was not well within. He looked, nevertheless, with an air of indolent curiosity on the ceremony of the governor of the gaol handing over his body to the sheriff and taking the customary receipt therefor ; meanwhile the heavy manacles were struck from the prisoner's ankles and wrists, and their place supplied by a strong black silk scarf furnished at the culprit's request for the purpose of pinioning him, in lieu of the ordinary cord.

The convict glanced around : his eye rested on Sir Albert, and he intimated a request to the sheriff that he might be permitted a minute's converse with a gentleman whom he saw present. The chaplain officiously interposed ; but a short phrase, and a determined look from Turpin silenced the intermeddler, and the sheriff, looking at his watch, remarked that the conversation must be indeed a brief one.

Sir Albert, acquainted with Turpin's wish, drew near.

" Sir Albert, on such an occasion as this we must waive all ceremony. Deeply do I feel the consideration shown by you in being here at this unhappy trial. A paper which, with the permission of the sheriff, I will commit to your hands, contains the requests of a dying man."

No. 40.

The paper was handed to Sir Albert, who, with mingled surprise and emotion perused its contents.

Turpin with scrutinising gaze watched each movement of the reader's features; Sir Albert folded the paper and looked dubiously at him.

" I see you think the requests in that writing strange, but they arise from no motive or feeling of levity. I have, perhaps I may *now* say it, elevated myself above my fellow men to an indeed bad eminence—perchance, had fate willed otherwise, I had been celebrated, instead of infamous, to future time—it is too late to think on *that*. Have I your word that the desires expressed in that writing shall be complied with? say, and I feel safe in your promise."

Sir Albert was too much surprised to argue or expostulate.

" I respectfully repeat my —"

" They *shall* be complied with."

" Enough; farewell!" and Turpin quickly ascended the short ladder, entered the fatal cart, and took up his place between the clergyman and executioner; the latter, pipe in mouth, coolly seating himself on the coffin, looked up in the face of the living man destined in a short hour to be borne back a lifeless clod within it.

The procession was formed, the word " forward" given, and it slowly moved forth from the frowning portal. A loud and confused murmur, like the distant roar of a heavy surf, rose as the opening gates and solemn clang of the death-bell announced the coming forth of the cavalcade.

Sir Albert stood with the paper yet clasped in his hand, watching with fixed eye till the last of the train had disappeared from beneath the arch, as if expecting some recognition or signal from the prisoner; but he turned not his head from the moment that he bade him farewell. Sir Albert was recalled from his momentary absence of mind by finding himself surrounded by several gentlemen whom intimacy or acquaintance entitled to be curious.

" So, Sir Albert," said a rubicund, bottle-nosed, fox-hunting baronet, of his neighbourhood; " he ha' left you executor; excuse the liberty, but may I ask if the gentleman has made you sole legatee to all his estates in reversion, when the sheriff has done with 'em?" added he, with a chuckle at his clumsy attempt to be facetious.

" Why, Sir Harbottle," said Sir Albert recovering himself; " I must confess, if you see any subject of jest in the affair, that I *am* sole executor of as singular a will as dying man ever penned; but I was at that moment recalling the little I have known of the strange, eventful life of that unfortunate culprit." So saying, Sir Albert seemed about to move away from the group; but old Sir Harbottle receiving a monitory nudge on the elbow from one of the inquisitive bystanders, returned to the charge, with a determination not to be thus fobbed off.

" Must beg your pardon, Sir Alby; but don't think you're a bit more communicative to your old friends than you need be; what's the will about, eh? no such secret in it, surely, but what your old friends here may be made partners in, I suppose? eh? Come, the will, my boy, the will; or, if you demur at showing it us, we'll take your word for the contents; which must be out of the common run to throw such a cool, steady, soldier as you off your guard, as we saw you just now."

" There is no secret in the will," said Sir Albert slowly; " yet I shall certainly not allow the solemn requests of a dying man, albeit that man is a felon, to become the topic of idle jest or light discourse. Nevertheless," for he saw that the bystanders looked somewhat ashamed at his reproof, " I will communicate its effect: Firstly, I am desired to forward certain tokens and things of trifling value to a lady—you smile, but let that pass; out of other property, long since resigned by the felon, and enjoyed by others, I am requested to bestow a sum on a woman who has for some time past been considered as his wife—and lastly, for the document is short, there is a curious clause, and one which, please God, I will perform—it runs thus: ' Acknowledging fully the justness of this, my last sentence, and conscious how I have deserved it—though still feeling a wish that the offence for which I forfeit my life had been less ignominious—I desire that none may weep the death I die, since my country has demanded my blood; therefore, as none should mourn, it is my last wish, that the good friend whom I entrust with this will comply with my desire, that no outward mockery of woe may mark my passage to my last rest, but that six young unmarried maidens, dressed in bridal white, may follow me to the grave; and to each of them be given the garments for the occasion, and a gratuity for their kind offices.' "*

Sir Albert paused, and looked round at his curious and attentive auditory, and as he regarded their constrained solemnity he could scarcely forbear a smile.

" And do ye mean to zee all this doon, Sir Albert," asked a jolly Yorkshireman, the cultivator of his patrimonial acres, and whose wealth entitled him to some standing in society.

" I have passed my word," was Sir Albert's brief reply.

" Well," observed Sir Harbottle, " it will be a new sort of a sight for the people of York." There was a pause, which the old baronet ended by exclaiming,—" Now, gentlemen, which of you are for Knavesmire? though we've time enough yet, for the crowd will keep them from moving very fast."

" Not I," said Sir Albert: the rest, without a remark on his refusal, mounted their horses, and, avoiding the crowded road, were on the ground long before the head of the cavalcade reached its destination; where, leaving them, we will return to the principal actor in this law-made tragedy.

He had passed a few yards along the narrow way, and had cleared Ousegate and the city, when, turning to the clergyman, Turpin addressed a few words to him in a low tone, intimating an intention to make a disclosure of certain facts in his misspent life: but his intention was foiled, for scarcely had he began, when an unwonted commotion agitated the mighty sea of heads. He looked round upon the wavering crowd as it reeled to and fro, and soon perceived a knot of men, whose determined purpose in forcing a passage through the dense crowd, occasioned the tumult and outcries of those thrust aside or driven forward by their violence. The throng approached, and amid the knot, Dick saw a female, borne by two stout fellows, whom he had no difficulty in recognizing as Madge—a deep frown knit his brow, and he bit his lip. The woman caught his eye, and stretched out her hands towards him— the crowd divided; " Let her bid un good bye," shouted a chorus of voices, among which, that of Dave Clank, the quondam gaoler, was distinguishable.

* This is a fact: the coffin of Turpin was followed by six young women attired in white. He does not seem, however, to have been the only hero of the gallows-tree, thus singularly attended. At least the old flash song, beginning,—" In the County of Wicklow, I was born," contains the following lines :—

      " With six young maidens to bear up my pall,
      Let them have green ribbons and white favours all,' &c.

Though it is more than probable, as a similar desire is expressed in other songs besides the one above quoted, (generally known as " The Roving Blade,") that all the traditions had one common origin, now impossible to be ascertained, were it even worth the trouble of the search.

He appeared to be the leader of the party, by his stout oaken cudgel, and holding the place of pioneer. "Let her to un, will 'ee," exclaimed he, dealing his thwacks to right and left with hearty goodwill. Madge was brought close to the culprit by the friends of the discharged turnkey, who with sinewy arms cleared for her a passage. Turpin looked at her with a cold, fixed, and steady eye : despair was written on her countenance—wild, senseless, agonizing despair: his colour changed.

"Do you wish to speak with her?" said the Sheriff, mildly, riding close to the wheel; "say aye, or my men must beat them off—we cannot suffer these obstructions.—Back, there! back!" The functionary waved his hand, and the party slightly receded before the pressure of the constables.

"Oh Richard! Richard!" screamed the wretched woman.

Jan Reeves, on whom, since Dave Clank's dereliction of duty, the office of chief turnkey had devolved, now stept up ; touching his hat to the Sheriff, he said—"There's some impurdence i' thot, Sir Walter ; yon's t'e wench as tried on t'e rescue, and w'ud ha' dropt in for a lumbering* on'y for lawyer Double's findin' t'e flor in—"

"Stand clear, there!" shouted the constables, laying their staves on the heads of the second and third ranks, while they pushed the foremost on the breast : a judicious method, seeing that by striking the front men, your constable may get a counter-hit, while with staff and arm, his reach is greater than those behind. We take this to be a point worthy the consideration of all policemen.—But to return.

"I'm dom'd," exclaimed Davie, "if we do stond back, till—"

Dick had distinctly heard the few words of Jan Reeves, and was more than ever perplexed.—"Oh, Richard! Richard!" again struck upon his ear, and he made a sign to the Sheriff.

"It is a great indulgence," said that gentleman, "but it shall be granted ;—Officers! permit the woman to have speech with the prisoner!" And he rode into the press, toward the spot where Madge stood, surrounded and supported by her small knot of adherents.

A mighty shout arose as the mob observed that a female, heedless of the thousands of gazing eyes, stood resting on the condemned man's shoulder : the most distant needed no interpreter of the scene before them. Woman's affection is ever a moving sight, but doubly so, when we see it in the darkest hour of man's adversity and trial. It matters not the character, the dark crimes, or the abandoned life of the actors in such scenes ; perhaps it is the more striking on that very account.

The writer of these pages knows not that he ever experienced a more choking sensation than that produced on the occasion of an execution at the Old Bailey, some years since.—The wretched man, young in years but old in crime, suffered for *uttering* not *forging*, certain characters on a scrap of watered tissue paper, "with intent to defraud the Governor and Company, &c." The horrid preparations were all made, the finish put to the adjusting of the rope, the minister of the gospel (!!) dropped his handkerchief, as the signal for public murder—the bolt was drawn, when, from near the foot of the scaffold, arose a cry so piercing, so unearthly, that it was pain to the very sense of hearing, and a female, who must have fallen heavily but for the dense crowd, was borne forth on the arms of some bystanders. A neighbouring public-house received the fainting woman, and it will be long before he forgets the piteous aspect, the wild, imploring, helpless look of the despairing wretch. Yet, she

* Imprisonment.

was a common outcast—a vile, polluted thing—one of those beings to whom novel-mongers, and drama-concoctors, allow neither hearts nor sympathies. He enquired subsequently the fate of the poor wretch, and found that her feelings had overwhelmed her reason, and that, after three months of wretched heedlessness and insanity, the outcast paramour of the felon had destroyed herself by drowning, remained unowned for some days, at a parish bone-house, and then found (happy she) a pauper-grave.

Loud and long was the murmur of that mighty flood of voices, as it poured forth its full tide of applause. There is a solemnity, a vastness, a choral fulness in the grand diapason of a myriad human voices, which no instrumental imitation can ever approach, much more reach ; the hum, the booming roar of a vast crowd, must be heard to be understood, must be observed with listening ear to be appreciated : from the shrill treble to the deepest bass each note is blended in the mighty and onorous swell, and so rose the involuntary expression of the sympathy of that vast assemblage.

But the two most concerned heeded them not. For the thunder, though "like unto the voice of many waters," they had no ear, and pursued their brief colloquy as though none were present but themselves. The explanation was short: the death of Roger had severed all clue to the mysterious failure ; Madge had been rigorously excluded from all communication with Turpin ; the attempted rescue had been the cause of her own imprisonment ; and here she was to share the last hour of trial ; participating in the bitter dregs of the cup of death and separation, and showing by tears, sobs and looks, such as never *were* or *could be* feigned, the strength of woman's affection—the powerful softness, the invincible tenderness, the strong weakness of woman's heart !

Jan Reeves stood a close listener during the short interview, and filled up each hiatus of Madge's explanations and extenuations, by taking to himself, in a by-conversation with the sheriff, the whole credit of detecting the plotted escape. Though short, the conversation satisfied Turpin that he had egregiously misjudged her, and he asked her forgiveness for his injurious suspicions. The wretched woman threw herself on his breast and sobbed aloud.

Several minutes had now elapsed ; the more distant of the crowd were growing impatient of the, to them, long delay, and the roar of impatience to witness the bloody sacrifice, rose long and loud, drowning the former shouts of applause—so fickle are your mighty masses, so incapable is a mob of deliberative consistency. The tide was turned, and the growl of the monster for his postponed meal succeeded ; the sheriff, too, seemed of opinion that the interview had lasted long enough : at a signal from his hand, Madge was torn from her hold, and borne from the cart, which again moved onward amid the living tide.

Knavesmire is reached ; and in that vast expanse of upturned faces you shall see but one expression—that of curious eagerness to feast its owner's eyes on the brutal scene. The cavalcade struggles slowly through the dense mass ; the clergyman reads aloud the solemn ritual appointed by the Church for the burial of the dead—and now he stands beneath the triple tree, with the victim at his side—Dick mounts the steps of the ladder whose rounds he shall no more descend—his right leg trembles in the momentary re-action of overwrought firmness, but, with a sudden stamp of pride, the fated man steadies the shuddering nerves, whose shrinking might shame him in the last act, and tell to thousands of gaping admirers that this stoicism was but assumed. Turpin, we say, stamped his foot, and stood on the frail plank whose support alone divided him from death.   The clergyman again proffered his services, but he declined them ; and beckoning towards him the sheriff and the topsman, thus spoke :—

"I shall not address the multitude here, after the custom of many offenders. My regret is that I suffer for so base a crime ; I had rather it had been for some offence more fitted to my character, and my career. To you, Mr. Sheriff, as concealment can no longer serve me, I wish, in the presence of this reverend gentleman, here to confess the deed which lies heaviest on my mind. It would take long, even if there were time, to relate my many robberies.— In none did I ever shed blood, though life I have taken in self-defence. It avails me not now to conceal it, but the murder, if so you please to call it, of the ranger's man, on Epping Forest, was the act of this hand. I am justly sentenced, and fear not to meet my fate. There are some requests, which a kind friend of mine has consented to see executed ;—and now, having cleared my breast of all that I deem necessary, may God pardon my many sins, and receive my soul."*

The last word had scarcely left his lips, and the topsman was about to mount, in order to complete the final arrangements of the toilet of death, and draw the cap over the eyes of the highwayman, when his intention was suddenly forestalled :—a short ejaculatory prayer breathed from the lips of the dying man —the crowd stood tiptoe with expectancy ;—but before the cart had time to move away, he flung himself from his foot-hold with fearless energy.— The mob shouted,—a jerk—a spasm—a choking sob—a convulsive shudder, and the soul of the daring highwayman flew to its awful doom !—Yes ! there, sluggishly and slowly swaying to and fro in the passing wind, hung the inanimate corse, so late instinct with life, passion, and vigour ; and the gratified multitude turned slowly from the spot, jesting, gossipping, and laughing. You might have guessed that plain the scene of some glorious rejoicing, some wake, festival, or fair ; in one place a gaping circle of bumpkins listened to the exaggerations and lies of a leather-lunged vendor of the cheap printed sheets, then the staple literature of our remote districts, who retailed a whole cento of the exploits of robbers, from Ishmael downwards, all of which he affiliated on the dangling corse that once was Turpin ; finishing each extraordinary narrative by holding up his blue-looking broad sheet, " containing," as he phrased it, "a full, true, and purtickler haccount of the birth, parintage, and hedication, life, cha-rak-ter, and be-ha-vi-er, last dying speech and confession, of that most notoriousest robber, Dick Turpin ; together with a copy of werses writ by him on the wery night afore his hexecution ; likewise a letter to his beloved wife, and other facs and 'ticklers too numerous to mention, all for the small charge of one ha' penny !"   Near him two amphibious-looking animals, a cross between the gipsey and the sailor, in tattered clothes, with shoeless feet, roared from their hoarse throats some ear-splitting-chaunt about the miseries of " them as sails the salt-sea hocean ;" while vendors of brandy-balls, nuts, apples, hot pudding, &c., plied their several vocations in the motley group.

As we have before said, you might have deemed that plain the scene of

---

* This is substantially the narrative and confession, given in the early life of Turpin, 8vo. York, 1739, in the British Museum. He threw himself from the ladder, as above described. The stealing of his body, its recovery, and second burial by the mob, are also authenticated by the above book, published at the very place of his execution, within a twelvemonth of that event.

some festival or fair, had not that one black and ominous object cast its gloom upon the scene : yes there, amid this ribald riot, and drunken confusion—for itinerant vendors of spirits, with bottle in hand, were rife among the mob— the frowning gallows with its unconscious burden presided over the orgies : a potent example—an instructive lesson—a solemn warning—a sagacious moni- tor—a mighty monument of legislative wisdom ! Yet for a century from the time we are writing of, parliamentary sages were to be found, who practically regarded the gibbet and the rope as the protectors of property, the efficient vindicators of the law, and who seem to have classed the hangman among the " best possible public instructors !"

The time appointed expired ; the body was cut down, and delivered to Madge, who conveyed it back to the city, followed still by a large crowd ; though it bore but a small proportion to that which had escorted the living man to his violent death. That evening and the morn of the following day the corpse lay at the ' Blue Boar,' in Castlegate, and at noon, on the Sabbath, again surrounded by a multitude of spectators, and followed by six maidens, the remains of Turpin were conveyed to their last home, in the churchyard of St. George's, without Fishergate postern ; but, as if even the grave was not destined to receive him peacefully, another and more tumultuous funeral awaited them.

*   *   *   *   *   *   *   *   *

It was a dark and cloudy evening ; the wind sighed heavily and mournfully among the trees of the churchyard, and slight spits of rain foretold a shower. The last of the indifferent spectators of that strange funeral procession had departed, yet there remained *one*—a woman, closely muffled in a hood and cloak, near the sheltering wall which bounded the field of death, where, beneath the grassy hillocks,

> Each in his narrow cell for ever laid,
> The rude forefathers of the hamlet sleep :—

She was there she knew not why. Some strange, undefinable presentiment hung over her ; one of those vague imaginings which assail us, when death, mysterious, inexplicable death, is the subject of our thoughts, and when our waking reason, prostrated by the stunning blow of some mighty and over- whelming grief, gives way and surrenders itself to the wildest fancies. There stood she, the one living being amid that concourse of dead ; rooted there amid pleasing horrors, revelling in a " luxury of woe," and framing in her dis- ordered brain a thousand fantasies, extravagant, unnatural, absurd, (so she felt them to be) yet still rising as vivid and irresistible as they were unbidden. Now her love for Turpin—anon some tenderness which had passed between them, some kindness till now forgotten—she spoke with the dead, who replied ; she started at the well-known voice and glanced fearfully around. The dull yew- trees waved heavily—her eye ranged over the tiny verdant mounds, till they rested on one brown-heap hard by, and then she clasped her hands, and wept bitterly. "Shall I return home ?" thought she ; " no ! I will watch here ; yet what can it avail *him ?* I'll watch, though ; for I feel sure—something tells me—I know not what !" and she struck her throbbing forehead with her hand. Some dark object moving beneath the dark shade of the trees now attracted her attention : fear seized her soul ; for not only the guilty—and guilty indeed she was—feel superstitious terrors. Her breath seemed suspended, and her heart almost ceased to beat, as she saw, in the doubtful obscurity, the form approach the spot where she was standing. Common sense, that most uncom- mon gift in emergencies, might have relieved her from her apprehensions, had she been in a frame of mind to have deliberately scanned the actions of the object of her dread. He approached---for man it was---until within a few yards of the grave, and, disappearing suddenly behind a tombstone, a circumstance by no means calculated to reassure her, she heard a fall, as of something thrown heavily on the ground. Her suspense, however, was not of long duration; for, in another minute, two other men entered from another quarter of the churchyard.

"Hist! hoy! Ned, is that you?" asked the fellow from behind the stone. A short low whistle was the reply, and the dreaded ghost came forth, armed with a mattock, a shovel, and a sack; it was the grave-digger of the burial-ground! A lantern was produced by one of the newcomers from beneath his cloak, and placed close to the foot of a grave, and the sack so placed around it as to conceal its light, all but one narrow stream which shone along the recent grave of the highwayman. Madge could, however, see enough of two of them to guess by their habiliments that they were not exactly of the lower rank.

"Now Ned," asked one in a loud whisper, "is all ready?"

"Aye, aye, zur!" was the muttered reply; and all was again silent, but the dull sound of the new laid earth, as two of the party tossed it aside from the grave, while the third kept a sharp look out.---The truth now flashed upon her; they were about to steal *his* body: yet, how should she act---she would run and give an alarm---she watched another minute, and although the grave, as she supposed, could not be a quarter dug out, some white object---yes it must be *he*- -was being dragged slowly from the earth.---Madge rushed forward, heedless of the consequences. "For God's sake!" was all she uttered, before the man on watch rushed behind her, and seized her in his arms: a faint scream was stifled by the tight pressure of her ample hood, which the man pressed on her mouth with one hand, while he grasped her waist tightly with the other.

"Why what the devil have we got here?" said he, as his comrades joined him; "the thief's doxy, by goles! what, in the name of old scratch, shall we do with her?"

Madge struggled, and again sent forth a cry.

"Oh, oh, 'tis all of no use," said the man who held her; "d----d unlucky, though---aint it?"

"Gag her, tie her, and shove her into the grave," suggested his companion; "I wouldn't lose our chance, now we've gone so far, for the best twenty guineas ever coined."

"No, no," replied the man who held her, "that would be rather too strong, poor devil :---just bind a handkerchief over her mouth, tie her hands, and blindfold her eyes, and I'll bet a trifle we manage her."

It was done while being talked of, for Madge was too feeble to offer much resistance.

"Now then!" and away they led the blindfolded Madge, she knew not whither. They did not go above a hundred yards; though she felt assured, by being lifted over a stile, that they had left the church-yard. She found herself led into a barn, for that it was so she could tell by the smell of hay, and here, seating her upon a truss, one of the party left, while the other remained to keep guard: an hour elapsed, and the man returned, the word "all right," was whispered, and, after threatening her with vengeance if she dared to stir till morning, or raise the least alarm, they departed; returning several times at an interval of a minute or two to repeat their menaces. Madge, however, was not so easily daunted; half an hour more passed away: they were certainly gone; and after several attempts, having succeeded in shifting the bandage from her eyes, she hastened towards her lodging with the speed of fear. The events of the last few days had made Madge a public character. Passing an alehouse, for the day's excitement had given an unwonted bustle to all places of public resort, she entered, her hands still fast-bound, to relieve herself from her painful thraldom. There were still remaining many rustic tipplers therein, and great was the surprise and strong the indignation of the assembly on hearing the tale of the violation of the grave of Turpin; for if there is one thing more than another which excites the abhorrence of the lower classes, it is the subjecting of the relics of mortality to the knife of the dissector. True it is that we have somewhat worn out this absurd prejudice, and that the example of some of our wisest and most humane men—who have left, during life, their remains for the furtherance of the cause of science—has abated this feeling, yet it still acts strongly upon the ignorant; and if it prevail so generally among them NOW, ten times more powerfully did it sway the people in the time of Turpin.

"A'm dong'd if a' woant make one to stop they doct'rin' chaps fra' cootting 'un up, arter he ha' had a Christun berrin," exclaimed one.

The declaration was loudly applauded by the rest; and each of the half-fuddled rustics vied with his fellow in being loudest in his declarations of vengeance on the resurrectionists.

"A'd loike to ha' the coottin' oop o' sum o' thae: Lor' bless 'ee, they care no more aboot carvin' an' slashin' o' Christians, nor Pollaxe, t' butcher, do aboot dead carves. A'd loike a grip o' sum o' thae 'spital coves; wouldn't I—" and the speaker wound up his wish with a pantomimic motion of his hands, similar to the process of killing rabbits.

"Doan't stand a-talkin' here, then—let's be off at once," suggested another; and a forward movement was made along the passage.

> Inspiring, bold John Barleycorn,
> What dangers canst thou make us scorn:
> Wi' tippenny we fear na evil,
> Wi' usquebaugh we'll face the devil;

and this feeling pervaded the indignant Yorkshiremen.

"Ay, ay," suggested one of the soberest of the fellows; "but how the dickins are ye to foind oot whar they chaps ha' stowed 'un?"

This was a poser, and they all looked at Madge as if expecting a solution of the query. She was too overjoyed at this unexpected reinforcement of rescuers to refuse the proffered service, and said:—

"Can one of you fetch Dave Clank hither: he knows the grave-digger, and so do I; but —" She hesitated a moment.

"What, ould Neddy Slug, dost mean?" asked two or three in a breath.

"The same," answered Madge: "he was one who helped to take him from the ground."

We will not soil our page with the exulting execrations which followed this important piece of information.

"Ho! ho! he wor in it, wor he? we'll foind 'un roight soon; he lives doon here hard by. We'll root 'un oot, never fear: by gum, that be a good 'un—ho! ho! measter Neddy, we'll be doon on 'ee in no toime: coom on, lads! Do ye goa and fetch Clank, Robin lad: we'll ha' 'un, and bury 'un, if he be to be found i' York."

A short delay took place, during which each sought his oaken cudgel; and

No. 41.

such as had them not, were supplied with other weapons of offence and defence. Dave Clank was soon at the spot, for he had not gone to rest, having remained up anxiously searching for Madge, whose departure from her lodging, shortly after her return from the funeral, had somewhat alarmed him.   In a few minutes they were thundering at the door of the humble dwelling of the grave-digger.   That worthy had not returned to his loving wife, who, alarmed at the noise outside, ventured to enquire the cause of the disturbance from the casement.

"We want t'e ould mon—and we'll ha' him oot," cried the disturbers.

In vain did mistress Slug remonstrate, and assure the party that he was not at home—nothing but a search would satisfy them ; and terrified by their menaces, she at length opened the door—and a glorious search they had. Not a cup-board, bed, or chest, escaped them ; and they were holding a council as to what next should be done, when a shout was raised outside.

"Here he be! here he be! Oh you 'tarnal ould bla'guard!" and poor Slug, pale with affright, was dragged in to his own hearthstone.

Threats, followed by an ugly thump or two, and the infuriated aspects of his assailants, soon extorted from the terrified Slug the names of his accomplices ;—and away hied the party, gathering strength and numbers as they passed along, to the house of the delinquent doctor.

Mr. —— had just turned in for a snooze, when he was unpleasantly turned out by a dreadful assault upon the door of his mansion.   With night-cap on head he enquired the cause of the tumult, and was very shortly satisfied as to its cause.

Loud, long, and heavy, rattled cudgels and stones upon his door, which was, fortunately for his personal safety, one of the stoutest.

"Run, Nicholas!" cried the alarmed professor of healing ; "out at the back-door—quick! Haste to the city watch ; alarm the neighbourhood— here's a riot ; we shall all be murdered."

Nicholas made his exit through the back premises : the rapidly increasing mob became impatient.

"Dom him, whoy doan't 'ee brake the door in ?" asked a fellow, advancing with a huge stone between his two hands: "stand clear there !" and he delivered the ponderous missile full against the centre of the lock—the stout hasp flew, and the passage was instantly filled with the rioters.   The slighter doors within soon yielded—the surgery was entered, and there lay the stark corse, the object of their search.   Mr. Sawbone prudently retreated to the roof on the forcible entry, for he well knew that the consequences of his body-snatching—or rather, that of his subordinates—might be anything but pleasant.

To raise the body from the tressels, with the board upon which it lay, was but the work of a moment, and it was steadily placed on the shoulders of four stout men.

"Hurrah! hurrah!" resounded from the rioters, as they made their way along the passage with their burden.

At this very juncture a magistrate, accompanied by a number of the ancient watch and ward, reached the spot, and were shortly followed by a corporal's guard from the castle.   The civil force were soon driven back, and the worshipful gentleman, who knew not the cause of the disturbance, warned the populace in the king's name to desist.   That it was a riot he saw—and that the house of the respectable Esculapius had been broken open was also evident; and he commanded the four soldiers—for the more distant of the mob were still wreaking their vengeance upon the doctor's windows—to suppress the tumult and apprehend the ringleaders. Backed by the soldiery, the watch made a desperate rush:—cracked crowns were at a discount; stones flew in all directions; cudgels flourished; and the scale of the contest hung long doubtful—numbers at length prevailed. The constables were beaten off; and the soldiers having gained the passage of the house, which the populace, who had now achieved their object, had quitted, the rioters went on their way shouting and rejoicing.

It was a strange scene. There, in the midst of that uproarious assemblage, surrounded by flaring torches, and borne along with bursts of triumph and discordant yells of defiance, moved that white and ghastly object—its bearers staggering to and fro, as the pressure of the multitude impelled them. The churchyard is again filled with crowds; imprecations, shouts, lamentation, strike harshly on the dull ear of night; the ancient solitary owl, whose nightly vigil in the ivy-mantled tower or the sombre yew-tree was thus unwontedly disturbed, stretches its downy wing, and flies scared from its peaceful domain; the red lights gleam on the moss grown grave-stones; and in the heart of this confusion and tumult, were the remains of the bold Dick Turpin again consigned to their mother earth.

* * * * * * * * *

Near the quiet little village of Sibbertoft, in Leicestershire, some thirty years after that torch-light funeral, a stranger stopped at a little cottage, at the door of which sat an elderly female plying her wheel. The day was sultry, and the woman, with mild courtesy, proffered him a glass of whey: he accepted it, and rode forward. Struck with her melancholy aspect, her neat mourning attire, and her placid manner, on arriving at his inn, he enquired who that solitary widow might be. The answer was soon given. She lived alone—few cared to seek her company, and she intruded it on no one—she lived on a small stipend, regularly paid to her by a gentleman who lived in the north of England, and was—the WIDOW OF DICK TURPIN THE HIGHWAYMAN.

THE END.

SHORTLY WILL BE PUBLISHED,

*In Weekly Numbers and Monthly Parts, embellished with
Numerous Engravings,*

CLAUDE DUVAL:

A HISTORICAL NOVEL.

BY THE AUTHOR OF DICK TURPIN.

Orders received by all Booksellers and Newsmen.